the
narrative
sensibility

the narrative sensibility

an introduction to fiction

Reloy Garcia and
Lloyd Hubenka

Creighton University

DAVID McKAY COMPANY, INC.
NEW YORK

THE NARRATIVE SENSIBILITY:
AN INTRODUCTION TO FICTION

MANUFACTURED IN THE UNITED STATES OF AMERICA

Developmental Editor: Gordon T. R. Anderson

Editorial and Design Supervision: Nicole Benevento

Design: Angela Foote

Cover Photography: Angela Foote

Production and Manufacturing Supervision: Donald W. Strauss

Composition: Maryland Linotype Company

Printing and Binding: The Maple Press Company, Inc.

Library of Congress Cataloging in Publication Data

Main entry under title:

The narrative sensibility.

    1. Fiction—Collections. I. Garcia, Reloy.
II. Hubenka, Lloyd J.
PZ1.N23   [PN6014]   808.83   75-33664
ISBN 0-679-30295-6

Acknowledgments

For permission to reprint selections in this book the editors thank the following:

Sherwood Anderson, "Death in the Woods." Reprinted by permission of Harold Ober Associates Incorporated. Copyright 1926 American Mercury, Inc. Renewed 1953 by Eleanor Copenhaver Anderson.

James Baldwin, "The Man Child." Excerpted from *Going to Meet the Man* by James Baldwin. Copyright © 1965 by James Baldwin. Reprinted by permission of the publisher, The Dial Press.

John Barth, "Title." Copyright © 1967 by Yale University. From *Lost in the Funhouse* by John Barth. Reprinted by permission of Doubleday & Company, Inc.

Phyllis Bentley, for excerpts from *Some Observations on the Art of Narrative*. Copyright 1946 by The Macmillan Company. Reprinted by permission of A. D. Peters and Company.

Gordon Bergquist, for permission to use his translation of "The Pardoner's Exemplum" from *Canterbury Tales* by Geoffrey Chaucer. Copyright © 1976 by Gordon Bergquist.

Heinrich Böll, "Action Will Be Taken." From *18 Stories* by Heinrich Böll. Copyright © 1966 by Heinrich Böll. Used with permission of the publisher McGraw-Hill Book Company.

Ivan Bunin, "The Gentleman From San Francisco." From *The Gentleman From San Francisco and Other Stories*, by Ivan Bunin, translated by Bernard Guilbert Guerney. Copyright 1923 and renewed 1951 by Alfred A. Knopf, Inc. Reprinted by permission of the publisher.

Michel Butor, "Welcome to Utah." From *Mobile* by Michel Butor. Translation copyright © 1963 by Simon & Schuster, Inc. for the translation by Richard Howard; © 1962 Editions Gallimard for the original French edition. Reprinted by permission of the publisher and Georges Borchardt, Inc.

Joseph Conrad, Preface to *The Nigger of the Narcissus*. From *Joseph Conrad: Three Great Tales*. By permission of J. M. Dent & Sons Ltd. and the Trustees of the Joseph Conrad Estate.

Joseph Conrad, "The Secret Sharer." From *'Twixt Land and Sea* by Joseph Conrad. Reprinted by permission of J. M. Dent & Sons Ltd. and the Trustees of the Joseph Conrad Estate.

Julio Cortazar, "Blow-Up." From *End of the Game and Other Stories*, by Julio Cortazar, translated by Paul Blackburn. Copyright © 1967 by Random House, Inc. Reprinted by permission of Pantheon Books, a Division of Random House, Inc.

Stephen Crane, "The Open Boat." Reprinted from *Stephen Crane: An Omnibus*, edited by Robert Wooster Stallman and published by Alfred A. Knopf, Inc.

Fyodor Dostoevsky, "A Christmas Tree and a Wedding." Reprinted with permission of Macmillan Publishing Co., Inc. from *White Nights and Other Stories* by Fyodor Dostoevsky. Translated from the Russian by Constance Garnett. Published in the United States by Macmillan Publishing Co., Inc. and in Britain by William Heinemann Ltd., Publishers.

William Faulkner, "A Rose for Emily." Copyright 1930 and renewed 1958 by William Faulkner. Reprinted from *Collected Stories of Faulkner*, by William Faulkner, by permission of Random House, Inc.

William Faulkner, Nobel Prize Acceptance Speech. Reprinted from *The Faulkner Reader*, Copyright 1954 by William Faulkner (Random House, Inc.)

E. M. Forster, Excerpt from *Aspects of the Novel*. Reprinted by permission of Harcourt Brace Jovanovich, Inc. and Edward Arnold (Publishers) Ltd.

Inc. and Calder and Boyars Ltd. Copyright © 1968 by Grove Press, Inc. Translated by Bruce Morrissette.

Philip Roth, "Novotny's Pain." First appeared in *The New Yorker*, Oct. 27, 1962, The New Yorker Magazine, Inc. Reprinted by permission of the author.

Hernando Téllez, "Just Lather, That's All." Translated by Donald A. Yates. Reprinted by permission of the estate of Hernando Téllez.

Leo Tolstoy, "The Death of Ivan Ilych." From *The Death of Ivan Ilych and Other Stories* by Leo Tolstoy, translated by Louise and Aylmer Maude and published by Oxford University Press. Reprinted by permission of the publisher.

Emmett Williams, for permission to reprint "an opera," copyright © 1960, 1974 by Emmett Williams. First published in English in *Breakthrough Fictioneers*, edited by Richard Kostelanetz (New York: Something Else Press, 1973).

Virginia Woolf, "The Mark on the Wall." From *A Haunted House and Other Stories* by Virginia Woolf, copyright, 1944, 1972, by Harcourt Brace Jovanovich, Inc. and reprinted by their permission, the Author's Literary Estate, and The Hogarth Press.

Virginia Woolf, "Modern Fiction." From *The Common Reader* by Virginia Woolf, copyright, 1925, by Harcourt Brace Jovanovich, Inc.; copyright, 1953, by Leonard Woolf. Reprinted by permission of the publishers.

Virginia Woolf, Excerpt from *To the Lighthouse* by Virginia Woolf, copyright, 1927, by Harcourt Brace Jovanovich, Inc.; copyright, 1955, by Leonard Woolf. Reprinted by permission of the publishers.

Virginia Woolf, Excerpts from *Mrs. Dalloway* by Virginia Woolf, copyright, 1925, by Harcourt Brace Jovanovich, Inc.; copyright, 1953, by Leonard Woolf. Reprinted by permission of the publishers.

Like everything we do, The Narrative Sensibility *is dedicated to our wives; to Mary Lynn Strecker, typist and friend; to our colleagues in the English Department at Creighton University; and to the many anonymous reviewers whose constructive criticism helped to shape this book. In addition, we owe a special debt to Mr. Guy Jones, whose early confidence in the manuscript assured its eventual publication. This book bears his imprint.*

contents

part two/masters of modern fiction 55

part three/the novella or short novel 269

part four/beyond the safety zone: new directions in experimental fiction 379

part one
the roots
of fiction

Introductory courses in fiction often begin with stories composed in the nineteenth century, usually with a short story by Edgar Allan Poe (1809–49), the first great practitioner of the form. While fiction as we know it was first written more than a century ago, short fiction did not grow in a hothouse of such recent construction: its roots stretch thousands of years back, deep into the rich soil of the distant past, and into many countries. Short fiction has its origins in times when the demarcation line between verse and prose was less clear than it is now, when the oral tradition influenced all written forms.

In a sense, then, the study that ignores the roots of fiction, or pays only lip service to it in a passing reference, belies the long evolution which has led to fiction as we know it today. Early prose was very diverse in its forms, themes, and intents. In "The Roots of Fiction" section of *The Narrative Sensibility* we have included several types and examples of early fiction. The *fable*, represented here by "The Lion-Makers," is a brief story that employs animal characters to develop a moral point. The *character sketch*, such as Theophrastus's "The Miser" (*ca.* 325 B.C.), is a caricature that retains the spirit of real characters who inspired it.

And while the Bible is generally read for its literal or symbolic truths, students of literature must also acknowledge it as a wealth of short narratives, of which "Samson and Delilah" and the *parable* of "The Good

Samaritan" are included in this collection. Another influential predecessor of the modern short story is the *collection*, and from *The Thousand and One Nights* (tenth century A.D.), we have selected "The Lady and Her Five Suitors" to illustrate the cycle of stories Scheherazade told the Caliph Harun-al-Rashid to forestall her death and win his love. The *fabliau*, which had its origins in thirteenth-century France and is an ancestor of the modern "dirty story," is compact of form, pithy in wit, and realistic in nature; it tells a bawdy story, often in coarse language, culminating in an unlikely but comical climax. Often such *fabliaux*, the most famous of which is Chaucer's "The Miller's Tale," from *The Canterbury Tales* (1387–95), make light of religion or the clergy. Boccaccio's *The Decameron* (1353) provides us with such a *fabliau*, "The Path to Sainthood." From Chaucer we have selected "The Pardoner's Exemplum" to illustrate the form of the *exemplum*, a short narrative with a moral or instructive intention and ofen employed in sermons. Indeed, "The Pardoner's Exemplum" is a standard medieval sermon on the evils of the tavern.

The rogue, or *picaro*, as he is called in Spanish, is the heart of the *picaresque tale* or novel, the most famous example of which is *Don Quixote* (1605), from which we have translated "The Windmill Episode." In the picaresque story a roguish hero stumbles his way through a series of loosely related, realistic comic episodes, sometimes on the way to virtue, sometimes to satire. The *allegorical narrative*, such as John Bunyan's "Vanity Fair" (1678), has an undisguised moral purpose: to show how man must transcend this world to gain the next. Allegory (see *Glossary*) slights characterization at the expense of the sermon, often making a character an embodiment of a virtue or a vice, such as Good Deeds or Temptation.

Two final examples serve to illustrate the wide range and richness of pre-nineteenth-century prose. One is the *periodical sketch*, the most famous example of which is *The Spectator*, a group of more than five hundred eighteenth-century commentaries on everything of interest to the keen and urbane writers, Joseph Addison and Richard Steele. The period sketch stands midway between the newspaper and fiction, employing elements of both. Interestingly, period sketches often provided a *persona*, or mask character, through which the writer could express his own views, either directly or ironically. *Satire* is the final example. In "The Land of the Brobdingnags," from *Gulliver's Travels* (1726), Jonathan Swift shows how satire can be directed at men and institutions while delighting the very objects of attack. *Gulliver's Travels*, of course, is mistakenly considered a book for children in our time. In its own century, it was a mirror for misguided individuals, all of them adults.

The examples of early prose in this section, then, can be defined by certain general characteristics while being different from one another. As a rule, their controlling principle is theme, not plot or time or character or context. The plots are episodic, the time chronological. The works assume a basic world order and often a body of acquired mythological, historical, and Biblical knowledge; there is a fixed relationship between the author and his work, the author and his reader, and the reader and the work. Finally, this early literature is almost always didactic in nature, even when it does not seem to be so. Deep character studies and psychological analyses have no role here. And, in a technical sense, these works are not experimental in form or in treatment of time. Hopefully, the samples which follow illustrate the general validity of these observations and, as well, the interesting range of types of stories and themes which delight us even now—the Biblical tale, the chronicle, the romance, the parable, the exemplum, the dirty story with a moral pit, the knight-errant's adventure. By the time Washington Irving and Edgar Allan Poe had taken up the pen, they had accumulated considerable debts to storytellers they would never know.

THE LION-MAKERS
A Fable from the *Panchantra*
(*ca.* 500 B.C.)

Even men of learning and noble birth are sometimes devoid of common-sense. For, true is the saying:—

> Book-learning people rightly cherish;
> But common sense is best of all to me.
> Bereft of common sense you shall perish,
> Like to the Lion-makers three.

"How was that?" said the Man-with-the-wheel. And the Gold-magician narrated:

In a certain place there dwelt four brahman youths in the greatest friendship. Three of them had got to the further shore of the ocean of science, but were devoid of common-sense; while the fourth had common-sense only, and no mind for science. Now once upon a time these friends took counsel together, and said, "Of what profit is science, if we cannot go with it to some foreign country and win the favor of princes and make our fortune? Therefore to the Eastern Country let us go." And so it came to pass.

Now after they had gone a little way, the eldest spoke: "There is one among us, the fourth, who has no learning, but only common-sense; and a man can't get presents from kings by common-sense without learning. Not a whit will I give him of all that I gain; so let him go home." And the second said, "Ho there, Common Sense! get you homeward, for you have no learning!" But the third made answer, "Alas, it is not fitting so to do: for we have played together since we were boys. So let him come along too. He's a noble fellow, and shall have a share in the riches that we win."

On then they went together, till in a jungle they saw the bones of a dead lion. Then spoke the first: "Ha! now we can put our book-learning to the test. Here lies some sort of a dead creature: by the power of our learning we'll bring it to life. I'll put the bones together." And that then he did with zeal. The second added flesh, blood, and hide. But just as the third was breathing the breath of life into it, Common Sense stopped him and said, "Hold: this is a lion that you are turning out. If you make him alive, he will kill every one of us." Thereupon made answer the other, "Fie, stupid! is learning to be fruitless in my hands?" "Well, then," said Common Sense, "just wait a bit till I climb a tree."

Thereupon the lion was brought to life. But the instant this was done, he sprang up and killed the three. Afterwards Common Sense climbed down and went home.

Therefore, concluded the Gold-magician, therefore I say:—

> Book-learning people rightly cherish;
> But common sense is best of all to me.
> Bereft of common sense you shall perish,
> Like to the Lion-makers three.

SAMSON AND DELILAH
Old Testament, Book of Judges 13–16

Then the Israelites again did what was evil in the sight of the Lord; so that the Lord delivered them into the power of the Philistines for forty years.

Now there was a certain man of Zorah, belonging to the Danite clan, whose name was Manoah. His wife was barren and childless; but the angel of the Lord appeared to the woman, and said to her,

"See now, although you have been barren and childless, you are going to conceive, and bear a son. Now then, take care not to drink wine or liquor, nor to eat anything unclean; for you are going to conceive, and bear a son. A razor is not to be used on his head; for the boy is to be a Nazirite to God from conception. He it is who will take the lead in saving Israel from the power of the Philistines."

Then the woman came and told her husband, saying,

"A man of God came to me, whose appearance was like that of an angel of God, very awe-inspiring. I did not ask him where he came from, nor did he tell me his name; but he said to me, 'You are going to conceive, and bear a son; now then, do not drink wine or liquor, nor eat anything unclean; for the boy is to be a Nazirite to God from conception to the day of his death.' "

Then Manoah besought the Lord, and said,

"Pray, O Lord, let the man of God whom thou didst send come back to us, and teach us what to do for the boy that is to be born."

So God acceded to Manoah's request, and the angel of God came back to the woman while she was sitting in the field, her husband Manoah not being with her. Then the woman ran quickly to tell her husband.

"The man who came to me the other day has just appeared to me!" she said to him.

So Manoah rose and followed his wife, and coming to the man, said to him,

"Are you the man who spoke to my wife?"

"I am," he said.

"In case your promise come true," said Manoah, "what is to be the boy's training and his vocation?"

The angel of the Lord said to Manoah,

"The woman must abstain from everything of which I spoke to her. She must not eat any of the products of the grapevine, nor drink wine or liquor, nor eat anything unclean. All that I commanded her she must observe."

Then Manoah said to the angel of the Lord,

"Pray allow us to detain you, that we may prepare a kid for you."

But the angel of the Lord said to Manoah,

"Though you detain me, I will not taste your food; but if you are going to make a burnt-offering, offer it up to the Lord." (For Manoah did not know that he was the angel of the Lord.)

Then Manoah said to the angel of the Lord,

"What is your name, that we may properly honor you when your promise comes true?"

"Why do you ask for my name," the angel of the Lord said to him, "seeing that it is ineffable."

Then Manoah took the kid, along with the cereal-offering, and offered it up on the rock to the Lord, who performed wonders while Manoah and his wife looked on; when the flame ascended from the altar heavenward, the angel of the Lord ascended in the flame of the altar, while Manoah and his wife looked on, and fell on their faces to the ground. (The angel of the

Lord never again appeared to Manoah and his wife.) Then Manoah knew that he was the angel of the Lord; so Manoah said to his wife,

"We shall certainly die; for we have seen God!"

But his wife said to him,

"If the Lord had meant to kill us, he would not have accepted a burnt-offering and a cereal-offering from us, nor would he have showed us all these things, nor would he have told us such a thing as he did just now."

So the woman bore a son, and called his name Samson. The boy grew up, and the Lord blessed him; but the spirit of the Lord first stirred him up at Mahaneh-dan, between Zorah and Eshtaol.

Samson went down to Timnah, and saw a woman at Timnah, one of the Philistine women. When he came back, he told his father and mother.

"I saw a woman at Timnah," he said, "one of the Philistine women; now then, get her for me in marriage."

But his father and mother said to him,

"Is there no woman among the girls of your own kinsmen or among all my people, that you must go and get a wife from the uncircumcised Philistines?"

But Samson said to his father,

"Get her for me; for she is the one that suits me."

His father and mother did not know, however, that it was at the instigation of the Lord that he was picking a quarrel with the Philistines; for at that time the Philistines held sway over Israel.

Then Samson went down with his father and mother to Timnah, and just as they reached the vineyards of Timnah, a young lion came roaring at him. Then the spirit of the Lord came rushing upon him, so that he split it open as one might split a kid, although he had nothing at all in his hands. However, he did not tell his father and mother what he had done. So he went down, and talked to the woman, and she suited Samson. When he returned after a while to marry her, he turned aside to look at the remains of the lion, and there was a swarm of bees in the carcass of the lion, and honey. So he scraped it out into his hands, and ate it as he went along. When he returned to his father and mother, he gave them some to eat, but he did not tell them that it was out of the carcass of the lion that he had scraped the honey.

When his father went down to the woman, Samson made a feast there; for so bridegrooms were accustomed to do. As soon as they saw him, they selected thirty companions to accompany him. To them Samson said,

"Let me propound you a riddle; if you can but solve it for me in the seven days of the feast, and find it out, I will give you thirty linen robes and thirty festal garments; but if you are unable to tell me the solution, then you must give me thirty linen robes and thirty festal garments."

"Propound your riddle," they said to him, "let us hear it!"

So he said to them,

"Out of the eater came something to eat,
And out of the strong came something sweet."

When they could not solve the riddle after three days, they said to Samson's wife on the fourth day,

"Coax your husband to solve the riddle for us, lest we burn up you and your father's house. Was it to impoverish us that you invited us here?"

So Samson's wife wept on his shoulder, and said,

"You simply hate me and do not love me at all. You have propounded a riddle to my countrymen without telling me the solution."

He said to her,

"Why I haven't told my father or mother; so should I tell you?"

But she wept on his shoulder through the seven days that they kept the feast, until finally on the seventh day he told her, since she pressed him so hard. Then she told the riddle to her countrymen; and on the seventh day, as he was about to enter the bridal chamber, the men of the city said to him,

"What is sweeter than honey,
And what is stronger than a lion?"

He said to them,

"If you had not ploughed with this heifer of mine,
You would not have found out this riddle of mine."

Then the spirit of the Lord came rushing upon him, so that he went down to Askelon, and killing thirty of them, he despoiled them, and gave the festal garments to those who had solved the riddle. Then, blazing with anger, he went up to his father's house, and Samson's wife went to his rival, who had been a rival to him.

After a while, however, in the time of wheat harvest, Samson paid a visit to his wife with a kid.

"I am going into the bridal chamber to my wife," he said.

But her father would not let him go in.

"I thought of course that you must simply hate her," her father said, "so I gave her to your rival. Is her younger sister not better than she? Take her instead."

Then Samson said of them,

"This time I am going to get even with the Philistines; for I am going to do them harm."

So Samson went and caught three hundred foxes; he then procured torches, and turning tail to tail, he put a torch between each pair of tails. Then, setting the torches on fire, he turned the foxes loose in the standing grain of the Philistines, and burnt up both the shocks and the standing grain, and also the vineyards and olive groves.

"Who has done this?" said the Philistines.

So the Philistines went up, and burned up her and her father's house.

"Samson, the son-in-law of the Timnite," it was said, "because his wife was taken away and given to his rival."

Then Samson said to them,

"You can never do such a thing as this without my taking revenge on you; but after this I will quit."

So he smote them hip and thigh with great slaughter; then he went down, and lived in a cleft of the crag Etam.

Then the Philistines came up, and encamped in Judah, and made a raid on Lehi.

"Why have you come up against us?" said the Judeans.

"We have come up to take Samson prisoner," they said, "that we may do to him as he did to us."

So three thousand of the Judeans went down to the cleft of the crag Etam, and said to Samson,

"Do you not know that the Philistines hold sway over us? What ever have you done to us?"

"As they did to me," he replied, "so have I done to them."

"We have come down to take you prisoner," they said to him, "to turn you over to the Philistines."

"Swear to me that you will not fall upon me yourselves," Samson said to them.

"No," they responded, "we will but take you prisoner, and turn you over to them, but we will not kill you."

So they bound him with two new ropes, and brought him up from the crag. As he reached Lehi, the Philistines came shouting to meet him. Then the spirit of the Lord came rushing upon him, so that the ropes on his arms became like flax that has caught on fire, and his bonds melted off his hands; and finding a fresh jawbone of an ass, he put out his hand, and seizing it, felled a thousand men with it. Then Samson said,

"With the red ass's jawbone I have dyed them red;
With the red ass's jawbone I have felled a thousand men."

As he finished speaking, he threw the jawbone away; hence that place came to be called Ramath-lehi, the hill of the jawbone. Then he became very thirsty, so he called to the Lord, saying,

"Thou hast vouchsafed this great victory by thy servant, and am I now to die of thirst, and fall by the hands of the uncircumcised?"

Then God split open the mortar that is at Lehi, and water gushed out of it; and when he drank, his spirits rose, and he revived. That is how its name came to be called En-hakkor, the spring of the caller, which is at Lehi to this day. So he governed Israel in the time of the Philistines for twenty years.

Samson went to Gaza, and seeing a harlot there, had intercourse with her. When the Gazaites were told, "Samson has come here," they came around, and lay in wait for him all night at the gate of the city. They kept quiet all night, saying, "As soon as morning dawns, we will kill him." Samson lay until midnight; but at midnight he rose, and taking hold of the doors of the city gate and the two gateposts, he pulled them up, together with the bar, and putting them on his shoulder, he carried them to the top of the hill that faces Hebron.

Afterwards he fell in love with a woman in the valley of Sorek, whose name was Delilah. Then the Philistine tyrants came to her, and said to her,

"Coax him, and find out why his strength is so great, and how we can overpower him and bind him helpless, and we will each give you eleven hundred shekels of silver."

So Delilah said to Samson,

"Do tell me why your strength is so great, and how you can be bound helpless?"

Samson said to her,

"If I were to be bound with seven fresh bowstrings that have not been dried, I should become weak, and be like any other man."

Then the Philistine tyrants brought her seven fresh bowstrings that had not been dried, and she bound him with them. Then, having men lie in wait in the inner room, she said to him,

"The Philistines are on you, Samson!"

But he snapped the bowstrings, as a strand of tow is snapped when it comes near fire. So the source of his strength was not discovered.

Then Delilah said to Samson,

"There, you have trifled with me, and told me lies! Do tell me now how you can be bound."

So he said to her,

"If I were but bound with new ropes that have not been used, I should become weak, and be like any other man."

So Delilah took new ropes, and bound him with them. Then she said to him,

"The Philistines are on you, Samson!"

(Meanwhile men were lying in wait in the inner room.)

But he snapped them off his arms like thread.

Then Delilah said to Samson,

"Up to now you have trifled with me, and told me lies. Tell me how you can be bound."

So he said to her,

"If you were to weave the seven locks of my head into the web, and beat them in with the pin, I should become weak, and be like any other man."

So when he was asleep, Delilah took the seven locks of his head and wove them into the web, and beat them in with the pin. Then she said to him,

"The Philistines are on you, Samson!"

But he awoke from his sleep, and pulled up both the loom and the web.

Then she said to him,

"How can you say, 'I love you,' when you do not confide in me? Three times already you have trifled with me, and have not told me why your strength is so great."

At last, after she had pressed him with her words continually, and urged him, he got tired to death of it, and told her his whole secret.

"A razor has never been used on my head," he said to her; "for I have been a Nazirite to God from conception. If I were to be shaved, my strength would leave me; I should become weak, and be like any other man."

When Delilah saw that he had told her his whole secret, she sent for the Philistine tyrants, saying,

"Come up this once; for he has told me his whole secret."

So the Philistine tyrants came to her, and brought the money in their hands. Then she put him to sleep on her knees, and summoning a man, she had him shave off the seven locks of his head, so that he became quite helpless, and his strength left him. Then she said,

"The Philistines are on you, Samson!"

He awoke from his sleep, and thought, "I shall get off as I have done over and over again, and shake myself free"—not knowing that the Lord had left him. Then the Philistines seized him, and gouged out his eyes, and bringing him down to Gaza, they bound him with bronze shackles, and he spent his time grinding in the prison. But the hair of his head began to grow again as soon as it had been shaved off.

Now the Philistine tyrants gathered to offer a great sacrifice to their god Dagon, and for merry-making, saying, "Our god has delivered our enemy Samson into our power!"

When the people saw him, they praised their god; "For," said they, "our god has delivered our enemy into our hands, the devastator of our lands, and him who slew us in bands."

When they were in high spirits, they said,

"Summon Samson, that he may make sport for us!"

So Samson was summoned from the prison, and made sport before them. When they had stationed him between the pillars, Samson said to the attendant who was holding his hand,

"Put me so that I can feel the pillars on which the building is supported, that I may lean against them."

Now the building was full of men and women, and all the Philistine tyrants were there; and on the roof there were about three thousand men and women, looking on while Samson made sport. Then Samson cried to the Lord, saying,

"O Lord God, pray remember me, and give me strength just this one time, O God, to wreak vengeance but once upon the Philistines for my two eyes!"

Then Samson grasped the two middle pillars on which the building was supported, one with his right hand and the other with his left, and braced himself against them.

"Let me die with the Philistines!" said Samson.

Then he pulled with all his might, so that the building fell in upon the tyrants and all the people that were in it. So those that he killed at his death were more than those that he had killed during his life.

Then his kinsmen and all his father's household came down, and took him up; and bringing him away, they buried him between Zorah and Eshtaol, in the tomb of his father Manoah. He had governed Israel for twenty years.

THE MISER (*ANELEUTHERIA*)*
The Character Sketches of Theophrastus
(*ca.* 372–286 B.C.)

The miser is one who neglects his honor whenever it involves spending. If he should win a prize for sponsoring a tragedy, he will dedicate to Dionysus only a wooden crown with his own name and no other inscribed upon it. And when the Assembly asks for public contributions, he remains silent or sneaks out the back door. At his daughter's wedding feast he will sell the sacrificial meat (except for the portion that goes to the priest), and makes arrangements with those he has hired to serve at the banquet to have them eat at their own homes. And when he sponsors a boat for the state, he will use the navigator's blanket to save the wear on his own. The miser will not send his children to school on certain feast days, but pretend that they are ill so that he will not have to contribute money. On his way home from the market place, he carries the meats

---

* Translators Note: In accord with the wishes of the editors, I have prepared here a "free" translation intended to capture the spirit of Theophrastus's sketch, not a scholarly redaction.

and vegetables in his coat rather than purchasing a basket. And when his coat is at the cleaner's, he simply stays at home. If his friends are taking up a collection for some worthy purpose, he will take side streets to avoid them.

His wife, who has brought a large dowry, is not allowed to have a maid; instead, he gets a little girl to assist her. Although his shoes are old clodhoppers, he insists that they are yet very durable. He arises very early to do his own house cleaning. And when he sits down, he will carefully arrange his outer garment so as not to sit on it, thus saving wear and tear.

Translated by James Karabatsos

THE PARABLE OF THE GOOD SAMARITAN
New Testament,
Luke 10:30–37

And Jesus said, A certain man went down from Jerusalem to Jericho, and fell among thieves, which stripped him of his raiment, and wounded him, and departed, leaving him half dead.

And by chance there came down a certain priest that way; and when he saw him, he passed by on the other side.

And likewise a Levite, when he was at the place, came and looked on him, and passed by on the other side.

But a certain Samaritan, as he journeyed, came where he was; and when he saw him, he had compassion on him,

And went to him, and bound up his wounds, pouring in oil and wine, and set him on his own beast, and brought him to an inn, and took care of him.

And on the morrow when he departed, he took out two pence, and gave them to the host, and said unto him, Take care of him: and whatsoever thou spendest more, when I come again, I will repay thee.

Which now of these three, thinkest thou, was neighbor unto him that fell among the thieves?

And he said, he that showed mercy on him. Then said Jesus unto him, Go, and do thou likewise.

THE LADY AND HER FIVE SUITORS

The Arabian Tale,

from *The Thousand and One Nights*

$\mathbf{A}$ woman of the daughters of the merchants was married to a man who was a great traveler. It chanced once that he set out for a far country and was absent so long that his wife, from pure ennui, fell in love with a handsome young man of the sons of the merchants, and they loved each other with exceeding love. One day the youth quarreled with another man, who lodged a complaint against him with the Chief of Police, and he cast him into prison. When the news came to the merchant's wife, his mistress, she well nigh lost her wits; then she arose and donning her richest clothes repaired to the house of the Chief of Police. She saluted him and presented a written petition to this purport: "He thou hast clapped in jail is my brother such and such, who fell out with such an one; and those who testified against him bore false witness. He hath been wrongfully imprisoned, and I have none other to come in to me nor to provide for my support; therefore I beseech thee of thy grace to release him."

When the magistrate had read the paper, he cast his eyes on her and fell in love with her forthright; so he said to her, "Go into the house, till I bring him before me; then I will send for thee and thou shalt take him." "O my lord," replied she, "I have none to protect me save Almighty Allah! I am a stranger and may not enter any man's abode." Quoth the Wali, "I will not let him go, except thou come to my home and I take my will of thee." Rejoined she, "If it must be so, thou must needs come to my lodging and sit and sleep the siesta and rest the whole day there." "And where is thy abode?" asked he; and she answered, "In such a place," and appointed him for such a time. Then she went out from him, leaving his heart taken with love of her, and she repaired to the Kazi of the city to whom she said, "O our lord the Kazi!" He exclaimed, "Yes!" and she continued, "Look into my case, and thy reward be with Allah the Most High!" Quoth he, "Who hath wronged thee?" and quoth she, "O my lord, I have a brother and I have none but that one, and it is on his account that I come to thee; because the Wali hath imprisoned him for a criminal and men have borne false witness against him that he is a wrongdoer; and I beseech thee to intercede for him with the Chief of Police."

When the Kazi looked on her, he fell in love with her forthright and said to her, "Enter the house and rest awhile with my handmaids whilst I send to the Wali to release thy brother. If I knew the money-fine which is upon him, I would pay it out of my own purse, so I may have my desire of thee, for thou pleasest me with thy sweet speech." Quoth she, "If thou, O my lord, do thus, we must not blame others." Quoth he, "An thou wilt not come in, wend thy ways." Then said she, "An thou wilt have it so, O our lord, it will be privier and better in my place than in thine, for here are slave girls and eunuchs and goers-in and comers-out, and indeed I am a woman who wotteth naught of this fashion; but need compelleth." Asked the Kazi, "And where is thy house?"; and she answered, "In such a place," and appointed him for the same day and time as the Chief of Police. Then she went out from him to the Wazir, to whom she proffered her petition for the release from prison of her brother who was absolutely necessary to her; but he also required her of herself, saying, "Suffer me to have my will of thee and I will set thy brother free." Quoth she, "An thou wilt have it so, be it in my house, for there it will be privier both for me and for thee. It is not far distant and thou knowest that which behoveth us women of cleanliness and adornment." Asked he, "Where is thy house?" "In such a place," answered she and appointed him for the same time as the two others.

Then she went out from him to the King of the city and told him her story and sought of him her brother's release. "Who imprisoned him?" inquired he; and she replied, " 'Twas thy Chief of Police." When the King heard her speech, it transpierced his heart with the arrows of love and he bade her enter the palace with him, that he might send to the Kazi and release her brother. Quoth she, "O King, this thing is easy to thee, whether I will or nill; and if the King will indeed have this of me, it is of my good fortune; but, if he come to my house, he will do me the more honor by setting step therein." Quoth the King, "We will not cross thee in this." So she appointed him for the same time as the three others, and told him where her house was.

Then she left him and, betaking herself to a man which was a carpenter, said to him, "I would have thee make me a cabinet with four compartments one above other, each with its door for locking up. Let me know thy hire and I will give it thee." Replied he, "My price will be four dinars; but, O noble lady and well-protected, if thou wilt vouchsafe me thy favors, I will ask nothing of thee." Rejoined she, "An there be no help but that thou have it so, then make thou five compartments with their padlocks"; and she appointed him to bring it exactly on the day required. Said he, "It is well; sit down, O my lady, and I will make it for thee forthright, and after I will come to thee at my leisure." So she sat down by him, whilst he fell to work on the cabinet, and when he had made an end of it she chose to see it at once carried home and set up in the sitting chamber. Then she took four gowns and carried them to the dyer, who dyed them each of a different color; after which she applied herself to making ready meat and drink, fruits, flowers and perfumes.

Now, when the appointed trysting day came, she donned her costliest dress and adorned herself and scented herself, then spread the sitting room with various kinds of rich carpets and sat down to await who should come. And behold, the Kazi was the first to appear, preceding the rest; and when she saw him, she rose to her feet and kissed the ground before him; then, taking him by the hand, made him sit down by her on the couch and lay with him and fell to jesting and toying with him. By and by, he would have her do his desire, but she said, "O my lord, doff thy clothes and turband and assume this yellow cassock and this headkerchief, whilst I bring thee meat and drink; and after thou shalt win thy will." So saying, she took his clothes and turband and clad him in the cassock and the kerchief; but hardly had she done this, when lo! there came a knocking at the door. Asked he, "Who is that rapping at the door?" and she answered, "My husband." Quoth the Kazi, "What is to be done, and where shall I go?" Quoth she, "Fear nothing, I will hide thee in this cabinet"; and he, "Do as seemeth good to thee." So she took him by the hand and, pushing him into the lowest compartment, locked the door upon him.

Then she went to the house door, where she found the Wali; so she kissed the ground before him and, taking his hand, brought him into the salon, where she made him sit down and said to him, "O my lord, this house is thy house; this place is thy place, and I am thy handmaid; thou shalt pass all this day with me; wherefore do thou doff thy clothes and don this red gown, for it is a sleeping gown." So she took away his clothes and made him assume the red gown and set on his head an old patched rag she had by her; after which she sat by him on the divan and she sported with him while he toyed with her awhile, till he put out his hand to her. Whereupon she said to him, "O our lord, this day is thy day and none shall share in it with thee; but first, of thy favor and benevolence, write me an order for my brother's release from jail that my heart may be at ease." Quoth he, "Hearkening and obedience; on my head and eyes be it!" and wrote a letter to his treasurer, saying: "As soon as this communication shall reach thee, do thou set such an one free, without stay or delay; neither answer the bearer a word." Then he sealed it and she took it from him, after which she began to toy again with him on the divan when, behold, someone knocked at the door. He asked, "Who is that?" and she answered, "My husband." "What shall I do?" said he, and she, "Enter this cabinet, till I send him away and return to thee." So she clapped him into the second compartment from the bottom and padlocked the door on him; and meanwhile the Kazi heard all they said.

Then she went to the house door and opened it, whereupon, lo! the Wazir entered. She kissed the ground before him and received him with all honor and worship, saying, "O my lord, thou exaltest us by thy coming to our house; Allah never deprive us of the light of thy countenance!" Then she seated him on the divan and said to him, "O my lord, doff thy heavy dress and turband and don these lighter vestments." So he put off his clothes and turband and she clad him in a blue cassock and a tall red bonnet, and said to him, "Erst thy garb was that of the Wazirate; so leave it to its own time and don this light gown, which is better fitted for carousing and making merry and sleep." Thereupon she began to play with him and he with her, and he would have done his desire of her; but she put him off, saying, "O my lord, this shall not fail us." As they were talking there came a knocking at the door, and the Wazir asked her, "Who is that?"; to which she answered, "My husband." Quoth he, "What is to be done?" Quoth she, "Enter this cabinet, till I get rid of him and come back to thee and fear thou nothing." So she put him in the third compartment and locked the door on him, after which she went out and opened the house door when, lo and behold! in came the King.

As soon as she saw him she kissed the ground before him and, taking him by the hand, led him into the salon and seated him on the divan at the upper end. Then said she to him, "Verily, O King, thou dost us high honor, and if we brought thee to gift the world and all that therein is, it would not be worth a single one of thy steps us-ward." And when he had taken his seat upon the divan she said, "Give me leave to speak one word." "Say what thou wilt," answered he, and she said, "O my lord, take thine ease and doff thy dress and turband." Now his clothes were worth a thousand dinars; and when he put them off she clad him in a patched gown, worth at the very most ten dirhams, and fell to talking and jesting with him; all this while the folk in the cabinet hearing everything that passed, but not daring to say a word. Presently, the King put his hand to her neck and sought to do his desire of her; when she said, "This thing shall not fail us, but I had first promised myself to entertain thee in this sitting chamber, and I have that which shall content thee." Now, as they were speaking, someone knocked at the door and he asked her, "Who is that?" "My husband," answered she; and he, "Make him go away of his own good will, or I will fare forth to him and send him away perforce." Replied she, "Nay, O my lord, have patience till I send him away by my skillful contrivance." "And I, how shall I do?" inquired the King; whereupon she took him by the hand and, making him enter the fourth compartment of the cabinet, locked it upon him. Then she went out and opened the house door, when behold, the carpenter entered and saluted her.

Quoth she, "What manner of thing is this cabinet thou hast made me?" "What aileth it, O my lady?" asked he, and she answered, "The top compartment is too strait." Rejoined he, "Not so"; and she, "Go in thyself and see; it is not wide enough for thee." Quoth he, "It is wide enough for four," and entered the fifth compartment, whereupon she locked the door on him. Then she took the letter of the Chief of Police and carried it to the treasurer who, having read and understood it, kissed it and delivered her lover to her. She told him all she had done and he said, "And how shall we act now?" She answered, "We will remove hence to another city, for after this work there is no tarrying for us here." So the twain packed up what goods they had and, loading them on camels, set out forthright for another city.

Meanwhile, the five abode each in his compartment of the cabinet without eating or drinking three whole days, during which time they held their water, until at last the carpenter could retain his no longer; so he staled on the King's head, and the King urined on the Wazir's head, and the Wazir piddled on the Wali and the Wali pissed on the head of the Kazi; whereupon the Judge cried out and said, "What nastiness is this? Doth not what strait we are in suffice us, but you must make water upon us?" The Chief of Police recognized the Kazi's voice and answered, saying aloud, "Allah increase thy reward, O Kazi!" And when the Kazi heard him, he knew him for the Wali. Then the Chief of Police lifted up his voice and said, "What means this nastiness?" and the Wazir answered, saying, "Allah increase thy reward, O Wali!" whereupon he knew him to be the Minister. Then the Wazir lifted up his voice and said, "What means this nastiness?" But when the King heard and recognized his Minister's voice, he held his peace and concealed his affair. Then said the Wazir, "May God damn this woman for her dealing with us! She hath brought hither all the Chief Officers of the State, except the King." Quoth the King, "Hold your peace, for I was the first to fall into the toils of this lewd strumpet." Whereat cried the carpenter, "And I, what have I done? I made her a cabinet for four gold pieces, and when I came to seek my hire, she tricked me into entering this compartment and locked the door on me." And they fell to talking with one another, diverting the King and doing away his chagrin.

Presently the neighbors came up to the house and, seeing it deserted, said one to other, "But yesterday our neighbor, the wife of such an one, was in it; but now no sound is to be heard therein nor is soul to be seen. Let us break open the doors and see how the case stands, lest it come to the ears of the Wali or the King and we be cast into prison and regret not doing this thing before." So they broke open the doors and entered the salon, where they saw a large wooden cabinet and heard men within groaning for hunger and thirst. Then said one of them, "Is there a Jinni in this cabinet?" and his fellow, "Let us heap fuel about it and burn it with fire." When the Kazi heard this, he bawled out to them, "Do it not!" And they said to one another, "Verily the Jinn make believe to be mortals and speak with men's voices." Thereupon the Kazi repeated somewhat of the Sublime Koran and said to the neighbors, "Draw near to the cabinet wherein we are." So they drew near, and he said, "I am so and so the Kazi, and ye are such an one and such an one, and we are here a company." Quoth the neighbors, "Who brought you here?" And he told them the whole case from beginning to end. Then they fetched a carpenter, who opened the five doors and let out Kazi, Wazir, Wali, King and carpenter in their queer disguises; and each, when he saw how the others were accoutred, fell a-laughing at them.

Translated by Sir Richard Burton

THE PATH TO SAINTHOOD

The Fourth Tale of the Third Day
in *The Decameron* (1353)
by Giovanni Boccaccio
(1313–1375)

> *Friar Felipe shows his friend Puccio the path to sainthood*
> *by means of a certain penance; his friend Puccio performs*
> *the penance, and in this manner Friar Felipe diverts*
> *himself with his friend's wife.*

When Filomena had finished her story and Dioneo had praised her wit lavishly, the Queen smilingly glanced at Pánfilo, and said:

"And now Pánfilo will entertain our ears with a delightful story."

He quickly responded that he would be pleased to do so, and expressed himself in the following manner:

"There are many people, my lady, who, while they make great efforts to get to paradise, take their neighbors there as well: this is precisely what happened to a neighbor of ours not long ago, as you will hear.

"I have heard that near San Pancracio there lived a good and wealthy man named Puccio de Rinieri who, having devoted himself completely to prayer, became a tertiary of San Francisco, and thus became known as Brother Puccio; since he had no one to provide for but his wife and a maid, and since he had no need to work, he attended church a great deal. Being ingenuous and good-hearted, he said his prayers faithfully, attended daily mass, fasted frequently, and subjugated his body to the spirit; there were even rumors that he was one of those who flagellate themselves.

"His wife, whose name was Isabetta, was a young woman of twenty-eight or thirty years of age, sprightly and plump as an apple; it was not known if because of her husband's sanctity or because of his old age she fasted and abstained, frequently longer than she would have liked; and when she wanted to partake of the fruits of matrimony, her husband would lecture her on the life of Christ, or Friar Anastasio's sermons, or of Mary Magdalene's laments, and of other things of this manner.

"About that time, a young and handsome Franciscan monk named

Friar Felipe returned to San Pancracio from Paris. This young priest, who was of quick wit and very knowledgeable, soon struck up a close friendship with Brother Puccio.

"Since the saintly Friar Felipe resolved his religious doubts, Brother Puccio occasionally invited him to lunch or dinner, according to whatever time it was; for her part and out of love for Brother Puccio, Isabetta befriended Friar Felipe as well. The monk thus visited Brother Puccio's home from time to time, and upon noticing the wife's plump sprightliness, he determined what it was that he himself was in need of; in order to save Brother Puccio some strenuous efforts, he concluded that he should take his place. And glancing at her intently, at length he planted in her mind the seed that had taken root in his; when he noticed that he had accomplished this, he did all he could to please her. Yet, although she was favorably disposed to his desires, there seemed no way to satisfy them, for Isabetta could not risk being seen with the monk, and Brother Puccio was always at home; all this upset Friar Felipe very much. After great and extensive deliberation, he devised a plan by which he could be with her in her own home without arousing Brother Puccio's suspicions.

"One day, when Brother Puccio was visiting him, the monk said to him: 'I have noted, Brother Puccio, that your great desire is to become a saint and although the path you have chosen will take you to that end, there is another path which is much shorter; it is this path that the Pope and his prelates use, but they do not want it made public lest the priesthood, which lives on charity, disappear, since the laity would have no need to donate anything. But since you are my friend and have given me a great deal, and since I believe that you would never tell anyone about it, I will reveal to you the path to sainthood.'

"Brother Puccio, burning with desire to know this, begged him to reveal the path to him and, swearing never to breathe a word to anyone, vowed to take the path, if indeed he could follow it.

" 'Since you promise so solemnly,' said the monk, 'I will reveal it to you. You must know that the Church Fathers unanimously agree that anyone who aspires to sainthood should do the penance you are about to hear, but listen carefully: I do not say that after you have done the penance you will not sin again, but that all the sins you have committed up to the hour of penance will be absolved; and, further, that the sins you commit afterward will not damn you, but, on the contrary, will be washed away with holy water, just as is done with venial sins. It is to your advantage, then, to carefully consider your sins before you begin your penance; and then you must endure a rigorous fast and abstinence for forty days, during which you must refrain from touching the flesh of woman, either your own wife or that of another.

" 'Further, it is to your advantage to have in your home some place from which you can see the sky at night; and at the hour of evening prayer go to that retreat, where you should have a wide and large table upon which you can lie, with your feet on the floor, and with your arms out-stretched on pegs in the position of crucifixion; there you must remain immobile until dawn. If you could read, I would teach you special prayers, but since you cannot read, you must pray three hundred Our Fathers and three hundred Hail Marys in reverence to the Trinity; and, while looking at the sky, think about the Passion of Christ and remember that you are in the same position as he was on the Cross. Then, when the bells ring for morning prayers, if you wish you may go to bed, but fully dressed; next morning you must go to church and hear at least three masses, say fifty Our Fathers and a like number of Hail Marys, and then you may conduct your daily business, if you have any; then eat and return to church, where you must recite special and indispensable prayers, which I will teach you. When it is time for evening prayers, you must begin again. Having done this, at the end of your penance you will have experienced the marvelous effects of sanctity, even as I have done, provided you have walked the path with complete devotion.'

"Then Brother Puccio said: 'The path is neither so difficult nor so long,' and after receiving the monk's authorization, he made the necessary preparations and told his wife.

"She understood clearly the implications of the penance and, considering the plan well conceived, she told Brother Puccio that she approved of this and all the other good deeds he was doing to save his soul, and that she would help him in any way she could.

"The following Sunday, Brother Puccio began his penance, and the monk, having reached agreement with Isabetta, came to dinner every evening under cover of dark; there he dined and wined, and bedded until the bells rang for morning prayers, at which time he arose and Brother Puccio returned to his bed.

"It happened that the place Brother Puccio chose for his retreat was the room next to the bedroom, and the two rooms were separated by a thin wall. Since Friar Felipe and Isabetta made considerable movement and noise, Brother Puccio thought he felt the floor tremble and, having completed one hundred Our Fathers, he paused and called to his wife, asking what she was doing.

"The wife, who was of a playful nature, replied: 'But my love, I am stirring as much as I possibly can.'

" 'Stirring?' asked Puccio. 'What does all this stirring mean?'

"Laughing, the lady, who was a woman of wit with good reason to laugh, answered: 'But my love, how can you not know what this means. I have heard you say a thousand times: "He who does not sup from the pot during the day will stir at night." '

"Brother Puccio thus believed that she stirred because she had fasted and, full of good faith, responded: 'I told you, my dear, not to fast, but since you insisted, now you must try not to think of it, and rest; you stir so much in bed that the whole house trembles.'

" 'Try not to think about it,' answered the wife. 'I know what I am about. I must find the path to paradise, even as you do.'

Thus Brother Puccio quieted down and returned to his prayers.

"From that night on, the Friar and Isabetta slept in another room, and when the Friar left, Isabetta returned to her bed where, soon after, Brother Puccio would join her. In this manner Brother Puccio continued his penance, and the monk and the wife their stirring. Often the wife remarked jokingly to the Friar:

" 'Brother Puccio does the penance and we get to paradise.'

"And, since the wife enjoyed the fasting and the stirring and became so accustomed to the repast offered by the monk, she found the means by which to enjoy the fruits he offered for a long time. And, in order that my closing remarks will not differ from my opening ones, I repeat that Brother Puccio walked the path to sainthood but his wife and the monk reached paradise."

Translated by Elvira Garcia

THE PARDONER'S EXEMPLUM
from *The Canterbury Tales*
by Geoffrey Chaucer
(1340?–1400)

"The Pardoner's Exemplum" is taken from what amounts to a standard medieval sermon on the evils of the tavern. It is important to note that, although it appears singly here, it is best understood in context. The Pardoner's tale is preceded by the Physician's tale, a woeful tale of suicide and attempted rape. The Host, Harry Bailey, has just called upon the Pardoner to change the tone by telling a tale of mirth and joy. Instead, the Pardoner, a religious con man, tells how he bilks the faithful with the following story.

Once upon a time in Flanders, there was a group of young men who practiced such debaucheries as wild parties and gambling, and who frequented whorehouses and taverns. Day and night, to the accompaniment of harps, lutes, and guitars, they danced and diced while eating and drinking more than was good for them. Thus, through these disgusting excesses, they did the work of the devil in the very temples of the devil. Their oaths were so great and so damnable that it was grim indeed to hear them curse. Our Blessed Lord's body they tore to shreds—they thought the Jews hadn't done it enough—and each of them laughed at the others' sins. And then, in order to make the fires of lechery, which is closely allied to gluttony, burn even higher, on would come the trim and shapely dancing girls, the girls selling fruit, the singers with their harps, the whores, and the candy vendors—all of whom are the very agents of the devil!

.   .   .

Three of these wastrels, then, were drinking very early one morning in a tavern. As they sat there, they heard a bell tolling as a corpse was being carried to its grave. One of them called to his young servant, "Hurry out there and find out whose corpse is passing by—and make sure you get his name right!"

"Sir," said the boy, "that's not necessary; I was told two hours before you came. As a matter of fact, he was an old friend of yours; he was killed suddenly last night as he sat dead drunk at his bench. A silent thief, whom men called Death and who kills all the people in this country, came and cut his heart in two with his spear and went on his way without a single word. He has slain a thousand during this plague; and, master, before you meet him, I think it would be advisable to be very careful with such a foe. My mother always taught me: Be ready to meet him at any time. I'll say no more."

"By Holy Mary!" said the innkeeper, "the child knows what he's talking about! I believe Death's home is in a good-sized village, not over a mile from here, because he has killed man, woman, child, servant, and page there this past year. You would be well advised to be very careful, lest he harm you."

"By God's arms!" the rascal said, "is it then so dangerous to meet him? By God's honorable bones! I promise to seek him out in the lanes and the streets! Listen, my friends, we three are as one! Let each of us hold out his hand to the others; let us all become brothers, and we will slay this false traitor, Death! He that slays so many shall himself be slain, by God's dignity, before night falls!"

Together, then, these three pledged to live and die for each other, as though they were all born brothers. Then up they jumped, all drunken in their rage, and went out toward that village of which the innkeeper had told them. They swore many a horrible oath and tore Christ's blessed body all apart. Death shall be dead!—if only they can catch him.

When they had gone about half a mile, just as they were about to climb over a stile, they met a poor old man, who with humble dignity greeted them, saying, "Good gentlemen, God be with you!"

The proudest of these three revelers replied, "Hey, you old yokel, why are you all wrapped up except for your face? Why have you lived so long and to such a great age?"

The old man looked him in the face and said, "Because I can find no one, neither in city nor village, even though I were to walk as far as India, who will trade his youth for my years. Therefore, I must keep my age for as long as it is God's will. Death, alas, will not take my life, and thus I walk like a restless prisoner, constantly knocking with my staff on the ground which is my mother's gate, saying, 'Dear mother, let me in! Look how my flesh and blood and skin waste away! Alas, when shall my bones find rest? Mother, I would exchange with you my strongbox, that I've kept for so long in my bedroom, for a shroud to wrap myself in!' But she will not grant me that favor, and that is why my face is so pale and withered.

"But, good gentlemen, it is most discourteous of you to speak harshly to an old man, unless he has offended you in word or deed. In the Good Book it is written: 'You should rise before an old man whose hairs are white upon his head.' Therefore, let me give you this advice: Do no more harm to an old man than you would want men to do to you in your old age—if you should live so long. And now, God be with you, wherever you walk or ride; I must go on wherever I am called."

"No, old man! By God, you won't leave yet," the second gambler replied at once. "You won't get away so lightly, by Saint John! You spoke just now of that traitor Death who is killing all our friends in this country. Since you are his spy, tell us where he is, or, I promise you by God and by the Holy Sacrament, you shall pay for it! It seems likely, you false thief, that you are one of those that wants to kill us young people."

"Now, gentlemen," he said, "if you are so eager to find Death, turn up this crooked path; by my faith, I left him in that grove there under a tree, and there he will be waiting; your boasting won't make him hide at all. Do you see that oak tree? Just there you will find him. May the God that redeemed mankind save you—and improve you!"

When the old man finished speaking, the three revelers ran to the tree, and there they found what seemed to be nearly eight bushels of fine, round, golden florins. Then they no longer searched for Death, but, being entranced with the sight of the bright shiny coins, they sat down beside the precious hoard.

The worst of the three was the first to speak. "Brothers," he said, "though I often joke and play the fool, I've got some common sense—so listen to me. Fortune has given us this treasure so that we can lead our lives in joy and merriment. And since it came easily, that's the way we'll spend it. By God's precious dignity! Who would have thought that we would have such good luck today!

"You realize that all this gold is ours. Now if only we can carry it from here to my house, or to yours, then we would be in great shape. But certainly we can't do that during the day. People would say we were great thieves and would hang us for our own treasure. This treasure must be moved by night as carefully and as quietly as possible. Therefore, I think we ought to draw straws and see who gets the short one; the one who does must run into town and secretly get us some bread and wine. The other two will carefully guard the treasure, and, if he isn't too late, when night comes we can carry this treasure to wherever we agree upon as the best place."

One of them held the straws in his fist and had the others draw to see who would get the short straw. It fell to the youngest of them, and he headed for the town at once.

But as soon as he was gone, one of the two said to the other, "You know perfectly well that you are my sworn brother; let me tell you something for your own good: Our companion is gone. Now here is this great pile of gold, to be divided among the three of us. But if I could arrange it so that it would be divided among just two of us, wouldn't I be doing you a good turn?"

"I don't know how you could do that," replied the other. "He knows perfectly well that the gold is here with the two of us. What would we do? What would we say to him?"

"If you can keep a secret," said the first rascal, "I'll tell you briefly what we can do to bring it off."

"I agree," said the other. "I give you my word I won't betray you."

"Now," said the first, "you realize that there are two of us—and two are stronger than one! When he sits down, then right away you get up as though you were going to wrestle with him; and while you are wrestling with him in fun, I'll run him through from side to side and you do the same with your dagger. Then, my dear friend, all this gold will be divided between you and me, and we can satisfy all our desires and play at dice whenever we want." Thus it was that these two rascals agreed to murder the third.

Meanwhile, the youngest, who had gone to the town, was turning over and over in his mind the beauty of the bright new florins. "Oh Lord," he said, "if only I could have this treasure all to myself, there would be nobody under God's heaven that would lead as gay a life as I would." Then the Devil, who found the young man's way of life such that he had God's permission to bring him low, put into his mind the idea of buying poison in order to kill his two companions. He was completely determined to murder them both and never to repent. He didn't wait a moment longer but went to a druggist in the town and begged him to sell him some poison so that he could put down his rats; he also claimed that there was a weasel in his yard which had slain his chickens, and he wanted to get revenge, if he could, on the vermin that bothered him at night.

The druggist replied, "God save my soul, I've got just the thing. Any creature in the whole world that eats or drinks of this mixture, even if he takes no more than a piece the size of a grain of wheat, will quickly die.

This poison is so strong and so violent, that he will die in less time than it takes to walk a mile."

The young rascal grabbed the box of poison in his hand and ran into the next street and there borrowed three large bottles from a man. In two of these he poured his poison, while he kept the third clean for his own drink. He planned to spend all night in hard labor carrying out the gold. And when he had filled his three large bottles with wine he returned to his companions.

What need is there to talk about it any more? The two killed him just as they had planned it out. And when that was over, one of them said, "Let's sit down, have a drink, and enjoy ourselves; we can bury his body later." And as he spoke, he took up one of the bottles with the poison and had a drink and gave it to his companion to drink from—and soon they both fell dead.

Translated by Gordon Bergquist

THE TWO ROGUES
An Elizabethan Tale
(*ca.* 1567)
by Thomas Harman

There was not long since two rogues that always did associate themselves together and would never separate themselves unless it were for some especial causes, for they were sworn brothers, and they were both of one age and much like of favor. These two traveling into East Kent reported unto an alehouse, being wearied with traveling, saluting with short courtesy when they came into the house such as they saw sitting there, in which company was the parson of the parish, and calling for a pot of the best ale sat down at the table's end. The liquor liked them so well that they had pot upon pot, and sometimes for a little good manner would drink and offer the cup to such as they best fancied and, to be short, they sat out all the company, for each man departed home about their business.

When they had well refreshed themselves, then these rousy rogues requested the good man of the house with his wife to sit down and drink with them, of whom they inquired what priest the same was and where he dwelt. Then they feigning that they had an uncle a priest, and that he should dwell in these parts, which by all presumptions it should be he, and that they came of purpose to speak with him, but because they had not seen him since they were six years old, they durst not be bold to take acquaintance of him until they were farther instructed of the truth, and began to inquire of his name and how long he had dwelt there, and how far his house was off from the place they were in, the goodwife of the house, thinking them honest men without deceit, because they so far inquired of their kinsman, was but of a good zealous natural intent, showed them cheerfully that he was an honest man and well beloved in the parish and of good wealth, and had been there resident fifteen years at the least.

"But," saith she, "are you brothers?"

"Yea, surely," said they, "we have been both in one belly and were twins."

"Mercy God!" quoth this foolish woman, "it may well be, for ye be not much unlike," and went unto her hall window calling these young men unto her, and looking out pointed with her finger and showed them the house standing alone, no house near the same by almost a quarter of a mile.

"That," said she, "is your uncle's house."

"Nay," saith one of them, "he is not only my uncle but also my godfather."

"It may well be," quoth she. "Nature will bind him to be the better unto you."

"Well," quoth they, "we be weary and mean not to trouble our uncle tonight, but tomorrow, God willing, we will see him and do our duty. But, I pray you, doth our uncle occupy husbandry? What company hath he in his house?"

"Alas!" saith she, "but one old woman and a boy. He hath no occupying at all. Tush," quoth this goodwife, "you be madmen. Go to him this night, for he hath better lodging for you than I have, and yet I speak foolishly against mine own profit, for by your tarrying here I should gain the more by you."

"Now, by my troth," quoth one of them, "we thank you, good hostess, for your wholesome counsel, and we mean to do as you will us. We will pause a while and by that time it will be almost night, and I pray you give us a reckoning."

So mannerly paying for that they took, bade their host and hostess farewell with taking leave of the cup, marched merely out of the doors toward this parson's house, viewed the same well round about, and passed by two bowshots off into a young wood where they lay consulting what they should do until midnight.

Quoth one of them, of sharper wit and subtler than the other, to his fellow: "Thou seest that this house is stone walled about, and that we cannot well break in, in any part thereof. Thou seest also that the windows be thick of mullions, that there is no creeping in between, wherefore we must of necessity use some policy when strength will not serve. I have a horse lock here about me," saith he, "and this I hope shall serve our turn."

So when it was about twelve of the clock, they came to the house and lurked near unto his chamber window. The dog of the house barked that with the noise this priest waketh out of his sleep and began to cough and hem. Then one of these rogues steps forth nearer the window and maketh a rueful and pitiful noise, requiring for Christ's sake some relief that was both hungry and thirsty and was like to lie without the doors all night and die for cold, unless he were relieved by him with some small piece of money.

"Where dwellest thou?" quoth this parson.

"Alas, sir," saith this rogue, "I have small dwelling, and have come out of my way, and I should now," saith he, "go to any town now at this time of night, they would set me in the stocks and punish me."

"Well, well," quoth this pitiful parson, "away from my house. Either lie in some of my outhouses until the morning, and hold, here is a couple of pence for thee."

"A God reward you," quoth this rogue, "and in Heaven may you find it."

The parson opened his window and thrusteth out his arm to give his alms to this rogue that came whining to receive it, and quickly taketh hold of his hand and calleth his fellow to him, which was ready at hand with the horse lock and clappeth the same about the wrist of his arm that the mullions standing so close together for strength, that for his life he could not pluck in his arm again, and made him believe, unless he would at the least give him three pounds, they would smite off his arm from the body, so that this poor parson in fear to lose his hand, called up his old woman that lay in the loft over him, and willed her to take out all the money he had, which was four marks, which he said was all the money in his house, for he had lent six pounds to one of his neighbors not four days before.

"Well," quoth they, "master parson, if you have no more, upon this condition we will take off the lock that you will drink twelve pence for our sakes tomorrow at the alehouse where we found you and thank the good-wife for the good cheer she made us."

He promised faithfully that he would do so, so they took off the lock and went their way so far ere it was day that the parson could never have any understanding more of them. Now this parson sorrowfully slumbering that night between fear and hope, though it was but folly to make two sorrows of one, he used contentation for his remedy, not forgetting in the morning to perform his promise, but went betimes to his neighbor that kept tippling, and asked angrily where the same two men were that drank with her yesterday.

"Which two men?" quoth this goodwife.

"The strangers that came in when I was at your house with my neighbors yesterday."

"What! Your nephews?" quoth she.

"My nephews?" quoth this parson. "I trow thou art mad."

"Nay, by God," quoth this wife, "as sober as you, for they told me faithfully that you were their uncle, but, in faith, are you not so indeed, for, by my troth, they are strangers to me? I never saw them before."

"Oh, out upon them!" quoth the parson, "they be false thieves, and this night they compelled me to give them all the money in my house."

"*Benedicite!*" quoth this goodwife, "and have they so indeed? As I shall answer before God, one of them told me besides that you were godfather to him and that he trusted to have your blessing before he departed."

"What! did he?" quoth this parson. "A halter bless him for me!"

"Methinketh, by the Mass, by your countenance you looked so wildly when you came in," quoth this goodwife, "that something was amiss."

"I use not to jest," quoth this parson, "when I speak so earnestly."

"Why, all your sorrows go with it," quoth this goodwife, "and sit down here and I will fill a fresh pot of ale to make you merry again."

"Yea," saith this parson, "fill in and give me some meat, for they made me swear and promise them faithfully that I should drink twelve-pence with you this day."

"What! did they?" quoth she. "Now, by the marry Mass, they be merry knaves! I warrant you they mean to buy no land with your money. But how could they come unto you in the night, your doors being shut fast? Your house is very strong."

Then this parson showed her all the whole circumstance how he gave them his alms out at the window, they made such lamentable cry that it pitied him to the heart, for he saw but one when he put out his hand at the window.

"Be ruled by me," quoth this goodwife.

"Wherein?" quoth this parson.

"Ever by my troth speak no more of it. When they shall understand of it in the parish, they will but laugh you to scorn."

"Why, then," quoth this parson, "the devil go with it, and there an end!"

THE WINDMILL EPISODE

A Picaresque Tale
from *Don Quixote de la Mancha*
by Miguel de Cervantes Saavedra
(1547–1616)

Concerning the success enjoyed by the gallant knight Don Quixote in the incredible adventure of the windmills, and other episodes worthy of note.

At that time they came upon thirty or forty windmills which are common in that land, and as Don Quixote saw them, he said to his squire, "Luck is guiding our fortunes far better than we could ever desire because, as thou seest there, dear Sancho Panza, there are thirty or more angry giants whom I shall engage in combat and kill, and with whose possessions we shall become rich; this is a holy battle, and it is a service to God to eliminate such bad seeds from the face of the earth."

"What giants?" asked Sancho Panza.

"Those thou seest over there," answered his master, "with long arms, some as long as two leagues."

"Look, your grace, those are not giants, but windmills, and what appear to be arms are the sails of the windmill, which—when turned by the wind—make the mill's stone move."

"It seems," answered Don Quixote, "that thou art little versed in the subtleties of adventure; they are giants, and if thou art afraid, leave the battle area and pray, while I begin a fearful battle against horrendous odds."

And saying this, he spurred his horse Rocinante, heedless of the admonitions of his squire Sancho, who warned him repeatedly that doubtless they were windmills and not giants. But, so convinced was he that they were giants, that he did not even hear his squire's voice, and did not realize what the windmills were even when he was very close to them, saying aloud, "Do not flee, ye vile and cowardly creatures, for it is only one gallant knight alone who challenges ye."

At this moment a breeze began to blow and the large sails began to move. Seeing this, Don Quixote said:

"Even if ye move more arms than those of the giant Briareus, ye will pay for this."

And saying this, while entrusting his soul to his Lady Dulcinea and asking her support amidst such dangers, and well protected by his round shield with his lance on its rest, atop the galloping Rocinante he attacked the first windmill; as he struck its sail with his lance, the wind turned the sail with such fury that it broke the lance to pieces, knocking the horse and knight to the ground. Sancho Panza rushed to his aid as fast as his donkey could carry him, but such was the blow that Don Quixote had received that he was unable to move.

"Lord in heaven," said Sancho, "did I not warn your grace what he was doing, that these were only windmills, and that one could only ignore that fact if some wild and fanciful idea entered one's head?"

"Hush, my dear Sancho," answered Don Quixote, "the affairs of warfare are subject to continual change, more so than any other thing; the more I think of it, and this is doubtless the truth, the wicked and cunning magician Frestón, who invaded my quarters and stole my books, transformed these giants into windmills in order to deprive me of the glory of defeating them in combat, such is his hatred for me; but, ultimately, his evil arts can have little effect against the goodness of my sword."

"God's will be done," answered Sancho Panza. And with Sancho's assistance Don Quixote again mounted Rocinante, who was half sway-backed. And discussing their latest adventure, they continued on the road to the Port of Lápice, sure to find there many and varied adventures, since Lápice was a busy port. But Quixote was saddened by the loss of his lance, and discussing this with his squire he said:

"I remember reading of a Spanish knight named Diego Perez de Vargas who, having had his sword broken in battle, tore a heavy branch from a huge oak tree and performed such awesome feats that day and crushed so many Moors that he got the nickname of Machuca [Crusher], and henceforward he and his descendants were called Vargas y Machuca, I tell thee this because I am planning to break off a similar branch from the first oak tree that I see, and with it I am going to perform such great deeds that thou shalt count thyself fortunate to have seen them and to be a witness to events of such incredible magnitude."

"May God be with you," said Sancho. "I believe it exactly as your grace describes it; but straighten out a little, for you are tilting sideways. It must be the effects of the fall your grace suffered of late."

"That is true," answered Don Quixote, "and if I do not complain it is because knights are not permitted to complain of any wound, even if one's entrails were to fall from it."

"If that is true, I have nothing to say," answered Sancho, "but God knows I would rest more easily if your grace would complain when something hurts him. As far as I am concerned, I am going to complain at the least pain I might suffer, unless that business about not complaining applies to squires as well!"

Don Quixote could not help but laugh at his squire's simpleness; and so he declared to him that he could complain whenever and however he chose; for he had never read otherwise in the code of chivalry. Then Sancho told him that it was time to eat. His master answered that he did not yet feel like eating, but that he himself could do so whenever he chose. With this permission, Sancho made himself as comfortable as he could on his donkey, and eating from his knapsack, he trailed behind his master. At intervals he would raise his wineskin with such pleasure that the most cultured keeper of the lowliest inn in Malaga could have envied him. And while he sipped his wine thus, he did not remember any commitments made by his master, nor did he consider the search for adventures a chore but a diversion, regardless of their danger.

In conclusion, they spent that night in a forest, and from a tree Don Quixote tore a dry branch that would serve him as a lance, and on it he put the remaining piece of metal from the broken one. That night Don Quixote did not sleep the whole night, thinking of his Lady Dulcinea, in accord with what he had read in his books, where knights spent many sleepless nights in forests and deserts, entertained only by thoughts of their ladies. Sancho Panza did not pass his evening in like manner, for he had a stomach filled not with chicory water; he slept deeply, and neither the sun upon his face nor the songs of morning birds, joyfully greeting the morning, could awaken him. So his master did. Upon awakening, he reached for his wineskin, which he found slightly slimmer than the night before, much to his dismay, for he saw no way that this deficiency could soon be remedied. Don Quixote did not want breakfast either, since—as it was mentioned earlier—he sustained himself on sweet memories. They resumed their interrupted trip to the Port of Lápice, arriving there at three in the afternoon.

Upon seeing the town, Don Quixote said, "Here, brother Sancho Panza, we can plunge our arms up to the elbows in what is called adventure. But be cautioned that thou must never take up thy sword to assist me, no matter the danger, unless against gross people, in which case thou mayst well help me; for it is written in the laws of chivalry that only a knight may engage another knight in combat."

"Naturally, master," answered Sancho, "your grace will be obeyed in this as in all things; and, besides, I am a pacifist and an enemy of disputes and quarrels. Of course, if it comes to defending myself I shall take those laws into little account, for both divine and human laws allow one to defend oneself against whomever might want to wrong one."

"I agree," answered Don Quixote, "but in helping me against knights thou must keep in check thy natural instinct."

"So I shall," answered Sancho, "just as I observe the holiness of Sunday."

While they were talking, two monks from San Benito appeared on the road upon two steeds of the size of mules. The monks wore sunshades and shaded themselves with umbrellas. Some distance behind them was a coach accompanied by four or five horsemen and two grooms on foot. As it was learned later, in the coach was a lady from Biscay on her way to Seville to join her husband, who had recently been commissioned to the Indias on a very important assignment. The monks were not in her party, although they were on the same road. But as soon as Don Quixote espied them, he said to his squire:

"Either I am mistaken or this will be the most fabulous adventure ever seen; because those black hulks over there doubtless are enchanters who have kidnapped and detain a princess in that coach, and it is imperative to undo this wrong with all my power."

"This will be worse than the windmills," said Sancho. "Your grace, those are monks from San Benito, and the coach must belong to travelers. Consider well before you act so that the devil does not mislead you."

"I have already told thee, Sancho," answered Don Quixote, "that thou knowest very little about the matter of adventures; what I say is the truth and now thou shalt see."

And saying this, he advanced and stood in the middle of the road, blocking the path of the monks, and when they came close enough to hear him, he pronounced loudly:

"Ye diabolical and gigantic beings, release at once the princess ye detain by force in that coach, or prepare for an early death as a just punishment for your misdeeds."

The monks reined in their mounts, astonished at Don Quixote's appearance and statements, to which they answered:

"Sir knight, we are neither demons nor giants, but two simple monks from San Benito about their own business, and we do not know whether or not there are kidnapped princesses in the coach which follows us."

"No trickery or excuses, for I already know ye well, ye treacherous scoundrels," said Don Quixote.

And without waiting for a response, he spurred Rocinante, and with his lance held low he attacked the first monk with such fury that if the monk had not let himself fall from the mule, he would have fallen unwillingly and been badly wounded if not dead. The second monk, who saw the way his comrade was being treated, furiously spurred his mule, who began to run through the field faster than the wind.

Sancho Panza, seeing the fallen monk, dismounted and began to attack him, taking off his religious garments. At this moment, two of the monk's servants arrived and asked him why he was undressing him. Sancho answered that these were his legitimate spoils of war from the great victory that his master Don Quixote had won. The servants, who did not enjoy mockery and who knew nothing of the spoils of war, and seeing that Don Quixote was then talking to the travelers accompanying the coach, attacked Sancho and knocked him down, leaving him breathless and unconscious on the ground. Seizing his opportunity, the monk hastily mounted his steed and, fearful, intimidated, and pale, sped off toward his comrade, who was waiting a short distance away to see the outcome of the affair; and so they continued their journey, crossing themselves repeatedly, as if the devil himself were following them.

Meanwhile, Don Quixote was addressing the lady in the carriage, saying:

"My gracious lady, your person may now go where you wish; the arrogance of your kidnappers lies vanquished on the ground, a victim of the strength of this arm. So that you will not be kept in suspense as to the identity of your liberator, be it known that my name is Don Quixote, Man of la Mancha, knight and adventurer, and prisoner only of the Lady Dulcinea of Toboso; as payment for the service I have rendered, I ask only that you return to Toboso to tell my lady who has liberated you."

All of this was overheard by a squire from Biscay who accompanied the carriage, seeing not only that Don Quixote would not permit the coach to pass, but that he also spoke of a return to Toboso, the squire approached Don Quixote and, grabbing his lance, told him in a base dialect:

"Get out of here, O horseman, as bad a shape as you're in; by the God who created me, you're as good as dead if you don't let that coach pass by or I'm not from Biscay."

Don Quixote understood him very well, and with great calm answered:

"If thou wert a gentleman or a knight, as obviously thou art not, I would already have punished thy folly and boldness, thou captured creature."

"Me not a gentleman? I swear to God as a Christian that you're lying. Put down your lance and sword and you'll take to me like a cat to water. I'm a Biscayan, noble on sea or land by the devil, and you're lyin' if you say different."

"As the grammarian Agrajes said," answered Don Quixote, " 'Now thou shalt learn.' "

And, throwing his lance aside and taking up his sword and shield, he attacked the squire, determined to take his life. When the squire saw him come forward, he could do nothing other than take up his own sword, not even able to dismount from his unpredictable and mulish mount, which was not a trustworthy steed for such combat, being but a lowly and untrained beast. Fortunately for the squire, he was near the coach, from which he took a large cushion to use as a shield, and the two warriors engaged in mortal combat. The others attempted to separate them, but the squire raged that if they did not let him finish the battle, he himself would kill his lady and anyone else who got in his way. The lady, awed and afraid at the spectacle, had her driver move the carriage a short distance away, from where she watched the rigorous battle, during which the squire slashed over the shield and wounded Don Quixote on the shoulder, a blow so terrible that it would have sliced Don Quixote to the waist if he had not been otherwise protected. Don Quixote, feeling the pain of that outrageous blow, wailed loudly:

"Oh my Lady Dulcinea, mistress of my heart, flower of beauty, come to the aid of this your poor knight who is in this critical moment only to satisfy your goodness!"

Saying this, he raised his sword and shield and assaulted the squire, risking all on a single strike.

The squire quickly saw both his courage and strategy, and decided to do the same as Don Quixote; and thus he prepared himself for the assault, protected by his cushion and unable to make his mount move here or there; in truth, the mule, unused to such adventures, was simply too exhausted to move. Don Quixote, as it was said, advanced against the squire with his sword raised high, determined to open up his middle; the squire raised his sword high as well, and shielded himself with his pillow, while fearful spectators awaited the fury of the imminent blows. Meanwhile, the lady in the carriage, together with her maids, was offering a thousand prayers to all the saints in heaven for God's deliverance from the great danger they were in.

The unfortunate thing about all of this is that at this point the original recorder of this tale leaves the battle pending, explaining that he could find no further record of the exploits of Don Quixote than what has just been narrated. It is true that the present author could hardly believe that such an intriguing story could be forgotten, or that the people of La Mancha were so little inquisitive that they would not have in their files or records additional papers treating of this famous knight; with this in mind, he did not despair of determining the outcome of this pleasant story, and with the help of heaven he discovered that outcome in a manner to be revealed in the next chapter.

Translated by Elvira Garcia

VANITY FAIR
from *Pilgrim's Progress*
by John Bunyan
(1628–88)

Pilgrim's Progress *is John Bunyan's allegory of man's journey through a life of lust, deceit, greed, and temptation of every order. Only by transcending the material world and the body can man reach heaven, the Celestial City.*

Then I saw in my dream that when they were got out of the wilderness, they presently saw a town before them, and the name of that town is Vanity; and at the town there is a fair kept, called Vanity Fair: it is kept all the year long; it beareth the name of Vanity Fair, because the town where it is kept is lighter than vanity; and also because all that is there sold, or that cometh thither, is vanity. As is the saying of the wise, "all that cometh is vanity."

This fair is no new-erected business, but a thing of ancient standing; I will show you the original of it.

Almost five thousand years ago there were pilgrims walking to the Celestial City, as these two honest persons are, and Beelzebub, Apollyon, and Legion, with their companions, perceiving by the path that the pilgrims made that their way to the city lay through this town of Vanity, they contrived here to set up a fair; a fair wherein should be sold all sorts of vanity, and that it should last all the year long: therefore at this fair are all such merchandise sold, as houses, lands, trades, places, honors, preferments, titles, countries, kingdoms, lusts, pleasures, and delights of all sorts, as whores, bawds, wives, husbands, children, masters, servants, lives, blood, bodies, souls, silver, gold, pearls, precious stones, and what not.

And, moreover, at this fair there are at all times to be seen jugglings, cheats, games, plays, fools, apes, knaves, and rogues, and that of every kind.

Here are to be seen too, and that for nothing, thefts, murders, adulteries, false swearers, and that of a blood-red color.

And as in other fairs of less moment there are the several rows and streets under their proper names, where such and such wares are vended;

so here likewise you have the proper places, rows, streets (viz. countries and kingdoms), where the wares of this fair are soonest to be found. Here is the Britain Row, the French Row, the Italian Row, the Spanish Row, the German Row, where several sorts of vanities are to be sold. But as in other fairs some one commodity is as the chief of all the fair, so the ware of Rome and her merchandise is greatly promoted in this fair; only our English nation, with some others, have taken a dislike thereat.

Now, as I said, the way to the Celestial City lies just through this town where this lusty fair is kept; and he that will go to the city, and yet not go through this town, must needs "go out of the world." The Prince of princes Himself, when here, went through this town to His own country, and that upon a fair day too; yea, and as I think, it was Beelzebub, the chief lord of this fair, that invited Him to buy of his vanities; yea, would have made Him lord of the fair, would He but have done him reverence as He went through the town. Yea, because He was such a person of honor, Beelzebub had Him from street to street, and showed Him all the kingdoms of the world in a little time, that he might, if possible, allure the Blessed One to cheapen and buy some of his vanities; but He had no mind to the merchandise, and therefore left the town without laying out so much as one farthing upon these vanities. This fair therefore is an ancient thing, of long standing, and a very great fair. Now these pilgrims, as I said, must needs go through this fair. Well, so they did: but behold, even as they entered into the fair, all the people in the fair were moved, and the town itself as it were in a hubbub about them; and that for several reasons: for,

First, The pilgrims were clothed with such kind of raiment as was diverse from the raiment of any that traded in that fair. The people therefore of the fair made a great gazing upon them: some said they were fools, some they were bedlams, and some they are outlandish men.

Secondly, And as they wondered at their apparel, so they did likewise at their speech; for few could understand what they said; they naturally spoke the language of Canaan, but they that kept the fair were the men of this world; so that from one end of the fair to the other they seemed barbarians each to the other.

Thirdly, But that which did not a little amuse the merchandisers was that these pilgrims set very light by all their wares; they cared not so much as to look upon them; and if they called upon them to buy, they would put their fingers in their ears and cry, "Turn away mine eyes from beholding vanity," and look upward, signifying that their trade and traffic was in heaven.

One chanced mockingly, beholding the carriage of the men, to say unto them, What will ye buy? But they, looking gravely upon him, answered, "We buy the truth." At that there was an occasion taken to despise the men the more; some mocking, some taunting, some speaking reproachfully, and some calling upon others to smite them. At last things came to a hubbub and great stir in the fair, insomuch that all order was confounded. Now was word presently brought to the great one of the fair, who quickly came down and deputed some of his most trusty friends to take these men into examination, about whom the fair was almost overturned. So the men were brought to examination; and they that sat upon them asked them whence they came, whither they went, and what they did there in such an unusual garb? The men told them that they were pilgrims and strangers in the world, and that they were going to their own country, which was the heavenly Jerusalem, and that they had given no occasion to the men of the town, nor yet to the merchandisers, thus to abuse them, and to let them in their journey, except it was for that, when one asked them what they would buy, they said they would buy the truth. But they that were appointed to examine them did not believe them to be any other than bedlams and mad, or else such as came to put all things into a confusion in the fair. Therefore they took them and beat them, and besmeared them with dirt, and then put them into the cage, that they might be made a spectacle to all the men of the fair.

> Behold Vanity Fair! the pilgrims there
> Are chained and stoned beside;
> Even so it was our Lord passed here,
> And on Mount Calvary died.

There therefore they lay for some time and were made the objects of any man's sport, or malice, or revenge, the great one of the fair laughing still at all that befell them. But the men being patient and not rendering railing for railing, but contrariwise blessing, and giving good words for bad and kindness for injuries done, some men in the fair that were more observing and less prejudiced than the rest, began to check and blame the baser sort for their continual abuses done by them to the men; they therefore in angry manner let fly at them again, counting them as bad as the men in the cage, and telling them that they seemed confederates and should be made partakers of their misfortunes. The other replied that for aught they could see, the men were quiet, and sober, and intended nobody any harm; and that there were many that traded in their fair that were more worthy to be put into the cage, yea, and pillory too, than were the men they had abused. Thus after divers words had passed on both sides (the men behaving themselves all the while very wisely and soberly before them) they fell to some blows among themselves and did harm one to another. Then were these two poor men brought before their examiners again, and there charged as being guilty of the late hubbub that had been in the fair. So they beat them pitifully, and hanged irons upon them, and led them in chains up and down the fair, for an example and a terror to others, lest any should speak in their behalf or join themselves unto them. But Christian and Faithful behaved themselves yet more wisely, and received the ignominy and shame that was cast upon them with so much meekness and patience that it won to their side (though but few in comparison of the rest) several of the men in the fair. This put the other party yet into greater rage, insomuch that they concluded the death of these two men. Wherefore they threatened that neither cage nor irons should serve their turn, but that they should die for the abuse they had done and for deluding the men of the fair.

Then were they remanded to the cage again, until further order should be taken with them. So they put them in and made their feet fast in the stocks.

Here also they called again to mind what they had heard from their faithful friend Evangelist, and were the more confirmed in their way and sufferings by what he told them would happen to them. They also now comforted each other that whose lot it was to suffer, even he should have the best of it; therefore each man secretly wished that he might have that preferment: but committing themselves to the all-wise disposal of him that ruleth all things, with much content they abode in the condition in which they were, until they should be otherwise disposed of.

Then a convenient time being appointed, they brought them forth to their trial in order to their condemnation. When the time was come, they were brought before their enemies and arraigned. The judge's name was Lord Hategood. Their indictment was one and the same in substance, though somewhat varying in form; the contents whereof were this:

"That they were enemies to and disturbers of their trade; that they had made commotions and divisions in the town, and had won a party to their own most dangerous opinions, in contempt of the law of their prince."

> Now, Faithful, play the man, speak for thy God:
> Fear not the wickeds' malice; nor their rod!
> Speak boldly, man, the truth is on thy side:
> Die for it, and to life in triumph ride.

Then Faithful began to answer, that he had only set himself against that which hath set itself against Him that is higher than the highest. And, said he, as for disturbance, I make none, being myself a man of peace; the parties that were won to us were won by beholding our truth and innocence, and they are only turned from the worse to the better. And as to the king you talk of, since he is Beelzebub, the enemy of our Lord, I defy him and all his angels.

Then proclamation was made that they that had aught to say for their lord the king against the prisoner at the bar should forthwith appear and give in their evidence. So there came in three witnesses, to wit, Envy, Superstition, and Pickthank. They were then asked if they knew the prisoner at the bar, and what they had to say for their lord the king against him.

Then stood forth Envy and said to this effect: My Lord, I have known this man a long time, and will attest upon my oath before this honorable bench that he is—

JUDGE: Hold, give him his oath. (So they sware him.)

Then he said, My Lord, this man, notwithstanding his plausible name, is one of the vilest men in our country. He neither regardeth prince nor people, law nor custom; but doth all that he can to possess all men with certain of his disloyal notions, which he in the general calls principles of faith and holiness. And, in particular, I heard him once myself affirm that Christianity and the customs of our town of Vanity were diametrically opposite and could not be reconciled. By which saying, my Lord, he doth at once not only condemn all our laudable doings, but us in the doing of them.

JUDGE: Then did the judge say to him, Hast thou any more to say?

ENVY: My Lord, I could say much more, only I would not be tedious to the court. Yet, if need be, when the other gentlemen have given in their evidence, rather than anything shall be wanting that will dispatch him, I will enlarge my testimony against him. So he was bid to stand by.

Then they called Superstition, and bid him look upon the prisoner. They also asked what he could say for their lord the king against him. Then they sware him; so he began.

SUPER.: My Lord, I have no great acquaintance with this man, nor do I desire to have further knowledge of him; however, this I know, that he is a very pestilent fellow, from some discourse that the other day I had with him in this town; for then talking with him, I heard him say that our religion was naught, and such by which a man could by no means please God. Which sayings of his, my Lord, your Lordship very well knows what necessarily thence will follow, to wit, that we do still worship in vain, are yet in our sins, and finally shall be damned; and this is that which I have to say.

Then was Pickthank sworn and bid say what he knew in behalf of their lord and king against the prisoner at the bar.

PICK.: My Lord, and you gentleman all, this fellow I have known of a long time, and have heard him speak things that ought not to be spoke; for he hath railed on our noble prince Beelzebub, and hath spoken contemptibly of his honorable friends, whose names are the Lord Old Man, the Lord Carnal Delight, the Lord Luxurious, the Lord Desire of Vainglory, my old Lord Lechery, Sir Having Greedy, with all the rest of our nobility; and he hath said, moreover, that if all men were of his mind, if possible, there is not one of these noblemen should have any longer a being in this town. Besides, he hath not been afraid to rail on you, my Lord, who are now appointed to be his judge, calling you an ungodly villain, with many other such like vilifying terms, with which he hath bespattered most of the gentry of our town.

When this Pickthank had told his tale, the judge directed his speech to the prisoner at the bar, saying, Thou runagate, heretic, and traitor, hast thou heard what these honest gentlemen have witnessed against thee?

FAITH.: May I speak a few words in my own defense?

JUDGE: Sirrah, sirrah, thou deservest to live no longer, but to be slain immediately upon the place; yet that all men may see our gentleness toward thee, let us hear what thou, vile runagate, hast to say.

FAITH.: 1. I say then in answer to what Mr. Envy hath spoken, I never said aught but this, That what rule, or laws, or custom, or people, were flat against the Word of God, are diametrically opposite to Christianity. If I have said amiss in this, convince me of my error, and I am ready here before you to make my recantation.

2. As to the second, to wit, Mr. Superstition, and his charge against me, I said only this, That in the worship of God there is required a Divine faith; but there can be no Divine faith without a Divine revelation of the will of God. Therefore whatever is thrust into the worship of God that is not agreeable to Divine revelation cannot be done but by a human faith, which faith will not be profitable to eternal life.

3. As to what Mr. Pickthank hath said, I say (avoiding terms, as that I am said to rail and the like) that the prince of this town, with all the rabblement, his attendants, by this gentleman named, are more fit for a being in hell, than in this town and country: and so the Lord have mercy upon me!

Then the judge called to the jury (who all this while stood by, to hear and observe): Gentlemen of the jury, you see this man about whom so great an uproar hath been made in this town. You have also heard what these worthy gentlemen have witnessed against him. Also you have heard his reply and confession. It lieth now in your breasts to hang him or save his life; but yet I think meet to instruct you into our law.

There was an Act made in the days of Pharaoh the Great, servant to our prince, that lest those of a contrary religion should multiply and grow too strong for him, their males should be thrown into the river. There was also an Act made in the days of Nebuchadnezzar the Great, another of his servants, that whosoever would not fall down and worship his golden image should be thrown into a fiery furnace. There was also an Act made in the days of Darius, that whoso for some time called upon any god but him should be cast into the lions' den. Now the substance of these laws this rebel has broken, not only in thought (which is not to be borne), but also in word and deed; which must therefore needs be intolerable.

For that of Pharaoh, his law was made upon a supposition, to prevent mischief, no crime being yet apparent; but here is a crime apparent. For the second and third, you see he disputeth against our religion; and for the treason he hath confessed, he deserveth to die the death.

Then went the jury out, whose names were, Mr. Blind-man, Mr. No-good, Mr. Malice, Mr. Love-lust, Mr. Live-loose, Mr. Heady, Mr. High-mind, Mr. Enmity, Mr. Liar, Mr. Cruelty, Mr. Hate-light, and Mr. Implacable; who every one gave in his private verdict against him among themselves, and afterward unanimously concluded to bring him in guilty before the judge. And first, among themselves, Mr. Blind-man, the foreman, said, I see clearly that this man is a heretic. Then said Mr. No-good, Away with such a fellow from the earth. Ay, said Mr. Malice, for I hate the very looks of him. Then said Mr. Love-lust, I could never endure him. Nor I, said Mr. Live-loose, for he would always be condemning my way. Hang him, hang him, said Mr. Heady. A sorry scrub, said Mr. High-mind. My heart riseth against him, said Mr. Enmity. He is a rogue, said Mr. Liar. Hanging is too good for him, said Mr. Cruelty. Let us dispatch him out of the way, said Mr. Hate-light. Then said Mr. Implacable, Might I have all the world given me, I could not be reconciled to him; therefore let us forthwith bring him in guilty of death. And so they did; therefore he was presently condemned to be had from the place where he was, to the place from whence he came, and there to be put to the most cruel death that could be invented.

They therefore brought him out, to do with him according to their law; and first they scourged him, then they buffeted him, then they lanced his flesh with knives; after that they stoned him with stones, then pricked him with their swords; and last of all they burned him to ashes at the stake. Thus came Faithful to his end. Now I saw that there stood behind the multitude a chariot and a couple of horses, waiting for Faithful, who (so soon as his adversaries had dispatched him) was taken up into it, and straightway was carried up through the clouds, with sound of trumpet, the nearest way to the Celestial Gate.

> Brave Faithful, bravely done in word and deed;
> Judge, witnesses, and jury have, instead
> Of overcoming thee, but shown their rage;
> When they are dead, thou'lt live from age to age.

But as for Christian, he had some respite, and was remanded back to prison. So he there remained for a space; but He that overrules all things, having the power of their rage in His own hand, so wrought it about that Christian for that time escaped them and went his way; and as he went he sang, saying,

> Well, Faithful, thou hast faithfully professed
> Unto thy Lord; with whom thou shalt be blest,
> When faithless ones, with all their vain delights,
> Are crying out under their hellish plights,
> Sing, Faithful, sing, and let thy name survive;
> For though they killed thee, thou are yet alive.

Now I saw in my dream that Christian went not forth alone, for there was one whose name was Hopeful (being made so by the beholding of Christian and Faithful in their words and behavior, in their sufferings at the fair), who joined himself unto him, and entering into a brotherly covenant, told him that he would be his companion. Thus one died to bear testimony to the truth, and another rises out of his ashes to be a companion with Christian in his pilgrimage. This Hopeful also told Christian that there were many more of the men in the fair, that would take their time and follow after.

FROM THE SPECTATOR

Joseph Addison and Richard Steele

(1711)

The following selection is from The Spectator, *a group of better than five hundred periodical essays written by Joseph Addison and Richard Steele in the early eighteenth century. One aim of these essays, as Addison himself says, was "to enliven morality with wit and to temper wit with morality"; another aim was to convey to the reader, after the manner of Montaigne, the personal reflections of the author on whatever subject was uppermost in his mind, usually with the intention of enlightening the reader for his moral benefit. But the eighteenth-century idea of good manners prevented Addison and Steele from speaking to the reader in their own persons; hence, as a vehicle through which to convey their views on moral matters and contemporary manners, they created* a persona, *Mr. Spectator, much as Swift does in* Gulliver's Travels *(but admittedly for different reasons). The two authors, however, did not stop there. Using devices found in Plato's* Dialogues *and Theophrastus's* Characters, *Addison and Steele created a host of characters who exemplify their views and who are revealed through their speech and actions as well as by what Mr. Spectator says about them. As a result, the Spectator papers have a vividness and a dramatic quality about them rarely attained in the eighteenth-century periodical essay. In this the second number of* The Spectator, *Mr. Spectator introduces the reader to the members of the Spectator Club. The quote that immediately*

*precedes the selection is from the preceding paper and
describes very aptly the way Addison and Steele must have
conceived of their roles.*

Thus I live in the world, rather as a Spectator of Mankind,
than as one of the species; by which means I have made myself a speculative
statesman, soldier, merchant, and artizan, without ever meddling with any
practical part in life. I am very well versed in the theory of an husband, or a
father, and can discern the errors in the economy, business and diversion of
others, better than those who are engaged in them; as standers-by discover
blots, which are apt to escape those who are in the game. I never espoused
any party with violence, and am resolved to observe an exact neutrality between the Whigs and Tories, unless I shall be forced to declare myself by
the hostilities of either side. In short, I have acted in all the parts of my
life as a looker-on, which is the character I intend to preserve in this paper.

No. 2
[Steele.]   Friday, March 2.
————*Ast alii sex*
Vel plures uno conclamant ore.—Juvenal
    Satires, VII, 167.

The first of our society is a gentleman of Worcestershire, of ancient descent, a baronet, his name Sir ROGER DE COVERLEY. His great
grandfather was inventor of that famous country-dance which is called
after him. All who know that shire are very well acquainted with the parts
and merits of Sir ROGER. He is a gentleman that is very singular in his
behaviour, but his singularities proceed from his good sense, and are contradictions to the manners of the world, only as he thinks the world is in
the wrong. However, this humour creates him no enemies, for he does
nothing with sourness or obstinacy, and his being unconfined to modes and
forms, makes him but the readier and more capable to please and oblige
all who know him. When he is in town he lives in Soho Square: It is said,
he keeps himself a bachelor by reason he was crossed in love, by a perverse beautiful widow of the next county to him. Before this disappointment, Sir ROGER was what you call a fine gentleman, had often supped
with my Lord Rochester and Sir George Etherege, fought a duel upon his
first coming to town, and kicked Bully Dawson in a public coffee-house for
calling him youngster. But being ill used by the above-mentioned widow,
he was very serious for a year and a half; and though, his temper being
naturally jovial, he at last got over it, he grew careless of himself, and

never dressed afterwards; he continues to wear a coat and doublet of the same cut that were in fashion at the time of his repulse, which, in his merry humours, he tells us has been in and out twelve times since he first wore it. 'Tis said Sir ROGER grew humble in his desires after he had forgot this cruel beauty, insomuch that it is reported he has frequently offended in point of chastity with beggars and gypsies: but this is looked upon by his friends rather as matter of raillery than truth. He is now in his fifty-sixth year, cheerful, gay, and hearty, keeps a good house both in town and country; a great lover of mankind; but there is such a mirthful cast in his behaviour, that he is rather beloved than esteemed: His tenants grow rich, his servants look satisfied, all the young women profess love to him, and the young men are glad of his company. When he comes into a house he calls the servants by their names, and talks all the way up stairs to a visit. I must not omit that Sir ROGER is a Justice of the Quorum: that he fills the chair at a Quarter Session with great abilities, and three months ago gained universal applause by explaining a passage in the Game Act.

The gentleman next in esteem and authority among us, is another bachelor, who is a member of the Inner Temple; a man of great probity, wit, and understanding; but he has chosen his place of residence rather to obey the direction of an old humoursome father, than in pursuit of his own inclinations. He was placed there to study the laws of the land, and is the most learned of any of the house in those of the stage. Aristotle and Longinus are much better understood by him than Littleton or Coke. The father sends up every post questions relating to marriage-articles, leases, and tenures, in the neighbourhood; all which questions he agrees with an attorney to answer and take care of in the lump. He is studying the passions themselves, when he should be inquiring into the debates among men which arise from them. He knows the argument of each of the orations of Demosthenes and Tully, but not one Case in the Reports of our own Courts. No one ever took him for a fool, but none, except his intimate friends, know he has a great deal of wit. This turn makes him at once both disinterested and agreeable. As few of his thoughts are drawn from business, they are most of them fit for conversation. His taste of books is a little too just for the age he lives in; he has read all, but approves of very few. His familiarity with the customs, manners, actions, and writings of the ancients, makes him a very delicate observer of what occurs to him in the present world. He is an excellent critic, and the time of the play is his hour of business; exactly at five he passes through New Inn, crosses through Russell Court, and takes a turn at Will's till the play begins; he has his shoes rubbed and his periwig powdered at the barber's as you go into the Rose. It is for the good of the audience when he is at a play, for the actors have an ambition to please him.

The person of next consideration is Sir ANDREW FREEPORT, a merchant of great eminence in the city of London. A person of indefatigable industry, strong reason, and great experience. His notions of trade are noble and generous, and (as every rich man has usually some sly way of jesting, which would make no great figure were he not a rich man) he calls the Sea the British Common. He is acquainted with commerce in all its parts, and will tell you that it is a stupid and barbarous way to extend dominion by arms; for true power is to be got by arts and industry. He will often argue, that if this part of our trade were well cultivated, we should gain from one nation; and if another, from another. I have heard him prove, that diligence makes more lasting acquisitions than valour, and that sloth has ruined more nations than the sword. He abounds in several frugal maxims, among which the greatest favourite is, "A penny saved is a penny got." A general trader of good sense, is pleasanter company than a general scholar; and Sir ANDREW having a natural unaffected eloquence, the perspicuity of his discourse gives the same pleasure that wit would in another man. He has made his fortunes himself; and says that England may be richer than other kingdoms, by as plain methods as he himself is richer than other men; though at the same time I can say this of him, that there is not a point in the compass but blows home a ship in which he is an owner.

Next to Sir ANDREW in the clubroom sits Captain SENTRY, a gentleman of great courage, good understanding, but invincible modesty. He is one of those that deserve very well, but are very awkward at putting their talents within the observation of such as should take notice of them. He was some years a captain, and behaved himself with great gallantry in several engagements, and at several sieges; but having a small estate of his own, and being next heir to Sir ROGER, he has quitted a way of life in which no man can rise suitably to his merit, who is not something of a courtier as well as a soldier. I have heard him often lament, that in a profession where merit is placed in so conspicuous a view, impudence should get the better of modesty. When he has talked to this purpose I never heard him make a sour expression, but frankly confess that he left the world, because he was not fit for it. A strict honesty and an even regular behaviour, are in themselves obstacles to him that must press through crowds, who endeavour at the same end with himself, the favour of a commander. He will however in his way of talk excuse generals for not disposing according to men's desert, or inquiring into it: for, says he, that great man who has a mind to help me, has as many to break through to come at me, as I have to come at him. Therefore he will conclude that the man who would make a figure, especially in a military way, must get over all false modesty, and assist his patron against the importunity of other pretenders by a proper assurance in his own vindication. He says it is a civil cowardice to be backward in asserting what you ought to expect, as it is a military fear to be slow in attacking when it is your duty. With this candour does the gentleman speak of himself and others. The same frankness runs through all his conversation. The military part of his life has furnished him with many adventures, in the relation of which he is very agreeable to the company; for he is never overbearing, though accustomed to command men in the utmost degree below him; nor ever too obsequious, from an habit of obeying men highly above him.

But that our society may not appear a set of humourists unacquainted with the gallantries and pleasures of the age, we have among us the gallant WILL HONEYCOMB, a gentleman who according to his years should be in the decline of his life, but having ever been very careful of his person, and always had a very easy fortune, time has made but very little impression, either by wrinkles on his forehead or traces in his brain. His person is well turned, of a good height. He is very ready at that sort of discourse with which men usually entertain women. He has all his life dressed very well, and remembers habits as others do men. He can smile when one speaks to him, and laughs easily. He knows the history of every mode, and can inform you from which of the French king's wenches our wives and daughters had this manner of curling their hair, that way of placing their hoods; whose frailty was covered by such a sort of petticoat, and whose vanity to show her foot made that part of the dress so short in such a year. In a word all his conversation and knowledge has been in the female world. As other men of his age will take notice to you what such a minister said upon such and such an occasion, he will tell you when the Duke of Monmouth danced at court such a woman was then smitten, another was taken with him at the head of his troop in the Park. In all these important relations, he has ever about the same time received a kind glance or a blow of a fan from some celebrated beauty, mother of the present Lord Such-a-one. If you speak of a young commoner that said a lively thing in the House, he starts up, "He has good blood in his veins, Tom Mirabell begot him, the rogue cheated me in that affair; that young fellow's mother used me more like a dog than any woman I ever made advances to." This way of talking of his very much enlivens the conversation among us of a more sedate turn, and I find there is not one of the company, but my self, who rarely speak at all, but speaks of him as of that sort of man who is usually called a well-bred fine gentleman. To conclude his character, where women are not concerned, he is an honest worthy man.

I cannot tell whether I am to account him whom I am next to speak of as one of our company; for he visits us but seldom, but when he does it adds to every man else a new enjoyment of himself. He is a clergyman, a very philosophic man, of general learning, great sanctity of life, and the most exact good breeding. He has the misfortune to be of a very weak constitution, and consequently cannot accept of such cares and business as preferments in his function would oblige him to. He is therefore among divines what a chamber-counsellor is among lawyers. The probity of his mind, and the integrity of his life, create him followers, as being eloquent or loud advances others. He seldom introduces the subject he speaks upon; but we are so far gone in years that he observes, when he is among us, an earnestness to have him fall on some divine topic, which he always treats with much authority, as one who has no interests in this world, as one who is hastening to the object of all his wishes, and conceives hope from his decays and infirmities. These are my ordinary companions.

THE LAND OF THE BROBDINGNAGS
Chapter 6 of *Gulliver's Travels*
by Jonathan Swift
(1667–1745)

This episode is taken from Gulliver's voyage to the land of the race of highly civilized giants, the Brobdingnags. Here Gulliver, the persona *or fictitious author of the* Travels, *explains to the King of the Brobdingnags the "glories" of European civilization. Gulliver's Travels, of course, can be taken on two levels: first as merely a fable for children, but more properly as a savage satire on the nature of man and an indictment of his institutions.*

Several Contrivances of the Author to please the King and Queen. He shews his Skill in Musick. The King enquires into the State of Europe, *which the Author relates to him. The King's Observations thereon.*

I used to attend the King's Levee once or twice a Week, and had often seen him under the Barber's Hand, which indeed was at first very terrible to behold. For, the Razor was almost twice as long as an ordinary Scythe. His Majesty, according to the Custom of the Country, was only shaved twice a Week. I once prevailed on the Barber to give me some of the Suds or Lather, out of which I picked Forty or Fifty of the strongest Stumps of Hair. I then took a Piece of fine Wood, and cut it like the Back of a Comb, making several Holes in it at equal Distance, with as small a Needle as I could get from *Glumdalclitch*. I fixed in the Stumps so artificially, scraping and sloping them with my Knife towards the Points; that I made a very tolerable Comb; which was a seasonable Supply, my own being so much broken in the Teeth, that it was almost useless: Neither did I know any Artist in that Country so nice and exact, as would undertake to make me another.

And this puts me in mind of an Amusement wherein I spent many of my leisure Hours. I desired the Queen's Woman to save for me the Combings of her Majesty's Hair, whereof in time I got a good Quantity; and consulting with my Friend the Cabinet-maker, who had received general Orders to do little Jobs for me; I directed him to make two Chair-frames, no larger than those I had in my Box, and then to bore little Holes with a fine Awl round those Parts where I designed the Backs and Seats; through these Holes I wove the strongest Hairs I could pick out, just after the Manner of Cane-chairs in *England*. When they were finished, I made a Present of them to her Majesty, who kept them in her Cabinet, and used to shew them for Curiosities; as indeed they were the Wonder of every one who beheld them. The Queen would have had me sit upon one of these Chairs, but I absolutely refused to obey her; protesting I would rather dye a Thousand Deaths than place a dishonourable Part of my Body on those precious Hairs that once adorned her Majesty's Head. Of these Hairs (as I had always a Mechanical Genius) I likewise made a neat little purse about five Foot long, with her Majesty's Name decyphered in Gold Letters; which I gave to *Glumdalclitch*, by the Queen's Consent. To say the Truth, it was more for Shew than Use, being not of Strength to bear the Weight of the larger Coins; and therefore she kept nothing in it, but some little Toys that Girls are fond of.

The King, who delighted in Musick, had frequent Consorts at Court, to which I was sometimes carried, and set in my Box on a Table to hear them: But, the Noise was so great, that I could hardly distinguish the Tunes. I am confident, that all the Drums and Trumpets of a Royal Army, beating and sounding together just as your Ears, could not equal it. My Practice was to have my Box removed from the Places where the Performers sat, as far as I could; then to shut the Doors and Windows of it, and draw the Window-Curtains; after which I found their Musick not disagreeable.

I had learned in my Youth to play a little upon the Spinet; *Glumdalclitch* kept one in her Chamber, and a Master attended twice a Week to teach her: I call it a Spinet, because it somewhat resembled that Instrument, and was play'd upon in the same Manner. A Fancy came into my Head, that I would entertain the King and Queen with an *English* Tune upon this Instrument. But this appeared extremely difficult: For, the Spinet was near sixty Foot long, each Key being almost a Foot wide; so that, with my Arms extended, I could not reach to above five Keys; and to press them down required a good smart Stroak with my Fist, which would be too great a Labour, and to no Purpose. The Method I contrived was this. I prepared two round Sticks about the Bigness of common Cudgels; they were thicker at one End than the other; and I covered the thicker End with a Piece of a Mouse's Skin, that by rapping on them, I might neither

Damage the Tops of the Keys, nor interrupt the Sound. Before the Spinet, a Bench was placed about four Foot below the Keys, and I was put upon the Bench. I ran sideling upon it that way and this, as fast as I could, banging the proper Keys with my two Sticks; and made a Shift to play a Jigg to the great Satisfaction of both their Majesties: But, it was the most violent Exercise I ever underwent, and yet I could not strike above sixteen Keys, nor, consequently, play the Bass and Treble together, as other Artists do; which was a great Disadvantage to my Performance.

The King, who as I before observed, was a Prince of excellent Understanding, would frequently order that I should be brought in my Box, and set upon the Table in his Closet. He would then command me to bring one of my Chairs out of the Box, and sit down within three Yards Distance upon the Top of the Cabinet; which brought me almost to a Level with his Face. In this Manner I had several Conversations with him. I one Day took the Freedom to tell his Majesty, that the Contempt he discovered towards *Europe*, and the rest of the World, did not seem answerable to those excellent Qualities of Mind, that he was Master of. That, Reason did not extend itself with the Bulk of the Body: On the Contrary, we observed in our Country, that the tallest Persons were usually least provided with it. That among other Animals, Bees and Ants had the Reputation of more Industry, Art, and Sagacity than many of the larger Kinds. And that, as inconsiderable as he took me to be, I hoped I might live to do his Majesty some signal Service. The King heard me with Attention; and began to conceive a much better Opinion of me than he had ever before. He desired I would give him as exact an Account of the Government of *England* as I possibly could; because, as fond as Princes commonly are of their own Customs (for so he conjectured of other Monarchs by my former Discourses) he should be glad to hear of any Thing that might deserve Imitation.

Imagine with thy Self, courteous Reader, how often I then wished for the Tongue of *Demosthenes* or *Cicero*, that might have enabled me to celebrate the Praise of my own dear native Country in a Style equal to its Merits and Felicity.

I began my Discourse by informing his Majesty, that our Dominions consisted of two Islands, which composed three mighty Kingdoms under one Sovereign, besides our Plantations in *America*. I dwelt long upon the Fertility of our Soil, and the Temperature of our Climate. I then spoke at large upon the Constitution of an *English* Parliament, partly made up of an illustrious Body called the House of Peers, Persons of the noblest Blood, and of the most ancient and ample Patrimonies. I described that extraordinary Care always taken of their Education in Arts and Arms, to qualify them for being Counsellors born to the King and Kingdom; to have a Share in the Legislature, to be Members of the highest Court of Judicature from whence there could be no Appeal; and to be Champions always ready for the Defence of their Prince and Country by their Valour, Conduct and

Fidelity. That these were the Ornament and Bulwark of the Kingdom; worthy Followers of their most renowned Ancestors, whose Honour had been the Reward of their Virtue; from which their Posterity were never once known to degenerate. To these were joined several holy Persons, as part of that Assembly, under the Title of Bishops; whose peculiar Business it is, to take care of Religion, and of those who instruct the People therein. These were searched and sought out through the whole Nation, by the Prince and wisest Counsellors, among such of the Priesthood, as were most deservedly distinguished by the Sanctity of their Lives, and the Depth of their Erudition; who were indeed the spiritual Fathers of the Clergy and the People.

That, the other Part of the Parliament consisted of an Assembly called the House of Commons; who were all principal Gentlemen, *freely* picked and culled out by the People themselves, for their great Abilities, and Love of their Country, to represent the Wisdom of the whole Nation. And, these two Bodies make up the most august Assembly in *Europe*; to whom, in Conjunction with the Prince, the whole Legislature is committed.

I then descended to the Courts of Justice, over which the Judges, those venerable Sages and Interpreters of the Law, presided, for determining the disputed Rights and Properties of Men, as well as for the Punishment of Vice, and Protection of Innocence. I mentioned the prudent Management of our Treasury; the Valour and Atchievements of our Forces by Sea and Land. I computed the Number of our People, by reckoning how many Millions there might be of each Religious Sect, or Political Party among us. I did not omit even our Sports and Pastimes, or any other Particular which I thought might redound to the Honour of my Country. And, I finished all with a brief historical Account of Affairs and Events in *England* for about an hundred Years past.

This Conversation was not ended under five Audiences, each of several Hours; and the King heard the Whole with great Attention; frequently taking Notes of what I spoke, as well as Memorandums of what Questions he intended to ask me.

When I had put an End to these long Discourses, his Majesty in a sixth Audience consulting his Notes, proposed many Doubts, Queries, and Objections, upon every Article. He asked, what Methods were used to cultivate the Minds and Bodies of our young Nobility; and in what kind of Business they commonly spent the first and teachable Part of their Lives. What Course was taken to supply that Assembly, when any noble Family became extinct. What Qualifications were necessary in those who are to be created new Lords: Whether the Humour of the Prince, a Sum of Money to a Court-Lady, or a Prime Minister; or a Design of strengthening a Party opposite to the publick Interest, ever happened to be Motives in those Advancements. What Share of Knowledge these Lords had in the Laws of their Country, and how they came by it, so as to enable them to decide the Properties of their Fellow-Subjects in the last Resort. Whether they were always so free from Avarice, Partialities, or Want, that a Bribe, or some other sinister View, could have no Place among them. Whether those holy Lords I spoke of, were constantly promoted to that Rank upon Account of their Knowledge in religious Matters, and the Sanctity of their Lives, had never been Compliers with the Times, while they were common Priests; or slavish prostitute Chaplains to some Nobleman, whose Opinions they continued servilely to follow after they were admitted into that Assembly.

He then desired to know, what Arts were practised in electing those whom I called Commoners. Whether, a Stranger with a strong Purse might not influence the vulgar Voters to chuse him before their own Landlord, or the most considerable Gentleman in the Neighbourhood. How it came to pass, that People were so violently bent upon getting into this Assembly, which I allowed to be a great Trouble and Expence, often to the Ruin of their Families, without any Salary or Pension: Because this appeared such an exalted Strain of Virtue and publick Spirit, that his Majesty seemed to doubt it might possibly not be always sincere: And he desired to know, whether such zealous Gentlemen could have any Views of refunding themselves for the Charges and Trouble they were at, by sacrificing the publick Good to the Designs of a weak and vicious Prince, in Conjunction with a corrupted Ministry. He multiplied his Questions and sifted me thoroughly upon every Part of this Head; proposing numberless Enquiries and Objections, which I think it not prudent or convenient to repeat.

Upon what I said in relation to our Courts of Justice, his Majesty desired to be satisfied in several Points: And, this I was the better able to do, having been formerly almost ruined by a long Suit in Chancery, which was decreed for me with Costs. He asked, what Time was usually spent in determining between Right and Wrong; and what Degree of Expence. Whether Advocates and Orators had Liberty to plead in Causes manifestly known to be unjust, vexatious, or oppressive. Whether Party in Religion or Politicks were observed to be of any Weight in the Scale of Justice. Whether those pleading Orators were Persons educated in the general Knowledge of Equity; or only in provincial, national, and other local Customs. Whether they or their Judges had any Part in penning those Laws, which they assumed the Liberty of interpreting and glossing upon at their Pleasure. Whether they had ever at different Times pleaded for and against the same Cause, and cited Precedents to prove contrary Opinions. Whether they were a rich or a poor Corporation. Whether they received any pecuniary Reward for pleading or delivering their Opinions. And particularly whether they were ever admitted as Members in the lower Senate.

He fell next upon the Management of our Treasury; and said, he thought my Memory had failed me, because I computed our Taxes at about five or six Millions a Year; and when I came to mention the Issues, he found they sometimes amounted to more than double; for, the Notes he had taken were very particular in this Point; because he hoped, as he told me, that the Knowledge of our Conduct might be useful to him; and he could not be deceived in his Calculations. But, if what I told him were true, he was still at a Loss how a Kingdom could run out of its Estate like a private Person. He asked me, who were our Creditors? and, where we found Money to pay them? He wondered to hear me talk of such chargeable and extensive Wars; that, certainly we must be a quarrelsome People, or live among very bad Neighbours; and that our Generals must needs be richer than our Kings. He asked, what Business we had out of our own Islands, unless upon the Score of Trade or Treaty, or to defend the Coasts with our Fleet. Above all, he was amazed to hear me talk of a mercenary standing Army in the Midst of Peace, and among a free People. He said, if we were governed by our own Consent in the Persons of our Representatives, he could not imagine of whom we were afraid, or against whom we were to fight; and would hear my Opinion, whether a private Man's House might not better be defended by himself, his Children, and Family; than by half a Dozen Rascals picked up at a Venture in the Streets, for small Wages, who might get an Hundred Times more by cutting their Throats.

He laughed at my odd Kind of Arithmetick (as he was pleased to call it) in reckoning the Numbers of our People by a Computation drawn from the several Sects among us in Religion and Politicks. He said, he knew no Reason, why those who entertain Opinions prejudicial to the Publick, should be obliged to change, or should not be obliged to conceal them. And, as it was Tyranny in any Government to require the first, so it was Weakness not to enforce the second: For, a Man may be allowed to keep Poisons in his Closet, but not to vend them about as Cordials.

He observed, that among the Diversions of our Nobility and Gentry, I had mentioned Gaming. He desired to know at what Age this Entertainment was usually taken up, and when it was laid down. How much of their Time it employed; whether it ever went so high as to affect their Fortunes. Whether mean vicious People, by their Dexterity in that Art, might not arrive at great Riches, and sometimes keep our very Nobles in Dependance, as well as habituate them to vile Companions; wholly take them from the Improvement of their Minds, and force them by the losses they received, to learn and practice that infamous Dexterity upon others.

He was perfectly astonished with the historical Account I gave him of our Affairs during the last Century; protesting it was only an Heap of Conspiracies, Rebellions, Murders, Massacres, Revolutions, Banishments; the very worst Effects that Avarice, Faction, Hypocrisy, Perfidiousness, Cruelty, Rage, Madness, Hatred, Envy, Lust, Malice, and Ambition could produce.

His Majesty in another Audience, was at the Pains to recapitulate the Sum of all I had spoken; compared the Questions he made, with the Answers I had given; then taking me into his Hands, and stroaking me gently, delivered himself in these Words, which I shall never forget, nor the Manner he spoke them in. My little Friend *Grildrig*; you have made a most admirable Panegyrick upon your Country. You have clearly proved that

Ignorance, Idleness, and Vice are the proper Ingredients for qualifying a Legislator. That Laws are best explained, interpreted, and applied by those whose Interest and Abilities lie in perverting, confounding, and eluding them. I observe among you some Lines of an Institution, which in its Original might have been tolerable; but these half erased, and the rest wholly blurred and blotted by Corruptions. It doth not appear from all you have said, how any one Perfection is required towards the Procurement of any one Station among you; much less that Men are ennobled on Account of their Virtue, that Priests are advanced for their Piety or Learning, soldiers for their Conduct or Valour, Judges for their Integrity, Senators for the Love of their Country, or Counsellors for their Wisdom. As for yourself (continued the King) who have spent the greatest Part of your Life in travelling; I am well disposed to hope you may hitherto have escaped many Vices of your Country. But, by what I have gathered from your own Relation, and the Answers I have with much Pains wringed and extorted from you; I cannot but conclude the Bulk of your Natives, to be the most pernicious Race of little odious Vermin that Nature ever suffered to crawl upon the Surface of the Earth.

part two
masters of
modern fiction

THE BIRTH AND EVOLUTION
OF MODERN SHORT FICTION

The roots of fiction were not only diverse and interesting in their own right; they were a necessary prologue to the coming of the short story, as we know it, in the nineteenth century. That the eighteenth century saw the rise of the novel is to acknowledge that the son gained his reputation before the father, for the medieval *novella*, or short tale, is to the novel as father is to son.

Significantly the nineteenth century was not only a great age of fiction, but of criticism as well; interestingly, often the most perceptive critics were writers first, such as Edgar Allan Poe and Nathaniel Hawthorne. This meant that the writer explained his newly evolving theories as he wrote, analyzing almost simultaneously what he had written. Although nineteenth-century writers were still at variance on what to call the short story, or even what it was supposed to do, they found a community of expression in a "new" form.

Many modern critics regard Edgar Allan Poe as the father of the modern short story. With Poe, the form dropped the shackles of didacticism and directed its vision at the world outside, discovering wonder and terror in what people see and do. Poe said in 1842 that "the tale proper . . . affords unquestionably the fairest field for the exercise of the loftiest talent, which can be afforded by the wide domains of mere prose." To him, "unity of impression" distinguished the short story among prose forms. Thus, he regarded the short story as second only to the rhymed poem of proper length (about an hour's reading time) in fulfilling the "demands of high genius." More than any other early modern, Poe helped to fulfill those extraordinary demands.

By the time of Poe's early death the accelerating momentum of the short story could not be diminished, stilled, or reversed. Nor was this "new" mode purely American. Guy de Maupassant (1850–1893), Henry James (1843–1916), James Joyce (1882–1941), D. H. Lawrence (1885–1930), and many others beyond American shores helped bring the short story to its fruition in the nineteenth and twentieth centuries. In an age of prose, the short story challenged the novel for prominence. With some justice, our era has been called "the age of short fiction."

The short story found many masters before so-called traditional fiction came under attack by the avant-garde writers of more recent times (see part 4, "Beyond the Safety Zone"). Thus it is erroneous to claim that in the nineteenth and twentieth centuries the short story finally found a form; it found *many* forms, all living comfortably under the umbrella term "the short story." The selections in this part capture the short story in but a handful of its many masks: the sketch, the horror story, the well-made story, the allegorical tale, the detective story, and so on. The diversity of the short story came to be its strength, its very range a testament to a newly found wealth of sources and authors.

YOUNG GOODMAN BROWN
by Nathaniel Hawthorne
(1804–64)

Young Goodman Brown came forth at sunset into the street at Salem village; but put his head back, after crossing the threshold, to exchange a parting kiss with his young wife. And Faith, as the wife was aptly named, thrust her own pretty head into the street, letting the wind play with the pink ribbons of her cap while she called to Goodman Brown.

"Dearest heart," whispered she, softly and rather sadly, when her lips were close to his ear, "prithee put off your journey until sunrise and sleep in your own bed tonight. A lone woman is troubled with such dreams and such thoughts that she's afeared of herself sometimes. Pray tarry with me this night, dear husband, of all nights in the year."

"My love and my Faith," replied young Goodman Brown, "of all nights in the year, this one night must I tarry away from thee. My journey, as thou callest it, forth and back again, must needs be done 'twixt now and sunrise. What, my sweet wife, dost thou doubt me already, and we but three months married?"

"Then God bless you!" said Faith, with the pink ribbons; "and may you find all well when you come back."

"Amen!" cried Goodman Brown. "Say thy prayers, dear Faith, and go to bed at dusk, and no harm will come to thee."

So they parted; and the young man pursued his way until, being about to turn the corner by the meeting-house, he looked back and saw the head of Faith still peeping after him with a melancholy air, in spite of her pink ribbons.

"Poor little Faith!" thought he, for his heart smote him. "What a wretch am I to leave her on such an errand! She talks of dreams, too. Methought as she spoke there was trouble in her face, as if a dream had warned her what work is to be done tonight. But no, no; 'twould kill her to think it. Well, she's a blessed angel on earth; and after this one night I'll cling to her skirts and follow her to heaven."

With this excellent resolve for the future, Goodman Brown felt himself justified in making more haste on his present evil purpose. He had taken a dreary road, darkened by all the gloomiest trees of the forest, which barely stood aside to let the narrow path creep through, and closed immediately behind. It was all as lonely as could be; and there is this peculiarity in such a solitude, that the traveler knows not who may be concealed by the innumerable trunks and the thick boughs overhead; so that with lonely footsteps he may yet be passing through an unseen multitude.

"There may be a devilish Indian behind every tree," said Goodman Brown to himself; and he glanced fearfully behind him as he added, "What if the devil himself should be at my very elbow!"

His head being turned back, he passed a crook of the road, and, looking forward again, beheld the figure of a man, in grave and decent attire, seated at the foot of an old tree. He arose at Goodman Brown's approach and walked onward side by side with him.

"You are late, Goodman Brown," said he. "The clock of the Old South was striking as I came through Boston, and that is full fifteen minutes agone."

"Faith kept me back a while," replied the young man, with a tremor in his voice, caused by the sudden appearance of his companion, though not wholly unexpected.

It was now deep dusk in the forest, and deepest in that part of it where these two were journeying. As nearly as could be discerned, the second traveler was about fifty years old, apparently in the same rank of life as Goodman Brown, and bearing a considerable resemblance to him, though perhaps more in expression than features. Still they might have been taken for father and son. And yet, though the elder person was as simply clad as the younger, and as simple in manner too, he had an indescribable air of one who knew the world, and who would not have felt abashed at the governor's dinner table or in King William's court, were it possible that his affairs should call him thither. But the only thing about him that could be fixed upon as remarkable was his staff, which bore the likeness of a great black snake, so curiously wrought that it might almost be seen to twist and wriggle itself like a living serpent. This, of course, must have been an ocular deception, assisted by the uncertain light.

"Come, Goodman Brown," cried his fellow-traveler, "this is a dull pace for the beginning of a journey. Take my staff, if you are so soon weary."

"Friend," said the other, exchanging his slow pace for a full stop, "having kept covenant by meeting thee here, it is my purpose now to return whence I came. I have scruples touching the matter thou wot'st of."

"Sayest thou so?" replied he of the serpent, smiling apart. "Let us walk on, nevertheless, reasoning as we go; and if I convince thee not thou shalt turn back. We are but a little way in the forest yet."

"Too far! too far!" exclaimed the goodman, unconsciously resuming his walk. "My father never went into the woods on such an errand, nor his father before him. We have been a race of honest men and good Christians since the days of the martyrs; and shall I be the first of the name of Brown that ever took this path and kept—"

"Such company thou wouldst say," observed the elder person, interpreting his pause. "Well said, Goodman Brown! I have been as well acquainted with your family as with ever a one among the Puritans; and that's no trifle to say. I helped your grandfather, the constable, when he lashed the Quaker woman so smartly through the streets of Salem; and it was I that brought your father a pitch-pine knot, kindled at my own hearth, to set fire to an Indian village, in King Philip's war. They were my good friends, both; and many a pleasant walk have we had along this path, and returned merrily after midnight. I would fain be friends with you for their sake."

"If it be as thou sayest," replied Goodman Brown, "I marvel they never spoke of these matters; or, verily, I marvel not, seeing that the least rumor of the sort would have driven them from New England. We are a people of prayer, and good works to boot, and abide no such wickedness."

"Wickedness or not," said the traveler with the twisted staff, "I have a very general acquaintance here in New England. The deacons of many a church have drunk the communion wine with me; the selectmen of divers towns make me their chairman; and a majority of the Great and General Court are firm supporters of my interest. The governor and I, too—but these are state secrets."

"Can this be so?" cried Goodman Brown, with a stare of amazement at his undisturbed companion. "Howbeit, I have nothing to do with the governor and council; they have their own ways, and are no rule for a simple husbandman like me. But, were I to go on with thee, how should I meet the eye of that good old man, our minister, at Salem village? Oh, his voice would make me tremble both Sabbath day and lecture day."

Thus far the elder traveler had listened with due gravity; but now burst into a fit of irrepressible mirth, shaking himself so violently that his snake-like staff actually seemed to wiggle in sympathy.

"Ha! ha! ha!" shouted he again and again; then composing himself, "Well, go on, Goodman Brown, go on; but, prithee, don't kill me with laughing."

"Well, then, to end the matter at once," said Goodman Brown, considerably nettled, "there is my wife, Faith. It would break her dear little heart; and I'd rather break my own."

"Nay, if that be the case," answered the other, "e'en go thy ways, Goodman Brown. I would not for twenty old women like the one hobbling before us that Faith should come to any harm."

As he spoke he pointed his staff at a female figure on the path, in whom Goodman Brown recognized a very pious and exemplary dame, who had taught him his catechism in youth, and was still his moral and spiritual adviser, jointly with the minister and Deacon Gookin.

"A marvel, truly, that Goody Cloyse should be so far in the wilderness at nightfall," said he. "But with your leave, friend. I shall take a cut through the woods until we have left this Christian woman behind. Being a stranger to you, she might ask whom I was consorting with and wither I was going."

"Be it so," said his fellow-traveler. "Betake you to the woods, and let me keep the path."

Accordingly the young man turned aside, but took care to watch his companion, who advanced softly along the road until he had come within a staff's length of the old dame. She, meanwhile, was making the best of her way, with singular speed for so aged a woman, and mumbling some indistinct words—a prayer, doubtless—as she went. The traveler put forth his staff and touched her withered neck with what seemed the serpent's tail.

"The devil!" screamed the pious old lady.

"Then Goody Cloyse knows her old friend?" observed the traveler, confronting her and leaning on his writhing stick.

"Ah, forsooth, and is it your worship indeed?" cried the good dame. "Yea, truly is it, and in the very image of my old gossip, Goodman Brown, the grandfather of the silly fellow that now is. But—would your worship believe it?—my broomstick hath strangely disappeared, stolen, as I suspect, by that unhanged witch, Goody Cory, and that, too, when I was all anointed with the juice of smallage, and cinquefoil, and wolf's bane—"

"Mingled with fine wheat and the fat of a new-born babe," said the shape of old Goodman Brown.

"Ah, your worship knows the recipe," cried the old lady, cackling aloud. "So, as I was saying, being all ready for the meeting, and no horse to ride on, I made up my mind to foot it; for they tell me there is a nice young man to be taken into communion tonight. But now your good worship will lend me your arm, and we shall be there in a twinkling."

"That can hardly be," answered her friend. "I may not spare you my arm, Goody Cloyse; but here is my staff, if you will."

So saying, he threw it down at her feet, where, perhaps, it assumed life, being one of the rods which its owner had formerly lent to the Egyptian magi. Of this fact, however, Goodman Brown could not take cognizance. He had cast up his eyes in astonishment, and, looking down again, beheld neither Goody Cloyse nor the serpentine staff, but his fellow-traveler alone, who waited for him as calmly as if nothing had happened.

"That old woman taught me my catechism," said the young man; and there was a world of meaning in this simple comment.

They continued to walk onward, while the elder traveler exhorted his companion to make good speed and persevere in the path, discoursing so aptly that his arguments seemed rather to spring up in the bosom of his auditor than to be suggested by himself. As they went, he plucked a branch of maple to serve for a walking stick, and began to strip it of the twigs and little boughs, which were wet with evening dew. The moment his fingers touched them they became strangely withered and dried up as with a week's sunshine. Thus the pair proceeded, at a good free pace, until suddenly, in a gloomy hollow of the road, Goodman Brown sat himself down on the stump of a tree and refused to go any farther.

"Friend," said he, stubbornly, "my mind is made up. Not another step will I budge on this errand. What if a wretched old woman do choose to go to the devil when I thought she was going to heaven: is that any reason why I should quit my dear Faith and go after her?"

"You will think better of this by and by," said his acquaintance, composedly. "Sit here and rest yourself a while; and when you feel like moving again, there is my staff to help you along."

Without more words, he threw his companion the maple stick, and was as speedily out of sight as if he had vanished into the gloom. The young man sat a few moments by the roadside, applauding himself greatly, and thinking with how clear a conscience he should meet the minister in his morning walk, nor shrink from the eye of good old Deacon Gookin. And what calm sleep would be his that very night; which was to have been spent so wickedly, but so purely and sweetly now, in the arms of Faith! Amidst these pleasant and praiseworthy meditations, Goodman Brown heard the tramp of horses along the road, and deemed it advisable to conceal himself within the verge of the forest, conscious of the guilty purpose that had brought him thither, though now so happily turned from it.

On came the hoof tramps and the voices of the riders, two grave old voices, conversing soberly as they drew near. These mingled sounds appeared to pass along the road, within a few yards of the young man's hiding-place; but, owing doubtless to the depth of the gloom at that particular spot, neither the travelers nor their steeds were visible. Though their figures brushed the small boughs by the wayside, it could not be seen that they intercepted, even for a moment, the faint gleam from the strip of bright sky athwart which they must have passed. Goodman Brown alternately crouched and stood on tiptoe, pulling aside the branches and thrusting forth his head as far as he durst without discerning so much as a shadow. It vexed him the more, because he could have sworn, were such a thing possible, that he recognized the voices of the minister and Deacon Gookin, jogging along quietly, as they were wont to do, when bound to some ordination or ecclesiastical council. While yet within hearing, one of the riders stopped to pluck a switch.

"Of the two, reverend sir," said the voice like the deacon's, "I had rather miss an ordination dinner than tonight's meeting. They tell me that some of our community are to be here from Falmouth and beyond, and others from Connecticut and Rhode Island, besides several of the Indian powwows, who, after their fashion know almost as much deviltry as the best of us. Moreover, there is a goodly young woman to be taken into communion."

"Mighty well, Deacon Gookin!" replied the solemn old tones of the minister. "Spur up, or we shall be late. Nothing can be done, you know, until I get on the ground."

The hoofs clattered again; and the voices, talking so strangely in the empty air, passed on through the forest, where no church had ever been gathered or solitary Christian prayed. Whither, then, could these holy men be journeying so deep into the heathen wilderness? Young Goodman Brown caught hold of a tree for support, being ready to sink down on the ground, faint and overburdened with the heavy sickness of his heart. He looked up to the sky, doubting whether there really was a heaven above him. Yet there was the blue arch, and the stars brightening in it.

"With heaven above and Faith below, I will yet stand firm against the devil!" cried Goodman Brown.

While he still gazed upward into the deep arch of the firmament and had lifted his hands to pray, a cloud, though no wind was stirring, hurried across the zenith and hid the brightening stars. The blue sky was still visible, except directly overhead, where this black mass of cloud was sweeping swiftly northward. Aloft in the air, as if from the depths of the cloud, came a confused and doubtful sound of voices. Once the listener fancied that he could distinguish the accents of townspeople of his own, men and women, both pious and ungodly, many of whom he had met at the communion table, and had seen others rioting at the tavern. The next moment, so indistinct were the sounds, he doubted whether he had heard aught but the murmur of the old forest, whispering without a wind. Then came a stronger swell of those familiar tones, heard daily in the sunshine at Salem village, but never until now from a cloud of night. There was one voice, of a young woman, uttering lamentations, yet with an uncertain sorrow, and entreating for some favor, which, perhaps, it would grieve her to obtain; and all the unseen multitude, both saints and sinners, seemed to encourage her onward.

"Faith!" shouted Goodman Brown, in a voice of agony and desperation; and the echoes of the forest mocked him, crying, "Faith! Faith!" as if bewildered wretches were seeking her all through the wilderness.

The cry of grief, rage, and terror was yet piercing the night, when the unhappy husband held his breath for a response. There was a scream, drowned immediately in a louder murmur of voices, fading into far-off laughter, as the dark cloud swept away, leaving the clear and silent sky above Goodman Brown. But something fluttered lightly down through the air and caught on the branch of a tree. The young man seized it, and beheld a pink ribbon.

"My Faith is gone!" cried he, after one stupefied moment. "There is no good on earth; and sin is but a name. Come, devil; for to thee is this world given."

And, maddened with despair, so that he laughed loud and long, did Goodman Brown grasp his staff and set forth again, at such a rate that he seemed to fly along the forest path rather than to walk or run. The road grew wilder and drearier and more faintly traced, and vanished at length, leaving him in the heart of the dark wilderness, still rushing onward with the instinct that guides mortal man to evil. The whole forest was peopled with frightful sounds—the creaking of the trees, the howling of wild beasts, and the yell of Indians; while sometimes the wind tolled like a distant church bell, and sometimes gave a broad roar around the traveler, as if all Nature were laughing him to scorn. But he was himself the chief horror of the scene, and shrank not from its other horrors.

"Ha! ha! ha!" roared Goodman Brown when the wind laughed at him. "Let us hear which will laugh loudest. Think not to frighten me with your deviltry. Come witch, come wizard, come Indian powwow, come devil himself, and here comes Goodman Brown. You may as well fear him as he fear you."

In truth, all through the haunted forest there could be nothing more frightful than the figure of Goodman Brown. On he flew among the black pines, brandishing his staff with frenzied gestures, now giving vent to an inspiration of horrid blasphemy, and now shouting forth such laughter as set all the echoes of the forest laughing like demons around him. The fiend in his own shape is less hideous than when he rages in the breast of man. Thus sped the demoniac on his course, until, quivering among the trees, he saw a red light before him, as when the felled trunks and branches of a clearing have been set on fire, and throw up their lurid blaze against the sky, at the hour of midnight. He paused, in a lull of the tempest that had driven him onward, and heard the swell of what seemed a hymn, rolling solemnly from a distance with the weight of many voices. He knew the tune; it was a familiar one in the choir of the village meeting-house. The verse died heavily away, and was lengthened by a chorus, not of human voices, but of all the sounds of the benighted wilderness pealing in awful harmony together. Goodman Brown cried out, and his cry was lost to his own ear by its unison with the cry of the desert.

In the interval of silence he stole forward until the light glared full upon his eyes. At one extremity of an open space, hemmed in by the dark wall of the forest, arose a rock, bearing some rude, natural resemblance either to an altar or a pulpit, and surrounded by four blazing pines, their tops aflame, their stems untouched, like candles at an evening meeting. The mass of foliage that had overgrown the summit of the rock was all on fire, blazing high into the night and fitfully illuminating the whole field. Each pendent twig and leafy festoon was in a blaze. As the red light arose and fell, a numerous congregation alternately shone forth, then disappeared in shadow, and again grew, as it were, out of the darkness, peopling the heart of the solitary woods at once.

"A grave and dark-clad company," quoth Goodman Brown.

In truth they were such. Among them, quivering to and fro between gloom and splendor, appeared faces that would be seen next day at the council board of the province, and others which, Sabbath after Sabbath, looked devoutly heavenward, and benignantly over the crowded pews, from the holiest pulpits in the land. Some affirm that the lady of the governor was there. At least there were high dames well known to her, and wives of honored husbands, and widows, a great multitude, and ancient maidens, all of excellent repute, and fair young girls, who trembled lest their mothers should espy them. Either the sudden gleams of light flashing over the obscure field bedazzled Goodman Brown, or he recognized a score of the church members of Salem village famous for their especial sanctity. Good old Deacon Gookin had arrived, and waited at the skirts of that venerable saint, his revered pastor. But, irreverently consorting with these grave, reputable, and pious people, these elders of the church, these chaste dames and dewy virgins, there were men of dissolute lives and women of spotted fame, wretches given over to all mean and filthy vice, and suspected even of horrid crimes. It was strange to see that the good shrank not from the wicked, nor were the sinners abashed by the saints. Scattered also among their palefaced enemies were the Indian priests, or powwows, who had often scared their native forest with more hideous incantations than any known to English witchcraft.

"But where is Faith?" thought Goodman Brown; and, as hope came into his heart, he trembled.

Another verse of the hymn arose, a slow and mournful strain, such as the pious love, but joined to words which expressed all that our nature can conceive of sin, and darkly hinted at far more. Unfathomable to mere mortals is the lore of fiends. Verse after verse was sung; and still the chorus of the desert swelled between like the deepest tone of a mighty organ; and with the final peal of that dreadful anthem there came a sound, as if the roaring wind, the rushing streams, the howling beasts, and every other voice of the unconcerted wilderness were mingling and according with the voice of guilty man in homage to the prince of all. The four blazing pines threw up a loftier flame, and obscurely discovered shapes and visages of horror on the smoke wreaths above the impious assembly. At the same moment the fire on the rock shot redly forth and formed a glowing arch above its base, where now appeared a figure. With reverence be it spoken, the figure bore no slight similitude, both in garb and manner, to some grave divine of the New England churches.

"Bring forth the converts!" cried a voice that echoed through the field and rolled into the forest.

At the word, Goodman Brown stepped forth from the shadow of the trees and approached the congregation, with whom he felt a loathful brotherhood by the sympathy of all that was wicked in his heart. He could have well-nigh sworn that the shape of his own dead father beckoned him to advance, looking downward from a smoke wreath, while a woman, with dim features of despair, threw out her hand to warn him back. Was it his mother? But he had no power to retreat one step, nor to resist, even in thought, when the minister and good old Deacon Gookin seized his arms and led him to the blazing rock. Thither came also the slender form of a veiled female, led between Goody Cloyse, that pious teacher of the cate-chism, and Martha Carrier, who had received the devil's promise to be queen of hell. A rampant hag was she. And there stood the proselytes beneath the canopy of fire.

"Welcome, my children," said the dark figure, "to the communion of your race. Ye have found thus young your nature and your destiny. My children, look behind you!"

They turned; and flashing forth, as it were, in a sheet of flame, the fiend worshippers were seen; the smile of welcome gleamed darkly on every visage.

"There," resumed the sable form, "are all whom ye have reverenced from youth. Ye deemed them holier than yourselves, and shrank from your own sin, contrasting it with their lives of righteousness and prayerful as-pirations heavenward. Yet here are they all in my worshipping assembly. This night it shall be granted you to know their secret deeds: how hoary-bearded elders of the church have whispered wanton words to the young maids of their households; how many a woman, eager for widows' weeds, has given her husband a drink at bedtime and let him sleep his last sleep in her bosom; how beardless youths have made haste to inherit their fathers' wealth: and how fair damsels—blush not, sweet ones—have dug little graves in the garden, and bidden me, the sole guest, to an infant's funeral. By the sympathy of your human hearts for sin ye shall scent out all the places—whether in church, bedchamber, street, field, or forest—where crime has been committed, and shall exult to behold the whole earth one stain of guilt, one mighty blood spot. Far more than this. It shall be yours to penetrate, in every bosom, the deep mystery of sin, the fountain of all wicked arts, and which inexhaustibly supplies more evil impulses than human power—than my power at its utmost—can make manifest in deeds. And now, my children, look upon each other."

They did so; and, by the blaze of the hell-kindled torches, the wretched man beheld his Faith, and the wife her husband, trembling before that unhallowed altar.

"Lo, there ye stand, my children," said the figure, in a deep and solemn tone, almost sad with its despairing awfulness, as if his once angelic nature could yet mourn for our miserable race. "Depending upon one another's hearts, ye had still hoped that virtue were not all a dream. Now are ye undeceived. Evil is the nature of mankind. Evil must be your only happiness. Welcome again, my children, to the communion of your race."

"Welcome," repeated the fiend worshippers, in one cry of despair and triumph.

And there they stood, the only pair, as it seemed, who were yet hesitating on the verge of wickedness in this dark world. A basin was hollowed, naturally, in the rock. Did it contain water, reddened by the lurid light? or was it blood? or, perchance, a liquid flame? Herein did the shape of evil dip his hand and prepare to lay the mark of baptism upon their foreheads, that they might be partakers of the mystery of sin, more conscious of the secret guilt of others, both in deed and thought, than they could now be of their own. The husband cast one look at his pale wife, and Faith at him. What polluted wretches would the next glance show them to each other, shuddering alike at what they disclosed and what they saw!

"Faith! Faith!" cried the husband, "look up to heaven, and resist the wicked one."

Whether Faith obeyed he knew not. Hardly had he spoken when he found himself amid calm night and solitude, listening to a roar of the wind which died heavily away through the forest. He staggered against the rock, and felt it chill and damp; while a hanging twig, that had been all on fire, besprinkled his cheek with the coldest dew.

The next morning young Goodman Brown came slowly into the street of Salem village, staring around him like a bewildered man. The good old minister was taking a walk along the graveyard to get an appetite for breakfast and meditate his sermon, and bestowed a blessing, as he passed, on Goodman Brown. He shrank from the venerable saint as if to avoid an anathema. Old Deacon Gookin was at domestic worship, and the holy words of his prayer were heard through the open window. "What God doth the wizard pray to?" quoth Goodman Brown. Goody Cloyse, that excellent old Christian, stood in the early sunshine at her own lattice, catechizing a little girl who had brought her a pint of morning's milk. Goodman Brown snatched away the child as from the grasp of the fiend himself. Turning the corner by the meeting-house, he spied the head of Faith, with the pink ribbons, gazing anxiously forth, and bursting into such joy at sight of him that she skipped along the street and almost kissed her husband before the whole village. But Goodman Brown looked sternly and sadly into her face, and passed on without a greeting.

Had Goodman Brown fallen asleep in the forest and only dreamed a wild dream of a witch-meeting?

Be it so if you will; but, alas! it was a dream of evil omen for young Goodman Brown. A stern, a sad, a darkly meditative, a distrustful, if not a desperate man did he become from the night of that fearful dream. On the Sabbath day, when the congregation were singing a holy psalm, he could not listen because an anthem of sin rushed loudly upon his ear and drowned all the blessed strain. When the minister spoke from the pulpit with power and fervid eloquence, and, with his hand on the open Bible, of the sacred truths of our religion, and of saint-like lives and triumphant deaths, and of future bliss or misery unutterable, then did Goodman Brown turn pale, dreading lest the roof should thunder down upon the gray blasphemer and his hearers. Often, awaking suddenly at midnight, he shrank from the bosom of Faith; and at morning or eventide, when the family knelt down at prayer, he scowled and muttered to himself, and gazed sternly at his wife, and turned away. And when he had lived long, and was borne to his grave a hoary corpse, followed by Faith, an aged woman, and children and grandchildren, a goodly procession, besides neighbors not a few, they carved no hopeful verse upon his tombstone, for his dying hour was gloom.

THE TELL-TALE HEART
by Edgar Allan Poe
(1809–49)

True!—nervous—very, very dreadfully nervous I had been and am; but why *will* you say that I am mad? The disease had sharpened my senses—not destroyed—not dulled them. Above all was the sense of hearing acute. I heard all things in the heaven and in the earth. I heard many things in hell. How, then, am I mad? Hearken! and observe how healthily—how calmly I can tell you the whole story.

It is impossible to say how first the idea entered my brain; but once conceived, it haunted me day and night. Object there was none. Passion there was none. I loved the old man. He had never wronged me. He had never given me insult. For his gold I had no desire. I think it was his eye! yes, it was this! He had the eye of a vulture—a pale blue eye, with a film over it. Whenever it fell upon me, my blood ran cold; and so by degrees—very gradually—I made up my mind to take the life of the old man, and thus rid myself of the eye forever.

Now this is the point. You fancy me mad. Madmen know nothing. But you should have seen *me*. You should have seen how wisely I proceeded—with what caution—with what foresight—with what dissimulation I went to work! I was never kinder to the old man than during the whole week before I killed him. And every night, about midnight, I turned the latch of his door and opened it—oh so gently! And then, when I had made an opening sufficient for my head, I put in a dark lantern, all closed, closed, so that no light shone out, and then I thrust in my head. Oh, you would have laughed to see how cunningly I thrust it in! I moved it slowly—very, very slowly, so that I might not disturb the old man's sleep. It took me an hour to place my whole head within the opening so far that I could see him as he lay upon his bed. Ha!—would a madman have been so wise as this? And then, when my head was well in the room, I undid the lantern cautiously—oh, so cautiously—cautiously (for the hinges creaked)—I undid it just so much that a single thin ray fell upon the vulture eye. And this I did for seven long nights—every night just at midnight—but I found the eye always closed; and so it was impossible to do the work; for it was not the old man who vexed me, but his Evil Eye. And every morning, when the day broke, I went boldly into the chamber, and spoke courageously to him, calling him by name in a hearty tone, and inquiring how he had passed the night. So you see he would have been a very profound old man, indeed, to suspect that every night, just at twelve, I looked in upon him while he slept.

Upon the eighth night I was more than usually cautious in opening the door. A watch's minute hand moves more quickly than did mine. Never before that night, had I *felt* the extent of my own powers—of my sagacity. I could scarcely contain my feelings of triumph. To think that there I was, opening the door, little by little, and he not even to dream of my secret deeds or thoughts. I fairly chuckled at the idea; and perhaps he heard me; for he moved on the bed suddenly, as if startled. Now you may think that I drew back—but no. His room was as black as pitch with the thick darkness (for the shutters were close fastened, through fear of robbers), and so I knew that he could not see the opening of the door, and I kept pushing it on steadily, steadily.

I had my head in, and was about to open the lantern, when my thumb slipped upon the tin fastening, and the old man sprang up in bed, crying out—"Who's there?"

I kept quite still and said nothing. For a whole hour I did not move a muscle, and in the meantime I did not hear him lie down. He was still sitting up in the bed listening; just as I have done, night after night, hearkening to the death watches in the wall.

Presently I heard a slight groan, and I knew it was the groan of mortal terror. It was not a groan of pain or of grief—oh, no!—it was the low stifled sound that arises from the bottom of the soul when overcharged with awe. I knew the sound well. Many a night, just at midnight, when all the world slept, it has welled up from my own bosom, deepening, with its dreadful echo, the terrors that distracted me. I say I knew it well. I knew what the old man felt, and pitied him, although I chuckled at heart. I knew that he had been lying awake ever since the first slight noise, when he had turned in the bed. His fears had been ever since growing upon him. He had been trying to fancy them causeless, but could not. He had been saying to himself—"It is nothing but the wind in the chimney—it is only a mouse crossing the floor," or "it is merely a cricket which has made a single chirp." Yes, he had been trying to comfort himself with these suppositions: but he had found all in vain. *All in vain*; because Death, in approaching him had stalked with his black shadow before him, and enveloped the victim. And it was the mournful influence of the unperceived shadow that caused him to feel—although he neither saw nor heard—to *feel* the presence of my head within the room.

When I had waited a long time, very patiently, without hearing him lie down, I resolved to open a little—a very, very little crevice in the lantern. So I opened it—you cannot imagine how stealthily, stealthily— until, at length, a simple dim ray, like the thread of the spider, shot from out the crevice and fell full upon the vulture eye.

It was open—wide, wide open—and I grew furious as I gazed upon it. I saw it with perfect distinctness—all a dull blue, with a hideous veil over it that chilled the very marrow in my bones, but I could see nothing else of the old man's face or person: for I had directed the ray as if by instinct, precisely upon the damned spot.

And have I not told you that what you mistake for madness is but over acuteness of the senses?—now, I say, there came to my ears a low, dull, quick sound, such as a watch makes when enveloped in cotton. I knew *that* sound well, too. It was the beating of the old man's heart. It increased my fury, as the beating of a drum stimulates the soldier into courage.

But even yet I refrained and kept still. I scarcely breathed. I held the lantern motionless. I tried how steadily I could maintain the ray upon the eye. Meantime the hellish tattoo of the heart increased. It grew quicker and quicker, and louder and louder every instant. The old man's terror *must* have been extreme! It grew louder, I say louder every moment!—do you mark me well? I have told you that I am nervous: so I am. And now at the dead hour of the night, amid the dreadful silence of that old house, so strange a noise as this excited me to uncontrollable terror. Yet, for some minutes longer I refrained and stood still. But the beating grew louder, louder! I thought the heart must burst. And now a new anxiety seized me—the sound would be heard by a neighbor! The old man's hour had come! With a loud yell, I threw open the lantern and leaped into the room. He shrieked once—once only. In an instant I dragged him to the floor, and pulled the heavy bed over him. I then smiled gaily, to find the deed so far done. But, for many minutes, the heart beat on with a muffled sound. This, however, did not vex me; it would not be heard through the wall. At length it ceased. The old man was dead. I removed the bed and examined the corpse. Yes, he was stone, stone dead. I placed my hand upon the heart and held it there many minutes. There was no pulsation. He was stone dead. His eye would trouble me no more.

If still you think me mad, you will think so no longer when I describe the wise precautions I took for the concealment of the body. The night waned, and I worked hastily, but in silence. First of all I dismembered the corpse. I cut off the head and the arms and the legs.

I then took up three planks from the flooring of the chamber, and deposited all between the scantlings. I then replaced the boards so cleverly, so cunningly, that no human eye—not even *his*—could have detected any thing wrong. There was nothing to wash out—no stain of any kind—no blood-spot whatever. I had been too wary for that. A tub had caught all—ha! ha!

When I had made an end of these labors, it was four o'clock—still dark as midnight. As the bell sounded the hour, there came a knocking at the street door. I went down to open it with a light heart, for what had I *now* to fear? There entered three men, who introduced themselves, with perfect suavity, as officers of the police. A shriek had been heard by a neighbor during the night; suspicion of foul play had been aroused; information had been lodged at the police office, and they (the officers) had been deputed to search the premises.

I smiled, for *what* had I to fear? I bade the gentlemen welcome. The shriek, I said, was my own in a dream. The old man, I mentioned, was absent in the country. I took my visitors all over the house. I bade them search—search *well*. I led them, at length, to *his* chamber. I showed them his treasures, secure, undisturbed. In the enthusiasm of my confidence, I brought chairs into the room, and desired them *here* to rest from their fatigues, while I myself, in the wild audacity of my perfect triumph, placed my own seat upon the very spot beneath which reposed the corpse of the victim.

The officers were satisfied. My *manner* had convinced them. I was singularly at ease. They sat, and while I answered cheerily, they chatted of familiar things. But, ere long, I felt myself getting pale and wished them gone. My head ached, and I fancied a ringing in my ears: but still they sat and still chatted. The ringing became more distinct—it continued and became more distinct: I talked more freely to get rid of the feeling: but it continued and gained definiteness—until, at length, I found that the noise was *not* within my ears.

No doubt I now grew *very* pale; but I talked more fluently, and with a heightened voice. Yet the sound increased—and what could I do? It was *a low, dull, quick sound—much such a sound as a watch makes when enveloped in cotton.* I gasped for breath—and yet the officers heard it not. I talked more quickly—more vehemently; but the noise steadily increased. I arose and argued about trifles, in a high key and with violent gesticulations; but the noise steadily increased. Why *would* they not be gone? I paced the floor to and fro with heavy strides, as if excited to fury by the observations of the men—but the noise steadily increased. Oh God! what *could* I do? I foamed—I raved—I swore! I swung the chair upon which I had been sitting, and grated it upon the boards, but the noise arose over all and continually increased. It grew louder—louder—*louder!* And still the men chatted pleasantly, and smiled. Was it possible they heard not? Almighty God!—no, no! They heard!—they suspected!—they *knew!*—they were making a mockery of my horror—this I thought, and this I think. But anything was better than this agony! Anything was more tolerable than this derision! I could bear those hypocritical smiles no longer! I felt that I must scream or die! and now—again!—hard! louder! louder! louder! *louder!*

"Villains!" I shrieked, "dissemble no more! I admit the deed!—tear up the planks! here, here!—it is the beating of his hideous heart!"

BARTLEBY
by Herman Melville
(1819–91)

I am a rather elderly man. The nature of my avocations, for the last thirty years, has brought me into more than ordinary contact with what would seem an interesting and somewhat singular set of men, of whom, as yet, nothing, that I know of, has ever been written—I mean, the law-copyists, or scriveners. I have known very many of them, professionally and privately, and, if I pleased, could relate divers histories, at which good-natured gentlemen might smile, and sentimental souls might weep. But I waive the biographies of all other scriveners, for a few passages in the life of Bartleby, who was a scrivener, the strangest I ever saw, or heard of. While, of other law-copyists, I might write the complete life, of Bartleby nothing of that sort can be done. I believe that no materials exist, for a full and satisfactory biography of this man. It is an irreparable loss to literature. Bartleby was one of those beings of whom nothing is ascertainable, except from the original sources, and, in his case, those are very small. What my own astonished eyes saw of Bartleby, *that* is all I know of him, except, indeed, one vague report, which will appear in the sequel.

Ere introducing the scrivener, as he first appeared to me, it is fit I make some mention of myself, my *employés*, my business, my chambers and general surroundings; because some such description is indispensable to an adequate understanding of the chief character about to be presented. Imprimis: I am a man who, from his youth upwards, has been filled with a profound conviction that the easiest way of life is the best. Hence, though I belong to a profession proverbially energetic and nervous, even to turbulence, at times, yet nothing of that sort have I ever suffered to invade my peace. I am one of those unambitious lawyers who never addresses a jury, or in any way draws down public applause; but, in the cool tranquillity of a snug retreat, do a snug business among rich men's bonds, and mortgages, and title-deeds. All who know me, consider me an eminently *safe* man. The late John Jacob Astor, a personage little given to poetic enthusiasm, had no hesitation in pronouncing my first grand point to be prudence; my next, method. I do not speak it in vanity, but simply record the fact, that I was not unemployed in my profession by the late John Jacob Astor; a name which, I admit, I love to repeat; for it hath a rounded and orbicular sound to it, and rings like unto bullion. I will freely add, that I was not insensible to the late John Jacob Astor's good opinion.

Some time prior to the period at which this little history begins, my avocations had been largely increased. The good old office, now extinct in the State of New York, of a Master in Chancery, had been conferred upon me. It was not a very arduous office, but very pleasantly remunerative. I seldom lose my temper; much more seldom indulge in dangerous indignation at wrongs and outrages; but, I must be permitted to be rash here, and declare, that I consider the sudden and violent abrogation of the office of Master in Chancery, by the new Constitution, as a ——— premature act; inasmuch as I had counted upon a life-lease of the profits, whereas I only received those of a few short years. But this is by the way.

My chambers were upstairs, at No. ——— Wall Street. At one end, they looked upon the white wall of the interior of a spacious sky-light shaft, penetrating the building from top to bottom.

This view might have been considered rather tame than otherwise, deficient in what landscape painters call "life." But, if so, the view from the other end of my chambers offered, at least, a contrast, if nothing more. In that direction, my windows commanded an unobstructed view of a lofty brick wall, black by age and everlasting shade; which wall required no spyglass to bring out its lurking beauties, but, for the benefit of all nearsighted spectators, was pushed up to within ten feet of my window panes. Owing to the great height of the surrounding buildings, and my chambers being on the second floor, the interval between this wall and mine not a little resembled a huge square cistern.

At the period just preceding the advent of Bartleby, I had two persons as copyists in my employment, and a promising lad as an office-boy. First, Turkey; second, Nippers; third, Ginger Nut. These may seem names, the like of which are not usually found in the Directory. In truth, they were nicknames, mutually conferred upon each other by my three clerks, and were deemed expressive of their respective persons or characters. Turkey was a short, pursy Englishman, of about my own age—that is, somewhere not far from sixty. In the morning, one might say, his face was of a fine florid hue, but after twelve o'clock, meridian—his dinner hour—it blazed like a grate full of Christmas coals; and continued blazing—but, as it were, with a gradual wane—till six o'clock P.M., or thereabouts; after which, I saw no more of the proprietor of the face, which, gaining its meridian with the sun, seemed to set with it, to rise, culminate, and decline the following day, with the like regularity and undiminished glory. There are many singular coincidences I have known in the course of my life, not the least among which was the fact, that, exactly when Turkey displayed his fullest beams from his red and radiant countenance, just then, too, at that critical moment, began the daily period when I considered his business capacities as seriously disturbed for the remainder of the twenty-four hours. Not that he was absolutely idle, or averse to business, then; far from it. The difficulty was, he was apt to be altogether too energetic. There was a strange, inflamed, flurried, flighty recklessness of activity about him. He would be incautious in dipping his pen into his inkstand. All his blots upon my documents were dropped there after twelve o'clock, meridian. Indeed, not only would he be reckless, and sadly given to making blots in the afternoon, but, some days, he went further, and was rather noisy. At such times, too, his face flamed with augmented blazonry, as if cannel coal had been heaped on anthracite. He made an unpleasant racket with his chair; spilled his sand-box; in mending his pens, impatiently split them all to pieces, and threw them on the floor in a sudden passion; stood up, and leaned over his table, boxing his papers about in a most indecorous manner, very sad to behold in an elderly man like him. Nevertheless, as he was in many ways a most valuable person to me, and all the time before twelve o'clock, meridian, was the quickest, steadiest creature, too, accomplishing a great deal of work in a style not easily to be matched—for these reasons, I was willing to overlook his eccentricities, though, indeed, occasionally, I remonstrated with him. I did this very gently, however, because, though the civilest, nay, the blandest and most reverential of men in the morning, yet, in the afternoon, he was disposed, upon provocation, to be slightly rash with his tongue—in fact, insolent. Now, valuing his morning services as I did, and resolved not to lose them—yet, at the same time, made uncomfortable by his inflamed ways after twelve o'clock—and being a man of peace, unwilling by my admonitions to call forth unseemly retorts from him. I took upon me, one Saturday noon (he was always worse on Saturdays), to hint to him, very kindly, that, perhaps, now that he was growing old, it might be well to abridge his labors; in short, he need not come to my chambers after twelve o'clock, but, dinner over, had best go home to his lodgings, and rest himself till tea-time. But no; he insisted upon his afternoon devotions. His countenance became intolerably fervid, as he oratorically assured me—gesticulating with a long ruler at the other end of the room—that if his services in the morning were useful, how indispensable, then, in the afternoon?

"With submission, sir," said Turkey, on this occasion, "I consider myself your right-hand man. In the morning I but marshal and deploy my columns; but in the afternoon I put myself at their head, and gallantly charge the foe, thus"—and he made a violent thrust with the ruler.

"But the blots, Turkey," intimated I.

"True; but, with submission, sir, behold these hairs! I am getting old. Surely, sir, a blot or two of a warm afternoon is not to be severely urged against gray hairs. Old age—even if it blot the page—is honorable. With submission, sir, we *both* are getting old."

This appeal to my fellow-feeling was hardly to be resisted. At all events, I saw that go he would not. So, I made up my mind to let him stay, resolving, nevertheless, to see to it that, during the afternoon, he had to do with my less important papers.

Nippers, the second on my list, was a whiskered, sallow, and, upon the whole, rather piratical-looking young man, of about five and twenty. I always deemed him the victim of two evil powers—ambition and indigestion. The ambition was evinced by a certain impatience of the duties of a mere copyist, an unwarrantable usurpation of strictly professional affairs, such as the original drawing up of legal documents. The indigestion seemed betokened in an occasional nervous testiness and grinning irritability, causing the teeth to audibly grind together over mistakes committed in copying; unnecessary maledictions, hissed, rather than spoken, in the heat of business; and especially by a continual discontent with the height of the table where he worked. Though of a very ingenious mechanical turn, Nippers could never get this table to suit him. He put chips under it, blocks of various sorts, bits of pasteboard, and at last went so far as to attempt an exquisite adjustment, by final pieces of folded blotting-paper. But no invention would answer. If, for the sake of easing his back, he brought the table lid at a sharp angle well up towards his chin, and wrote there like a man using the steep roof of a Dutch house for his desk, then he declared that it stopped the circulation in his arms. If now he lowered the table to his waistbands, and stooped over it in writing, then there was a sore aching in his back. In short, the truth of the matter was, Nippers knew not what he wanted. Or, if he wanted anything, it was to be rid of a scrivener's table altogether. Among the manifestations of his diseased ambition was a fondness he had for receiving visits from certain ambiguous-looking fellows in seedy coats, whom he called his clients. Indeed, I was aware that not only was he, at times, considerable of a ward-politician, but he occasionally did a little business at the Justices' courts, and was not unknown on the steps of the Tombs. I have good reason to believe, however, that one individual who called upon him at my chambers, and who, with a grand air, he insisted was his client, was no other than a dun, and the alleged title-deed, a bill. But, with all his failings, and the annoyances he caused me, Nippers, like his compatriot Turkey, was a very useful man to me; wrote a neat, swift hand; and, when he chose, was not deficient in a gentlemanly sort of deportment. Added to this, he always dressed in a gentlemanly sort of way; and so, incidentally, reflected credit upon my chambers. Whereas, with respect to Turkey, I had much ado to keep him from being a reproach to me. His clothes were apt to look oily, and smell of eating-houses. He wore his pantaloons very loose and baggy in summer. His coats were execrable; his hat not to be handled. But while the hat was a thing of indifference to me, inasmuch as his natural civility and deference, as a dependent Englishman, always led him to doff it the moment he entered the room, yet his coat was another matter. Concerning his coats, I reasoned with him; but with no effect. The truth was, I suppose, that a man with so small an income could not afford to sport such a lustrous face and a lustrous coat at one and the same time. As Nippers once observed, Turkey's money went chiefly for red ink. One winter day, I presented Turkey with a highly respectable-looking coat of my own—a padded gray coat, of a most comfortable warmth, and which buttoned straight up from the knee to the neck. I thought Turkey would appreciate the favor, and abate his rashness and obstreperousness of afternoons. But no; I verily believe that buttoning himself up in so downy and blanket-like a coat had a pernicious effect upon him—upon the same principle that too much oats are bad for horses. In fact, precisely as a rash, restive horse is said to feel his oats, so Turkey felt his coat. It made him insolent. He was a man whom prosperity harmed.

Though, concerning the self-indulgent habits of Turkey, I had my own private surmises, yet, touching Nippers, I was well persuaded that, whatever might be his faults in other respects, he was, at least, a temperate young man. But, indeed, nature herself seemed to have been his vintner, and, at his birth, charged him so thoroughly with an irritable, brandy-like disposition, that all subsequent potations were needless. When I consider how, amid the stillness of my chambers, Nippers would sometimes impatiently rise from his seat, and stooping over his table, spread his arms wide apart, seize the whole desk, and move it, and jerk it, with a grim, grinding motion on the floor, as if the table were a perverse voluntary agent, intent on thwarting and vexing him, I plainly perceive that, for Nippers, brandy-and-water were altogether superfluous.

It was fortunate for me that, owing to its peculiar cause—indigestion —the irritability and consequent nervousness of Nippers were mainly observable in the morning, while in the afternoon he was comparatively mild. So that, Turkey's paroxysms only coming on about twelve o'clock, I never had to do with their eccentricities at one time. Their fits relieved each other, like guards. When Nippers's was on, Turkey's was off; and vice versa. This was a good natural arrangement, under the circumstances.

Ginger Nut, the third on my list, was a lad, some twelve years old. His father was a car-man, ambitious of seeing his son on the bench instead of a cart, before he died. So he sent him to my office, as student at law, errand-boy, cleaner and sweeper, at the rate of one dollar a week. He had a little desk to himself, but he did not use it much. Upon inspection, the drawer exhibited a great array of the shells of various sorts of nuts. Indeed, to this quick-witted youth, the whole noble science of the law was contained in a nut-shell. Not the least among the employments of Ginger Nut, as well as one which he discharged with the most alacrity, was his duty as cake and apple purveyor for Turkey and Nippers. Copying law-papers being proverbially a dry, husky sort of business, my two scriveners were fain to moisten their mouths very often with Spitzenbergs, to be had at the numerous stalls nigh the Custom House and Post Office. Also, they sent Ginger Nut very frequently for that peculiar cake—small, flat, round, and very spicy—after which he had been named by them. Of a cold morning, when business was but dull, Turkey would gobble up scores of these cakes, as if they were mere wafers—indeed, they sell them at the rate of six or eight for a penny—the scrape of his pen blending with the crunching of the crisp particles in his mouth. Of all the fiery afternoon blunders and flurried rashnesses of Turkey, was his once moistening a ginger-cake between his lips, and clapping it on to a mortage, for a seal. I came within an ace of dismissing him then. But he mollified me by making an oriental bow, and saying—

"With submission, sir, it was generous of me to find you in stationery on my own account."

Now my original business—that of a conveyancer and title hunter, and drawer-up of recondite documents of all sorts—was considerably increased by receiving the master's office. There was now great work for scriveners. Not only must I push the clerks already with me, but I must have additional help.

In answer to my advertisement, a motionless young man one morning stood upon my office threshold, the door being open, for it was summer. I can see that figure now—pallidly neat, pitiably respectable, incurably forlorn! It was Bartleby.

After a few words touching his qualifications, I engaged him, glad to have among my corps of copyists a man of so singularly sedate an aspect, which I thought might operate beneficially upon the flighty temper of Turkey, and the fiery one of Nippers.

I should have stated before that ground glass folding-doors divided my premises into two parts, one of which was occupied by my scriveners, the other by myself. According to my humor, I threw open these doors, or closed them. I resolved to assign Bartleby a corner by the folding-doors, but on my side of them, so as to have this quiet man within easy call, in case any trifling thing was to be done. I placed his desk close up to a small side-window in that part of the room, a window which originally had afforded a lateral view of certain grimy back-yards and bricks, but which, owing to subsequent erections, commanded at present no view at all, though it gave some light. Within three feet of the panes was a wall, and the light came down from far above, between two lofty buildings, as from a very small opening in a dome. Still further to a satisfactory arrangement, I procured a high green folding screen, which might entirely isolate Bartleby from my sight, though not remove him from my voice. And thus, in a manner, privacy and society were conjoined.

At first, Bartleby did an extraordinary quantity of writing. As if long famishing for something to copy, he seemed to gorge himself on my documents. There was no pause for digestion. He ran a day and night line, copying by sun-light and by candle-light. I should have been quite delighted with his application, had he been cheerfully industrious. But he wrote on silently, palely, mechanically.

It is, of course, an indispensable part of a scrivener's business to verify the accuracy of his copy, word by word. Where there are two or more scriveners in an office, they assist each other in this examination, one reading from the copy, the other holding the original. It is a very dull, wearisome, and lethargic affair. I can readily imagine that, to some sanguine temperaments, it would be altogether intolerable. For example, I cannot credit that the mettlesome poet Byron would have contentedly sat down with Bartleby to examine a law document of, say five hundred pages, closely written in a crimpy hand.

Now and then, in the haste of business, it had been my habit to assist in comparing some brief document myself, calling Turkey or Nippers for this purpose. One object I had, in placing Bartleby so handy to me behind the screen, was, to avail myself of his services on such trivial occasions. It was on the third day, I think, of his being with me, and before any necessity had arisen for having his own writing examined, that, being much hurried to complete a small affair I had in hand, I abruptly called to Bartleby. In my haste and natural expectancy of instant compliance, I sat with my head bent over the original on my desk, and my right hand sideways, and somewhat nervously extended with the copy, so that, immediately upon emerging from his retreat, Bartleby might snatch it and proceed to business without the least delay.

In this very attitude did I sit when I called to him, rapidly stating what it was I wanted him to do—namely, to examine a small paper with me. Imagine my surprise, nay, my consternation, when, without moving from his privacy, Bartleby, in a singularly mild, firm voice, replied, "I would prefer not to."

I sat awhile in perfect silence, rallying my stunned faculties. Immediately it occurred to me that my ears had deceived me, or Bartleby had entirely misunderstood my meaning. I repeated my request in the clearest tone I could assume; but in quite as clear a one came the previous reply, "I would prefer not to."

"Prefer not to," echoed I, rising in high excitement, and crossing the room with a stride. "What do you mean? Are you moon-struck? I want you to help me compare this sheet here—take it," and I thrust it towards him.

"I would prefer not to," said he.

I looked at him steadfastly. His face was leanly composed; his gray eye dimly calm. Not a wrinkle of agitation rippled him. Had there been the least uneasiness, anger, impatience or impertinence in his manner; in other words, had there been any thing ordinarily human about him, doubtless I should have violently dismissed him from the premises. But as it was, I should have as soon thought of turning my pale plaster-of-paris bust of Cicero out of doors. I stood gazing at him awhile, as he went on with his own writing, and then reseated myself at my desk. This is very strange, thought I. What had one best do? But my business hurried me. I concluded to forget the matter for the present, reserving it for my future leisure. So calling Nippers from the other room, the paper was speedily examined.

A few days after this, Bartleby concluded four lengthy documents, being quadruplicates of a week's testimony taken before me in my High Court of Chancery. It became necessary to examine them. It was an important suit, and great accuracy was imperative. Having all things arranged, I called Turkey, Nippers, and Ginger Nut from the next room, meaning to place the four copies in the hands of my four clerks, while I should read from the original. Accordingly, Turkey, Nippers, and Ginger Nut had taken their seats in a row, each with his document in his hand, when I called to Bartleby to join this interesting group.

"Bartleby! quick, I am waiting."

I heard a slow scrape of his chair legs on the uncarpeted floor, and soon he appeared standing at the entrance of his hermitage.

"What is wanted?" said he, mildly.

"The copies, the copies," said I, hurriedly. "We are going to examine them. There"—and I held towards him the fourth quadruplicate.

"I would prefer not to," he said, and gently disappeared behind the screen.

For a few moments I was turned into a pillar of salt, standing at the head of my seated column of clerks. Recovering myself, I advanced towards the screen, and demanded the reason for such extraordinary conduct.

"*Why* do you refuse?"

"I would prefer not to."

With any other man I should have flown outright into a dreadful passion, scorned all further words, and thrust him ignominiously from my presence. But there was something about Bartleby that not only strangely disarmed me, but, in a wonderful manner, touched and disconcerted me. I began to reason with him.

"These are your own copies we are about to examine. It is labor saving to you, because one examination will answer for your four papers. It is common usage. Every copyist is bound to help examine his copy. Is it not so? Will you not speak? Answer!"

"I prefer not to," he replied in a flutelike tone. It seemed to me that, while I had been addressing him, he carefully revolved every statement that I made; fully comprehended the meaning; could not gainsay the irresistible conclusion; but, at the same time, some paramount consideration prevailed with him to reply as he did.

"You are decided, then, not to comply with my request—a request made according to common usage and common sense?"

He briefly gave me to understand, that on that point my judgment was sound. Yes: his decision was irreversible.

It is not seldom the case that, when a man is browbeaten in some unprecedented and violently unreasonable way, he begins to stagger in his own plainest faith. He begins, as it were, vaguely to surmise that, wonderful as it may be, all the justice and all the reason is on the other side. Accordingly, if any disinterested persons are present, he turns to them for some reinforcement of his own faltering mind.

"Turkey," said I, "what do you think of this? Am I not right?"

"With submission, sir," said Turkey, in his blandest tone, "I think that you are."

"Nippers," said I, "what do *you* think of it?"

"I think I should kick him out of the office."

(The reader, of nice perceptions, will here perceive that, it being morning, Turkey's answer is couched in polite and tranquil terms, but Nippers replies in ill-tempered ones. Or, to repeat a previous sentence, Nippers's ugly mood was on duty, and Turkey's off.)

"Ginger Nut," said I, willing to enlist the smallest suffrage in my behalf, "what do *you* think of it?"

"I think, sir, he's a little *luny*," replied Ginger Nut, with a grin.

"You hear what they say," said I, turning towards the screen, "come forth and do your duty."

But he vouchsafed no reply. I pondered a moment in sore perplexity. But once more business hurried me. I determined again to postpone the consideration of this dilemma to my future leisure. With a little trouble we made out to examine the papers without Bartleby, though at every page or two Turkey deferentially dropped his opinion, that this proceeding was quite out of the common; while Nippers, twitching in his chair with a dyspeptic nervousness, ground out, between his set teeth, occasional hissing maledictions against the stubborn oaf behind the screen. And for his

(Nippers's) part, this was the first and the last time he would do another man's business without pay.

Meanwhile Bartleby sat in his hermitage, oblivious to everything but his own peculiar business there.

Some days passed, the scrivener being employed upon another lengthy work. His late remarkable conduct led me to regard his ways narrowly. I observed that he never went to dinner; indeed, that he never went anywhere. As yet I had never, of my personal knowledge, known him to be outside of my office. He was a perpetual sentry in the corner. At about eleven o'clock though, in the morning, I noticed that Ginger Nut would advance towards the opening in Bartleby's screen, as if silently beckoned thither by a gesture invisible to me where I sat. The boy would then leave the office, jingling a few pence, and reappear with a handful of ginger-nuts, which he delivered in the hermitage, receiving two of the cakes for his trouble.

He lives, then, on ginger-nuts, thought I; never eats a dinner, properly speaking; he must be a vegetarian, then; but no! he never eats even vegetables, he eats nothing but ginger-nuts. My mind then ran on in reveries concerning the probable effects upon the human constitution of living entirely on ginger-nuts. Ginger-nuts are so called, because they contain ginger as one of their peculiar constituents, and the final flavoring one. Now, what was ginger? A hot, spicy thing. Was Bartleby hot and spicy? Not at all. Ginger, then, had no effect upon Bartleby. Probably he preferred it should have none.

Nothing so aggravates an earnest person as a passive resistance. If the individual so resisted be of a not inhumane temper, and the resisting one perfectly harmless in his passivity, then, in the better moods of the former, he will endeavor charitably to construe to his imagination what proves impossible to be solved by his judgment. Even so, for the most part, I regarded Bartleby and his ways. Poor fellow! thought I, he means no mischief; it is plain he intends no insolence; his aspect sufficiently evinces that his eccentricities are involuntary. He is useful to me. I can get along with him. If I turn him away, the chances are he will fall in with some less-indulgent employer, and then he will be rudely treated, and perhaps driven forth miserably to starve. Yes. Here I can cheaply purchase a delicious self-approval. To befriend Bartleby; to humor him in his strange willfulness, will cost me little or nothing, while I lay up in my soul what will eventually prove a sweet morsel for my conscience. But this mood was not invariable with me. The passiveness of Bartleby sometimes irritated me. I felt strangely goaded on to encounter him in new opposition—to elicit some angry spark from him answerable to my own. But, indeed, I might as well have essayed to strike fire with my knuckles against a bit of Windsor soap. But one afternoon the evil impulse in me mastered me, and the following little scene ensued:

"Bartleby," said I, "when those papers are all copied, I will compare them with you."

"I would prefer not to."

"How? Surely you do not mean to persist in that mulish vagary?"

No answer.

I threw open the folding-doors near by, and, turning upon Turkey and Nippers, exclaimed:

"Bartleby a second time says, he won't examine his papers. What do you think of it, Turkey?"

It was afternoon, be it remembered. Turkey sat glowing like a brass boiler; his bald head steaming; his hands reeling among his blotted papers.

"Think of it?" roared Turkey; "I think I'll just step behind his screen, and black his eyes for him!"

So saying, Turkey rose to his feet and threw his arms into a pugilistic position. He was hurrying away to make good his promise, when I detained him, alarmed at the effect of incautiously rousing Turkey's combativeness after dinner.

"Sit down, Turkey," said I, "and hear what Nippers has to say. What do you think of it, Nippers? Would I not be justified in immediately dismissing Bartleby?"

"Excuse me, that is for you to decide, sir. I think his conduct quite unusual, and, indeed, unjust, as regards Turkey and myself. But it may only be a passing whim."

"Ah," exclaimed I, "you have strangely changed your mind, then— you speak very gently of him now."

"All beer," cried Turkey; "gentleness is effects of beer—Nippers and I dined together today. You see how gentle *I* am, sir. Shall I go and black his eyes?"

"You refer to Bartleby, I suppose. No, not today, Turkey," I replied; "pray, put up your fists."

I closed the doors, and again advanced towards Bartleby. I felt additional incentives tempting me to my fate. I burned to be rebelled against again. I remembered that Bartleby never left the office.

"Bartleby," said I, "Ginger Nut is away; just step around to the Post Office, won't you? (it was but a three minutes' walk), and see if there is anything for me."

"I would prefer not to."

"You *will* not?"

"I *prefer* not."

I staggered to my desk, and sat there in a deep study. My blind inveteracy returned. Was there any other thing in which I could procure myself to be ignominiously repulsed by this lean, penniless wight?—my hired clerk? What added thing is there, perfectly reasonable, that he will be sure to refuse to do?

"Bartleby!"

No answer.

"Bartleby," in a louder tone.

No answer.

"Bartleby," I roared.

Like a very ghost, agreeable to the laws of magical invocation, at the third summons, he appeared at the entrance of his hermitage.

"Go to the next room, and tell Nippers to come to me."

"I prefer not to," he respectfully and slowly said, and mildly disappeared.

"Very good, Bartleby," said I, in a quiet sort of serenely severe self-possessed tone, intimating the unalterable purpose of some terrible retribution very close at hand. At the moment I half intended something of the kind. But upon the whole, as it was drawing towards my dinner-hour, I thought it best to put on my hat and walk home for the day, suffering much from perplexity and distress of mind.

Shall I acknowledge it? The conclusion of this whole business was, that it soon became a fixed fact of my chambers, that a pale young scrivener, by the name of Bartleby, had a desk there; that he copied for me at the usual rate of four cents a folio (one hundred words); but he was permanently exempt from examining the work done by him, that duty being transferred to Turkey and Nippers, out of compliment, doubtless, to their superior acuteness; moreover, said Bartleby was never, on any account, to be dispatched on the most trivial errand of any sort; and that even if entreated to take upon him such a matter, it was generally understood that he would "prefer not to"—in other words, that he would refuse point-blank.

As days passed on, I became considerably reconciled to Bartleby. His steadiness, his freedom from all dissipation, his incessant industry (except when he chose to throw himself into a standing reverie behind his screen), his great stillness, his unalterableness of demeanor under all circumstances, made him a valuable acquisition. One prime thing was this—*he was always there*—first in the morning, continually through the day, and the last at night. I had a singular confidence in his honesty. I felt my most precious papers perfectly safe in his hands. Sometimes, to be sure, I could not, for the very soul of me, avoid falling into sudden spasmodic passions with him. For it was exceeding difficult to bear in mind all the time those strange peculiarities, privileges, and unheard of exemptions, forming the tacit stipulations on Bartleby's part under which he remained in my office. Now and then, in the eagerness of dispatching pressing business, I would inadvertently summon Bartleby, in a short, rapid tone, to put his finger, say, on the incipient tie of a bit of red tape with which I was about compressing some papers. Of course, from behind the screen the usual answer, "I prefer not to," was sure to come; and then, how could a human creature, with the common infirmities of our nature, refrain from bitterly exclaiming upon such perverseness—such unreasonableness. However, every added repulse of this sort which I received only tended to lessen the probability of my repeating the inadvertence.

Here it must be said, that according to the custom of most legal gentlemen occupying chambers in densely populated law buildings, there were several keys to my door. One was kept by a woman residing in the attic, which person weekly scrubbed and daily swept and dusted my apartments. Another was kept by Turkey for convenience sake. The third I sometimes carried in my own pocket. The fourth I knew not who had.

Now, one Sunday morning I happened to go to Trinity Church, to hear a celebrated preacher, and finding myself rather early on the ground I thought I would walk around to my chambers for a while. Luckily I had my key with me; but upon applying it to the lock, I found it resisted by something inserted from the inside. Quite surprised, I called out; when to my consternation a key was turned from within; and thrusting his lean visage at me, and holding the door ajar, the apparition of Bartleby appeared, in his shirt sleeves, and otherwise in a strangely tattered deshabille, saying quietly that he was sorry, but he was deeply engaged just then, and—preferred not admitting me at present. In a brief word or two, he moreover added, that perhaps I had better walk around the block two or three times, and by that time he would probably have concluded his affairs.

Now, the utterly unsurmised appearance of Bartleby, tenanting my law-chambers of a Sunday morning, with his cadaverously gentlemanly *nonchalance*, yet withal firm and self-possessed, had such a strange effect upon me, that incontinently I slunk away from my own door, and did as desired. But not without sundry twinges of impotent rebellion against the mild effrontery of this unaccountable scrivener. Indeed, it was his wonderful mildness chiefly, which not only disarmed me but unmanned me as it were. For I consider that one, for the time, is a sort of unmanned when he tranquilly permits his hired clerk to dictate to him, and order him away from his own premises. Furthermore, I was full of uneasiness as to what Bartleby could possibly be doing in my office in his shirt sleeves, and in an otherwise dismantled condition of a Sunday morning. Was anything amiss going on? Nay, that was out of the question. It was not to be thought of for a moment that Bartleby was an immoral person. But what could he be doing there?—copying? Nay again, whatever might be his eccentricities Bartleby was an eminently decorous person. He would be the last man to sit down to his desk in any state approaching to nudity. Besides, it was Sunday; and there was something about Bartleby that forbade the supposition that he would by any secular occupation violate the proprieties of the day.

Nevertheless, my mind was not pacified; and full of a restless curiosity, at last I returned to the door. Without hindrance I inserted my key, opened it, and entered. Bartleby was not to be seen. I looked round anxiously, peeped behind his screen; but it was very plain that he was gone. Upon more closely examining the place, I surmised that for an indefinite period Bartleby must have ate, dressed, and slept in my office, and that, too, without plate, mirror, or bed. The cushioned seat of a rickety old sofa in one corner bore the faint impress of a lean, reclining form. Rolled away under his desk, I found a blanket; under the empty grate, a blacking box and brush; on a chair, a tin basin, with soap and a ragged towel; in a newspaper a few crumbs of ginger-nuts and a morsel of cheese. Yes, thought I, it is evident enough that Bartleby has been making his home here, keeping bachelor's hall all by himself. Immediately then the thought came sweeping across me, what miserable friendlessness and loneliness are here revealed! His poverty is great; but his solitude, how horrible! Think of it. Of a Sunday, Wall Street is deserted as Petra; and every night of every day it is an emptiness. This building, too, which of weekdays hums with industry and life, at nightfall echoes with sheer vacancy, and all through Sunday is forlorn. And here Bartleby makes his home; sole spectator of a solitude which he has seen all populous—a sort of innocent and transformed Marius brooding among the ruins of Carthage!

For the first time in my life a feeling of over-powering stinging melancholy seized me. Before, I had never experienced aught but a not unpleasing sadness. The bond of a common humanity now drew me irresistibly to gloom. A fraternal melancholy! For both I and Bartleby were sons of Adam. I remembered the bright silks and sparkling faces I had seen that day, in gala trim, swan-like sailing down the Mississippi of Broadway; and I contrasted them with the pallid copyist, and thought to myself, Ah, happiness courts the light, so we deem the world is gay; but misery hides aloof, so we deem that misery there is none. These sad fancyings—chimeras, doubtless, of a sick and silly brain—led on to other and more special thoughts, concerning the eccentricities of Bartleby. Presentiments of strange discoveries hovered round me. The scrivener's pale form appeared to me laid out, among uncaring strangers, in its shivering winding sheet.

Suddenly I was attracted by Bartleby's closed desk, the key in open sight left in the lock.

I mean no mischief, seek the gratification of no heartless curiosity, thought I; besides, the desk is mine, and its contents, too, so I will make bold to look within. Everything was methodically arranged, the papers smoothly placed. The pigeon holes were deep, and removing the files of documents, I groped into their recesses. Presently I felt something there, and dragged it out. It was an old bandanna handkerchief, heavy and knotted. I opened it, and saw it was a savings bank.

I now recalled all the quiet mysteries which I had noted in the man. I remembered that he never spoke but to answer; that, though at intervals he had considerable time to himself, yet I had never seen him reading—no, not even a newspaper; that for long periods he would stand looking out, at his pale window behind the screen, upon the dead brick wall; I was quite sure he never visited any refectory or eating house; while his pale face clearly indicated that he never drank beer like Turkey, or tea and coffee even, like other men; that he never went anywhere in particular that I could learn; never went out for a walk, unless, indeed, that was the case at present; that he had declined telling who he was, or whence he came, or whether he had any relatives in the world; that though so thin and pale, he never complained of ill health. And more than all, I remembered a certain unconscious air of pallid—how shall I call it?—of pallid haughtiness, say, or rather an austere reserve about him, which had positively awed me into my tame compliance with his eccentricities, when I had feared to ask him to do the slightest incidental thing for me, even though I might know, from his long-continued motionlessness, that behind his screen he must be standing in one of those dead-wall reveries of his.

Revolving all these things, and coupling them with the recently discovered fact, that he made my office his constant abiding place and home, and not forgetful of his morbid moodiness; revolving all these things, a prudential feeling began to steal over me. My first emotions had been those of pure melancholy and sincerest pity; but just in proportion as the forlornness of Bartleby grew and grew to my imagination, did that same melancholy merge into fear, that pity into repulsion. So true it is, and so terrible, too, that up to a certain point the thought or sight of misery enlists our best affections; but, in certain special cases, beyond that point it does not. They err who would assert that invariably this is owing to the inherent selfishness of the human heart. It rather proceeds from a certain hopelessness of remedying excessive and organic ill. To a sensitive being, pity is not seldom pain. And when at last it is perceived that such pity cannot lead to effectual succor, common sense bids the soul be rid of it. What I saw that morning persuaded me that the scrivener was the victim of innate and incurable disorder. I might give alms to his body; but his body did not pain him; it was his soul that suffered, and his soul I could not reach.

I did not accomplish the purpose of going to Trinity Church that morning. Somehow, the things I had seen disqualified me for the time from church-going. I walked homeward, thinking what I would do with Bartleby. Finally, I resolved upon this—I would put certain calm questions to him the next morning, touching his history, etc., and if he declined to answer them openly and unreservedly (and I supposed he would prefer not), then to give him a twenty dollar bill over and above whatever I might owe him, and tell him his services were no longer required; but that if in any other way I could assist him, I would be happy to do so, especially if he desired to return to his native place, wherever that might be, I would willingly help to defray the expenses. Moreover, if, after reaching home, he found himself at any time in want of aid, a letter from him would be sure of a reply.

The next morning came.

"Bartleby," said I, gently calling to him behind his screen.

No reply.

"Bartleby," said I, in a still gentler tone, "come here; I am not going to ask you to do anything you would prefer not to do—I simply wish to speak to you."

Upon this he noiselessly slid into view.

"Will you tell me, Bartleby, where you were born?"

"I would prefer not to."

"Will you tell me *anything* about yourself?"

"I would prefer not to."

"But what reasonable objection can you have to speak to me? I feel friendly towards you."

He did not look at me while I spoke, but kept his glance fixed upon my bust of Cicero, which, as I then sat, was directly behind me, some six inches above my head."

"What is your answer, Bartleby," said I, after waiting a considerable time for a reply, during which his countenance remained immovable, only there was the faintest conceivable tremor of the white attenuated mouth.

"At present I prefer to give no answer," he said, and retired into his hermitage.

It was rather weak in me I confess, but his manner, on this occasion, nettled me. Not only did there seem to lurk in it a certain calm disdain, but his perverseness seemed ungrateful, considering the undeniable good usage and indulgence he had received from me.

Again I sat ruminating what I should do. Mortified as I was at his behavior, and resolved as I had been to dismiss him when I entered my office, nevertheless I strangely felt something superstitious knocking at my heart, and forbidding me to carry out my purpose, and denouncing me for a villain if I dared to breathe one bitter word against this forlornest of mankind. At last, familiarly drawing my chair behind his screen, I sat down and said: "Bartleby, never mind, then, about revealing your history; but let me entreat you, as a friend, to comply as far as may be with the usages of this office. Say now, you will help to examine papers tomorrow or next day: in short, say now, that in a day or two you will begin to be a little reasonable:—say so, Bartleby."

"At present I would prefer not to be a little reasonable," was his mildly cadaverous reply.

Just then the folding-doors opened, and Nippers approached. He seemed suffering from an unusually bad night's rest, induced by severer indigestion than common. He overheard those final words of Bartleby.

"*Prefer not*, eh?" gritted Nippers—"I'd *prefer* him, if I were you, sir," addressing me—"I'd *prefer* him; I'd give him preferences, the stubborn mule! What is it, sir, pray, that he *prefers* not to do now?"

Bartleby moved not a limb.

"Mr. Nippers," said I, "I'd prefer that you would withdraw for the present."

Somehow, of late, I had got into the way of involuntarily using this word "prefer" upon all sorts of not exactly suitable occasions. And I trembled to think that my contact with the scrivener had already and seriously affected me in a mental way. And what further and deeper aberration might it not yet produce? This apprehension had not been without efficacy in determining me to summary measures.

As Nippers, looking very sour and sulky, was departing, Turkey blandly and deferentially approached.

"With submission, sir," said he, "yesterday I was thinking about Bartleby here, and I think that if he would but prefer to take a quart of good ale every day, it would do much towards mending him, and enabling him to assist in examining his papers."

"So you have got the word, too," said I, slightly excited.

"With submission, what word, sir," asked Turkey, respectfully crowding himself into the contracted space behind the screen, and by so doing, making me jostle the scrivener. "What word, sir?"

"I would prefer to be left alone here," said Bartleby, as if offended at being mobbed in his privacy.

"*That's* the word, Turkey," said I—"*that's* it."

"Oh, *prefer*? oh yes—queer word I never use it myself. But, sir, as I was saying, if he would but prefer—"

"Turkey," interrupted I, "you will please withdraw."

"Oh, certainly, sir, if you prefer that I should."

As he opened the folding-door to retire, Nippers at his desk caught a glimpse of me, and asked whether I would prefer to have a certain paper copied on blue paper or white. He did not in the least roguishly accent the word prefer. It was plain that it involuntarily rolled from his tongue. I thought to myself, surely I must get rid of a demented man, who already has in some degree turned the tongues, if not the heads, of myself and clerks. But I thought it prudent not to break the dismission at once.

The next day I noticed that Bartleby did nothing but stand at his window in his dead-walled reverie. Upon asking him why he did not write, he said that he had decided upon doing no more writing.

"Why, how now? what next?" exclaimed I, "do no more writing?"

"No more."

"And what is the reason?"

"Do you not see the reason for yourself," he indifferently replied.

I looked steadfastly at him, and perceived that his eyes looked dull and glazed. Instantly it occurred to me, that his unexampled diligence in copying by his dim window for the first few weeks of his stay with me might have temporarily impaired his vision.

I was touched. I said something in condolence with him. I hinted that of course he did wisely in abstaining from writing for a while; and urged him to embrace that opportunity of taking wholesome exercise in the open air. This, however, he did not do. A few days after this, my other clerks being absent, and being in a great hurry to dispatch certain letters by the mail, I thought that, having nothing else earthly to do, Bartleby would surely be less inflexible than usual, and carry these letters to the post-office. But he blankly declined. So, much to my inconvenience, I went myself.

Still added days went by. Whether Bartleby's eyes improved or not, I could not say. To all appearance, I thought they did. But when I asked him if they did, he vouchsafed no answer. At all events, he would do no copying. At last, in reply to my urgings, he informed me that he had permanently given up copying.

"What!" exclaimed I; "suppose your eyes should get entirely well—better than ever before—would you not copy then?"

"I have given up copying," he answered, and slid aside.

He remained as ever, a fixture in my chamber. Nay—if that were possible—he became still more of a fixture than before. What was to be done? He would do nothing in the office; why should he stay there? In plain fact, he had now become a millstone to me, not only useless as a necklace, but afflictive to bear. Yet I was sorry for him. I speak less than truth when I say that, on his own account, he occasioned me uneasiness. If he would but have named a single relative or friend, I would instantly have written, and urged their taking the poor fellow away to some convenient retreat. But he seemed alone, absolutely alone in the universe. A bit of wreck in the mid-Atlantic. At length, necessities connected with my business tyrannized over all other considerations. Decently as I could, I told Bartleby that in six days time he must unconditionally leave the office. I warned him to take measures, in the interval, for procuring some other abode. I offered to assist him in this endeavor, if he himself would but take the first step towards a removal. "And when you finally quit me, Bartleby," added I, "I shall see that you go not away entirely unprovided. Six days from this hour, remember."

At the expiration of that period, I peeped behind the screen, and lo! Bartleby was there.

I buttoned up my coat, balanced myself; advanced slowly towards him, touched his shoulder, and said, "The time has come; you must quit this place; I am sorry for you; here is money; but you must go."

"I would prefer not," he replied, with his back still towards me.

"You *must*."

He remained silent.

Now I had an unbounded confidence in this man's common honesty. He had frequently restored to me sixpences and shillings carelessly dropped upon the floor, for I am apt to be very reckless in such shirt-button affairs. The proceeding, then, which followed will not be deemed extraordinary.

"Bartleby," said I, "I owe you twelve dollars on account; here are thirty-two; the odd twenty are yours—Will you take it?" and I handed the bills towards him.

But he made no motion.

"I will leave them here, then," putting them under a weight on the table. Then taking my hat and cane and going to the door, I tranquilly turned and added—"After you have removed your things from these offices, Bartleby, you will of course lock the door—since every one is now gone for the day but you—and if you please, slip your key underneath the mat, so that I may have it in the morning. I shall not see you again; so good-by to you. If, hereafter, in your new place of abode, I can be of any service to you, do not fail to advise me by letter. Good-by, Bartleby, and fare you well."

But he answered not a word; like the last column of some ruined temple, he remained standing mute and solitary in the middle of the otherwise deserted room.

As I walked home in a pensive mood, my vanity got the better of my pity. I could not but highly plume myself on my masterly management in getting rid of Bartleby. Masterly I call it, and such it must appear to any dispassionate thinker. The beauty of my procedure seemed to consist in its perfect quietness. There was no vulgar bullying, no bravado of any sort, no choleric hectoring, and striding to and fro across the apartment, jerking out vehement commands for Bartleby to bundle himself off with his beggarly traps. Nothing of the kind. Without loudly bidding Bartleby depart— as an inferior genius might have done—I *assumed* the ground that depart he must; and upon that assumption built all I had to say. The more I thought over my procedure, the more I was charmed with it. Nevertheless, next morning, upon awakening, I had my doubts—I had somehow slept off the fumes of vanity. One of the coolest and wisest hours a man has, is just after he awakes in the morning. My procedure seemed as sagacious as ever—but only in theory. How it would prove in practice—there was the rub. It was truly a beautiful thought to have assumed Bartleby's departure; but, after all, that assumption was simply my own, and none of Bartleby's. The great point was, not whether I had assumed that he would quit me, but whether he would prefer so to do. He was more a man of preferences than assumptions.

After breakfast, I walked down town, arguing the probabilities pro and con. One moment I thought it would prove a miserable failure, and Bartleby would be found all alive at my office as usual; the next moment it seemed certain that I should find his chair empty. And so I kept veering about. At the corner of Broadway and Canal Street, I saw quite an excited group of people standing in earnest conversation.

"I'll take odds he doesn't," said a voice as I passed.

"Doesn't go?—done!" said I, "put up your money."

I was instinctively putting my hand in my pocket to produce my own, when I remembered that this was an election day. The words I had overheard bore no reference to Bartleby, but to the success or non-success of some candidate for the mayoralty. In my intent frame of mind, I had, as it were, imagined that all Broadway shared in my excitement, and were debating the same question with me. I passed on, very thankful that the uproar of the street screened my momentary absent-mindedness.

As I had intended, I was earlier than usual at my office door. I stood listening for a moment. All was still. He must be gone. I tried the knob. The door was locked. Yes, my procedure had worked to a charm; he indeed must be vanished. Yet a certain melancholy mixed with this: I was almost sorry for my brilliant success. I was fumbling under the door mat for the key, which Bartleby was to have left there for me, when accidentally my knee knocked against a panel, producing a summoning sound, and in response a voice came to me from within—"Not yet; I am occupied."

It was Bartleby.

I was thunderstruck. For an instant I stood like the man who, pipe in mouth, was killed one cloudless afternoon long ago in Virginia, by summer lightning; at his own warm open window he was killed, and remained leaning out there upon the dreamy afternoon, till some one touched him, when he fell.

"Not gone!" I murmured at last. But again obeying that wondrous ascendancy which the inscrutable scrivener had over me, and from which ascendancy, for all my chafing, I could not completely escape, I slowly went downstairs and out into the street, and while walking round the block, considered what I should next do in this unheard of perplexity. Turn the man out by an actual thrusting I could not; to drive him away by calling him hard names would not do; calling in the police was an unpleasant idea; and yet, permit him to enjoy his cadaverous triumph over me— this, too, I could not think of. What was to be done? or, if nothing could be done, was there anything further that I could *assume* in the matter? Yes, as before I had prospectively assumed that Bartleby would depart, so now I might retrospectively assume that departed he was. In the legitimate carrying out of this assumption, I might enter my office in a great hurry, and pretending not to see Bartleby at all, walk straight against him as if he were air. Such a proceeding would in a singular degree have the appearance of a home-thrust. It was hardly possible that Bartleby could withstand such an application of the doctrine of assumptions. But upon second thoughts the success of the plan seemed rather dubious. I resolved to argue the matter over with him again.

"Bartleby," said I, entering the office, with a quietly severe expression, "I am seriously displeased. I am pained, Bartleby. I had thought better of you. I had imagined you of such a gentlemanly organization, that in any delicate dilemma a slight hint would suffice—in short, an assumption. But it appears I am deceived. Why," I added, unaffectedly starting, "you have not even touched that money yet," pointing to it, just where I had left it the evening previous.

He answered nothing.

"Will you, or will you not, quit me?" I now demanded in a sudden passion, advancing close to him.

"I would prefer *not* to quit you," he replied, gently emphasizing the *not*.

"What earthly right have you to stay here? Do you pay any rent? Do you pay my taxes? Or is this property yours?"

He answered nothing.

"Are you ready to go on and write now? Are your eyes recovered? Could you copy a small paper for me this morning? or help examine a few lines? or step round to the post-office? In a word, will you do anything at all, to give a coloring to your refusal to depart the premises?"

He silently retired into his hermitage.

I was now in such a state of nervous resentment that I thought it but prudent to check myself at present from further demonstrations. Bartleby and I were alone. I remembered the tragedy of the unfortunate Adams and the still more unfortunate Colt in the solitary office of the latter; and how poor Colt, being dreadfully incensed by Adams, and imprudently permitting himself to get wildly excited, was at unawares hurried into his fatal act—an act which certainly no man could possibly deplore more than the actor himself. Often it had occurred to me in my ponderings upon the subject, that had that altercation taken place in the public street, or at a private residence, it would not have terminated as it did. It was the circumstance of being alone in a solitary office, upstairs, of a building entirely unhallowed by humanizing domestic associations—an uncarpeted office, doubtless, of a dusty, haggard sort of appearance—this it must have been, which greatly helped to enhance the irritable desperation of the hapless Colt.

But when this old Adam of resentment rose in me and tempted me concerning Bartleby, I grappled him and threw him. How? Why, simply by recalling the divine injunction: "A new commandment give I unto you, that ye love one another." Yes, this it was that saved me. Aside from higher considerations, charity often operates as a vastly wise and prudent principle—a great safeguard to its possessor. Men have committed murder for jealousy's sake, and anger's sake, and hatred's sake, and selfishness' sake, and spiritual pride's sake; but no man, that ever I heard of, ever committed a diabolical murder for sweet charity's sake. Mere self-interest, then, if no better motive can be enlisted, should, especially with high-tempered men, prompt all beings to charity and philanthropy. At any rate, upon the occasion in question, I strove to drown my exasperated feelings towards the scrivener by benevolently construing his conduct. Poor fellow, poor fellow! thought I, he don't mean anything; and besides, he has seen hard times, and ought to be indulged.

I endeavored, also, immediately to occupy myself, and at the same time to comfort my despondency. I tried to fancy, that in the course of the morning, at such time as might prove agreeable to him, Bartleby, of his own free accord, would emerge from his hermitage and take up some decided line of march in the direction of the door. But no. Half-past twelve o'clock came; Turkey began to glow in the face, overturn his inkstand, and become generally obstreperous; Nippers abated down into quietude and courtesy; Ginger Nut munched his noon apple; and Bartleby remained standing at his window in one of his profoundest dead-wall reveries. Will it be credited? Ought I to acknowledge it? That afternoon I left the office without saying one further word to him.

Some days now passed, during which, at leisure intervals I looked a little into "Edwards on the Will," and "Priestly on Necessity." Under the circumstances, those books induced a salutary feeling. Gradually I slid into the persuasian that these troubles of mine, touching the scrivener, had been all predestinated from eternity, and Bartleby was billeted upon me for some mysterious purpose of an allwise Providence, which it was not for a mere mortal like me to fathom. Yes, Bartleby, stay there behind your screen, thought I; I shall persecute you no more; you are harmless and noiseless as any of these old chairs; in short, I never feel so private as when I know you are here. At last I see it, I feel it; I penetrate to the predestinated purpose of my life. I am content. Others may have loftier parts to enact; but my mission in this world, Bartleby, is to furnish you with office-room for such period as you may see fit to remain.

I believe that this wise and blessed frame of mind would have continued with me, had it not been for the unsolicited and uncharitable remarks obtruded upon me by my professional friends who visited the rooms. But thus it often is, that the constant friction of illiberal minds wears out at last the best resolves of the more generous. Though to be sure, when I reflected upon it, it was not strange that people entering my office should be struck by the peculiar aspect of the unaccountable Bartleby, and so be tempted to throw out some sinister observations concerning him. Sometimes an attorney, having business with me, and calling at my office, and finding no one but the scrivener there, would undertake to obtain some sort of precise information from him touching my whereabouts; but without heeding his idle talk, Bartleby would remain standing immovable in the middle of the room. So after contemplating him in that position for a time, the attorney would depart, no wiser than he came.

Also, when a reference was going on, and the room full of lawyers and witnesses, and business driving fast, some deeply occupied legal gentleman present, seeing Bartleby wholly unemployed, would request him to run round to his (the legal gentleman's) office and fetch some papers for him. Thereupon, Bartleby would tranquilly decline, and yet remain idle as before. Then the lawyer would give a great stare, and turn to me. And what could I say? At last I was made aware that all through the circle of my professional acquaintance, a whisper of wonder was running round, having reference to the strange creature I kept at my office. This worried me very much. And as the idea came upon me of his possibly turning out a long-lived man, and keep occupying my chambers, and denying my authority; and perplexing my visitors; and scandalizing my professional reputation; and casting a general gloom over the premises; keeping soul and body together to the last upon his savings (for doubtless he spent but half a dime a day), and in the end perhaps outlive me, and claim possession of my office by right of his perpetual occupancy: as all these dark anticipations crowded upon me more and more, and my friends continually intruded their relentless remarks upon the apparition in my room; a great change was wrought in me. I resolved to gather all my faculties together, and forever rid me of this intolerable incubus.

Ere revolving any complicated project, however, adapted to this end, I first simply suggested to Bartleby the propriety of his permanent departure. In a calm and serious tone, I commended the idea to his careful and mature consideration. But, having taken three days to meditate upon it, he apprised me, that his original determination remained the same; in short, that he still preferred to abide with me.

What shall I do? I now said to myself, buttoning up my coat to the last button. What shall I do? what ought I to do? what does conscience say I *should* do with this man, or, rather, ghost. Rid myself of him, I must; go, he shall. But how? You will not thrust him, the poor, pale, passive mortal —you will not thrust such a helpless creature out of your door? you will not dishonor yourself by such cruelty? No, I will not, I cannot do that, Rather would I let him live and die here, and then mason up his remains in the wall. What, then, will you do? For all your coaxing, he will not budge. Bribes he leaves under your own paper-weight on your table; in short, it is quite plain that he prefers to cling to you.

Then something severe, something unusual must be done. What! surely you will not have him collared by a constable, and commit his innocent pallor to the common jail? And upon what ground could you procure such a thing to be done?—a vagrant, is he? What! he a vagrant, a wanderer, who refuses to budge? It is because he will *not* be a vagrant, then, that you seek to count him *as* a vagrant. That is too absurd. No visible means of support: there I have him. Wrong again: for indubitably he *does* support himself, and that is the only unanswerable proof that any man can show of his possessing the means so to do. No more, then. Since he will not quit me, I must quit him. I will change my offices; I will move elsewhere, and give him fair notice, that if I find him on my new premises I will then proceed against him as a common trespasser.

Acting accordingly, next day I thus addressed him: "I find these chambers too far from the City Hall; the air is unwholesome. In a word, I propose to remove my offices next week, and shall no longer require your services. I tell you this now, in order that you may seek another place."

He made no reply, and nothing more was said.

On the appointed day I engaged carts and men, proceeded to my chambers, and, having but little furniture, everything was removed in a few hours. Throughout, the scrivener remained standing behind the screen, which I directed to be removed the last thing. It was withdrawn; and, being folded up like a huge folio, left him the motionless occupant of a naked room. I stood in the entry watching him a moment, while something from within me upbraided me.

I re-entered, with my hand in my pocket—and—and my heart in my mouth.

"Good-by, Bartleby; I am going—good-by, and God some way bless you; and take that," slipping something in his hand. But it dropped upon the floor, and then—strange to say—I tore myself from him whom I had so longed to be rid of.

Established in my new quarters, for a day or two I kept the door locked, and started at every footfall in the passages. When I returned to my rooms, after any little absence, I would pause at the threshold for an instant, and attentively listen, ere applying my key. But these fears were needless. Bartleby never came nigh me.

I thought all was going well, when a perturbed-looking stranger visited me, inquiring whether I was the person who had recently occupied rooms at No. —— Wall Street.

Full of forebodings, I replied that I was.

"Then, sir," said the stranger, who proved a lawyer, "you are responsible for the man you left there. He refuses to do any copying; he refuses to do anything; he says he prefers not to; and he refuses to quit the premises."

"I am very sorry, sir," said I, with assumed tranquillity, but an inward tremor, "but, really, the man you allude to is nothing to me—he is no relation or apprentice of mine, that you should hold me responsible for him."

"In mercy's name, who is he?"

"I certainly cannot inform you. I know nothing about him. Formerly I employed him as a copyist; but he has done nothing for me now for some time past."

"I shall settle him, then—good morning, sir."

Several days passed, and I heard nothing more; and, though I often felt a charitable prompting to call at the place and see poor Bartleby, yet a certain squeamishness, of I know not what, withheld me.

All is over with him, by this time, thought I, at last, when, through another week, no further intelligence reached me. But, coming to my room the day after, I found several persons waiting at my door in a high state of nervous excitement.

"That's the man—here he comes," cried the foremost one, whom I recognized as the lawyer who had previously called upon me alone.

"You must take him away, sir, at once," cried a portly person among them, advancing upon me, and whom I knew to be the landlord of No.

—— Wall Street. "These gentlemen, my tenants, cannot stand it any longer; Mr. B——," pointing to the lawyer, "has turned him out of his room, and he now persists in haunting the building generally, sitting upon the banisters of the stairs by day, and sleeping in the entry by night. Everybody is concerned; clients are leaving the offices; some fears are entertained of a mob; something you must do, and that without delay."

Aghast at this torrent, I fell back before it, and would fain have locked myself in my new quarters. In vain I persisted that Bartleby was nothing to me—no more than to any one else. In vain—I was the last person known to have anything to do with him, and they held me to the terrible account. Fearful, then, of being exposed in the papers (as one person present obscurely threatened), I considered the matter, and, at length, said, that if the lawyer would give me a confidential interview with the scrivener, in his (the lawyer's) own room, I would, that afternoon, strive my best to rid them of the nuisance they complained of.

Going up stairs to my old haunt, there was Bartleby silently sitting upon the banister at the landing.

"What are you doing here, Bartleby?" said I.

"Sitting upon the banister," he mildly replied.

I motioned him into the lawyer's room, who then left us.

"Bartleby," said I, "are you aware that you are the cause of great tribulation to me, by persisting in occupying the entry after being dismissed from the office?"

No answer.

"Now one of two things must take place. Either you must do something, or something must be done to you. Now what sort of business would you like to engage in? Would you like to re-engage in copying for some one?"

"No; I would prefer not to make any change."

"Would you like a clerkship in a dry-goods store?"

"There is too much confinement about that. No, I would not like a clerkship; but I am not particular."

"Too much confinement," I cried, "why you keep yourself confined all the time!"

"I would prefer not to take a clerkship," he rejoined, as if to settle that little item at once.

"How would a bartender's business suit you? There is no trying of the eyesight in that."

"I would not like it at all; though, as I said before, I am not parular."

His unwonted wordiness inspirited me. I returned to the charge.

"Well, then, would you like to travel through the country collecting bills for the merchants? That would improve your health."

"No, I would prefer to be doing something else."

"How, then, would going as a companion to Europe, to entertain some young gentleman with your conversation—how would that suit you?"

"Not at all. It does not strike me that there is anything definite about that. I like to be stationary. But I am not particular."

"Stationary you shall be, then," I cried, now losing all patience, and, for the first time in all my exasperating connection with him, fairly flying into a passion. "If you do not go away from these premises before night, I shall feel bound—indeed, I *am* bound—to—to—to quit the premises myself!" I rather absurdly concluded, knowing not with what possible threat to try to frighten his immobility into compliance. Despairing of all further efforts, I was precipitately leaving him, when a final thought occurred to me—one which had not been wholly unindulged before.

"Bartleby," said I, in the kindest tone I could assume under such exciting circumstances, "will you go home with me now—not to my office, but my dwelling—and remain there till we can conclude upon some convenient arrangement for you at our leisure? Come, let us start now, right away."

"No: at present I would prefer not to make any change at all."

I answered nothing; but, effectually dodging every one by the suddenness and rapidity of my flight, rushed from the building, ran up Wall Street towards Broadway, and jumping into the first omnibus, was soon removed from pursuit. As soon as tranquillity returned, I distinctly perceived that I had now done all that I possibly could, both in respect to the demands of the landlord and his tenants, and with regard to my own desire and sense of duty, to benefit Bartleby, and shield him from rude persecution. I now strove to be entirely care-free and quiescent; and my conscience justified me in the attempt; though, indeed, it was not so successful as I could have wished. So fearful was I of being again hunted out by the incensed landlord and his exasperated tenants, that, surrendering my business to Nippers for a few days, I drove about the upper part of the town and through the suburbs, in my rockaway; crossed over to Jersey City and Hoboken, and paid fugitive visits to Manhattanville and Astoria. In fact, I almost lived in my rockaway for the time.

When again I entered my office, lo, a note from the landlord lay upon the desk. I opened it with trembling hands. It informed me that the writer had sent to the police, and had Bartleby removed to the Tombs as a vagrant. Moreover, since I knew more about him than any one else, he wished me to appear at that place, and make a suitable statement of the facts. These tidings had a conflicting effect upon me. At first I was indignant; but, at last, almost approved. The landlord's energetic, summary disposition, had led him to adopt a procedure which I do not think I would have decided upon myself; and yet, as a last resort, under such peculiar circumstances, it seemed the only plan.

As I afterwards learned, the poor scrivener, when told that he must be conducted to the Tombs, offered not the slightest obstacle, but, in his pale, unmoving way, silently acquiesced.

Some of the compassionate and curious bystanders joined the party; and headed by one of the constables arm in arm with Bartleby, the silent procession filed its way through all the noise, and heat, and joy of the roaring thoroughfares at noon.

The same day I received the note, I went to the Tombs, or, to speak more properly, the Halls of Justice. Seeking the right officer, I stated the purpose of my call, and was informed that the individual I described was, indeed, within. I then assured the functionary that Bartleby was a perfectly honest man, and greatly to be compassionated, however unaccountably eccentric. I narrated all I knew, and closed by suggesting the idea of letting him remain in as indulgent confinement as possible, till something less harsh might be done—though, indeed, I hardly knew what. At all events, if nothing else could be decided upon the alms-house must receive him. I then begged to have an interview.

Being under no disgraceful charge, and quite serene and harmless in all his ways, they had permitted him freely to wander about the prison, and, especially, in the inclosed grass-platted yards thereof. And so I found him there, standing all alone in the quietest of the yards, his face towards a high wall, while all around, from the narrow slits of the jail windows, I thought I saw peering out upon him the eyes of murderers and thieves.

"Bartleby!"

"I know you," he said, without looking round—"and I want nothing to say to you."

"It was not I that brought you here, Bartleby," said I, keenly pained at his implied suspicion. "And to you, this should not be so vile a place. Nothing reproachful attaches to you by being here. And see, it is not so sad a place as one might think. Look, there is the sky, and here is the grass."

"I know where I am," he replied, but would say nothing more, and so I left him.

As I entered the corridor again, a broad meat-like man, in an apron, accosted me, and, jerking his thumb over his shoulder, said—"Is that your friend?"

"Yes."

"Does he want to starve? If he does, let him live on the prison fare, that's all."

"Who are you?" asked I, not knowing what to make of such an unofficially speaking person in such a place.

"I am the grub-man. Such gentlemen as have friends here, hire me to provide them with something good to eat."

"Is this so?" said I, turning to the turnkey.

He said it was.

"Well, then," said I, slipping some silver into the grub-man's hands (for so they called him), "I want you to give particular attention to my friend there; let him have the best dinner you can get. And you must be as polite to him as possible."

"Introduce me, will you?" said the grub-man, looking at me with an expression which seemed to say he was all impatience for an opportunity to give a specimen of his breeding.

Thinking it would prove of benefit to the scrivener, I acquiesced; and, asking the grub-man his name, went up with him to Bartleby.

"Bartleby, this is a friend; you will find him very useful to you."

"Your sarvant, sir, your sarvant," said the grub-man, making a low salutation behind his apron. "Hope you find it pleasant here, sir; nice grounds—cool apartments—hope you'll stay with us sometime—try to make it agreeable. What will you have for dinner today?"

"I prefer not to dine today," said Bartleby, turning away. "It would disagree with me; I am unused to dinners." So saying, he slowly moved to the other side of the inclosure, and took up a position fronting the dead-wall.

"How's this?" said the grub-man, addressing me with a stare of astonishment. "He's odd, ain't he?"

"I think he is a little deranged," said I, sadly.

"Deranged? deranged is it? Well, now, upon my word, I thought that friend of yourn was a gentleman forger; they are always pale and genteel-like, them forgers. I can't help pity 'em—can't help it, sir. Did you know Monroe Edwards?" he added, touchingly, and paused. Then, laying his hand piteously on my shoulder, sighed, "he died of consumption at Sing-Sing. So you weren't acquainted with Monroe?"

"No, I was never socially acquainted with any forgers. But I cannot stop longer. Look to my friend yonder. You will not lose by it. I will see you again."

Some few days after this, I again obtained admission to the Tombs, and went through the corridors in quest of Bartleby; but without finding him.

"I saw him coming from his cell not long ago," said a turnkey, "may be he's gone to loiter in the yards."

So I went in that direction.

"Are you looking for the silent man?" said another turnkey, passing me. "Yonder he lies—sleeping in the yard there. 'Tis not twenty minutes since I saw him lie down."

The yard was entirely quiet. It was not accessible to the common prisoners. The surrounding walls, of amazing thickness, kept off all sounds behind them. The Egyptian character of the masonry weighed upon me with its gloom. But a soft imprisoned turf grew under foot. The heart of the eternal pyramids, it seemed, wherein, by some strange magic, through the clefts, grass-seed, dropped by birds, had sprung.

Strangely huddled at the base of the wall, his knees drawn up, and lying on his side, his head touching the cold stones, I saw the wasted Bartleby. But nothing stirred. I paused; then went close up to him, stooped over, and saw that his dim eyes were open; otherwise he seemed profoundly sleeping. Something prompted me to touch him. I felt his hand, when a tingling shiver ran up my arm and down my spine to my feet.

The round face of the grub-man peered upon me now. "His dinner is ready. Won't he dine today, either? Or does he live without dining?"

"Lives without dining," said I, and closed the eyes.

"Eh!—He's asleep, ain't he?"

"With kings and counselors," murmured I.

There would seem little need for proceeding further in this history. Imagination will readily supply the meagre recital of poor Bartleby's interment. But, ere parting with the reader, let me say, that if this little narrative has sufficiently interested him, to awaken curiosity as to who Bartleby was, and what manner of life he led prior to the present narrator's making his acquaintance, I can only reply, that in such curiosity I fully share, but am wholly unable to gratify it. Yet here I hardly know whether I should divulge one little item of rumor, which came to my ear a few months after the scrivener's decease. Upon what basis it rested, I could never ascertain; and hence, how true it is I cannot now tell. But, inasmuch as this vague report has not been without a certain suggestive interest to me, however sad, it may prove the same with some others; and so I will briefly mention it. The report was this: that Bartleby had been a subordinate clerk in the Dead Letter Office at Washington, from which he had been suddenly removed by a change in the administration. When I think over this rumor, hardly can I express the emotions which seize me. Dead letters! does it not sound like dead men? Conceive a man by nature and misfortune prone to a pallid hopelessness, can any business seem more fitted to heighten it than that of continually handling these dead letters, and assorting them for the flames? For by the cart-load they are annually burned. Sometimes from out the folded paper the pale clerk takes a ring—the finger it was meant for, perhaps, moulders in the grave; a bank-note sent in swiftest charity— he whom it would relieve, nor eats nor hungers any more; pardon for those who died despairing; hope for those who died unhoping; good tidings for those who died stifled by unrelieved calamities. On errands of life, these letters speed to death.

Ah, Bartleby! Ah, humanity!

A CHRISTMAS TREE AND A WEDDING

by Fyodor Dostoevsky

(1821–81)

The other day I saw a wedding . . . but no, I had better tell you about the Christmas tree. The wedding was nice, I liked it very much; but the other incident was better. I don't know how it was that, looking at that wedding, I thought of that Christmas tree. This was what happened. Just five years ago, on New Year's Eve, I was invited to a children's party. The giver of the party was a well-known and businesslike personage, with connections, with a large circle of acquaintances, and a good many schemes on hand, so that it may be supposed that this party was an excuse for getting the parents together and discussing various interesting matters in an innocent, casual way. I was an outsider; I had no interesting matter to contribute, and so I spent the evening rather independently. There was another gentleman present who was, I fancied, of no special rank or family, and who, like me, had simply turned up at this family festivity. He was the first to catch my eye. He was a tall, lanky man, very grave and very correctly dressed. But one could see that he was in no mood for merry-making and family festivity; whenever he withdrew into a corner he left off smiling and knitted his bushy black brows. He had not a single acquaintance in the party except his host. One could see that he was fearfully bored, but that he was valiantly keeping up the part of a man perfectly happy and enjoying himself. I learned afterward that this was a gentleman from the provinces, who had a critical and perplexing piece of business in Petersburg, who had brought a letter of introduction to our host, for whom our host was, by no means *con amore*, using his interest, and whom he had invited, out of civility, to his children's party. He did not play cards, cigars were not offered him, everyone avoided entering into conversation with him, most likely recognizing the bird from its feathers: and so my gentleman was forced to sit the whole evening stroking his whiskers simply to have something to do with his hands. His whiskers were certainly very fine. But he stroked them so zealously that, looking at him, one might have supposed that the whiskers were created first and the gentleman only attached to them in order to stroke them.

In addition to this individual who assisted in this way at our host's family festivity (he had five fat, well-fed boys), I was attracted, too, by another gentleman. But he was quite of a different sort. He was a personage. He was called Yulian Mastakovitch. From the first glance one could see that he was an honored guest, and stood in the same relation to our host as our host stood in relation to the gentleman who was stroking his whiskers. Our host and hostess said no end of polite things to him, waited on him hand and foot, pressed him to drink, flattered him, brought their visitors up to be introduced to him, but did not take him to be introduced to anyone else. I noticed that tears glistened in our host's eyes when he remarked about the party that he had rarely spent an evening so agreeably. I felt as it were frightened in the presence of such a personage, and so, after admiring the children, I went away into a little parlor, which was quite empty, and sat down in an arbor of flowers which filled up almost half the room.

The children were all incredibly sweet, and resolutely refused to model themselves on the "grown-ups," regardless of all the admonitions of their governesses and mammas. They stripped the Christmas tree to the last sweetmeat in the twinkling of an eye, and had succeeded in breaking half the playthings before they knew what was destined for which. Particularly charming was a black-eyed, curly-headed boy, who kept trying to shoot me with his wooden gun. But my attention was still more attracted by his sister, a girl of eleven, quiet, dreamy, pale, with big, prominent, dreamy eyes, exquisite as a little Cupid. The children hurt her feelings in some way, and so she came away from them to the same empty parlor in which I was sitting, and played with her doll in the corner. The visitors respectfully pointed out her father, a wealthy contractor, and someone whispered that three hundred thousand rubles were already set aside for her dowry. I turned round to glance at the group who were interested in such a circumstance, and my eye fell on Yulian Mastakovitch, who, with his hands behind his back and his head on one side, was listening with the greatest attention to these gentlemen's idle gossip. Afterward I could not help admiring the discrimination of the host and hostess in the distribution of the children's presents. The little girl, who had already a portion of three hundred thousand rubles, received the costliest doll. Then followed presents diminishing in value in accordance with the rank of the parents of these happy children; finally, the child of lowest degree, a thin, freckled red-haired little boy of ten, got nothing but a book of stories about the marvels of nature and tears of devotion, etc., without pictures or even woodcuts. He was the son of a poor widow, the governess of the children of the house, an oppressed and scared little boy. He was dressed in a short jacket of inferior nankin. After receiving his book he walked round the other toys for a long time; he longed to play with the other children, but did not dare; it was evident that he already felt and understood his position. I love watching children. Their first independent approaches to life are extremely interesting. I noticed that the red-haired boy was so fascinated by the costly toys of the other children, especially by a theater in which he certainly longed to take some part, that he made up his mind to sacrifice his dignity. He smiled and began playing with the other children, he gave away his apple to a fat-faced little boy who had a mass of goodies tied up in a pocket handkerchief already, and even brought himself to carry another boy on his back, simply not to be turned away from the theater, but an insolent youth gave him a heavy thump a minute later. The child did not dare to cry. Then the governess, his mother, made her appearance, and told him not to interfere with the other children's playing. The boy went away to the same room in which was the little girl. She let him join her, and the two set to work very eagerly dressing the expensive doll.

I had been sitting more than half an hour in the ivy arbor, listening to the little prattle of the red-haired boy and the beauty with the dowry of three hundred thousand, who was nursing her doll, when Yulian Mastakovitch suddenly walked into the room. He had taken advantage of the general commotion following a quarrel among the children to step out of the drawing room. I had noticed him a moment before talking very cordially to the future heiress's papa, whose acquaintance he had just made, of the superiority of one branch of the service over another. Now he stood in hesitation and seemed to be reckoning something on his fingers.

"Three hundred . . . three hundred," he was whispering. "Eleven . . . twelve . . . thirteen," and so on. "Sixteen—five years! Supposing it is at four percent—five times twelve is sixty; yes, to that sixty . . . well, in five years we may assume it will be four hundred. Yes! . . . But he won't stick to four percent, the rascal. He can get eight or ten. Well, five hundred, let us say, five hundred at least . . . that's certain; well, say a little more for frills. H'm! . . ."

His hesitation was at an end, he blew his nose and was on the point of going out of the room when he suddenly glanced at the little girl and stopped short. He did not see me behind the pots of greenery. It seemed to me that he was greatly excited. Either his calculations had affected his imagination or something else, for he rubbed his hands and could hardly stand still. This excitement reached its utmost limit when he stopped and bent another resolute glance at the future heiress. He was about to move forward, but first looked round, then moving on tiptoe, as though he felt guilty, he advanced toward the children. He approached with a little smile, bent down and kissed her on the head. The child, not expecting this attack, uttered a cry of alarm.

"What are you doing here, sweet child?" he asked in a whisper, looking round and patting the girl's cheek.

"We are playing."

"Ah! With him?" Yulian Mastakovitch looked askance at the boy. "You had better go into the drawing room, my dear," he said to him.

The boy looked at him open-eyed and did not utter a word. Yulian Mastakovitch looked round him again, and again bent down to the little girl.

"And what is this you've got—a dolly, dear child?" he asked.

"Yes, a dolly," answered the child, frowning, and a little shy.

"A dolly . . . and do you know, dear child, what your dolly is made of?"

"I don't know . . ." the child answered in a whisper, hanging her head.

"It's made of rags, darling. You had better go into the drawing room to your playmates, boy," said Yulian Mastakovitch, looking sternly at the boy. The boy and girl frowned and clutched at each other. They did not want to be separated.

"And do you know why they gave you that doll?" asked Yulian Mastakovitch, dropping his voice to a softer and softer tone.

"I don't know."

"Because you have been a sweet and well-behaved child all the week."

At this point Yulian Mastakovitch, more excited than ever, speaking in most dulcet tones, asked at last, in a hardly audible voice choked with emotion and impatience—

"And will you love me, dear little girl, when I come and see your papa and mamma?"

Saying this, Yulian Mastakovitch tried once more to kiss "the dear little girl," but the red-haired boy, seeing that the little girl was on the point of tears, clutched her hand and began whimpering from sympathy for her. Yulian Mastakovitch was angry in earnest.

"Go away, go away from here, go away!" he said to the boy. "Go into the drawing room! Go in there to your playmates!"

"No, he needn't, he needn't! You go away," said the little girl. "Leave him alone, leave him alone," she said, almost crying.

Someone made a sound at the door. Yulian Mastakovitch instantly raised his majestic person and took alarm. But the red-haired boy was even more alarmed than Yulian Mastakovitch; he abandoned the little girl and, slinking along by the wall, stole out of the parlor into the dining room. To avoid arousing suspicion, Yulian Mastokovitch, too, went into the dining room. He was as red as a lobster, and, glancing into the looking glass, seemed to be ashamed at himself. He was perhaps vexed with himself for his impetuosity and hastiness. Possibly, he was at first so much impressed by his calculations, so inspired and fascinated by them, that in spite of his seriousness and dignity he made up his mind to behave like a boy, and directly approach the object of his attentions, even though she could not be really the object of his attentions for another five years at least. I followed the estimable gentleman into the dining room and there beheld a strange spectacle. Yulian Mastakovitch, flushed with vexation and anger, was frightening the red-haired boy, who, retreating from him, did not know where to run in his terror.

"Go away; what are you doing here? Go away, you scamp; are you after the fruit here, eh? Get along, you naughty boy! Get along, you sniveler, to your playmates!"

The panic-stricken boy in his desperation tried creeping under the table. Then his persecutor, in a fury, took out his large batiste handkerchief and began flicking it under the table at the child, who kept perfectly quiet. It must be observed that Yulian Mastakovitch was a little inclined to be fat. He was a sleek, red-faced, solidly built man, paunchy, with thick legs; what is called a fine figure of a man, round as a nut. He was perspiring, breathless, and fearfully flushed. At last he was almost rigid, so great was his indignation and perhaps—who knows?—his jealousy. I burst into loud laughter. Yulian Mastakovitch turned round and, in spite of all his consequence, was overcome with confusion. At that moment from the opposite door our host came in. The boy crept out from under the table and wiped his elbows and his knees. Yulian Mastakovitch hastened to put to his nose the handkerchief which he was holding in his hand by one end.

Our host looked at the three of us in some perplexity; but as a man who knew something of life, and looked at it from a serious point of view, he at once availed himself of the chance of catching his visitor by himself.

"Here, this is the boy," he said, pointing to the red-haired boy, "for whom I had the honor to solicit your influence."

"Ah!" said Yulian Mastakovitch, who had hardly quite recovered himself.

"The son of my children's governess," said our host, in a tone of a petitioner, "a poor woman, the widow of an honest civil servant; and therefore . . . and therefore, Yulian Mastakovitch, if it were possible . . ."

"Oh, no, no!" Yulian Mastakovitch made haste to answer; "no, excuse me, Filip Alexyevitch, it's quite impossible. I've made inquiries; there's no vacancy, and if there were, there are twenty applicants who have far more claim than he. . . . I am very sorry, very sorry. . . ."

"What a pity," said our host. "He is a quiet, well-behaved boy."

"A great rascal, as I notice," answered Yulian Mastakovitch, with a nervous twist of his lip. "Get along, boy; why are you standing there? Go to your playmates," he said, addressing the child.

At that point he could not contain himself, and glanced at me out of one eye. I, too, could not contain myself, and laughed straight in his face. Yulian Mastakovitch turned away at once, and in a voice calculated to reach my ear, asked who was that strange young man? They whispered together and walked out of the room. I saw Yulian Mastakovitch afterward shaking his head incredulously as our host talked to him.

After laughing to my heart's content I returned to the drawing room. There the great man, surrounded by fathers and mothers of families, including the host and hostess, was saying something very warmly to a lady to whom he had just been introduced. The lady was holding by the hand the little girl with whom Yulian Mastakovitch had had the scene in the parlor a little while before. Now he was launching into praises and raptures over the beauty, the talents, the grace, and the charming manners of the charming child. He was unmistakably making up to the mamma. The mother listened to him almost with tears of delight. The father's lips were smiling. Our host was delighted at the general satisfaction. All the guests, in fact, were sympathetically gratified; even the children's games were checked that they might not hinder the conversation: the whole atmosphere was saturated with reverence. I heard afterward the mamma of the interesting child, deeply touched, beg Yulian Mastakovitch, in carefully chosen phrases, to do her the special honor of bestowing upon them the precious gift of his acquaintance, and heard with what unaffected delight Yulian Mastakovitch accepted the invitation, and how afterward the guests, dispersing in different directions, moving away with the greatest propriety, poured out to one another the most touchingly flattering comments upon the contractor, his wife, his little girl, and, above all, upon Yulian Mastakovitch.

"Is that gentleman married?" I asked, almost aloud, of one of my acquaintances, who was standing nearest to Yulian Mastakovitch. Yulian Mastakovitch flung a searching and vindictive glance at me.

"No!" answered my acquaintance, chagrined to the bottom of his heart by the awkwardness of which I had intentionally been guilty. . . .

I passed lately by a certain church; I was struck by the crowd of people in carriages. I heard people talking of the wedding. It was a cloudy day, it was beginning to sleet. I made my way through the crowd at the door and saw the bridegroom. He was a sleek, well-fed, round, paunchy man, very gorgeously dressed up. He was running fussily about, giving orders. At last the news passed through the crowd that the bride was coming. I squeezed my way through the crowd and saw a marvelous beauty, who could scarcely have reached her first season. But the beauty was pale and melancholy. She looked preoccupied; I even fancied that her eyes were red with recent weeping. The classic severity of every feature of her face gave a certain dignity and seriousness to her beauty. But through that sternness and dignity, through that melancholy, could be seen the look of childish innocence; something indescribably naïve, fluid, youthful, which seemed mutely begging for mercy.

People were saying that she was only just sixteen. Glancing attentively at the bridegroom, I suddenly recognized him as Yulian Mastakovitch, whom I had not seen for five years. I looked at her. My God! I began to squeeze my way as quickly as I could out of the church. I heard people saying in the crowd that the bride was an heiress, that she had a dowry of five hundred thousand . . . and a trousseau worth ever so much.

"It was a good stroke of business, though!" I thought as I made my way into the street.

Translated by Constance Garnett

PASTE

by Henry James

(1843–1916)

I've found a lot more things," her cousin said to her the day after the second funeral; "they're up in her room—but they're things I wish *you'd* look at."

The pair of mourners, sufficiently stricken, were in the garden of the vicarage together, before luncheon, waiting to be summoned to that meal, and Arthur Prime had still in his face the intention, she was moved to call it rather than the expression, of feeling something or other. Some such appearance was in itself of course natural within a week of his stepmother's death, within three of his father's; but what was most present to the girl, herself sensitive and shrewd, was that he seemed somehow to brood without sorrow, to suffer without what she in her own case would have called pain. He turned away from her after this last speech—it was a good deal his habit to drop an observation and leave her to pick it up without assistance. If the vicar's widow, now in her turn finally translated, had not really belonged to him it was not for want of her giving herself, so far as he ever would take her; and she had lain for three days all alone at the end of the passage, in the great cold chamber of hospitality, the dampish greenish room where visitors slept and where several of the ladies of the parish had, without effect, offered, in pairs and successions, piously to watch with her. His personal connection with the parish was now slighter than ever, and he had really not waited for this opportunity to show the ladies what he thought of them. She felt that she herself had, during her doleful month's leave from Bleet, where she was governess, rather taken her place in the same snubbed order; but it was presently, none the less, with a better little hope of coming in for some remembrance, some relic, that she went up to look at the things he had spoken of, the identity of which, as a confused cluster of bright objects on a table in the darkened room, shimmered at her as soon as she had opened the door.

They met her eyes for the first time, but in a moment, before touching them, she knew them as things of the theatre, as very much too fine to have been with any verisimilitude things of the vicarage. They were too dreadfully good to be true, for her aunt had had no jewels to speak of, and these were coronets and girdles, diamonds, rubies and sapphires. Flagrant tinsel and glass, they looked strangely vulgar, but if after the first queer shock of them she found herself taking them up it was for the very proof, never yet so distinct to her, of a far-off faded story. An honest widowed cleric with a small son and a large sense of Shakespeare had, on a brave latitude of habit as well as of taste—since it implied his having in very fact dropped deep into the "pit"—conceived for an obscure actress several years older than himself an admiration of which the prompt offer of his reverend name and hortatory hand was the sufficiently candid sign. The response had perhaps in those dim years, so far as eccentricity was concerned, even bettered the proposal, and Charlotte, turning the tale over, had long since drawn from it a measure of the career renounced by the undistinguished comedienne—doubtless also tragic, or perhaps panto-mimic, at a pinch—of her late uncle's dreams. This career couldn't have been eminent and must much more probably have been comfortless.

"You see what it is—old stuff of the time she never liked to mention."

Our young woman gave a start; her companion had after all rejoined her and had apparently watched a moment her slightly scared recognition. "So I said to myself," she replied. Then to show intelligence, yet keep clear of twaddle: "How peculiar they look!"

"They look awful," said Arthur Prime. "Cheap gilt, diamonds as big as potatoes. These are trappings of a ruder age than ours. Actors do themselves better now."

"Oh now," said Charlotte, not to be less knowing, "actresses have real diamonds."

"Some of them." Arthur spoke dryly.

"I mean the bad ones—the nobodies too."

"Oh some of the nobodies have the biggest. But Mamma wasn't of that sort."

"A nobody?" Charlotte risked.

"Not a nobody to whom somebody—well, not a nobody with diamonds. It isn't all worth, this trash, five pounds."

There was something in the old gewgaws that spoke to her, and she continued to turn them over. "They're relics. I think they have their melancholy and even their dignity."

Arthur observed another pause. "Do you care for them?" he then asked. "I mean," he promptly added, "as a souvenir."

"Of you?" Charlotte threw off.

"Of me? What have I to do with it? Of your poor dead aunt who was so kind to you," he said with virtuous sternness.

"Well, I'd rather have them than nothing."

"Then please take them," he returned in a tone of relief which expressed somehow more of the eager than of the gracious.

"Thank you." Charlotte lifted two or three objects up and set them down again. Though they were lighter than the materials they imitated they were so much more extravagant that they struck her in truth as rather an awkward heritage, to which she might have preferred even a matchbox or a penwiper. They were indeed shameless pinchbeck. "Had you any idea she had kept them?"

"I don't at all believe she *had* kept them or knew they were there, and I'm very sure my father didn't. They had quite equally worked off any tenderness for the connection. These odds and ends, which she thought had been given away or destroyed, had simply got thrust into a dark corner and been forgotten."

Charlotte wondered. "Where then did you find them?"

"In that old tin box"—and the young man pointed to the receptacle from which he had dislodged them and which stood on a neighbouring chair. "It's rather a good box still, but I'm afraid I can't give you *that*."

The girl took no heed of the box; she continued only to look at the trinkets. "What corner had she found?"

"She hadn't 'found' it," her companion sharply insisted; "she had simply lost it. The whole thing had passed from her mind. The box was on the top shelf of the old school-room closet, which, until one put one's head into it from a step-ladder, looked, from below, quite cleared out. The door's narrow and the part of the closet to the left goes well into the wall. The box had stuck there for years."

Charlotte was conscious of a mind divided and a vision vaguely troubled, and once more she took up two or three of the subjects of this revelation; a big bracelet in the form of a gilt serpent with many twists and beady eyes, a brazen belt studded with emeralds and rubies, a chain, of flamboyant architecture, to which, at the Theatre Royal Little Peddlington, Hamlet's mother must have been concerned to attach the portrait of the successor to Hamlet's father. "Are you very sure they're not really worth something? Their mere weight alone—!" she vaguely observed, balancing a moment a royal diadem that might have crowned one of the creations of the famous Mrs. Jarley.

But Arthur Prime, it was clear, had already thought the question over and found the answer easy. "If they had been worth anything to speak of she would long ago have sold them. My father and she had unfortunately never been in a position to keep any considerable value locked up." And while his companion took in the obvious force of this he went on with a flourish just marked enough not to escape her: "If they're worth anything at all—why you're only the more welcome to them."

Charlotte had now in her hand a small bag of faded figured silk—one of those antique conveniences that speak to us, in terms of evaporated camphor and lavender, of the part they have played in some personal history; but though she had for the first time drawn the string she looked much more at the young man than at the questionable treasure it appeared to contain. "I shall like them. They're all I have."

"All you have—?"

"That belonged to her."

He swelled a little, then looked about him as if to appeal—as against her avidity—to the whole poor place. "Well, what else do you want?"

"Nothing. Thank you very much." With which she bent her eyes on the article wrapped, and now only exposed, in her superannuated satchel —a string of large pearls, such a shining circle as might once have graced the neck of a provincial Ophelia and borne company to a flaxen wig. "This perhaps *is* worth something. Feel it." And she passed him the necklace, the weight of which she had gathered for a moment into her hand.

He measured it in the same way with his own, but remained quite detached. "Worth at most thirty shillings."

"Not more?"

"Surely not if it's paste?"

"But *is* it paste?"

He gave a small sniff of impatience. "Pearls nearly as big as filberts?"

"But they're heavy," Charlotte declared.

"No heavier than anything else." And he gave them back with an allowance for her simplicity. "Do you imagine for a moment they're real?"

She studied them a little, feeling them, turning them round. "Mightn't they possibly be?"

"Of that size—stuck away with that trash?"

"I admit it isn't likely," Charlotte presently said. "And pearls are so easily imitated."

"That's just what—to a person who knows—they're not. These have no lustre, no play."

"No—they *are* dull. They're opaque."

"Besides," he lucidly enquired, "how could she ever come by them?"

"Mightn't they have been a present?"

Arthur stared at the question as if it were almost improper. "Because actresses are exposed—?" He pulled up, however, not saying to what, and before she could supply the deficiency had, with the sharp ejaculation of "No, they mightn't!" turned his back on her and walked away. His manner made her feel she had probably been wanting in tact, and before he returned to the subject, the last thing that evening, she had satisfied herself of the ground of his resentment. They had been talking of her departure the next morning, the hour of her train and the fly that would come for her, and it was precisely these things that gave him his effective chance. "I really can't allow you to leave the house under the impression that my stepmother was at *any* time of her life the sort of person to allow herself to be approached—"

"With pearl necklaces and that sort of thing?" Arthur had made for her somehow the difficulty that she couldn't show him she understood him without seeming pert.

It at any rate only added to his own gravity. "That sort of thing, exactly."

"I didn't think when I spoke this morning—but I see what you mean."

"I mean that she was beyond reproach," said Arthur Prime.

"A hundred times yes."

"Therefore if she couldn't, out of her slender gains, ever have paid for a row of pearls—"

"She couldn't, in that atmosphere, ever properly have had one? Of course she couldn't. I've seen perfectly since our talk," Charlotte went on, "that the string of beads isn't even as an imitation very good. The little clasp itself doesn't seem even gold. With false pearls, I suppose," the girl mused, "it naturally wouldn't be."

"The whole thing's rotten paste," her companion returned as if to have done with it. "If it were *not*, and she had kept it all these years hidden—"

"Yes?" Charlotte sounded as he paused.

"Why I shouldn't know what to think!"

"Oh I see." She had met him with a certain blankness, but adequately enough, it seemed, for him to regard the subject as dismissed; and there was no reversion to it between them before, on the morrow, when she had with difficulty made a place for them in her trunk, she carried off these florid survivals.

At Bleet she found small occasion to revert to them and, in an air charged with such quite other references, even felt, after she had laid them away, much enshrouded, beneath various piles of clothing, that they formed a collection not wholly without its note of the ridiculous. Yet she was never, for the joke, tempted to show them to her pupils, though Gwendolen and Blanche in particular always wanted, on her return, to know what she had brought back; so that without an accident by which the case was quite changed they might have appeared to enter on a new phase of interment. The essence of the accident was the sudden illness, at the last moment, of Lady Bobby, whose advent had been so much counted on to spice the five days' feast laid out for the coming of age of the eldest son of the house; and its equally marked effect was the dispatch of a pressing message, in quite another direction, to Mrs. Guy, who, could she by a miracle be secured—she was always engaged ten parties deep—might be trusted to supply, it was believed, an element of exuberance scarcely less potent. Mrs. Guy was already known to several of the visitors already on the scene, but she wasn't yet known to our young lady, who found her, after many wires and counter-wires had at last determined the triumph of her arrival, a strange charming little red-haired black-dressed woman, a person with the face of a baby and the authority of a commodore. She took on the spot the discreet, the exceptional young governess into the confidence of her designs and, still more, of her doubts; intimating that it was a policy she almost always promptly pursued.

"Tomorrow and Thursday are all right," she said frankly to Charlotte on the second day, "but I'm not half-satisfied with Friday."

"What improvement then do you suggest?"

"Well, my strong point, you know, is *tableaux vivants*."

"Charming. And what is your favourite character?"

"Boss!" said Mrs. Guy with decision; and it was very markedly under that ensign that she had, within a few hours, completely planned her campaign and recruited her troop. Every word she uttered was to the point, but none more so than, after a general survey of their equipment, her final enquiry of Charlotte. She had been looking about, but half-appeased, at the muster of decoration and drapery. "We shall be dull. We shall want more colour. You've nothing else?"

Charlotte had a thought. "No—I've *some* things."

"Then why don't you bring them?"

The girl weighed it. "Would you come to my room?"

"No," said Mrs. Guy—"bring them tonight to mine."

So Charlotte, at the evening's end, after candlesticks had flickered through brown old passages bedward, arrived at her friend's door with the burden of her aunt's relics. But she promptly expressed a fear. "Are they too garish?"

When she had poured them out on the sofa Mrs. Guy was but a minute, before the glass, in clapping on the diadem. "Awfully jolly—we can do Ivanhoe!"

"But they're only glass and tin."

"Larger than life they are, *rather*!—which is exactly what's wanted for tableaux. *Our* jewels, for historic scenes, don't tell—the real thing falls short. Rowena must have rubies as big as eggs. Leave them with me," Mrs. Guy continued—"they'll inspire me. Good night."

The next morning she was in fact—yet very strangely—inspired. "Yes, *I'll* do Rowena. But I don't, my dear, understand."

"Understand what?"

Mrs. Guy gave a very lighted stare. "How do you come to have such things?"

Poor Charlotte smiled. "By inheritance."

"Family jewels?"

"They belonged to my aunt, who died some months ago. She was on the stage a few years in early life, and these are a part of her trappings."

"She left them to you?"

"No; my cousin, her stepson, who naturally has no use for them, gave them to me for remembrance of her. She was a dear kind thing, always so nice to me, and I was fond of her."

Mrs. Guy had listened with frank interest. "But it's *he* who must be a dear kind thing!"

Charlotte wondered. "You think so?"

"Is *he*," her friend went on, "also 'always so nice' to you?"

The girl, at this, face to face there with the brilliant visitor in the deserted breakfast-room, took a deeper sounding. "What is it?"

"Don't you know?"

Something came over her. "The pearls—?" But the question fainted on her lips.

Charlotte found herself flushing. "They're *not* paste?"

"Haven't you looked at them?"

She was conscious of two kinds of embarrassment. "*You* have?"

"Very carefully."

"And they're real?"

Mrs. Guy became slightly mystifying and returned for all answer: "Come again, when you've done with the children, to my room."

Our young woman found she had done with the children that morning so promptly as to reveal to them a new joy, and when she reappeared before Mrs. Guy this lady had already encircled a plump white throat with the only ornament, surely, in all the late Mrs. Prime's—the effaced Miss Bradshaw's—collection, in the least qualified to raise a question. If Charlotte had never yet once, before the glass, tied the string of pearls about her own neck, this was because she had been capable of no such stoop to approved "imitation"; but she had now only to look at Mrs. Guy to see that, so disposed, the ambiguous objects might have passed for frank originals. "What in the world have you done to them?"

"Only handled them, understood them, admired them and put them on. That's what pearls want; they want to be worn—it wakes them up. They're alive, don't you see? How *have* these been treated? They must have been buried, ignored, despised. They were half-dead. Don't you *know* about pearls?" Mrs. Guy threw off as she fondly fingered the necklace.

"How *should* I? Do *you*?

"Everything. These were simply asleep, and from the moment I really touched them—well," said their wearer lovingly, "it only took one's eye!"

"It took more than mine—though I did just wonder; and than Arthur's," Charlotte brooded. She found herself almost panting. "Then their value?"

"Oh their value's excellent."

The girl, for a deep contemplative moment, took another plunge into the wonder, the beauty and the mystery. "Are you *sure*?"

Her companion wheeled round for impatience. "Sure? For what kind of an idiot, my dear, do you take me?"

It was beyond Charlotte Prime to say. "For the same kind as Arthur—and as myself," she could only suggest. "But my cousin didn't know. He thinks they're worthless."

"Because of the rest of the lot? Then your cousin's an ass. But what—if, as I understood you, he gave them to you—has he to do with it?"

"Why if he gave them to me as worthless and they turn out precious—!"

"You must give them back? I don't see that—if he was such a noodle. He took the risk."

Charlotte fed, in fancy, on the pearls, which decidedly were exquisite, but which at the present moment somehow presented themselves much more as Mrs. Guy's than either as Arthur's or as her own. "Yes—he did take it; even after I had distinctly hinted to him that they looked to me different from the other pieces."

"Well then!" said Mrs. Guy with something more than triumph—with a positive odd relief.

But it had the effect of making our young woman think with more intensity. "Ah you see he thought they couldn't be different, because—so peculiarly—they shouldn't be."

"Shouldn't? I don't understand."

"Why how would she have got them?"—so Charlotte candidly put it.

"She? Who?" There was a capacity in Mrs. Guy's tone for a sinking of persons—!

"Why the person I told you of: his stepmother, my uncle's wife—among whose poor old things, extraordinarily thrust away and out of sight, he happened to find them."

Mrs. Guy came a step nearer to the effaced Miss Bradshaw. "Do you mean she may have stolen them?"

"No. But she had been an actress."

"Oh well then," cried Mrs. Guy, "wouldn't that be just how?"

"Yes, except that she wasn't at all a brilliant one, nor in receipt of large pay." The girl even threw off a nervous joke. "I'm afraid she couldn't have been our Rowena."

Mrs. Guy took it up. "Was she very ugly?"

"No. She may very well, when young, have looked rather nice."

"Well then!" was Mrs. Guy's sharp comment and fresh triumph.

"You mean it was a present? That's just what he so dislikes the idea of her having received—a present from an admirer capable of going such lengths."

"Because she wouldn't have taken it for nothing? *Speriamo*—that she wasn't a brute. The 'length' her admirer went was the length of a whole row. Let us hope she was just a little kind!"

"Well," Charlotte went on, "that she was 'kind' might seem to be shown by the fact that neither her husband, nor his son, nor I, his niece, knew or dreamed of her possessing anything so precious; by her having kept the gift all the rest of her life beyond discovery—out of sight and protected from suspicion."

"As if, you mean"—Mrs. Guy was quick—"she had been wedded to it and yet was ashamed of it? Fancy," she laughed while she manipulated the rare beads, "being ashamed of *these*!"

"But you see she had married a clergyman."

"Yes, she must have been 'rum.' But at any rate he had married *her*. What did he suppose?"

"Why that she had never been of the sort by whom such offerings are encouraged."

"Ah my dear, the sort by whom they're *not!*" But Mrs. Guy caught herself up. "And her stepson thought the same?"

"Overwhelmingly."

"Was he then, if only her stepson—"

"So fond of her as that comes to? Yes; he had never known, consciously, his real mother, and, without children of her own, she was very patient and nice with him. And *I* liked her so," the girl pursued, "that at the end of ten years, in so strange a manner, to 'give her away'—"

"Is impossible to you? Then don't!" said Mrs. Guy with decision.

"Ah but if they're real I can't keep them!" Charlotte, with her eyes on them, moaned in her impatience. "It's too difficult."

"Where's the difficulty, if he has such sentiments that he'd rather sacrifice the necklace than admit it, with the presumption it carries with it, to be genuine? You've only to be silent."

"And keep it? How can *I* ever wear it?"

"You'd have to hide it, like your aunt?" Mrs. Guy was amused. "You can easily sell it."

Her companion walked round her for a look at the affair from behind. The clasp was certainly, doubtless intentionally, misleading, but everything else was indeed lovely. "Well, I must think. Why didn't *she* sell them?" Charlotte broke out in her trouble.

Mrs. Guy had an instant answer. "Doesn't that prove what they secretly recalled to her? You've only to be silent!" she ardently repeated.

"I must think—I must think!"

Mrs. Guy stood with her hands attached but motionless. "Then you want them back?"

As if with the dread of touching them Charlotte retreated to the door. "I'll tell you tonight."

"But may I wear them?"

"Meanwhile?"

"This evening—at dinner."

It was a sharp selfish pressure of this that really, on the spot, determined the girl; but for the moment, before closing the door on the question, she only said: "As you like!"

They were busy much of the day with preparation and rehearsal, and at dinner that evening the concourse of guests were such that a place among them for Miss Prime failed to find itself marked. At the time the company rose she was therefore alone in the school-room, where, towards eleven o'clock, she received a visit from Mrs. Guy. This lady's white shoulders heaved, under the pearls, with an emotion that the very red lips which formed, as if the full effect, the happiest opposition of colour, were not slow to translate. "My dear, you should have seen the sensation—they've had a success!"

Charlotte, dumb a moment, took it all in. "It *is* as if they knew it—they're more and more alive. But so much the worse for both of us! I can't," she brought out with an effort, "be silent."

"You mean to return them?"

"If I don't I'm a thief."

Mrs. Guy gave her a long hard look: what was decidedly not of the baby in Mrs. Guy's face was a certain air of established habit in the eyes. Then, with a sharp little jerk of her head and a backward reach of her bare beautiful arms, she undid the clasp and, taking off the necklace, laid it on the table. "If you do you're a goose."

"Well, of the two—!" said our young lady, gathering it up with a sigh. And as if to get it, for the pang it gave, out of sight as soon as possible, she shut it up, clicking the lock, in the drawer of her own little table; after which, when she turned again, her companion looked naked and plain without it. "But what will you say?" it then occurred to her to demand.

"Downstairs—to explain?" Mrs. Guy was after all trying at least to keep her temper. "Oh I'll put on something else and say the clasp's broken. And you won't of course name *me* to him," she added.

"As having undeceived me? No—I'll say that, looking at the thing more carefully, it's my own private idea."

"And does he know how little you really know?"

"As an expert—surely. And he has always much the conceit of his own opinion."

"Then he won't believe you—as he so hates to. He'll stick to his judgement and maintain his gift, and we shall have the darlings back!" With which reviving assurance Mrs. Guy kissed her young friend for good-night.

She was not, however, to be gratified or justified by any prompt event, for, whether or no paste entered into the composition of the ornament in question, Charlotte shrank from the temerity of dispatching it to town by post. Mrs. Guy was thus disappointed of the hope of seeing the business settled—"by return," she had seemed to expect—before the end of the revels. The revels, moreover, rising to a frantic pitch, pressed for all her attention, and it was at last only in the general confusion of leave-taking that she made, parenthetically, a dash at the person in the whole company with whom her contact had been most interesting.

"Come, what will you take for them?"

"The pearls? Ah, you'll have to treat with my cousin."

Mrs. Guy, with quick intensity, lent herself. "Where then does he live?"

"In chambers in the Temple. You can find him."

"But what's the use, if *you* do neither one thing nor the other?"

"Oh I *shall* do the 'other,' " Charlotte said: "I'm only waiting till I go up. You want them so awfully?" She curiously, solemnly again, sounded her.

"I'm dying for them. There's a special charm in them—I don't know what it is: they tell so their history."

"But what do you know of that?"

"Just what they themselves say. It's all *in* them—and it comes out. They breathe a tenderness—they have the white glow of it. My dear," hissed Mrs. Guy in supreme confidence and as she buttoned her glove—"they're things of love!"

"Oh!" our young woman vaguely exclaimed.

"They're things of passion!"

"Mercy!" she gasped, turning short off. But these words remained, though indeed their help was scarce needed, Charlotte being in private face to face with a new light, as she by this time felt she must call it, on the dear dead kind colourless lady whose career had turned so sharp a corner in the middle. The pearls had quite taken their place as a revelation. She might have received them for nothing—admit that; but she couldn't have kept them so long and so unprofitably hidden, couldn't have enjoyed them only in secret, for nothing; and she had mixed them in her reliquary with false things in order to put curiosity and detection off the scent. Over this strange fact poor Charlotte interminably mused: it became more touching, more attaching for her than she could now confide to any ear. How bad or how happy—in the sophisticated sense of Mrs. Guy and the young man at the Temple—the effaced Miss Bradshaw must have been to have had to be so mute! The little governess at Bleet put on the necklace now in secret sessions; she wore it sometimes under her dress; she came to feel verily a haunting passion for it. Yet in her penniless state she would have parted with it for money; she gave herself also to dreams of what in this direction it would do for her. The sophistry of her so often saying to herself that Arthur had after all definitely pronounced her welcome to any gain from his gift that might accrue—this trick remained innocent, as she perfectly knew it for what it was. Then there was always the possibility of his—as she could only picture it—rising to the occasion. Mightn't he have a grand magnanimous moment?—mightn't he just say "Oh I couldn't of course have afforded to let you have it if I had known; but since you *have* got it, and have made out the truth by your own wit, I really can't screw myself down to the shabbiness of taking it back"?

She had, as it proved, to wait a long time—to wait till, at the end of several months, the great house of Bleet had, with due deliberation, for the season, transferred itself to town; after which, however, she fairly snatched at her first freedom to knock, dressed in her best and armed with her disclosure, at the door of her doubting kinsman. It was still with doubt and not quite with the face she had hoped that he listened to her story. He had turned pale, she thought, as she produced the necklace, and he appeared above all disagreeably affected. Well, perhaps there was reason, she more than ever remembered; but what on earth was one, in close touch with the fact, to do? She had laid the pearls on his table, where, without his having at first put so much as a finger to them, they met his hard cold stare.

"I don't believe in them," he simply said at last.

"That's exactly then," she returned with some spirit, "what I wanted to hear!"

She fancied that at this his colour changed; it was indeed vivid to her afterwards—for she was to have a long recall of the scene—that she had made him quite angrily flush. "It's a beastly unpleasant imputation, you know!"—and he walked away from her as he had always walked at the vicarage.

"It's none of *my* making, I'm sure," said Charlotte Prime. "If you're afraid to believe they're real—"

"Well?"—and he turned, across the room, sharp round at her.

"Why it's not my fault."

He said nothing more, for a moment, on this; he only came back to the table. "They're what I originally said they were. They're rotten paste."

"Then I may keep them?"

"No. I want a better opinion."

"Than your own?"

"Than *your* own." He dropped on the pearls another queer stare; then, after a moment, bringing himself to touch them, did exactly what she had herself done in the presence of Mrs. Guy at Bleet—gathered them together, marched off with them to a drawer, put them in and clicked the key. "You say I'm afraid," he went on as he again met her; "but I shan't be afraid to take them to Bond Street."

"And if the people say they're real—?"

He had a pause and then his strangest manner. "They won't say it! They shan't!"

There was something in the way he brought it out that deprived poor Charlotte, as she was perfectly aware, of any manner at all. "Oh!" she simply sounded, as she had sounded for her last word to Mrs. Guy; and within a minute, without more conversation, she had taken her departure.

A fortnight later she received a communication from him, and toward the end of the season one of the entertainments in Eaton Square was graced by the presence of Mrs. Guy. Charlotte was not at dinner, but she came down afterwards, and this guest, on seeing her, abandoned a very beautiful young man on purpose to cross and speak to her. The guest displayed a lovely necklace and had apparently not lost her habit of overflowing with the pride of such ornaments.

"Do you see?" She was in high joy.

They were indeed splendid pearls—so far as poor Charlotte could feel that she knew, after what had come and gone, about such mysteries. The poor girl had a sickly smile. "They're almost as fine as Arthur's."

"Almost? Where, my dear, are your eyes? They *are* 'Arthur's'!" After which, to meet the flood of crimson that accompanied her young friend's start: "I tracked them—after your folly, and, by miraculous luck, recognised them in the Bond Street window to which he had disposed of them."

"*Disposed* of them?" Charlotte gasped. "He wrote me that I had insulted his mother and that the people had shown him he was right—had pronounced them utter paste."

Mrs. Guy gave a stare. "Ah I told you he wouldn't bear it! No. But I had, I assure you," she wound up, "to drive my bargain!"

Charlotte scarce heard or saw; she was full of her private wrong. "He wrote me," she panted, "that he had smashed them."

Mrs. Guy could only wonder and pity. "He's really morbid!" But it wasn't quite clear which of the pair she pitied; though the young person employed in Eaton Square felt really morbid too after they had separated and she found herself full of thought. She even went the length of asking herself what sort of a bargain Mrs. Guy had driven and whether the marvel of the recognition in Bond Street had been a veracious account of the matter. Hadn't she perhaps in truth dealt with Arthur directly? It came back to Charlotte almost luridly that she had had his address.

A COWARD
by Guy de Maupassant
(1850–93)

He was known in society as "the handsome Signoles." His name was Viscount Gontran Joseph de Signoles.

An orphan and the possessor of a sufficient fortune, he cut a dash, as they say. He had style and presence, sufficient fluency of speech to make people think him clever, a certain natural grace, an air of nobility and pride, a gallant mustache and a gentle eye, which the women like.

He was in great demand in the salons, much sought after by fair dancers; and he aroused in his own sex that smiling animosity which they always feel for men of an energetic figure. He had been suspected of several love affairs well adapted to cause a young bachelor to be much esteemed. He passed a happy, unconcerned life, in a comfort of mind which was most complete. He was known to be a skillful fencer, and with the pistol even more adept.

"If I ever fight a duel," he would say, "I shall choose the pistol. With that weapon I am sure of killing my man."

Now, one evening, when he had accompanied to the theater two young lady friends of his, whose husbands also were of the party, he invited them, after the play, to take an ice at Tortoni's. They had been at the café but a few moments, when he noticed that a man sitting at a table near by was staring persistently at one of his fair neighbors. She seemed annoyed and uneasy, and lowered her eyes. At last she said to her husband:

"That man is staring me out of countenance. I don't know him; do you?"

The husband, who had noticed nothing, raised his eyes, and answered: "No, not at all."

The young woman continued, half smiling, half vexed:

"It is very unpleasant; that man is spoiling my ice."

The husband shrugged his shoulders:

"Pshaw! don't pay any attention to him. If we had to bother our heads about all the impertinent fellows we meet, we should never have done."

But the viscount had risen abruptly. He could not suffer that stranger to spoil an ice which he had offered. It was to him that the affront was paid, since it was through him and for him that his friends had entered the café, so that the affair was his concern, and his alone.

He walked toward the man and said to him:

"You have a way of looking at those ladies, monsieur, that I cannot tolerate. I beg you to be so kind as to stare less persistently."

The other retorted:

"You may go to the devil!"

"Take care, monsieur," said the viscount, with clenched teeth; "you will force me to pass bounds."

The gentleman answered but one word, a foul word, that rang from one end of the café to the other, and caused every guest to give a sudden start, as if moved by a hidden spring. Those whose backs were turned wheeled round; all the others raised their heads; three waiters whirled about on their heels like tops; the two women at the desk gave a jump, then turned completely round, like automata obedient to the same crank.

Profound silence ensued. Suddenly a sharp sound cracked in the air. The viscount had slapped his adversary. Everyone rose to interfere. Cards were exchanged between the two.

When the viscount had returned to his apartment he paced the floor for several minutes, with great, quick strides. He was too much agitated to reflect. A single thought hovered over his mind—"a duel"—without arousing any emotion whatsoever. He had done what he should have done; he had shown himself to be what he ought to be. His conduct would be discussed and approved; people would congratulate him. He said aloud, speaking as one speaks when one's thoughts are in great confusion:

"What a brute the fellow was!"

Then he sat down and began to consider. He must find seconds, in the morning. Whom should he choose? He thought over those of his acquaintances who were the most highly esteemed and the best known. He decided at last upon the Marquis de la Tour-Noire and the Colonel Bourdin—a great noble and a soldier—excellent! Their names would sound well in the papers. He discovered that he was thirsty, and he drank three glasses of water in rapid succession; then he resumed his pacing of the floor. He felt full of energy. If he blustered a little, seemed determined to carry the thing through, demanded rigorous and dangerous conditions, insisted upon a serious duel, very serious and terrible, his adversary would probably back down and apologize.

He picked up the card, which he had drawn from his pocket and tossed on the table, and read it again, as he had read it in a glance at the café, and again in the cab, by the glimmer of every street lamp, on his way home. "Georges Lamil, 51 Rue Moncey." Nothing more.

He examined these assembled letters, which seemed to him mysterious, full of vague meaning. Georges Lamil! Who was this man? What was his business? Why had he stared at that lady in such a way? Was it not disgusting that a stranger, an unknown, should cause such a change in one's life, because it had pleased him to fasten his eyes insolently upon a lady?

And the viscount again exclaimed aloud:

"What a brute!"

Then he stood perfectly still, thinking, his eyes still glued to the card. There arose within him a fierce anger against that bit of paper—a malevolent sort of rage, blended with a strange feeling of discomfort. What a stupid business! He took a penknife that lay open to his hand, and stuck it through the middle of the printed name, as if he were stabbing someone.

So he must fight! Should he choose swords, or pistols?—for he deemed himself the insulted party. He ran less risk with the sword; but with the pistol he had a chance of making his opponent withdraw. A duel with swords is rarely fatal, mutual prudence preventing the combatants from engaging near enough to each other for a point to enter very deep. With the pistol his life was seriously endangered; but he might in that way come out of the affair with all the honors, and without coming to a meeting.

"I must be firm," he said. "He will be afraid."

The sound of his voice made him tremble, and he looked about him. He felt extremely nervous. He drank another glass of water, then began to undress for bed.

As soon as he was in bed he blew out the light and shut his eyes.

He thought:

"I have all day tomorrow to arrange my affairs. I must sleep now, so that I may be calm."

He was very warm under the bedclothes, but he could not manage to doze off. He twisted and turned, lay on his back five minutes, then changed to the left side, then rolled over on his right.

He was still thirsty. He got up again, to drink. Then a disquieting thought occurred to him:

"Can it be that I am afraid?"

Why did his heart begin to beat wildly at every familiar sound in the room? When the clock was about to strike, the faint whirring of the spring making ready made him jump; and then he had to keep his mouth open for several seconds to breathe, the oppression was so great.

He commenced to argue with himself concerning the possibility of this thing:

"Am I afraid?"

No, of course he was not afraid, as he had determined to carry the thing through, as his mind was fully made up to fight, and not to tremble. But he felt so profoundly troubled that he asked himself the question:

"Is it possible to be afraid in spite of one's self?"

And that doubt, that disquietude, that dread took possession of him; if some force stronger than his will, a dominating, irresistible power should conquer him, what would happen? Yes, what could happen? He certainly would go to the ground, inasmuch as he had made up his mind to go there. But suppose his hand should tremble? Suppose he should faint? And he thought of his position, of his reputation, of his name.

And suddenly a strange fancy seized him to get up, in order to look in the mirror. He relit his candle. When he saw the reflection of his face in the polished glass, he could hardly recognize himself, and it seemed to him that he had never seen this man before. His eyes appeared enormous; and he was certainly pale—yes, very pale.

He remained standing in front of the mirror. He put out his tongue as if to test the state of his health, and of a sudden this thought burst into his mind like a bullet:

"The day after tomorrow, at this time, I may be dead."

And his heart began to beat furiously again.

"The day after tomorrow, at this time, I may be dead. This person in front of me, this I, whom I am looking at in this mirror, will be no more! What! I am standing here, looking at myself, conscious that I am a living man; and in twenty-four hours I shall be lying on that bed, dead, with my eyes closed, cold, lifeless, gone!"

He turned toward the bed, and he distinctly saw himself lying on his back, between the very sheets that he had just left. He had the hollow cheeks that dead bodies have, and that slackness of the hands that will never stir more.

Thereupon he conceived a fear of his bed, and, in order to avoid looking at it, passed into his smoking room. He mechanically took a cigar, lighted it, and began to pace the floor anew. He was cold; he walked to the bell cord to wake his valet; but he stopped, with his hand halfway to the cord.

"That fellow will see that I am afraid."

And he did not ring, but made the fire himself. His hands trembled slightly, with a nervous shudder, when they touched anything. His brain was in a whirl; his troubled thoughts became fugitive, sudden, melancholy; a sort of intoxication seized on his spirit as if he had been drunk.

And ceaselessly he asked himself:

"What am I going to do? What will become of me?"

His whole body quivered, shaken by jerky tremblings. He got up, went to the window, and drew aside the curtains. The day was breaking, a summer's day. The rosy sky made rosy the city, the roofs, and the walls. A great burst of light, like a caress from the rising sun, enveloped the awaking world; and with that glimmer, a sudden, enlivening, brutal hope seized on the heart of the viscount. How insane he was to have allowed himself to be so struck down by terror, even before anything was decided, before his seconds had met those of Georges Lamil, before he knew whether he was really to fight!

He made his toilet, dressed himself, and left the house with a firm step.

As he walked, he said to himself again and again:

"I must be firm, very firm. I must prove that I am not afraid."

His seconds, the marquis and the colonel, placed themselves at his disposal, and after warmly shaking his hand, discussed the conditions.

The colonel asked:

"Do you desire a serious duel?"

"Very serious," the viscount replied.

"You insist upon pistols?"

"Yes."

"Do you leave us at liberty to make the other arrangements?"

The viscount articulated with a dry, jerky voice:

"Twenty paces, firing at the word, lifting the arm instead of lowering it. Shots to be exchanged until someone is badly wounded."

"Those are excellent conditions," said the colonel, in a tone of satisfaction. "You are a good shot; the chances are all in your favor."

And they separated. The viscount returned home to wait for them. His agitation, which had been temporarily allayed, increased from moment to moment. He felt along his arms and legs, in his chest, a sort of shudder, an incessant vibration; he could not keep still, either sitting or standing. He had only a trace of moisture in his mouth, and he moved his tongue noisily every second, as if to unglue it from his palate.

He tried to breakfast, but he could not eat. Thereupon it occurred to him to drink to renew his courage, and he ordered a small decanter of rum, from which he gulped down six little glasses, one after another. A warmth, like that caused by a burn, invaded his whole frame, followed as soon by a giddiness of the soul.

"I have found the way," he thought; "now it is all right."

But in an hour he had emptied the decanter, and his agitation became intolerable. He was conscious of a frantic longing to throw himself on the floor, to cry, to bite. Evening fell.

A ring at the bell caused him such a feeling of suffocation that he had not the strength to rise and receive his seconds.

He did not dare even to talk to them any longer—to say: "How do you do?," to utter a single word, for fear that they would divine everything from the trembling of his voice.

"Everything is arranged according to the conditions that you fixed," said the colonel. "At first, your adversary claimed the privileges of the insulted party, but he gave way almost immediately and assented to everything. His seconds are two military men."

The viscount said:

"Thank you."

The marquis added:

"Excuse us if we stay but a moment, but we still have a thousand things to attend to. We must have a good doctor, as the duel is not to stop until somebody is severely wounded; and you know there's no trifling with bullets. We must arrange about the place, too—near a house to which the wounded man may be taken if necessary, etc.; in short, we still have two or three hours' work before us."

The viscount succeeded in articulating a second time:

"Thank you."

The colonel asked:

"You are all right? quite calm?"

"Yes, quite calm, thanks."

The two men withdrew.

When he was alone once more it seemed to him that he was going mad. His servant having lighted the lamps, he seated himself at his table to write some letters. After tracing at the top of a page: "This is my Will," he rose with a jump and walked away, feeling incapable of putting two ideas together, of forming any resolution, of deciding any question whatsoever.

So he was really going to fight! It was no longer possible for him to avoid it. What on earth was taking place in him? He wanted to fight; his purpose and determination to do so were firmly fixed; and yet he knew full well that, despite all the effort of his mind and all the tension of his will, he would be unable to retain even the strength necessary to take him to the place of meeting. He tried to fancy the combat, his own attitude, and the bearing of his adversary.

From time to time his teeth chattered with a little dry noise. He tried to read, and took up Châteauvillard's dueling code. Then he asked himself:

"Has my opponent frequented the shooting galleries? Is he well known? What's his class? How can I find out?"

He remembered Baron de Vaux's book on pistol shooters, and he looked it through from end to end. Georges Lamil's name was not mentioned. But if the fellow were not a good shot, he would not have assented so readily to that dangerous weapon and those fatal conditions! As he passed a table, he opened the case by Gastinne Renette, took out one of the pistols, then stood as if he were about to fire, and raised his arm. But he was trembling from head to foot, and the barrel shook in all directions.

Then he said to himself:

"It is impossible. I cannot fight like this!"

He regarded the little hole, black and deep, at the end of the barrel, the hole that spits out death; he thought of the dishonor, of the whispered comments at the clubs, of the laughter in the salons, of the disdain of the women, of the allusions in the newspapers, of the insults which cowards would throw in his face.

He continued to gaze at the weapon, and as he raised the hammer, he saw the priming glitter beneath it like a little red flame. The pistol had been left loaded, by chance, by oversight. And he experienced a confused, inexplicable joy thereat.

If he did not display in the other's presence the calm and noble bearing suited to the occasion, he would be lost forever. He would be disgraced, branded with the sign of infamy, hunted from society! And that calm and bold bearing he could not command—he knew it, he felt it. And yet he was really brave, because he wanted to fight! He was brave, because—. The thought that grazed his mind was never completed; opening his mouth wide, he suddenly thrust the barrel of the pistol into the very bottom of his throat and pressed upon the trigger.

When his valet ran in, alarmed by the report, he found him on his back, dead. The blood had spattered the white paper on the table, and made a great red stain under the four words:

"This is my Will."

THE MAN WITH THE FLOWER IN HIS MOUTH

by Luigi Pirandello
(1867–1936)

"Ah! Well, I mean— That is—you seem a good-natured sort of man. Have you missed your train?"

"By a minute! I get to the station. And there it is, going out before my very eyes!"

"You might have run after it!"

"True enough. It's ridiculous, I know. Good Heavens, I'd have managed it all right, if I hadn't been cluttered up with all those parcels. Parcels and packets of all sorts and sizes! I was loaded worse than a packhorse! Oh, these women! Nothing but errands, errands! They're never-ending! Do you know, it took me fully three minutes after I got out of the taxi, to loop all those parcels onto my finger! Two parcels to every finger!"

"You must have looked a fine sight! Do you know what I'd have done? I'd have left them all in the taxi!"

"And what about my wife? Oh, yes! And what about my daughters? And all their bosom friends!"

"Weeping and wailing and gnashing of teeth, eh? I'd have enjoyed myself no end!"

"That's because you—well, I suppose it's because you don't know what women get like when they're on holiday in the country!"

"Oh yes, I do know. I said that just now, precisely because I do know. They all say they won't need a thing."

"Is that all they say? They're quite capable of maintaining even that they go into the country in order to save money! Then, no sooner have they got to some place at the back of beyond— The uglier the place is, the more wretched and filthy it is, the more frenziedly they insist on livening it up by decking themselves out in all their frills and fal-lals! Oh, women, my dear fellow! But, when all's said and done, that's the way God made them! 'My dear, if you *should* be running into town, I really need such-and-such a thing—and some of that other stuff too. . . . Oh, yes! You might also—if it's not too much trouble. . . .' Charming, isn't it, the way they say, 'If it's not too much trouble'? 'And then, since you're there anyway, on your way back . . .' 'But, my dear, how do you expect me to get through all that business for you in three hours?' 'What was that you said? Why, by taking a taxi!' The awful thing is that, only intending to spend three hours in town, I came away without the keys to my house here."

"Oh, wonderful! So . . .?"

"So I left that small mountain of parcels and packets in the cloakroom at the station. Then I went along to a restaurant and had some dinner. Finally, so as to give my temper a chance to cool down a little, I went to a theater. The heat was killing! When I came out, I said to myself, 'Well, what shall I do now? It's twelve o'clock already. I can get the first train back at four. Barely three hours left for sleep. It's not worth the expense.' So I came here. This café doesn't shut, does it?"

"No, it doesn't shut. So you've left all those parcels in the cloakroom at the station?"

"Why do you ask me that? Don't you think they're safe there? They were all well tied up."

"No, that wasn't what I meant. H'm! Well tied up. Yes, I can imagine. Tied up with that special art which shop assistants put into the wrapping up of purchases. What wonderful hands they have! They pick up a fine large sheet of double-thickness paper, all pink and shiny. It's a joy to behold in itself! It's so smooth that you almost feel that you'd like to put it up to your face. Just to feel its cool caressing touch. Well, they spread it out on the counter—and then, in the most self-possessed manner in the world, they put your piece of cloth, all neatly folded, exactly in the middle of it. First of all, with the back of their hand, they bring up one edge of the paper from underneath. Then they bring the other down from on top to meet the first, and so deftly, so gracefully, make the narrowest of folds— one they don't really need—put in, as it were, for sheer love of the art. Then, first at one end, then at the other, they fold the corners in to make two triangles. The points are turned under. They reach out a hand for the string. Pull out just the length they'll need. And tie up your parcel so quickly, that you haven't even time to admire their dexterity, before they're presenting you with it. With a little loop all ready for you to put your finger through."

"H'm! H'm! It's easy to see that you've paid a great deal of attention to shop assistants."

"I? My dear fellow, I spend whole days at a time watching them. I am capable of standing quite still for a whole hour, looking into a shop through the window. By so doing I am able to forget myself. To myself I seem to be—I should really very much like to be—that silk material over there; that strip of braid; the red or blue ribbon that the girls in the haberdashery department— After they've measured it out on the yard-stick, have you noticed what they do? They twist it in a figure-eight round the thumb and little finger of their left hand before they wrap it up. I watch the customers, men and women alike, as they come out from the shop with their parcels dangling from their fingers, or in their hands, or under their arms. I follow them with my eyes. Until I lose sight of them, imagining— Oh, how many things I imagine! You can have no conception! But it helps me. Doing that helps me."

"*Helps* you? Forgive my asking. But *what* helps you?"

"Attaching myself like that. With my imagination, I mean, to life. Like a creeper to the bars of an iron railing. Ah, never letting my imagina-tion rest for a single moment. Holding on—holding on with it to the lives of others. But not to the lives of people I know! No! No! I couldn't do that! If I do try, a feeling of utter weariness comes over me. Oh, if only you knew! A feeling of absolute nausea! I hold on to the lives of strangers, upon whom my imagination can work freely but not capriciously. On the con-trary, it takes into account even the slightest characteristic, the slightest appearance of reality to be observed in this person or in that. And if you only knew how my imagination works; how hard it works! If you could only realize just how far I succeed in putting myself inside these people! I see the house of such-and-such a person, or such-and-such another. I live in it. I feel myself completely at home in it. I even get to the point of noticing—do you know that faint smell which lurks in a house? Every single house has its own particular smell. It's there in your house; in mine. But in our own house, of course, we're no longer aware of it, because it is the breath of our very life itself. Do I make myself clear? Ah, yes. I see you agree with me."

"Yes, I agree, because, I mean, you must experience a great deal of pleasure, imagining all these things."

"Pleasure? I?"

"Yes. I imagine . . ."

"Tell me something. Have you ever been to see a good doctor?"

"Who, me? No! Why do you ask? There's nothing the matter with me!"

"Oh, don't start getting agitated! I only ask because I want to know whether you've ever seen the rooms in those good doctors' houses where the patients sit and wait for their turn to go in."

"Oh, yes. As a matter of fact, it did so happen once that I had to go with one of my daughters. She was having a bit of trouble with her nerves."

"Good. Please don't think I'm trying to be inquisitive. What I mean is, those rooms— Have you ever looked at them really attentively? A black, old-fashioned, horsehair sofa. Those stuffed chairs, which all too often don't match one another. Those little armchairs; secondhand stuff, picked up quite at random, just put in there for the patients. It doesn't really belong to the house at all! The doctor has quite another sort of room for himself and for his wife's friends. A fine, handsome, sumptuously furnished drawing room. Can't you just imagine how it would shriek to high heaven if you were to bring one of the chairs—stuffed or otherwise—out of that drawing room, and set it down in the patients' waiting room? This sort of furniture is good enough for in here. It's not showy but it's honest-to-goodness, solid, hard-wearing stuff. What I should like to know is whether you looked attentively at the chair or armchair in which you sat, waiting. That time you went with your daughter."

"Did I . . .? Well, to tell you the truth, no!"

"Of course not. Because you weren't ill. But quite often not even the sick notice, all wrapped up as they are in the illness from which they're suffering. Yet, how often do some of them sit there intently watching their fingers tracing meaningless patterns on the polished arm of the chair in which they're sitting! Their thoughts are miles away, and they see . . . nothing! But what a strange effect it has on us afterward, when we cross that room again, on coming out from our consultation, and see our chair once more. The chair on which, but a short while before, we were sitting, waiting for the verdict on our as yet unnamed disease. And find it occupied by another patient. He too with his secret disease. Or empty, impassively there, waiting for someone else—anyone at all—to come and occupy it. But what were we talking about? Oh, yes, of course. The pleasure we derive from imagining things. But why on earth should I immediately have started thinking about a chair in one of those rooms at the doctor's, where the patients sit and wait for their turn to go in and see him?"

"Well, yes. To tell you the truth . . ."

"You don't see the connection? Neither do I. But the fact is, that certain mental associations of images . . . among them associations of things that are poles apart, are so peculiar to each one of us, and determined by reasons and experiences which are so highly individual, that we should no longer understand one another were we not to forbid ourselves to make use of them when speaking to one another. Nothing more illogical, often, than these analogies. But the connection, perhaps, may be this. . . . Look! Would those chairs derive any pleasure from imagining who might be the next patient to come and sit on them, while waiting for his turn to see the doctor? From imagining what disease might be lurking there inside him? Where he will go, what he will do after his consultation? No, no pleasure at all. That's how it is with me, too! No pleasure at all! So many patients come, and they, poor chairs, are there to be occupied. Well, mine is a similar occupation. Now this thing occupies me, now that. At the present moment you are occupying me. And, believe me, I derive not the slightest pleasure from thinking about how you've missed your train, about how your family's waiting for you in the country. Nor do I derive any pleasure from all the vexation that I can imagine you to be feeling."

"And, let me tell you, I do feel pretty fed up!"

"Thank God, then, that being fed up is all you've got to complain about! There are some of us that have worse to contend with, my dear fellow. I tell you—I need to attach myself with my imagination to the lives of other people. But only like this. Without pleasure, without taking the slightest interest in it. Rather—well, just the reverse. Like this; so that I can feel all the vexation of life. So that I can condemn it as foolish and empty and quite in vain. And really, since that's what it's like, it oughtn't to cause anyone the slightest concern if it were brought to an end. And this, you realize, is something that has to be demonstrated most clearly! Proof upon proof; example after example. Implacably we must make ourselves appreciate this fact! Because, my dear fellow, although we don't know of what substance it is made, it's here. Here! We all feel it here, like an anguish in the throat. The taste of life—the taste *for* life! That is never satisfied—that never can be satisfied—because life, even as we're in the very act of living it, is always so ravenously hungering after itself, that it never lets itself be fully tasted! Its savor is in the past, the past that remains living within us. The taste for life comes to us from there. From the memories that hold us bound—but bound to *what*? To this folly of ours, to this mass of vexations, to so many stupid illusions, so many insipid occupations. Yes! Yes! What now, here on earth, seems to be folly; what now seems tedious and irritating, and— Well, you get to the point where you say, that what is now, for us, a disaster, a real disaster—yes, oh yes!—at a distance of four, five, ten years, who knows what flavor it will have acquired? What taste these tears will have? And life! Oh, God! Why, the mere thought of losing it . . . Especially when one knows that it's only a question of days— There . . . can you see? There! There, I say! At the corner—can you see that shadow? There, she's hidden herself again!"

"What? Who? Who was it?"

"Didn't you see her? She's hidden herself again now."

"A woman?"

"Yes, my wife."

"Oh, your wife?"

"She watches over me from a distance. And, do you know, sometimes I almost feel like going over to her and kicking her! But it wouldn't be any use. She's like one of those stray dogs. The more you kick them, the closer they stick to your heels. Obstinate creatures! You can't possibly imagine what that woman is suffering on my account. She doesn't eat, she doesn't sleep any longer. Night and day she follows me around, like this, at a distance. And she might at least brush her clothes every now and again! And that old shoe of a hat she wears! She no longer looks like a woman. She looks more like a rag doll! And her hair—well, the white dust has settled there at her temples. *Forever.* And she's only just thirty-four. She makes me so terribly angry! Oh, you'd never believe how angry! There come times when I round on her. Hurl myself at her. And shout in her face, 'Idiot!' shaking her furiously. She just takes it all. She stands there, looking at me with such an expression in her eyes . . . such an expression in her eyes, that I feel a savage desire to choke the life out of her coming into my fingers. And from her, not a flicker! She just waits for me to get a little way off, and then she starts following me again at a distance. There! Look! She's stuck her head round the corner again!"

"Poor woman!"

"What do you mean, 'poor woman'? Do you realize what she'd like me to do? She'd like me to stay at home. Quietly and peacefully. She'd like to coddle me with all her most loving and heartfelt care. She'd like me to enjoy the perfect order of all the rooms, the polish on all the furniture, that mirror-like silence that there was at first in my house. Measured out by the tick-tock of the grandfather clock in the dining room. That's what she'd like! Now, I ask you—in order to make you understand the absurdity— No, why do I say absurdity? The macabre ferocity of what she wants! I ask you! Do you think it at all possible that the houses of Avezzano, the houses of Messina, knowing about the earthquake that was, in a short time from then, to send them crashing down in ruins, would have found it possible to stay where they were? So peacefully there in the light of the moon, ordered in their nice straight lines along the roads, flanking the squares, obedient to the master plan of the Municipal Housing Committee. My God, houses though they were, for all their bricks and mortar, they'd have found some way of escaping! Just imagine the people of Avezzano, the people of Messina, undressing themselves quite unconcernedly to go to bed. Neatly folding their clothes, putting their shoes outside the door, and burying themselves under the bedclothes. Enjoying the cool freshness of their clean sheets. And all this in the knowledge that within a few hours they'd be dead. Does it seem possible to you?"

"But perhaps your wife—"

"Please. Do let me say what—! If death, my dear fellow, were like one of those strange, loathsome insects that somebody—all unexpectedly —finds walking up his sleeve. You're going along the street, another passer-by suddenly stops you, and cautiously, with his thumb and forefinger outstretched, says to you, 'Excuse me, but may I . . . ? You, my dear sir, have death upon you.' And with his outstretched thumb and forefinger he picks it off you, and throws it away. Oh, that would be magnificent! But death is not like one of those strange, loathsome insects. So many people who pass by, coolly, unconcernedly—quite unpreoccupied with one another—perhaps they too have death upon them. . . . No one sees it. . . . And they go on thinking calmly and peacefully about what they will do tomorrow. Or the day after. Now I . . . Look here. . . . Come over here! Over here; under this light. Come on! I want to show you something. Look, *here*. Under my moustache. Here. Can you see a purplish spot? Do you know what its name is? Ah, it's one of the prettiest names—prettier than a picture! *Epithelioma*, they call it. . . . You say it! Then you'll hear how lovely it sounds! *Epithelioma*. . . . Death, do you understand? It has passed this way. It has planted this flower in my mouth, saying 'Keep it, my friend! I shall come this way again in nine or ten months' time.' Now tell me whether—with this flower in my mouth—I can stay at home peacefully and quietly. As that unfortunate woman would like me to. I scream at her, 'Oh yes, I see! You'd like me to kiss you?' 'Yes, kiss me!' But do you know what she did the other week? She took a pin and made a scratch. Here, on her lip. Then she took my head in her hands, and wanted to kiss me—to kiss me on the mouth. Because, so she says, she wants to die with me! She's mad. I can't stay at home. I need to stand in front of the shop windows, gazing in, admiring the dexterity of the shop assistants. Because, you understand, if there is one single moment of emptiness within me— You do understand, don't you? I might even kill all the life in someone I don't know. Just as if it were nothing at all. . . . Take out a revolver and kill someone who, like you, has had the bad luck to miss his train. . . . No! No! Don't be afraid, my dear fellow! I'm only joking! I'm going now. If it ever came to that, it'd be myself I'd kill, rather than— But these days there are some fine apricots to be had—how do *you* eat them? Skin and all, am I right? You split them in half. Then you squeeze the halves between your thumb and forefinger, till they lengthen out, and look just like two juicy lips. Oh, how lovely! My best wishes to your wife and daughters in the country. I can just picture them. . . . Dressed in blue and white. Seated in the shade of a tree. In a beautiful green field. . . . Do me a favor— Tomorrow morning, when you get back. I imagine that the village where you're staying is some little way from the station. It'll be dawn; you can make the rest of your journey on foot. The first tuft of grass by the roadside—count the number of blades for me. The number of those blades will be the number of days that I have yet to live. But I beg you—please choose a fine large tuft. Good night!"

Translated by Frederick May

THE OPEN BOAT
A Tale Intended to Be after the Fact.
Being the Experience of Four Men
from the Sunk Steamer *Commodore*.
by Stephen Crane
(1871–1900)

None of them knew the color of the sky. Their eyes glanced level, and were fastened upon the waves that swept toward them. These waves were of the hue of slate, save for the tops, which were of foaming white, and all of the men knew the colors of the sea. The horizon narrowed and widened, and dipped and rose, and at all times its edge was jagged with waves that seemed thrust up in points like rocks. Many a man ought to have a bathtub larger than the boat which here rode upon the sea. These waves were most wrongfully and barbarously abrupt and tall, and each froth-top was a problem in small-boat navigation.

The cook squatted in the bottom and looked with both eyes at the six inches of gunwale which separated him from the ocean. His sleeves were rolled over his fat forearms, and the two flaps of his unbuttoned vest dangled as he bent to bail out the boat. Often he said: "Gawd! That was a narrow clip." As he remarked it he invariably gazed eastward over the broken sea.

The oiler, steering with one of the two oars in the boat, sometimes raised himself suddenly to keep clear of water that swirled in over the stern. It was a thin little oar and it seemed often ready to snap.

The correspondent, pulling at the other oar, watched the waves and wondered why he was there.

The injured captain, lying in the bow, was at this time buried in that profound dejection and indifference which comes, temporarily at least, to even the bravest and most enduring when, willy nilly, the firm fails, the army loses, the ship goes down. The mind of the master of a vessel is rooted deep in the timbers of her, though he command for a day or a decade, and this captain had on him the stern impression of a scene in the grays of dawn of seven turned faces, and later a stump of a topmast with a white ball on it that slashed to and fro at the waves, went low and lower, and down. Thereafter there was something strange in his voice. Although steady, it was deep with mourning, and of a quality beyond oration or tears.

"Keep 'er a little more south, Billie," said he.

" 'A little more south,' sir," said the oiler in the stern.

A seat in this boat was not unlike the seat upon a bucking broncho, and by the same token, a broncho is not much smaller. The craft pranced and reared, and plunged like an animal. As each wave came, and she rose for it, she seemed like a horse making at a fence outrageously high. The manner of her scramble over these walls of water is a mystic thing, and, moreover, at the top of them were ordinarily these problems in white water, the foam racing down from the summit of each wave, requiring a new leap, and a leap from the air. Then, after scornfully bumping a crest, she would slide, and race, and splash down a long incline, and arrive bobbing and nodding in front of the next menace.

A singular disadvantage of the sea lies in the fact that after success-fully surmounting one wave you discover that there is another behind it just as important and just as nervously anxious to do something effective in the way of swamping boats. In a ten-foot dinghy one can get an idea of the resources of the sea in the line of waves that is not probable to the average experience which is never at sea in a dinghy. As each slatey wall of water approached, it shut all else from the view of the men in the boat, and it was not difficult to imagine that this particular wave was the final outburst of the ocean, the last effort of the grim water. There was a terrible grace in the move of the waves, and they came in silence, save for the snarling of the crests.

In the wan light, the faces of the men must have been gray. Their eyes must have glinted in strange ways as they gazed steadily astern. Viewed from a balcony, the whole thing would doubtless have been weirdly pic-turesque. But the men in the boat had no time to see it, and if they had had leisure there were other things to occupy their minds. The sun swung steadily up the sky, and they knew it was broad day because the color of the sea changed from slate to emerald-green, streaked with amber lights, and the foam was like tumbling snow. The process of the breaking day was unknown to them. They were aware only of this effect upon the color of the waves that rolled toward them.

In disjointed sentences the cook and the correspondent argued as to the difference between a lifesaving station and a house of refuge. The cook had said: "There's a house of refuge just north of the Mosquito Inlet

Light, and as soon as they see us, they'll come off in their boat and pick us up."

"As soon as who sees us?" said the correspondent.

"The crew," said the cook.

"Houses of refuge don't have crews," said the correspondent. "As I understand them, they are only places where clothes and grub are stored for the benefit of shipwrecked people. They don't carry crews."

"Oh, yes, they do," said the cook.

"No, they don't," said the correspondent.

"Well, we're not there yet, anyhow," said the oiler, in the stern.

"Well," said the cook, "perhaps it's not a house of refuge that I'm thinking of as being near Mosquito Inlet Light. Perhaps it's a lifesaving station."

"We're not there yet," said the oiler, in the stern.

II

As the boat bounced from the top of each wave, the wind tore through the hair of the hatless men, and as the craft plopped her stern down again the spray splashed past them. The crest of each of these waves was a hill, from the top of which the men surveyed, for a moment, a broad tumultuous expanse, shining and wind-riven. It was probably splendid. It was probably glorious, this play of the free sea, wild with lights of emerald and white and amber.

"Bully good thing it's an on-shore wind," said the cook. "If not, where would we be? Wouldn't have a show."

"That's right," said the correspondent.

The busy oiler nodded his assent.

Then the captain, in the bow, chuckled in a way that expressed humor, contempt, tragedy, all in one. "Do you think we've got much of a show now, boys?" said he.

Whereupon the three were silent, save for a trifle of hemming and hawing. To express any particular optimism at this time they felt to be childish and stupid, but they all doubtless possessed this sense of the situation in their mind. A young man thinks doggedly at such times. On the other hand, the ethics of their condition was decidedly against any open suggestion of hopelessness. So they were silent.

"Oh, well," said the captain, soothing his children, "we'll get ashore all right."

But there was that in his tone which made them think, so the oiler quoth: "Yes! If this wind holds!"

The cook was bailing: "Yes! If we don't catch hell in the surf."

Canton flannel gulls flew near and far. Sometimes they sat down on the sea, near patches of brown seaweed that rolled on the waves with a movement like carpets on a line in a gale. The birds sat comfortably in groups, and they were envied by some in the dinghy, for the wrath of the sea was no more to them than it was to a covey of prairie chickens a thousand miles inland. Often they came very close and stared at the men with black beadlike eyes. At these times they were uncanny and sinister in their unblinking scrutiny, and the men hooted angrily at them, telling them to be gone. One came, and evidently decided to alight on the top of the captain's head. The bird flew parallel to the boat and did not circle, but made short sidelong jumps in the air in chicken-fashion. His black eyes were wistfully fixed upon the captain's head. "Ugly brute," said the oiler to the bird. "You look as if you were made with a jack knife." The cook and the correspondent swore darkly at the creature. The captain naturally wished to knock it away with the end of the heavy painter; but he did not dare do it, because anything resembling an emphatic gesture would have capsized this freighted boat, and so with his open hand, the captain gently and carefully waved the gull away. After it had been discouraged from the pursuit the captain breathed easier on account of his hair, and others breathed easier because the bird struck their minds at this time as being somehow gruesome and ominous.

In the meantime the oiler and the correspondent rowed. And also they rowed.

They sat together in the same seat, and each rowed an oar. Then the oiler took both oars; then the correspondent took both oars; then the oiler; then the correspondent. They rowed and they rowed. The very ticklish part of the business was when the time came for the reclining one in the stern to take his turn at the oars. By the very last star of truth, it is easier to steal eggs from under a hen than it was to change seats in the dinghy. First the man in the stern slid his hand along the thwart and moved with care, as if he were of Sèvres. Then the man in the rowing seat slid his hand along the other thwart. It was all done with the most extraordinary care. As the two sidled past each other, the whole party kept watchful eyes on the coming wave, and the captain cried: "Look out now! Steady there!"

The brown mats of seaweed that appeared from time to time were like islands, bits of earth. They were traveling, apparently, neither one way nor the other. They were, to all intents, stationary. They informed the men in the boat that it was making progress slowly toward the land.

The captain, rearing cautiously in the bow, after the dinghy soared on a great swell, said that he had seen the lighthouse at Mosquito Inlet. Presently the cook remarked that he had seen it. The correspondent was at the oars then, and for some reason he too wished to look at the lighthouse, but his back was toward the far shore and the waves were important, and for some time he could not seize an opportunity to turn his head. But at last there came a wave more gentle than the others, and when at the crest of it he swiftly scoured the western horizon.

"See it?" said the captain.

"No," said the correspondent slowly, "I didn't see anything."

"Look again," said the captain. He pointed. "It's exactly in that direction."

At the top of another wave, the correspondent did as he was bid, and this time his eyes chanced on a small still thing on the edge of the swaying horizon. It was precisely like the point of a pin. It took an anxious eye to find a lighthouse so tiny.

"Think we'll make it, captain?"

"If this wind holds and the boat don't swamp, we can't do much else," said the captain.

The little boat, lifted by each towering sea, and splashed viciously by the crests, made progress that in the absence of seaweed was not apparent to those in her. She seemed just a wee thing wallowing, miraculously top-up, at the mercy of five oceans. Occasionally, a great spread of water, like white flames, swarmed into her.

"Bail her, cook," said the captain serenely.

"All right, captain," said the cheerful cook.

III

It would be difficult to describe the subtle brotherhood of men that was here established on the seas. No one said that it was so. No one mentioned it. But it dwelt in the boat, and each man felt it warm him. They were a captain, an oiler, a cook, and a correspondent, and they were friends, friends in a more curiously iron-bound degree than may be common. The hurt captain, lying against the water jar in the bow, spoke always in a low voice and calmly, but he could never command a more ready and swiftly obedient crew than the motley three of the dinghy. It was more than a mere recognition of what was best for the common safety. There was surely in it a quality that was personal and heartfelt. And after this devotion to the commander of the boat there was this comradeship that the correspondent, for instance, who had been taught to be cynical of men, knew even at the time was the best experience of his life. But no one said that it was so. No one mentioned it.

"I wish we had a sail," remarked the captain, "We might try my overcoat on the end of an oar and give you two boys a chance to rest." So the cook and the correspondent held the mast and spread wide the overcoat. The oiler steered, and the little boat made good way with her new rig. Sometimes the oiler had to scull sharply to keep a sea from breaking into the boat, but otherwise sailing was a success.

Meanwhile the lighthouse had been growing slowly larger. It had now almost assumed color, and appeared like a little gray shadow on the sky. The man at the oars could not be prevented from turning his head rather often to try for a glimpse of this little gray shadow.

At last, from the top of each wave the men in the tossing boat could see land. Even as the lighthouse was an upright shadow on the sky, this land seemed but a long black shadow on the sea. It certainly was thinner than paper. "We must be about opposite New Smyrna," said the cook, who had coasted this shore often in schooners. "Captain, by the way, I believe they abandoned that lifesaving station there about a year ago."

"Did they?" said the captain.

The wind slowly died away. The cook and the correspondent were not now obliged to slave in order to hold high the oar. But the waves continued their old impetuous swooping at the dinghy, and the little craft, no longer under way, struggled woundily over them. The oiler or the correspondent took the oars again.

Shipwrecks are à propos of nothing. If men could only train for them and have them occur when the men had reached pink condition, there would be less drowning at sea. Of the four in the dinghy none had slept any time worth mentioning for two days and two nights previous to embarking in the dinghy, and in the excitement of clambering about the deck of a foundering ship they had also forgotten to eat heartily.

For these reasons, and for others, neither the oiler nor the correspondent was fond of rowing at this time. The correspondent wondered ingenuously how in the name of all that was sane could there be people who thought it amusing to row a boat. It was not an amusement; it was a diabolical punishment, and even a genius of mental aberrations could never conclude that it was anything but a horror to the muscles and a crime against the back. He mentioned to the boat in general how the amusement of rowing struck him, and the weary-faced oiler smiled in full sympathy. Previously to the foundering, by the way, the oiler had worked double-watch in the engine room of the ship.

"Take her easy, now, boys," said the captain. "Don't spend yourselves. If we have to run a surf you'll need all your strength, because we'll sure have to swim for it. Take your time."

Slowly the land arose from the sea. From a black line it became a line of black and a line of white, trees and sand. Finally, the captain said that he could make out a house on the shore. "That's the house of refuge, sure," said the cook. "They'll see us before long, and come out after us."

The distant lighthouse reared high. "The keeper ought to be able to make us out now, if he's looking through a glass," said the captain. "He'll notify the lifesaving people."

"None of those other boats could have got ashore to give word of the wreck," said the oiler, in a low voice. "Else the lifeboat would be out hunting us."

Slowly and beautifully the land loomed out of the sea. The wind came again. It had veered from the northeast to the southeast. Finally, a new sound struck the ears of the men in the boat. It was the low thunder of the surf on the shore. "We'll never be able to make the lighthouse now," said the captain. "Swing her head a little more north, Billie," said he.

" 'A little more north,' sir," said the oiler.

Whereupon the little boat turned her nose once more down the wind, and all but the oarsman watched the shore grow. Under the influence of this expansion doubt and direful apprehension was leaving the minds of the men. The management of the boat was still most absorbing, but it could not prevent a quiet cheerfulness. In an hour, perhaps, they would be ashore.

Their backbones had become thoroughly used to balancing in the boat, and they now rode this wild colt of a dinghy like circus men. The correspondent thought that he had been drenched to the skin, but happening to feel in the top pocket of his coat, he found therein eight cigars. Four of them were soaked with seawater; four were perfectly scathless. After a search, somebody produced three dry matches, and thereupon the four waifs rode impudently in their little boat, and with an assurance of an impending rescue shining in their eyes, puffed at the big cigars and judged well and ill of all men. Everybody took a drink of water.

IV

"Cook," remarked the captain, "there don't seem to be any signs of life about your house of refuge."

"No," replied the cook. "Funny they don't see us!"

A broad stretch of lowly coast lay before the eyes of the men. It was of dunes topped with dark vegetation. The roar of the surf was plain, and sometimes they could see the white lip of a wave as it spun up the beach. A tiny house was blocked out black upon the sky. Southward, the slim lighthouse lifted its little gray length.

Tide, wind, and waves were swinging the dinghy northward. "Funny they don't see us," said the men.

The surf's roar was here dulled, but its tone was, nevertheless, thunderous and mighty. As the boat swam over the great rollers, the men sat listening to this roar. "We'll swamp sure," said everybody.

It is fair to say here that there was not a lifesaving station within twenty miles in either direction, but the men did not know this fact, and in consequence they made dark and opprobrious remarks concerning the eyesight of the nation's lifesavers. Four scowling men sat in the dinghy and surpassed records in the invention of epithets.

"Funny they don't see us."

The lightheartedness of a former time had completely faded. To their sharpened minds it was easy to conjure pictures of all kinds of incompetency and blindness and, indeed, cowardice. There was the shore of the populous land, and it was bitter and bitter to them that from it came no sign.

"Well," said the captain, ultimately, "I suppose we'll have to make a try for ourselves. If we stay out here too long, we'll none of us have strength left to swim after the boat swamps."

And so the oiler, who was at the oars, turned the boat straight for the shore. There was a sudden tightening of muscle. There was some thinking.

"If we don't all get ashore—" said the captain. "If we don't all get ashore, I suppose you fellows know where to send news of my finish?"

They then briefly exchanged some addresses and admonitions. As for the reflections of the men, there was a great deal of rage in them. Perchance they might be formulated thus: "If I am going to be drowned—if I am going to be drowned—if I am going to be drowned, why in the name of the seven mad gods who rule the sea, was I allowed to come thus far and contemplate sand and trees ? Was I brought here merely to have my nose dragged away as I was about to nibble the sacred cheese of life? It is preposterous. If this old ninny-woman, Fate, cannot do better than this, she should be deprived of the management of men's fortunes. She is an old hen who knows not her intention. If she has decided to drown me, why did she not do it in the beginning and save me all this trouble? The whole affair is absurd. . . . But no, she cannot mean to drown me. She dare not drown me. She cannot drown me. Not after all this work." Afterward the man might have had an impulse to shake his fist at the clouds: "Just you drown me, now, and then hear what I call you!"

The billows that came at this time were more formidable. They seemed always just about to break and roll over the little boat in a turmoil of foam. There was a preparatory and long growl in the speech of them. No mind unused to the sea would have concluded that the dinghy could ascend these sheer heights in time. The shore was still afar. The oiler was a wily surfman. "Boys," he said swiftly, "she won't live three minutes more, and we're too far out to swim. Shall I take her to sea again, captain?"

"Yes! Go ahead!" said the captain.

This oiler, by a series of quick miracles, and fast and steady oarsmanship, turned the boat in the middle of the surf and took her safely to sea again.

There was a considerable silence as the boat bumped over the furrowed sea to deeper water. Then somebody in gloom spoke. "Well, anyhow, they must have seen us from the shore by now."

The gulls went in slanting flight up the wind toward the gray desolate east. A squall, marked by dingy clouds, and clouds brick-red, like smoke from a burning building, appeared from the southeast.

"What do you think of those lifesaving people? Ain't they peaches?"

"Funny they haven't seen us."

"Maybe they think we're out here for sport! Maybe they think we're fishin'. Maybe they think we're damned fools."

It was a long afternoon. A changed tide tried to force them southward, but the wind and wave said northward. Far ahead, where coastline, sea, and sky formed their mighty angle, there were little dots which seemed to indicate a city on the shore.

"St. Augustine?"

The captain shook his head. "Too near Mosquito Inlet."

And the oiler rowed, and then the correspondent rowed. Then the oiler rowed. It was a weary business. The human back can become the seat of more aches and pains than are registered in books for the composite anatomy of a regiment. It is a limited area, but it can become the theater of innumerable muscular conflicts, tangles, wrenches, knots, and other comforts.

"Did you ever like to row, Billie?" asked the correspondent.

"No," said the oiler. "Hang it!"

When one exchanged the rowing seat for a place in the bottom of the boat, he suffered a bodily depression that caused him to be careless of everything save an obligation to wiggle one finger. There was cold sea-water swashing to and fro in the boat, and he lay in it. His head, pillowed on a thwart, was within an inch of the swirl of a wave crest, and sometimes a particularly obstreperous sea came in-board and drenched him once more. But these matters did not annoy him. It is almost certain that if the boat had capsized he would have tumbled comfortably out upon the ocean as if he felt sure that it was a great soft mattress.

"Look! There's a man on the shore!"

"Where?"

"There! See 'im? See 'im?"

"Yes, sure! He's walking along."

"Now he's stopped. Look! He's facing us!"

"He's waving at us!"

"So he is! By thunder!"

"Ah, now we're all right! Now we're all right! There'll be a boat out here for us in half an hour."

"He's going on. He's running. He's going up to that house there."

The remote beach seemed lower than the sea, and it required a searching glance to discern the little black figure. The captain saw a float-ing stick and they rowed to it. A bath towel was by some weird chance in the boat, and, tying this on the stick, the captain waved it. The oarsman did not dare turn his head, so he was obliged to ask questions.

"What's he doing now?"

"He's standing still again. He's looking, I think. . . . There he goes again. Toward the house. . . . Now he's stopped again."

"Is he waving at us?"

"No, not now! He was, though."

"Look! There comes another man!"

"He's running."

"Look at him go, would you."

"Why, he's on a bicycle. Now he's met the other man. They're both waving at us. Look!"

"There comes something up the beach."

"What the devil is that thing?"

"Why, it looks like a boat."

"Why, certainly it's a boat."

"No, it's on wheels."

"Yes, so it is. Well, that must be the lifeboat. They drag them along shore on a wagon."

"That's the lifeboat, sure."

"No, by——, it's—it's an omnibus."

"I tell you it's a lifeboat."

"It is not! It's an omnibus. I can see it plain. See? One of these big hotel omnibuses."

"By thunder, you're right. It's an omnibus, sure as fate. What do you suppose they are doing with an omnibus? Maybe they are going around collecting the life-crew, hey?"

"That's it, likely. Look! There's a fellow waving a little black flag. He's standing on the steps of the omnibus. There come those other two fellows. Now they're all talking together. Look at the fellow with the flag. Maybe he ain't waving it."

"That ain't a flag, is it? That's his coat. Why, certainly, that's his coat."

"So it is. It's his coat. He's taken it off and is waving it around his head. But would you look at him swing it."

"Oh, say, there isn't any lifesaving station there. That's just a winter resort hotel omnibus that has brought over some of the boarders to see us drown."

"What's that idiot with the coat mean? What's he signaling, anyhow?"

"It looks as if he were trying to tell us to go north. There must be a lifesaving station up there."

"No! He thinks we're fishing. Just giving us a merry hand. See? Ah, there, Willie!"

"Well, I wish I could make something out of those signals. What do you suppose he means?"

"He don't mean anything. He's just playing."

"Well, if he'd just signal us to try the surf again, or to go to sea and wait, or go north, or go south, or go to hell—there would be some reason in it. But look at him. He just stands there and keeps his coat revolving like a wheel. The ass!"

"There come more people."

"Now there's quite a mob. Look! Isn't that a boat?"

"Where? Oh, I see where you mean. No, that's no boat."

"That fellow is still waving his coat."

"He must think we like to see him do that. Why don't he quit it? It don't mean anything."

"I don't know. I think he is trying to make us go north. It must be that there's a lifesaving station there somewhere."

"Say, he ain't tired yet. Look at 'im wave."

"Wonder how long he can keep that up. He's been revolving his coat ever since he caught sight of us. He's an idiot. Why aren't they getting men to bring a boat out? A fishing boat—one of those big yawls—could come out here all right. Why don't he do something?"

"Oh, it's all right, now."

"They'll have a boat out here for us in less than no time, now that they've seen us."

A faint yellow tone came into the sky over the low land. The shadows on the sea slowly deepened. The wind bore coldness with it, and the men began to shiver.

"Holy smoke!" said one, allowing his voice to express his impious mood, "if we keep on monkeying out here! If we've got to flounder out here all night!"

"Oh, we'll never have to stay here all night! Don't you worry. They've seen us now, and it won't be long before they'll come chasing out after us."

The shore grew dusky. The man waving a coat blended gradually into this gloom, and it swallowed in the same manner the omnibus and the group of people. The spray, when it dashed uproariously over the side, made the voyagers shrink and swear like men who were being branded.

"I'd like to catch the chump who waved the coat. I feel like soaking him one, just for luck."

"Why? What did he do?"

"Oh, nothing, but then he seemed so damned cheerful."

In the meantime the oiler rowed, and then the correspondent rowed, and then the oiler rowed. Gray-faced and bowed forward, they mechanically, turn by turn, plied the leaden oars. The form of the lighthouse had vanished from the southern horizon, but finally a pale star appeared, just lifting from the sea. The streaked saffron in the west passed before the all-merging darkness, and the sea to the east was black. The land had vanished, and was expressed only by the low and drear thunder of the surf.

"If I am going to be drowned—if I am going to be drowned—if I am going to be drowned, why, in the name of the seven mad gods who rule the sea, was I allowed to come thus far and contemplate sand and trees? Was I brought here merely to have my nose dragged away as I was about to nibble the sacred cheese of life?"

The patient captain, drooped over the water jar, was sometimes obliged to speak to the oarsman.

"Keep her head up! Keep her head up!"

" 'Keep her head up,' sir." The voices were weary and low.

This was surely a quiet evening. All save the oarsman lay heavily and listlessly in the boat's bottom. As for him, his eyes were just capable of noting the tall black waves that swept forward in a most sinister silence, save for an occasional subdued growl of a crest.

The cook's head was on a thwart, and he looked without interest at the water under his nose. He was deep in other scenes. Finally he spoke. "Billie," he murmured, dreamfully, "what kind of pie do you like best?"

V

"Pie," said the oiler and the correspondent, agitatedly. "Don't talk about those things, blast you!"

"Well," said the cook, "I was just thinking about ham sandwiches and—"

A night on the sea in an open boat is a long night. As darkness settled finally, the shine of the light, lifting from the sea in the south, changed to full gold. On the northern horizon a new light appeared, a small bluish gleam on the edge of the waters. These two lights were the furniture of the world. Otherwise there was nothing but waves.

Two men huddled in the stern, and distances were so magnificent in the dinghy that the rower was enabled to keep his feet partly warmed by thrusting them under his companions. Their legs indeed extended far under the rowing seat until they touched the feet of the captain forward. Sometimes, despite the efforts of the tired oarsman, a wave came piling into the boat, an icy wave of the night, and the chilling water soaked them anew. They would twist their bodies for a moment and groan, and sleep the dead sleep once more, while the water in the boat gurgled about them as the craft rocked.

The plan of the oiler and the correspondent was for one to row until he lost the ability, and then arouse the other from his seawater couch in the bottom of the boat.

The oiler plied the oars until his head drooped forward, and the overpowering sleep blinded him. And he rowed yet afterward. Then he touched a man in the bottom of the boat, and called his name. "Will you spell me for a little while?" he said, meekly.

"Sure, Billie," said the correspondent, awakening and dragging himself to a sitting position. They exchanged places carefully, and the oiler, cuddling down in the seawater at the cook's side, seemed to go to sleep instantly.

The particular violence of the sea had ceased. The waves came without snarling. The obligation of the man at the oars was to keep the boat headed so that the tilt of the rollers would not capsize her, and to preserve her from filling when the crests rushed past. The black waves were silent and hard to be seen in the darkness. Often one was almost upon the boat before the oarsman was aware.

In a low voice the correspondent addressed the captain. He was not sure that the captain was awake, although this iron man seemed to be always awake. "Captain, shall I keep her making for that light north, sir?"

The same steady voice answered him. "Yes. Keep it about two points off the port bow."

The cook had tied a life belt around himself in order to get even the warmth which this clumsy cork contrivance could donate, and he seemed almost stove-like when a rower, whose teeth invariably chattered wildly as soon as he ceased his labor, dropped down to sleep.

The correspondent, as he rowed, looked down at the two men sleeping underfoot. The cook's arm was around the oiler's shoulders, and, with their fragmentary clothing and haggard faces, they were the babes of the sea, a grotesque rendering of the old babes in the wood.

Later he must have grown stupid at his work, for suddenly there was a growling of water, and a crest came with a roar and a swash into the boat, and it was a wonder that it did not set the cook afloat in his life belt. The cook continued to sleep, but the oiler sat up, blinking his eyes and shaking with the new cold.

"Oh, I'm awful sorry, Billie," said the correspondent contritely.

"That's all right, old boy," said the oiler, and lay down again and was asleep.

Presently it seemed that even the captain dozed, and the correspondent thought that he was the one man afloat on all the oceans. The wind had a voice as it came over the waves, and it was sadder than the end.

There was a long, loud swishing astern of the boat, and a gleaming trail of phosphorescence, like blue flame, was furrowed on the black waters. It might have been made by a monstrous knife.

Then there came a stillness, while the correspondent breathed with the open mouth and looked at the sea.

Suddenly there was another swish and another long flash of bluish light, and this time it was alongside the boat, and might almost have been reached with an oar. The correspondent saw an enormous fin speed like a shadow through the water, hurling the crystalline spray and leaving the long glowing trail.

The correspondent looked over his shoulder at the captain. His face was hidden, and he seemed to be asleep. He looked at the babes of the sea. They certainly were asleep. So, being bereft of sympathy, he leaned a little way to one side and swore softly into the sea.

But the thing did not then leave the vicinity of the boat. Ahead or astern, on one side or the other, at intervals long or short, fled the long sparkling streak, and there was to be heard the whirroo of the dark fin. The speed and power of the thing was greatly to be admired. It cut the water like a gigantic and keen projectile.

The presence of this biding thing did not affect the man with the same horror that it would if he had been a picnicker. He simply looked at the sea dully and swore in an undertone.

Nevertheless, it is true that he did not wish to be alone. He wished one of his companions to awaken by chance and keep him company with it. But the captain hung motionless over the water jar, and the oiler and the cook in the bottom of the boat were plunged in slumber.

VI

"If I am going to be drowned—if I am going to be drowned—if I am going to be drowned, why, in the name of the seven mad gods who rule the sea, was I allowed to come thus far and contemplate sand and trees?"

During this dismal night, it may be remarked that a man would conclude that it was really the intention of the seven mad gods to drown him, despite the abominable injustice of it. For it was certainly an abominable injustice to drown a man who had worked so hard, so hard. The man felt it would be a crime most unnatural. Other people had drowned at sea since galleys swarmed with painted sails, but still—

When it occurs to a man that nature does not regard him as important, and that she feels she would not maim the universe by disposing of him, he at first wishes to throw bricks at the temple, and he hates deeply the fact that there are no bricks and no temples. Any visible expression of nature would surely be pelleted with his jeers.

Then, if there be no tangible thing to hoot he feels, perhaps, the desire to confront a personification and indulge in pleas, bowed to one knee, and with hands supplicant, saying: "Yes, but I love myself."

A high cold star on a winter's night is the word he feels that she says to him. Thereafter he knows the pathos of his situation.

The men in the dinghy had not discussed these matters, but each had, no doubt, reflected upon them in silence and according to his mind. There was seldom any expression upon their faces save the general one of complete weariness. Speech was devoted to the business of the boat.

To chime the notes of his emotion, a verse mysteriously entered the correspondent's head. He had even forgotten that he had forgotten this verse, but it suddenly was in his mind.

"A soldier of the Legion lay dying in Algiers,
There was a lack of woman's nursing, there was dearth of woman's tears;
But a comrade stood beside him, and he took the comrade's hand,
And he said: 'I shall never see my own, my native land.' "

In his childhood, the correspondent had been made acquainted with the fact that a soldier of the Legion lay dying in Algiers, but he had never regarded the fact as important. Myriads of his school fellows had informed him of the soldier's plight, but the dinning had naturally ended by making him perfectly indifferent. He had never considered it his affair that a soldier of the Legion lay dying in Algiers, nor had it appeared to him as a matter for sorrow. It was less to him than the breaking of a pencil's point.

Now, however, it quaintly came to him as a human, living thing. It was no longer merely a picture of a few throes in the breast of a poet, meanwhile drinking tea and warming his feet at the grate; it was an actuality—stern, mournful, and fine.

The correspondent plainly saw the soldier. He lay on the sand with his feet out straight and still. While his pale left hand was upon his chest in an attempt to thwart the going of his life, the blood came between his fingers. In the far Algerian distance, a city of low square forms was set against a sky that was faint with the last sunset hues. The correspondent, plying the oars and dreaming of the slow and slower movements of the lips of the soldier, was moved by a profound and perfectly impersonal comprehension. He was sorry for the soldier of the Legion who lay dying in Algiers.

The thing which had followed the boat and waited had evidently grown bored at the delay. There was no longer to be heard the slash of the cut-water, and there was no longer the flame of the long trail. The light in the north still glimmered, but it was apparently no nearer to the boat. Sometimes the boom of the surf rang in the correspondent's ears, and he turned the craft seaward then and rowed harder. Southward, some one had evidently built a watch-fire on the beach. It was too low and too far to be seen, but it made a shimmering, roseate reflection upon the bluff back of it, and this could be discerned from the boat. The wind came stronger, and sometimes a wave suddenly raged out like a mountain cat, and there was to be seen the sheen and sparkle of a broken crest.

The captain, in the bow, moved on his water jar and sat erect. "Pretty long night," he observed to the correspondent. He looked at the shore. "Those lifesaving people take their time."

"Did you see that shark playing around?"

"Yes, I saw him. He was a big fellow, all right."

"Wish I had known you were awake."

Later the correspondent spoke into the bottom of the boat.

"Billie!" There was a slow and gradual disentanglement. "Billie, will you spell me?"

"Sure," said the oiler.

As soon as the correspondent touched the cold comfortable seawater in the bottom of the boat, and had huddled close to the cook's life belt he was deep in sleep, despite the fact that his teeth played all the popular airs. This sleep was so good to him that it was but a moment before he heard a voice call his name in a tone that demonstrated the last stages of exhaustion. "Will you spell me?"

"Sure, Billie."

The light in the north had mysteriously vanished, but the correspondent took his course from the wide-awake captain.

Later in the night they took the boat farther out to sea, and the captain directed the cook to take one oar at the stern and keep the boat facing the seas. He was to call out if he should hear the thunder of the surf. This plan enabled the oiler and the correspondent to get respite together. "We'll give those boys a chance to get into shape again," said the captain. They curled down and, after a few preliminary chatterings and trembles, slept once more the dead sleep. Neither knew they had bequeathed to the cook the company of another shark, or perhaps the same shark.

As the boat caroused on the waves, spray occasionally bumped over the side and gave him a fresh soaking, but this had no power to break their repose. The ominous slash of the wind and the water affected them as it would have affected mummies.

"Boys," said the cook, with the notes of every reluctance in his voice, "she's drifted in pretty close. I guess one of you had better take her to sea again." The correspondent, aroused, heard the crash of the toppled crests.

As he was rowing, the captain gave him some whisky-and-water, and this steadied the chills out of him. "If I ever get ashore and anybody shows me even a photograph of an oar—"

At last there was a short conversation.

"Billie. . . . Billie, will you spell me?"

"Sure," said the oiler.

VII

When the correspondent again opened his eyes, the sea and the sky were each of the gray hue of the dawning. Later, carmine and gold was painted upon the waters. The morning appeared finally, in its splendor, with a sky of pure blue, and the sunlight flamed on the tips of the waves.

On the distant dunes were set many little black cottages, and a tall white windmill reared above them. No man, nor dog, nor bicycle appeared on the beach. The cottages might have formed a deserted village.

The voyagers scanned the shore. A conference was held in the boat. "Well," said the captain, "if no help is coming we might better try a run through the surf right away. If we stay out here much longer we will be too weak to do anything for ourselves at all." The others silently acquiesced in this reasoning. The boat was headed for the beach. The correspondent wondered if none ever ascended the tall wind-tower, and if then they never looked seaward. This tower was a giant, standing with its back to the plight of the ants. It represented in a degree, to the correspondent, the serenity of nature amid the struggles of the individual—nature in the wind, and nature in the vision of men. She did not seem cruel to him then, nor beneficent, nor treacherous, nor wise. But she was indifferent, flatly indifferent. It is, perhaps, plausible that a man in this situation, impressed with the unconcern of the universe, should see the innumerable flaws of his life, and have them taste wickedly in his mind and wish for another chance. A distinction between right and wrong seems absurdly clear to him, then, in this new ignorance of the grave-edge, and he understands that if he were given another opportunity he would mend his conduct and his words, and be better and brighter during an introduction or at a tea.

"Now, boys," said the captain, "she is going to swamp, sure. All we can do is to work her in as far as possible, and then when she swamps, pile out and scramble for the beach. Keep cool now, and don't jump until she swamps sure."

The oiler took the oars. Over his shoulders he scanned the surf. "Captain," he said, "I think I'd better bring her about, and keep her head-on to the seas and back her in."

"All right, Billie," said the captain. "Back her in." The oiler swung the boat then and, seated in the stern, the cook and the correspondent were obliged to look over their shoulders to contemplate the lonely and indifferent shore.

The monstrous in-shore rollers heaved the boat high until the men were again enabled to see the white sheets of water scudding up the slanted beach. "We won't get in very close," said the captain. Each time a man could wrest his attention from the rollers, he turned his glance toward the shore, and in the expression of the eyes during this contemplation there was a singular quality. The correspondent, observing the others, knew that they were not afraid, but the full meaning of their glances was shrouded.

As for himself, he was too tired to grapple fundamentally with the fact. He tried to coerce his mind into thinking of it, but the mind was dominated at this time by the muscles, and the muscles said they did not care. It merely occurred to him that if he should drown it would be a shame.

There were no hurried words, no pallor, no plain agitation. The men simply looked at the shore. "Now, remember to get well clear of the boat when you jump," said the captain.

Seaward the crest of a roller suddenly fell with a thunderous crash, and the long white comber came roaring down upon the boat.

"Steady now," said the captain. The men were silent. They turned their eyes from the shore to the comber and waited. The boat slid up the incline, leaped at the furious top, bounced over it, and swung down the long back of the wave. Some water had been shipped and the cook bailed it out.

But the next crest crashed also. The tumbling, boiling flood of white water caught the boat and whirled it almost perpendicular. Water swarmed in from all sides. The correspondent had his hands on the gunwale at this time, and when the water entered at that place he swiftly withdrew his fingers, as if he objected to wetting them.

The little boat, drunken with this weight of water, reeled and snuggled deeper into the sea.

"Bail her out, cook! Bail her out," said the captain.

"All right, captain," said the cook.

"Now, boys, the next one will do for us, sure," said the oiler. "Mind to jump clear of the boat."

The third wave moved forward, huge, furious, implacable. It fairly swallowed the dinghy, and almost simultaneously the men tumbled into the sea. A piece of life belt had lain in the bottom of the boat, and as the correspondent went overboard he held this to his chest with his left hand.

The January water was icy, and he reflected immediately that it was colder than he had expected to find it on the coast of Florida. This appeared to his dazed mind as a fact important enough to be noted at the time. The coldness of the water was sad; it was tragic. This fact was somehow so mixed and confused with his opinion of his own situation that it seemed almost a proper reason for tears. The water was cold.

When he came to the surface he was conscious of little but the noisy water. Afterward he saw his companions in the sea. The oiler was ahead in the race. He was swimming strongly and rapidly. Off to the correspondent's left, the cook's great white and corked back bulged out of the water, and in the rear the captain was hanging with his one good hand to the keel of the overturned dinghy.

There is a certain immovable quality to a shore, and the correspondent wondered at it amid the confusion of the sea.

It seemed also very attractive, but the correspondent knew that it was a long journey, and he paddled leisurely. The piece of life preserver lay under him, and sometimes he whirled down the incline of a wave as if he were on a hand-sled.

But finally he arrived at a place in the sea where travel was beset with difficulty. He did not pause swimming to inquire what manner of current had caught him, but there his progress ceased. The shore was set before him like a bit of scenery on a stage, and he looked at it and understood with his eyes each detail of it.

As the cook passed, much farther to the left, the captain was calling to him, "Turn over on your back, cook! Turn over on your back and use the oar."

"All right, sir." The cook turned on his back, and, paddling with an oar, went ahead as if he were a canoe.

Presently the boat also passed to the left of the correspondent with the captain clinging with one hand to the keel. He would have appeared like a man raising himself to look over a board fence, if it were not for the extraordinary gymnastics of the boat. The correspondent marveled that the captain could still hold to it.

They passed on, nearer to shore—the oiler, the cook, the captain— and following them went the water jar, bouncing gaily over the seas.

The correspondent remained in the grip of this strange new enemy—a current. The shore, with its white slope of sand and its green bluff, topped with little silent cottages, was spread like a picture before him. It was very near to him then, but he was impressed as one who in a gallery looks at a scene from Brittany or Holland.

He thought: "I am going to drown? Can it be possible? Can it be possible? Can it be possible?" Perhaps an individual must consider his own death to be the final phenomenon of nature.

But later a wave perhaps whirled him out of this small, deadly current, for he found suddenly that he could again make progress toward the shore. Later still, he was aware that the captain, clinging with one hand to the keel of the dinghy, had his face turned away from the shore and toward him, and was calling his name. "Come to the boat! Come to the boat!"

In his struggle to reach the captain and the boat, he reflected that when one gets properly wearied, drowning must really be a comfortable arrangement, a cessation of hostilities accompanied by a large degree of relief, and he was glad of it, for the main thing in his mind for some months had been horror of the temporary agony. He did not wish to be hurt.

Presently he saw a man running along the shore. He was undressing with most remarkable speed. Coat, trousers, shirt, everything flew magically off him.

"Come to the boat," called the captain.

"All right, captain." As the correspondent paddled, he saw the captain let himself down to bottom and leave the boat. Then the correspondent performed his one little marvel of the voyage. A large wave caught him and flung him with ease and supreme speed completely over the boat and far beyond it. It struck him even then as an event in gymnastics, and a true miracle of the sea. An overturned boat in the surf is not a plaything to a swimming man.

The correspondent arrived in water that reached only to his waist, but his condition did not enable him to stand for more than a moment. Each wave knocked him into a heap, and the undertow pulled at him.

Then he saw the man who had been running and undressing, and undressing and running, come bounding into the water. He dragged ashore the cook, and then waded toward the captain, but the captain waved him away, and sent him to the correspondent. He was naked, naked as a tree in winter, but a halo was about his head, and he shone like a saint. He gave a strong pull, and a long drag, and a bully heave at the correspondent's hand. The correspondent, schooled in the minor formulas, said: "Thanks, old man." But suddenly the man cried: "What's that?" He pointed a swift finger. The correspondent said: "Go."

In the shallows, face downward, lay the oiler. His forehead touched sand that was periodically, between each wave, clear of the sea.

The correspondent did not know all that transpired afterward. When he achieved safe ground he fell, striking the sand with each particular part of his body. It was as if he had dropped from a roof, but the thud was grateful to him.

It seems that instantly the beach was populated with men with blankets, clothes, and flasks, and women with coffeepots and all the remedies sacred to their minds. The welcome of the land to the men from the sea was warm and generous, but a still and dripping shape was carried slowly up the beach, and the land's welcome for it could only be the different and sinister hospitality of the grave.

When it came night, the white waves paced to and fro in the moonlight, and the wind brought the sound of the great sea's voice to the men on shore, and they felt that they could then be interpreters.

THE GENTLEMAN FROM SAN FRANCISCO

by Ivan Bunin
(1870–1953)

"Alas, alas, that great city Babylon, that mighty city!"
—Revelation of St. John

The gentleman from San Francisco—neither at Naples nor on Capri could anyone recall his name—with his wife and daughter, was on his way to Europe, where he intended to stay for two whole years, solely for the pleasure of it.

He was firmly convinced that he had a full right to a rest, enjoyment, a long comfortable trip, and what not. This conviction had a twofold reason: first he was rich, and second, despite his fifty-eight years, he was just about to enter the stream of life's pleasures. Until now he had not really lived, but simply existed, to be sure—fairly well, yet putting off his fondest hopes for the future. He toiled unweariedly—the Chinese, whom he imported by thousands for his works, knew full well what it meant—and finally he saw that he had made much, and that he had nearly come up to the level of those whom he had once taken as a model, and he decided to catch his breath. The class of people to which he belonged was in the habit of beginning its enjoyment of life with a trip to Europe, India, Egypt. He made up his mind to do the same. Of course, it was first of all himself that he desired to reward for the years of toil, but he was also glad for his wife and daughter's sake. His wife was never distinguished by any extraordinary impressionability, but then, all elderly American women are ardent travelers. As for his daughter, a girl of marriageable age, and somewhat sickly—travel was the very thing she needed. Not to speak of the benefit to her health, do not happy meetings occur during travels? Abroad, one may chance to sit at the same table with a prince, or examine frescoes side by side with a multimillionaire.

The itinerary the Gentleman from San Francisco planned out was an extensive one. In December and January he expected to relish the sun of southern Italy, monuments of antiquity, the tarantella, serenades of wandering minstrels, and that which at his age is felt most keenly—the love, not entirely disinterested though, of young Neapolitan girls. The Carnival days he planned to spend at Nice and Monte Carlo, which at that time of the year is the meeting place of the choicest society, the society upon which depend all the blessings of civilization: the cut of dress suits, the stability of thrones, the declaration of wars, the prosperity of hotels. Some of these people passionately give themselves over to automobile and boat races, others to roulette, others, again, busy themselves with what is called flirtation, and others shoot pigeons, which soar so beautifully from the dovecote, hover a while over the emerald lawn, on the background of the forget-me-not colored sea, and then suddenly hit the ground, like little white lumps. Early March he wanted to devote to Florence, and at Easter, to hear the Miserere in Paris. His plans also included Venice, Paris, bull-baiting at Seville, bathing on the British Islands, also Athens, Constantinople, Palestine, Egypt, and even Japan, of course, on the way back. . . . And at first things went very well indeed.

It was the end of November, and all the way to Gibraltar the ship sailed across seas which were either clad by icy darkness or swept by storms carrying wet snow. But there were no accidents, and the vessel did not even roll. The passengers—all people of consequence—were numerous, and the steamer, the famous *Atlantis*, resembled the most expensive European hotel with all improvements: a night refreshment-bar, Oriental baths, even a newspaper of its own. The manner of living was a most aristocratic one; passengers rose early, awakened by the shrill voice of a bugle, filling the corridors at the gloomy hour when the day broke slowly and sulkily over the grayish-green watery desert, which rolled heavily in the fog. After putting on their flannel pajamas, they took coffee, chocolate, cocoa; they seated themselves in marble baths, went through their exercises, whetting their appetites and increasing their sense of well-being, dressed for the day, and had their breakfast. Till eleven o'clock they were supposed to stroll on the deck, breathing in the chill freshness of the ocean, or they played table-tennis, or other games which arouse the appetite. At eleven o'clock a collation was served consisting of sandwiches and bouillon, after which people read their newspapers, quietly waiting for luncheon, which was more nourishing and varied than the breakfast. The next two hours were given to rest; all the decks were crowded then with steamer chairs, on which the passengers, wrapped in plaids, lay stretched, dozing lazily, or watching the cloudy sky and the foamy-fringed water hillocks flashing beyond the sides of the vessel. At five o'clock, refreshed and gay, they drank strong, fragrant tea; at seven the sound of the bugle announced a dinner of nine courses. . . . Then the Gentleman from San Francisco, rubbing his hands in an onrush of vital energy, hastened to his luxurious stateroom to dress.

In the evening, all the decks of the *Atlantis* yawned in the darkness, shone with their innumerable fiery eyes, and a multitude of servants worked with increased feverishness in the kitchens, dishwashing compartments, and wine cellars. The ocean, which heaved about the sides of the ship, was dreadful, but no one thought of it. All had faith in the controlling power of the captain, a red-headed giant, heavy and very sleepy, who, clad in a uniform with broad golden stripes, looked like a huge idol, and but rarely emerged, for the benefit of the public, from his mysterious retreat. On the forecastle, the siren gloomily roared or screeched in a fit of mad rage, but few of the diners heard the siren: its hellish voice was covered by the sounds of an excellent string orchestra, which played ceaselessly and exquisitely in a vast hall, decorated with marble and spread with velvety carpets. The hall was flooded with torrents of light, radiated by crystal lusters and gilt chandeliers: it was filled with a throng of bejeweled ladies in low-necked dresses, of men in dinner coats, graceful waiters, and deferential maîtres d'hôtel. One of these—who accepted wine orders exclusively—wore a chain on his neck like some lord-mayor. The evening dress, and the ideal linen, made the Gentleman from San Francisco look very young. Dry-skinned, of average height, strongly though irregularly built, glossy with thorough washing and cleaning, and moderately animated, he sat in the golden splendor of this palace. Near him stood a bottle of amber-colored Johannisberg, and goblets of most delicate glass and of varied sizes, surmounted by a frizzled bunch of fresh hyacinths. There was something Mongolian in his yellowish face with its trimmed silvery moustache; his large teeth glimmered with gold fillings, and his strong, bald head had a dull glow, like old ivory. His wife, a big, broad and placid woman, was dressed richly, but in keeping with her age. Complicated, but light, transparent, and innocently immodest was the dress of his daughter, tall and slender, with magnificent hair gracefully combed; her breath was sweet with violet-scented tablets, and she had a number of tiny and most delicate pink dimples near her lips and between her slightly powdered shoulder blades. . . .

The dinner lasted two whole hours, and was followed by dances in the dancing hall, while the men—the Gentleman from San Francisco among them—made their way to the refreshment bar, where Negroes in red jackets and with eyeballs like shelled hard-boiled eggs, waited on them. There, with their feet on tables, smoking Havana cigars, and drinking themselves purple in the face, they settled the destinies of nations on the basis of the latest political and stock-exchange news. Outside, the ocean tossed up black mountains with a thud; and the snowstorm hissed furiously in the rigging grown heavy with slush; the ship trembled in every limb, struggling with the storm and ploughing with difficulty the shifting and seething mountainous masses that threw far and high their foaming tails; the siren groaned in agony, choked by storm and fog; the watchmen in their towers froze and almost went out of their minds under the super-human stress of attention. Like the gloomy and sultry mass of the inferno, like its last, ninth circle, was the submersed womb of the steamer, where monstrous furnaces yawned with red-hot open jaws, and emitted deep, hooting sounds, and where the stokers, stripped to the waist, and purple with reflected flames, bathed in their own dirty, acid sweat. And here, in the refreshment bar, carefree men, with their feet, encased in dancing shoes, on the table, sipped cognac and liqueurs, swam in waves of spiced smoke, and exchanged subtle remarks, while in the dancing hall everything sparkled and radiated light, warmth and joy. The couples now turned around in a waltz, now swayed in the tango; and the music, sweetly shame-less and sad, persisted in its ceaseless entreaties. . . . There were many persons of note in this magnificent crowd: an ambassador, a dry, modest old man; a great millionaire, shaved, tall, of an indefinite age, who, in his old-fashioned dress coat, looked like a prelate; also a famous Spanish writer, and an international belle, already slightly faded and of dubious morals. There was also among them a loving pair, exquisite and refined, whom everybody watched with curiosity and who did not conceal their bliss; he danced only with her, sang—with great skill—only to her ac-companiment, and they were so charming, so graceful. The captain alone knew that they had been hired by the company at a good salary to play at love, and that they had been sailing now on one, now on another steamer, for quite a long time.

In Gibraltar everybody was gladdened by the sun, and by the weather which was like early spring. A new passenger appeared aboard the *Atlan-tis* and aroused everybody's interest. It was the crown prince of an Asiatic state, who traveled incognito, a small man, very nimble, though looking as if made of wood, broad-faced, narrow-eyed, in gold-rimmed glasses, some-what disagreeable because of his long moustache, which was sparse like that of a corpse, but otherwise—charming, plain, modest. In the Medi-terranean the breath of winter was again felt. The seas were heavy and motley like a peacock's tail, and the waves, stirred up by the gay gusts of the tramontane, tossed their white crests under a sparkling and perfectly clear sky. Next morning, the sky grew paler and the skyline misty. Land was near. Then Ischia and Capri came in sight, and one could descry, through an opera glass, Naples, looking like pieces of sugar strewn at the foot of an indistinct dove-colored mass, and above them, a snow-covered chain of distant mountains. The decks were crowded, many ladies and gentlemen put on light fur coats; Chinese servants, bandy-legged youths—

with pitch-black braids down to the heels and with girlish, thick eyelashes —always quiet and speaking in a whisper, were carrying to the foot of the staircases, plaid wraps, canes, and crocodile-leather valises and handbags. The daughter of the Gentleman from San Francisco stood near the prince, who, by a happy chance, had been introduced to her the evening before, and feigned to be looking steadily at something far off, which he was pointing out to her, while he was, at the same time, explaining something, saying something rapidly and quietly. He was so small that he looked like a boy among other men, and he was not handsome at all. And then there was something strange about him; his glasses, derby and coat were most commonplace, but there was something horse-like in the hair of his sparse moustache, and the thin, tanned skin of his flat face looked as though it were somewhat stretched and varnished. But the girl listened to him, and so great was her excitement that she could hardly grasp the meaning of his words, her heart palpitated with incomprehensible rapture and with pride that he was standing and speaking with her and nobody else. Everything about him was different; his dry hands, his clean skin, under which flowed ancient kingly blood, even his lights shoes and his European dress, plain, but singularly tidy—everything held an inexplicable fascination and engendered thoughts of love. And the Gentleman from San Francisco, himself, in a silk hat, gray leggings, patent-leather shoes, kept eyeing the famous beauty who was standing near him, a tall, stately blonde, with eyes painted according to the latest Parisian fashion, and a tiny, bent peeled-off pet-dog, to whom she addressed herself. And the daughter, in a kind of vague perplexity, tried not to notice him.

Like all wealthy Americans he was very liberal when traveling, and believed in the complete sincerity and good-will of those who so painstakingly fed him, served him day and night, anticipating his slightest desire, protected him from dirt and disturbance, hauled things for him, hailed carriers, and delivered his luggage to hotels. So it was everywhere, and it had to be so at Naples. Meanwhile, Naples grew and came nearer. The musicians, with their shining brass instruments, had already formed a group on the deck, and all of a sudden deafened everybody with the triumphant sounds of a ragtime march. The giant captain, in his full uniform, appeared on the bridge and, like a gracious Pagan idol, waved his hands to the passengers—and it seemed to the Gentleman from San Francisco—as it did to all the rest—that for him alone thundered the march, so greatly loved by proud America, and that him alone did the captain congratulate on the safe arrival. And when the *Atlantis* had finally entered the port and all its many-decked mass leaned against the quay, and the gangplank began to rattle heavily—what a crowd of porters, with their assistants, in caps with golden galloons, what a crowd of various boys and husky ragamuffins with pads of colored postal cards attacked the Gentleman from San Francisco, offering their services! With kindly contempt he grinned at these beggars, and, walking toward the automobile of the hotel where the prince might stop, muttered between his teeth, now in English, now in Italian—"Go away! Via . . ."

Immediately, life at Naples began to follow a set routine. Early in the morning breakfast was served in the gloomy dining room, swept by a wet draft from the open windows looking upon a stony garden, while outside the sky was cloudy and cheerless, and a crowd of guides swarmed at the door of the vestibule. Then came the first smiles of the warm roseate sun, and from the high suspended balcony, a broad vista unfolded itself: Vesuvius, wrapped to its base in radiant morning vapors; the pearly ripple, touched to silver, of the bay, the delicate outline of Capri in the skyline; tiny asses dragging two-wheeled buggies along the soft, sticky embankment, and detachments of little soldiers marching somewhere to the tune of cheerful and defiant music.

Next on the day's program was a slow automobile ride along crowded, narrow, and damp corridors of streets, between high, many-windowed buildings. It was followed by visits to museums, lifelessly clean and lighted evenly and pleasantly, but as though with the dull light cast by snow; then to churches, cold, smelling of wax, always alike; a majestic entrance, closed by a ponderous, leather curtain, and inside—a vast void, silence, quiet flames of seven-branched candlesticks, sending forth a red glow from where they stood at the farther end, on the bedecked altar—a lonely, old woman lost among the dark wooden benches, slippery gravestones under the feet, and somebody's *Descent from the Cross*, infallibly famous. At one o'clock—luncheon, on the mountain of San Martius, where at noon the choicest people gathered, and where the daughter of the Gentleman from San Francisco once almost fainted with joy, because it seemed to her that she saw the prince in the hall, although she had learned from the newspapers that he had temporarily left for Rome. At five o'clock it was customary to take tea at the hotel, in a smart *salon*, where it was far too warm because of the carpets and the blazing fireplaces; and then came dinner time—and again did the mighty, commanding voice of the gong resound throughout the building, again did silk rustle and the mirrors reflect files of ladies in low-necked dresses ascending the staircases, and again the splendid palatial dining hall opened with broad hospitality, and again the musicians' jackets formed red patches on the estrade, and the black figures of the waiters swarmed around the maître d'hôtel, who, with extraordinary skill, poured a thick pink soup into plates. . . . As everywhere, the dinner was the crown of the day. People dressed for it as for a wedding, and so abundant was it in food, wines, mineral waters, sweets and fruits, that about eleven o'clock in the evening chambermaids would carry to all the rooms hot-water bags.

That year, however, December did not happen to be a very propitious one. The doormen were abashed when people spoke to them about the weather, and shrugged their shoulders guiltily, mumbling that they could not recollect such a year, although, to tell the truth, it was not the first year they mumbled those words, usually adding that "things are terrible every-where"; that unprecedented showers and storms had broken out on the Riviera, that it was snowing in Athens, that Aetna, too, was all blocked up with snow, and glowed brightly at night, and that tourists were fleeing from Palermo to save themselves from the cold spell. . . .

That winter, the morning sun daily deceived Naples; toward noon the sky would invariably grow gray, and a light rain would begin to fall, growing thicker and duller. Then the palms at the hotel porch glistened disagreeably like wet tin, the town appeared exceptionally dirty and con-gested, the museums too monotonous, the cigars of the drivers in their rubber raincoats, which flattened in the wind like wings, intolerably stink-ing, and the energetic flapping of their whips over their thin-necked nags—obviously false. The shoes of the signors, who cleaned the streetcar tracks, were in a frightful state, the women who splashed in the mud, with black hair unprotected from the rain, were ugly and short legged, and the humid-ity mingled with the foul smell of rotting fish, that came from the foaming sea, was simply disheartening. And so, early-morning quarrels began to break out between the Gentleman from San Francisco and his wife; and their daughter now grew pale and suffered from headaches, and now be-came animated, enthusiastic over everything, and at such times was lovely and beautiful. Beautiful were the tender, complex feelings which her meet-ing with the ungainly man aroused in her—the man in whose veins flowed unusual blood, for, after all, it does not matter what in particular stirs up a maiden's soul: money, or fame, or nobility of birth. . . . Everybody as-sured the tourists that it was quite different at Sorrento and on Capri, that lemon trees were blossoming there, that it was warmer and sunnier there, the morals purer, and the wine less adulterated. And the family from San Francisco decided to set out with all their luggage for Capri. They planned to settle down at Sorrento, but first to visit the island, tread the stones where stood Tiberius's palaces, examine the fabulous wonders of the Blue Grotto, and listen to the bagpipers of Abruzzi, who roam about the island during the whole month preceding Christmas and sing the praises of the Madonna.

On the day of departure—a very memorable day for the family from San Francisco—the sun did not appear even in the morning. A heavy winter fog covered Vesuvius down to its very base and hung like a gray curtain low over the leaden surge of the sea, hiding it completely at a distance of half a mile. Capri was completely out of sight, as though it had never existed on this earth. And the little steamboat which was making for the island tossed and pitched so fiercely that the family lay prostrated on the sofas in the miserable cabin of the little steamer, with their feet wrapped in plaids and their eyes shut because of their nausea. The older lady suffered, as she thought, most; several times she was overcome with seasickness, and it seemed to her then she was dying, but the chamber-maid, who repeatedly brought her the basin, and who for many years, in heat and in cold, had been tossing on these waves, ever on the alert, ever kindly to all—the chambermaid only laughed. The lady's daughter was frightfully pale and kept a slice of lemon between her teeth. Not even the hope of an unexpected meeting with the prince at Sorrento, where he planned to arrive on Christmas, served to cheer her. The Gentleman from San Francisco, who was lying on his back, dressed in a large overcoat and a big cap, did not loosen his jaws throughout the voyage. His face grew dark, his moustache white, and his head ached heavily; for the last few days, because of the bad weather, he had drunk far too much in the evenings.

And the rain kept on beating against the rattling window panes, and water dripped down from them on the sofas; the howling wind attacked the masts, and sometimes, aided by a heavy sea, it laid the little steamer on its side, and then something below rolled about with a rattle.

While the steamer was anchored at Castellamare and Sorrento, the situation was more cheerful; but even here the ship rolled terribly, and the coast with all its precipices, gardens and pines, with its pink and white hotels and hazy mountains clad in curling verdure, flew up and down as if it were on swings. The rowboats hit against the sides of the steamer, the sailors and the deck passengers shouted at the top of their voices, and somewhere a baby screamed as if it were being crushed to pieces. A wet wind blew through the door, and from a wavering barge flying the flag of the Hotel Royal, an urchin kept on unwearyingly shouting "Kgoyal-al! Hotel Kgoyal-al! . . ." inviting tourists. And the Gentleman from San Francisco felt like the old man that he was—and it was with weariness and animosity that he thought of all these "Royals," "Splendids," "Excelsiors," and of all those greedy bugs, reeking with garlic, who are called Italians. Once, during a stop, having opened his eyes and half-risen from the sofa, he noticed in the shadow of the rock beach a heap of stone huts, miserable, mildewed through and through, huddled close by the water, near boats, rags, tin boxes, and brown fishing nets—and as he remembered that this was the very Italy he had come to enjoy, he felt a great despair. . . . Finally, in twilight, the black mass of the island began to grow nearer, as though burrowed through at the base by red fires, the wind grew softer, warmer, more fragrant; from the dock lanterns huge golden serpents flowed down the tame waves which undulated like black oil. . . . Then, suddenly, the anchor rumbled and fell with a splash into the water, the fierce yells of the boatman filled the air—and at once everyone's heart grew easy. The electric lights in the cabin grew more brilliant, and there came a desire to eat, drink, smoke, move. . . . Ten minutes later the family from San Francisco found themselves in a large ferryboat; fifteen minutes later they trod the stones of the quay, and then seated themselves in a small lighted car, which, with a buzz, started to ascend the slope, while vineyard stakes, half-ruined stone fences, and wet, crooked lemon trees, in spots shielded by straw sheds, with their glimmering orange-colored fruit

and thick glossy foliage, were sliding down past the open car windows. . . .
After rain, the earth smells sweetly in Italy, and each of her islands has a
fragrance of its own.

The island of Capri was dark and damp on that evening. But for a
while it grew animated and lit up, in spots, as always in the hour of the
steamer's arrival. On the top of the hill, at the station of the *funiculaire*,
there stood already the crowd of those whose duty it was to receive properly the Gentleman from San Francisco. The rest of the tourists hardly
deserved any attention. There were a few Russians, who had settled on
Capri, untidy, absent-minded people, absorbed in their bookish thoughts,
spectacled, bearded, with the collars of their cloth overcoats raised. There
was also a company of long-legged, long-necked, round-headed German
youths in Tyrolean costume, and with linen bags on their backs, who need
no one's services, are everywhere at home, and are by no means liberal in
their expenses. The Gentleman from San Francisco, who kept quietly aloof
from both the Russians and the Germans, was noticed at once. He and his
ladies were hurriedly helped from the car, a man ran before them to show
them the way, and they were again surrounded by boys and those thickset
Caprean peasant women, who carry on their heads the trunks and valises
of wealthy travelers. Their tiny, wooden footstools rapped against the
pavement of the small square, which looked almost like an opera square,
and over which an electric lantern swung in the damp wind; the gang of
urchins whistled like birds and turned somersaults, and as the Gentleman
from San Francisco passed among them, it all looked like a stage scene; he
went first under some kind of medieval archway, beneath houses huddled
close together, and then along a steep echoing lane which led to the hotel
entrance, flooded with light. At the left, a palm tree raised its tuft above
the flat roofs, and higher up, blue stars burned in the black sky. And again
things looked as though it was in honor of the guests from San Francisco
that the stony damp little town had awakened on its rocky island in the
Mediterranean, that it was they who had made the owner of the hotel so
happy and beaming, and that the Chinese gong, which had sounded the
call to dinner through all the floors as soon as they entered the lobby, had
been waiting only for them.

The owner, an elegant young man, who met the guests with a polite
and exquisite bow, for a moment startled the Gentleman from San Francisco. Having caught sight of him, the Gentleman from San Francisco
suddenly recollected that on the previous night, among other confused
images which disturbed his sleep, he had seen this very man. His vision
resembled the hotel keeper to a dot, had the same head, the same hair,
shining and scrupulously combed, and wore the same frock coat with
rounded skirts. Amazed, he almost stopped for a while. But as there was
not a mustard seed of what is called mysticism in his heart, his surprise
subsided at once; in passing the corridor of the hotel he jestingly told his
wife and daughter about this strange coincidence of dream and reality. His

daughter alone glanced at him with alarm, longing suddenly compressed her heart, and such a strong feeling of solitude on this strange, dark island seized her that she almost began to cry. But, as usual, she said nothing about her feeling to her father.

A person of high dignity, Rex XVII, who had spent three entire weeks on Capri, had just left the island, and the guests from San Francisco were given the apartments he had occupied. At their disposal was put the most handsome and skillful chambermaid, a Belgian, with a figure rendered slim and firm by her corset, and with a starched cap, shaped like a small, indented crown; and they had the privilege of being served by the most well-appearing and portly footman, a black, fiery-eyed Sicilian, and by the quickest waiter, the small, stout Luigi, who was a fiend at cracking jokes and had changed many places in his life. Then the maître d'hôtel, a Frenchman, gently rapped at the door of the American gentleman's room. He came to ask whether the gentleman and the ladies would dine, and in case they would, which he did not doubt, to report that there was to be had that day lobsters, roast beef, asparagus, pheasants, etc., etc.

The floor was still rocking under the Gentleman from San Francisco —so seasick had the wretched Italian steamer made him—yet, he slowly, though awkwardly, shut the window which had banged when the maître d'hôtel entered, and which let in the smell of the distant kitchen and wet flowers in the garden, and answered with slow distinctiveness, that they would dine, that their table must be placed farther away from the door, in the depth of the hall, that they would have local wine and champagne, moderately dry and but slightly cooled. The maître d'hôtel approved the words of the guest in various intonations, which all meant, however, only one thing; there is and can be no doubt that the desires of the Gentleman from San Francisco are right, and that everything would be carried out, in exact conformity with his words. At last he inclined his head and asked delicately:

"Is that all, sir?"

And having received in reply a slow "Yes," he added that today they were going to have the tarantella danced in the vestibule by Carmella and Giuseppe, known to all Italy and to "the entire world of tourists."

"I saw her on postcard pictures," said the Gentleman from San Francisco in a tone of voice which expressed nothing. "And this Giuseppe, is he her husband?"

"Her cousin, sir," answered the maître d'hôtel.

The Gentleman from San Francisco tarried a little, evidently musing on something, but said nothing, then dismissed him with a nod of his head.

Then he started making preparations, as though for a wedding: he turned on all the electric lamps, and filled the mirrors with reflections of light and the sheen of furniture, and opened trunks; he began to shave and to wash himself, and the sound of his bell was heard every minute in the corridor, crossing with other impatient calls which came from the rooms of his wife and daughter. Luigi, in his red apron, with the ease characteristic of stout people, made funny faces at the chambermaids, who were dashing by with tile buckets in their hands, making them laugh until the tears came. He rolled head over heels to the door, and, tapping with his knuckles, asked with feigned timidity and with an obsequiousness which he knew how to render idiotic:

"Ha sonata, Signore?" (Did you ring, sir?)

And from behind the door a slow, grating, insultingly polite voice answered:

"Yes, come in."

What did the Gentleman from San Francisco think and feel on that evening forever memorable to him? It must be said frankly: absolutely nothing exceptional. The trouble is that everything on this earth appears too simple. Even had he felt anything deep in his heart, a premonition that something was going to happen, he would have imagined that it was not going to happen so soon, at least not at once. Besides, as is usually the case just after seasickness is over, he was very hungry, and he anticipated with real delight the first spoonful of soup, and the first gulp of wine; therefore, he was performing the habitual process of dressing, in a state of excitement which left no time for reflection.

Having shaved and washed himself, and dexterously put in place a few false teeth, he then, standing before the mirror, moistened and vigorously plastered what was left of his thick pearly colored hair, close to his tawny-yellow skull. Then he put on, with some effort, a tight-fitting undershirt of cream-colored silk, fitted tight to his strong, aged body with its waist swelling out because of an abundant diet; and he pulled black silk socks and patent-leather dancing shoes on his dry feet with their fallen arches. Squatting down, he set right his black trousers, drawn high by means of silk suspenders, adjusted his snow-white shirt with its bulging front, put the buttons into the shining cuffs, and began the painful process of hunting up the front button under the hard collar. The floor was still swaying under him, the tips of his fingers hurt terribly, the button at times painfully pinched the flabby skin in the depression under his Adam's apple, but he persevered, and finally, with his eyes shining from the effort, his face blue because of the narrow collar which squeezed his neck, he triumphed over the difficulties—and all exhausted, he sat down before the pier glass, his reflected image repeating itself in all the mirrors.

"It's terrible!" he muttered, lowering his strong, bald head and making no effort to understand what was terrible; then, with a careful and habitual gesture, he examined his short fingers with gouty calluses in the joints, and their large, convex, almond-colored nails, and repeated with conviction, "It's terrible!"

But here the stentorian voice of the second gong sounded throughout the house, as in a heathen temple. And having risen hurriedly, the Gentleman from San Francisco drew his tie more taut and firm around his collar, and pulled together his abdomen by means of a tight waistcoat, put on a dinner coat, set to rights the cuffs, and for the last time he examined himself in the mirror. . . . This Carmella, tawny as a mulatto, with fiery eyes, in a dazzling dress in which orange-color predominated, must be an extraordinary dancer—it occurred to him. And cheerfully leaving his room, he walked on the carpet, to his wife's chamber, and asked in a loud tone of voice if they would be long.

"In five minutes, papa!" answered cheerfully and gaily a girlish voice. "I am combing my hair."

"Very well," said the Gentleman from San Francisco.

And thinking of her wonderful hair, streaming on her shoulders, he slowly walked down along corridors and staircases, spread with red velvet carpets—looking for the library. The servants he met hugged the walls, and he walked by as if not noticing them. An old lady, late for dinner, already bowed with years, with milk-white hair, yet bare-necked, in a light-gray silk dress, hurried at top speed, but she walked in a mincing, funny, hen-like manner, and he easily overtook her. At the glass door of the dining hall where the guests had already gathered and started eating, he stopped before the table crowded with boxes of matches and Egyptian cigarettes, took a great Manila cigar, and threw three liras on the table. On the winter veranda he glanced into the open window; a stream of soft air came to him from the darkness, the top of the old palm loomed up before him afar off, with its boughs spread among the stars and looking gigantic, and the distant even noise of the sea reached his ear. In the library room, snug, quiet, a German in round silver-bowed glasses and with crazy, wondering eyes—stood turning the rustling pages of a newspaper. Having coldly eyed him, the Gentleman from San Francisco seated himself in a deep leather armchair near a lamp under a green hood, put on his pince-nez and twitching his head because of the collar which choked him, hid himself from view behind a newspaper. He glanced at a few headlines, read a few lines about the interminable Balkan war, and turned over the page with an habitual gesture. Suddenly, the lines blazed up with a glassy sheen, the veins of his neck swelled, his eyes bulged out, the pince-nez fell from his nose. . . . He dashed forward, wanted to swallow air—and made a wild, rattling noise; his lower jaw dropped, dropped on his shoulder and began to shake, the shirt-front bulged out—and the whole body, writhing, the heels catching in the carpet, slowly fell to the floor in a desperate struggle with an invisible foe. . . .

Had not the German been in the library, this frightful accident would have been quickly and adroitly hushed up. The body of the Gentleman from San Francisco would have been rushed away to some far corner— and none of the guests would have known of the occurrence. But the German dashed out of the library with outcries and spread the alarm all over the house. And many rose from their meal, upsetting chairs, others growing pale, ran along the corridors to the library, and the question, asked in many languages, was heard: "What is it? What has happened?" And no one was able to answer it clearly, no one understood anything, for until this very day men still wonder most at death and most absolutely refuse to believe in it. The owner rushed from one guest to another, trying to keep back those who were running and soothe them with hasty assurances, that this was nothing, a mere trifle, a little fainting spell by which a Gentleman from San Francisco had been overcome. But no one listened to him, many saw how the footman and waiters tore from the gentleman his tie, collar, waistcoat, the rumpled evening coat, and even—for no visible reason—the dancing shoes from his black silk-covered feet. And he kept on writhing. He obstinately struggled with death, he did not want to yield to the foe that attacked him so unexpectedly and grossly. He shook his head, emitted rattling sounds like one throttled, and turned up his eyeballs like one drunk with wine. When he was hastily brought into Number 43—the smallest, worst, dampest, and coldest room at the end of the lower corridor—and stretched on the bed—his daughter came running, her hair falling over her shoulders, the skirts of her dressing gown thrown open, with bare breasts raised by the corset. Then came his wife, big, heavy, almost completely dressed for dinner, her mouth round with terror.

In a quarter of an hour all was well again in good trim at the hotel. But the evening was irreparably spoiled. Some tourists returned to the dining hall and finished their dinner, but they kept silent, and it was obvious that they took the accident as a personal insult, while the owner went from one guest to another, shrugging his shoulders in impotent and appropriate irritation, feeling like one innocently victimized, assuring everyone that he understood perfectly well "how disagreeable this is," and giving his word that he would take all "the measures that are within his power" to do away with the trouble. Yet it was found necessary to cancel the tarantella. The unnecessary electric lamps were put out, most of the guests left for the beer hall, and it grew so quiet in the hotel that one could distinctly hear the tick-tock of the clock in the lobby, where a lonely parrot babbled something in its expressionless manner, stirring in its cage, and trying to fall asleep with its paw clutching the upper perch in a most absurd manner. The Gentleman from San Francisco lay stretched in a cheap iron bed, under coarse woolen blankets, dimly lighted by a single gas-burner fastened in the ceiling. An icebag slid down on his wet, cold forehead. His blue, already lifeless face grew gradually cold; the hoarse, rattling noise which came from his mouth, lighted by the glimmer of the golden fillings, gradually weakened. It was not the Gentleman from San Francisco that was emitting those weird sounds; he was no more— someone else did it. His wife and daughter, the doctor, the servants were standing and watching him apathetically. Suddenly, that which they expected and feared happened. The rattling sound ceased. And slowly, slowly, in everybody's sight a pallor stole over the face of the dead man, and his features began to grow thinner and more luminous, beautiful with the beauty that he had long shunned and that became him well. . . .

The proprietor entered. *"Gia é morto,"* whispered the doctor to him. The proprietor shrugged his shoulders indifferently. The older lady, with tears slowly running down her cheeks, approached him and said timidly that now the deceased must be taken to his room.

"O no, madam," answered the proprietor politely, but without any amiability and not in English, but in French. He was no longer interested in the trifle which the guests from San Francisco could now leave at his cash-office. "This is absolutely impossible," he said, and added in the form of an explanation that he valued this apartment highly, and if he satisfied her desire, this would become known over Capri and the tourists would begin to avoid it.

The girl, who had looked at him strangely, sat down, and with her handkerchief to her mouth, began to cry. Her mother's tears dried up at once, and her face flared up. She raised her tone, began to demand, using her own language and still unable to realize that the respect for her was absolutely gone. The proprietor, with dignity, cut her short: "If madam does not like the ways of this hotel, he dare not detain her." And he firmly announced that the corpse must leave the hotel that very day, at dawn, that the police had been informed, that an agent would call immediately and attend to all the necessary formalities. . . . "Is it possible to get on Capri at least a plain coffin?" madam asks. . . . Unfortunately not; by no means, and as for making one, there will be no time. It will be necessary to arrange things some other way. . . . For instance, he gets English soda-water in big, oblong boxes. . . . The partitions could be taken out from such a box. . . .

By night, the whole hotel was asleep. A waiter opened the window in Number 43—it faced a corner of the garden where a consumptive banana tree grew in the shadow of a high stone wall set with broken glass on the top—turned out the electric light, locked the door, and went away. The deceased remained alone in the darkness. Blue stars looked down at him from the black sky, the cricket in the wall started his melancholy, carefree song. In the dimly lighted corridor two chambermaids were sitting on the windowsill, mending something. Then Luigi came in, in slippered feet, with a heap of clothes on his arm.

"Pronto?" he asked in a stage whisper, as if greatly concerned, directing his eyes toward the terrible door, at the end of the corridor. And waving his free hand in that direction, *"Partenza!"* he cried out in a whisper, as if seeing off a train—and the chambermaids, choking with noiseless laughter, put their heads on each other's shoulders.

Then, stepping softly, he ran to the door, slightly rapped at it, and inclining his ear, asked most obsequiously in a subdued tone of voice:

"Ha sonata, Signore?"

And, squeezing his throat and thrusting his lower jaw forward, he answered himself in a drawling, grating, sad voice, as if from behind the door:

"Yes, come in. . . ."

At dawn, when the window panes in Number 43 grew white, and a damp wind rustled in the leaves of the banana tree, when the pale-blue morning sky rose and stretched over Capri, and the sun, rising from behind the distant mountains of Italy, touched into gold the pure, clearly outlined summit of Monte Solaro, when the masons, who mended the paths for the tourists on the island, went out to their work—an oblong box was brought to room Number 43. Soon it grew very heavy and painfully pressed against the knees of the assistant doorman who was conveying it in a one-horse carriage along the white highroad which winded on the slopes, among stone fences and vineyards, all the way down to the seacoast. The driver, a sickly man, with red eyes, in an old short-sleeved coat and in worn-out shoes, had a drunken headache; all night long he had played dice at the eating house—and he kept on flogging his vigorous little horse. According to Sicilian custom, the animal was heavily burdened with decorations: all sorts of bells tinkled on the bridle, which was ornamented with colored woolen fringes; there were bells also on the edge of the high saddle; and a bird's feather, two feet long, stuck in the trimmed crest of the horse, nodded up and down. The driver kept silence: he was depressed by his wrongheadedness and vices, by the fact that last night he had lost in gambling all the copper coins with which his pockets had been full— neither more nor less than four liras and forty centesimi. But on such a morning, when the air is so fresh, and the sea stretches nearby, and the sky is serene with a morning serenity—a headache passes rapidly and one becomes carefree again. Besides, the driver was also somewhat cheered by the unexpected earnings which the Gentleman from San Francisco, who bumped his dead head against the walls of the box behind his back, had brought him. The little steamer, shaped like a great bug, which lay far down, on the tender and brilliant blue, filling to the brim the Neapolitan bay, was blowing the signal of departure—and the sounds swiftly re-sounded all over Capri. Every bend of the island, every ridge and stone was seen as distinctly as if there were no air between heaven and earth. Near the quay the driver was overtaken by the head doorman who con-ducted in an auto the wife and daughter of the Gentleman from San Francisco. Their faces were pale and their eyes sunken with tears and a sleepless night. And in ten minutes the little steamer was again stirring up the water and picking its way toward Sorrento and Castellamare, carrying the American family away from Capri forever. . . . Meanwhile, peace and rest were restored on the island.

Two thousand years ago there had lived on that island a man who became utterly entangled in his own brutal and filthy actions. For some unknown reason he usurped the rule over millions of men and found himself bewildered by the absurdity of his power, while the fear that someone might kill him unawares made him commit deeds inhuman beyond all measure. And mankind has forever retained his memory, and those who, taken together, now rule the world, as incomprehensibly and, essentially, as cruelly as he did—come from all the corners of the earth to look at the remnants of the stone house he inhabited, which stands on one of the steepest cliffs of the island. On that wonderful morning the tourists, who had come to Capri for precisely that purpose, were still asleep in the various hotels, but tiny long-eared asses under red saddles were already being led to the hotel entrances. Americans and Germans, men and women, old and young, after having arisen and breakfasted heartily, were to scramble on them, and the old beggar-women of Capri, with sticks in their sinewy hands, were again to run after them along stony, mountainous paths, all the way up to the summit of Monte Tiberia. The dead old man from San Francisco, who had planned to keep the tourists company but who had, instead, only scared them by reminding them of death, was already shipped to Naples, and soothed by this, the travelers slept soundly, and silence reigned over the island. The stores in the little town were still closed, with the exception of the fish and greens market on the tiny square. Among the plain people who filled it, going about their business, stood idly by, as usual, Lorenzo, a tall old boatman, a carefree reveler and once a handsome man, famous all over Italy, who had many times served as a model for painters. He had brought and already sold—for a song—two big sea-crawfish, which he had caught at night and which were rustling in the apron of Don Cataldo, the cook of the hotel where the family from San Francisco had been lodged—and now Lorenzo could stand calmly until nightfall, wearing princely airs, showing off his rags, his clay pipe with its long reed mouthpiece, and his red woolen cap, tilted on one ear. Meanwhile, among the precipices of Monte Solare, down the ancient Phoenician road, cut in the rocks in the form of a gigantic staircase, two Abruzzi mountaineers were coming from Anacapri. One carried under his leather mantle a bagpipe, a large goat's skin with two pipes; the other, something in the nature of a wooden flute. They walked, and the entire country, joyous, beautiful, sunny, stretched below them; the rocky shoulders of the island, which lay at their feet, the fabulous blue in which it swam, the shining morning vapors over the sea westward, beneath the dazzling sun, and the wavering masses of Italy's mountains, both near and distant, whose beauty human word is powerless to render. . . . Midway they slowed up. Overshadowing the road stood, in a grotto of the rock wall of Monte Solare, the Holy Virgin, all radiant, bathed in the warmth and the splendor of the sun. The rust of her snow-white plaster-of-paris vestures and queenly crown was touched into gold, and there were meekness and mercy in her eyes raised toward the heavens, toward the eternal and beatific abode of her thrice-blessed Son. They bared their heads, applied the pipes to their lips, and praises flowed on, candid and humbly-joyous, praises to the sun and the morning, to Her, the Immaculate Intercessor for all who suffer in this evil and beautiful world, and to Him who had been born of her womb in the cavern of Bethlehem, in a hut of lovely shepherds in distant Judea.

As for the body of the dead Gentleman from San Francisco, it was on its way home, to the shores of the New World, where a grave awaited it. Having undergone many humiliations and suffered much human neglect, having wandered about a week from one port warehouse to another, it finally got on that same famous ship which had brought the family, such a short while ago and with such a pomp, to the Old World. But now he was concealed from the living: in a tar-coated coffin he was lowered deep into the black hold of the steamer. And again did the ship set out on its far sea journey. At night it sailed by the island of Capri, and, for those who watched it from the island, its lights slowly disappearing in the dark sea, it seemed infinitely sad. But there, on the vast steamer, in its lighted halls shining with brilliance and marble, a noisy dancing party was going on, as usual.

On the second and the third night there was again a ball—this time in mid-ocean, during the furious storm sweeping over the ocean, which roared like a funeral mass and rolled up mountainous seas fringed with mourning silvery foam. The Devil, who from the rocks of Gibraltar, the stony gateway of two worlds, watched the ship vanish into night and storm, could hardly distinguish from behind the snow the innumerable fiery eyes of the ship. The Devil was as huge as a cliff, but the ship was even bigger, a many-storied, many-stacked giant, created by the arrogance of the New Man with the old heart. The blizzard battered the ship's rigging and its broad-necked stacks, whitened with snow, but it remained firm, majestic—and terrible. On its uppermost deck, amidst a snowy whirlwind there loomed up in loneliness the cozy, dimly lighted cabin, where, only half awake, the vessel's ponderous pilot reigned over its entire mass, bearing the semblance of a pagan idol. He heard the wailing moans and the furious screeching of the siren, choked by the storm, but the nearness of that which was behind the wall and which in the last account was incomprehensible to him, removed his fears. He was reassured by the thought of the large, armored cabin, which now and then was filled with mysterious rumbling sounds and with the dry creaking of blue fires, flaring up and exploding around a man with a metallic headpiece, who was eagerly catching the indistinct voices of the vessels that hailed him, hundreds of miles away. At the very bottom, in the underwater womb of the *Atlantis*, the huge mass of tanks and various other machines, their steel parts shining dully, wheezed with steam and oozed hot water and oil; here was the gigantic kitchen, heated by hellish furnaces, where the motion of the vessel was being generated; here seethed those forces terrible in their concentration which were transmitted to the keel of the vessel, and into that endless round tunnel, which was lighted by electricity, and looked like a gigantic cannon barrel, where slowly, with a punctuality and certainty that crushes the human soul, a colossal shaft was revolving in its oily nest, like a living monster stretching in its lair. As for the middle part of the *Atlantis*, its warm, luxurious cabins, dining rooms, and halls, they radiated light and joy, were astir with a chattering smartly dressed crowd, were filled with the fragrance of fresh flowers, and resounded with a string orchestra. And again did the slender supple pair of hired lovers painfully turn and twist and at times clash convulsively amid the splendor of lights, silks, diamonds, and bare feminine shoulders: she—a sinfully modest pretty girl, with lowered eyelashes and an innocent hairdressing, he—a tall, young man, with black hair, looking as if it were pasted, pale with powder, in most exquisite patent-leather shoes, in a narrow, long-skirted dress coat— a beautiful man resembling a leech. And no one knew that this couple had long since been weary of torturing themselves with a feigned beatific torture under the sounds of shamefully melancholy music; nor did anyone know what lay deep, deep, beneath them, on the very bottom of the hold, in the neighborhood of the gloomy and sultry maw of the ship, that heavily struggled with the ocean, the darkness, and the storm. . . .

Translated by A. Yarmolinsky

DEATH IN THE WOODS
by Sherwood Anderson
(1876–1941)

She was an old woman and lived on a farm near the town in which I lived. All country and small-town people have seen such old women, but no one knows much about them. Such an old woman comes into town driving an old worn-out horse or she comes afoot carrying a basket. She may own a few hens and have eggs to sell. She brings them in a basket and takes them to a grocer. There she trades them in. She gets some salt pork and some beans. Then she gets a pound or two of sugar and some flour.

Afterward she goes to the butcher's and asks for some dog-meat. She may spend ten or fifteen cents, but when she does she asks for something. Formerly the butchers gave liver to anyone who wanted to carry it away. In our family we were always having it. Once one of my brothers got a whole cow's liver at the slaughterhouse near the fair grounds in our town. We had it until we were sick of it. It never cost a cent. I have hated the thought of it ever since.

The old farm woman got some liver and a soup bone. She never visited with anyone, and as soon as she got what she wanted she lit out for home. It made quite a load for such an old body. No one gave her a lift. People drive right down a road and never notice an old woman like that.

There was such an old woman who used to come into town past our house one summer and fall when I was a young boy and was sick with what was called inflammatory rheumatism. She went home later carrying a heavy pack on her back. Two or three large gaunt-looking dogs followed at her heels.

The old woman was nothing special. She was one of the nameless ones that hardly anyone knows, but she got into my thoughts. I have just suddenly now, after all these years, remembered her and what happened. It is a story. Her name was Grimes, and she lived with her husband and son in a small unpainted house on the bank of a small creek four miles from town.

The husband and son were a tough lot. Although the son was but twenty-one, he had already served a term in jail. It was whispered about that the woman's husband stole horses and ran them off to some other county. Now and then, when a horse turned up missing, the man had also disappeared. No one ever caught him. Once, when I was loafing at Tom Whitehead's livery-barn, the man came there and sat on the bench in front. Two or three other men were there, but no one spoke to him. He sat for a few minutes and then got up and went away. When he was leaving he turned around and stared at the men. There was a look of defiance in his eyes. "Well, I have tried to be friendly. You don't want to talk to me. It has been so wherever I have gone in this town. If, some day, one of your fine horses turns up missing, well, then what?" He did not say anything actually. "I'd like to bust one of you on the jaw," was about what his eyes said. I remember how the look in his eyes made me shiver.

The old man belonged to a family that had had money once. His name was Jake Grimes. It all comes back clearly now. His father, John Grimes, had owned a sawmill when the country was new, and had made money. Then he got to drinking and running after women. When he died there wasn't much left.

Jake blew in the rest. Pretty soon there wasn't any more lumber to cut and his land was nearly all gone.

He got his wife off a German farmer, for whom he went to work one June day in the wheat harvest. She was a young thing then and scared to death. You see, the farmer was up to something with the girl—she was, I think, a bound girl and his wife had her suspicions. She took it out on the girl when the man wasn't around. Then, when the wife had to go off to town for supplies, the farmer got after her. She told young Jake that nothing really ever happened, but he didn't know whether to believe it or not.

He got her pretty easy himself, the first time he was out with her. He wouldn't have married her if the German farmer hadn't tried to tell him where to get off. He got her to go riding with him in his buggy one night when he was threshing on the place, and then he came for her the next Sunday night.

She managed to get out of the house without her employer's seeing, but when she was getting into the buggy he showed up. It was almost dark, and he just popped up suddenly at the horse's head. He grabbed the horse by the bridle and Jake got out his buggy whip.

They had it out all right! The German was a tough one. Maybe he didn't care whether his wife knew or not. Jake hit him over the face and shoulders with the buggy whip, but the horse got to acting up and he had to get out.

Then the two men went for it. The girl didn't see it. The horse started to run away and went nearly a mile down the road before the girl got him stopped. Then she managed to tie him to a tree beside the road. (I wonder how I know all this. It must have stuck in my mind from small-town tales when I was a boy.) Jake found her there after he got through with the German. She was huddled up in the buggy seat, crying, scared to death. She told Jake a lot of stuff, how the German had tried to get her, how he chased her once into the barn, how another time, when they happened to be alone in the house together, he tore her dress open clear down the front. The German, she said, might have got her that time if he hadn't heard his old woman drive in at the gate. She had been off to town for supplies. Well, she would be putting the horse in the barn. The German managed to sneak off to the fields without his wife seeing. He told the girl he would kill her if she told. What could she do? She told a lie about ripping her dress in the barn when she was feeding the stock. I remember now that she was a bound girl and did not know where her father and mother were. Maybe she did not have any father. You know what I mean.

Such bound children were often enough cruelly treated. They were children who had no parents, slaves really. There were very few orphan homes then. They were legally bound into some home. It was a matter of pure luck how it came out.

II

She married Jake and had a son and daughter, but the daughter died.

Then she settled down to feed stock. That was her job. At the German's place she had cooked the food for the German and his wife. The wife was a strong woman with big hips and worked most of the time in the fields with her husband. She fed them and fed the cows in the barn, fed the pigs, the horses and the chickens. Every moment of every day, as a young girl, was spent feeding something.

Then she married Jake Grimes and he had to be fed. She was a slight thing, and when she had been married for three or four years, and after the two children were born, her slender shoulders became stooped.

Jake always had a lot of big dogs around the house, that stood near the unused sawmill near the creek. He was always trading horses when he wasn't stealing something and had a lot of poor bony ones about. Also he kept three or four pigs and a cow. They were all pastured in the few acres left of the Grimes place and Jake did little enough work.

He went into debt for a threshing outfit and ran it for several years, but it did not pay. People did not trust him. They were afraid he would steal the grain at night. He had to go a long way off to get work and it cost too much to get there. In the winter he hunted and cut a little firewood, to be sold in some nearby town. When the son grew up he was just like the father. They got drunk together. If there wasn't anything to eat in the house when they came home the old man gave his old woman a cut over the head. She had a few chickens of her own and had to kill one of them in a hurry. When they were all killed she wouldn't have any eggs to sell when she went to town, and then what would she do?

She had to scheme all her life about getting things fed, getting the pigs fed so they would grow fat and could be butchered in the fall. When they were butchered her husband took most of the meat off to town and sold it. If he did not do it first the boy did. They fought sometimes and when they fought the old woman stood aside trembling.

She had got the habit of silence anyway—that was fixed. Sometimes, when she began to look old—she wasn't forty yet—and when the husband and son were both off trading horses or drinking or hunting or stealing, she went around the house and the barnyard muttering to herself.

How was she going to get everything fed?—that was her problem. The dogs had to be fed. There wasn't enough hay in the barn for the horses and the cow. If she didn't feed the chickens how could they lay eggs? Without eggs to sell how could she get things in town, things she had to have to keep the life of the farm going? Thank heaven, she did not have to feed her husband—in a certain way. That hadn't lasted long after their marriage and after the babies came. Where he went on his long trips she did not know. Sometimes he was gone from home for weeks, and after the boy grew up they went off together.

They left everything at home for her to manage and she had no money. She knew no one. No one ever talked to her in town. When it was winter she had to gather sticks of wood for her fire, had to try to keep the stock fed with very little grain.

The stock in the barn cried to her hungrily, the dogs followed her about. In the winter the hens laid few enough eggs. They huddled in the corners of the barn and she kept watching them. If a hen lays an egg in the barn in the winter and you do not find it, it freezes and breaks.

One day in winter the old woman went off to town with a few eggs and the dogs followed her. She did not get started until nearly three o'clock and the snow was heavy. She hadn't been feeling very well for several days and so she went muttering along, scantily clad, her shoulders stooped. She had an old grain bag in which she carried her eggs, tucked away down in the bottom. There weren't many of them, but in winter the price of eggs is up. She would get a little meat in exchange for the eggs, some salt pork, a little sugar, and some coffee perhaps. It might be the butcher would give her a piece of liver.

When she had got to town and was trading in her eggs the dogs lay by the door outside. She did pretty well, got the things she needed, more than she had hoped. Then she went to the butcher and he gave her some liver and some dog meat.

It was the first time anyone had spoken to her in a friendly way for a long time. The butcher was alone in his shop when she came in and was annoyed by the thought of such a sick-looking old woman out on such a day. It was bitter cold and the snow, that had let up during the afternoon, was falling again. The butcher said something about her husband and her son, swore at them, and the old woman stared at him, a look of mild surprise in her eyes as he talked. He said that if either the husband or the son were going to get any of the liver or the heavy bones with scraps of meat hanging to them that he had put into the grain bag, he'd see him starve first.

Starve, eh? Well, things had to be fed. Men had to be fed, and the horses that weren't any good but maybe could be traded off, and the poor thin cow that hadn't given any milk for three months.

Horses, cows, pigs, dogs, men.

III

The old woman had to get back before darkness came if she could. The dogs followed at her heels, sniffing at the heavy grain bag she had fastened on her back. When she got to the edge of town she stopped by a fence and tied the bag on her back with a piece of rope she had carried in her dress pocket for just that purpose. That was an easier way to carry it. Her arms ached. It was hard when she had to crawl over fences and once she fell over and landed in the snow. The dogs went frisking about. She had to struggle to get to her feet again, but she made it. The point of climbing over the fences was that there was a short cut over a hill and through a woods. She might have gone around by the road, but it was a mile farther that way. She was afraid she couldn't make it. And then, besides, the stock had to be fed. There was a little hay left and a little corn. Perhaps her husband and son would bring some home when they came. They had driven off in the only buggy the Grimes family had, a rickety thing, a rickety horse hitched to the buggy, two other rickety horses led by halters. They were going to trade horses, get a little money if they could. They might come home drunk. It would be well to have something in the house when they came back.

The son had an affair on with a woman at the county seat, fifteen miles away. She was a rough enough woman, a tough one. Once, in the summer, the son had brought her to the house. Both she and the son had been drinking. Jake Grimes was away and the son and his woman ordered the old woman about like a servant. She didn't mind much; she was used to it. Whatever happened she never said anything. That was her way of getting along. She had managed that way when she was a young girl at the German's and ever since she had married Jake. That time her son brought his woman to the house they stayed all night, sleeping together just as though they were married. It hadn't shocked the old woman, not much. She had got past being shocked early in life.

With the pack on her back she went painfully along across an open field, wading in the deep snow, and got into the woods.

There was a path, but it was hard to follow. Just beyond the top of the hill, where the woods was thickest, there was a small clearing. Had someone once thought of building a house there? The clearing was as large as a building lot in town, large enough for a house and a garden. The path ran along the side of the clearing, and when she got there the old woman sat down to rest at the foot of a tree.

It was a foolish thing to do. When she got herself placed, the pack against the tree's trunk, it was nice, but what about getting up again? She worried about that for a moment and then quietly closed her eyes.

She must have slept for a time. When you are about so cold you can't get any colder. The afternoon grew a little warmer and the snow came thicker than ever. Then after a time the weather cleared. The moon even came out.

There were four Grimes dogs that had followed Mrs. Grimes into town, all tall gaunt fellows. Such men as Jake Grimes and his son always keep just such dogs. They kick and abuse them, but they stay. The Grimes dogs, in order to keep from starving, had to do a lot of foraging for themselves, and they had been at it while the old woman slept with her back to the tree at the side of the clearing. They had been chasing rabbits in the woods and in adjoining fields and in their ranging had picked up three other farm dogs.

After a time all the dogs came back to the clearing. They were excited about something. Such nights, cold and clear and with a moon, do things to dogs. It may be that some old instinct, come down from the time when they were wolves and ranged the woods in packs on winter nights, comes back into them.

The dogs in the clearing, before the old woman, had caught two or three rabbits and their immediate hunger had been satisfied. They began to play, running in circles in the clearing. Round and round they ran, each dog's nose at the tail of the next dog. In the clearing, under the snow-laden trees and under the wintry moon they made a strange picture, running thus silently, in a circle their running had beaten in the soft snow. The dogs made no sound. They ran around and around in the circle.

It may have been that the old woman saw them doing that before she died. She may have awakened once or twice and looked at the strange sight with dim old eyes.

She wouldn't be very cold now, just drowsy. Life hangs on a long time. Perhaps the old woman was out of her head. She may have dreamed of her girlhood at the German's, and before that, when she was a child and before her mother lit out and left her.

Her dreams couldn't have been very pleasant. Not many pleasant things had happened to her. Now and then one of the Grimes dogs left the running circle and came to stand before her. The dog thrust his face close to her face. His red tongue was hanging out.

The running of the dogs may have been a kind of death ceremony. It may have been that the primitive instinct of the wolf, having been aroused in the dogs by the night and the running, made them somehow afraid.

"Now we are no longer wolves. We are dogs, the servants of men. Keep alive, man! When man dies we become wolves again."

When one of the dogs came to where the old woman sat with her back against the tree and thrust his nose close to her face he seemed satisfied and went back to run with the pack. All the Grimes dogs did it at some time during the evening, before she died. I knew all about it afterward, when I grew to be a man, because once in a woods in Illinois, on another winter night, I saw a pack of dogs act just like that. The dogs were waiting for me to die as they had waited for the old woman that night when I was a child, but when it happened to me I was a young man and had no intention whatever of dying.

The old woman died softly and quietly. When she was dead and when one of the Grimes dogs had come to her and had found her dead all the dogs stopped running.

They gathered about her.

Well, she was dead now. She had fed the Grimes dogs when she was alive, what about now?

There was the pack on her back, the grain bag containing the piece of salt pork, the liver the butcher had given her, the dog meat, the soup bones. The butcher in town, having been suddenly overcome with a feeling of pity, had loaded her grain bag heavily. It had been a big haul for the old woman.

It was a big haul for the dogs now.

IV

One of the Grimes dogs sprang suddenly out from among the others and began worrying the pack on the old woman's back. Had the dogs really been wolves that one would have been the leader of the pack. What he did, all the others did.

All of them sank their teeth into the grain bag the old woman had fastened with ropes to her back.

They dragged the old woman's body out into the open clearing. The worn-out dress was quickly torn from her shoulders. When she was found, a day or two later, the dress had been torn from her body clear to the hips, but the dogs had not touched her body. They had got the meat out of the grain bag, that was all. Her body was frozen stiff when it was found, and the shoulders were so narrow and the body so slight that in death it looked like the body of some charming young girl.

Such things happened in towns of the Middle West, on farms near town, when I was a boy. A hunter out after rabbits found the old woman's body and did not touch it. Something, the beaten round path in the little snow-covered clearing, the silence of the place, the place where the dogs had worried the body trying to pull the grain bag away or tear it open—something startled the man and he hurried off to town.

I was in Main Street with one of my brothers who was town newsboy and who was taking the afternoon papers to the stores. It was almost night.

The hunter came into a grocery and told his story. Then he went to a hardware shop and into a drugstore. Men began to gather on the sidewalks. Then they started out along the road to the place in the woods.

My brother should have gone on about his business of distributing papers but he didn't. Everyone was going to the woods. The undertaker went and the town marshal. Several men got on a dray and rode out to where the path left the road and went into the woods, but the horses weren't very sharply shod and slid about on the slippery roads. They made no better time than those of us who walked.

The town marshal was a large man whose leg had been injured in the Civil War. He carried a heavy cane and limped rapidly along the road. My brother and I followed at his heels, and as we went other men and boys joined the crowd.

It had grown dark by the time we got to where the old woman had left the road but the moon had come out. The marshal was thinking there might have been a murder. He kept asking the hunter questions. The hunter went along with his gun across his shoulders, a dog following at his heels. It isn't often a rabbit hunter has a chance to be so conspicuous. He was taking full advantage of it, leading the procession with the town marshal. "I didn't see any wounds. She was a beautiful young girl. Her face was buried in the snow. No, I didn't know her." As a matter of fact, the hunter had not looked closely at the body. He had been frightened. She might have been murdered and someone might spring out from behind a tree and murder him. In a woods, in the late afternoon, when the trees are all bare and there is white snow on the ground, when all is silent, something creepy steals over the mind and body. If something strange or un- canny has happened in the neighborhood all you think about is getting away from there as fast as you can.

The crowd of men and boys had got to where the old woman had crossed the field and went, following the marshal and the hunter, up the slight incline and into the woods.

My brother and I were silent. He had his bundle of papers in a bag slung across his shoulder. When he got back to town he would have to go on distributing his papers before he went home to supper. If I went along, as he had no doubt already determined I should, we would both be late. Either mother or our older sister would have to warm our supper.

Well, we would have something to tell. A boy did not get such a chance very often. It was lucky we just happened to go into the grocery when the hunter came in. The hunter was a country fellow. Neither of us had ever seen him before.

Now the crowd of men and boys had got to the clearing. Darkness comes quickly on such winter nights, but the full moon made everything clear. My brother and I stood near the tree, beneath which the old woman had died.

She did not look old, lying there in that light, frozen and still. One of the men turned her over in the snow and I saw everything. My body trembled with some strange mystical feeling and so did my brother's. It might have been the cold.

Neither of us had ever seen a woman's body before. It may have been the snow, clinging to the frozen flesh, that made it look so white and lovely, so like marble. No woman had come with the party from town; but one of the men, he was the town blacksmith, took off his overcoat and spread it over her. Then he gathered her into his arms and started off to town, all the others following silently. At that time no one knew who she was.

V

I had seen everything, had seen the oval in the snow, like a miniature race track, where the dogs had run, had seen how the men were mystified, had seen the white bare young-looking shoulders, had heard the whispered comments of the men.

The men were simply mystified. They took the body to the under- taker's, and when the blacksmith, the hunter, the marshal and several others had got inside they closed the door. If father had been there perhaps he could have got in, but we boys couldn't.

I went with my brother to distribute the rest of his papers and when we got home it was my brother who told the story.

I kept silent and went to bed early. It may have been I was not satisfied with the way he told it.

Later, in the town, I must have heard other fragments of the old woman's story. She was recognized the next day and there was an investigation.

The husband and son were found somewhere and brought to town and there was an attempt to connect them with the woman's death, but it did not work. They had perfect enough alibis.

However, the town was against them. They had to get out. Where they went I never heard.

I remember only the picture there in the forest, the men standing about, the naked girlish-looking figure, face down in the snow, the tracks made by the running dogs and the clear cold winter sky above. White fragments of clouds were drifting across the sky. They went racing across the little open space among the trees.

The scene in the forest had become for me, without my knowing it, the foundation for the real story I am now trying to tell. The fragments, you see, had to be picked up slowly, long afterward.

Things happened. When I was a young man I worked on the farm of a German. The hired girl was afraid of her employer. The farmer's wife hated her.

I saw things at that place. Once later, I had a half-uncanny, mystical adventure with dogs in an Illinois forest on a clear, moonlit winter night. When I was a schoolboy, and on a summer day, I went with a boy friend out along a creek some miles from town and came to the house where the old woman had lived. No one had lived in the house since her death. The doors were broken from the hinges; the window lights were all broken. As the boy and I stood in the road outside, two dogs, just roving farm dogs no doubt, came running around the corner of the house. The dogs were tall, gaunt fellows and came down to the fence and glared through at us, standing in the road.

The whole thing, the story of the old woman's death, was to me as I grew older like music heard from far off. The notes had to be picked up slowly one at a time. Something had to be understood.

The woman who died was one destined to feed animal life. Anyway, that is all she ever did. She was feeding animal life before she was born, as a child, as a young woman working on the farm of the German, after she married, when she grew old and when she died. She fed animal life in cows, in chickens, in pigs, in horses, in dogs, in men. Her daughter had died in childhood and with her one son she had no articulate relations. On the night when she died she was hurrying homeward, bearing on her body food for animal life.

She died in the clearing in the woods and even after her death continued feeding animal life.

You see it is likely that, when my brother told the story, that night when we got home and my mother and sister sat listening, I did not think he got the point. He was too young and so was I. A thing so complete has its own beauty.

I shall not try to emphasize the point. I am only explaining why I was dissatisfied then and have been ever since. I speak of that only that you may understand why I have been impelled to try to tell the simple story over again.

THE MARK ON THE WALL
by Virginia Woolf
(1882–1941)

Perhaps it was the middle of January in the present year that I first looked up and saw the mark on the wall. In order to fix a date it is necessary to remember what one saw. So now I think of the fire; the steady film of yellow light upon the page of my book; the three chrysanthemums in the round glass bowl on the mantelpiece. Yes, it must have been the winter time, and we had just finished our tea, for I remember that I was smoking a cigarette when I looked up and saw the mark on the wall for the first time. I looked up through the smoke of my cigarette and my eye lodged for a moment upon the burning coals, and that old fancy of the crimson flag flapping from the castle tower came into my mind, and I thought of the cavalcade of red knights riding up the side of the black rock. Rather to my relief the sight of the mark interrupted the fancy, for it is an old fancy, an automatic fancy, made as a child perhaps. The mark was a small round mark, black upon the white wall, about six or seven inches above the mantelpiece.

How readily our thoughts swarm upon a new object, lifting it a little way, as ants carry a blade of straw so feverishly, and then leave it. . . . If that mark was made by a nail, it can't have been for a picture, it must have been for a miniature—the miniature of a lady with white powdered curls, powder-dusted cheeks, and lips like red carnations. A fraud of course, for the people who had this house before us would have chosen pictures in that way—an old picture for an old room. That is the sort of people they were—very interesting people, and I think of them so often, in such queer places, because one will never see them again, never know what happened next. They wanted to leave this house because they wanted to change their style of furniture, so he said, and he was in process of saying that in his opinion art should have ideas behind it when we were torn asunder, as one is torn from the old lady about to pour out tea and the young man about to hit the tennis ball in the back garden of the suburban villa as one rushes past in the train.

But for that mark, I'm not sure about it; I don't believe it was made by a nail after all; it's too big, too round, for that. I might get up, but if I got up and looked at it, ten to one I shouldn't be able to say for certain; because once a thing's done, no one ever knows how it happened. Oh! dear me, the mystery of life; the inaccuracy of thought! The ignorance of humanity! To show how very little control of our possessions we have— what an accidental affair this living is after all our civilization—let me just count over a few of the things lost in one lifetime, beginning, for that seems always the most mysterious of losses—what cat would gnaw, what rat would nibble—three pale blue canisters of book-binding tools? Then there were the bird cages, the iron hoops, the steel skates, the Queen Anne coal-scuttle, the bagatelle board, the hand organ—all gone, and jewels, too. Opals and emeralds, they lie about the roots of turnips. What a scraping paring affair it is to be sure! The wonder is that I've any clothes on my back, that I sit surrounded by solid furniture at this moment. Why, if one wants to compare life to anything, one must liken it to being blown through the Tube at fifty miles an hour—landing at the other end without a single hairpin in one's hair! Shot out at the feet of God entirely naked! Tumbling head over heels in the asphodel meadows like brown paper parcels pitched down a shoot in the post office! With one's hair flying back like the tail of a race-horse. Yes, that seems to express the rapidity of life, the perpetual waste and repair; all so casual, all so haphazard. . . .

But after life. The slow pulling down of thick green stalks so that the cup of the flower, as it turns over, deluges one with purple and red light. Why, after all, should one not be born there as one is born here, helpless, speechless, unable to focus one's eyesight, groping at the roots of the grass, at the toes of the Giants? As for saying which are trees, and which are men and women, or whether there are such things, that one won't be in a condition to do for fifty years or so. There will be nothing but spaces of light and dark, intersected by thick stalks, and rather higher up perhaps, rose-shaped blots of an indistinct colour—dim pinks and blues—which will, as time goes on, become more definite, become—I don't know what. . . .

And yet that mark on the wall is not a hole at all. It may even be caused by some round black substance, such as a small rose leaf, left over from the summer, and I, not being a very vigilant housekeeper—look at the dust on the mantelpiece, for example, the dust which, so they say, buried Troy three times over, only fragments of pots utterly refusing an- nihilation, as one can believe.

The tree outside the window taps very gently on the pane. . . . I want to think quietly, calmly, spaciously, never to be interrupted, never to have to rise from my chair, to slip easily from one thing to another, without any sense of hostility, or obstacle. I want to sink deeper and deeper, away from the surface, with its hard separate facts. To steady myself, let me catch hold of the first idea that passes . . . Shakespeare. . . . Well, he will do as well as another. A man who sat himself solidly in an arm-chair, and looked into the fire, so— A shower of ideas fell perpetually from some very high Heaven down through his mind. He leant his forehead on his hand, and people, looking in through the open door—for this scene is supposed to take place on a summer's evening— But how dull this is, this historical fiction! It doesn't interest me at all. I wish I could hit upon a pleasant track of thought, a track indirectly reflecting credit upon myself, for those are the pleasantest thoughts, and very frequent even in the minds of modest mouse-coloured people, who believe genuinely that they dislike to hear their own praises. They are not thoughts directly praising oneself; that is the beauty of them; they are thoughts like this:

"And then I came into the room. They were discussing botany. I said how I'd seen a flower growing on a dust heap on the site of an old house in Kingsway. The seed, I said, must have been sown in the reign of Charles the First. What flowers grew in the reign of Charles the First?" I asked— (But I don't remember the answer.) Tall flowers with purple tassels to them perhaps. And so it goes on. All the time I'm dressing up the figure of myself in my own mind, lovingly, steathily, not openly adoring it, for if I did that, I should catch myself out, and stretch my hand at once for a book in self-protection. Indeed, it is curious how instinctively one protects the image of oneself from idolatry or any other handling that could make it ridiculous, or too unlike the original to be believed in any longer. Or is it not so very curious after all? It is a matter of great importance. Suppose the looking-glass smashes, the image disappears, and the romantic figure with the green of forest depths all about it is there no longer, but only that shell of a person which is seen by other people—what an airless, shallow, bald, prominent world it becomes! A world not to be lived in. As we face each other in omnibuses and underground railways we are looking into the mirror; that accounts for the vagueness, the gleam of glassiness, in our eyes. And the novelists in future will realize more and more the importance of these reflections, for of course there is not one reflection but an almost infinite number; those are the depths they will explore, those the phantoms they will pursue, leaving the description of reality more and more out of their stories, taking a knowledge of it for granted, as the Greeks did and Shakespeare perhaps—but these generalizations are very worthless. The military sound of the word is enough. It recalls leading articles, cabinet ministers—a whole class of things indeed which, as a child, one thought the thing itself, the standard thing, the real thing, from which one could not depart save at the risk of nameless damnation. Generalizations bring back somehow Sunday in London, Sunday afternoon walks, Sunday luncheons, and also ways of speaking of the dead, clothes, and habits—like the habit of sitting all together in one room until a certain hour, although nobody liked it. There was a rule for everything. The rule for tablecloths at that particular period was that they should be made of tapestry with little yellow compartments marked upon them, such as you may see in photographs of the carpets in the corridors of the royal palaces. Tablecloths of a different kind were not real tablecloths. How shocking, and yet how wonderful it was to discover that these real things, Sunday luncheons, Sunday walks, country houses, and tablecloths were not entirely real, were indeed half phantoms, and the damnation which visited the disbeliever in them was only a sense of illegitimate freedom. What now takes the place of those things I wonder, those real standard things? Men perhaps, should you be a woman; the masculine point of view which governs our lives, which sets the standard, which establishes Whitaker's Table of Precedency, which has become, I suppose, since the war, half a phantom to many men and women, which soon, one may hope, will be laughed into the dustbin where the phantoms go, the mahogany sideboards and the Landseer prints, Gods and Devils, Hell and so forth, leaving us all with an intoxicating sense of illegitimate freedom—if freedom exists. . . .

In certain lengths that mark on the wall seems actually to project from the wall. Nor is it entirely circular. I cannot be sure, but it seems to cast a perceptible shadow, suggesting that if I ran my finger down that strip of the wall it would, at a certain point, mount and descend a small tumulus, a smooth tumulus like those barrows on the South Downs which are, they say, either tombs or camps. Of the two I should prefer them to be tombs, desiring melancholy like most English people, and finding it natural at the end of a walk to think of the bones stretched beneath the turf. . . . There must be some book about it. Some antiquary must have dug up those bones and given them a name. . . . What sort of a man is an antiquary, I wonder? Retired Colonels for the most part, I daresay, leading parties of aged labourers to the top here, examining clods of earth and stone, and getting into correspondence with the neighbouring clergy, which, being opened at breakfast time, gives them a feeling of importance, and the comparison of arrow-heads necessitates cross-country journeys to the county towns, an agreeable necessity both to them and to their elderly wives, who wish to make them plum jam or to clean out the study, and have every reason for keeping that great question of the camp or the tomb in perpetual suspension, while the Colonel himself feels agreeably philosophic in accumulating evidence on both sides of the question. It is true that he does finally incline to believe in the camp; and, being opposed, indites a pamphlet which he is about to read at the quarterly meeting of the local society when a stroke lays him low, and his last conscious thoughts are not of wife or child, but of the camp and that arrow-head there, which is now in the case at the local museum, together with the foot of a Chinese murderess, a handful of Elizabethan nails, a great many

Tudor clay pipes, a piece of Roman pottery, and the wineglass that Nelson drank out of—proving I really don't know what.

No, no, nothing is proved, nothing is known. And if I were to get up at this very moment and ascertain that the mark on the wall is really—what shall we say?—the head of a gigantic old nail, driven in two hundred years ago, which has now, owing to the patient attrition of many generations of housemaids, revealed its head above the coat of paint, and is taking its first view of modern life in the sight of a white-walled fire-lit room, what should I gain?— Knowledge? Matter for further speculation? I can think sitting still as well as standing up. And what is knowledge? What are our learned men save the descendants of witches and hermits who crouched in caves and in woods brewing herbs, interrogating shrew-mice and writing down the language of the stars? And the less we honour them as our superstitions dwindle and our respect for beauty and health of mind increases. . . . Yes, one could imagine a very pleasant world. A quiet, spacious world, with the flowers so red and blue in the open fields. A world without professors or specialists or house-keepers with the profiles of policemen, a world which one could slice with one's thought as a fish slices the water with his fin, grazing the stems of the water-lilies, hanging suspended over nests of white sea eggs. . . . How peaceful it is down here, rooted in the centre of the world and gazing up through the grey waters, with their sudden gleams of light, and their reflections—if it were not for Whitaker's Almanack—if it were not for the Table of Precedency!

I must jump up and see for myself what that mark on the wall really is—a nail, a rose-leaf, a crack in the wood?

Here is nature once more at her old game of self-preservation. This train of thought, she perceives, is threatening mere waste of energy, even some collision with reality, for who will ever be able to lift a finger against Whitaker's Table of Precedency? The Archbishop of Canterbury is followed by the Lord High Chancellor; the Lord High Chancellor is followed by the Archbishop of York. Everybody follows somebody, such is the philosophy of Whitaker; and the great thing is to know who follows whom. Whitaker knows, and let that, so Nature counsels, comfort you, instead of enraging you; and if you can't be comforted, if you must shatter this hour of peace, think of the mark on the wall.

I understand Nature's game—her prompting to take action as a way of ending any thought that threatens to excite or to pain. Hence, I suppose, comes our slight contempt for men of action—men, we assume, who don't think. Still, there's no harm in putting a full stop to one's disagreeable thoughts by looking at a mark on the wall.

Indeed, now that I have fixed my eyes upon it, I feel that I have grasped a plank in the sea; I feel a satisfying sense of reality which at once turns the two Archbishops and the Lord High Chancellor to the shadows of shades. Here is something definite, something real. Thus, waking from a midnight dream of horror, one hastily turns on the light and lies quiescent, worshipping the chest of drawers, worshipping solidity, worshipping reality, worshipping the impersonal world which is a proof of some existence other than ours. That is what one wants to be sure of. . . . Wood is a pleasant thing to think about. It comes from a tree; and trees grow, and we don't know how they grow. For years and years they grow, without paying any attention to us, in meadows, in forests, and by the side of rivers—all things one likes to think about. The cows swish their tails beneath them on hot afternoons; they paint rivers so green that when a moorhen dives one expects to see its feathers all green when it comes up again. I like to think of the fish balanced against the stream like flags blown out; and of water-beetles slowly raising domes of mud upon the bed of the river. I like to think of the tree itself: first of the close dry sensation of being wood; then the grinding of the storm; then the slow, delicious ooze of sap; I like to think of it, too, on winter's nights standing in the empty field with all leaves close-furled, nothing tender exposed to the iron bullets of the moon, a naked mast upon an earth that goes tumbling, tumbling, all night long. The song of birds must sound very loud and strange in June; and how cold the feet of insects must feel upon it, as they make laborious progresses up the creases of the bark, or sun themselves upon the thin green awning of the leaves, and look straight in front of them with diamond-cut red eyes. . . . One by one the fibres snap beneath the immense cold pressure of the earth, then the last storm comes and, falling, the highest branches drive deep into the ground again. Even so, life isn't done with; there are a million patient, watchful lives still for a tree, all over the world, in bedrooms, in ships, on the pavement, lining rooms, where men and women sit after tea, smoking cigarettes. It is full of peaceful thoughts, happy thoughts, this tree. I should like to take each one separately—but something is getting in the way. . . . Where was I? What has it all been about? A tree? A river? The Downs? Whitaker's Almanack? The fields of asphodel? I can't remember a thing. Everything's moving, falling, slipping, vanishing. . . . There is a vast upheaval of matter. Someone is standing over me and saying:

"I'm going out to buy a newspaper."

"Yes?"

"Though it's no good buying newspapers. . . . Nothing ever happens. Curse this war; God damn this war! . . . All the same, I don't see why we should have a snail on our wall."

Ah, the mark on the wall! It was a snail.

A FRAGMENT OF STAINED GLASS
by D. H. Lawrence
(1885–1930)

*This story is an allegory or parable on the Fall of Man.
In Lawrence's scheme the Renaissance marks modern man's
acquisition of consciousness and loss of innocence. Hence,
here he telescopes Edenic time and the Renaissance. The
limping authority figure, often a Vicar, is a devil figure.*

Beauvale is, or was, the largest parish in England. It is
thinly populated, only just netting the stragglers from shoals of houses in
three large mining villages. For the rest, it holds a great tract of woodland,
fragment of old Sherwood, a few hills of pasture and arable land, three
collieries, and, finally, the ruins of a Cistercian abbey. These ruins lie in a
still rich meadow at the foot of the last fall of woodland, through whose
oaks shines a blue of hyacinths, like water, in Maytime. Of the abbey,
there remains only the east wall of the chancel standing, a wild thick mass
of ivy weighting one shoulder, while pigeons perch in the tracery of the
lofty window. This is the window in question.

The vicar of Beauvale is a bachelor of forty-two years. Quite early in
life some illness caused a slight paralysis of his right side, so that he drags
a little, and so that the right corner of his mouth is twisted up into his
cheek with a constant grimace, unhidden by a heavy moustache. There is
something pathetic about this twist on the vicar's countenance: his eyes
are so shrewd and sad. It would be hard to get near to Mr. Colbran.
Indeed, now, his soul has some of the twist to his face, so that, when he is
not ironical, he is satiric. Yet a man of more complete tolerance and
generosity scarcely exists. Let the boors mock him, he merely smiles on
the other side, and there is no malice in his eyes, only a quiet expression of
waiting till they have finished. His people do not like him, yet none could
bring forth an accusation against him, save that "You never can tell when
he's having you."

I dined the other evening with the vicar in his study. The room
scandalises the neighbourhood because of the statuary which adorns it: a
Laocoön and other classic copies, with bronze and silver Italian Renaissance works. For the rest, it is all dark and tawny.

Mr. Colbran is an archæologist. He does not take himself seriously, however, in his hobby, so that nobody knows the worth of his opinions on the subject.

"Here you are," he said to me after dinner. "I've found another paragraph for my great work."

"What's that?" I asked.

"Haven't I told you I was compiling a Bible of the English people— the Bible of their hearts—their exclamations in presence of the unknown? I've found a fragment at home, a jump at God from Beauvale."

"Where?" I asked, startled.

The vicar closed his eyes whilst looking at me.

"Only on parchment," he said.

Then, slowly, he reached for a yellow book, and read, translating as he went:

"Then, while we chanted, came a crackling at the window, at the great east window, where hung our Lord on the Cross. It was a malicious coveitous Devil wrathed by us, rended the lovely image of the glasse. We saw the iron clutches of the fiend pick the window, and a face flaming red like fire in a basket did glower down on us. Our hearts melted away, our legs broke, we thought to die. The breath of the wretch filled the chapel.

"But our dear Saint, etc., etc., came hastening down heaven to defend us. The fiend began to groan and bray—he was daunted and beat off.

"When the sun up-rose, and it was morning, some went out in dread upon the thin snow. There the figure of our Saint was broken and thrown down, whilst in the window was a wicked hole as from the Holy Wounds the Blessed Blood was run out at the touch of the Fiend, and on the snow was the Blood, sparkling like gold. Some gathered it up for the joy of this House. . . ."

"Interesting," I said. "Where's it from?"

"Beauvale records—fifteenth century."

"Beauvale Abbey," I said; "they were only very few, the monks. What frightened them, I wonder."

"I wonder," he repeated.

"Somebody climbed up," I supposed, "and attempted to get in."

"What?" he exclaimed, smiling.

"Well, what do you think?"

"Pretty much the same," he replied. "I glossed it out for my book."

"Your great work? Tell me."

He put a shade over the lamp so that the room was almost in darkness.

"Am I more than a voice?" he asked.

"I can see your hand," I replied. He moved entirely from the circle of light. Then his voice began, sing-song, sardonic:

"I was a serf at Rollestoun's, Newthorpe Manor, master of the stables, I was. One day a horse bit me as I was grooming him. He was an old enemy of mine. I fetched him a blow across the nose. Then, when he got a chance, he lashed out at me and caught me a gash over the mouth. I snatched at a hatchet and cut his head. He yelled, fiend as he was, and strained for me with all his teeth bare. I brought him down.

"For killing him they flogged me till they thought I was dead. I was sturdy, because we horse-serfs got plenty to eat. I was sturdy, but they flogged me till I did not move. The next night I set fire to the stables, and the stables set fire to the house. I watched and saw the red flame rise and look out of the window, I saw the folk running, each for himself, master no more than one of a frightened party. It was freezing, but the heat made me sweat. I saw them all turn again to watch, all rimmed with red. They cried, all of them, when the roof went in, when the sparks splashed up at rebound. They cried then like dogs at the bagpipes howling. Master cursed me, till I laughed as I lay under a bush quite near.

"As the fire went down I got frightened. I ran for the woods with fire blazing in my eyes and crackling in my ears. For hours I was all fire. Then I went to sleep under the bracken. When I woke it was evening. I had no mantle, was frozen stiff. I was afraid to move, lest all the sores of my back should be broken like thin ice. I lay still until I could bear my hunger no longer. I moved then to get used to the pain of movement, when I began to hunt for food. There was nothing to be found but hips.

"After wandering about till I was faint I dropped again in the bracken. The boughs above me creaked with frost. I started and looked round. The branches were like hair among the starlight. My heart stood still. Again there was a creak, creak, and suddenly a whoop, that whistled in fading. I fell down in the bracken like dead wood. Yet, by the peculiar whistling sound at the end, I knew it was only the ice bending or tightening in the frost. I was in the woods above the lake, only two miles from the Manor. And yet, when the lake whooped hollowly again, I clutched the frozen soil, every one of my muscles as stiff as the stiff earth. So all the night long I dare not move my face, but pressed it flat down, and taut I lay as if pegged down and braced.

"When morning came still I did not move, I lay still in a dream. By afternoon my ache was such it enlivened me. I cried, rocking my breath in the ache of moving. Then again I became fierce. I beat my hands on the rough bark to hurt them, so that I should not ache so much. In such a rage I was I swung my limbs to torture till I fell sick with pain. Yet I fought the hurt, fought it and fought by twisting and flinging myself, until it was overcome. Then the evening began to draw on. All day the sun had not loosened the frost. I felt the sky chill again towards afternoon. Then I knew the night was coming, and, remembering the great space I had just come through, horrible so that it seemed to have made me another man, I fled across the wood.

"But in my running I came upon the oak where hanged five bodies. There they must hang, bar-stiff, night after night. It was a terror worse than any. Turning, blundering through the forest, I came out where the trees thinned, where only hawthorns, ragged and shaggy, went down to the lake's edge.

"The sky across was red, the ice on the water glistened as if it were warm. A few wild geese sat out like stones on the sheet of ice. I thought of Martha. She was the daughter of the miller at the upper end of the lake. Her hair was red like beech leaves in a wind. When I had gone often to the mill with the horses she had brought me food.

" 'I thought,' said I to her, ' 'twas a squirrel sat on your shoulder. 'Tis your hair fallen loose.'

" 'They call me the fox,' she said.

" 'Would I were your dog,' said I. She would bring me bacon and good bread, when I called at the mill with the horses. The thought of cakes of bread and of bacon made me reel as if drunk. I had torn at the rabbit-holes, I had chewed wood all day. In such a dimness was my head that I felt neither the soreness of my wounds nor the cuts of thorns on my knees, but stumbled towards the mill, almost past fear of man and death, panting with fear of the darkness that crept behind me from trunk to trunk.

"Coming to the gap in the wood, below which lay the pond, I heard no sound. Always I knew the place filled with the buzz of water, but now it was silent. In fear of this stillness I ran forward, forgetting myself, forgetting the frost. The wood seemed to pursue me. I fell, just in time, down by a shed wherein were housed the few wintry pigs. The miller came riding in on his horse, and the barking of dogs was for him. I heard him curse the day, curse his servant, curse me, whom he had been out to hunt, in his rage of wasted labour, curse all. As I lay I heard inside the shed a sucking. Then I knew that the sow was there, and that the most of her sucking pigs would be already killed for to-morrow's Christmas. The miller, from fore-thought to have young at that time, made profit by his sucking pigs that were sold for the midwinter feast.

"When in a moment all was silent in the dusk, I broke the bar and came into the shed. The sow grunted, but did not come forth to discover me. By and by I crept in towards her warmth. She had but three young left, which now angered her, she being too full of milk. Every now and again she slashed at them and they squealed. Busy as she was with them, I in the darkness advanced towards her. I trembled so that scarce dared I trust myself near her, for long dared not put my naked face towards her. Shuddering with hunger and fear, I at last fed of her, guarding my face with my arm. Her own full young tumbled squealing against me, but she, feeling her ease, lay grunting. At last, I, too, lay drunk, swooning.

"I was roused by the shouting of the miller. He, angered by his daughter who wept, abused her, driving her from the house to feed the swine. She came, bowing under a yoke, to the door of the shed. Finding the pin broken she stood afraid, then, as the sow grunted, she came cautiously in. I took her with my arm, my hand over her mouth. As she struggled against my breast my heart began to beat loudly. At last she knew it was I. I clasped her. She hung in my arms, turning away her face, so that I kissed her throat. The tears blinded my eyes, I know not why, unless it were the hurt of my mouth, wounded by the horse, was keen.

" 'They will kill you,' she whispered.

" 'No,' I answered.

"And she wept softly. She took my head in her arms and kissed me, wetting me with her tears, brushing me with her keen hair, warming me through.

" 'I will not go away from here,' I said. 'Bring me a knife, and I will defend myself.'

" 'No,' she wept. 'Ah, no!'

"When she went I lay down, pressing my chest where she had rested on the earth, lest being alone were worse emptiness than hunger.

"Later she came again. I saw her bend in the doorway, a lanthorn hanging in front. As she peered under the redness of her falling hair, I was afraid of her. But she came with food. We sat together in the dull light. Sometimes still I shivered and my throat would not swallow.

" 'If,' said I, 'I eat all this you have brought me, I shall sleep till somebody finds me.'

"Then she took away the rest of the meat.

" 'Why,' said I, 'should I not eat?' She looked at me in tears of fear.

" 'What?' I said, but still she had no answer. I kissed her, and the hurt of my wounded mouth angered me.

" 'Now there is my blood,' said I, 'on your mouth.' Wiping her smooth hand over her lips, she looked thereat, then at me.

" 'Leave me,' I said, 'I am tired.' She rose to leave me.

" 'But bring a knife,' I said. Then she held the lanthorn near my face, looking as at a picture.

" 'You look to me,' she said, 'like a stirk that is roped for the axe. Your eyes are dark, but they are wide open.'

" 'Then I will sleep,' said I, 'but will not wake too late.'

" 'Do not stay here,' she said.

" 'I will not sleep in the wood,' I answered, and it was my heart that spoke, 'for I am afraid. I had better be afraid of the voice of man and dogs, than the sounds in the woods. Bring me a knife, and in the morning I will go. Alone will I not go now.'

" 'The searchers will take you,' she said.

" 'Bring me a knife,' I answered.

" 'Ah, go,' she wept.

" 'Not now—I will not—'

"With that she lifted the lanthorn, lit up her own face and mine. Her blue eyes dried of tears. Then I took her to myself, knowing she was mine.

" 'I will come again,' she said.

"She went, and I folded my arms, lay down and slept.

"When I woke, she was rocking me wildly to rouse me.

" 'I dreamed,' said I, 'that a great heap, as if it were a hill, lay on me and above me.'

"She put a cloak over me, gave me a hunting-knife and a wallet of food, and other things I did not note. Then under her own cloak, she hid the lanthorn.

" 'Let us go,' she said, and blindly I followed her.

"When I came out into the cold someone touched my face and my hair.

" 'Ha!' I cried, 'who now—?' Then she swiftly clung to me, hushed me.

" 'Someone has touched me,' I said aloud, still dazed with sleep.

" 'Oh, hush!' she wept. ' 'Tis snowing.' The dogs within the house began to bark. She fled forward, I after her. Coming to the ford of the stream she ran swiftly over, but I broke through the ice. Then I knew where I was. Snowflakes, fine and rapid, were biting at my face. In the wood there was no wind nor snow.

" 'Listen,' said I to her, 'listen, for I am locked up with sleep.'

" 'I hear roaring overhead,' she answered. 'I hear in the trees like great bats squeaking.'

" 'Give me your hand,' said I.

"We heard many noises as we passed. Once as there up-rose a whiteness before us, she cried aloud.

" 'Nay,' said I, 'do not untie thy hand from mine,' and soon we were crossing fallen snow. But ever and again she started back from fear.

" 'When you draw back my arm,' I said, angry, 'you loosen a weal on my shoulder.'

"Thereafter she ran by my side like a fawn beside its mother.

" 'We will cross the valley and gain the stream,' I said. 'That will lead us on its ice as on a path deep into the forest. There we can join the outlaws. The wolves are driven from this part. They have followed the driven deer.'

"We came directly on a large gleam that shaped itself up among flying grains of snow.

" 'Ah!' she cried, and she stood amazed.

"Then I thought we had gone through the bounds into faery realm, and I was no more a man. How did I know what eyes were gleaming at me between the snow, what cunning spirits in the draughts of air? So I waited for what would happen, and I forgot her, that she was there. Only I could feel the spirits whirling and blowing about me.

"Whereupon she clung upon me, kissing me lavishly, and, were dogs or men or demons come upon us at that moment, she had let us be stricken down, nor heeded not. So we moved forward to the shadow that shone in colours upon the passing snow. We found ourselves under a door of light which shed its colours mixed with snow. This Martha had never seen, nor I, this door open for a red and brave issuing like fires. We wondered.

" 'It is faery," she said, and after a while, 'Could one catch such— Ah, no!'

"Through the snow shone bushes of red and blue.

" 'Could one have such a little light like a red flower—only a little, like a rose-berry scarlet on one's breast!—then one were singled out as Our Lady.'

"I flung off my cloak and my burden to climb up the face of the shadow. Standing on rims of stone, then in pockets of snow, I reached upward. My hand was red and blue, but I could not take the stuff. Like colour of a moth's wing it was on my hand, it flew on the increasing snow. I stood higher on the head of a frozen man, reached higher my hand. Then I felt the bright stuff cold. I could not pluck it off. Down below she cried to me to come again to her. I felt a rib that yielded, I struck at it with my knife. There came a gap in the redness. Looking through, I saw below as it were white stunted angels, with sad faces lifted in fear. Two faces they had each, and round rings of hair. I was afraid. I grasped the shining red, I pulled. Then the cold man under me sank, so I fell as if broken on to the snow.

"Soon I was risen again, and we were running downwards towards the stream. We felt ourselves eased when the smooth road of ice was beneath us. For a while it was resting, to travel thus evenly. But the wind blew round us, the snow hung upon us, we leaned us this way and that, towards the storm. I drew her along, for she came as a bird that stems lifting and swaying against the wind. By and by the snow came smaller, there was no wind in the wood. Then I felt nor labour, nor cold. Only I knew the darkness drifted by on either side, that overhead was a lane of paleness where a moon fled us before. Still, I can feel the moon fleeing from me, can feel the trees passing round me in slow dizzy reel, can feel the hurt of my shoulder and my straight arm torn with holding her. I was following the moon and the stream, for I knew where the water peeped from its burrow in the ground there were shelters of the outlaw. But she fell, without sound or sign.

"I gathered her up and climbed the bank. There all round me hissed the larchwood, dry beneath, and laced with its dry-fretted cords. For a little way I carried her into the trees. Then I laid her down till I cut flat hairy boughs. I put her in my bosom on this dry bed, so we swooned together through the night. I laced her round and covered her with myself, so she lay like a nut within its shell.

"Again, when morning came, it was pain of cold that woke me. I groaned, but my heart was warm as I saw the heap of red hair in my arms. As I looked at her, her eyes opened into mine. She smiled—from out of her smile came fear. As if in a trap she pressed back her head.

" 'We have no flint,' said I.

" 'Yes—in the wallet, flint and steel and tinder-box,' she answered.

" 'God yield you blessing,' I said.

"In a place a little open I kindled a fire of larch boughs. She was afraid of me, hovering near, yet never crossing a space.

" 'Come,' said I, 'let us eat this food.'

" 'Your face,' she said, 'is smeared with blood.'

"I opened out my cloak.

" 'But come,' said I, 'you are frosted with cold.'

"I took a handful of snow in my hand, wiping my face with it, which then I dried on my cloak.

" 'My face is no longer painted with blood. You are no longer afraid of me. Come here then, sit by me while we eat.'

"But as I cut the cold bread for her, she clasped me suddenly, kissing me. She fell before me, clasped my knees to her breast, weeping. She laid her face down to my feet, so that her hair spread like a fire before me. I wondered at the woman. 'Nay,' I cried. At that she lifted her face to me from below. 'Nay,' I cried, feeling my tears fall. With her head on my breast, my own tears rose from their source, wetting my cheek and her hair, which was wet with the rain of my eyes.

"Then I remembered and took from my bosom the coloured light of that night before. I saw it was black and rough.

" 'Ah,' said I, 'this is magic.'

" 'The black stone!' she wondered.

" 'It is magic,' she answered.

" 'Shall I throw it?' said I, lifting the stone, 'shall I throw it away, for fear?'

" 'It shines!' she cried, looking up, 'it shines like the eye of a creature at night, the eye of a wolf in the doorway.'

" ' 'Tis magic,' I said, 'let me throw it from us.' But nay, she held my arm.

" 'It is red and shining,' she cried.

" 'It is a bloodstone,' I answered. 'It will hurt us, we shall die in blood.'

" 'But give it to me,' she answered.

" 'It is red of blood,' I said.

" 'Ah, give it to me,' she called.

" 'It is my blood," I said.

" 'Give it,' she commanded, low.

" 'It is my life-stone,' I said.

" 'Give it me,' she pleaded.

"I gave it her. She held it up, she smiled, she smiled in my face, lifting her arms to me. I took her with my mouth, her mouth, her white throat. Nor she ever shrank, but trembled with happiness.

"What woke us, when the woods were filling again with shadow, when the fire was out, when we opened our eyes and looked up as if drowned, into the light which stood bright and thick on the tree-tops, what woke us was the sound of wolves. . . ."

"Nay," said the vicar, suddenly rising, "they lived happily ever after." "No," I said.

THE CHILDREN'S CAMPAIGN
by Pär Lagerkvist
(b. 1891)

Even the children at that time received military training, were assembled in army units and exercised just as though on active service, had their own headquarters and annual maneuvers when everything was conducted as in a real state of war. The grownups had nothing directly to do with this training; the children actually exercised themselves and all command was entrusted to them. The only use made of adult experience was to arrange officers' training courses for especially suitable boys, who were chosen with the greatest care and who were then put in charge of the military education of their comrades in the ranks.

These schools were of high standing and there was hardly a boy throughout the land who did not dream of going to them. But the entrance tests were particularly hard; not only a perfect physique was required but also a highly developed intelligence and character. The age of admission was six to seven years and the small cadets then received an excellent training, both purely military and in all other respects, chiefly the further molding of character. It was also greatly to one's credit in after life to have passed through one of these schools. It was really on the splendid foundation laid here that the quality, organization and efficiency of the child army rested.

Thereafter, as already mentioned, the grownups in no way interfered but everything was entrusted to the children themselves. No adult might meddle in the command, in organizational details or matters of promotion. Everything was managed and supervised by the children; all decisions, even the most vital, being reached by their own little general staff. No one over fourteen was allowed. The boys then passed automatically into the first age group of the regular troops with no mean military training already behind them.

The large child army, which was the object of the whole nation's love and admiration, amounted to three army corps of four divisions: infantry, light field artillery, medical and service corps. All physically fit boys were enrolled in it and a large number of girls belonged to it as nurses, all volunteers.

Now it so happened that a smaller, quite insignificant nation behaved in a high-handed and unseemly way toward its powerful neighbor, and the insult was all the greater since this nation was by no means an equal. Indignation was great and general and, since people's feelings were running high, it was necessary to rebuke the malapert and at the same time take the chance to subjugate the country in question. In this situation the child army came forward and through its high command asked to be charged with the crushing and subduing of the foe. The news of this caused a sensation and a wave of fervor throughout the country. The proposal was given serious consideration in supreme quarters and as a result the commission was given, with some hesitation, to the children. It was in fact a task well suited to this army, and the people's obvious wishes in the matter had also to be met, if possible.

The Foreign Office therefore sent the defiant country an unacceptable ultimatum and, pending the reply, the child army was mobilized within twenty-four hours. The reply was found to be unsatisfactory and war was declared immediately.

Unparalleled enthusiasm marked the departure for the front. The intrepid little youngsters had green sprigs in the barrels of their rifles and were pelted with flowers. As is so often the case, the campaign was begun in the spring, and this time the general opinion was that there was something symbolic in it. In the capital the little commander in chief and chief of general staff, in the presence of huge crowds, made a passionate speech to the troops in which he expressed the gravity of the hour and his conviction of their unswerving valor and willingness to offer their lives for their country.

The speech, made in a strong voice, aroused the greatest ecstasy. The boy—who had a brilliant career behind him and had reached his exalted position at the age of only twelve and a half—was acclaimed with wild rejoicing and from this moment was the avowed hero of the entire nation. There was not a dry eye and those of the many mothers especially shone with pride and happiness. For them it was the greatest day in their lives. The troops marched past below fluttering banners, each regiment with its music corps at the head. It was an unforgettable spectacle.

There were also many touching incidents, evincing a proud patriotism, as when a little four-year-old, who had been lifted up on his mother's arm so that he could see, howled with despair and shouted, "I want to go, too. I want to go, too!" while his mother tried to hush him, explaining that he was too small. "Small am I, eh?" he exclaimed, punching her face so that her nose bled. The evening papers were full of such episodes showing the mood of the people and of the troops who were so sure of victory. The big march past was broadcast and the c in c's speech, which had been recorded, was broadcast every evening during the days that followed at 7:15 P.M.

Military operations had already begun, however, and reports of victory began to come in at once from the front. The children had quickly taken the offensive and on one sector of the front had inflicted a heavy defeat on the enemy, seven hundred dead and wounded and over twelve hundred prisoners, while their own losses amounted to only a hundred or so fallen. The victory was celebrated at home with indescribable rejoicing and with thanksgiving services in the churches. The newspapers were filled with accounts of individual instances of valor and pictures several columns wide of the high command, of which the leading personalities, later so well-known, began to appear now for the first time. In their joy, mothers and aunts sent so much chocolate and other sweets to the army that headquarters had to issue a strict order that all such parcels were, for the time being at any rate, forbidden, since they had made whole regiments unfit for battle and these in their turn had nearly been surrounded by the enemy.

For the child army was already far inside enemy territory and still managed to keep the initiative. The advance sector did retreat slightly in order to establish contact with its wings but only improved its positions by so doing. A stalemate ensued in the theater of war for some time after this.

During July, however, troops were concentrated for a big attack along the whole line and huge reserves—the child army's, in comparison with those of its opponent, were almost inexhaustible—were mustered to the front. The new offensive, which lasted for several weeks, resulted, too, in an almost decisive victory for the whole army, even though casualties were high. The children defeated the enemy all along the line but did not manage to pursue him and thereby exploit their success to the full, because he was greatly favored by the fact that his legs were so much longer, an advantage of which he made good use. By dint of forced marches, however, the children finally succeeded in cutting the enemy's right flank to pieces. They were now in the very heart of the country and their outposts were only a few days' march from the capital.

It was a pitched battle on a big scale and the newspapers had enormous headlines every day which depicted the dramatic course of events. At set hours the radio broadcast the gunfire and a résumé of the position. The war correspondents described in rapturous words and vivid colors the state of affairs at the front—the children's incredible feats, their indomitable courage and self-sacrifice, the whole morale of the army. It was no exaggeration. The youngsters showed the greatest bravery; they really behaved like heroes. One only had to see their discipline and contempt of death during an attack, as though they had been grown-up men at least.

It was an unforgettable sight to see them storm ahead under murderous machine gun fire and the small medical orderlies dart nimbly forward and pick them up as they fell. Or the wounded and dying who were moved behind the front, those who had had a leg shot away or their bellies ripped open by a bayonet so that their entrails hung out—but without one sound of complaint crossing their small lips. The hand-to-hand fighting had been very fierce and a great number of children fell in this, while they were superior in the actual firing. Losses were estimated at 4,000 on the enemy side and 7,000 among the children, according to the secret reports. The victory had been hard won but all the more complete.

This battle became very famous and was also of far greater importance than any previously. It was now clear beyond all doubt that the children were incomparably superior in tactics, discipline and individual courage. At the same time, however, it was admitted by experts that the enemy's headlong retreat was very skillfully carried out, that his strength was evidently in defense and that he should not be underrated too much. Toward the end, also, he had unexpectedly made a stubborn resistance which had prevented any further penetration.

This observation was not without truth. In actual fact the enemy was anything but a warlike nation, and indeed his forces found it very difficult to hold their own. Nevertheless, they improved with practice during the fighting and became more efficient as time went on. This meant that they caused the children a good deal of trouble in each succeeding battle. They also had certain advantages on their side. As their opponents were so small, for instance, it was possible after a little practice to spit several of them on the bayonet at once, and often a kick was enough to fell them to the ground.

But against this, the children were so much more numerous and also braver. They were everywhere. They swarmed over one and in between one's legs and the unwarlike people were nearly demented by all these small monsters who fought like fiends. Little fiends was also what they were generally called—not without reason—and this name was even adopted in the children's homeland, but there it was a mark of honor and a pet name. The enemy troops had all their work cut out merely defending themselves. At last, however, they were able to check the others' advance and even venture on one or two counterattacks. Everything then came to a standstill for a while and there was a breathing space.

The children were now in possession of a large part of the country. But this was not always so easy. The population did not particularly like them and proved not to be very fond of children. It was alleged that snipers fired on the boys from houses and that they were ambushed when they moved in small detachments. Children had even been found impaled on stakes or with their eyes gouged out, so it was said. And in many cases these stories were no doubt true. The population had quite lost their heads, were obviously goaded into a frenzy, and as they were of little use as a warlike nation and their cruelty could therefore find no natural outlet, they tried to revenge themselves by atrocities. They felt overrun by all the foreign children as by troublesome vermin and, being at their wits' end, they simply killed whenever they had the chance. In order to put an end to these outrages the children burned one village after the other and shot hundreds of people daily, but this did not improve matters. The despicable deeds of these craven guerrillas caused them endless trouble.

At home, the accounts of all this naturally aroused the most bitter resentment. People's blood boiled to think that their small soldiers were treated in this way by those who had nothing to do with the war, by barbarous civilians who had no notion of established and judicial forms. Even greater indignation was caused, however, by an incident that occurred inside the occupied area some time after the big summer battle just mentioned.

A lieutenant who was out walking in the countryside came to a stream where a large, fat woman knelt washing clothes. He asked her the way to a village close by. The woman, who probably suspected him of evil intent, retorted, "What are you doing here? You ought to be at home with your mother." Whereupon the lieutenant drew his saber to kill her, but the woman grabbed hold of him and, putting him over her knee, thwacked him black and blue with her washboard so that he was unable to sit down for several days afterward. He was so taken aback that he did nothing, armed though he was to the teeth. Luckily no one saw the incident, but there were orders that all outrages on the part of the population were to be reported to headquarters. The lieutenant therefore duly reported what had happened to him. True, it gave him little satisfaction, but as he had to obey orders he had no choice. And so it all came out.

The incident aroused a storm of rage, particularly among those at home. The infamous deed was a humiliation for the country, an insult which nothing could wipe out. It implied a deliberate violation by this militarily ignorant people of the simplest rules of warfare. Everywhere, in the press, in propaganda speeches, in ordinary conversation, the deepest contempt and disgust for the deed was expressed. The lieutenant who had so flagrantly shamed the army had his officer's epaulettes ripped off in front of the assembled troops and was declared unworthy to serve any longer in the field. He was instantly sent home to his parents, who belonged to one of the most noted families but who now had to retire into obscurity in a remote part of the country.

The woman, on the other hand, became a heroic figure among her people and the object of their rapturous admiration. During the whole of the war she and her deed were a rallying national symbol which people looked up to and which spurred them on to further effort. She subsequently became a favorite motif in the profuse literature about their desperate struggle for freedom; a vastly popular figure, brought to life again and again as time passed, now in a rugged, everyday way which appealed to the man in the street, now in heroic female form on a grandiose scale, to become gradually more and more legendary, wreathed in saga and myth.

In some versions she was shot by the enemy; in others she lived to a ripe old age, loved and revered by her people.

This incident, more than anything else, helped to increase the bad feelings between the two countries and to make them wage the war with ever greater ruthlessness. In the late summer, before the autumn rains began, both armies, ignorant of each other's plans, simultaneously launched a violent offensive, which devastated both sides. On large sectors of the front the troops completely annihilated each other so that there was not a single survivor left. Any peaceful inhabitants thereabouts who were still alive and ventured out of their cellars thought that the war was over, because all were slain.

But soon new detachments came up and began fighting again. Great confusion arose in other quarters from the fact that in the heat of attack men ran past each other and had to turn around in order to go on fighting; and that some parts of the line rushed ahead while others came behind, so that the troops were both in front of and behind where they should have been and time and again attacked each other in the rear. The battle raged in this way with extreme violence and shots were fired from all directions at once.

When at last the fighting ceased and stock was taken of the situation, it appeared that no one had won. On both sides there was an equal number of fallen, 12,924, and after all attacks and retreats the position of the armies was exactly the same as at the start of the battle. It was agreed that both should claim the victory. Thereafter the rain set in and the armies went to earth in trenches and put up barbed wire entanglements.

The children were the first to finish their trenches, since they had had more to do with that kind of thing, and settled down in them as best they could. They soon felt at home. Filthy and lousy, they lived there in the darkness as though they had never done anything else. With the adaptability of children they quickly got into the way of it. The enemy found this more difficult; he felt miserable and homesick for the life above ground to which he was accustomed. Not so the children. When one saw them in their small gray uniforms, which were caked thick with mud, and their small gas masks, one could easily think they had been born to this existence. They crept in and out of the holes down into the earth and scampered about the passages like mice. When their burrows were attacked they were instantly up on the parapet and snapped back in blind fury. As the months passed, this hopeless, harrowing life put endurance to an increasingly severe test. But they never lost courage or the will to fight.

For the enemy the strain was often too much; the glaring pointlessness of it all made many completely apathetic. But the little ones did not react like this. Children are really more fitted for war and take more pleasure in it, while grownups tire of it after a while and think it is boring. The boys continued to find the whole thing exciting and they wanted to go on living as they were now. They also had a more natural herd instinct; their unity and camaraderie helped them a great deal, made it easier to hold out.

But, of course, even they suffered great hardship. Especially when winter set in with its incessant rain, a cold sleet which made everything sodden and filled the trenches with mud. It was enough to unman anyone. But it would never have entered their heads to complain. However bad things were, nothing could have made them admit it. At home everyone was very proud of them. All the cinemas showed parades behind the front and the little c-in-c and his generals pinning medals for bravery on their soldiers' breasts. People thought of them a great deal out there, of their little fiends, realizing that they must be having a hard time.

At Christmas, in particular, thoughts went out to them, to the lighted Christmas trees and all the sparkling childish eyes out in the trenches; in every home people sat wondering how they were faring. But the children did not think of home. They were soldiers out and out, absorbed by their duty and their new life. They attacked in several places on the morning of Christmas Eve, inflicting fairly big losses on the enemy in killed and wounded, and did not stop until it was time to open their parcels. They had the real fighting spirit which might have been a lesson even to adults.

There was nothing sentimental about them. The war had hardened and developed them, made them men. It did happen that one poor little chap burst into tears when the Christmas tree was lighted, but he was made the laughing-stock of them all. "Are you homesick for your mummy, you bastard?" they said, and kept on jeering at him all evening. He was the object of their scorn all through Christmas; he behaved suspiciously and tried to keep to himself. Once he walked a hundred yards away from the post and, because he might well have been thinking of flight, he was seized and court-martialed. He could give no reason for having absented himself and since he had obviously intended to desert he was shot.

If those at home had been fully aware of the morale out there, they need not have worried. As it was, they wondered if the children could really hold their ground and half regretted having entrusted them with the campaign, now that it was dragging on so long because of this nerve-racking stationary warfare. After the New Year help was even offered in secret, but it was rejected with proud indignation.

The morale of the enemy, on the other hand, was not so high. They did intend to fight to the last man, but the certainty of a complete victory was not so general as it should have been. They could not help thinking, either, how hopeless their fight really was; that in the long run they could not hold their own against these people who were armed to the very milk teeth, and this often dampened their courage.

Hardly had nature begun to come to life and seethe with the newly awakened forces of spring before the children started with incredible intensity to prepare for the decisive battle. Heavy mechanized artillery was brought up and placed in strong positions; huge troop movements went on night and day; all available fighting forces were concentrated in the very front lines. After murderous gunfire which lasted for six days, an attack was launched with great force and extreme skill. Individual bravery was, if possible, more dazzling than ever. The whole army was also a year older, and that means much at that age. But their opponents, too, were determined to do their utmost. They had assembled all their reserves, and their spirits, now that the rain had stopped and the weather was fine, were full of hope.

It was a terrible battle. The hospital trains immediately started going back from both sides packed with wounded and dying. Machine guns, tanks and gas played fearful havoc. For several days the outcome was impossible to foresee, since both armies appeared equally strong and the tide of battle constantly changed. The position gradually cleared, however. The enemy had expected the main attack in the center, but the child army turned out to be weakest there. Use was made of this, especially because they themselves were best prepared at this very point, and this part of the children's front was soon made to waver and was forced farther and farther back by repeated attack. Advantage was also taken of an ideal evening breeze from just the right quarter to gas the children in thousands. Encouraged by their victory, the troops pursued the offensive with all their might and with equal success.

The child army's retreat, however, turned out to be a stratagem, brilliantly conceived and carried out. Its center gave way more and more and the enemy, giving all his attention to this, forgot that at the same time he himself was wavering on both wings. In this way he ran his head into a noose. When the children considered that they had retreated far enough they halted, while the troops on the outermost wings, already far ahead, advanced swiftly until they met behind the enemy's back. The latter's entire army was thereby surrounded and in the grip of an iron hand. All the children's army had to do now was to draw the noose tighter. At last the gallant defenders had to surrender and let themselves be taken prisoner, which in fact they already were. It was the most disastrous defeat in history; not a single one escaped other than by death.

This victory became much more famous than any of the others and was eagerly studied at all military academies on account of its brilliantly executed, doubly effective encircling movement. The great general Sludelsnorp borrowed its tactics outright seventy years later at his victory over the Slivokvarks in the year 2048.

The war could not go on any longer now, because there was nothing left to fight, and the children marched to the capital with the imprisoned army between them to dictate the peace terms. These were handed over by the little commander in chief in the hall of mirrors in the stately old palace at a historic scene which was to be immortalized time and again in art and even now was reproduced everywhere in the weekly press. The film cameras whirred, the flashlights hissed and the radio broadcast the great moment to the world. The commander in chief, with austere and haughty mien and one foot slightly in front of the other, delivered the historic document with his right hand. The first and most important condition was the complete cession of the country, besides which the expenses of its capture were to be borne by the enemy, who thus had to pay the cost of the war on both sides, the last clause on account of the fact that he had been the challenging party and, according to his own admission, the cause of the war. The document was signed in dead silence, the only sound was the scratching of the fountain pen, which, according to the commentator's whisper, was solid gold and undoubtedly a future museum piece.

With this, everything was settled and the children's army returned to its own country, where it was received with indescribable rapture. Everywhere along the roads the troops were greeted with wild rejoicing, their homecoming was one long victory parade. The march into the capital and the dismissal there of the troops, which took place before vast crowds, were especially impressive. People waved and shouted in the streets as they passed, were beside themselves with enthusiasm, bands played, eyes were filled with tears of joy. Some of the loudest cheering was for the small invalids at the rear of the procession, blind and with limbs amputated, who had sacrificed themselves for their country. Many of them had already got small artificial arms and legs so that they looked just the same as before. The victory salute thundered, bayonets flashed in the sun. It was an unforgettable spectacle.

A strange, new leaf was written in the great book of history which would be read with admiration in time to come. The nation had seen many illustrious deeds performed, but never anything as proud as this. What these children had done in their devotion and fervent patriotism could never be forgotten.

Nor was it. Each spring, on the day of victory, school children marched out with flags in their hands to the cemeteries with all the small graves where the heroes rested under their small white crosses. The mounds were strewn with flowers and passionate speeches were made, reminding everyone of the glorious past, their imperishable honor and youthful, heroic spirit of self-sacrifice. The flags floated in the sun and the voices rang out clear as they sang their rousing songs, radiant childish eyes looking ahead to new deeds of glory.

Translated by Alan Blair

A ROSE FOR EMILY
by William Faulkner
(1897–1962)

I

When Miss Emily Grierson died, our whole town went to her funeral: the men through a sort of respectful affection for a fallen monument, the women mostly out of curiosity to see the inside of her house, which no one save an old manservant—a combined gardener and cook—had seen in at least ten years.

It was a big, squarish frame house that had once been white, decorated with cupolas and spires and scrolled balconies in the heavily lightsome style of the seventies, set on what had once been our most select street. But garages and cotton gins had encroached and obliterated even the august names of that neighborhood; only Miss Emily's house was left, lifting its stubborn and coquettish decay above the cotton wagons and the gasoline pumps—an eyesore among eyesores. And now Miss Emily had gone to join the representatives of those august names where they lay in the cedar-bemused cemetery among the ranked and anonymous graves of Union and Confederate soldiers who fell at the battle of Jefferson.

Alive, Miss Emily had been a tradition, a duty, and a care; a sort of hereditary obligation upon the town, dating from that day in 1894 when Colonel Sartoris, the mayor—he who fathered the edict that no Negro woman should appear on the streets without an apron—remitted her taxes, the dispensation dating from the death of her father on into perpetuity. Not that Miss Emily would have accepted charity. Colonel Sartoris invented an involved tale to the effect that Miss Emily's father had loaned money to the town, which the town, as a matter of business, preferred this way of repaying. Only a man of Colonel Sartoris' generation and thought could have invented it, and only a woman could have believed it.

When the next generation, with its more modern ideas, became mayors and aldermen, this arrangement created some little dissatisfaction. On the first of the year they mailed her a tax notice. February came, and there was no reply. They wrote her a formal letter, asking her to call at the sheriff's office at her convenience. A week later the mayor wrote her himself, offering to call or to send his car for her, and received in reply a note on paper of an archaic shape, in a thin, flowing calligraphy in faded ink, to the effect that she no longer went out at all. The tax notice was also enclosed, without comment.

They called a special meeting of the Board of Aldermen. A deputation waited upon her, knocked at the door through which no visitor had passed since she ceased giving china-painting lessons eight or ten years earlier. They were admitted by the old Negro into a dim hall from which a stairway mounted into still more shadow. It smelled of dust and disuse—a close, dank smell. The Negro led them into the parlor. It was furnished in heavy, leather-covered furniture. When the Negro opened the blinds of one window, a faint dust rose sluggishly about their thighs, spinning with slow motes in the single sun-ray. On a tarnished gilt easel before the fireplace stood a crayon portrait of Miss Emily's father.

They rose when she entered—a small, fat woman in black, with a thin gold chain descending to her waist and vanishing into her belt, leaning on an ebony cane with a tarnished gold head. Her skeleton was small and spare; perhaps that was why what would have been merely plumpness in another was obesity in her. She looked bloated, like a body long submerged in motionless water, and of that pallid hue. Her eyes, lost in the fatty ridges of her face, looked like two small pieces of coal pressed into a lump of dough as they moved from one face to another while the visitors stated their errand.

She did not ask them to sit. She just stood in the door and listened quietly until the spokesman came to a stumbling halt. Then they could hear the invisible watch ticking at the end of the gold chain.

Her voice was dry and cold. "I have no taxes in Jefferson. Colonel Sartoris explained it to me. Perhaps one of you can gain access to the city records and satisfy yourselves."

"But we have. We are the city authorities, Miss Emily. Didn't you get a notice from the sheriff, signed by him?"

"I received a paper, yes," Miss Emily said. "Perhaps he considers himself the sheriff. . . . I have no taxes in Jefferson."

"But there is nothing on the books to show that, you see. We must go by the—"

"See Colonel Sartoris. I have no taxes in Jefferson."

"But, Miss Emily—"

"See Colonel Sartoris." (Colonel Sartoris had been dead almost ten years.) "I have no taxes in Jefferson. Tobe!" The Negro appeared. "Show these gentlemen out."

II

So she vanquished them, horse and foot, just as she had vanquished their fathers thirty years before about the smell. That was two years after her father's death and a short time after her sweetheart—the one we believed would marry her—had deserted her. After her father's death she went out very little; after her sweetheart went away, people hardly saw her at all. A few of the ladies had the temerity to call, but were not received, and the only sign of life about the place was the Negro man—a young man then—going in and out with a market basket.

"Just as if a man—any man—could keep a kitchen properly," the ladies said; so they were not surprised when the smell developed. It was another link between the gross, teeming world and the high and mighty Griersons.

A neighbor, a woman, complained to the mayor, Judge Stevens, eighty years old.

"But what will you have me do about it, madam?" he said.

"Why, send her word to stop it," the woman said. "Isn't there a law?"

"I'm sure that won't be necessary," Judge Stevens said. "It's probably just a snake or a rat that nigger of hers killed in the yard. I'll speak to him about it."

The next day he received two more complaints, one from a man who came in diffident deprecation. "We really must do something about it, Judge. I'd be the last one in the world to bother Miss Emily, but we've got to do something." That night the Board of Aldermen met—three gray-beards and one younger man, a member of the rising generation.

"It's simple enough," he said. "Send her word to have her place cleaned up. Give her a certain time to do it in, and if she don't . . ."

"Dammit, sir," Judge Stevens said, "will you accuse a lady to her face of smelling bad?"

So the next night, after midnight, four men crossed Miss Emily's lawn and slunk about the house like burglars, sniffing along the base of the brickwork and at the cellar openings while one of them performed a regular sowing motion with his hand out of a sack slung from his shoulder. They broke open the cellar door and sprinkled lime there, and in all the outbuildings. As they recrossed the lawn, a window that had been dark was lighted and Miss Emily sat in it, the light behind her, and her upright torso motionless as that of an idol. They crept quietly across the lawn and into the shadow of the locusts that lined the street. After a week or two the smell went away.

That was when people had begun to feel really sorry for her. People in our town, remembering how old lady Wyatt, her great-aunt, had gone completely crazy at last, believed that the Griersons held themselves a little too high for what they really were. None of the young men were quite good enough for Miss Emily and such. We had long thought of them as a tableau; Miss Emily a slender figure in white in the background, her father a spraddled silhouette in the foreground, his back to her and clutching a horsewhip, the two of them framed by the back-flung front door. So when she got to be thirty and was still single, we were not pleased exactly, but vindicated; even with insanity in the family she wouldn't have turned down all of her chances if they had really materialized.

When her father died, it got about that the house was all that was left to her; and in a way, people were glad. At last they could pity Miss Emily. Being left alone, and a pauper, she had become humanized. Now she too would know the old thrill and the old despair of a penny more or less.

The day after his death all the ladies prepared to call at the house and offer condolence and aid, as is our custom. Miss Emily met them at the door, dressed as usual and with no trace of grief on her face. She told them that her father was not dead. She did that for three days, with the ministers calling on her, and the doctors, trying to persuade her to let them dispose of the body. Just as they were about to resort to law and force, she broke down, and they buried her father quickly.

We did not say she was crazy then. We believed she had to do that. We remembered all the young men her father had driven away, and we knew that with nothing left, she would have to cling to that which had robbed her, as people will.

III

She was sick for a long time. When we saw her again, her hair was cut short, making her look like a girl, with a vague resemblance to those angels in colored church windows—sort of tragic and serene.

The town had just let the contracts for paving the sidewalks, and in the summer after her father's death they began to work. The construction company came with niggers and mules and machinery, and a foreman named Homer Barron, a Yankee—a big, dark, ready man, with a big voice and eyes lighter than his face. The little boys would follow in groups to hear him cuss the niggers, and the niggers singing in time to the rise and fall of picks. Pretty soon he knew everybody in town. Whenever you heard a lot of laughing anywhere about the square, Homer Barron would be in the center of the group. Presently we began to see him and Miss Emily on Sunday afternoons driving in the yellow-wheeled buggy and the matched team of bays from the livery stable.

At first we were glad that Miss Emily would have an interest, because the ladies all said, "Of course a Grierson would not think seriously of a Northerner, a day laborer." But there were still others, older people, who said that even grief could not cause a real lady to forget *noblesse oblige*—without calling it *noblesse oblige*. They just said, "Poor Emily. Her kinsfolk should come to her." She had some kin in Alabama; but years ago her father had fallen out with them over the estate of old lady Wyatt, the crazy woman, and there was no communication between the two families. They had not even been represented at the funeral.

And as soon as the old people said, "Poor Emily," the whispering began. "Do you suppose it's really so?" they said to one another. "Of course it is. What else could . . ." This behind their hands; rustling of craned silk and satin behind jalousies closed upon the sun of Sunday afternoon as the thin, swift clop-clop-clop of the matched team passed: "Poor Emily."

She carried her head high enough—even when we believed that she was fallen. It was as if she demanded more than ever the recognition of her dignity as the last Grierson; as if it had wanted that touch of earthiness to reaffirm her imperviousness. Like when she bought the rat poison, the arsenic. That was over a year after they had begun to say "Poor Emily," and while the two female cousins were visiting her.

"I want some poison," she said to the druggist. She was over thirty then, still a slight woman, though thinner than usual, with cold, haughty black eyes in a face the flesh of which was strained across the temples and about the eyesockets as you imagine a lighthouse-keeper's face ought to look. "I want some poison," she said.

"Yes, Miss Emily. What kind? For rats and such? I'd recom—"

"I want the best you have. I don't care what kind."

The druggist named several. "They'll kill anything up to an elephant. But what you want is—"

"Arsenic," Miss Emily said. "Is that a good one?"

"Is . . . arsenic? Yes ma'am. But what you want—"

"I want arsenic."

The druggist looked down at her. She looked back at him, erect, her face like a strained flag. "Why, of course," the druggist said. "If that's what you want. But the law requires you to tell what you are going to use it for."

Miss Emily just stared at him, her head tilted back in order to look him eye for eye, until he looked away and went and got the arsenic and wrapped it up. The Negro delivery boy brought her the package; the druggist didn't come back. When she opened the package at home there was written on the box, under the skull and bones: "For rats."

IV

So the next day we all said, "She will kill herself"; and we said it would be the best thing. When she had first begun to be seen with Homer Barron, we had said, "She will marry him." Then we said, "She will persuade him yet," because Homer himself had remarked—he liked men, and it was known that he drank with the younger men in the Elk's Club— that he was not a marrying man. Later we said, "Poor Emily," behind the jalousies as they passed on Sunday afternoon in the glittering buggy, Miss Emily with her head high and Homer Barron with his hat cocked and a cigar in his teeth, reins and whip in a yellow glove.

Then some of the ladies began to say that it was a disgrace to the town and a bad example to the young people. The men did not want to interfere, but at last the ladies forced the Baptist minister—Miss Emily's people were Episcopal—to call upon her. He would never divulge what happened during that interview, but he refused to go back again. The next Sunday they again drove about the streets, and the following day the minister's wife wrote to Miss Emily's relations in Alabama.

So she had blood-kin under her roof again and we sat back to watch developments. At first nothing happened. Then we were sure that they were to be married. We learned that Miss Emily had been to the jeweler's and ordered a man's toilet set in silver, with the letters H.B. on each piece. Two days later we learned that she had bought a complete outfit of men's clothing, including a nightshirt, and we said, "They are married." We were really glad. We were glad because the two female cousins were even more Grierson than Miss Emily had ever been.

So we were not surprised when Homer Barron—the streets had been finished some time since—was gone. We were a little disappointed that there was not a public blowing-off, but we believed that he had gone on to prepare for Miss Emily's coming, or to give her a chance to get rid of the cousins. (By that time it was a cabal, and we were all Miss Emily's allies to help circumvent the cousins.) Sure enough, after another week they departed. And, as we had expected all along, within three days Homer Barron was back in town. A neighbor saw the Negro man admit him at the kitchen door at dusk one evening.

And that was the last we saw of Homer Barron. And of Miss Emily for some time. The Negro man went in and out with the market basket, but the front door remained closed. Now and then we would see her at a window for a moment, as the men did that night when they sprinkled the lime, but for almost six months she did not appear on the streets. Then we knew that this was to be expected too; as if that quality of her father which had thwarted her woman's life so many times had been too virulent and too furious to die.

When we next saw Miss Emily, she had grown fat and her hair was turning gray. During the next few years it grew grayer and grayer until it attained an even pepper-and-salt iron-gray, when it ceased turning. Up to the day of her death at seventy-four it was still that vigorous iron-gray, like the hair of an active man.

From that time on her front door remained closed, save for a period of six or seven years, when she was about forty, during which she gave lessons in china-painting. She fitted up a studio in one of the downstairs rooms, where the daughters and granddaughters of Colonel Sartoris' contemporaries were sent to her with the same regularity and in the same spirit that they were sent on Sundays with a twenty-five cent piece for the collection plate. Meanwhile her taxes had been remitted.

Then the newer generation became the backbone and the spirit of the town, and the painting pupils grew up and fell away and did not send their children to her with boxes of color and tedious brushes and pictures cut from the ladies' magazines. The front door closed upon the last one and remained closed for good. When the town got free postal delivery Miss

Emily alone refused to let them fasten the metal numbers above her door and attach a mailbox to it. She would not listen to them.

Daily, monthly, yearly we watched the Negro grow grayer and more stooped, going in and out with the market basket. Each December we sent her a tax notice, which would be returned by the post office a week later, unclaimed. Now and then we would see her in one of the downstairs windows—she had evidently shut up the top floor of the house—like the carven torso of an idol in a niche, looking or not looking at us, we could never tell which. Thus she passed from generation to generation—dear, inescapable, impervious, tranquil, and perverse.

And so she died. Fell ill in the house filled with dust and shadows, with only a doddering Negro man to wait on her. We did not even know she was sick; we had long since given up trying to get any information from the Negro. He talked to no one, probably not even to her, for his voice had grown harsh and rusty, as if from disuse.

She died in one of the downstairs rooms, in a heavy walnut bed with a curtain, her gray head propped on a pillow yellow and moldy with age and lack of sunlight.

V

The Negro met the first of the ladies at the front door and let them in, with their hushed, sibilant voices and their quick, curious glances, and then he disappeared. He walked right through the house and out the back and was not seen again.

The two female cousins came at once. They held the funeral on the second day, with the town coming to look at Miss Emily beneath a mass of bought flowers, with the crayon face of her father musing profoundly above the bier and the ladies sibilant and macabre; and the very old men—some in their brushed Confederate uniforms—on the porch and the lawn, talking of Miss Emily as if she had been a contemporary of theirs, believing that they had danced with her and courted her perhaps, confusing time with its mathematical progression, as the old do, to whom all the past is not a diminishing road, but, instead, a huge meadow which no winter ever quite touches, divided from them now by the narrow bottleneck of the most recent decade of years.

Already we knew that there was one room in that region above stairs which no one had seen in forty years, and which would have to be forced. They waited until Miss Emily was decently in the ground before they opened it.

The violence of breaking down the door seemed to fill this room with pervading dust. A thin, acrid pall as of the tomb seemed to lie everywhere upon this room decked and furnished as for a bridal: upon the valance curtains of faded rose color, upon the rose-shaded lights, upon the dressing table, upon the delicate array of crystal and the man's toilet things backed with tarnished silver, silver so tarnished that the monogram was obscured.

Among them lay a collar and tie, as if they had just been removed, which, lifted, left upon the surface a pale crescent in the dust. Upon a chair hung the suit, carefully folded; beneath it the two mute shoes and the discarded socks.

The man himself lay in the bed.

For a long while we just stood there, looking down at the profound and fleshless grin. The body had apparently once laid in the attitude of an embrace, but now the long sleep that outlasts love, that conquers even the grimace of love, had cuckolded him. What was left of him, rotted beneath what was left of the nightshirt, had become inextricable from the bed in which he lay; and upon him and upon the pillow beside him lay that even coating of the patient and biding dust.

Then we noticed that in the second pillow was the indentation of a head. One of us lifted something from it, and leaning forward, that faint and invisible dust dry and acrid in the nostrils, we saw a long strand of iron-gray hair.

SOLDIER'S HOME
by Ernest Hemingway
(1899–1961)

Krebs went to the war from a Methodist college in Kansas. There is a picture which shows him among his fraternity brothers, all of them wearing exactly the same height and style collar. He enlisted in the Marines in 1917 and did not return to the United States until the second division returned from the Rhine in the summer of 1919.

There is a picture which shows him on the Rhine with two German girls and another corporal. Krebs and the corporal look too big for their uniforms. The German girls are not beautiful. The Rhine does not show in the picture.

By the time Krebs returned to his home town in Oklahoma the greeting of heroes was over. He came back much too late. The men from the town who had been drafted had all been welcomed elaborately on their return. There had been a great deal of hysteria. Now the reaction had set in. People seemed to think it was rather ridiculous for Krebs to be getting back so late, years after the war was over.

At first Krebs, who had been at Belleau Wood, Soissons, the Champagne, St. Mihiel and in the Argonne, did not want to talk about the war at all. Later he felt the need to talk but no one wanted to hear about it. His town had heard too many atrocity stories to be thrilled by actualities.

Krebs found that to be listened to at all he had to lie, and after he had done this twice he, too, had a reaction against the war and against talking about it. A distaste for everything that had happened to him in the war set in because of the lies he had told. All of the times that had been able to make him feel cool and clear inside himself when he thought of them; the times so long back when he had done the one thing, the only thing for a man to do, easily and naturally, when he might have done something else, now lost their cool, valuable quality and then were lost themselves.

His lies were quite unimportant lies and consisted in attributing to himself things other men had seen, done or heard of, and stating as facts certain apocryphal incidents familiar to all soldiers. Even his lies were not sensational at the pool room. His acquaintances, who had heard detailed accounts of German women found chained to machine guns in the Argonne forest and who could not comprehend, or were barred by their patriotism from interest in, any German machine gunners who were not chained, were not thrilled by his stories.

Krebs acquired the nausea in regard to experience that is the result of untruth or exaggeration, and when he occasionally met another man who had really been a soldier and they talked a few minutes in the dressing room at a dance he fell into the easy pose of the old soldier among other soldiers: that he had been badly, sickeningly frightened all the time. In this way he lost everything.

During this time, it was late summer, he was sleeping late in bed, getting up to walk down town to the library to get a book, eating lunch at home, reading on the front porch until he became bored and then walking down through the town to spend the hottest hours of the day in the cool dark of the pool room. He loved to play pool.

In the evening he practiced on his clarinet, strolled down town, read and went to bed. He was still a hero to his two young sisters. His mother would have given him breakfast in bed if he had wanted it. She often came in when he was in bed and asked him to tell her about the war, but her attention always wandered. His father was non-committal.

Before Krebs went away to the war he had never been allowed to drive the family motor car. His father was in the real estate business and always wanted the car to be at his command when he required it to take clients out into the country to show them a piece of farm property. The car always stood outside the First National Bank building where his father had an office on the second floor. Now, after the war, it was still the same car.

Nothing was changed in the town except that the young girls had grown up. But they lived in such a complicated world of already defined alliances and shifting feuds that Krebs did not feel the energy or the courage to break into it. He liked to look at them, though. There were so many good-looking young girls. Most of them had their hair cut short. When he went away only little girls wore their hair like that or girls that were fast. They all wore sweaters and shirt waists with round Dutch collars. It was a pattern. He liked to look at them from the front porch as they walked on the other side of the street. He liked to watch them walking under the shade of the trees. He liked the round Dutch collars above their sweaters. He liked their silk stockings and flat shoes. He liked their bobbed hair and the way they walked.

When he was in town their appeal to him was not very strong. He did not like them when he saw them in the Greek's ice cream parlor. He did not want them themselves really. They were too complicated. There was something else. Vaguely he wanted a girl but he did not want to have to work to get her. He would have liked to have a girl but he did not want to have to spend a long time getting her. He did not want to get into the intrigue and the politics. He did not want to have to do any courting. He did not want to tell any more lies. It wasn't worth it.

He did not want any consequences. He did not want any consequences ever again. He wanted to live along without consequences. Besides he did not really need a girl. The army had taught him that. It was all right to pose as though you had to have a girl. Nearly everybody did that. But it wasn't true. You did not need a girl. That was the funny thing. First a fellow boasted how girls mean nothing to him, that he never thought of them, that they could not touch him. Then a fellow boasted that he could not get along without girls, that he had to have them all the time, that he could not go to sleep without them.

That was all a lie. It was all a lie both ways. You did not need a girl unless you thought about them. He learned that in the army. Then sooner or later you always got one. When you were really ripe for a girl you always got one. You did not have to think about it. Sooner or later it would come. He had learned that in the army.

Now he would have liked a girl if she had come to him and not wanted to talk. But here at home it was all too complicated. He knew he could never get through it all again. It was not worth the trouble. That was the thing about French girls and German girls. There was not all this talking. You couldn't talk much and you did not need to talk. It was simple and you were friends. He thought about France and then he began to think about Germany. On the whole he had liked Germany better. He did not want to leave Germany. He did not want to come home. Still, he had come home. He sat on the front porch.

He liked the girls that were walking along the other side of the street. He liked the look of them much better than the French girls or the German girls. But the world they were in was not the world he was in. He would like to have one of them. But it was not worth it. They were such a nice pattern. He liked the pattern. It was exciting. But he would not go through all the talking. He did not want one badly enough. He liked to look at them all, though. It was not worth it. Not now when things were getting good again.

He sat there on the porch reading a book on the war. It was a history and he was reading about all the engagements he had been in. It was the most interesting reading he had ever done. He wished there were more maps. He looked forward with a good feeling to reading all the really good histories when they would come out with good detail maps. Now he was really learning about the war. He had been a good soldier. That made a difference.

One morning after he had been home about a month his mother came into his bedroom and sat on the bed. She smoothed her apron.

"I had a talk with your father last night, Harold," she said, "and he is willing for you to take the car out in the evenings."

"Yeah?" said Krebs, who was not fully awake. "Take the car out? Yeah?"

"Yes. Your father has felt for some time that you should be able to take the car out in the evenings whenever you wished but we only talked it over last night."

"I'll bet you made him," Krebs said.

"No. It was your father's suggestion that we talk the matter over."

"Yeah. I'll bet you made him," Krebs sat up in bed.

"Will you come down to breakfast, Harold?" his mother said.

"As soon as I get my clothes on," Krebs said.

His mother went out of the room and he could hear her frying something downstairs while he washed, shaved and dressed to go down into the dining-room for breakfast. While he was eating breakfast his sister brought in the mail.

"Well, Hare," she said. "You old sleepyhead. What do you ever get up for?"

Krebs looked at her. He liked her. She was his best sister.

"Have you got the paper?" he asked.

She handed him the Kansas City *Star* and he shucked off its brown wrapper and opened it to the sporting page. He folded the *Star* open and propped it against the water pitcher with his cereal dish to steady it, so he could read while he ate.

"Harold," his mother stood in the kitchen doorway, "Harold, please don't muss up the paper. Your father can't read his *Star* if it's been mussed."

"I won't muss it," Krebs said.

His sister sat down at the table and watched him while he read.

"We're playing indoor over at school this afternoon," she said. "I'm going to pitch."

"Good," said Krebs. "How's the old wing?"

"I can pitch better than lots of the boys. I tell them all you taught me. The other girls aren't much good."

"Yeah?" said Krebs.

"I tell them all you're my beau. Aren't you my beau, Hare?"

"You bet."

"Couldn't your brother really be your beau just because he's your brother?"

"I don't know."

"Sure you know. Couldn't you be my beau, Hare, if I was old enough and if you wanted to?"

"Sure. You're my girl now."

"Am I really your girl?"

"Sure."

"Do you love me?"

"Uh, huh."

"Will you love me always?"

"Sure."

"Will you come over and watch me play indoor?"

"Maybe."

"Aw, Hare, you don't love me. If you loved me, you'd want to come over and watch me play indoor."

Krebs' mother came into the dining room from the kitchen. She carried a plate with two fried eggs and some crisp bacon on it and a plate of buckwheat cakes.

"You run along, Helen," she said. "I want to talk to Harold."

She put the eggs and bacon down in front of him and brought in a jug of maple syrup for the buckwheat cakes. Then she sat down across the table from Krebs.

"I wish you'd put down the paper a minute, Harold," she said.

Krebs took down the paper and folded it.

"Have you decided what you are going to do yet, Harold?" his mother said, taking off her glasses.

"No," said Krebs.

"Don't you think it's about time?" His mother did not say this in a mean way. She seemed worried.

"I hadn't thought about it," Krebs said.

"God has some work for everyone to do," his mother said. "There can be no idle hands in His Kingdom."

"I'm not in His Kingdom," Krebs said.

"We are all of us in His Kingdom."

Krebs felt embarrassed and resentful as always.

"I've worried about you so much, Harold," his mother went on. "I know the temptations you must have been exposed to. I know how weak men are. I know what your own dear grandfather, my own father, told us about the Civil War and I have prayed for you. I pray for you all day long, Harold."

Krebs looked at the bacon fat hardening on his plate.

"Your father is worried, too," his mother went on. "He thinks you have lost your ambition, that you haven't got a definite aim in life. Charley

Simmons, who is just your age, has a good job and is going to be married. The boys are all settling down; they're all determined to get somewhere; you can see that boys like Charley Simmons are on their way to being really a credit to the community."

Krebs said nothing.

"Don't look that way, Harold," his mother said. "You know we love you and I want to tell you for your own good how matters stand. Your father does not want to hamper your freedom. He thinks you should be allowed to drive the car. If you want to take some of the nice girls out riding with you, we are only too pleased. We want you to enjoy yourself. But you are going to have to settle down to work, Harold. Your father doesn't care what you start in at. All work is honorable as he says. But you've got to make a start at something. He asked me to speak to you this morning and then you can stop in and see him at his office."

"Is that all?" Krebs said.

"Yes. Don't you love your mother, dear boy?"

"No," Krebs said.

His mother looked at him across the table. Her eyes were shiny. She started crying.

"I don't love anybody," Krebs said.

It wasn't any good. He couldn't tell her, he couldn't make her see it. It was silly to have said it. He had only hurt her. He went over and took hold of her arm. She was crying with her head in her hands.

"I didn't mean it," he said. "I was just angry at something. I didn't mean I didn't love you."

His mother went on crying. Krebs put his arm on her shoulder.

"Can't you believe me, mother?"

His mother shook her head.

"Please, please, mother. Please believe me."

"All right," his mother said chokily. She looked up at him. "I believe you, Harold."

Krebs kissed her hair. She put her face up to him.

"I'm your mother," she said. "I held you next to my heart when you were a tiny baby."

Krebs felt sick and vaguely nauseated.

"I know, Mummy," he said. "I'll try and be a good boy for you."

"Would you kneel and pray with me, Harold?" his mother asked.

They knelt down beside the dining-room table and Krebs' mother prayed.

"Now, you pray, Harold," she said.

"I can't," Krebs said.

"Try, Harold."

"I can't."

"Do you want me to pray for you?"

"Yes."

So his mother prayed for him and then they stood up and Krebs kissed his mother and went out of the house. He had tried so to keep his life from being complicated. Still, none of it had touched him. He had felt sorry for his mother and she had made him lie. He would go to Kansas City and get a job and she would feel all right about it. There would be one more scene maybe before he got away. He would not go down to his father's office. He would miss that one. He wanted his life to go smoothly. It had just gotten going that way. Well, that was all over now, anyway. He would go over to the schoolyard and watch Helen play indoor baseball.

THANK YOU, M'AM
by Langston Hughes
(b. 1902)

She was a large woman with a large purse that had everything in it but a hammer and nails. It had a long strap, and she carried it slung across her shoulder. It was about eleven o'clock at night, dark, and she was walking alone, when a boy ran up behind her and tried to snatch her purse. The strap broke with the sudden single tug the boy gave it from behind. But the boy's weight and the weight of the purse combined caused him to lose his balance. Instead of taking off full blast as he had hoped, the boy fell on his back on the sidewalk and his legs flew up. The large woman simply turned around and kicked him right square in his blue-jeaned sitter. Then she reached down, picked the boy up by his shirt front, and shook him until his teeth rattled.

After that the woman said, "Pick up my pocketbook, boy, and give it here."

She still held him tightly. But she bent down enough to permit him to stoop and pick up her purse. Then she said, "Now ain't you ashamed of yourself?"

Firmly gripped by his shirt front, the boy said, "Yes'm."

The woman said, "What did you want to do it for?"

The boy said, "I didn't aim to."

She said, "You a lie!"

By that time two or three people passed, stopped, turned to look, and some stood watching.

"If I turn you loose, will you run?" asked the woman.

"Yes'm," said the boy.

"Then I won't turn you loose," said the woman. She did not release him.

"Lady, I'm sorry," whispered the boy.

"Um-hum! Your face if dirty. I got a great mind to wash your face for you. Ain't you got nobody home to tell you to wash your face?"

"No'm," said the boy.

"Then it will get washed this evening," said the large woman, starting up the street, dragging the frightened boy behind her.

He looked as if he were fourteen or fifteen, frail and willow-wild, in tennis shoes and blue jeans.

The woman said, "You ought to be my son. I would teach you right from wrong. Least I can do right now is to wash your face. Are you hungry?"

"No'm," said the being-dragged boy. "I just want you to turn me loose."

"Was I bothering *you* when I turned that corner?" asked the woman.

"No'm."

"But you put yourself in contact with *me*," said the woman. "If you think that that contact is not going to last awhile, you got another thought coming. When I get through with you, sir, you are going to remember Mrs. Luella Bates Washington Jones."

Sweat popped out on the boy's face and he began to struggle. Mrs. Jones stopped, jerked him around in front of her, put a half nelson about his neck, and continued to drag him up the street. When she got to her door, she dragged the boy inside, down a hall, and into a large kitchenette-furnished room at the rear of the house. She switched on the light and left the door open. The boy could hear other roomers laughing and talking in the large house. Some of their doors were open, too, so he knew he and the woman were not alone. The woman still had him by the neck in the middle of her room.

She said, "What is your name?"

"Roger," answered the boy.

"Then, Roger, you go to that sink and wash your face," said the woman, whereupon she turned him loose—at last. Roger looked at the door—looked at the woman—looked at the door—*and went to the sink*.

"Let the water run until it gets warm," she said. "Here's a clean towel."

"You gonna take me to jail?" asked the boy, bending over the sink.

"Not with that face, I would not take you nowhere," said the woman. "Here I am trying to get home to cook me a bite to eat, and you snatch my pocketbook! Maybe you ain't been to your supper either, late as it be. Have you?"

"There's nobody home at my house," said the boy.

"Then we'll eat," said the woman. "I believe you're hungry—or been hungry—to try to snatch my pocketbook!"

"I want a pair of blue suede shoes," said the boy.

"Well, you didn't have to snatch *my* pocketbook to get some suede shoes," said Mrs. Luella Bates Washington Jones. "You could of asked me."

"M'am?"

The water dripping from his face, the boy looked at her. There was a long pause. A very long pause. After he had dried his face, and not knowing what else to do, dried it again, the boy turned around, wondering what next. The door was open. He could make a dash for it down the hall. He could, run, run, run, *run!*

The woman was sitting on the daybed. After a while she said, "I were young once and I wanted things I could not get."

There was another long pause. The boy's mouth opened. Then he frowned, not knowing he frowned.

The woman said, "Um-hum! You thought I was going to say *but*, didn't you? You thought I was going to say, *but I didn't snatch people's pocketbooks*. Well, I wasn't going to say that." Pause. Silence. "I have done things, too, which I would not tell you, son—neither tell God, if He didn't already know. Everybody's got something in common. So you set down while I fix us something to eat. You might run that comb through your hair so you will look presentable."

In another corner of the room behind a screen was a gas plate and an icebox. Mrs. Jones got up and went behind the screen. The woman did not watch the boy to see if he was going to run now, nor did she watch her purse, which she left behind her on the daybed. But the boy took care to sit on the far side of the room, away from the purse, where he thought she could easily see him out of the corner of her eye if she wanted to. He did not trust the woman *not* to trust him. And he did not want to be mistrusted now.

"Do you need somebody to go to the store," asked the boy, "maybe to get some milk or something?"

"Don't believe I do," said the woman, "unless you just want sweet milk yourself. I was going to make cocoa out of this canned milk I got here."

"That will be fine," said the boy.

She heated some lima beans and ham she had in the icebox, made the cocoa, and set the table. The woman did not *ask* the boy anything about where he lived, or his folks, or anything else that would embarrass him. Instead, as they ate, she told him about her job in a hotel beauty shop that stayed open late, what the work was like, and how all kinds of women came in and out, blondes, redheads, and Spanish. Then she cut him a half of her ten-cent cake.

"Eat some more, son," she said.

When they were finished eating, she got up and said, "Now here, take this ten dollars and buy yourself some blue suede shoes. And next time, do not make the mistake of latching onto *my* pocketbook *nor nobody else's*—because shoes got by devilish ways will burn your feet. I got to get my rest now. But from here on in, son, I hope you will behave yourself."

She led him down the hall to the front door and opened it. "Good night! Behave yourself, boy!" she said, looking out into the street as he went down the steps.

The boy wanted to say something other than, "Thank you, m'am," to Mrs. Luella Bates Washington Jones, but although his lips moved, he couldn't even say that as he turned at the foot of the barren stoop and looked up at the large woman in the door. Then she shut the door.

JUDAS
by Frank O'Connor
(1903–66)

I'll forget a lot of things before I forget that night. As I was going out the mother said: "Sure, you won't be late, Jerry?" and I only laughed at her and said: "Am I ever late?" As I went down the road I was thinking it was months since I had taken her to the pictures. You might think that funny, Michael John, but after the father's death we were thrown together a lot. And I knew she hated being alone in the house after dark.

At the same time I had troubles of my own. You see, Michael John, being an only child, I never knocked round with girls the way others did. All the chaps in the office went with girls, or at any rate they let on they did. They said: "Who was the old doll I saw you with last night, Jerry? Aha, Jerry, you'd better mind yourself, boy, or you'll be getting into trouble!" Paddy Kinnane, for instance, talked like that, and he never saw how it upset me. I think he thought it was a great compliment. It wasn't until years after that I began to suspect that Paddy's acquaintance with dolls was about of one kind with my own.

Then I met Kitty Doherty. Kitty was a hospital nurse, and all the chaps in the office said a fellow should never go with hospital nurses—they knew too much. I knew when I met Kitty that that was a lie. She was a well-educated, superior girl; she lived up the river in a posh locality, and her mother was on all sorts of councils and committees. She was small and wiry; a good-looking girl, always in good humor, and when she talked, she hopped from one thing to another like a robin on a frosty morning.

Anyway, she had me dazzled. I used to meet her in the evenings up the river road, as if I was walking there by accident and very surprised to see her. "Fancy meeting you!" I'd say, or "Well, well, isn't this a great surprise?" Then we'd stand talking for half an hour and I'd see her home. Several times she asked me in, but I was too nervous. I knew I'd lose my head, break the china, use some dirty word, and then go home and cut my throat. Of course, I never asked her to come to the pictures or anything like that. I knew she was above that. My only hope was that if I waited long enough I might be able to save her from drowning, the White Slave Traffic, or something of the sort. That would show in a modest, dignified way how I felt about her. Of course, I knew at the same time I ought to stay at home more with the mother, but the very thought that I might be missing an opportunity like that would be enough to spoil a whole evening on me.

This night in particular I was nearly distracted. It was three weeks since I'd seen Kitty. You know what three weeks are at that age. I was sure that at the very least the girl was dying and asking for me and that no one knew my address. A week before, I'd felt I simply couldn't bear it any longer, so I made an excuse and went down to the post office. I rang up the hospital and asked for her. I fully expected them to say that she was dead, and I got a shock when the girl at the other end asked my name. "I'm afraid," I said, "I'm a stranger to Miss Doherty, but I have an important message for her." Then I got completely panic-stricken. What could a girl like Kitty make of a damned deliberate lie like that? What else was it but a trap laid by an old and cunning hand. I held the receiver out and looked at it. "Moynihan," I said to it, "you're mad. An asylum, Moynihan, is the only place for a fellow like you." Then I heard her voice, not in my ear at all, but in the telephone booth as if she were standing before me, and I nearly dropped the receiver with terror. I put it to my ear and asked in a disguised voice: "Who is that speaking, please?" "This is Kitty Doherty," she said rather impatiently. "Who are you?" "I am Monsieur Bertrand," said I, speaking in what I hoped was a French accent. "I am afraid I have de wrong number." Then I put down the receiver carefully and thought how nice it would be if only I had a penknife handy to cut my throat with. It's funny, but from the moment I met Kitty I was always coveting sharp things like razors and penknives.

After that an awful idea dawned on my mind. Of course, I should have thought of it before, but, as you've probably guessed, I wasn't exactly knowledgeable. I began to see that I wasn't meeting Kitty for the very good reason that Kitty didn't want to meet me. That filled me with terror. I examined my conscience to find out what I might have said to her. You know what conscience is at that age. I remembered every remark I'd made and they were all brutal, indecent or disgusting. I had talked of Paddy Kinnane as a fellow who "went with dolls." What could a pure-minded girl think of a chap who naturally used such a phrase except—what, unfortunately, was true—that he had a mind like a cesspit.

It was a lovely summer evening, with views of hillsides and fields between the gaps in the houses, and that raised my spirits a bit. Maybe I was wrong, maybe she hadn't found out the sort I was and wasn't avoiding me, maybe we might meet and walk home together. I walked the full length of the river road and back, and then started off to walk it again. The crowds were thinning out as fellows and girls slipped off up the lanes or down to the river. As the streets went out like lamps about me I grew desperate. I saw clearly that she was avoiding me; that she knew I wasn't the quiet, good-natured chap I let on to be but a volcano of brutality and lust. "Lust, lust, lust!" I hissed to myself, clenching my fists.

Then I glanced up and saw her on a tram. I forgot instantly about the lust and smiled and waved my cap at her, but she was looking ahead and didn't see me. I ran after the car, intending to jump on it, to sit on one of the back seats on top and then say as she was getting off: "Fancy meeting you here!" (Trams were always a bit of a problem. If you sat beside a girl and paid for her, it might be considered forward; if you didn't it looked mean. I never quite knew.) But as if the driver knew what was in my mind, he put on speed and away went the tram, tossing and screeching down the straight, and I stood panting in the middle of the road, smiling as if missing a tram was the best joke in the world and wishing all the time I had the penknife and the courage to use it. My position was hopeless. Then I must have gone a bit mad, for I started to race the tram. There were still lots of people out walking, and they stared after me, so I lifted my fists to my chest in the attitude of a professional runner and dropped into a comfortable stride which I hoped vaguely would delude them into the belief that I was in training for a big race.

Between the running and the halts I just managed to keep the tram in view all the way through town and out at the other side. When I saw Kitty get off and go up a hilly street I collapsed and was just able to drag myself after her. When she went into a house on a terrace I sat on the curb with my head between my knees till the panting stopped. At any rate I felt safe. I could now walk up and down before the house till she came out, and accost her with an innocent smile and say: "Fancy meeting you!"

But my luck was dead out that night. As I was walking up and down out of range of the house I saw a tall chap come strolling up at the opposite side and my heart sank. It was Paddy Kinnane.

"Hullo, Jerry," he chuckled with that knowing grin he put on whenever he wanted to compliment you on being discovered in a compromising situation, "what are you doing here?"

"Ah, just waiting for a chap I had a date with, Paddy," I said, trying to sound casual.

"Begor," said Paddy, "you look to me more like a man that was waiting for an old doll. Still waters run deep. . . . What time are you supposed to be meeting him?"

"Half eight," I said at random.

"Half eight?" said Paddy in surprise. " 'Tis nearly nine now."

"I know," said I, "but as I waited so long I may as well give him another few minutes."

"Ah, I'll wait along with you," said Paddy, leaning against the wall and taking out a packet of fags. "You might find yourself stuck by the end of the evening. There's people in this town and they have no consideration for anyone."

That was Paddy all out; no trouble was too much for him if he could do you a good turn.

"As he kept me so long," I said hastily, "I don't think I'll bother with him. It only struck me this very minute that there's a chap up the Asragh road that I have to see on urgent business. You'll excuse me, Paddy. I'll tell you about it another time."

And away I went hell for leather to the tram. When I reached the tram-stop below Kitty's house I sat on the river wall in the dusk. The moon was rising, and every quarter of an hour the trams came grunting and squeaking over the old bridge and then went black out while the conductors switched the trolleys. I stood on the curb in the moonlight searching for Kitty. Then a bobby came along, and as he seemed to be watching me, I slung slowly off up the hill and stood against a wall in the shadow. There was a high wall at the other side too, and behind it the roofs of a house shining in the moon. Every now and then a tram would come in and people would pass in the moonlight, and the snatches of conversation I caught were like the warmth from an open door to the heart of a homeless man. It was quite clear now that my position was hopeless. The last tram came and went, and still there was no Kitty and still I hung on.

Then I heard a woman's step. I couldn't even pretend to myself that it might be Kitty till she shuffled past me with that hasty little walk of hers. I started and called out her name; she glanced over her shoulder and, seeing a man emerging from the shadow, took fright and ran. I ran too, but she put on speed and began to outdistance me. At that I despaired. I stood on the pavement and shouted after her at the top of my voice.

"Kitty!" I cried. "Kitty, for God's sake, wait for me!"

She ran a few steps further and then halted, turned, and came back slowly down the path.

"Jerry Moynihan!" she whispered, lifting her two arms to her breasts as if I had found her with nothing on. "What in God's name are you doing here?"

I was summoning up strength to tell her that I just happened to be taking a stroll in that direction and was astonished to see her when I realized the improbability of it and began to cry instead. Then I laughed. I suppose it was nerves. But Kitty had had a bad fright and now that she was getting over it she was as cross as two sticks.

"What's wrong with you, I say," she snapped. "Are you out of your senses or what?"

"Well, you see," I stammered awkwardly, half in dread I was going to cry again, "I didn't see you in town."

"No," she replied with a shrug, "I know you didn't. I wasn't out. What about it?"

"I thought it might be something I said to you," I said desperately.

"No," said Kitty candidly, "it wasn't anything to do with you. It's Mother."

"Why?" I asked almost joyously. "Is there something wrong with her?"

"I don't mean that," said Kitty impatiently. "It's just that she made such a fuss, I felt it wasn't worth it."

"But what did she make a fuss about?" I asked.

"About you, of course," said Kitty in exasperation. "What did you think?"

"But what did I do?" I asked, clutching my head. This was worse than anything I'd ever imagined. This was terrible.

"You didn't do anything," said Kitty, "but people were talking about us. And you wouldn't come in and be introduced to her like anyone else. I know she's a bit of a fool, and her head is stuffed with old nonsense about her family. I could never see that they were different to anyone else, and anyway, she married a commercial herself, so she has nothing much to boast about. Still, you needn't be so superior. There's no obligation to buy, you know."

I didn't. There were cold shivers running through me. I had thought of Kitty as a secret between God, herself, and me and that she only knew the half of it. Now it seemed I didn't even know the half. People were talking about us! I was superior! What next?

"But what has she against me?" I asked despairingly.

"She thinks we're doing a tangle, of course," snapped Kitty as if she was astonished at my stupidity, "and I suppose she imagines you're not grand enough for a great-great-grandniece of Daniel O'Connell. I told her you were a different sort of fellow entirely and above all that sort of thing, but she wouldn't believe me. She said I was a deep, callous, crafty little intriguer and that I hadn't a drop of Daniel O'Connell's blood in my veins." Kitty began to giggle at the thought of herself as an intriguer.

"That's all she knows," I said bitterly.

"I know," said Kitty with a shrug. "The woman has no sense. And anyway she has no reason to think I'm telling lies. Cissy and I always had fellows, and we spooned with them all over the shop under her very nose, so why should she think I'm lying to her now?"

At that I began to laugh like an idiot. This was worse than appalling. This was a nightmare. Kitty, whom I had thought so angelic, talking in cold blood about "spooning" with fellows all over the house. Even the bad women in the books I'd read didn't talk about love in that cold-blooded way. Madame Bovary herself had at least the decency to pretend that she didn't like it. It was like another door opening on the outside world, but Kitty thought I was laughing at her and started to apologize.

"Of course I had no sense," she said. "You're the first fellow I ever met that treated me properly. The others only wanted to fool around with me, and now because I don't like it, Mother thinks I'm getting stuck-up. I told her I liked you better than any fellow I knew, but that I'd grown out of all that sort of thing."

"And what did she say to that?" I asked fiercely. It was—how can I describe it?—like a man who'd lived all his life in a dungeon getting into the sunlight for the first time and afraid of every shadow.

"Ah, I told you the woman was silly," said Kitty, getting embarrassed.

"Go on!" I shouted. "I want to know everything. I insist on knowing everything."

"Well," said Kitty with a demure little grin, "she said you were a deep, designing guttersnipe who knew exactly how to get round feather-pated little idiots like me. . . . You see," she added with another shrug, "it's quite hopeless. The woman is common. She doesn't understand."

"But I tell you she does understand," I shouted frantically. "She understands better than you do. I only wish to God I was deep and designing so that I'd have some chance with you."

"Do you really?" asked Kitty, opening her eyes wide. "To tell you the truth," she added after a moment, "I thought you were a bit keen the first time, but then I didn't know. When you didn't kiss me or anything, I mean."

"God," I said bitterly, "when I think of what I've been through in the past couple of weeks!"

"I know," said Kitty, biting her lip. "I was the same." And then we said nothing for a few moments.

"You're sure you're serious?" she asked suspiciously.

"I tell you, girl," I shouted, "I was on the point of committing suicide."

"What good would that be?" she asked with another shrug, and then she looked at me and laughed outright—the little jade!

It is all as clear in my mind as if it had happened last night. I told Kitty about my prospects. She didn't care, but I insisted on telling her. It was as if a stone had been lifted off my heart, and I went home in the moonlight singing. Then I heard the clock strike, and the singing stopped. I remembered the mother at home, waiting, and began to run again. This was desperation too, but a different sort.

The door was ajar and the kitchen in darkness. I saw her sitting before the fire by herself, and just as I was going to throw my arms about her, I smelt Kitty's perfume round me and was afraid to go near her. God help us, as if it would have told her anything!

"Hallo, Mum," I said with a laugh, rubbing my hands, "you're all in darkness."

"You'll have a cup of tea?" she said.

"I might as well," said I.

"What time is it?" she said, lighting the gas. "You're very late."

"Ah, I met a fellow from the office," I said, but at the same time I was stung by the complaint in her tone.

"You frightened me," she said with a little whimper. "I didn't know what happened to you. What kept you at all?"

"Oh, what do you think?" I said, goaded into retorting. "Drinking and blackguarding as usual."

I could have bitten my tongue off when I'd said it; it sounded so cruel, as if some stranger had said it instead of me. She turned to me for a moment with a frightened stare as if she was seeing the stranger too, and somehow I couldn't bear it.

"God Almighty," I said, "a fellow can have no life in his own house," and away with me upstairs.

I lit the candle, undressed and got into bed. I was wild. A chap could be a drunkard and blackguard and not be made to suffer more reproach than I was for being late one single night. That, I felt, was what you got for being a good son.

"Jerry," she called from the foot of the stairs, "will I bring you up your cup?"

"I don't want it now, thanks," I said.

I heard her give a heavy sigh and turn away. Then she locked the two doors front and back. She didn't wash up, and I knew my cup of tea was standing there on the table with a saucer on top in case I changed my mind. She came slowly up the stairs, and she walked like an old woman. I blew out the candle before she reached the landing in case she came into ask me if I wanted anything else, and the moonlight came in the attic window and brought me memories of Kitty. But every time I tried to imagine her face while she grinned up at me, waiting for me to kiss her, it was the mother's face that came up with that look like a child's when you strike him the first time—as if he suddenly saw the stranger in you. I remembered all our life together from the night the father—God rest him!—died; our early Mass on Sunday; our visits to the pictures; our plans for the future, and Christ, Michael John, it was as if I was inside her mind and she sitting by the fire, waiting for the blow to fall! And now it had fallen, and I was a stranger to her, and nothing I ever did could make us the same to each other again. There was something like a cannon-ball stuck in my chest, and I lay awake till the cocks started crowing. Then I couldn't bear it any longer. I went out on to the landing and listened.

"Are you awake, Mother?" I asked in a whisper.

"What is it, Jerry?" she said in alarm, and I knew she hadn't slept any more than I had.

"I only came to say I was sorry," I said, opening the room door, and then as I saw her sitting up in bed under the Sacred Heart lamp, the cannon-ball burst inside me and I began to bawl like a kid.

"Oh, child, child," she cried out, "what are you crying for at all, my little boy?" and she spread out her arms to me. I went to her and she hugged me and rocked me just as she did when I was only a nipper. "Oh, oh, oh," she was saying to herself in a whisper, "my storeen bawn, my little man!"—all the names she hadn't called me since I was a kid. That was all we said. I couldn't bring myself to tell her what I'd done, and she wouldn't confess to me that she was jealous; all she could do was to try and comfort me for the way I'd hurt her, to make up to me for the nature she'd given me. "My storeen bawn," she said. "My little man!"

THE MAN CHILD
by James Baldwin
(b. 1924)

As the sun began preparing for her exit, and he sensed the waiting night, Eric, blond and eight years old and dirty and tired, started homeward across the fields. Eric lived with his father, who was a farmer and the son of a farmer, and his mother, who had been captured by his father on some far-off, unblessed, unbelievable night, who had never since burst her chains. She did not know that she was chained anymore than she knew that she lived in terror of the night. One child was in the churchyard, it would have been Eric's little sister and her name would have been Sophie: for a long time, then, his mother had been very sick and pale. It was said that she would never, really, be better, that she would never again be as she had been. Then, not long ago, there had begun to be a pounding in his mother's belly, Eric had sometimes been able to hear it when he lay against her breast. His father had been pleased. *I did that*, said his father, big, laughing, dreadful, and red, and Eric knew how it was done, he had seen the horses and the blind and dreadful bulls. But then, again, his mother had been sick, she had had to be sent away, and when she came back the pounding was not there anymore, nothing was there anymore. His father laughed less, something in his mother's face seemed to have gone to sleep forever.

Eric hurried, for the sun was almost gone and he was afraid the night would catch him in the fields. And his mother would be angry. She did not really like him to go wandering off by himself. She would have forbidden it completely and kept Eric under her eye all day but in this she was overruled: Eric's father liked to think of Eric as being curious about the world and as being daring enough to explore it, with his own eyes, by himself.

His father would not be at home. He would be gone with his friend, Jamie, who was also a farmer and the son of a farmer, down to the tavern. This tavern was called The Rafters. They went each night, as his father said, imitating an Englishman he had known during a war, *to destruct The Rafters, sir.* They had been destructing The Rafters long before Eric had kicked in his mother's belly, for Eric's father and Jamie had grown up together, gone to war together, and survived together—never, apparently, while life ran, were they to be divided. They worked in the fields all day together, the fields which belonged to Eric's father. Jamie had been forced to sell his farm and it was Eric's father who had bought it.

Jamie had a brown and yellow dog. This dog was almost always with him; whenever Eric thought of Jamie he thought also of the dog. They had always been there, they had always been together: in exactly the same way, for Eric, that his mother and father had always been together, in exactly the same way that the earth and the trees and the sky were together. Jamie and his dog walked the country roads together, Jamie walking slowly in the way of country people, seeming to see nothing, heads lightly bent, feet striking surely and heavily on the earth, never stumbling. He walked as though he were going to walk to the other end of the world and knew it was a long way but knew that he would be there by the morning. Sometimes he talked to his dog, head bent a little more than usual and turned to one side, a slight smile playing about the edges of his granite lips; and the dog's head snapped up, perhaps he leapt upon his master, who cuffed him down lightly, with one hand. More often he was silent. His head was carried in a cloud of blue smoke from his pipe. Through this cloud, like a ship on a foggy day, loomed his dry and steady face. Set far back, at an unapproachable angle, were those eyes of his, smoky and thoughtful, eyes which seemed always to be considering the horizon. He had the kind of eyes which no one had ever looked into—except Eric, only once. Jamie had been walking these roads and across these fields, whistling for his dog in the evenings as he turned away from Eric's house, for years, in silence. He had been married once, but his wife had run away. Now he lived alone in a wooden house and Eric's mother kept his clothes clean and Jamie always ate at Eric's house.

Eric had looked into Jamie's eyes on Jamie's birthday. They had had a party for him. Eric's mother had baked a cake and filled the house with flowers. The doors and windows of the great kitchen all stood open on the yard and the kitchen table was placed outside. The ground was not muddy as it was in winter, but hard, dry, and light brown. The flowers his mother so loved and so labored for flamed in their narrow borders against the stone wall of the farmhouse; and green vines covered the grey stone wall at the far end of the yard. Beyond this wall were the fields and barns, and Eric could see, quite far away, the cows nearly motionless in the bright green pasture. It was a bright, hot, silent day, the sun did not seem to be moving at all.

This was before his mother had had to be sent away. Her belly had been beginning to grow big, she had been dressed in blue, and had seemed —that day, to Eric—younger than she was ever to seem again.

Though it was still early when they were called to table, Eric's father and Jamie were already tipsy and came across the fields, shoulders touching, laughing, and telling each other stories. To express disapproval and also, perhaps, because she had heard their stories before and was bored, Eric's mother was quite abrupt with them, barely saying, "Happy Birthday, Jamie" before she made them sit down. In the nearby village church bells rang as they began to eat.

It was perhaps because it was Jamie's birthday that Eric was held by something in Jamie's face. Jamie, of course, was very old. He was thirty-four today, even older than Eric's father, who was only thirty-two. Eric wondered how it felt to have so many years and was suddenly, secretly glad that he was only eight. For today, Jamie *looked* old. It was perhaps the one additional year which had done it, this day, before their very eyes—a metamorphosis which made Eric rather shrink at the prospect of becoming nine. The skin of Jamie's face, which had never before seemed so, seemed wet today, and that rocky mouth of his was loose; loose was the word for everything about him, the way his arms and shoulders hung, the way he sprawled at the table, rocking slightly back and forth. It was not that he was drunk. Eric had seen him much drunker. Drunk, he became rigid, as though he imagined himself in the army again. No. He was old. It had come upon him all at once, today, on his birthday. He sat there, his hair in his eyes, eating, drinking, laughing now and again, and in a very strange way, and teasing the dog at his feet so that it sleepily growled and snapped all through the birthday dinner.

"Stop that," said Eric's father.

"Stop what?" asked Jamie.

"Let that stinking useless dog alone. Let him be quiet."

"Leave the beast alone," said Eric's mother—very wearily, sounding as she often sounded when talking to Eric.

"Well, now," said Jamie, grinning, and looking first at Eric's father and then at Eric's mother, "it *is* my beast. And a man's got a right to do as he likes with whatever's his."

"That dog's got a right to bite you, too," said Eric's mother, shortly.

"This dog's not going to bite me," said Jamie, "he knows I'll shoot him if he does."

"That dog knows you're not going to shoot him," said Eric's father. "Then you *would* be all alone."

"All alone," said Jamie, and looked around the table. "All alone." He lowered his eyes to his plate. Eric's father watched him. He said, "It's pretty serious to be all alone at *your* age." He smiled. "If I was you, I'd start thinking about it."

"I'm thinking about it," said Jamie. He began to grow red.

"No, you're not," said Eric's father, "you're dreaming about it."

"Well, goddammit," said Jamie, even redder now, "it isn't as though I haven't tried!"

"Ah," said Eric's father, "that was a *real* dream, that was. I used to pick *that* up on the streets of town every Saturday night."

"Yes," said Jamie. "I bet you did."

"I didn't think she was as bad as all that," said Eric's mother, quietly. "*I* liked her. I was surprised when she ran away."

"Jamie didn't know how to keep her," said Eric's father. He looked at Eric and chanted: "*Jamie, Jamie, pumpkin-eater, had a wife and couldn't keep her!*" At this, Jamie at last looked up, into the eyes of Eric's father. Eric laughed again, more shrilly, out of fear. Jamie said:

"Ah, yes, you can talk, you can."

"It's not my fault," said Eric's father, "if you're getting old—and haven't got anybody to bring you your slippers when night comes—and no pitter-patter of little feet—"

"Oh, leave Jamie alone," said Eric's mother, "he's *not* old, leave him alone."

Jamie laughed a peculiar, high, clicking laugh which Eric had never heard before, which he did not like, which made him want to look away and, at the same time, want to stare. "Hell, no," said Jamie, "I'm not old. I can still do all the things we used to do." he put his elbows on the table, grinning. "I haven't ever told you, have I, about the things we used to do?"

"No, you haven't," said Eric's mother, "and I certainly don't want to hear about them now."

"He wouldn't tell you anyway," said Eric's father, "he knows what I'd do to him if he did."

"Oh, sure, sure," said Jamie, and laughed again. He picked up a bone from his plate. "Here," he said to Eric, "why don't you feed my poor mistreated dog?"

Eric took the bone and stood up, whistling for the dog; who moved away from his master and took the bone between his teeth. Jamie watched with a smile and opened the bottle of whiskey and poured himself a drink. Eric sat on the ground beside the dog, beginning to be sleepy in the bright, bright sun.

"Little Eric's getting big," he heard his father say.

"Yes," said Jamie, "they grow fast. It won't be long now."

"Won't be long *what*?" he heard his father ask.

"Why, before he starts skirt-chasing like his Daddy used to do," said

Jamie. There was mild laughter at the table in which his mother did not join; he heard instead, or thought he heard, the familiar, slight, exasperated intake of her breath. No one seemed to care whether he came back to the table or not. He lay on his back, staring up at the sky, wondering—wondering what he would feel like when he was old—and fell asleep.

When he awoke his head was in his mother's lap, for she was sitting on the ground. Jamie and his father were still sitting at the table; he knew this from their voices, for he did not open his eyes. He did not want to move or speak. He wanted to remain where he was, protected by his mother, while the bright day rolled on. Then he wondered about the uncut birthday cake. But he was sure, from the sound of Jamie's voice, which was thicker now, that they had not cut it yet; or if they had, they had certainly saved a piece for him.

"—ate himself just as full as he could and then fell asleep in the sun like a little animal," Jamie was saying, and the two men laughed. His father—though he scarcely ever got as drunk as Jamie did, and had often carried Jamie home from The Rafters—was a little drunk, too.

Eric felt his mother's hand on his hair. By opening his eyes very slightly he would see, over the curve of his mother's thigh, as through a veil, a green slope far away and beyond it the everlasting, motionless sky.

"—she was a no-good *bitch*," said Jamie.

"She was beautiful," said his mother, just above him.

Again, they were talking about Jamie's wife.

"Beauty!" said Jamie, furious. "Beauty doesn't keep a house clean. Beauty doesn't keep a bed warm, neither."

Eric's father laughed. "You were so—poetical—in those days, Jamie," he said. "Nobody thought you cared much about things like that. I guess she thought you didn't care, either."

"I cared," said Jamie, briefly.

"In fact," Eric's father continued. "I *know* she thought you didn't care."

"*How* do you know?" asked Jamie.

"She told me," Eric's father said.

"What do you mean," asked Jamie, "what do you mean, she told you?"

"I mean just that. She told me."

Jamie was silent.

"In those days," Eric's father continued after a moment, "all you did was walk around the woods by yourself in the daytime and sit around The Rafters in the evenings with me."

"You two were always together then," said Eric's mother.

"Well," said Jamie, harshly, "at least that hasn't changed."

"Now, you know," said Eric's father, gently, "it's not the same. Now I got a wife and kid—and another one coming—"

Eric's mother stroked his hair more gently, yet with something in her touch more urgent, too, and he knew that she was thinking of the child who lay in the churchyard, who would have been his sister.

"Yes," said Jamie, "you really got it all fixed up, you did. You got it all—the wife, the kid, the house, and all the land."

"I didn't steal your farm from you. It wasn't my fault you lost it. I gave you a better price for it than anybody else would have done."

"I'm not blaming you. I know all the things I have to thank you for."

There was a short pause, broken, hesitantly, by Eric's mother. "What I don't understand," she said, "is why, when you went away to the city, you didn't *stay* away. You didn't really have anything to keep you here."

There was the sound of a drink being poured. Then, "No. I didn't have nothing—*really*—to keep me here. Just all the things I ever knew— all the things—*all* the things—I ever cared about."

"A man's not supposed to sit around and mope," said Eric's father, wrathfully, "for things that are over and dead and finished, things that can't *ever* begin again, that can't ever be the same again. That's what I mean when I say you're a dreamer—and if you hadn't kept on dreaming so long, you might not be alone now."

"Ah, well," said Jamie, mildly, and with a curious rush of affection in his voice, "I know you're the giant-killer, the hunter, the lover—the real old Adam, that's you. I know you're going to cover the earth. I know the world depends on men like you."

"And you're damn right," said Eric's father, after an uneasy moment.

Around Eric's head there was a buzzing, a bee, perhaps, a blue-fly, or a wasp. He hoped that his mother would see it and brush it away, but she did not move her hand. And he looked out again, through the veil of his eyelashes, at the slope and the sky, and then saw that the sun had moved and that it would not be long now before she would be going.

"—just like you already," Jamie said.

"You think my little one's like me?" Eric knew that his father was smiling—he could almost feel his father's hands.

"Looks like you, walks like you, talks like you," said Jamie.

"*And* stubborn like you," said Eric's mother.

"Ah, yes," said Jamie, and sighed. "You married the stubbornest, most determined—most selfish—man I know."

"I didn't know you felt that way," said Eric's father. He was still smiling.

"I'd have warned you about him," Jamie added, laughing, "if there'd been time."

"Everyone who knows you feels that way," said Eric's mother, and Eric felt a sudden brief tightening of the muscle in her thigh.

"Oh, *you*," said Eric's father, "I know *you* feel that way, women like to feel that way, it makes them feel important. But," and he changed to the teasing tone he took so persistently with Jamie today, "I didn't know my fine friend, Jamie, here—"

It was odd how unwilling he was to open his eyes. Yet, he felt the sun on him and knew that he wanted to rise from where he was before the sun went down. He did not understand what they were talking about this afternoon, these grown-ups he had known all his life; by keeping his eyes closed he kept their conversation far from him. And his mother's hand lay on his head like a blessing, like protection. And the buzzing had ceased, the bee, the blue-fly, or the wasp seemed to have flown away.

"—if it's a boy this time," his father said, "we'll name it after you."

"That's touching," said Jamie, "but that really won't do me—or the kid—a hell of a lot of good."

"Jamie can get married and have kids of his own any time he decides to," said Eric's mother.

"No," said his father, after a long pause, "Jamie's thought about it too long."

And, suddenly, he laughed and Eric sat up as his father slapped Jamie on the knee. At the touch, Jamie leaped up, shouting, spilling his drink and overturning his chair, and the dog beside Eric awoke and began to bark. For a moment, before Eric's unbelieving eyes, there was nothing in the yard but noise and flame.

His father rose slowly and stared at Jamie. "What the matter with you?"

"What's the matter with me!" mimicked Jamie, "what's the matter with me? What the hell do you care what's the matter with me! What the hell have you been riding me for all day like this? What do you want? What do you *want?*"

"I want you to learn to hold your liquor for one thing," said his father, coldly. The two men stared at each other. Jamie's face was red and ugly and tears stood in his eyes. The dog, at his legs, kept up a furious prancing and barking. Jamie bent down and, with one hand, with all his might, slapped his dog, which rolled over, howling, and ran away to hide itself under the shadows of the far grey wall.

Then Jamie stared again at Eric's father, trembling, and pushed his hair back from his eyes.

"You better pull yourself together," Eric's father said. And, to Eric's mother. "Get him some coffee. He'll be all right."

Jamie set his glass on the table and picked up the overturned chair. Eric's mother rose and went into the kitchen. Eric remained sitting on the ground, staring at the two men, his father and his father's best friend, who had become so unfamiliar. His father, with something in his face which Eric had never before seen there, a tenderness, a sorrow—or perhaps it was, after all, the look he sometimes wore when approaching a calf he was about to slaughter—looked down at Jamie where he sat, head bent, at the table. "You take things too hard," he said. "You always have. I was only teasing you for your own good."

Jamie did not answer. His father looked over to Eric, and smiled.

"Come on," he said. "You and me are going for a walk."

Eric, passing on the side of the table farthest from Jamie, went to his father and took his hand.

"Pull yourself together," his father said to Jamie. "We're going to cut your birthday cake as soon as me and the little one come back."

Eric and his father passed beyond the gray wall where the dog still whimpered, out into the fields. Eric's father was walking too fast and Eric stumbled on the uneven ground. When they had gone a little distance his father abruptly checked his pace and looked down at Eric, grinning.

"I'm sorry," he said. "I guess I said we were going for a walk, not running to put out a fire."

"What's the matter with Jamie?" Eric asked.

"Oh," said his father, looking westward where the sun was moving, pale orange now, making the sky ring with brass and copper and gold— which, like a magician, she was presenting only to demonstrate how variously they could be transformed—"Oh," he repeated, "there's nothing wrong with Jamie. He's been drinking a lot," and he grinned down at Eric, "and he's been sitting in the sun—you know, his hair's not as thick as yours," and he ruffled Eric's hair, "and I guess birthdays make him nervous. Hell," he said, "they make me nervous, too."

"Jamie's *very* old," said Eric, "isn't he?"

His father laughed. "Well, butch, he's not exactly ready to fall into the grave yet—he's going to be around awhile, is Jamie. Hey," he said, and looked down at Eric again, "you must think I'm an old man, too."

"Oh," said Eric, quickly, "I know you're not as old as Jamie."

His father laughed again. "Well, thank you, son. That shows real confidence. I'll try to live up to it."

They walked in silence for a while and then his father said, not looking at Eric, speaking to himself, it seemed, or to the air: "No, Jamie's not so old. He's not as old as he should be."

"How old *should* he be?" asked Eric.

"Why," said his father, "he ought to be his age," and, looking down at Eric's face, he burst into laughter again.

"Ah," he said, finally, and put his hand on Eric's head again, very gently, very sadly, "don't you worry now about what you don't understand. The time is coming when you'll have to worry—but that time hasn't come yet."

Then they walked till they came to the steep slope which led to the railroad tracks, down, down, far below them, where a small train seemed to be passing forever through the countryside, smoke, like the very definition of idleness, blowing out of the chimney stack of the toy locomotive.

Eric thought, resentfully, that he scarcely ever saw a train pass when he came here alone. Beyond the railroad tracks was the river where they sometimes went swimming in the summer. The river was hidden from them now by the high bank where there were houses and where tall trees grew.

"And this," said his father, "is where your land ends."

"What?" said Eric.

His father squatted on the ground and put one hand on Eric's shoulder. "You know all the way we walked, from the house?" Eric nodded. "Well," said his father, "that's your land."

Eric looked back at the long way they had come, feeling his father watching him.

His father, with a pressure on his shoulder made him turn; he pointed: "And over there. It belongs to you." He turned him again. "And that," he said, "that's yours, too."

Eric stared at his father. "Where does it end?" he asked.

His father rose. "I'll show you that another day," he said. "But it's further than you can walk."

They started walking slowly, in the direction of the sun.

"When did it get to be mine?" asked Eric.

"The day you were born," his father said, and looked down at him and smiled.

"My father," he said, after a moment, "had some of this land—and when he died, it was mine. He held onto it for me. And I did my best with the land I had, and I got some more. I'm holding onto it for you."

He looked down to see if Eric was listening. Eric was listening, staring at his father and looking around him at the great countryside.

"When I get to be a real old man," said his father, "even older than old Jamie there—you're going to have to take care of all this. When I die it's going to be yours." He paused and stopped; Eric looked up at him. "When you get to be a big man, like your Papa, you're going to get married and have children. And all this is going to be theirs."

"And when *they* get married?" Eric prompted.

"All this will belong to *their* children," his father said.

"Forever?" cried Eric.

"Forever," said his father.

They turned and started walking toward the house.

"Jamie," Eric asked at last, "how much land has *he* got?"

"Jamie doesn't have any land," his father said.

"Why not?" asked Eric.

"He didn't take care of it," his father said, "and he lost it."

"Jamie doesn't have a wife anymore, either, does he?" Eric asked.

"No," said his father. "He didn't take care of her, either."

"And he doesn't have any little boy," said Eric—very sadly.

"No," said his father. Then he grinned. "But *I* have."

"*Why* doesn't Jamie have a little boy?" asked Eric.

His father shrugged. "Some people do, Eric, some people don't."

"Will I?" asked Eric.

"Will you what?" asked his father.

"Will I get married and have a little boy?"

His father seemed for a moment both amused and checked. He looked down at Eric with a strange, slow smile. "Of course you will," he said at last. "Of course you will." And he held out his arms. "Come," he said, "climb up. I'll ride you on my shoulders home."

So Eric rode on his father's shoulders through the wide green fields which belonged to him, into the yard which held the house which would hear the first cries of his children. His mother and Jamie sat at the table talking quietly in the silver sun. Jamie had washed his face and combed his hair, he seemed calmer, he was smiling.

"Ah," cried Jamie, "the lord, the master of this house arrives! And bears on his shoulders the prince, the son, and heir!" He described a flourish, bowing low in the yard. "My lords! Behold your humble, most properly chastised servant, desirous of your—compassion, your love, and your forgiveness!"

"Frankly," said Eric's father, putting Eric on the ground, "I'm not sure that this is an improvement." He looked at Jamie and frowned and grinned. "Let's cut that cake."

Eric stood with his mother in the kitchen while she lit the candles— thirty-five, one, as they said, to grow on, though Jamie, surely, was far past the growing age—and followed her as she took the cake outside. Jamie took the great, gleaming knife and held it with a smile.

"Happy Birthday!" they cried—only Eric said nothing—and then Eric's mother said, "You have to blow out the candles, Jamie, before you cut the cake."

"It looks so pretty the way it is," Jamie said.

"Go ahead," said Eric's father, and clapped him on the back, "be a man."

Then the dog, once more beside his master, awoke, growling, and this made everybody laugh. Jamie laughed loudest. Then he blew out the candles, all of them at once, and Eric watched him as he cut the cake. Jamie raised his eyes and looked at Eric and it was at this moment, as the suddenly blood-red sun was striking the topmost tips of the trees, that Eric had looked into Jamie's eyes. Jamie smiled that strange smile of an old man and Eric moved closer to his mother.

"The first piece for Eric," said Jamie, then, and extended it to him on the silver blade.

That had been near the end of summer, nearly two months ago. Very shortly after the birthday party, his mother had fallen ill and had had to be taken away. Then his father spent more time than ever at The Rafters; he and Jamie came home in the evenings, stumbling drunk. Sometimes, during the time that his mother was away, Jamie did not go home at all, but spent the night at the farm house; and once or twice Eric had awakened in the middle of the night, or near dawn, and heard Jamie's footsteps walking up and down, walking up and down, in the big room downstairs. It had been a strange and dreadful time, a time of waiting, stillness, and silence. His father rarely went into the fields, scarcely raised himself to give orders to his farm hands—it was unnatural, it was frightening, to find him around the house all day, and Jamie was there always, Jamie and his dog. Then one day Eric's father told him that his mother was coming home but that she would not be bringing him a baby brother or sister, not this time, nor in any time to come. He started to say something more, then looked at Jamie who was standing by, and walked out of the house. Jamie followed him slowly, his hands in his pockets and his head bent. From the time of the birthday party, as though he were repenting of that outburst, or as though it had frightened him, Jamie had become more silent than ever.

When his mother came back she seemed to have grown older—old; she seemed to have shrunk within herself, away from them all, even, in a kind of storm of love and helplessness, away from Eric; but, oddly, and most particularly, away from Jamie. It was in nothing she said, nothing she did—or perhaps it was in everything she said and did. She washed and cooked for Jamie as before, took him into account as much as before as a part of the family, made him take second helpings at the table, smiled good night to him as he left the house—it was only that something had gone out of her familiarity. She seemed to do all that she did out of memory and from a great distance. And if something had gone out of her ease, something had come into it, too, a curiously still attention, as though she had been startled by some new aspect of something she had always known. Once or twice at the supper table, Eric caught her regard bent on Jamie, who, obliviously, ate. He could not read her look, but it reminded him of that moment at the birthday party when he had looked into Jamie's eyes. She seemed to be looking at Jamie as though she were wondering why she had not looked at him before; or as though she were discovering, with some surprise, that she had never really liked him but also felt, in her weariness and weakness, that it did not really matter now.

Now, as he entered the yard, he saw her standing in the kitchen doorway, looking out, shielding her eyes against the brilliant setting sun.

"Eric!" she cried, wrathfully, as soon as she saw him, "I've been looking high and low for you for the last hour. You're getting old enough to have some sense of responsibility and I wish you wouldn't worry me so when you know I've not been well."

She made him feel guilty at the same time that he dimly and resentfully felt that justice was not all on her side. She pulled him to her, turning his face up toward hers, roughly, with one hand.

"You're filthy," she said, then. "Go around to the pump and wash your face. And hurry, so I can give you your supper and put you to bed."

And she turned and went into the kitchen, closing the door lightly behind her. He walked around to the other side of the house, to the pump.

On a wooden box next to the pump was a piece of soap and a damp rag. Eric picked up the soap, not thinking of his mother, but thinking of the day gone by, already half asleep: and thought of where he would go tomorrow. He moved the pump handle up and down and the water rushed out and wet his socks and shoes—this would make his mother angry, but he was too tired to care. Nevertheless, automatically, he moved back a little. He held the soap between his hands, his hands beneath the water.

He had been many places, he had walked a long way and seen many things that day. He had gone down to the railroad tracks and walked beside the tracks for a while, hoping that a train would pass. He kept telling himself that he would give the train one more last chance to pass; and when he had given it a considerable number of last chances, he left the railroad bed and climbed a little and walked through the high, sweet meadows. He walked through a meadow where there were cows and they looked at him dully with their great dull eyes and moo'd among each other about him. A man from the far end of the field saw him and shouted, but Eric could not tell whether it was someone who worked for his father or not and so he turned and ran away, ducking through the wire fence. He passed an apple tree, with apples lying all over the ground—he wondered if the apples belonged to him, if he were still walking on his own land or had gone past it—but he ate an apple anyway and put some in his pockets, watching a lone brown horse in a meadow far below him nibbling at the grass and flicking his tail. Eric pretended that he was his father and was walking through the fields as he had seen his father walk, looking it all over calmly, pleased, knowing that everything he saw belonged to him. And he stopped and pee'd as he had seen his father do, standing widelegged and heavy in the middle of the fields; he pretended at the same time to be smoking and talking, as he had seen his father do. Then, having watered the ground, he walked on, and all the earth, for that moment, in Eric's eyes, seemed to be celebrating Eric.

Tomorrow he would go away again, somewhere. For soon it would be winter, snow would cover the ground, he would not be able to wander off alone.

He held the soap between his hands, his hands beneath the water; then he heard a low whistle behind him and a rough hand on his head and the soap fell from his hands and slithered between his legs onto the ground.

He turned and faced Jamie, Jamie without his dog.

"Come on, little fellow," Jamie whispered. "We got something in the barn to show you."

"Oh, did the calf come yet?" asked Eric—and was too pleased to wonder why Jamie whispered.

"Your Papa's there," said Jamie. And then: "Yes. Yes, the calf is coming now."

And he took Eric's hand and they crossed the yard, past the closed kitchen door, past the stone wall and across the field, into the barn.

"But *this* isn't where the cows are!" Eric cried. He suddenly looked up at Jamie, who closed the barn door behind them and looked down at Eric with a smile.

"No," said Jamie, "that's right. No cows here." And he leaned against the door as though his strength had left him. Eric saw that his face was wet, he breathed as though he had been running.

"Let's go see the cows," Eric whispered. Then he wondered why he was whispering and was terribly afraid. He stared at Jamie, who stared at him.

"In a minute," Jamie said, and stood up. He had put his hands in his pockets and now he brought them out and Eric stared at his hands and began to move away. He asked, "Where's my Papa?"

"Why," said Jamie, "he's down at The Rafters, I guess. I have to meet him there soon."

"I have to go," said Eric. "I have to eat my supper." He tried to move to the door, but Jamie did not move. "I have to go," he repeated, and, as Jamie moved toward him the tight ball of terror in his bowels, in his throat, swelled and rose, exploded, he opened his mouth to scream but Jamie's fingers closed around his throat. He stared, stared into Jamie's eyes.

"That won't do you any good," said Jamie. And he smiled. Eric struggled for breath, struggled with pain and fright. Jamie relaxed his grip a little and moved one hand and stroked Eric's tangled hair. Slowly, wondrously, his face changed, tears came into his eyes and rolled down his face.

Eric groaned—perhaps because he saw Jamie's tears or because his throat was so swollen and burning, because he could not catch his breath, because he was so frightened—he began to sob in great, unchildish gasps. "Why do you hate my father?"

"I love your father," Jamie said. But he was not listening to Eric. He was far away—as though he were struggling, toiling inwardly up a tall, tall mountain. And Eric struggled blindly, with all the force of his desire to live, to reach him, to stop him before he reached the summit.

"Jamie," Eric whispered, "you can have the land. You can have all the land."

Jamie spoke, but not to Eric: "I don't want the land."

"I'll be your little boy," said Eric. "I'll be your little boy forever and forever and forever—and you can have the land and you can live forever! Jamie!"

Jamie had stopped weeping. He was watching Eric.

"We'll go for a walk tomorrow," Eric said, "and I'll show it to you, all of it—really and truly—if you kill my father I can be your little boy and we can have it all!"

"This land," said Jamie, "will belong to no one."

"Please!" cried Eric, "oh, please! Please!"

He heard his mother singing in the kitchen. Soon she would come out to look for him. The hands left him for a moment. Eric opened his mouth to scream, but the hands then closed around his throat.

Mama. Mama.

The singing was further and further away. The eyes looked into his, there was a question in the eyes, the hands tightened. Then the mouth began to smile. He had never seen such a smile before. He kicked and kicked.

Mama. Mama. Mama. Mama. Mama.

Far away, he heard his mother call him.

Mama.

He saw nothing, he knew that he was in the barn, he heard a terrible breathing near him, he thought he heard the sniffling of beasts, he remembered the sun, the railroad tracks, the cows, the apples, and the ground. He thought of tomorrow—he wanted to go away again somewhere tomorrow. *I'll take you with me,* he wanted to say. He wanted to argue the question, the question he remembered in the eyes—wanted to say, *I'll tell my Papa you're hurting me.* Then terror and agony and darkness overtook him, and his breath went violently out of him. He dropped on his face in the straw in the barn, his yellow head useless on his broken neck.

Night covered the countryside and here and there, like emblems, the lights of houses glowed. A woman's voice called, "Eric! Eric!"

Jamie reached his wooden house and opened his door; whistled, and his dog came bounding out of darkness, leaping up on him; and he cuffed it down lightly, with one hand. Then he closed the door and started down the road, his dog beside him, his hands in his pockets. He stopped to light his pipe. He heard singing from The Rafters, then he saw the light; soon, the lights and the sound of singing diminished behind him. When Jamie no longer heard the singing, he began to whistle the song that he had heard.

A GOOD MAN IS HARD TO FIND

by Flannery O'Connor

(1925–64)

The grandmother didn't want to go to Florida. She wanted to visit some of her connections in east Tennessee and she was seizing at every chance to change Bailey's mind. Bailey was the son she lived with, her only boy. He was sitting on the edge of his chair at the table, bent over the orange sports section of the *Journal*. "Now look here, Bailey," she said, "see here, read this," and she stood with one hand on her thin hip and the other rattling the newspaper at his bald head. "Here this fellow that calls himself The Misfit is aloose from the Federal Pen and headed toward Florida and you read what it says he did to these people. Just you read it. I wouldn't take my children in any direction with a criminal like that aloose in it. I couldn't answer to my conscience if I did."

Bailey didn't look up from his reading so she wheeled around then and faced the children's mother, a young woman in slacks, whose face was as broad and innocent as a cabbage and was tied around with a green head-kerchief that had two points on the top like rabbit's ears. She was sitting on the sofa, feeding the baby his apricots out of a jar. "The children have been to Florida before," the old lady said. "You all ought to take them somewhere else for a change so they would see different parts of the world and be broad. They never have been to east Tennessee."

The children's mother didn't seem to hear her but the eight-year-old boy, John Wesley, a stocky child with glasses, said, "If you don't want to go to Florida, why dontcha stay at home?" He and the little girl, June Star, were reading the funny papers on the floor.

"She wouldn't stay at home to be queen for a day," June Star said without raising her yellow head.

"Yes, and what would you do if this fellow, The Misfit, caught you?" the grandmother asked.

"I'd smack his face," John Wesley said.

"She wouldn't stay at home for a million bucks," June Star said. "Afraid she'd miss something. She has to go everywhere we go."

"All right, Miss," the grandmother said. "Just remember that the next time you want me to curl your hair."

June Star said her hair was naturally curly.

The next morning the grandmother was the first one in the car, ready to go. She had her big black valise that looked like the head of a hippopotamus in one corner, and underneath it she was hiding a basket with Pitty Sing, the cat, in it. She didn't intend for the cat to be left alone in the house for three days because he would miss her too much and she was afraid he might brush against one of the gas burners and accidentally asphyxiate himself. Her son, Bailey, didn't like to arrive at a motel with a cat.

She sat in the middle of the back seat with John Wesley and June Star on either side of her. Bailey and the children's mother and the baby sat in front and they left Atlanta at eight forty-five with the mileage on the car at 55890. The grandmother wrote this down because she thought it would be interesting to say how many miles they had been when they got back. It took them twenty minutes to reach the outskirts of the city.

The old lady settled herself comfortably, removing her white cotton gloves and putting them up with her purse on the shelf in front of the back window. The children's mother still had on slacks and still had her head tied up in a green kerchief, but the grandmother had on a navy blue straw sailor hat with a bunch of white violets on the brim and a navy blue dress with a small white dot in the print. Her collars and cuffs were white organdy trimmed with lace and at her neckline she had pinned a purple spray of cloth violets containing a sachet. In case of an accident, anyone seeing her dead on the highway would know at once that she was a lady.

She said she thought it was going to be a good day for driving, neither too hot nor too cold, and she cautioned Bailey that the speed limit was fifty-five miles an hour and that the patrolmen hid themselves behind billboards and small clumps of trees and sped out after you before you had a chance to slow down. She pointed out interesting details of the scenery: Stone Mountain; the blue granite that in some places came up to both sides of the highway; the brilliant red clay banks slightly streaked with purple; and the various crops that made rows of green lace-work on the ground. The trees were full of silver-white sunlight and the meanest of them sparkled. The children were reading comic magazines and their mother had gone back to sleep.

"Let's go through Georgia fast so we won't have to look at it much," John Wesley said.

"If I were a little boy," said the grandmother, "I wouldn't talk about my native state that way. Tennessee has the mountains and Georgia has the hills."

"Tennessee is just a hillbilly dumping ground," John Wesley said, "and Georgia is a lousy state too."

"You said it," June Star said.

"In my time," said the grandmother, folding her thin veined fingers, "children were more respectful of their native states and their parents and everything else. People did right then. Oh look at the cute little pickaninny!" she said and pointed to a Negro child standing in the door of a shack. "Wouldn't that make a picture, now?" she asked and they all turned and looked at the little Negro out of the back window. He waved.

"He didn't have any britches on," June Star said.

"He probably didn't have any," the grandmother explained. "Little niggers in the country don't have things like we do. If I could paint, I'd paint that picture," she said.

The children exchanged comic books.

The grandmother offered to hold the baby and the children's mother passed him over the front seat to her. She set him on her knee and bounced him and told him about the things they were passing. She rolled her eyes and screwed up her mouth and stuck her leathery thin face into his smooth bland one. Occasionally he gave her a faraway smile. They passed a large cotton field with five or six graves fenced in the middle of it, like a small island. "Look at the graveyard!" the grandmother said, pointing it out. "That was the old family burying ground. That belonged to the plantation."

"Where's the plantation?" John Wesley asked.

"Gone With the Wind," said the grandmother. "Ha. Ha."

When the children finished all the comic books they had brought, they opened the lunch and ate it. The grandmother ate a peanut butter sandwich and an olive and would not let the children throw the box and the paper napkins out the window. When there was nothing else to do they played a game by choosing a cloud and making the other two guess what shape it suggested. John Wesley took one the shape of a cow and June Star guessed a cow and John Wesley said, no, an automobile, and June Star said he didn't play fair, and they began to slap each other over the grandmother.

The grandmother said she would tell them a story if they would keep quiet. When she told a story, she rolled her eyes and waved her head and was very dramatic. She said once when she was a maiden lady she had been courted by a Mr. Edgar Atkins Teagarden from Jasper, Georgia. She said he was a very good-looking man and a gentleman and that he brought her a watermelon every Saturday afternoon with his initials cut in it, E.A.T. Well, one Saturday, she said, Mr. Teagarden brought the watermelon and there was nobody at home and he left it on the front porch and returned in his buggy to Jasper, but she never got the watermelon, she said, because a nigger boy ate it when he saw the initials, E.A.T.! This story tickled John Wesley's funny bone and he giggled and giggled but June Star didn't think it was any good. She said she wouldn't marry a man that just brought her a watermelon on Saturday. The grandmother said she would have done well to marry Mr. Teagarden because he was a gentleman and had bought Coca-Cola stock when it first came out and that he had died only a few years ago, a very wealthy man.

They stopped at The Tower for barbecued sandwiches. The Tower was a part stucco and part wood filling station and dance hall set in a clearing outside of Timothy. A fat man named Red Sammy Butts ran it and there were signs stuck here and there on the building and for miles up and down the highway saying, TRY RED SAMMY'S FAMOUS BARBECUE. NONE LIKE FAMOUS RED SAMMY'S! RED SAM! THE FAT BOY WITH THE HAPPY LAUGH. A VETERAN! RED SAMMY'S YOUR MAN!

Red Sammy was lying on the bare ground outside The Tower with his head under a truck while a gray monkey about a foot high, chained to a small chinaberry tree, chattered nearby. The monkey sprang back into the tree and got on the highest limb as soon as he saw the children jump out of the car and run toward him.

Inside, The Tower was a long dark room with a counter at one end and tables at the other and dancing space in the middle. They all sat down at a board table next to the nickelodeon and Red Sam's wife, a tall burnt-brown woman with hair and eyes lighter than her skin, came and took their order. The children's mother put a dime in the machine and played "The Tennessee Waltz," and the grandmother said that tune always made her want to dance. She asked Bailey if he would like to dance but he only glared at her. He didn't have a naturally sunny disposition like she did and trips made him nervous. The grandmother's brown eyes were very bright. She swayed her head from side to side and pretended she was dancing in her chair. June Star said play something she could tap to so the children's mother put in another dime and played a fast number and June Star stepped out onto the dance floor and did her tap routine.

"Ain't she cute?" Red Sam's wife said, leaning over the counter. "Would you like to come be my little girl?"

"No I certainly wouldn't," June Star said. "I wouldn't live in a broken-down place like this for a million bucks!" and she ran back to the table.

"Ain't she cute?" the woman repeated, stretching her mouth politely.

"Aren't you ashamed?" hissed the grandmother.

Red Sam came in and told his wife to quit lounging on the counter and hurry up with these people's order. His khaki trousers reached just to his hip bones and his stomach hung over them like a sack of meal swaying under his shirt. He came over and sat down at a table nearby and let out a combination sigh and yodel. "You can't win," he said. "You can't win," and he wiped his sweating red face off with a gray handkerchief. "These days you don't know who to trust," he said. "Ain't that the truth?"

"People are certainly not nice like they used to be," said the grandmother.

"Two fellers come in here last week," Red Sammy said, "driving a Chrysler. It was a old beat-up car but it was a good one and these boys looked all right to me. Said they worked at the mill and you know I let them fellers charge the gas they bought? Now why did I do that?"

"Because you're a good man!" the grandmother said at once.

"Yes'm, I suppose so," Red Sam said as if he were struck with this answer.

His wife brought the orders, carrying the five plates all at once without a tray, two in each hand and one balanced on her arm. "It isn't a soul in this green world of God's that you can trust," she said. "And I don't count nobody out of that, not nobody," she repeated, looking at Red Sammy.

"Did you read about that criminal, The Misfit, that's escaped?" asked the grandmother.

"I wouldn't be a bit surprised if he didn't attack this place right here," said the woman. "If he hears about it being here, I wouldn't be none surprised to see him. If he hears it's two cent in the cash register, I wouldn't be at all surprised if he . . ."

"That'll do," Red Sam said. "Go bring these people their Co'-Colas," and the woman went off to get the rest of the order.

"A good man is hard to find," Red Sammy said. "Everything is getting terrible. I remember the day you could go off and leave your screen door unlatched. Not no more."

He and the grandmother discussed better times. The old lady said that in her opinion Europe was entirely to blame for the way things were now. She said the way Europe acted you would think we were made of money and Red Sam said it was no use talking about it, she was exactly right. The children ran outside into the white sunlight and looked at the monkey in the lacy chinaberry tree. He was busy catching fleas on himself and biting each one carefully between his teeth as if it were a delicacy.

They drove off again into the hot afternoon. The grandmother took cat naps and woke up every few minutes with her own snoring. Outside of Toombsboro she woke up and recalled an old plantation that she had visited in this neighborhood once when she was a young lady. She said the house had six white columns across the front and that there was an avenue of oaks leading up to it and two little wooden trellis arbors on either side in front where you sat down with your suitor after a stroll in the garden. She recalled exactly which road to turn off to get to it. She knew that Bailey would not be willing to lose any time looking at an old house, but the more she talked about it, the more she wanted to see it once again and find out if the little twin arbors were still standing. "There was a secret panel in this house," she said craftily, not telling the truth but wishing that she were, "and the story went that all the family silver was hidden in it when Sherman came through but it was never found. . . ."

"Hey!" John Wesley said. "Let's go see it! We'll find it! We'll poke all the woodwork and find it! Who lives there? Where do you turn off at? Hey, Pop, can't we turn off there?"

"We never have seen a house with a secret panel!" June Star shrieked. "Let's go to the house with the secret panel! Hey Pop, can't we go see the house with the secret panel!"

"It's not far from here, I know," the grandmother said. "It wouldn't take over twenty minutes."

Bailey was looking straight ahead. His jaw was as rigid as a horse-shoe. "No," he said.

The children began to yell and scream that they wanted to see the house with the secret panel. John Wesley kicked the back of the front seat and June Star hung over her mother's shoulder and whined desperately into her ear that they never had any fun even on their vacation, that they could never do what THEY wanted to do. The baby began to scream and John Wesley kicked the back of the seat so hard that his father could feel the blows in his kidney.

"All right!" he shouted and drew the car to a stop at the side of the road. "Will you all shut up? Will you all just shut up for one second? If you don't shut up, we won't go anywhere."

"It would be very educational for them," the grandmother murmured.

"All right," Bailey said, "but get this: this is the only time we're going to stop for anything like this. This is the one and only time."

"The dirt road that you have to turn down is about a mile back," the grandmother directed. "I marked it when we passed."

"A dirt road," Bailey groaned.

After they had turned around and were headed toward the dirt road, the grandmother recalled other points about the house, the beautiful glass over the front doorway and the candle-lamp in the hall. John Wesley said that the secret panel was probably in the fireplace.

"You can't go inside this house," Bailey said. "You don't know who lives there."

"While you all talk to the people in front, I'll run around behind and get in a window," John Wesley suggested.

"We'll all stay in the car," his mother said.

They turned onto the dirt road and the car raced roughly along in a swirl of pink dust. The grandmother recalled the times when there were no paved roads and thirty miles was a day's journey. The dirt road was hilly and there were sudden washes in it and sharp curves on dangerous embankments. All at once they would be on a hill, looking down over the blue tops of trees for miles around, then the next minute, they would be in a red depression with the dust-coated trees looking down on them.

"This place had better turn up in a minute," Bailey said, "or I'm going to turn around."

The road looked as if no one had traveled on it in months.

"It's not much farther," the grandmother said and just as she said it, a horrible thought came to her. The thought was so embarrassing that she turned red in the face and her eyes dilated and her feet jumped up, upsetting her valise in the corner. The instant the valise moved, the newspaper top she had over the basket under it rose with a snarl and Pitty Sing, the cat, sprang onto Bailey's shoulder.

The children were thrown to the floor and their mother, clutching the baby, was thrown out the door onto the ground; the old lady was thrown into the front seat. The car turned over once and landed right-side-up in a gulch off the side of the road. Bailey remained in the driver's seat with the cat—gray-striped with a broad white face and an orange nose—clinging to his neck like a caterpillar.

As soon as the children saw they could move their arms and legs, they scrambled out of the car, shouting, "We've had an ACCIDENT!" The grandmother was curled up under the dashboard, hoping she was injured so that Bailey's wrath would not come down on her all at once. The horrible thought she had had before the accident was that the house she had remembered so vividly was not in Georgia but in Tennessee.

Bailey removed the cat from his neck with both hands and flung it out the window against the side of a pine tree. Then he got out of the car and started looking for the children's mother. She was sitting against the side of the red gutted ditch, holding the screaming baby, but she only had a cut down her face and a broken shoulder. "We've had an ACCIDENT!" the children screamed in a frenzy of delight.

"But nobody's killed," June Star said with disappointment as the grandmother limped out of the car, her hat still pinned to her head but the broken front brim standing up at a jaunty angle and the violet spray hanging off the side. They all sat down in the ditch, except the children, to recover from the shock. They were all shaking.

"Maybe a car will come along," said the children's mother hoarsely.

"I believe I have an injured organ," said the grandmother, pressing her side, but no one answered her. Bailey's teeth were clattering. He had on a yellow sport shirt with bright blue parrots designed on it and his face was as yellow as the shirt. The grandmother decided that she would not mention that the house was in Tennessee.

The road was about ten feet above and they could see only the tops of the trees on the other side of it. Behind the ditch they were sitting in there were more woods, tall and dark and deep. In a few minutes they saw a car some distance away on top of a hill, coming slowly as if the occupants were watching them. The grandmother stood up and waved both arms dramatically to attract their attention. The car continued to come on slowly, disappeared around a bend and appeared again, moving even slower, on top of the hill they had gone over. It was a big black battered hearse-like automobile. There were three men in it.

It came to a stop just over them and for some minutes, the driver looked down with a steady expressionless gaze to where they were sitting, and didn't speak. Then he turned his head and muttered something to the other two and they got out. One was a fat boy in black trousers and a red sweat shirt with a silver stallion embossed on the front of it. He moved around on the right side of them and stood staring, his mouth partly open in a kind of loose grin. The other had on khaki pants and a blue striped coat and a gray hat pulled down very low, hiding most of his face. He came around slowly on the left side. Neither spoke.

The driver got out of the car and stood by the side of it, looking down at them. He was an older man than the other two. His hair was just beginning to gray and he wore silver-rimmed spectacles that gave him a scholarly look. He had a long creased face and didn't have on any shirt or undershirt. He had on blue jeans that were too tight for him and was holding a black hat and a gun. The two boys also had guns.

"We've had an ACCIDENT!" the children screamed.

The grandmother had the peculiar feeling that the bespectacled man was someone she knew. His face was as familiar to her as if she had known him all her life but she could not recall who he was. He moved away from the car and began to come down the embankment, placing his feet carefully so that he wouldn't slip. He had on tan and white shoes and no socks, and his ankles were red and thin. "Good afternoon," he said. "I see you all had you a little spill."

"We turned over twice!" said the grandmother.

"Oncet," he corrected. "We seen it happen. Try their car and see will it run, Hiram," he said quietly to the boy with the gray hat.

"What you got that gun for?" John Wesley asked. "Whatcha gonna do with that gun?"

"Lady," the man said to the children's mother, "would you mind calling them children to sit down by you? Children make me nervous. I want all you to sit down right together there where you're at."

"What are you telling US what to do for?" June Star asked.

Behind them the line of woods gaped like a dark open mouth. "Come here," said their mother.

"Look here now," Bailey began suddenly, "we're in a predicament! We're in . . ."

The grandmother shrieked. She scrambled to her feet and stood staring. "You're The Misfit!" she said. "I recognized you at once!"

"Yes'm," the man said, smiling slightly as if he were pleased in spite of himself to be known, "but it would have been better for all of you, lady, if you hadn't of reckernized me."

Bailey turned his head sharply and said something to his mother that shocked even the children. The old lady began to cry and The Misfit reddened.

"Lady," he said, "don't you get upset. Sometimes a man says things he don't mean. I don't reckon he meant to talk to you thataway."

"You wouldn't shoot a lady, would you?" the grandmother said and removed the clean handkerchief from her cuff and began to slap at her eyes with it.

The Misfit pointed the toe of his shoe into the ground and made a little hole and then covered it up again. "I would hate to have to," he said.

"Listen," the grandmother almost screamed, "I know you're a good man. You don't look a bit like you have common blood. I know you must come from nice people!"

"Yes mam," he said, "finest people in the world." When he smiled he showed a row of strong white teeth. "God never made a finer woman than my mother and my daddy's heart was pure gold," he said. The boy with the red sweat shirt had come around behind them and was standing with his gun at his hip. The Misfit squatted down on the ground. "Watch them children, Bobby Lee," he said. "You know they make me nervous." He looked at the six of them huddled together in front of him and he seemed to be embarrassed as if he couldn't think of anything to say. "Ain't a cloud in the sky," he remarked, looking up at it. "Don't see no sun but don't seen no cloud neither."

"Yes, it's a beautiful day," said the grandmother. "Listen," she said, "You shouldn't call yourself The Misfit because I know you're a good man at heart. I can just look at you and tell."

"Hush!" Bailey yelled. "Hush! Everybody shut up and let me handle this!" He was squatting in the position of a runner about to sprint forward but he didn't move.

"I pre-chate that, lady," The Misfit said and drew a little circle in the ground with the butt of his gun.

"It'll take a half a hour to fix this here car," Hiram called, looking over the raised hood of it.

"Well, first you and Bobby Lee get him and that little boy to step over yonder with you," The Misfit said, pointing to Bailey and John Wesley. "The boys want to ask you something," he said to Bailey. "Would you mind stepping back in them woods there with them?"

"Listen," Bailey began, "we're in a terrible predicament! Nobody realizes what this is," and his voice cracked. His eyes were as blue and intense as the parrots on his shirt and he remained perfectly still.

The grandmother reached up to adjust her hat brim as if she were going to the woods with him but it came off in her hand. She stood staring at it and after a second she let it fall on the ground. Hiram pulled Bailey up by the arm as if he were assisting an old man. John Wesley caught hold of his father's hand and Bobby Lee followed. They went off toward the woods and just as they reached the dark edge, Bailey turned and supported himself against a gray naked pine trunk, he shouted, "I'll be back in a minute, Mamma, wait on me!"

"Come back this instant!" his mother shrilled but they all disappeared into the woods.

"Bailey Boy!" the grandmother called in a tragic voice but she found she was looking at The Misfit squatting on the ground in front of her. "I just know you're a good man," she said desperately. "You're not a bit common!"

"Nome, I ain't a good man," The Misfit said after a second as if he had considered her statement carefully, "but I ain't the worst in the world neither. My daddy said I was a different breed of dog from my brothers and sisters. 'You know,' Daddy said, 'it's some that can live their whole life out without asking about it and it's others has to know why it is, and this boy is one of the latters. He's going to be into everything!' " He put on his black hat and looked up suddenly and then away deep into the woods as if he were embarrassed again. "I'm sorry I don't have on a shirt before you ladies," he said, hunching his shoulders slightly. "We buried our clothes that we had on when we escaped and we're just making do until we can get better. We borrowed these from some folks we met," he explained.

"That's perfectly all right," the grandmother said. "Maybe Bailey has an extra shirt in his suitcase."

"I'll look and see terrectly," The Misfit said.

"Where are they taking him?" the children's mother screamed.

"Daddy was a card himself," The Misfit said. "You couldn't put anything over on him. He never got in trouble with the Authorities though. Just had the knack of handling them."

"You could be honest too if you'd only try," said the grandmother. "Think how wonderful it would be to settle down and live a comfortable life and not have to think about somebody chasing you all the time."

The Misfit kept scratching in the ground with the butt of his gun as if he were thinking about it. "Yes'm, somebody is always after you," he murmured.

The grandmother noticed how thin his shoulder blades were just behind his hat because she was standing up looking down on him. "Do you ever pray?" she asked.

He shook his head. All she saw was the black hat wiggle between his shoulder blades. "Nome," he said.

There was a pistol shot from the woods, followed closely by another. Then silence. The old lady's head jerked around. She could hear the wind move through the tree tops like a long satisfied insuck of breath. "Bailey Boy!" she called.

"I was a gospel singer for a while," The Misfit said. "I been most everything. Been in the arm service, both land and sea, at home and abroad, been twict married, been an undertaker, been with the railroads, plowed Mother Earth, been in a tornado, seen a man burnt alive oncet," and he looked up at the children's mother and the little girl who were sitting close together, their faces white and their eyes glassy; "I even seen a woman flogged," he said.

"Pray, pray," the grandmother began, "pray, pray . . ."

"I never was a bad boy that I remember of," The Misfit said in an almost dreamy voice, "but somewheres along the line I done something wrong and got sent to the penitentiary. I was buried alive," and he looked up and held her attention to him by a steady stare.

"That's when you should have started to pray," she said. "What did you do to get sent to the penitentiary that first time?"

"Turn to the right, it was a wall," The Misfit said, looking up again at the cloudless sky. "Turn to the left, it was a wall. Look up it was a ceiling, look down it was a floor. I forget what I done, lady. I set there and set there, trying to remember what it was I done and I ain't recalled it to this day. Oncet in a while, I would think it was coming to me, but it never come."

"Maybe they put you in by mistake," the old lady said vaguely.

"Nome," he said. "It wasn't no mistake. They had the papers on me."

"You must have stolen something," she said.

The Misfit sneered slightly. "Nobody had nothing I wanted," he said. "It was a head-doctor at the penitentiary said what I had done was kill my daddy but I known that for a lie. My daddy died in nineteen ought nineteen of the epidemic flu and I never had a thing to do with it. He was buried in the Mount Hopewell Baptist churchyard and you can go there and see for yourself."

"If you would pray," the old lady said, "Jesus would help you."

"That's right," The Misfit said.

"Well then, why don't you pray?" she asked trembling with delight suddenly.

"I don't want no hep," he said, "I'm doing all right by myself."

Bobby Lee and Hiram came ambling back from the woods. Bobby Lee was dragging a yellow shirt with bright blue parrots on it.

"Throw me that shirt, Bobby Lee," The Misfit said. The shirt came flying at him and landed on his shoulder and he put it on. The grandmother couldn't name what the shirt reminded her of. "No, lady," The Misfit said while he was buttoning it up, "I found out the crime don't matter. You can do one thing or you can do another, kill a man or take a tire off his car, because sooner or later you're going to forget what it was you done and just be punished for it."

The children's mother had begun to make heaving noises as if she couldn't get her breath. "Lady," he asked, "would you and that little girl like to step off yonder with Bobby Lee and Hiram and join your husband?"

"Yes, thank you," the mother said faintly. Her left arm dangled helplessly and she was holding the baby, who had gone to sleep, in the other. "Hep that lady up, Hiram," The Misfit said as she struggled to climb out of the ditch, "and Bobby Lee, you hold onto that little girl's hand."

"I don't want to hold hands with him," June Star said. "He reminds me of a pig."

The fat boy blushed and laughed and caught her by the arm and pulled her off into the woods after Hiram and her mother.

Alone with The Misfit, the grandmother found that she had lost her voice. There was not a cloud in the sky nor any sun. There was nothing around her but woods. She wanted to tell him that he must pray. She opened and closed her mouth several times before anything came out. Finally she found herself saying, "Jesus, Jesus," meaning, Jesus will help you, but the way she was saying it, it sounded as if she might be cursing.

"Yes'm," The Misfit said as if he agreed. "Jesus thown everything off balance. It was the same case with Him as with me except he hadn't committed any crime and they could prove I had committed one because they had the papers on me. Of course," he said, "they never shown me my papers. That's why I sign myself now. I said long ago, you get you a signature and sign everything you do and keep a copy of it. Then you'll know what you done and you can hold up the crime to the punishment and see do they match and in the end you'll have something to prove you ain't been treated right. I call myself The Misfit," he said, "because I can't make what all I done wrong fit what all I gone through in punishment."

There was a piercing scream from the woods, followed closely by a pistol report. "Does it seem right to you, lady, that one is punished a heap and another ain't punished at all?"

"Jesus!" the old lady cried. "You've got good blood! I know you wouldn't shoot a lady! I know you come from nice people! Pray! Jesus, you ought not to shoot a lady. I'll give you all the money I've got!"

"Lady," The Misfit said, looking beyond her far into the woods, "there never was a body that give the undertaker a tip."

There were two more pistol reports and the grandmother raised her head like a parched old turkey hen crying for water and called, "Bailey Boy, Bailey Boy!" as if her heart would break.

"Jesus was the only One that ever raised the dead," The Misfit continued, "and He shouldn't have done it. He thown everything off balance. If He did what He said, then it's nothing for you to do but throw away everything and follow Him, and if He didn't, then it's nothing for you to do but enjoy the few minutes you got left the best way you can—by killing somebody or burning down his house or doing some other meanness to him. No pleasure but meanness," he said and his voice had become almost a snarl.

"Maybe He didn't raise the dead," the old lady mumbled, not knowing what she was saying and feeling so dizzy that she sank down in the ditch with her legs twisted under her.

"I wasn't there so I can't say He didn't," The Misfit said. "I wisht I had of been there," he said, hitting the ground with his fist. "It ain't right I wasn't there because if I had of been there I would of known. Listen lady," he said in a high voice, "if I had of been there I would of known and I wouldn't be like I am now." His voice seemed about to crack and the grandmother's head cleared for an instant. She saw the man's face twisted close to her own as if he were going to cry and she murmured, "Why you're one of my babies. You're one of my own children!" She reached out and touched him on the shoulder. The Misfit sprang back as if a snake had bitten him and shot her three times through the chest. Then he put his gun down on the ground and took off his glasses and began to clean them.

Hiram and Bobby Lee returned from the woods and stood over the ditch, looking down at the grandmother who half sat and half lay in a puddle of blood with her legs crossed under her like a child's and her face smiling up at the cloudless sky.

Without his glasses, The Misfit's eyes were red-rimmed and pale and defenseless-looking. "Take her off and thow her where you thown the others," he said, picking up the cat that was rubbing itself against his leg.

"She was a talker, wasn't she?" Bobby Lee said, sliding down the ditch with a yodel.

"She would of been a good woman," The Misfit said, "if it had been somebody there to shoot her every minute of her life."

"Some fun!" Bobby Lee said.

"Shut up, Bobby Lee," The Misfit said. "It's no real pleasure in life."

JUST LATHER, THAT'S ALL
by Hernando Téllez
(1908–66)

He said nothing when he entered. I was passing the best of my razors back and forth on a strop. When I recognized him I started to tremble. But he didn't notice. Hoping to conceal my emotion, I continued sharpening the razor. I tested it on the meat of my thumb, and then held it up to the light. At that moment he took off the bullet-studded belt that his gun holster dangled from. He hung it up on a wall hook and placed his military cap over it. Then he turned to me, loosening the knot of his tie, and said, "It's hot as hell. Give me a shave." He sat in the chair.

I estimated he had a four-day beard. The four days taken up by the latest expedition in search of our troops. His face seemed reddened, burned by the sun. Carefully, I began to prepare the soap. I cut off a few slices, dropped them into the cup, mixed in a bit of warm water, and began to stir with the brush. Immediately the foam began to rise. "The other boys in the group should have this much beard, too." I continued stirring the lather.

"But we did all right, you know. We got the main ones. We brought back some dead, and we've got some others still alive. But pretty soon they'll all be dead."

"How many did you catch?" I asked.

"Fourteen. We had to go pretty deep into the woods to find them. But we'll get even. Not one of them comes out of this alive, not one."

He leaned back on the chair when he saw me with the lather-covered brush in my hand. I still had to put the sheet on him. No doubt about it, I was upset. I took a sheet out of a drawer and knotted it around my customer's neck. He wouldn't stop talking. He probably thought I was in sympathy with his party.

"The town must have learned a lesson from what we did the other day," he said.

"Yes," I replied, securing the knot at the base of his dark, sweaty neck.

"That was a fine show, eh?"

"Very good," I answered, turning back for the brush. The man closed his eyes with a gesture of fatigue and sat waiting for the cool caress of the soap. I had never had him so close to me. The day he ordered the whole town to file into the patio of the school to see the four rebels hanging there, I came face to face with him for an instant. But the sight of the mutilated bodies kept me from noticing the face of the man who had directed it all, the face I was now about to take into my hands. It was not an unpleasant face, certainly. And the beard, which made him seem a bit older than he was, didn't suit him badly at all. His name was Torres. Captain Torres. A man of imagination, because who else would have thought of hanging the naked rebels and then holding target practice on certain parts of their bodies? I began to apply the first layer of soap. With his eyes closed, he continued. "Without any effort I could go straight to sleep," he said, "but there's plenty to do this afternoon." I stopped the lathering and asked with a feigned lack of interest: "A firing squad?" "Something like that, but a little slower." I got on with the job of lathering his beard. My hands started trembling again. The man could not possibly realize it, and this was in my favor. But I would have preferred that he hadn't come. It was likely that many of our faction had seen him enter. And an enemy under one's roof imposes certain conditions. I would be obliged to shave that beard like any other one, carefully, gently, like that of any customer, taking pains to see that no single pore emitted a drop of blood. Being careful to see that the little tufts of hair did not lead the blade astray. Seeing that his skin ended up clean, soft, and healthy, so that passing the back of my hand over it I couldn't feel a hair. Yes, I was secretly a rebel, but I was also a conscientious barber, and proud of the preciseness of my profession. And this four-days' growth of beard was a fitting challenge.

I took the razor, opened up the two protective arms, exposed the blade and began the job, from one of the sideburns downward. The razor responded beautifully. His beard was inflexible and hard, not too long, but thick. Bit by bit the skin emerged. The razor rasped along, making its customary sound as fluffs of lather mixed with bits of hair gathered along the blade. I paused a moment to clean it, then took up the strop again to sharpen the razor, because I'm a barber who does things properly. The man, who had kept his eyes closed, opened them now, removed one of his hands from under the sheet, felt the spot on his face where the soap had been cleared off, and said, "Come to the school today at six o'clock." "The same thing as the other day?" I asked horrified. "It could be better," he replied. "What do you plan to do?" "I don't know yet. But we'll amuse ourselves." Once more he leaned back and closed his eyes. I approached him with the razor poised. "Do you plan to punish them all?" I ventured timidly. "All." The soap was drying on his face. I had to hurry. In the mirror I looked toward the street. It was the same as ever: the grocery store with two or three customers in it. Then I glanced at the clock: two-twenty in the afternoon. The razor continued on its downward stroke. Now from the other sideburn down. A thick, blue beard. He should have let it grow like some poets or priests do. It would suit him well. A lot of people wouldn't recognize him. Much to his benefit, I thought, as I attempted to cover the neck area smoothly. There, for sure, the razor had to be handled masterfully, since the hair, although softer, grew into little swirls. A curly beard. One of the tiny pores could be opened up and issue forth its pearl of blood. A good barber such as I prides himself on never allowing this to happen to a client. And this was a first-class client. How many of us had he ordered shot? How many of us had he ordered mutilated? It was better not to think about it. Torres did not know that I was his enemy. He did not know it nor did the rest. It was a secret shared by very few, precisely so that I could inform the revolutionaries of what Torres was doing in the town and of what he was planning each time he undertook a rebel-hunting excursion. So it was going to be very difficult to explain that I had him right in my hands and let him go peacefully—alive and shaved.

The beard was now almost completely gone. He seemed younger, less burdened by years than when he had arrived. I suppose this always happens with men who visit barber shops. Under the stroke of my razor Torres was being rejuvenated—rejuvenated because I am a good barber, the best in the town, if I may say so. A little more lather here, under his chin, on his Adam's apple, on this big vein. How hot it is getting! Torres must be sweating as much as I. But he is not afraid. He is a calm man, who is not even thinking about what he is going to do with the prisoners this afternoon. On the other hand I, with this razor in my hands, stroking and re-stroking this skin, trying to keep blood from oozing from these pores, can't even think clearly. Damn him for coming, because I'm a revolutionary and not a murderer. And how easy it would be to kill him. And he deserves it. Does he? No! What the devil! No one deserves to have someone else make the sacrifice of becoming a murderer. What do you gain by it? Nothing. Others come along and still others, and the first ones kill the second ones and they the next ones and it goes on like this until everything is a sea of blood. I could cut this throat just so, zip! zip! I wouldn't give him time to complain and since he has his eyes closed he wouldn't see the glistening knife blade or my glistening eyes. But I'm trembling like a real murderer. Out of his neck a gush of blood would spout onto the sheet, on the chair, on my hands, on the floor. I would have to close the door. And the blood would keep inching along the floor, warm, ineradicable, uncontainable, until it reached the street, like a little scarlet stream. I'm sure that one solid stroke, one deep incision, would prevent any pain. He wouldn't suffer. But what would I do with the body? Where would I hide it? I would have to flee, leaving all I have behind, and take refuge far away, far, far away. But they would follow until they found me. "Captain Torres' murderer. He slit his throat while he was shaving him—a coward." And then on the other side. "The avenger of us all. A name to remember. (And here they would mention my name.) He was the town barber. No one knew he was defending our cause."

And what of all this? Murderer or hero? My destiny depends on the edge of this blade. I can turn my hand a bit more, press a little harder on the razor, and sink it in. The skin would give way like silk, like rubber, like the strop. There is nothing more tender than human skin and the blood is always there, ready to pour forth. A blade like this doesn't fail. It is my best. But I don't want to be a murderer, no sir. You came to me for a shave. And I perform my work honorably. . . . I don't want blood on my hands. Just lather, that's all. You are an executioner and I am only a barber. Each person has his own place in the scheme of things. That's right. His own place.

Now his chin had been stroked clean and smooth. The man sat up and looked into the mirror. He rubbed his hands over his skin and felt it fresh, like new.

"Thanks," he said. He went to the hanger for his belt, pistol and cap. I must have been very pale; my shirt felt soaked. Torres finished adjusting the buckle, straightened his pistol in the holster and after automatically smoothing down his hair, he put on the cap. From his pants pocket he took out several coins to pay me for my services. And he began to head toward the door. In the doorway he paused for a moment, and turning to me he said:

"They told me that you'd kill me. I came to find out. But killing isn't easy. You can take my word for it." And he headed on down the street.

NOVOTNY'S PAIN
by Philip Roth
(b. 1933)

In the early months of the Korean War, a young man who had been studying to be a television cameraman in a night school just west of the Loop in Chicago was drafted into the army and almost immediately fell ill. He awoke one morning with a pain on the right side of his body, directly above the buttock. When he rolled over, it was as though whatever bones came together inside him there were not meeting as they should. The pain, however, was not what had awakened him; his eyes always opened themselves five minutes before the appearance in the barracks of the Charge of Quarters. Though there was much of army life that he had to grit his teeth to endure, he did not have to work at getting up on time; it simply happened to him. When it was necessary to grit his teeth, he gritted them and did what he was told. In that way, he was like a good many young men who suffered military life alongside him or had suffered it before him. His sense of shame was strong, as was his sense of necessity; the two made him dutiful.

Also, he was of foreign extraction, and though his hard-working family had not as yet grown fat off the fat of the land, it was nevertheless in their grain to feel indebted to this country. Perhaps if they had been a little fatter they would have felt less indebted. As it was, Novotny believed in fighting for freedom, but because what he himself wanted most from any government was that it should let him alone to live his life. His patriotism, then—his commitment to wearing this republic's uniform and carrying this republic's gun—was seriously qualified by his feeling of confinement and his feeling of loss, both of which were profound.

When the C.Q. got around to Novotny's bed that morning, he did not shine his flashlight into the soldier's eyes; he simply put a hand to his arm and said, "You better get yourself up, young trooper." Novotny was appreciative of this gentleness, and though, as he stepped from his bunk, the pain across his back was momentarily quite sharp, he met the day with his usual decision. Some mornings, making the decision required that he swallow hard and close his eyes, but he never failed to make it: *I am willing.* He did not know if any of those around him had equivalent decisions to make, because he did not ask. He did not mull much over motive. People were honest or dishonest, good or bad, himself included.

After dressing, he moved off with four others to the mess hall, where it was their turn to work for the day. It was still dark, and in the barracks the other recruits slept on. The previous day, the entire company had marched fifteen miserable miles with full packs, and then, when it was dark, they had dropped down on their stomachs and fired at pinpoints of light that flickered five hundred yards away and were supposed to be the gunfire of the enemy. Before they had climbed into trucks at midnight, they were ordered to attention and told in a high, whiny voice by their captain, a National Guardsman recently and unhappily called back to duty, that only one out of every fifty rounds they had fired had hit the targets. This news had had a strong effect upon the weary recruits, and the trucks had been silent all the way to the barracks, where it had been necessary for them to clean their rifles and scrape the mud from their boots before they flung themselves onto the springs of their bunks for a few hours' rest.

At the mess hall, the K.P.s were each served two large spoonfuls of army eggs and a portion of potatoes. The potatoes had not been cooked long enough, and the taste they left on the palate was especially disheartening at such an early hour, with no light outdoors and a cold wind blowing. But Novotny did not complain. For one thing, he was occupied with finding a comfortable position in which to sit and eat—he had the pain only when he twisted the wrong way. Besides, the food was on his tray to give him strength, not pleasure. Novotny did not skip meals, no matter how ill-prepared they were, for he did not want to lose weight and be unequal to the tasks assigned him.

Before entering the army, Novotny had worked for several years as an apprentice printer with a company that manufactured telephone books in Chicago. It had turned out to be dull work, and because he considered himself a bright and ambitious young man, he had looked around for a night school where he might learn a job with a future. He had settled on television, and for over a year he had been attending classes two evenings a week. He had a girl friend and a mother, to both of whom he had a strong attachment; his girl friend he loved, his mother he took care of. Novotny did not want to cause any trouble. On the other hand, he did not want to be killed. With his girl friend, he had been a man of passion; he dreamed of her often. He was thrifty, and had four hundred dollars in a savings account in the First Continental Bank on LaSalle Street in Chicago. He knew for a fact that he had been more adept at his work than anyone else in his television course. He hated the army because nothing he did there was for himself.

The labors of the K.P.s began at dawn, and at midnight—light having come and gone—they were still at it. The cooks had ordered the men around all day until five in the afternoon, when the Negro mess sergeant showed up. He hung his Eisenhower jacket on a hook, rolled up the sleeves of his shirt, and said, "As there is a regimental inspection tomorrow morning, we will now get ourselves down to the fine points of house-cleaning, gentlemens." The K.P.s had then proceeded to scrub the mess hall from floor to ceiling, inside and out.

A little after midnight, while Novotny was working away at the inside of a potato bin with a stiff brush and a bucket of hot, soapy water, the man working beside him began to cry. He said the sergeant was never going to let them go to sleep. The sergeant would be court-martialed for keeping them up like this. They would all get weak and sick. All Novotny knew of the fellow beside him was that his name was Reynolds and that he had been to college. Apparently, the mess sergeant only knew half that much, but that was enough; he came into the storeroom and saw Reynolds weeping into the empty potato bins. "College boy," he said, "wait'll they get you over in Korea." The sergeant delivered his words standing over them, looking down, and for the moment Novotny stopped feeling sorry for himself.

When the scrubbing was finished, Novotny and Reynolds had to carry back the potatoes, which were in garbage cans, and dump them into the bins. Reynolds began to explain to Novotny that he had a girl friend whom he was supposed to have called at ten-thirty. For some reason, Reynolds said, his not having been able to get to a phone had made him lose control. Novotny had, till then, been feeling superior to Reynolds. For all his resenting of the stupidity that had made them scrub out bins one minute so as to dump dirty potatoes back into them the next, he had been feeling somewhat in league with the sergeant. Now Reynolds' words broke through to his own unhappiness, and he was about to say a kind word to his companion when the fellow suddenly started crying again. Reynolds threw his hand up to cover his wet cheeks and dropped his end of the can. Novotny's body stiffened; with a great effort he yanked up on the can so that it wouldn't come down on Reynolds' toes. Pain cut deep across the base of Novotny's spine.

Later, he limped back to the barracks. He got into bed and counted up the number of hours he had spent scrubbing out what hadn't even needed to be scrubbed. At a dollar and a quarter an hour, he would have made over twenty dollars. Nineteen hours was as much night-school time as he had been able to squeeze into three weeks. He had known Rose Anne, his girl, for almost a year, but never had he spent nineteen consecutive hours in her company. Though once they had had twelve hours. . . . He had driven in his Hudson down to Champaign, where she was a freshman at the University of Illinois, and they had stayed together, in the motel room he had rented, from noon to midnight, not even going out for meals. He had driven her back to her dormitory, his shoelaces untied and wearing no socks. Never in his life had he been so excited.

The following week, he had been drafted.

After completing his eight weeks of basic training, Novotny was given a week's leave. His first evening home, his mother prepared a large meal and then sat down opposite him at the table and watched him eat it. After dinner, he stood under the hot shower for twenty minutes, letting the water roll over him. In his bedroom, he carefully removed the pins from a new white-on-white shirt and laid it out on the bedspread, along with a pair of Argyles, a silver tie clasp, cufflinks, and his blue suit. He polished his shoes—not for the captain's pleasure, but for his own—and chose a tie. Then he dressed for his date as he had learned to dress for a date from an article he had read in a Sunday picture magazine, while in high school, that he kept taped to the inside of his closet door. He had always collected articles having to do with how to act at parties, or dances, or on the job; his mother had never had any reason not to be proud of Novotny's behavior. She kissed him when he left the house, told him how handsome he looked, and then tears moved over her eyes as she thanked him for the government checks—for always having been a good son.

Novotny went to a movie with Rose Anne, and afterward he drove to the forest preserve where they remained until 2 A.M. In bed, later, he cursed the army. He awoke the following morning to find that the pain, which had not troubled him for some weeks, had returned. It came and went through the next day and the following night, when once again he saw Rose Anne. Two days later, he visited the family doctor, who said Novotny had strained a muscle, and gave him a diathermy treatment. On their last night together, Rose Anne said that if writing would help, she would write not just twice a day, as was her habit, but three times a day, even four. In the dark of the forest preserve, she told Novotny that she dreamed about his body; in the dark, he told her that he dreamed of hers.

He left her weeping into a Kleenex in her dim front hallway, and drove home in a mood darker than any he had ever known. He would be killed in Korea and never see Rose Anne again, or his mother. And how unfair—for he *had* been a good son. Following his father's death, he had worked every day after school, plus Wednesday nights and Saturdays. When he had been drafted, he had vowed he would do whatever they told him to do, no matter how much he might resent it. He had kept his mouth shut and become proficient at soldiering. The better he was at soldiering, the better chance he had of coming out alive and in one piece. But that night when he left Rose Anne, he felt he had no chance at all. He would leave some part of his body on the battlefield, or come home to Rose Anne in a box. Good as he had been—industrious, devoted, stern, sacrificing— he would never have the pleasure of being a husband, or a television cameraman, or a comfort to his mother in her old age.

Five days after his return to the post—where he was to receive eight weeks of advanced infantry training, preparatory to being shipped out—he went on sick call. He sat on a long bench in the barren waiting room, and while two sullen prisoners from the stockade mopped the floor around his feet, he had his temperature taken. There were thirteen men on sick call, and they all watched the floor being washed and held thermometers under their tongues. When Novotny got to see the medic, who sat outside the doctor's office, he told him that every time he twisted or turned or stepped down on his right foot, he felt a sharp pain just above the buttock on the right side of his body. Novotny was sent back to duty with three inches of tape across his back, and a packet of APC pills.

At mail call the following morning, Novotny received a letter from Rose Anne unlike any he had ever received from her before. It was not only that her hand was larger and less controlled than usual; it was what she said. She had written down, for his very eyes to see, all those things she dreamed about when she dreamed about his body. He saw, suddenly, scenes of passion that he and she were yet to enact, moments that would not merely repeat the past but would be even deeper, even more thrilling. Oh Rose Anne—how had he found her?

Novotny's company spent the afternoon charging around with fixed bayonets—crawling, jumping up, racing ahead, through fences, over housetops, down into trenches—screaming murderously all the while. At one point, leaping from a high wall, Novotny almost took his eye out with his own bayonet; he had been dreaming of his beautiful future.

The next morning, he walked stiffly to sick call and asked to see the doctor. When, in response to a question, he said it was his back that hurt him, the medic who was interviewing him replied sourly, "Everybody's back hurts." The medic told Novotny to take off his shirt so that he could lay on a few more inches of tape. Novotny asked if he could please see the doctor for just a minute. He was informed that the doctor was only seeing men with temperatures of a hundred or more. Novotny had no temperature, and he returned to his unit, as directed.

On the seventh weekend, with only one more week of training left, Novotny was given a seventy-two-hour pass. He caught a plane to Chicago and a bus to Champaign, carrying with him only a small ditty bag and Rose Anne's impassioned letter. Most of Friday, most of Saturday, and all day Sunday, Rose Anne wept, until Novotny was more miserable than he had ever imagined a man could be. On Sunday night, she held him in her arms and he proceeded to tell her at last of how he had been mistreated by the medic; till then he had not wanted to cause her more grief than she already felt. She stroked his hair while he told how he had not even been allowed to see a doctor. Rose Anne wept and said the medic should be shot. They had no right to send Novotny to Korea if they wouldn't even look after his health here at home. What would happen to him if his back started to act up in the middle of a battle? How could he take care of himself? She raised many questions—rational ones, irrational ones, but none that Novotny had not already considered himself.

Novotny traveled all night by train so as to be back at the base by reveille. He spent most of the next day firing a Browning automatic, and the following morning, when he was to go on K.P., he could not even lift himself from his bed, so cruel was the pain in his back.

In the hospital, the fellow opposite Novotny had been in a wheelchair for two years with osteomyelitis. Every few months, they shortened his legs; nevertheless, the disease continued its slow ascent. The man on Novotny's right had dropped a hand grenade in basic training and blown bits of both his feet off. Down at the end of Novotny's aisle lay a man who had had a crate full of ammunition tip off a truck onto him, and the rest of the men in the ward, many of whom were in the hospital to learn to use prosthetic devices, had been in Korea.

The day after Novotny was assigned to the ward, the man the crate had fallen on was wheeled away to be given a myelogram. He came back to the ward holding his head in his hands. As soon as Novotny was able to leave his bed, he made his way over to this fellow's bed, and because he had heard that the man's condition had been diagnosed as a back injury, he asked him how he was feeling. He got around to asking what a myelogram was, and why he had come back to the ward holding his head. The fellow was talkative enough, and told him that they had injected a white fluid directly into his spine and then X-rayed him as the fluid moved down along the vertebrae, so as to see if the spinal discs were damaged. He told Novotny that apparently it was the stuff injected into him that had given him the headache, but then he added that, lousy as he had felt, he considered himself pretty lucky. He had heard of cases, he said, where the needle had slipped. Novotny had himself heard of instances where doctors had left towels and sponges inside patients, so he could believe it. The man said that all the needle had to do was go off by a hairbreadth and it would wind up in the tangle of nerves leading into the spine. Two days later, two damaged discs were cut out of the man with the injured back, and three of his vertebrae were fused together. All through the following week he lay motionless in his bed.

One evening earlier, while Novotny was still restricted to bed, he had been visited by Reynolds. Reynolds had come around to say goodbye; the entire outfit was to be flown out the next day. Since Reynolds and Novotny hardly knew each other, they had been silent after Reynolds spoke of what was to happen to him and the others the following day. Then Reynolds had said that Novotny was lucky to have developed back trouble when he did; he wouldn't have minded a touch of it himself. Then he left.

When Novotny was out of bed and walking around, X-rays were taken of his back, and the doctors told him they showed no sign of injury or disease; there was a slight narrowing of the intervertebral space between what they referred to on the pictures as L-1 and L-2, but nothing to suggest damage to the disc—which was what Novotny had worked up courage to ask them about. The doctors took him into the examination room and bent him forward and backward. They ran a pin along his thigh and calf and asked if he felt any sensation. They laid him down on a table and, while they slowly raised his leg, asked if he felt any pain. When his leg was almost at a ninety-degree angle with his body, Novotny thought that he did feel his pain—he did, most certainly, remember the pain, and remembered the misery of no one's taking it seriously but himself. Then he thought of all the men around him who hobbled on artificial limbs during the day and moaned in their beds at night, and he said nothing. Consequently, they sent him back to duty.

He was shunted into an infantry company that was in its seventh week of advanced training. Two days before the company was to be shipped out, he awoke in the morning to discover that the pain had returned. He was able to limp to sick call, where he found on duty the unsympathetic medic, who, almost immediately upon seeing Novotny, began to unwind a roll of three-inch tape. Novotny raised an objection, and an argument ensued, which was settled when the doctor emerged from behind his door. He ordered Novotny into his office and had him strip. He told him to bend forward and touch his toes. Novotny tried, but could come only to within a few inches of them. The doctor looked over Novotny's medical record and then asked if he expected the army to stand on its head because one soldier couldn't touch his toes. He asked him what he expected the army to do for him. The doctor said there were plenty of G.I.s with sore backs in Korea. And with worse. Plenty worse.

Though the pain diminished somewhat during the day, it returned the next morning with increased severity. Novotny could by this time visualize his own insides—he saw the bone as white, and the spot where the pain was located as black. At breakfast, he changed his mind three times over, then went off to the first sergeant to ask permission to go on sick call. He had decided finally that if he did not go and have the condition taken care of within the next few days it would simply get worse and worse; surely there would be no time for medical attention, no proper facilities, while they were in transit to Korea. And, once in Korea, those in charge would surely be even more deaf to his complaints than they were here; there they would be deafened by the roar of cannons. The first sergeant asked Novotny what the matter was this time, and he answered that his back hurt. The first sergeant said what the medic had said the first day: "Everybody's back hurts." But he let him go.

At sick call, the doctor sat Novotny down and asked him what *he* thought was wrong with him. What the suffering soldier had begun to think was that perhaps he had cancer or leukemia. It was really in an effort to minimize his complaint that he said that maybe he had a slipped disc. The doctor said that if Novotny had slipped a disc he wouldn't even be able to walk around. Novotny suddenly found it difficult to breathe. What had he done in life to deserve this? What had he done, from the day he had grown out of short pants, but everything that was asked of him? He told the doctor that all he knew was that he had a pain. He tried to explain that taping it up didn't seem to work; the pain wasn't on the surface but deep inside his back. The doctor said it was deep inside his head. When the doctor told him to go back to duty like a man, Novotny refused.

Novotny was taken to the hospital, and to the office of the colonel in charge of orthopedics. He was a bald man with weighty circles under his eyes and a very erect carriage, who looked to have lived through a good deal. The colonel asked Novotny to sit down and tell him about the pain. Novotny, responding to a long-suffering quality in the man that seemed to him to demand respect, told him the truth: he had rolled over one morning during his basic training, and there it had been, deep and sharp. The colonel asked Novotny if he could think of anything at all that might have caused the pain. Novotny recounted what had happened on K.P. with Reynolds. The doctor asked if that had occurred before the morning he had awakened with the pain, or after it. Novotny admitted that it was after. But surely, he added, that must have aggravated the pain. The doctor said that that did not clear up the problem of where the pain had come from in the first place. He reminded Novotny that the X-rays showed nothing. He ordered Novotny to take off his hospital blues and stretch out on the examination table. By this time, of course, Novotny knew all the tests by heart; once, in fact, he anticipated what he was about to be asked to do, and the colonel gave him a strange look.

When the doctor was finished, he told Novotny that he had a lumbo-sacral strain with some accompanying muscle spasm. Nothing more. It was what they used to call a touch of lumbago. Novotny stood up to leave, and the colonel informed him that when he was released from the hospital he would have to appear at a summary court-martial for having refused to obey the doctor's order to return to duty. Novotny felt weak enough to faint. He was suddenly sorry he had ever opened his mouth. He was ashamed. He heard himself explaining to the colonel that he had refused to obey only because he had felt too sick to go back to duty. The colonel said it was for a trained doctor to decide how sick or well Novotny was. But, answered Novotny—hearing the gates to the stockade slamming shut behind him, imagining prison scenes so nasty even he couldn't endure them —but the doctor had made a mistake. As the colonel said, he *did* have a lumbosacral strain, and muscle spasm, too. In a steely voice, the colonel told him that there were men in Korea who had much worse. That was the statement to which Novotny had no answer; it was the statement that everyone finally made to him.

When they put him in traction, he had further premonitions of his court-martial and his subsequent internment in the stockade. He, Novotny, who had never broken a law in his life. What was happening? Each morning, he awoke at the foot of the bed, pulled there by the weights tied to his ankles and hanging to the floor. His limbs and joints ached day in and day out from being stretched. More than once, he had the illusion of being tortured for a crime he had not committed, although he knew that the traction was therapeutic. At the end of a week, the weights were removed and he was sent to the physical-therapy clinic, where he received heat treatments and was given a series of exercises to perform. Some days, the pain lessened almost to the point of disappearing. Other days, it was as severe as it had ever been. Then he believed that they would have to cut him open, and it would be the doctor at sick call who would be court-martialed instead of himself. When the pain was at its worst, he felt vindicated; but then, too, when it was at its worst he was most miserable.

He was only alone when he was in the bathroom, and it was there that he would try to bend over and touch his toes. He repeated and repeated this, as though it were a key to something. One day, thinking himself alone, he had begun to strain toward his toes when he was turned around by the voice of the osteomyelitis victim, who was sitting in the doorway in his wheelchair. "How's your backache, buddy?" he said, and wheeled sharply away. Everybody in the ward somehow knew bits of Novotny's history; nobody, nobody knew the whole story.

Nobody he didn't know liked him; and he stopped liking those he did know. His mother appeared at the hospital two weeks after his admittance. She treated him like a hero, leaving with him a shoebox full of baked goods and a Polish sausage. He could not bring himself to tell her about his court-martial; he could not disappoint her—and that made him angry. He was even glad to see her go, lonely as he was. Then, the following weekend, Rose Anne arrived. Everybody whistled when she walked down the ward. And he was furious at her—but for what? For being so desirable? So perfect? They argued, and Rose Anne went back to Champaign, bewildered. That night, the Negro fellow next to Novotny, who had lost his right leg in the battle of Seoul, leaned over the side of his bed and said to him, with a note in his voice more dreamy than malicious, "Hey, man, you got it made."

The next day, very early, Novotny went to the hospital library and searched the shelves until he found a medical encyclopedia. He looked up "slipped disc." Just as he had suspected, many of his own symptoms were recorded there. His heart beat wildly as he read of the difficulties of diagnosing a slipped disc, even with X-rays. Ah yes, only the myelogram was certain. He read on and on, over and over, symptoms, treatments, and drugs. One symptom he read of was a tingling sensation that ran down the back of the leg and into the foot, caused by pressure of the herniated disc on a nerve. The following morning, he awoke with a tingling sensation that ran down the back of his right leg and into his foot. Only momentarily was he elated; then it hurt.

On his weekly ward rounds, the colonel, followed by the nurse and the resident, walked up to each bed and talked to the patient; everyone waited his turn silently as in formation. The colonel examined stumps, incisions, casts, prosthetic devices, and then asked each man how he felt.

When he reached Novotny, he asked him to step out of bed and into the aisle, and there he had him reach down and touch his toes. Novotny tried, bending and bending. Someone in the ward called out, "Come on, Daddy, you can do it." Another voice called, "Push, Polack, *push*"—and then it seemed to him that all the patients in the ward were shouting and laughing, and the colonel was doing nothing to restrain them. "Ah, wait'll they get you in Korea"—and then suddenly the ward was silent, for Novotny was straightening up, his face a brilliant red. "I can't do it, sir," he said. "Does your back feel better?" the colonel asked. "Yes, sir." "Do you think we should send you back to duty?" "I've had a tingling sensation down the back of my right leg," Novotny said. "So?" the colonel asked. The ward was silent; Novotny decided not to answer.

In the afternoon, Novotny was called to the colonel's office. He walked there without too much difficulty—but then it was not unusual for the pain to come and go and come back again, with varying degrees of severity. Sometimes the cycle took hours, sometimes days, sometimes only minutes. It was enough to drive a man crazy.

In the colonel's office, Novotny was told that he was going to get another chance. Novotny was too young, the colonel said, not to be extended a little forgiveness for his self-concern. If he went back to duty, the charges against him would be dismissed and there would be no courtmartial. The colonel said that with a war on there was nothing to be gained by putting a good soldier behind bars. The colonel let Novotny know that he was impressed by his marksmanship record, which he had taken the trouble to look up in the company files.

When it was Novotny's turn to speak, he could only think to ask if the colonel believed the tingling sensation in his leg meant nothing at all. The colonel, making it obvious that it was patience he was displaying, asked Novotny what *he* thought it meant. Novotny said he understood it to be a symptom of a slipped disc. The colonel asked him how he knew that, and Novotny—hesitating only a moment, then going on with the truth, on and on with it—said that he had read it in a book. The colonel, his mouth turning down in disgust, asked Novotny if he was that afraid of going to Korea. Novotny did not know what to answer; he truly had not thought of it that way before. The colonel then asked him if he ever broke out in a cold sweat at night. Novotny said no—the only new symptom he had was the tingling in the leg. The colonel brought a fist down on his desk and told Novotny that the following day he was sending him over to see the psychiatrist. He could sit out the rest of the war in the nuthouse.

What to do? Novotny did not know. It was not a cold but a hot sweat that he was in all through dinner. In the evening, he walked to the Coke machine in the hospital basement, as lonely as he had ever been. A nurse passed him in the hall and smiled. She thought he was sick. He drank his Coke, but when he saw two wheelchairs headed his way he turned and moved up the stairs to the hospital library. He began to perspire again, and then he set about looking through the shelves for a book on psychology. Since he knew as little about psychology as he did about medicine, he had to look for a very long time. He did not want to ask for the help of the librarian, even though she was a civilian. At last he was able to pick out two books, and he sat down on the floor between the stacks, where nobody could see him.

Much of what he read he did not completely follow, but once in a while he came upon an anecdote, and in his frustration with the rest of the book, he would read that feverishly. He read of a woman in a European country who had imagined that she was pregnant. She had swelled up, and then, after nine months, she had had labor pains—but no baby. Because it had all been in her imagination. *Her imagination had made her swell up!* Novotny read this over several times. He was respectful of facts, and believed what he found in books. He did not believe that a man would take the time to sit down and write a book so as to tell other people lies.

When he walked back to the ward, his back seemed engulfed in flames. It was then that he became absorbed in the fantasy of reaching inside himself and cutting out of his body the offending circle of pain. He saw himself standing over his own naked back and twisting down on an instrument that resembled the little utensil that is sold in dime stores to remove the core of a grapefruit. In his bed, he could not find a position in which the pain could be forgotten or ignored. He got up and went to the phone booth, where he called long distance to Rose Anne. He could barely prevent himself from begging her to get on a plane and fly down to him that very night. And yet—the darkness, his fright, his fatigue were taking their toll—if it wasn't his back that was causing the pain, was it Rose Anne? Was he being punished for being so happy with her? Were they being punished for all that sex? Unlike his mother, he was not the kind of Catholic who believed in Hell; he was not the kind who was afraid of sex. All he wanted was his chance at life. That was all.

In the washroom, before he returned to bed, he tried to touch his toes. He forced himself down and down and down until his eyes were cloudy from pain and his fingers had moved to within an inch of the floor. But he could not keep his brain from working, and he did not know what to think. If a woman could imagine herself to be in labor, then for him, too, anything was possible. He leaned over the sink and looked into the mirror. With the aid of every truthful cell in his pained body, he admitted to his own face that he was—yes, he was—frightened of going to Korea. Terribly frightened. But wasn't everybody? He wondered if nothing could be wrong with him. He wondered if nothing he knew was so.

The next day, the psychiatrist asked Novotny if he felt nervous. He said he didn't. The psychiatrist asked if he had felt nervous before he had come into the army. Novotny said no, that he had been happy. He asked if

Novotny was afraid of high places, and if he minded being in crowds; he asked if he had any brothers and sisters, and which he liked better, his mother or his father. Novotny answered that his father was dead. He asked which Novotny had liked better before his father died. Novotny did not really care to talk about this subject, particularly to someone he didn't even know, but he had decided to be as frank and truthful with the psychiatrist as it was still possible for him to be—at least, he meant to tell him what he *thought* was the truth. Novotny answered that his father had been lazy and incompetent, and the family was finally better off with him gone. The psychiatrist then asked Novotny about Rose Anne. Novotny was frank. He asked Novotny if his back hurt when he was being intimate with Rose Anne. Novotny answered that sometimes it did and sometimes it didn't. He asked Novotny if, when it did hurt, they ceased being intimate. Novotny dropped his head. It was with a searing sense that some secret had been uncovered, something he himself had not even known, that he admitted that they did not. He simply could not bring himself, however, to tell the psychiatrist what exactly they did do when Novotny's back was at its worst. He said quickly that he planned to marry Rose Anne—that he had always known he would marry her. The psychiatrist asked where the couple would live, and Novotny said with his mother. When he asked Novotny why, Novotny said because he had to take care of her, too.

The psychiatrist made Novotny stand up, close his eyes, and try to touch the tips of his index fingers together. While Novotny's eyes were closed, the psychiatrist leaned forward and, in a whisper, asked if Novotny was afraid of dying. The weight of all that he had been put through in the past weeks came down upon the shoulder of the young soldier. He broke down and admitted to a fear of death. He began to weep and to say that he didn't want to die. The psychiatrist asked him if he hated the army, and he admitted that he did.

The psychiatrist's office was across the street from the main hospital, in the building the colonel had called the nuthouse. Novotny, full of shame, was led out of the building by an attendant with a large ring of keys hooked to his belt; he had to unlock three doors before Novotny got out to the street. He went out the rear door, just in sight of a volleyball game that was being played within a wire enclosure at the back of the building. To pull himself together before returning to the hostile cripples in the ward, Novotny watched the teams bat the ball back and forth over the net, and then he realized that they were patients who spent their days and nights inside the building from which he had just emerged. It occurred to him that the doctors were going to put him into the psychiatric hospital. Not because he was making believe he had a pain in his back—which, he had come to think, was really why they had been going to put him in the stockade—but precisely because he was *not* making believe. He was feeling a pain for which there was no cause. He had a terrible vision of Rose

Anne having to come here to visit him. She was only a young girl, and he knew that it would frighten her so much to be led through three locked doors that he would lose her. He was about to begin to lose things.

He pulled himself straight up—he had been stooping—and clenched his teeth and told himself that in a certain number of seconds the pain would be gone for good. He counted to thirty, and then took a step. He came down upon his right foot with only half his weight, but the pain was still there, so sharp that it made his eyes water. The volleyball smashed against the fence through which he was peering, and, trying to walk as he remembered himself walking when he was a perfectly healthy young man, a man with nothing to fear—a man, he thought, who had not even begun to know of all the confusion growing up inside him—he walked away.

The colonel had Novotny called to his office the following day. The night before, Novotny had got little sleep, but by dawn he had reached a decision. Now, though he feared the worst, he marched to the colonel's office with a plan of action held firmly in mind. When Novotny entered, the colonel asked him to sit down, and proceeded to tell him of his own experiences in the Second World War. He had flown with an airborne division at a time when he was only a little more than Novotny's age. He had jumped from a plane over Normandy and broken both his legs, and then been shot in the chest by a French farmer for a reason he still did not understand. The colonel said that he had returned from Korea only a week before Novotny had entered the hospital. He wished that Novotny could see what the men there were going through—he wished Novotny could be witness to the bravery and the courage and the comradery, and, too, to the misery and suffering. The misery of our soldiers and of those poor Koreans! He was not angry with Novotny personally; he was only trying to tell him something for his own good. Novotny was too young to make a decision that might disgrace him for the rest of his life. He told the young soldier that if he walked around with that back of his for a few weeks, if he just stopped *thinking* about it all the time, it would be as good as new. That, in actual fact, it was almost as good as new right now. He said that Novotny's trouble was that he was a passive-aggressive.

Novotny's voice was very thin when he asked the colonel what he meant. The colonel read to him what the psychiatrist had written. It was mostly the answers that Novotny had given to the psychiatrist's questions; some of it had to do with the way Novotny had sat, and the tone of his voice, and certain words he had apparently used. In the end, the report said that Novotny was a passive-aggressive and recommended he be given an administrative separation from the army, and the appropriate discharge. Novotny asked what that meant. The colonel replied that the appropriate discharge as far as he was concerned was "plain and simple"; he took down a book of regulations from a shelf behind him, and after flipping past several pages read to Novotny in a loud voice. " 'An undesirable discharge is an administrative separation from the service under conditions other than honorable. It is issued for unfitness, misconduct, or security reasons.' " He looked up, got no response, and, fiery-eyed, read further. " 'It is recognized that all enlisted personnel with behavior problems cannot be rehabilitated by proper leadership and/or psychiatric assistance. It is inevitable that a certain percentage of individuals entering the service subsequently will demonstrate defective moral habits, irresponsibility, inability to profit by experience—' " He paused to read the last phrase again, and then went on—" 'untrustworthiness, lack of regard for the rights of others, and inability to put off pleasures and impulses of the moment.' " He engaged Novotny's eye. " 'Often,' " he said, returning to the regulation, " 'these individuals show poor performance despite intelligence, superficial charm, and a readiness to promise improvement. The effective leader is able to rehabilitate only the percentage of persons with behavior problems who are amenable to leadership.' " He stopped. "You can say that again," he mumbled, and pushed the book forward on his desk so that it faced Novotny. "Unfitness, soldier," he said, tapping his finger on the page. "It's what we use to get the crackpots out—bed-wetters, homos, petty thieves, malingerers, and so on." He waited for Novotny to take in the page's contents, and while he did, the colonel made it clear that such a discharge followed a man through life. Novotny, raising his head slightly, asked again what a passive-aggressive was. The colonel looked into his eyes and said, "Just another kind of coward."

What Novotny had decided in bed the night before was to request a myelogram. Of course, there lived still in his imagination the man who had said that all the needle had to do was be off by a hairbreadth; he was convinced, in fact, that something like that was just what would happen to him, given the way things had begun to go in his life. But though such a prospect frightened him, he did not see that he had any choice. The truth had to be known, one way or the other. But when the colonel finished and waited for him to speak, he remained silent.

"What do you have against the army, Novotny?" the colonel asked. "What makes you so special?"

Novotny did not mention the myelogram. Why *should* he? Why should he have to take so much from people when he had an honest-to-God pain in his back? He was not imagining it, he was not making it up. He had practically ruptured himself when Reynolds had dropped the end of the can of potatoes. Maybe he had only awakened with a simple strain that first morning, but trying to keep the can from dropping on Reynolds' toes, he had done something serious to his back. That all the doctors were unable to give a satisfactory diagnosis did not make his pain any less real.

"You are a God-damned passive-aggressive, young man, what do you think of that?" the colonel said.

Novotny did not speak.

"You know how many people in America have low back pain?" the colonel demanded. "Something like fifteen per cent of the adult population of this country has low back pain—and what do you think they do, quit? Lay down on the job? What do you think a man does who has a family and responsibilities—stop supporting them? You know what your trouble is, my friend? You think life owes you something. You think something's coming to you. I spotted you right off, Novotny. You're going to get your way in this world. Everybody else can to to hell, just so long as you have your way. Imagine if all those men in Korea, if they all gave in to every little ache and pain. Imagine if that was what our troops had done at Valley Forge, or Okinawa. Then where would we all be? Haven't you ever heard of self-sacrifice? The average man, if you threatened him with this kind of discharge, would do just about anything he could to avoid it. But not you. Even if you have a pain, haven't you got the guts to go ahead and serve like everybody else? Well, answer me, yes or no?"

But Novotny would not answer. All he had done was answer people and tell them the truth, and what had it got him? What good was it, being good? What good was it, especially if at bottom you were bad anyway? What good was it, acting strong, if at bottom you were weak and couldn't *be* strong if you wanted to? With the colonel glaring across at him, the only solace Novotny had was to think that nobody knew any more about him than he himself did. Whatever anybody chose to call him didn't really mean a thing.

"Ah, get out of my sight," the colonel said. "People like you make me sick. Go ahead, join the bed-wetters and the queers. Get the hell out of here."

Within six days, the army had rid itself of Novotny. It took Novotny, however, a good deal more than six days to rid himself of infirmity—if he can be said ever to have rid himself of infirmity—or, at least, the threat of infirmity. During the next year, he missed days of work and evenings of night school, and spent numerous weekends on a mattress supported by a bedboard, where he rested and nursed away his pain. He went to one doctor who prescribed a set of exercises, and another who prescribed a steel brace, which Novotny bought but found so uncomfortable that he finally had to stick it away in the attic, though it had cost forty-five dollars. Another doctor, who had been recommended to him, listened to his story, then simply shrugged his shoulders; and still another told Novotny what the colonel had—that many Americans had low back ailments, that they were frequently of unknown origin, and that he would have to learn to live with it.

That, finally, was what he tried to do. Gradually, over the years, the pain diminished in severity and frequency, though even today he has an occasional bad week, and gets a twinge if he bends the wrong way or picks up something he shouldn't. He is married to Rose Anne and is employed as a television cameraman by an educational channel in Chicago. His mother lives with him and his wife in Park Forest. For the most part, he leads a quiet, ordinary sort of life, though his attachment to Rose Anne is still marked by an unusual passion. When the other men in Park Forest go bowling on Friday nights, Novotny stays home, for he tries not to put strains upon his body to which he has decided it is not equal. In a way, all the awfulness of those army days has boiled down to that—no bowling. There are nights, of course, when Novotny awakens from a dead sleep to worry in the dark about the future. What will happen to him? What won't? But surely those are questions he shares with all men, sufferers of low back pain and non-sufferers alike. Nobody has ever yet asked to see his discharge papers, so about that the colonel was wrong.

part three
the novella
or short novel

Few terms in the study of fiction are as elusive as *novella*; indeed, two of the three selections in this unit, Joseph Conrad's *The Secret Sharer* and James Joyce's *The Dead*, are often classified as long short stories rather than novellas. No clear boundary separates the short story from the novella. In their preface to *Ten Modern Short Novels*, Leo Hamalian and Edmond L. Volpe claim that length alone distinguishes the novella from the short story. Consequently, while acknowledging that some writers describe any work of fiction of about 30,000 words as a novella, Volpe and Hamalian so designate works between 15,000 and 40,000 words. Anything less they consider a short story, anything more a novel.

Even the origin of the term novella reveals its close relationship to the short story. In Italian, *novella* means "story," "short story," or "tale," definitions which emphasize the closeness of the short novel to the short story. Early collections of novellas which appeared even before the turn of the fourteenth century, such as *Cento Novelle Antiche*, culminated in perhaps the most famous book of novellas, Boccaccio's *Decameron* (1353), a collection of bawdy tales of unfaithful wives, ingenious lovers, and hypocritical priests. Strictly speaking, these novellas are short stories. But somewhere in its evolution the novella grew beyond the limits of a story which can be read easily at a single sitting.

Despite the fact that some critics consider length the only criterion that can "really serve to distinguish this form of fiction," the length of a work directly affects the number of characters a story will contain; the extent to which characters will be developed; the point of view an author will select; the structure of a work; the amount of time covered; and perhaps even the writing style.

A short story gains uniqueness from its directness and brevity, and usually aims at singleness of effect; it is the art of focus and revelation. Because the short story is restricted in how much space and time it can cover, it must reduce the number of characters and incidents to a minimum. It deals with fragments, with quick, brief glances at man's moral and psychological makeup. The short-story writer, consequently, asks that we take a good deal for granted. Often he begins near the "end" of a climactic period, depicting characters who are virtually "complete" as the story begins; they do not evolve or grow before our eyes. In the short story, then, theme is often more important than character or context. At the other end of the fiction spectrum, the novel is governed by different rules. It is the art of moral evolution; thus, it treats a more complex set of social and psychological relationships.

The short story, the novella, and the novel operate according to different patterns. Obviously, a large structure takes up more ground, uses more time and people, and needs different materials than does a small structure. The novelist can deal with whole generations, as Lawrence does in *Women in Love*, or with the growth of a single individual, as he does in *Sons and Lovers*, and as Joyce does in *A Portrait of the Artist as a Young Man*. The novelist can crowd his work with every manner of social type, as Dickens repeatedly does; he can travel from continent to continent, or move back or forward in time. In this sense, the novel is to the film or the epic as the short story is to the snapshot or lyric poem. Because of its added length, then, the novel is ideally suited to the revelation of context as well as character.

Like the short story, the novella follows conventions, however imprecise; thus, it is erroneous to say that the novella is merely a long short story. Nor is it merely a short novel, although it is often called that. In reality, it is midway between the short story and the novel, having at its disposal *either* directness, clarity, and limited scope *or* greater scope and multiplicity of focus. It has the capacity for more extensive psychological and contextual development than the short story, yet for less than the novel. It offers the fictionist a happy camp between both worlds of fiction, the short story and the novel.

THE DEATH OF IVAN ILYCH

by Leo Tolstoy

(1828–1910)

I

During an interval in the Melvinski trial in the large building of the Law Courts, the members and public prosecutor met in Ivan Egorovich Shebek's private room, where the conversation turned on the celebrated Krasovski case. Fëdor Vasilievich warmly maintained that it was not subject to their jurisdiction, Ivan Egorovich maintained the contrary, while Peter Ivanovich, not having entered into the discussion at the start, took no part in it but looked through the *Gazette* which had just been handed in.

"Gentlemen," he said, "Ivan Ilych has died!"

"You don't say so!"

"Here, read it yourself," replied Peter Ivanovich, handing Fëdor Vasilievich the paper still damp from the press. Surrounded by a black border were the words: "Praskovya Fëdorovna Golovina, with profound sorrow, informs relatives and friends of the demise of her beloved husband Ivan Ilych Golovin, Member of the Court of Justice, which occurred on February the 4th of this year 1882. The funeral will take place on Friday at one o'clock in the afternoon."

Ivan Ilych had been a colleague of the gentlemen present and was liked by them all. He had been ill for some weeks with an illness said to be incurable. His post had been kept open for him, but there had been conjectures that in case of his death Alexeev might receive his appointment, and that either Vinnikov or Shtabel would succeed Alexeev. So on receiving the news of Ivan Ilych's death the first thought of each of the gentlemen in that private room was of the changes and promotions it might occasion among themselves or their acquaintances.

"I shall be sure to get Shtabel's place or Vinnikov's," thought Fëdor Vasilievich. "I was promised that long ago, and the promotion means an extra eight hundred rubles a year for me beside the allowance."

"Now I must apply for my brother-in-law's transfer from Kaluga," thought Peter Ivanovich. "My wife will be very glad, and then she won't be able to say that I never do anything for her relations."

"I thought he would never leave his bed again," said Peter Ivanovich aloud. "It's very sad."

"But what really was the matter with him?"

"The doctors couldn't say—at least they could, but each of them said something different. When last I saw him I thought he was getting better."

"And I haven't been to see him since the holidays. I always meant to go."

"Had he any property?"

"I think his wife had a little—but something quite trifling."

"We shall have to go to see her, but they live so terribly far away."

"Far away from you, you mean. Everything's far away from your place."

"You see, he never can forgive my living on the other side of the river," said Peter Ivanovich, smiling at Shebek. Then, still talking of the distances between different parts of the city, they returned to the Court.

Besides considerations as to the possible transfers and promotions likely to result from Ivan Ilych's death, the mere fact of the death of a near acquaintance aroused, as usual, in all who heard of it the complacent feeling that, "it is he who is dead and not I."

Each one thought or felt, "Well, he's dead but I'm alive!" But the more intimate of Ivan Ilych's acquaintances, his so-called friends, could not help thinking also that they would now have to fulfill the very tiresome demands of propriety by attending the funeral service and paying a visit of condolence to the widow.

Fëdor Vasilievich and Peter Ivanovich had been his nearest acquaintances. Peter Ivanovich had studied law with Ivan Ilych and had considered himself to be under obligations to him.

Having told his wife at dinner-time of Ivan Ilych's death and of his conjecture that it might be possible to get her brother transferred to their circuit, Peter Ivanovich sacrificed his usual nap, put on his evening clothes, and drove to Ivan Ilych's house.

At the entrance stood a carriage and two cabs. Leaning against the wall in the hall downstairs near the cloakstand was a coffin lid covered with cloth of gold, ornamented with gold cord and tassels, that had been polished up with metal powder. Two ladies in black were taking off their fur cloaks. Peter Ivanovich recognized one of them as Ivan Ilych's sister, but the other was a stranger to him. His colleague Schwartz was just coming downstairs, but on seeing Peter Ivanovich enter he stopped and winked at him, as if to say: "Ivan Ilych has made a mess of things—not like you and me."

Schwartz's face, with his Piccadilly whiskers and his slim figure in evening dress, had as usual an air of elegant solemnity which contrasted with the playfulness of his character and had a special piquancy here, or so it seemed to Peter Ivanovich.

Peter Ivanovich allowed the ladies to precede him and slowly followed them upstairs. Schwartz did not come down but remained where he was, and Peter Ivanovich understood that he wanted to arrange where they should play bridge that evening. The ladies went upstairs to the widow's room, and Schwartz with seriously compressed lips but a playful look in his eyes, indicated by a twist of his eyebrows the room to the right where the body lay.

Peter Ivanovich, like everyone else on such occasions, entered feeling uncertain what he would have to do. All he knew was that at such times it is always safe to cross oneself. But he was not quite sure whether one should make obeisances while doing so. He therefore adopted a middle course. On entering the room he began crossing himself and made a slight movement resembling a bow. At the same time, as far as the motion of his head and arm allowed, he surveyed the room. Two young men—apparently nephews, one of whom was a high school pupil—were leaving the room, crossing themselves as they did so. An old woman was standing motionless, and a lady with strangely arched eyebrows was saying something to her in a whisper. A vigorous, resolute Church Reader, in a frock-coat, was reading something in a loud voice with an expression that precluded any contradiction. The butler's assistant, Gerasim, stepping lightly in front of Peter Ivanovich, was strewing something on the floor. Noticing this, Peter Ivanovich was immediately aware of a faint odor of a decomposing body.

The last time he had called on Ivan Ilych, Peter Ivanovich had seen Gerasim in the study. Ivan Ilych had been particularly fond of him and he was performing the duty of a sick nurse.

Peter Ivanovich continued to make the sign of the cross slightly inclining his head in an intermediate direction between the coffin, the Reader, and the icons on the table in a corner of the room. Afterward, when it seemed to him that this movement of his arm in crossing himself had gone on too long, he stopped and began to look at the corpse.

The dead man lay, as dead men always lie, in a specially heavy way, his rigid limbs sunk in the soft cushions of the coffin, with the head forever bowed on the pillow. His yellow waxen brow with bald patches over his sunken temples was thrust up in the way peculiar to the dead, the protruding nose seeming to press on the upper lip. He was much changed and had grown even thinner since Peter Ivanovich had last seen him, but, as is always the case with the dead, his face was handsomer and above all more dignified than when he was alive. The expression on the face said that what was necessary had been accomplished, and accomplished rightly. Besides this there was in that expression a reproach and a warning to the living. This warning seemed to Peter Ivanovich out of place, or at least not applicable to him. He felt a certain discomfort and so he hurriedly crossed himself once more and turned and went out of the door—too hurriedly and too regardless of propriety, as he himself was aware.

Schwartz was waiting for him in the adjoining room with legs spread wide apart and both hands toying with his top hat behind his back. The mere sight of that playful, well-groomed, and elegant figure refreshed Peter

Ivanovich. He felt that Schwartz was above all these happenings and would not surrender to any depressing influences. His very look said that this incident of a church service for Ivan Ilych could not be a sufficient reason for infringing the order of the session—in other words, that it would certainly not prevent his unwrapping a new pack of cards and shuffling them that evening while a footman placed four fresh candles on the table: in fact, that there was no reason for supposing that this incident would hinder their spending the evening agreeably. Indeed he said this in a whisper as Peter Ivanovich passed him, proposing that they should meet for a game at Fëdor Vasilievich's. But apparently Peter Ivanovich was not destined to play bridge that evening. Praskovya Fëdorovna (a short, fat woman who despite all efforts to the contrary had continued to broaden steadily from her shoulders downward and who had the same extraordinarily arched eyebrows as the lady who had been standing by the coffin), dressed all in black, her head covered with lace, came out of her own room with some other ladies, conducted them to the room where the dead body lay, and said: "The service will begin immediately. Please go in."

Schwartz making an indefinite bow, stood still, evidently neither accepting nor declining this invitation. Praskovya Fëdorovna, recognizing Peter Ivanovich, sighed, went close to him, took his hand, and said: "I know you were a true friend to Ivan Ilych . . ." and looked at him awaiting some suitable response. And Peter Ivanovich knew that, just as it had been the right thing to cross himself in that room, so what he had to do here was to press her hand, sigh, and say, "Believe me. . . ." So he did all this and as he did it felt that the desired result had been achieved: that both he and she were touched.

"Come with me. I want to speak to you before it begins," said the widow. "Give me your arm."

Peter Ivanovich gave her his arm and they went to the inner rooms, passing Schwartz, who winked at Peter Ivanovich compassionately.

"That does for our bridge! Don't object if we find another player. Perhaps you can cut in when you do escape," said his playful look.

Peter Ivanovich sighed still more deeply and despondently, and Praskovya Fëdorovna pressed his arm gratefully. When they reached the drawing room, upholstered in pink cretonne and lighted by a dim lamp, they sat down at the table—she on a sofa and Peter Ivanovich on a low pouffe, the springs of which yielded spasmodically under his weight. Praskovya Fëdorovna had been on the point of warning him to take another seat, but felt that such a warning was out of keeping with her present condition and so changed her mind. As he sat down on the pouffe Peter Ivanovich recalled how Ivan Ilych had arranged this room and had consulted him regarding this pink cretonne with green leaves. The whole room was full of furniture and knick-knacks, and on her way to the sofa the lace of the widow's black shawl caught on the carved edge of the table. Peter Ivanovich rose to detach it, and the springs of the pouffe, relieved of his weight, rose also and gave him a push. The widow began detaching her shawl herself, and Peter Ivanovich again sat down, suppressing the rebellious springs of the pouffe under him. But the widow had not quite freed herself and Peter Ivanovich got up again, and again the pouffe rebelled and even creaked. When this was all over she took out a clean cambric handkerchief and began to weep. The episode with the shawl and the struggle with the pouffe had cooled Peter Ivanovich's emotions and he sat there with a sullen look on his face. This awkward situation was interrupted by Sokolov, Ivan Ilych's butler, who came to report that the plot in the cemetery that Praskovya Fëdorovna had chosen would cost two hundred rubles. She stopped weeping and, looking at Peter Ivanovich with the air of a victim, remarked in French that it was very hard for her. Peter Ivanovich made a silent gesture signifying his full conviction that it must indeed be so.

"Please smoke," she said in a magnanimous yet crushed voice, and turned to discuss with Sokolov the price of the plot for the grave.

Peter Ivanovich while lighting his cigarette heard her inquiring very circumstantially into the prices of different plots in the cemetery and finally decide which she would take. When that was done she gave instructions about engaging the choir. Sokolov then left the room.

"I look after everything myself," she told Peter Ivanovich, shifting the albums that lay on the table; and noticing that the table was endangered by his cigarette ash, she immediately passed him an ashtray, saying as she did so: "I consider it an affectation to say that my grief prevents my attending to practical affairs. On the contrary, if anything can—I won't say console me, but—distract me, it is seeing to everything concerning him." She again took out her handkerchief as if preparing to cry, but suddenly, as if mastering her feeling, she shook herself and began to speak calmly. "But there is something I want to talk to you about."

Peter Ivanovich bowed, keeping control of the springs of the pouffe, which immediately began quivering under him.

"He suffered terribly the last few days."

"Did he?" said Peter Ivanovich.

"Oh, terribly! He screamed unceasingly, not for minutes but for hours. For the last three days he screamed incessantly. It was unendurable. I cannot understand how I bore it; you could hear him three rooms off. Oh, what I have suffered!"

"Is it possible that he was conscious all that time?" asked Peter Ivanovich.

"Yes," she whispered. "To the last moment. He took leave of us a quarter of an hour before he died, and asked us to take Volodya away."

The thought of the sufferings of this man he had known so intimately, first as a merry little boy, then as a schoolmate, and later as a grown-up colleague, suddenly struck Peter Ivanovich with horror, despite an unpleasant consciousness of his own and this woman's dissimulation. He again saw that brow, and that nose pressing down on the lip, and felt afraid for himself.

"Three days of frightful suffering and then death! Why, that might suddenly, at any time, happen to me," he thought, and for a moment felt terrified. But—he did not himself know how—the customary reflection at once occurred to him that this had happened to Ivan Ilych and not to him, and that it should not and could not happen to him, and to think that it could would be yielding to depression which he ought not to do, as Schwartz's expression plainly showed. After which reflection Peter Ivanovich felt reassured, and began to ask with interest about the details of Ivan Ilych's death, as though death was an accident natural to Ivan Ilych but certainly not to himself.

After many details of the really dreadful physical sufferings Ivan Ilych had endured (which details he learned only from the effect those sufferings had produced on Praskovya Fëdorovna's nerves) the widow apparently found it necessary to get to business.

"Oh, Peter Ivanovich, how hard it is! How terribly, terribly hard!" and she again began to weep.

Peter Ivanovich sighed and waited for her to finish blowing her nose. When she had done so he said, "Believe me . . ." and she again began talking and brought out what was evidently her chief concern with him— namely, to question him as to how she could obtain a grant of money from the government on the occasion of her husband's death. She made it appear that she was asking Peter Ivanovich's advice about her pension, but he soon saw that she already knew about that to the minutest detail, more even than he did himself. She knew how much could be got out of the government in consequence of her husband's death, but wanted to find out whether she could not possibly extract something more. Peter Ivanovich tried to think of some means of doing so, but after reflecting for a while and, out of propriety, condemning the government for its niggardliness, he said he thought that nothing more could be got. Then she sighed and evidently began to devise means of getting rid of her visitor. Noticing this, he put out his cigarette, rose, pressed her hand, and went out into the anteroom.

In the dining room where the clock stood that Ivan Ilych had liked so much and had bought at an antique shop, Peter Ivanovich met a priest and a few acquaintances who had come to attend the service, and he recognized Ivan Ilych's daughter, a handsome young woman. She was in black and her slim figure appeared slimmer than ever. She had a gloomy, determined, almost angry expression, and bowed to Peter Ivanovich as though he were in some way to blame. Behind her, with the same offended look, stood a wealthy young man, an examining magistrate, whom Peter Ivanovich also knew and who was her fiancé, as he had heard. He bowed mournfully to them and was about to pass into the death chamber, when from under the stairs appeared the figure of Ivan Ilych's schoolboy son, who was extremely like his father. He seemed a little Ivan Ilych, such as Peter Ivanovich remembered when they studied law together. His tear-stained eyes had in them the look that is seen in the eyes of boys of thirteen or fourteen who are not pure-minded. When he saw Peter Ivanovich he scowled morosely and shamefacedly. Peter Ivanovich nodded to him and entered the death chamber. The service began: candles, groans, incense, tears, and sobs. Peter Ivanovich stood looking gloomily down at his feet. He did not look once at the dead man, did not yield to any depressing influence, and was one of the first to leave the room. There was no one in the anteroom, but Gerasim darted out of the dead man's room, rummaged with his strong hands among the fur coats to find Peter Ivanovich's and helped him on with it.

"Well, friend Gerasim," said Peter Ivanovich, so as to say something. "It's a sad affair, isn't it?"

"It's God's will. We shall all come to it some day," said Gerasim, displaying his teeth—the even, white teeth of a healthy peasant—and, like a man in the thick of urgent work, he briskly opened the front door, called the coachman, helped Peter Ivanovich into the sledge, and sprang back to the porch as if in readiness for what he had to do next.

Peter Ivanovich found the fresh air particularly pleasant after the smell of incense, the dead body, and carbolic acid.

"Where to, sir?" asked the coachman.

"It's not too late even now. . . . I'll call round on Fëdor Vasilievich."

He accordingly drove there and found them just finishing the first rubber, so that it was quite convenient for him to cut in.

II

Ivan Ilych's life had been most simple and most ordinary and therefore most terrible.

He had been a member of the Court of Justice, and died at the age of forty-five. His father had been an official who after serving in various ministries and departments in Petersburg had made the sort of career which brings men to positions from which by reason of their long service they cannot be dismissed, though they are obviously unfit to hold any responsible position, and for whom therefore posts are especially created, which though fictitious carry salaries of from six to ten thousand rubles that are not fictitious, and in receipt of which they live on to a great age.

Such was the Privy Councillor and superfluous member of various superfluous institutions, Ilya Epimovich Golovin.

He had three sons, of whom Ivan Ilych was the second. The eldest son was following in his father's footsteps only in another department, and was already approaching that stage in the service at which a similar sine-cure would be reached. The third son was a failure. He had ruined his prospects in a number of positions and was now serving in the railway department. His father and brothers, and still more their wives, not merely disliked meeting him, but avoided remembering his existence unless compelled to do so. His sister had married Baron Greff, a Petersburg official of her father's type. Ivan Ilych was *le phénix de la famille* as people said. He was neither as cold and formal as his elder brother nor as wild as the younger, but was a happy mean between them—an intelligent, polished, lively and agreeable man. He had studied with his younger brother at the School of Law, but the latter had failed to complete the course and was expelled when he was in the fifth class. Ivan Ilych finished the course well. Even when he was at the School of Law he was just what he remained for the rest of his life: a capable, cheerful, good-natured, and sociable man, though strict in the fulfillment of what he considered to be his duty: and he considered his duty to be what was so considered by those in authority. Neither as a boy nor as a man was he a toady, but from early youth was by nature attracted to people of high station as a fly is drawn to the light, assimilating their ways and views of life and establishing friendly relations with them. All the enthusiasms of childhood and youth passed without leaving much trace on him; he succumbed to sensuality, to vanity, and latterly among the highest classes to liberalism, but always within limits which his instinct unfailingly indicated to him as correct.

At school he had done things which had formerly seemed to him very horrid and made him feel disgusted with himself when he did them; but when later on he saw that such actions were done by people of good position and that they did not regard them as wrong, he was able not exactly to regard them as right, but to forget about them entirely or not be at all troubled at remembering them.

Having graduated from the School of Law and qualified for the tenth rank of the civil service, and having received money from his father for his equipment, Ivan Ilych ordered himself clothes at Scharmer's, the fashionable tailor, hung a medallion inscribed *respice finem** on his watch-chain, took leave of his professor and the prince who was patron of the school, had a farewell dinner with his comrades at Donon's first-class restaurant, and with his new and fashionable portmanteau, linen, clothes, shaving and other toilet appliances, and a traveling rug, all purchased at the best shops, he set off for one of the provinces where, through his father's influence, he had been attached to the governor as an official for special service.

In the province Ivan Ilych soon arranged as easy and agreeable a position for himself as he had had at the School of Law. He performed his official tasks, made his career, and at the same time amused himself pleasantly and decorously. Occasionally he paid official visits to country districts, where he behaved with dignity both to his superiors and inferiors, and performed the duties entrusted to him, which related chiefly to the sectarians, with an exactness and incorruptible honesty of which he could not but feel proud.

* *respice finem:* look to the end.

In official matters, despite his youth and taste for frivolous gaiety, he was exceedingly reserved, punctilious, and even severe; but in society he was often amusing and witty, and always good-natured, correct in his manner, and *bon enfant*, as the governor and his wife—with whom he was like one of the family—used to say of him.

In the province he had an affair with a lady who made advances to the elegant young lawyer, and there was also a milliner; and there were carousals with aides-de-camp who visited the district, and after-supper visits to a certain outlying street of doubtful reputation; and there was too some obsequiousness to his chief and even to his chief's wife, but all this was done with such a tone of good breeding that no hard names could be applied to it. It all came under the heading of the French saying: *Il faut que jeunesse se passe.** It was all done with clean hands, in clean linen, with French phrases, and above all among people of the best society and consequently with the approval of people of rank.

So Ivan Ilych served for five years and then came a change in his official life. The new and reformed judicial institutions were introduced, and new men were needed. Ivan Ilych became such a new man. He was offered the post of examining magistrate, and he accepted it though the post was in another province and obliged him to give up the connections he had formed and to make new ones. His friends met to give him a send-off; they had a group photograph taken and presented him with a silver cigarette case, and he set off to his new post.

As examining magistrate Ivan Ilych was just as *comme il faut* and decorous a man, inspiring general respect and capable of separating his official duties from his private life, as he had been when acting as an official on special service. His duties now as examining magistrate were far more interesting and attractive than before. In his former position it had been pleasant to wear an undress uniform made by Scharmer, and to pass through the crowd of petitioners and officials who were timorously awaiting an audience with the governor, and who envied him as with free and easy gait he went straight into his chief's private room to have a cup of tea and a cigarette with him. But not many people had then been directly dependent on him—only police officials and the sectarians when he went on special missions—and he liked to treat them politely, almost as comrades, as if he were letting them feel that he who had the power to crush them was treating them in this simple, friendly way. There were then but few such people. But now, as an examining magistrate, Ivan Ilych felt that everyone without exception, even the most important and self-satisfied, was in his power, and that he need only write a few words on a sheet of paper with a certain heading, and this or that important, self-satisfied person would be brought before him in the role of an accused person or a witness, and if he did not choose to allow him to sit down, would have to

---

* *Il faut . . . passe:* You're only young once.

stand before him and answer his questions. Ivan Ilych never abused his power; he tried on the contrary to soften its expression, but the consciousness of it and of the possibility of softening its effect, supplied the chief interest and attraction of his office. In his work itself, especially in his examinations, he very soon acquired a method of eliminating all considerations irrelevant to the legal aspect of the case, and reducing even the most complicated case to a form in which it would be presented on paper only in its externals, completely excluding his personal opinion of the matter, while above all observing every prescribed formality. The work was new and Ivan Ilych was one of the first men to apply the new Code of 1864.

On taking up the post of examining magistrate in a new town, he made new acquaintances and connections, placed himself on a new footing, and assumed a somewhat different tone. He took up an attitude of rather dignified aloofness toward the provincial authorities, but picked out the best circle of legal gentlemen and wealthy gentry living in the town and assumed a tone of slight dissatisfaction with the government, of moderate liberalism, and of enlightened citizenship. At the same time, without at all altering the elegance of his toilet, he ceased shaving his chin and allowed his beard to grow as it pleased.

Ivan Ilych settled down very pleasantly in this new town. The society there, which inclined toward opposition to the Governor, was friendly, his salary was larger, and he began to play *vint*, which he found added not a little to the pleasure of life, for he had a capacity for cards, played good-humoredly, and calculated rapidly and astutely, so that he usually won.

After living there for two years he met his future wife, Praskovya Fëdorovna Mikhel, who was the most attractive, clever, and brilliant girl of the set in which he moved, and among other amusements and relaxations from his labors as examining magistrate, Ivan Ilych established light and playful relations with her.

While he had been an official on special service he had been accustomed to dance, but now as an examining magistrate it was exceptional for him to do so. If he danced now, he did it as if to show that though he served under the reformed order of things, and had reached the fifth official rank, yet when it came to dancing he could do it better than most people. So at the end of an evening he sometimes danced with Praskovya Fëdorovna, and it was chiefly during these dances that he captivated her. She fell in love with him. Ivan Ilych had at first no definite intention of marrying, but when the girl fell in love with him he said to himself: "Really, why shouldn't I marry?"

Praskovya Fëdorovna came of a good family, was not bad-looking, and had some little property. Ivan Ilych might have aspired to a more brilliant match, but even this was good. He had his salary, and she, he hoped, would have an equal income. She was well connected, and was a sweet, pretty, and thoroughly correct young woman. To say that Ivan Ilych married because he fell in love with Praskovya Fëdorovna and found that she sympathized with his views of life would be as incorrect as to say that he married because his social circle approved of the match. He was swayed by both these considerations: the marriage gave him personal satisfaction, and at the same time it was considered the right thing by the most highly placed of his associates.

So Ivan Ilych got married.

The preparations for marriage and the beginning of married life, with its conjugal caresses, the new furniture, new crockery, and new linen, were very pleasant until his wife became pregnant—so that Ivan Ilych had begun to think that marriage would not impair the easy, agreeable, gay and always decorous character of his life, approved of by society and regarded by himself as natural, but would even improve it. But from the first months of his wife's pregnancy, something new, unpleasant, depressing, and unseemly, and from which there was no way of escape, unexpectedly showed itself.

His wife, without any reason—*de gaieté de coeur** as Ivan Ilych expressed it to himself—began to disturb the pleasure and propriety of their life. She began to be jealous without any cause, expected him to devote his whole attention to her, found fault with everything, and made coarse and ill-mannered scenes.

At first Ivan Ilych hoped to escape from the unpleasantness of this state of affairs by the same easy and decorous relation to life that had served him heretofore: he tried to ignore his wife's disagreeable moods, continued to live in his usual easy and pleasant way, invited friends to his house for a game of cards, and also tried going out to his club or spending his evenings with friends. But one day his wife began upbraiding him so vigorously, using such coarse words, and continued to abuse him every time he did not fulfill her demands, so resolutely and with such evident determination not to give way till he submitted—that is, till he stayed at home and was bored just as she was—that he became alarmed. He now realized that matrimony—at any rate with Praskovya Fëdorovna—was not always conducive to the pleasures and amenities of life, but on the contrary often infringed both comfort and propriety, and that he must therefore entrench himself against such infringement. And Ivan Ilych began to seek for means of doing so. His official duties were the one thing that imposed upon Praskovya Fëdorovna, and by means of his official work and the duties attached to it he began struggling with his wife to secure his own independence.

With the birth of their child, the attempts to feed it and the various failures in doing so, and with the real and imaginary illnesses of mother and child, in which Ivan Ilych's sympathy was demanded but about which he understood nothing, the need of securing for himself an existence outside his family life became still more imperative.

* *de gaieté de coeur:* out of sheer wantonness.

As his wife grew more irritable and exacting and Ivan Ilych transferred the center of gravity of his life more and more to his official work, so did he grow to like his work better and became more ambitious than before.

Very soon, within a year of his wedding, Ivan Ilych had realized that marriage, though it may add some comforts to life, is in fact a very intricate and difficult affair toward which in order to perform one's duty, that is, to lead a decorous life approved of by society, one must adopt a definite attitude just as toward one's official duties.

And Ivan Ilych evolved such an attitude toward married life. He only required of it those conveniences—dinner at home, housewife, and bed—which it could give him, and above all that propriety of external forms required by public opinion. For the rest he looked for light-hearted pleasure and propriety, and was very thankful when he found them, but if he met with antagonism and querulousness he at once retired into his separate fenced-off world of official duties, where he found satisfaction.

Ivan Ilych was esteemed a good official, and after three years was made Assistant Public Prosecutor. His new duties, their importance, the possibility of indicting and imprisoning anyone he chose, the publicity his speeches received, and the success he had in all these things, made his work still more attractive.

More children came. His wife became more and more querulous and ill-tempered, but the attitude Ivan Ilych had adopted toward his home life rendered him almost impervious to her grumbling.

After seven years' service in that town he was transferred to another province as Public Prosecutor. They moved, but were short of money and his wife did not like the place they moved to. Though the salary was higher the cost of living was greater, besides which two of their children died and family life became still more unpleasant for him.

Praskovya Fëdorovna blamed her husband for every inconvenience they encountered in their new home. Most of the conversations between husband and wife, especially as to the children's education, led to topics which recalled former disputes, and those disputes were apt to flare up again at any moment. There remained only those rare periods of amorousness which still came to them at times but did not last long. These were islets at which they anchored for a while and then again set out upon that ocean of veiled hostility which showed itself in their aloofness from one another. This aloofness might have grieved Ivan Ilych had he considered that it ought not to exist, but he now regarded the position as normal, and even made it the goal at which he aimed in family life. His aim was to free himself more and more from those unpleasantnesses and to give them a semblance of harmlessness and propriety. He attained this by spending less and less time with his family, and when obliged to be at home he tried to safeguard his position by the presence of outsiders. The chief thing however was that he had his official duties. The whole interest of his life now centered in the official world and that interest absorbed him. The consciousness of his power, being able to ruin anybody he wished to ruin, the importance, even the external dignity of his entry into court, or meetings with his subordinates, his success with superiors and inferiors, and above all his masterly handling of cases, of which he was conscious—all this gave him pleasure and filled his life, together with chats with his colleagues, dinners, and bridge. So that on the whole Ivan Ilych's life continued to flow as he considered it should do—pleasantly and properly.

So things continued for another seven years. His eldest daughter was already sixteen, another child had died, and only one son was left, a schoolboy and a subject of dissension. Ivan Ilych wanted to put him in the School of Law, but to spite him Praskovya Fëdorovna entered him at the High School. The daughter had been educated at home and had turned out well: the boy did not learn badly either.

III

So Ivan Ilych lived for seventeen years after his marriage. He was already a Public Prosecutor of long standing, and had declined several proposed transfers while awaiting a more desirable post, when an unanticipated and unpleasant occurrence quite upset the peaceful course of his life. He was expecting to be offered the post of presiding judge in a university town, but Happe somehow came to the front and obtained the appointment instead. Ivan Ilych became irritable, reproached Happe, and quarreled both with him and with his immediate superiors—who became colder to him and again passed him over when other appointments were made.

This was in 1880, the hardest year of Ivan Ilych's life. It was then that it became evident on the one hand that his salary was insufficient for them to live on, and on the other that he had been forgotten, and not only this, but that what was for him the greatest and most cruel injustice appeared to others a quite ordinary occurrence. Even his father did not consider it his duty to help him. Ivan Ilych felt himself abandoned by everyone, and that they regarded his position with a salary of 3,500 rubles as quite normal and even fortunate. He alone knew that with the consciousness of the injustices done him, with his wife's incessant nagging, and with the debts he had contracted by living beyond his means, his position was far from normal.

In order to save money that summer he obtained leave of absence and went with his wife to live in the country at her brother's place.

In the country, without his work, he experienced ennui for the first time in his life, and not only ennui but intolerable depression, and he decided that it was impossible to go on living like that, and that it was necessary to take energetic measures.

Having passed a sleepless night pacing up and down the veranda, he decided to go to Petersburg and bestir himself, in order to punish those who had failed to appreciate him and to get transferred to another ministry.

Next day, despite many protests from his wife and her brother, he started for Petersburg with the sole object of obtaining a post with a salary of 5,000 rubles a year. He was no longer bent on any particular department, or tendency, or kind of activity. All he now wanted was an appointment to another post with a salary of 5,000 rubles, either in the administration, in the banks, with the railways, in one of the Empress Marya's Institutions, or even in the customs—but it had to carry with it a salary of 5,000 rubles and be in a ministry other than that in which they had failed to appreciate him.

And this quest of Ivan Ilych's was crowned with remarkable and unexpected success. At Kursk an acquaintance of his, F. I. Ilyin, got into the first-class carriage, sat down beside Ivan Ilych, and told him of a telegram just received by the Governor of Kursk announcing that a change was about to take place in the ministry: Peter Ivanovich was to be superseded by Ivan Semënovich.

The proposed change, apart from its significance for Russia, had a special significance for Ivan Ilych, because by bringing forward a new man, Peter Petrovich, and consequently his friend Zachar Ivanovich, it was highly favorable for Ivan Ilych, since Zachar Ivanovich was a friend and colleague of his.

In Moscow this news was confirmed, and on reaching Petersburg Ivan Ilych found Zachar Ivanovich and received a definite promise of an appointment in his former department of Justice.

A week later he telegraphed to his wife: "Zachar in Miller's place. I shall receive appointment on presentation of report."

Thanks to this change of personnel, Ivan Ilych had unexpectedly obtained an appointment in his former ministry which placed him two stages above his former colleagues besides giving him 5,000 rubles salary and 3,500 rubles for expenses connected with his removal. All his ill humor toward his former enemies and the whole department vanished, and Ivan Ilych was completely happy.

He returned to the country more cheerful and contented than he had been for a long time. Praskovya Fëdorovna also cheered up and a truce was arranged between them. Ivan Ilych told of how he had been feted by everybody in Petersburg, how all those who had been his enemies were put to shame and now fawned on him, how envious they were of his appointment, and how much everybody in Petersburg had liked him.

Praskovya Fëdorovna listened to all this and appeared to believe it. She did not contradict anything, but only made plans for their life in the town to which they were going. Ivan Ilych saw with delight that these plans were his plans, that he and his wife agreed, and that, after a stumble, his life was regaining its due and natural character of pleasant lightheartedness and decorum.

Ivan Ilych had come back for a short time only, for he had to take up his new duties on the 10th of September. Moreover, he needed time to settle into the new place, to move all his belongings from the province, and to buy and order many additional things: in a word, to make such arrangements as he had resolved on, which were almost exactly what Praskovya Fëdorovna too had decided on.

Now that everything had happened so fortunately, and that he and his wife were at one in their aims and moreover saw so little of one another, they got on together better than they had done since the first years of marriage. Ivan Ilych had thought of taking his family away with him at once, but the insistence of his wife's brother and her sister-in-law, who had suddenly become particularly amiable and friendly to him and his family, induced him to depart alone.

So he departed, and the cheerful state of mind induced by his success and by the harmony between his wife and himself, the one intensifying the other, did not leave him. He found a delightful house, just the thing both he and his wife had dreamed of. Spacious, lofty reception rooms in the old style, a convenient and dignified study, rooms for his wife and daughter, a study for his son—it might have been specially built for them. Ivan Ilych himself superintended the arrangements, chose the wallpapers, supplemented the furniture (preferably with antiques which he considered particularly *comme il faut*), and supervised the upholstering. Everything progressed and progressed and approached the ideal he had set himself: even when things were only half completed they exceeded his expectations. He saw what a refined and elegant character, free from vulgarity, it would all have when it was ready. On falling asleep he pictured to himself how the reception room would look. Looking at the yet unfinished drawing room he could see the fireplace, the screen, the whatnot, the little chairs dotted here and there, the dishes and plates on the walls, and the bronzes, as they would be when everything was in place. He was pleased by the thought of how his wife and daughter, who shared his taste in this matter, would be impressed by it. They were certainly not expecting as much. He had been particularly successful in finding, and buying cheaply, antiques which gave a particularly aristocratic character to the whole place. But in his letters he intentionally understated everything in order to be able to surprise them. All this so absorbed him that his new duties—though he liked his official work—interested him less than he had expected. Sometimes he even had moments of absentmindedness during the Court Sessions, and would consider whether he should have straight or curved cornices for his curtains. He was so interested in it all that he often did things himself, rearranging the furniture, or rehanging the curtains. Once when mounting a step ladder to show the upholsterer, who did not understand, how he wanted the hangings draped, he made a false step and slipped, but being a strong and agile man he clung on and only knocked his side against the knob of the window frame. The bruised place was painful but the pain soon passed, and he felt particularly bright and well just then. He wrote: "I feel fifteen years younger." He thought he would have everything ready by September, but it dragged on till mid-October. But the result was charming not only in his eyes but to everyone who saw it.

In reality it was just what is usually seen in the houses of people of moderate means who want to appear rich, and therefore succeed only in resembling others like themselves: there were damasks, dark wood, plants, rugs, and dull and polished bronzes—all the things people of a certain class have in order to resemble other people of that class. His house was so like the others that it would never have been noticed, but to him it all seemed to be quite exceptional. He was very happy when he met his family at the station and brought them to the newly furnished house all lit up, where a footman in a white tie opened the door into the hall decorated with plants, and when they went on into the drawing room and the study uttering exclamations of delight. He conducted them everywhere, drank in their praises eagerly, and beamed with pleasure. At tea that evening, when Praskovya Fëdorovna among other things asked him about his fall, he laughed and showed them how he had gone flying and had frightened the upholsterer.

"It's a good thing I'm a bit of an athlete. Another man might have been killed, but I merely knocked myself, just here; it hurts when it's touched, but it's passing off already—it's only a bruise."

So they began living in their new home—in which, as always happens, when they got thoroughly settled in they found they were just one room short—and with the increased income, which as always was just a little (some 500 rubles) too little, but it was all very nice.

Things went particularly well at first, before everything was finally arranged and while something had still to be done: this thing bought, that thing ordered, another thing moved, and something else adjusted. Though there were some disputes between husband and wife, they were both so well satisfied and had so much to do that it all passed off without any serious quarrels. When nothing was left to arrange it became rather dull and something seemed to be lacking, but they were then making acquaintances, forming habits, and life was growing fuller.

Ivan Ilych spent his mornings at the law court and came home to dinner, and at first he was generally in a good humor, though he occasionally became irritable just on account of his house. (Every spot on the tablecloth or the upholstery, and every broken window-blind string, irritated him. He had devoted so much trouble to arranging it all that every disturbance of it distressed him.) But on the whole his life ran its course as he believed life should do: easily, pleasantly, and decorously.

He got up at nine, drank his coffee, read the paper, and then put on his undress uniform and went to the law courts. There the harness in which he worked had already been stretched to fit him and he donned it without a hitch: petitioners, inquiries at the chancery, the chancery itself, and the sittings public and administrative. In all this the thing was to exclude everything fresh and vital, which always disturbs the regular course of official business, and to admit only official relations with people, and then only on official grounds. A man would come, for instance, wanting some information. Ivan Ilych, as one in whose sphere the matter did not lie, would have nothing to do with him: but if the man had some business with him in his official capacity, something that could be expressed on officially stamped paper, he would do everything, positively everything he could within the limits of such relations, and in doing so would maintain the semblance of friendly human relations, that is, would observe the courtesies of life. As soon as the official relations ended, so did everything else. Ivan Ilych possessed this capacity to separate his real life from the official side of affairs and not mix the two, in the highest degree, and by long practice and natural aptitude had brought it to such a pitch that sometimes, in the manner of a virtuoso, he would even allow himself to let the human and official relations mingle. He let himself do this just because he felt that he could at any time he chose resume the strictly official attitude again and drop the human relation. And he did it all easily, pleasantly, correctly, and even artistically. In the intervals between the sessions he smoked, drank tea, chatted a little about politics, a little about general topics, a little about cards, but most of all about official appointments. Tired, but with the feelings of a virtuoso—one of the first violins who has played his part in an orchestra with precision—he would return home to find that his wife and daughter had been out paying calls, or had a visitor, and that his son had been to school, had done his homework with his tutor, and was duly learning what is taught at High Schools. Everything was as it should be. After dinner, if they had no visitors, Ivan Ilych sometimes read a book that was being much discussed at the time, and in the evening settled down to work, that is, read official papers, compared the depositions of witnesses, and noted paragraphs of the Code applying to them. This was neither dull nor amusing. It was dull when he might have been playing bridge, but if no bridge was available it was at any rate better than doing nothing or sitting with his wife. Ivan Ilych's chief pleasure was giving little dinners to which he invited men and women of good social position, and just as his drawing room resembled all other drawing rooms so did his enjoyable little parties resemble all other such parties.

Once they even gave a dance. Ivan Ilych enjoyed it and everything went off well, except that it led to a violent quarrel with his wife about the cakes and sweets. Praskovya Fëdorovna had made her own plans, but Ivan Ilych insisted on getting everything from an expensive confectioner and ordered too many cakes, and the quarrel occurred because some of those cakes were left over and the confectioner's bill came to 45 rubles. It was a great and disagreeable quarrel. Praskovya Fëdorovna called him "a fool and an imbecile," and he clutched at his head and made angry allusions to divorce.

But the dance itself had been enjoyable. The best people were there, and Ivan Ilych had danced with Princess Trufonova, a sister of the distinguished founder of the Society "Bear My Burden."

The pleasures connected with his work were pleasures of ambition; his social pleasures were those of vanity; but Ivan Ilych's greatest pleasure was playing bridge. He acknowledged that whatever disagreeable incident happened in his life, the pleasure that beamed like a ray of light above everything else was to sit down to bridge with good players, not noisy partners, and of course to four-handed bridge (with five players it was annoying to have to stand out, though one pretended not to mind), to play a clever and serious game (when the cards allowed it) and then to have supper and drink a glass of wine. After a game of bridge, especially if he had won a little (to win a large sum was unpleasant), Ivan Ilych went to bed in specially good humor.

So they lived. They formed a circle of acquaintances among the best people and were visited by people of importance and by young folk. In their views as to their acquaintances, husband, wife and daughter were entirely agreed, and tacitly and unanimously kept at arm's length and shook off the shabby friends and relations who, with much show of affection, gushed into the drawing room with its Japanese plates on the walls. Soon these shabby friends ceased to obtrude themselves and only the best people remained in the Golovins' set.

Young men made up to Lisa, and Petrishchev, an examining magistrate and Dmitri Ivanovich Petrishchev's son and sole heir, began to be so attentive to her that Ivan Ilych had already spoken to Praskovya Fëdorovna about it, and considered whether they should not arrange a party for them, or get up some private theatricals.

So they lived, and all went well, without change, and life flowed pleasantly.

IV

They were all in good health. It could not be called ill health if Ivan Ilych sometimes said that he had a queer taste in his mouth and felt some discomfort in his left side.

But this discomfort increased and, though not exactly painful, grew into a sense of pressure in his side accompanied by ill humor. And his irritability became worse and worse and began to mar the agreeable, easy, and correct life that had established itself in the Golovin family. Quarrels between husband and wife became more and more frequent, and soon the ease and amenity disappeared and even the decorum was barely maintained. Scenes again became frequent, and very few of those islets remained on which husband and wife could meet without an explosion. Praskovya Fëdorovna now had good reason to say that her husband's temper was trying. With characteristic exaggeration she said he had always had a dreadful temper, and that it had needed all her good nature to put up with it for twenty years. It was true that now the quarrels were started by him. His bursts of temper always came just before dinner, often just as he began to eat his soup. Sometimes he noticed that a plate or dish was chipped, or the food was not right, or his son put his elbow on the table, or his daughter's hair was not done as he liked it, and for all this he blamed Praskovya Fëdorovna. At first she retorted and said disagreeable things to him, but once or twice he fell into such a rage at the beginning of dinner that she realized it was due to some physical derangement brought on by taking food, and so she restrained herself and did not answer, but only hurried to get the dinner over. She regarded this self-restraint as highly praiseworthy. Having come to the conclusion that her husband had a dreadful temper and made her life miserable, she began to feel sorry for herself, and the more she pitied herself the more she hated her husband. She began to wish he would die; yet she did not want him to die because then his salary would cease. And this irritated her against him still more. She considered herself dreadfully unhappy just because not even his death could save her, and though she concealed her exasperation, that hidden exasperation of hers increased his irritation also.

After one scene in which Ivan Ilych had been particularly unfair and after which he had said in explanation that he certainly was irritable but that it was due to his not being well, she said that if he was ill it should be attended to, and insisted on his going to see a celebrated doctor.

He went. Everything took place as he had expected and as it always does. There was the usual waiting and the important air assumed by the doctor, with which he was so familiar (resembling that which he himself assumed in court), and the sounding and listening, and the questions which called for answers that were foregone conclusions and were evidently unnecessary, and the look of importance which implied that "if only you put yourself in our hands we will arrange everything—we know indubitably how it has to be done, always in the same way for everybody alike." It was all just as it was in the law courts. The doctor put on just the same air toward him as he himself put on toward an accused person.

The doctor said that so-and-so indicated that there was so-and-so inside the patient, but if the investigaiton of so-and-so did not confirm this, then he must assume that and that. If he assumed that and that, then . . . and so on. To Ivan Ilych only one question was important: was his case serious or not? But the doctor ignored that inappropriate question. From his point of view it was not the one under consideration, the real question was to decide between a floating kidney, chronic catarrh, or appendicitis. It was not a question of Ivan Ilych's life or death, but one between a floating kidney and appendicitis. And that question the doctor solved brilliantly, as it seemed to Ivan Ilych, in favor of the appendix, with the reservation that should an examination of the urine give fresh indications the matter would be reconsidered. All this was just what Ivan Ilych had himself brilliantly accomplished a thousand times in dealing with men on trial. The doctor summed up just as brilliantly, looking over his spectacles triumphantly and even gaily at the accused. From the doctor's summing up Ivan Ilych concluded that things were bad, but that for the doctor, and perhaps for everybody else, it was a matter of indifference, though for him it was bad. And this conclusion struck him painfully, arousing in him a great feeling of pity for himself and of bitterness toward the doctor's indifference to a matter of such importance.

He said nothing of this, but rose, placed the doctor's fee on the table, and remarked with a sigh: "We sick people probably often put inappropriate questions. But tell me, in general, is this complaint dangerous, or not? . . ."

The doctor looked at him sternly over his spectacles with one eye, as if to say: "Prisoner, if you will not keep to the questions put to you, I shall be obliged to have you removed from the court."

"I have already told you what I consider necessary and proper. The analysis may show something more." And the doctor bowed.

Ivan Ilych went out slowly, seated himself disconsolately in his sledge, and drove home. All the way home he was going over what the doctor had said, trying to translate those complicated, obscure, scientific phrases into plain language and find in them an answer to the question: "Is my condition bad? Is it very bad? Or is there as yet nothing much wrong?" And it seemed to him that the meaning of what the doctor had said was that it was very bad. Everything in the streets seemed depressing. The cabmen, the houses, the passers-by, and the shops, were dismal. His ache, this dull gnawing ache that never ceased for a moment, seemed to have acquired a new and more serious significance from the doctor's dubious remarks. Ivan Ilych now watched it with a new and oppressive feeling.

He reached home and began to tell his wife about it. She listened, but in the middle of his account his daughter came in with her hat on, ready to go out with her mother. She sat down reluctantly to listen to this tedious story, but could not stand it long, and her mother too did not hear him to the end.

"Well, I am very glad," she said. "Mind now to take your medicine regularly. Give me the prescription and I'll send Gerasim to the chemist's." And she went to get ready to go out.

While she was in the room Ivan Ilych had hardly taken time to breathe, but he sighed deeply when she left it.

"Well," he thought, "perhaps it isn't so bad after all."

He began taking his medicine and following the doctor's directions, which had been altered after the examination of the urine. But then it happened that there was a contradiction between the indications drawn from the examination of the urine and the symptoms that showed themselves. It turned out that what was happening differed from what the doctor had told him, and that he had either forgotten, or blundered, or hidden something from him. He could not, however, be blamed for that, and Ivan Ilych still obeyed his orders implicitly and at first derived some comfort from doing so.

From the time of his visit to the doctor, Ivan Ilych's chief occupation was the exact fulfillment of the doctor's instructions regarding hygiene and the taking of medicine, and the observation of his pain and his excretions. His chief interests came to be people's ailments and people's health. When sickness, deaths, or recoveries were mentioned in his presence, especially when the illness resembled his own, he listened with agitation which he tried to hide, asked questions, and applied what he heard to his own case.

The pain did not grow less, but Ivan Ilych made efforts to force himself to think that he was better. And he could do this so long as nothing agitated him. But as soon as he had any unpleasantness with his wife, or a lack of success in his official work, or held bad cards at bridge, he was at once acutely sensible of his disease. He had formerly borne such mischances, hoping soon to adjust what was wrong, to master it and attain success, or make a grand slam. But now every mischance upset him and plunged him into despair. He would say to himself: "There now, just as I was beginning to get better and the medicine had begun to take effect, comes this accursed misfortune, or unpleasantness . . ." And he was furious with the mishap, or with the people who were causing the unpleasantness and killing him, for he felt that this fury was killing him but could not restrain it. One would have thought that it should have been clear to him that this exasperation with circumstances and people aggravated his illness, and that he ought therefore to ignore unpleasant occurrences. But he drew the very opposite conclusion: he said that he needed peace, and he watched for everything that might disturb it and became irritable at the slightest infringement of it. His condition was rendered worse by the fact that he read medical books and consulted doctors. The progress of his disease was so gradual that he could deceive himself when comparing one day with another—the difference was so slight. But when he consulted the doctors it seemed to him that he was getting worse, and even very rapidly. Yet despite this he was continually consulting them.

That month he went to see another celebrity, who told him almost the same as the first had done but put his questions rather differently, and the interview with this celebrity only increased Ivan Ilych's doubts and fears. A friend of a friend of his, a very good doctor, diagnosed his illness again quite differently from the others, and though he predicted recovery, his questions and suppositions bewildered Ivan Ilych still more and increased his doubts. A homoeopathist diagnosed the disease in yet another way, and prescribed medicine which Ivan Ilych took secretly for a week. But after a week, not feeling any improvement and having lost confidence both in the former doctor's treatment and in this one's, he became still more despondent. One day a lady acquaintance mentioned a cure effected by a wonder-working icon. Ivan Ilych caught himself listening attentively and beginning to believe that it had occurred. This incident alarmed him. "Has my mind really weakened to such an extent?" he asked himself. "Nonsense! It's all rubbish. I mustn't give way to nervous fears but having chosen a doctor must keep strictly to his treatment. That is what I will do. Now it's all settled. I won't think about it, but will follow the treatment seriously till summer, and then we shall see. From now there must be no more of this wavering!" This was easy to say but impossible to carry out. The pain in his side oppressed him and seemed to grow worse and more incessant, while the taste in his mouth grew stranger and stranger. It seemed to him that his breath had a disgusting smell, and he was conscious of a loss of appetite and strength. There was no deceiving himself: something terrible, new, and more important than anything before in his life, was taking place within him of which he alone was aware. Those about him did not understand or would not understand it, but thought everything in the world was going on as usual. That tormented Ivan Ilych more than anything. He saw that his household, especially his wife and daughter who were in a perfect whirl of visiting, did not understand anything of it and were annoyed that he was so depressed and so exacting, as if he were to blame for it. Though they tried to disguise it he saw that he was an obstacle in their path, and that his wife had adopted a definite line in regard to his illness and kept to it regardless of anything he said or did. Her attitude was this: "You know," she would say to her friends, "Ivan Ilych can't do as other people do, and keep to the treatment prescribed for him. One day he'll take his drops and keep strictly to his diet and go to bed in good time, but the next day unless I watch him he'll suddenly forget his medicine, eat sturgeon—which is forbidden—and sit up playing cards till one o'clock in the morning."

"Oh, come, when was that?" Ivan Ilych would ask in vexation. "Only once at Peter Ivanovich's."

"And yesterday with Shebek."

"Well, even if I hadn't stayed up, this pain would have kept me awake."

"Be that as it may you'll never get well like that, but will always make us wretched."

Praskovya Fëdorovna's attitude to Ivan Ilych's illness, as she expressed it both to others and to him, was that it was his own fault and was another of the annoyances he caused her. Ivan Ilych felt that this opinion escaped her involuntarily—but that did not make it easier for him.

At the law courts too, Ivan Ilych noticed, or thought he noticed, a strange attitude toward himself. It sometimes seemed to him that people were watching him inquisitively as a man whose place might soon be vacant. Then again, his friends would suddenly begin to chaff him in a friendly way about his low spirits, as if the awful, horrible, and unheard-of thing that was going on within him, incessantly gnawing at him and irresistibly drawing him away, was a very agreeable subject for jests. Schwartz in particular irritated him by his jocularity, vivacity, and *savoir faire*, which reminded him of what he himself had been ten years ago.

Friends came to make up a set and they sat down to cards. They dealt, bending the new cards to soften them, and he sorted the diamonds in his hand and found he had seven. His partner said "No trumps" and supported him with two diamonds. What more could be wished for? It ought to be jolly and lively. They would make a grand slam. But suddenly Ivan Ilych was conscious of that gnawing pain, that taste in his mouth, and it seemed ridiculous that in such circumstances he should be pleased to make a grand slam.

He looked at his partner, Mikhail Mikhaylovich, who rapped the table with his strong hand and instead of snatching up the tricks pushed the cards courteously and indulgently toward Ivan Ilych that he might have the pleasure of gathering them up without the trouble of stretching out his hand for them. "Does he think I am too weak to stretch out my arm?" thought Ivan Ilych, and forgetting what he was doing he over-trumped his partner, missing the grand slam by three tricks. And what was most awful of all was that he saw how upset Mikhail Mikhaylovich was about it but did not himself care. And it was dreadful to realize why he did not care.

They all saw that he was suffering, and said: "We can stop if you are tired. Take a rest." Lie down? No, he was not at all tired, and he finished the rubber. All were gloomy and silent. Ivan Ilych felt that he had diffused this gloom over them and could not dispel it. They had supper and went away, and Ivan Ilych was left alone with the consciousness that his life was poisoned and was poisoning the lives of others, and that this poison did not weaken but penetrated more and more deeply into his whole being.

With this consciousness, and with physical pain besides that terror, he must go to bed, often to lie awake the greater part of the night. Next morning he had to get up again, dress, go to the law courts, speak, and write; or if he did not go out, spend at home those twenty-four hours a day each of which was a torture. And he had to live thus all alone on the brink of an abyss, with no one who understood or pitied him.

V

So one month passed and then another. Just before the New Year his brother-in-law came to town and stayed at their house. Ivan Ilych was at the law courts and Praskovya Fëdorovna had gone shopping. When Ivan Ilych came home and entered his study he found his brother-in-law there —a healthy, florid man—unpacking his portmanteau himself. He raised his head on hearing Ivan Ilych's footsteps and looked up at him for a moment without a word. That stare told Ivan Ilych everything. His brother-in-law opened his mouth to utter an exclamation of surprise but checked himself, and that action confirmed it all.

"I have changed, eh?"

"Yes, there is a change."

And after that, try as he would to get his brother-in-law to return to the subject of his looks, the latter would say nothing about it. Praskovya

Fëdorovna came home and her brother went out to her. Ivan Ilych locked the door and began to examine himself in the glass, first full face, then in profile. He took up a portrait of himself taken with his wife, and compared it with what he saw in the glass. The change in him was immense. Then he bared his arms to the elbow, looked at them, drew the sleeves down again, sat down on an ottoman, and grew blacker than night.

"No, no, this won't do!" he said to himself, and jumped up, went to the table, took up some law papers and began to read them, but could not continue. He unlocked the door and went into the reception room. The door leading to the drawing room was shut. He approached it on tiptoe and listened.

"No, you are exaggerating!" Praskovya Fëdorovna was saying.

"Exaggerating! Don't you see it? Why, he's a dead man! Look at his eyes—there's no light in them. But what is it that is wrong with him?"

"No one knows. Nikolaevich [that was another doctor] said something, but I don't know what. And Leshchetitsky [this was the celebrated specialist] said quite the contrary . . ."

Ivan Ilych walked away, went to his own room, lay down, and began musing: "The kidney, a floating kidney." He recalled all the doctors had told him of how it detached itself and swayed about. And by an effort of imagination he tried to catch that kidney and arrest it and support it. So little was needed for this, it seemed to him. "No, I'll go to see Peter Ivanovich again." [That was the friend whose friend was a doctor.] He rang, ordered the carriage, and got ready to go.

"Where are you going, Jean?" asked his wife, with a specially sad and exceptionally kind look.

This exceptionally kind look irritated him. He looked morosely at her.

"I must go to see Peter Ivanovich."

He went to see Peter Ivanovich, and together they went to see his friend, the doctor. He was in, and Ivan Ilych had a long talk with him.

Reviewing the anatomical and physiological details of what in the doctor's opinion was going on inside him, he understood it all.

There was something, a small thing, in the vermiform appendix. It might all come right. Only stimulate the energy of one organ and check the activity of another, then absorption would take place and everything would come right. He got home rather late for dinner, ate his dinner, conversed cheerfully, but could not for a long time bring himself to go back to work in his room. At last, however, he went to his study and did what was necessary, but the consciousness that he had put something aside—an important, intimate matter which he would revert to when his work was done—never left him. When he had finished his work he remembered that this intimate matter was the thought of his vermiform appendix. But he did not give himself up to it, and went to the drawing room for tea. There were callers there, including the examining magistrate who was a desirable match for his daughter, and they were conversing, playing the piano, and singing. Ivan Ilych, as Praskovya Fëdorovna remarked, spent that evening more cheerfully than usual, but he never for a moment forgot that he had postponed the important matter of the appendix. At eleven o'clock he said good night and went to his bedroom. Since his illness he had slept alone in a small room next to his study. He undressed and took up a novel by Zola, but instead of reading it fell into thought, and in his imagination that desired improvement in the vermiform appendix occurred. There was the absorption and evacuation and the re-establishment of normal activity. "Yes, that's it!" he said to himself. "One need only assist nature, that's all." He remembered his medicine, rose, took it, and lay down on his back watching for the beneficent action of the medicine and for it to lessen the pain. "I need only take it regularly and avoid all injurious influences. I am already feeling better, much better." He began touching his side: it was not painful to the touch. "There, I really don't feel it. It's much better already." He put out the light and turned on his side . . . "The appendix is getting better, absorption is occurring." Suddenly he felt the old, familiar, dull, gnawing pain, stubborn and serious. There was the same familiar loathsome taste in his mouth. His heart sank and he felt dazed. "My God! My God!" he muttered. "Again, again! and it will never cease." And suddenly the matter presented itself in a quite different aspect. "Vermiform appendix! Kidney!" he said to himself. "It's not a question of appendix or kidney, but of life and . . . death. Yes, life was there and now it is going, going and I cannot stop it. Yes. Why deceive myself? Isn't it obvious to everyone but me that I'm dying, and that it's only a question of weeks, days . . . it may happen this moment. There was light and now there is darkness. I was here and now I'm going there! Where?" A chill came over him, his breathing ceased, and he felt only the throbbing of his heart.

"When I am not, what will there be? There will be nothing. Then where shall I be when I am no more? Can this be dying? No, I don't want to!" He jumped up and tried to light the candle, felt for it with trembling hands, dropped candle and candlestick on the floor, and fell back on his pillow.

"What's the use? It makes no difference," he said to himself, staring with wide-open eyes into the darkness. "Death. Yes, death. And none of them know or wish to know it, and they have no pity for me. Now they are playing." (He heard through the door the distant sound of a song and its accompaniment.) "It's all the same to them, but they will die too! Fools! I first, and they later, but it will be the same for them. And now they are merry . . . the beasts!"

Anger choked him and he was agonizingly, unbearably, miserable. "It is impossible that all men have been doomed to suffer this awful horror!" He raised himself.

"Something must be wrong. I must calm myself—must think it all over from the beginning." And he again began thinking. "Yes, the beginning of my illness: I knocked my side, but I was quite well that day and the next. It hurt a little, then rather more. I saw the doctor, then followed despondency and anguish, more doctors, and I drew nearer to the abyss. My strength grew less and I kept coming nearer and nearer, and now I have wasted away and there is no light in my eyes. I think of the appendix —but this is death! I think of mending the appendix, and all the while here is death! Can it really be death?" Again terror seized him and he gasped for breath. He leaned down and began feeling for the matches, pressing with his elbow on the stand beside the bed. It was in the way and hurt him, he grew furious with it, pressed on it still harder, and upset it. Breathless and in despair he fell on his back, expecting death to come immediately.

Meanwhile the visitors were leaving. Praskovya Fëdorovna was seeing them off. She heard something fall and came in.

"What has happened?"

"Nothing. I knocked it over accidentally."

She went out and returned with a candle. He lay there panting heavily, like a man who has run a thousand yards, and stared upward at her with a fixed look.

"What is it, Jean?"

"No . . . o . . . thing. I upset it." ("Why speak of it? She won't understand," he thought.)

And in truth she did not understand. She picked up the stand, lit his candle, and hurried away to see another visitor off. When she came back he still lay on his back, looking upward.

"What is it? Do you feel worse?"

"Yes."

She shook her head and sat down.

"Do you know, Jean, I think we must ask Leshchetitsky to come and see you here."

This meant calling in the famous specialist, regardless of expense. He smiled malignantly and said "No." She remained a little longer and then went up to him and kissed his forehead.

While she was kissing him he hated her from the bottom of his soul and with difficulty refrained from pushing her away.

"Good night. Please God you'll sleep."

"Yes."

VI

Ivan Ilych saw that he was dying, and he was in continual despair.

In the depth of his heart he knew he was dying, but not only was he not accustomed to the thought, he simply did not and could not grasp it.

The syllogism he had learned from Kiezewetter's Logic: "Caius is a man, men are mortal, therefore Caius is mortal," had always seemed to him correct as applied to Caius, but certainly not as applied to himself. That Caius—man in the abstract—was mortal, was perfectly correct, but he was not Caius, not an abstract man, but a creature quite, quite separate from all others. He had been little Vanya, with a mamma and a papa, with Mitya and Volodya, with the toys, a coachman and a nurse, afterward with Katenka and with all the joys, griefs, and delights of childhood, boyhood, and youth. What did Caius know of the smell of that striped leather ball Vanya had been so fond of? Had Caius kissed his mother's hand like that, and did the silk of her dress rustle so for Caius? Had he rioted like that at school when the pastry was bad? Had Caius been in love like that? Could Caius preside at a session as he did? "Caius really was mortal, and it was right for him to die; but for me, little Vanya, Ivan Ilych, with all my thoughts and emotions, it's altogether a different matter. It cannot be that I ought to die. That would be too terrible."

Such was his feeling.

"If I had to die like Caius, I should have known it was so. An inner voice would have told me so, but there was nothing of the sort in me and I and all my friends felt that our case was quite different from that of Caius. And now here it is!" he said to himself. "It can't be. It's impossible! But here it is. How is this? How is one to understand it?"

He could not understand it, and tried to drive this false, incorrect, morbid thought away and to replace it by other proper and healthy thoughts. But that thought, and not the thought only but the reality itself, seemed to come and confront him.

And to replace that thought he called up a succession of others, hoping to find in them some support. He tried to get back into the former current of thoughts that had once screened the thought of death from him. But strange to say, all that had formerly shut off, hidden, and destroyed, his consciousness of death, no longer had that effect. Ivan Ilych now spent most of his time in attempting to re-establish that old current. He would say to himself: "I will take up my duties again—after all I used to live by them." And banishing all doubts he would go to the law courts, enter into conversation with his colleagues, and sit carelessly as was his wont, scanning the crowd with a thoughtful look and leaning both his emaciated arms on the arms of his oak chair; bending over as usual to a colleague and drawing his papers nearer he would interchange whispers with him, and then suddenly raising his eyes and sitting erect would pronounce certain words and open the proceedings. But suddenly in the midst of those proceedings the pain in his side, regardless of the stage the proceedings had reached, would begin its own gnawing work. Ivan Ilych would turn his attention to it and try to drive the thought of it away, but without success. It would come and stand before him and look at him, and he would be petrified and the light would die out of his eyes, and he would again begin asking himself whether *It* alone was true. And his colleagues and subordinates would see with surprise and distress that he, the brilliant and subtle judge, was becoming confused and making mistakes. He would shake himself, try to pull himself together, manage somehow to bring the sitting to a close, and return home with the sorrowful consciousness that his judicial labors could not as formerly hide from him what he wanted them to hide, and could not deliver him from *It*. And what was worst of all was that *It* drew his attention to itself not in order to make him take some action but only that he should look at *It*, look it straight in the face: look at it and without doing anything, suffer inexpressibly.

And to save himself from this condition Ivan Ilych looked for consolations—new screens—and new screens were found and for a while seemed to save him, but then they immediately fell to pieces or rather became transparent, as if *It* penetrated them and nothing could veil *It*.

In these latter days he would go into the drawing room he had arranged—that drawing room where he had fallen and for the sake of which (how bitterly ridiculous it seemed) he had sacrificed his life—for he knew that his illness originated with that knock. He would enter and see that something had scratched the polished table. He would look for the cause of this and find that it was the bronze ornamentation of an album, that had got bent. He would take up the expensive album which he had lovingly arranged, and feel vexed with his daughter and her friends for their untidiness—for the album was torn here and there and some of the photographs turned upside down. He would put it carefully in order and bend the ornamentation back into position. Then it would occur to him to place all those things in another corner of the room, near the plants. He would call the footman, but his daughter or wife would come to help him. They would not agree, and his wife would contradict him, and he would dispute and grow angry. But that was all right, for then he did not think about *It*. *It* was invisible.

But then, when he was moving something himself, his wife would say: "Let the servants do it. You will hurt yourself again." And suddenly *It* would flash through the screen and he would see it. It was just a flash, and he hoped it would disappear, but he would involuntarily pay attention to his side. "It sits there as before, gnawing just the same!" And he could no longer forget *It*, but could distinctly see it looking at him from behind the flowers. "What is it all for?"

"It really is so! I lost my life over the curtain as I might have done when storming a fort. Is that possible? How terrible and how stupid. It can't be true! It can't, but it is."

He would go to his study, lie down, and again be alone with *It*: face to face with *It*. And nothing could be done with *It* except to look at it and shudder.

VII

How it happened it is impossible to say because it came about step by step, unnoticed, but in the third month of Ivan Ilych's illness, his wife, his daughter, his son, his acquaintances, the doctors, the servants, and above all he himself, were aware that the whole interest he had for other people was whether he would soon vacate his place, and at last release the living from the discomfort caused by his presence and be himself released from his sufferings.

He slept less and less. He was given opium and hypodermic injections of morphine, but this did not relieve him. The dull depression he experienced in a somnolent condition at first gave him a little relief, but only as something new, afterward it became as distressing as the pain itself or even more so.

Special foods were prepared for him by the doctors' orders, but all those foods became increasingly distasteful and disgusting to him.

For his excretions also special arrangements had to be made, and this was a torment to him every time—a torment from the uncleanliness, the unseemliness, and the smell, and from knowing that another person had to take part in it.

But just through this most unpleasant matter, Ivan Ilych obtained comfort. Gerasim, the butler's young assistant, always came in to carry the things out. Gerasim was a clean, fresh peasant lad, grown stout on town food and always cheerful and bright. At first the sight of him, in his clean Russian peasant costume, engaged in that disgusting task embarrassed Ivan Ilych.

Once when he got up from the commode too weak to draw up his trousers, he dropped into a soft armchair and looked with horror at his bare, enfeebled thighs with the muscles so sharply marked on them.

Gerasim with a firm light tread, his heavy boots emitting a pleasant smell of tar and fresh winter air, came in wearing a clean Hessian apron, the sleeves of his print shirt tucked up over his strong bare young arms; and refraining from looking at his sick master out of consideration for his feelings, and restraining the joy of life that beamed from his face, he went up to the commode.

"Gerasim!" said Ivan Ilych in a weak voice.

Gerasim started, evidently afraid he might have committed some blunder, and with a rapid movement turned his fresh, kind, simple young face which just showed the first downy signs of a beard.

"Yes, sir?"

"That must be very unpleasant for you. You must forgive me. I am helpless."

"Oh, why, sir," and Gerasim's eyes beamed and he showed his glistening white teeth, "what's a little trouble? It's a case of illness with you, sir."

And his deft strong hands did their accustomed task, and he went out of the room stepping lightly. Five minutes later he as lightly returned.

Ivan Ilych was still sitting in the same position in the armchair.

"Gerasim," he said when the latter had replaced the freshly washed utensil." "Please come here and help me." Gerasim went up to him. "Lift me up. It is hard for me to get up, and I have sent Dmitri away."

Gerasim went up to him, grasped his master with his strong arms deftly but gently, in the same way that he stepped—lifted him, supported him with one hand, and with the other drew up his trousers and would have set him down again, but Ivan Ilych asked to be led to the sofa. Gerasim, without an effort and without apparent pressure, led him, almost lifting him, to the sofa and placed him on it.

"Thank you. How easily and well you do it all!"

Gerasim smiled again and turned to leave the room. But Ivan Ilych felt his presence such a comfort that he did not want to let him go.

"One thing more, please move up that chair. No, the other one— under my feet. It is easier for me when my feet are raised."

Gerasim brought the chair, set it down gently in place, and raised Ivan Ilych's legs on to it. It seemed to Ivan Ilych that he felt better while Gerasim was holding up his legs.

"It's better when my legs are higher," he said. "Place that cushion under them."

Gerasim did so. He again lifted the legs and placed them, and again Ivan Ilych felt better while Gerasim held his legs. When he set them down Ivan Ilych fancied he felt worse.

"Gerasim," he said. "Are you busy now?"

"Not at all, sir," said Gerasim, who had learned from the townfolk how to speak to gentlefolk.

"What have you still to do?"

"What have I to do? I've done everything except chopping the logs for tomorrow."

"Then hold my legs up a bit higher, can you?"

"Of course I can. Why not?" And Gerasim raised his master's legs higher and Ivan Ilych thought that in that position he did not feel any pain at all.

"And how about the logs?"

"Don't trouble about that, sir. There's plenty of time."

Ivan Ilych told Gerasim to sit down and hold his legs, and began to talk to him. And strange to say it seemed to him that he felt better while Gerasim held his legs up.

After that Ivan Ilych would sometimes call Gerasim and get him to hold his legs on his shoulders, and he liked talking to him. Gerasim did it all easily, willingly, simply, and with a good nature that touched Ivan Ilych. Health, strength, and vitality in other people were offensive to him, but Gerasim's strength and vitality did not mortify but soothed him.

What tormented Ivan Ilych most was the deception, the lie, which for some reason they all accepted, that he was not dying but was simply ill, and that he only need keep quiet and undergo a treatment and then something very good would result. He however knew that do what they would nothing would come of it, only still more agonizing suffering and death. This deception tortured him—their not wishing to admit what they all knew and what he knew, but wanting to lie to him concerning his terrible condition, and wishing and forcing him to participate in that lie. Those lies—lies enacted over him on the eve of his death and destined to degrade this awful, solemn act to the level of their visitings, their curtains, their sturgeon for dinner—were a terrible agony for Ivan Ilych. And strangely enough, many times when they were going through their antics over him he had been within a hairbreadth of calling out to them: "Stop lying! You know and I know that I am dying. Then at least stop lying about it!" But he had never had the spirit to do it. The awful, terrible act of his dying was, he could see, reduced by those about him to the level of a casual, unpleasant, and almost indecorous incident (as if someone entered a drawing room diffusing an unpleasant odor) and this was done by that very decorum which he had served all his life long. He saw that no one felt for him, because no one even wished to grasp his position. Only Gerasim recognized it and pitied him. And so Ivan Ilych felt at ease only with him. He felt comforted when Gerasim supported his legs (sometimes all night long) and refused to go to bed, saying: "Don't you worry, Ivan Ilych. I'll get sleep enough later on," or when he suddenly became familiar and exclaimed: "If you weren't sick it would be another matter, but as it is, why should I grudge a little trouble?" Gerasim alone did not lie; everything showed that he alone understood the facts of the case and did not consider it necessary to disguise them, but simply felt sorry for his emaciated and enfeebled master. Once when Ivan Ilych was sending him away he even said straight out: "We shall all of us die, so why should I grudge a little trouble?"—expressing the fact that he did not think his work burdensome, because he was doing it for a dying man and hoped someone would do the same for him when his time came.

Apart from this lying, or because of it, what most tormented Ivan Ilych was that no one pitied him as he wished to be pitied. At certain moments after prolonged suffering he wished most of all (though he would have been ashamed to confess it) for someone to pity him as a sick child is pitied. He longed to be petted and comforted. He knew he was an important functionary, that he had a beard turning grey, and that therefore what he longed for was impossible, but still he longed for it. And in Gerasim's attitude towards him there was something akin to what he wished for, and so that attitude comforted him. Ivan Ilych wanted to weep, wanted to be petted and cried over, and then his colleague Shebek would come, and instead of weeping and being petted, Ivan Ilych would assume a serious, severe, and profound air, and by force of habit would express his opinion on a decision of the Court of Cassation and would stubbornly insist on that view. This falsity around him and within him did more than anything else to poison his last days.

VIII

It was morning. He knew it was morning because Gerasim had gone, and Peter the footman had come and put out the candles, drawn back one of the curtains, and begun quietly to tidy up. Whether it was morning or evening, Friday or Sunday, made no difference, it was all just the same: the gnawing, unmitigated, agonizing pain, never ceasing for an instant, the consciousness of life inexorably waning but not yet extinguished, the approach of that ever dreaded and hateful Death which was the only reality, and always the same falsity. What were days, weeks, hours, in such a case?

"Will you have some tea, sir?"

"He wants things to be regular, and wishes the gentlefolk to drink tea in the morning," thought Ivan Ilych, and only said "No."

"Wouldn't you like to move onto the sofa, sir?"

"He wants to tidy up the room, and I'm in the way. I am uncleanliness and disorder," he thought, and said only:

"No, leave me alone."

The man went on bustling about. Ivan Ilych stretched out his hand. Peter came up, ready to help.

"What is it, sir?"

"My watch."

Peter took the watch which was close at hand and gave it to his master.

"Half-past eight. Are they up?"

"No, sir, except Vladimir Ivanich" (the son) "who has gone to school. Praskovya Fëdorovna ordered me to wake her if you asked for her. Shall I do so?"

"No, there's no need to." "Perhaps I'd better have some tea," he thought, and added aloud: "Yes, bring me some tea."

Peter went to the door, but Ivan Ilych dreaded being left alone. "How can I keep him here? Oh yes, my medicine." "Peter, give me my medicine." "Why not? Perhaps it may still do me some good." He took a spoonful and swallowed it. "No, it won't help. It's all tomfoolery, all deception," he decided as soon as he became aware of the familiar, sickly, hopeless taste. "No, I can't believe in it any longer. But the pain, why this pain? If it would only cease just for a moment!" And he moaned. Peter turned toward him. "It's all right. Go and fetch me some tea."

Peter went out. Left alone Ivan Ilych groaned not so much with pain, terrible though that was, as from mental anguish. Always and for ever the same, always these endless days and nights. If only it would come quicker! If only *what* would come quicker? Death, darkness? . . . No, no! Anything rather than death!

When Peter returned with the tea on a tray, Ivan Ilych stared at him for a time in perplexity, not realizing who and what he was. Peter was disconcerted by that look and his embarrassment brought Ivan Ilych to himself.

"Oh, tea! All right, put it down. Only help me to wash and put on a clean shirt."

And Ivan Ilych began to wash. With pauses for rest, he washed his hands and then his face, cleaned his teeth, brushed his hair, and looked in the glass. He was terrified by what he saw, especially by the limp way in which his hair clung to his pallid forehead.

While his shirt was being changed he knew that he would be still more frightened at the sight of his body, so he avoided looking at it. Finally he was ready. He drew on a dressing gown, wrapped himself in a plaid, and sat down in the armchair to take his tea. For a moment he felt refreshed, but as soon as he began to drink the tea he was again aware of the same taste, and the pain also returned. He finished it with an effort, and then lay down stretching out his legs, and dismissed Peter.

Always the same. Now a spark of hope flashes up, then a sea of despair rages, and always pain; always pain, always despair, and always the same. When alone he had a dreadful and distressing desire to call someone, but he knew beforehand that with others present it would be still worse. "Another dose of morphine—to lose consciousness. I will tell him, the doctor, that he must think of something else. It's impossible, impossible, to go on like this."

An hour and another pass like that. But now there is a ring at the door bell. Perhaps it's the doctor? It is. He comes in fresh, hearty, plump, and cheerful, with that look on his face that seems to say: "There now, you're in a panic about something, but we'll arrange it all for you directly!" The doctor knows this expression is out of place here, but he has put it on once for all and can't take it off—like a man who has put on a frock coat in the morning to pay a round of calls.

The doctor rubs his hands vigorously and reassuringly.

"Brr! How cold it is! There's such a sharp frost; just let me warm myself!" he says, as if it were only a matter of waiting till he was warm, and then he would put everything right.

"Well now, how are you?"

Ivan Ilych feels that the doctor would like to say: "Well, how are your affairs?" but that even he feels that this would not do, and says instead: "What sort of a night have you had?"

Ivan Ilych looks at him as much as to say: "Are you really never ashamed of lying?" But the doctor does not wish to understand this question, and Ivan Ilych says: "Just as terrible as ever. The pain never leaves me and never subsides. If only something . . ."

"Yes, you sick people are always like that . . . There, now I think I am warm enough. Even Praskovya Fëdorovna, who is so particular, could find no fault with my temperature. Well, now I can say good morning," and the doctor presses his patient's hand.

Then, dropping his former playfulness, he begins with a most serious face to examine the patient, feeling his pulse and taking his temperature, and then begins the sounding and auscultation.

Ivan Ilych knows quite well and definitely that all this is nonsense and pure deception, but when the doctor, getting down on his knee, leans over him, putting the ear first higher then lower, and performs various gymnastic movements over him with a significant expression on his face, Ivan Ilych submits to it all as he used to submit to the speeches of the lawyers, though he knew very well that they were all lying and why they were lying.

The doctor, kneeling on the sofa, is still sounding him when Praskovya Fëdorovna's silk dress rustles at the door and she is heard scolding Peter for not having let her know of the doctor's arrival.

She comes in, kisses her husband, and at once proceeds to prove that she has been up a long time already, and only owing to a misunderstanding failed to be there when the doctor arrived.

Ivan Ilych looks at her, scans her all over, sets against her the whiteness and plumpness and cleanness of her hands and neck, the gloss of her hair, and the sparkle of her vivacious eyes. He hates her with his whole soul. And the thrill of hatred he feels for her makes him suffer from her touch.

Her attitude toward him and his disease is still the same. Just as the doctor had adopted a certain relation to his patient which he could not abandon, so had she formed one toward him—that he was not doing something he ought to do and was himself to blame, and that she reproached him lovingly for this—and she could not now change that attitude.

"You see he doesn't listen to me and doesn't take his medicine at the proper time. And above all he lies in a position that is no doubt bad for him—with his legs up."

She described how he made Gerasim hold his legs up.

The doctor smiled with a contemptuous affability that said: "What's to be done? These sick people do have foolish fancies of that kind, but we must forgive them."

When the examination was over the doctor looked at his watch, and then Praskovya Fëdorovna announced to Ivan Ilych that it was of course as he pleased, but she had sent today for a celebrated specialist who would examine him and have a consultation with Michael Danilovich (their regular doctor).

"Please don't raise any objections. I am doing this for my own sake," she said ironically, letting it be felt that she was doing it all for his sake and only said this to leave him no right to refuse. He remained silent, knitting his brows. He felt that he was so surrounded and involved in a mesh of falsity that it was hard to unravel anything.

Everything she did for him was entirely for her own sake, and she told him she was doing for herself what she actually was doing for herself, as if that was so incredible that he must understand the opposite.

At half-past eleven the celebrated specialist arrived. Again the sounding began and the significant conversations in his presence and in another room, about the kidneys and the appendix, and the questions and answers, with such an air of importance that again, instead of the real question of life and death which now alone confronted him, the question arose of the kidney and appendix which were not behaving as they ought to and would now be attacked by Michael Danilovich and the specialist and forced to mend their ways.

The celebrated specialist took leave of him with a serious though not hopeless look, and in reply to the timid question Ivan Ilych, with eyes glistening with fear and hope, put to him as to whether there was a chance of recovery, said that he could not vouch for it but there was a possibility. The look of hope with which Ivan Ilych watched the doctor out was so pathetic that Praskovya Fëdorovna, seeing it, even wept as she left the room to hand the doctor his fee.

The gleam of hope kindled by the doctor's encouragement did not last long. The same room, the same pictures, curtains, wallpaper, medicine bottles, were all there, and the same aching suffering body, and Ivan Ilych began to moan. They gave him a subcutaneous injection and he sank into oblivion.

It was twilight when he came to. They brought him his dinner and he swallowed some beef tea with difficulty, and then everything was the same again and night was coming on.

After dinner, at seven o'clock, Praskovya Fëdorovna came into the room in evening dress, her full bosom pushed up by her corset, and with traces of powder on her face. She had reminded him in the morning that they were going to the theater. Sarah Bernhardt was visiting the town and they had a box, which he had insisted on their taking. Now he had forgotten about it and her toilet offended him, but he concealed his vexation when he remembered that he had himself insisted on their securing a box and going because it would be an instructive and aesthetic pleasure for the children.

Praskovya Fëdorovna came in, self-satisfied but yet with a rather guilty air. She sat down and asked how he was, but, as he saw, only for the sake of asking and not in order to learn about it, knowing that there was nothing to learn—and then went on to what she really wanted to say: that she would not on any account have gone but that the box had been taken and Helen and their daughter were going, as well as Petrishchev (the examining magistrate, their daughter's fiancé) and that it was out of the question to let them go alone; but that she would have much preferred to sit with him for a while; and he must be sure to follow the doctor's orders while she was away.

"Oh, and Fëdor Petrovich" (the fiancé) "would like to come in. May he? And Lisa?"

"All right."

Their daughter came in in full evening dress, her fresh young flesh exposed (making a show of that very flesh which in his own case caused so much suffering), strong, healthy, evidently in love, and impatient with illness, suffering, and death, because they interfered with her happiness.

Fëdor Petrovich came in too, in evening dress, his hair curled à la Capoul, a tight stiff collar round his long sinewy neck, an enormous white shirt-front and narrow black trousers tightly stretched over his strong thighs. He had one white glove tightly drawn on, and was holding his opera hat in his hand.

Following him the schoolboy crept in unnoticed, in a new uniform, poor little fellow, and wearing gloves. Terribly dark shadows showed under his eyes, the meaning of which Ivan Ilych knew well.

His son had always seemed pathetic to him, and now it was dreadful to see the boy's frightened look of pity. It seemed to Ivan Ilych that Vasya was the only one besides Gerasim who understood and pitied him.

They all sat down and again asked how he was. A silence followed. Lisa asked her mother about the opera glasses, and there was an altercation between mother and daughter as to who had taken them and where they had been put. This occasioned some unpleasantness.

Fëdor Petrovich inquired of Ivan Ilych whether he had ever seen Sarah Bernhardt. Ivan Ilych did not at first catch the question, but then replied: "No, have you seen her before?"

"Yes, in *Adrienne Lecouvreur*."

Praskovya Fëdorovna mentioned some roles in which Sarah Bernhardt was particularly good. Her daughter disagreed. Conversation sprang up as to the elegance and realism of her acting—the sort of conversation that is always repeated and is always the same.

In the midst of the conversation Fëdor Petrovich glanced at Ivan Ilych and became silent. Ivan Ilych was staring with glittering eyes straight before him, evidently indignant with them. This had to be rectified, but it was impossible to do so. The silence had to be broken, but for a time no one dared to break it and they all became afraid that the conventional deception would suddenly become obvious and the truth become plain to all. Lisa was the first to pluck up courage and break that silence, but by trying to hide what everybody was feeling, she betrayed it.

"Well, if we are going it's time to start," she said, looking at her watch, a present from her father, and with a faint and significant smile at Fëdor Petrovich relating to something known only to them. She got up with a rustle of her dress.

They all rose, said good night, and went away.

When they had gone it seemed to Ivan Ilych that he felt better; the falsity had gone with them. But the pain remained—that same pain and that same fear that made everything monotonously alike, nothing harder and nothing easier. Everything was worse.

Again minute followed minute and hour followed hour. Everything remained the same and there was no cessation. And the inevitable end of it all became more and more terrible.

"Yes, send Gerasim here," he replied to a question Peter asked.

IX

His wife returned late at night. She came in on tiptoe, but he heard her, opened his eyes, and made haste to close them again. She wished to send Gerasim away and to sit with him herself, but he opened his eyes and said: "No, go away."

"Are you in great pain?"

"Always the same."

"Take some opium."

He agreed and took some. She went away.

Till about three in the morning he was in a state of stupefied misery. It seemed to him that he and his pain were being thrust into a narrow, deep black sack, but though they were pushed further and further in they could not be pushed to the bottom. And this, terrible enough in itself, was accompanied by suffering. He struggled but yet cooperated. And suddenly he broke through, fell, and regained consciousness. Gerasim was sitting at the foot of the bed dozing quietly, while he himself lay with his emaciated stockinged legs resting on Gerasim's shoulders; the same shaded candle was there and the same unceasing pain.

"Go away, Gerasim," he whispered.

"It's all right, sir. I'll stay awhile."

"No. Go away."

He removed his legs from Gerasim's shoulders, turned sideways onto his arm, and felt sorry for himself. He only waited till Gerasim had gone into the next room and then restrained himself no longer but wept like a child. He wept on account of his helplessness, his terrible loneliness, the cruelty of man, the cruelty of God, and the absence of God.

"Why hast Thou done all this? Why hast Thou brought me here? Why, why dost Thou torment me so terribly?"

He did not expect an answer and yet wept because there was no answer and could be none. The pain again grew more acute, but he did not stir and did not call. He said to himself: "Go on! Strike me! But what is it for? What have I done to Thee? What is it for?"

Then he grew quiet and not only ceased weeping but even held his breath and became all attention. It was as though he were listening not to an audible voice but to the voice of his soul, to the current of thoughts arising within him.

"What is it you want?" was the first clear conception capable of expression in words, that he heard.

"What do you want? What do you want?" he repeated to himself.

"What do I want? To live and not to suffer," he answered.

And again he listened with such concentrated attention that even his pain did not distract him.

"To live? How?" asked his inner voice.

"Why, to live as I used to—well and pleasantly."

"As you lived before, well and pleasantly?" the voice repeated.

And in imagination he began to recall the best moments of his pleasant life. But strange to say none of those best moments of his pleasant life now seemed at all what they had then seemed—none of them except the first recollections of childhood. There, in childhood, there had been something really pleasant with which it would be possible to live if it could return. But the child who had experienced that happiness existed no longer, it was like a reminiscence of somebody else.

As soon as the period began which had produced the present Ivan Ilych, all that had then seemed joys now melted before his sight and turned into something trivial and often nasty.

And the further he departed from childhood and the nearer he came to the present the more worthless and doubtful were the joys. This began with the School of Law. A little that was really good was still found there—there was lightheartedness, friendship, and hope. But in the upper classes there had already been fewer of such good moments. Then during the first years of his official career, when he was in the service of the Governor, some pleasant moments again occurred: they were the memories of love for a woman. Then all became confused and there was still less of what was good; later on again there was still less that was good, and the further he went the less there was. His marriage, a mere accident, then the disenchantment that followed it, his wife's bad breath and the sensuality and hypocrisy: then that deadly official life and those preoccupations about money, a year of it, and two, and ten, and twenty, and always the same thing. And the longer it lasted the more deadly it became. "It is as if I had been going downhill while I imagined I was going up. And that is really what it was. I was going up in public opinion, but to the same extent life was ebbing away from me. And now it is all done and there is only death."

"Then what does it mean? Why? It can't be that life is so senseless and horrible. But if it really has been so horrible and senseless, why must I die and die in agony? There is something wrong!"

"Maybe I did not live as I ought to have done," it suddenly occurred to him. "But how could that be, when I did everything properly?" he replied, and immediately dismissed from his mind this, the sole solution of all the riddles of life and death, as something quite impossible.

"Then what do you want now? To live? Live how? Live as you lived in the law courts when the usher proclaimed 'The judge is coming!' The judge is coming, the judge!" he repeated to himself. "Here he is, the judge. But I am not guilty!" he exclaimed angrily. "What is it for?" And he ceased crying, but turning his face to the wall continued to ponder on the same question: Why, and for what purpose, is there all this horror? But however much he pondered he found no answer. And whenever the thought occurred to him, as it often did, that it all resulted from his not having lived as he ought to have done, he at once recalled the correctness of his whole life and dismissed so strange an idea.

X

Another fortnight passed. Ivan Ilych now no longer left his sofa. He would not lie in bed but lay on the sofa, facing the wall nearly all the time. He suffered ever the same unceasing agonies and in his loneliness pondered always on the same insoluble question: "What is this? Can it be that it is Death?" And the inner voice answered: "Yes, it is Death."

"Why these sufferings?" And the voice answered, "For no reason—they just are so." Beyond and besides this there was nothing.

From the very beginning of his illness, ever since he had first been to see the doctor, Ivan Ilych's life had been divided between two contrary and alternating moods: now it was despair and the expectation of this uncomprehended and terrible death, and now hope and an intently interested observation of the functioning of his organs. Now before his eyes there was only a kidney or an intestine that temporarily evaded its duty, and now only that incomprehensible and dreadful death from which it was impossible to escape.

These two states of mind had alternated from the very beginning of his illness, but the further it progressed the more doubtful and fantastic became the conception of the kidney, and the more real the sense of impending death.

He had but to call to mind what he had been three months before and what he was now, to call to mind with what regularity he had been going downhill, for every possibility of hope to be shattered.

Latterly during that loneliness in which he found himself as he lay facing the back of the sofa, a loneliness in the midst of a populous town and surrounded by numerous acquaintances and relations but that yet could not have been more complete anywhere—either at the bottom of the sea or under the earth—during that terrible loneliness Ivan Ilych had lived only in memories of the past. Pictures of his past rose before him one after another. They always began with what was nearest in time and then went back to what was the most remote—to his childhood—and rested there. If he thought of the stewed prunes that had been offered him that day, his mind went back to the raw shriveled French plums of his childhood, their peculiar flavor and the flow of saliva when he sucked their stones, and along with the memory of that taste came a whole series of memories of those days: his nurse, his brother, and their toys. "No, I mustn't think of that . . . it is too painful," Ivan Ilych said to himself, and brought himself back to the present—to the button on the back of the sofa and the creases in its morocco. "Morocco is expensive, but it does not wear well: there had been a quarrel about it. It was a different kind of quarrel and a different kind of morocco that time when we tore father's portfolio and were punished, and Mamma brought us some tarts . . ." And again his thoughts dwelt on his childhood, and again it was painful and he tried to banish them and fix his mind on something else.

Then again together with that chain of memories another series passed through his mind—of how his illness had progressed and grown worse. There also the further back he looked the more life there had been. There had been more of what was good in life and more of life itself. The two merged together. "Just as the pain went on getting worse and worse, so my life grew worse and worse," he thought. "There is one bright spot there at the back, at the beginning of life, and afterward all becomes blacker and blacker and proceeds more and more rapidly—in inverse ratio to the square of the distance from death," thought Ivan Ilych. And the example of a stone falling downward with increasing velocity entered his mind. Life, a series of increasing sufferings, flies further and further toward its end—the most terrible suffering. "I am flying . . ." He shuddered, shifted himself, and tried to resist, but was already aware that resistance was impossible, and again with eyes weary of gazing but unable to cease seeing what was before them, he stared at the back of the sofa and waited —awaiting that dreadful fall and shock and destruction.

"Resistance is impossible!" he said to himself. "If I could only understand what it is all for! But that too is impossible. An explanation would be possible if it could be said that I have not lived as I ought to. But it is impossible to say that," and he remembered all the legality, correctitude, and propriety of his life. "That at any rate can certainly not be admitted," he thought, and his lips smiled ironically as if someone could see that smile and be taken in by it. "There is no explanation! Agony, death . . . What for?"

XI

Another two weeks went by in this way and during that fortnight an event occurred that Ivan Ilych and his wife had desired. Petrishchev formally proposed. It happened in the evening. The next day Praskovya Fëdorovna came into her husband's room considering how best to inform him of it, but that very night there had been a fresh change for the worse in his condition. She found him still lying on the sofa but in a different position. He lay on his back, groaning and staring fixedly in front of him.

She began to remind him of his medicines, but he turned his eyes toward her with such a look that she did not finish what she was saying; so great an animosity, to her in particular, did that look express.

"For Christ's sake let me die in peace!" he said.

She would have gone away, but just then their daughter came in and went up to say good morning. He looked at her as he had done at his wife, and in reply to her inquiry about his health said dryly that he would soon free them all of himself. They were both silent and after sitting with him for a while went away.

"Is it our fault?" Lisa said to her mother. "It's as if we were to blame! I am sorry for papa, but why should we be tortured?"

The doctor came at his usual time. Ivan Ilych answered "Yes" and "No," never taking his angry eyes from him, and at last said: "You know you can do nothing for me, so leave me alone."

"We can ease your sufferings."

"You can't even do that. Let me be."

The doctor went into the drawing room and told Praskovya Fëdorovna that the case was very serious and that the only resource left was opium to allay her husband's sufferings, which must be terrible.

It was true, as the doctor said, that Ivan Ilych's physical sufferings were terrible, but worse than the physical sufferings were his mental sufferings, which were his chief torture.

His mental sufferings were due to the fact that that night, as he looked at Gerasim's sleepy, good-natured face with its prominent cheekbones, the question suddenly occurred to him: "What if my whole life has really been wrong?"

It occurred to him that what had appeared perfectly impossible before, namely that he had not spent his life as he should have done, might after all be true. It occurred to him that his scarcely perceptible attempts to struggle against what was considered good by the most highly placed people, those scarcely noticeable impulses which he had immediately suppressed, might have been the real thing, and all the rest false. And his professional duties and the whole arrangement of his life and of his family, and all his social and official interests, might all have been false. He tried to defend all those things to himself and suddenly felt the weakness of what he was defending. There was nothing to defend.

"But if that is so," he said to himself, "and I am leaving this life with the consciousness that I have lost all that was given me and it is impossible to rectify it—what then?"

He lay on his back and began to pass his life in review in quite a new way. In the morning when he saw first his footman, then his wife, then his daughter, and then the doctor, their every word and movement confirmed to him the awful truth that had been revealed to him during the night. In them he saw himself—all that for which he had lived—and saw clearly that it was not real at all, but a terrible and huge deception which had hidden both life and death. This consciousness intensified his physical suffering tenfold. He groaned and tossed about, and pulled at his clothing which choked and stifled him. And he hated them on that account.

He was given a large dose of opium and became unconscious, but at noon his sufferings began again. He drove everybody away and tossed from side to side.

His wife came to him and said:

"Jean, my dear, do this for me. It can't do any harm and often helps. Healthy people often do it."

He opened his eyes wide.

"What? Take communion? Why? It's unnecessary! However . . ."

She began to cry.

"Yes, do, my dear. I'll send for our priest. He is such a nice man."

"All right. Very well," he muttered.

When the priest came and heard his confession, Ivan Ilych was softened and seemed to feel a relief from his doubts and consequently from his sufferings, and for a moment there came a ray of hope. He again began to think of the vermiform appendix and the possibility of correcting it. He received the sacrament with tears in his eyes.

When they laid him down again afterwards he felt a moment's ease, and the hope that he might live awoke in him again. He began to think of the operation that had been suggested to him. "To live! I want to live!" he said to himself.

His wife came to congratulate him after his communion, and when uttering the usual conventional words she added:

"You feel better, don't you?"

Without looking at her he said "Yes."

Her dress, her figure, the expression of her face, the tone of her voice, all revealed the same thing. "This is wrong, it is not as it should be. All you have lived for and still live for is falsehood and deception, hiding life and death from you." And as soon as he admitted that thought, his hatred and his agonizing physical suffering again sprang up, and with that suffering a consciousness of the unavoidable, approaching end. And to this was added a new sensation of grinding shooting pain and a feeling of suffocation.

The expression of his face when he uttered that "yes" was dreadful. Having uttered it, he looked her straight in the eyes, turned on his face with a rapidity extraordinary in his weak state and shouted:

"Go away! Go away and leave me alone!"

XII

From that moment the screaming began that continued for three days, and was so terrible that one could not hear it through two closed doors without horror. At the moment he answered his wife he realized that he was lost, that there was no return, that the end had come, the very end, and his doubts were still unsolved and remained doubts.

"Oh! Oh! Oh!" he cried in various intonations. He had begun by screaming "I won't!" and continued screaming on the letter *O*.

For three whole days, during which time did not exist for him, he struggled in that black sack into which he was being thrust by an invisible, resistless force. He struggled as a man condemned to death struggles in the hands of the executioner, knowing that he cannot save himself. And every moment he felt that despite all his efforts he was drawing nearer and nearer to what terrified him. He felt that his agony was due to his being thrust into that black hole and still more to his not being able to get right into it. He was hindered from getting into it by his conviction that his life had been a good one. That very justification of his life held him fast and prevented his moving forward, and it caused him most torment of all.

Suddenly some force struck him in the chest and side, making it still harder to breathe, and he fell through the hole and there at the bottom was a light. What had happened to him was like the sensation one sometimes experiences in a railway carriage when one thinks one is going backward while one is really going forward and suddenly becomes aware of the real direction.

"Yes, it was all not the right thing," he said to himself, "but that's no matter. It can be done. But what *is* the right thing?" he asked himself, and suddenly grew quiet.

This occurred at the end of the third day, two hours before his death. Just then his schoolboy son had crept softly in and gone up to the bedside. The dying man was still screaming and waving his arms. His hand fell on the boy's head, and the boy caught it, pressed it to his lips, and began to cry.

At that very moment Ivan Ilych fell through and caught sight of the light, and it was revealed to him that though his life had not been what it should have been, this could still be rectified. He asked himself, "What *is* the right thing?" and grew still, listening. Then he felt that someone was kissing his hand. He opened his eyes, looked at his son, and felt sorry for him. His wife came up to him and he glanced at her. She was gazing at him open-mouthed, with undried tears on her nose and cheek and a despairing look on her face. He felt sorry for her too.

"Yes, I am making them wretched," he thought. "They are sorry, but it will be better for them when I die." He wished to say this but had not the strength to utter it. "Besides, why speak? I must act," he thought. With a look at his wife he indicated his son and said: "Take him away . . . sorry for him . . . sorry for you too . . ." He tried to add, "forgive me," but said "forgo" and waved his hand, knowing that He whose understanding mattered would understand.

And suddenly it grew clear to him that what had been oppressing him and would not leave him was dropping away at once from two sides, from ten sides, and from all sides. He was sorry for them, he must act so as not to hurt them and free himself from these sufferings. "How good and how simple!" he thought. "And the pain?" he asked himself. "What has become of it? Where are you, pain?"

He turned his attention to it.

"Yes, here it is. Well, what of it? Let the pain be."

"And death . . . where is it?"

He sought his former accustomed fear of death and did not find it. "Where is it? What death?" There was no fear because there was no death. In place of death there was light.

"So that's what it is!" he suddenly exclaimed aloud. "What joy!"

To him all this happened in a single instant, and the meaning of that instant did not change. For those present his agony continued for another two hours. Something rattled in his throat, his emaciated body twitched, then the gasping and rattle became less and less frequent.

"It is finished!" said someone near him.

He heard these words and repeated them in his soul.

"Death is finished," he said to himself. "It is no more!"

He drew in a breath, stopped in the midst of a sigh, stretched out, and died.

Translated by Louise and Aylmer Maude

THE SECRET SHARER
by Joseph Conrad
(1857–1924)

On my right hand there were lines of fishing stakes resembling a mysterious system of half-submerged bamboo fences, incomprehensible in its division of the domain of tropical fishes, and crazy of aspect as if abandoned forever by some nomad tribe of fishermen now gone to the other end of the ocean; for there was no sign of human habitation as far as the eye could reach. To the left a group of barren islets, suggesting ruins of stone walls, towers, and blockhouses, had its foundations set in a blue sea that itself looked solid, so still and stable did it lie below my feet; even the track of light from the westering sun shone smoothly, without that animated glitter which tells of an imperceptible ripple. And when I turned my head to take a parting glance at the tug which had just left us anchored outside the bar, I saw the straight line of the flat shore joined to the stable sea, edge to edge, with a perfect and unmarked closeness, in one leveled floor half brown, half blue under the enormous dome of the sky. Corresponding in their significance to the islets of the sea, two small clumps of trees, one on each side of the only fault in the impeccable joint, marked the mouth of the river Meinam we had just left on the first preparatory stage of our homeward journey; and, far back on the inland level, a larger and loftier mass, the grove surrounding the great Paknam pagoda, was the only thing on which the eye could rest from the vain task of exploring the monotonous sweep of the horizon. Here and there gleams as of a few scattered pieces of silver marked the windings of the great river; and on the nearest of them, just within the bar, the tug steaming right into the land became lost to my sight, hull and funnel and masts, as though the impassive earth had swallowed her up without an effort, without a tremor. My eye followed the light cloud of her smoke, now here, now there, above the plain, according to the devious curves of the stream, but always fainter and farther away, till I lost it at last behind the miter-shaped hill of the great pagoda. And then I was left alone with my ship, anchored at the head of the Gulf of Siam.

She floated at the starting point of a long journey, very still in an immense stillness, the shadows of her spars flung far to the eastward by the setting sun. At that moment I was alone on her decks. There was not a sound in her—and around us nothing moved, nothing lived, not a canoe on the water, not a bird in the air, not a cloud in the sky. In this breathless pause at the threshold of a long passage we seemed to be measuring out fitness for a long and arduous enterprise, the appointed task of both our existences to be carried out, far from all human eyes, with only sky and sea for spectators and for judges.

There must have been some glare in the air to interfere with one's sight, because it was only just before the sun left us that my roaming eyes made out beyond the highest ridge of the principal islet of the group something which did away with the solemnity of perfect solitude. The tide of darkness flowed on swiftly; and with tropical suddenness a swarm of stars came out above the shadowy earth, while I lingered yet, my hand resting lightly on my ship's rail as if on the shoulder of a trusted friend. But, with all that multitude of celestial bodies staring down at one, the comfort of quiet communion with her was gone for good. And there were also disturbing sounds by this time—voices, footsteps forward; the steward flitted along the main deck, a busily ministering spirit; a hand bell tinkled urgently under the poop deck . . .

I found my two officers waiting for me near the supper table, in the lighted cuddy. We sat down at once, and as I helped the chief mate, I said:

"Are you aware that there is a ship anchored inside the islands? I saw her mastheads above the ridge as the sun went down."

He raised sharply his simple face, overcharged by a terrible growth of whisker, and emitted his usual ejaculations: "Bless my soul, sir! You don't say so!"

My second mate was a round-cheeked, silent young man, grave beyond his years, I thought; but as our eyes happened to meet I detected a slight quiver on his lips. I looked down at once. It was not my part to encourage sneering on board my ship. It must be said, too, that I knew very little of my officers. In consequence of certain events of no particular significance, except to myself, I had been appointed to the command only a fortnight before. Neither did I know much of the hands forward. All these people had been together for eighteen months or so, and my position was that of the only stranger on board. I mention this because it has some bearing on what is to follow. But what I felt most was my being a stranger to the ship; and if all the truth must be told, I was somewhat of a stranger to myself. The youngest man on board (barring the second mate), and untried as yet by a position of the fullest responsibility, I was willing to take the adequacy of the others for granted. They had simply to be equal to their tasks; but I wondered how far I should turn out faithful to that ideal conception of one's own personality every man sets up for himself secretly.

Meanwhile the chief mate, with an almost visible effect of collaboration on the part of his round eyes and frightful whiskers, was trying to evolve a theory of the anchored ship. His dominant trait was to take all things into earnest consideration. He was of a painstaking turn of mind. As he used to say, he "liked to account to himself" for practically everything that came in his way, down to a miserable scorpion he had found in his cabin a week before. The why and the wherefore of that scorpion—how it got on board and came to select his room rather than the pantry (which was a dark place and more what a scorpion would be partial to), and how on earth it managed to drown itself in the inkwell of his writing desk—had exercised him infinitely. The ship within the islands was much more easily accounted for; and just as we were about to rise from the table he made his pronouncement. She was, he doubted not, a ship from home lately arrived. Probably she drew too much water to cross the bar except at the top of spring tides. Therefore she went into that natural harbor to wait for a few days in preference to remaining in an open roadstead.

"That's so," confirmed the second mate, suddenly, in his slightly hoarse voice. "She draws over twenty feet. She's the Liverpool ship *Sephora* with a cargo of coal. Hundred and twenty-three days from Cardiff."

We looked at him in surprise.

"The tugboat skipper told me when he came on board for your letters, sir," explained the young man. "He expects to take her up the river the day after tomorrow."

After thus overwhelming us with the extent of his information he slipped out of the cabin. The mate observed regretfully that he "could not account for that young fellow's whims." What prevented him telling us all about it at once, he wanted to know.

I detained him as he was making a move. For the last two days the crew had had plenty of hard work, and the night before they had very little sleep. I felt painfully that I—a stranger—was doing something unusual when I directed him to let all hands turn in without setting an anchor watch. I proposed to keep on deck myself till one o'clock or thereabouts. I would get the second mate to relieve me at that hour.

"He will turn out the cook and the steward at four," I concluded, "and then give you a call. Of course at the slightest sign of any sort of wind we'll have the hands up and make a start at once."

He concealed his astonishment. "Very well, sir." Outside the cuddy he put his head in the second mate's door to inform him of my unheard-of-caprice to take a five hours' anchor watch on myself. I heard the other raise his voice incredulously: "What? The captain himself?" Then a few more murmurs, a door closed, then another. A few moments later I went on deck.

My strangeness, which had made me sleepless, had prompted that unconventional arrangement, as if I had expected in those solitary hours of the night to get on terms with the ship of which I knew nothing, manned by men of whom I knew very little more. Fast alongside a wharf, littered like any ship in port with a tangle of unrelated things, invaded by unrelated shore people, I had hardly seen her yet properly. Now, as she lay cleared for sea, the stretch of her main deck seemed to me very fine under the stars. Very fine, very roomy for her size, and very inviting. I descended the poop and paced the waist, my mind picturing to myself the coming passage through the Malay Archipelago, down the Indian Ocean, and up the Atlantic. All its phases were familiar enough to me, every characteristic, all the alternatives which were likely to face me on the high seas—everything! . . . except the novel responsibility of command. But I took heart from the reasonable thought that the ship was like other ships, the men like other men, and that the sea was not likely to keep any special surprises expressly for my discomfiture.

Arrived at that comforting conclusion, I bethought myself of a cigar and went below to get it. All was still down there. Everybody at the after end of the ship was sleeping profoundly. I came out again on the quarter-deck, agreeably at ease in my sleeping suit on that warm breathless night, barefooted, a glowing cigar in my teeth, and, going forward, I was met by the profound silence of the fore end of the ship. Only as I passed the door of the forecastle I heard a deep, quiet, trustful sigh of some sleeper inside. And suddenly I rejoiced in the great security of the sea as compared with the unrest of the land, in my choice of that untempted life presenting no disquieting problems, invested with an elementary moral beauty by the absolute straightforwardness of its appeal and by the singleness of its purpose.

The riding light in the fore-rigging burned with a clear, untroubled, as if symbolic, flame, confident and bright in the mysterious shades of the night. Passing on my way aft along the other side of the ship, I observed that the rope side ladder, put over, no doubt, for the master of the tug when he came to fetch away our letters, had not been hauled in as it should have been. I became annoyed at this, for exactitude in small matters is the very soul of discipline. Then I reflected that I had myself peremptorily dismissed my officers from duty, and by my own act had prevented the anchor watch being formally set and things properly attended to. I asked myself whether it was wise ever to interfere with the established routine of duties even from the kindest of motives. My action might have made me appear eccentric. Goodness only knew how that absurdly whiskered mate would "account" for my conduct, and what the whole ship thought of that informality of their new captain. I was vexed with myself.

Not from compunction certainly, but, as it were mechanically, I proceeded to get the ladder in myself. Now a side ladder of that sort is a light affair and comes in easily, yet my vigorous tug, which should have brought it flying on board, merely recoiled upon my body in a totally unexpected jerk. What the devil! . . . I was so astounded by the immovableness of that ladder that I remained stock-still, trying to account for it to myself like that imbecile mate of mine. In the end, of course, I put my head over the rail.

The side of the ship made an opaque belt of shadow on the darkling glassy shimmer of the sea. But I saw at once something elongated and pale floating very close to the ladder. Before I could form a guess a faint flash of phosphorescent light, which seemed to issue suddenly from the naked body of a man, flickered in the sleeping water with the elusive, silent play of summer lightning in a night sky. With a gasp I saw revealed to my stare a pair of feet, the long legs, a broad livid back immersed right up to the neck in a greenish cadaverous glow. One hand, awash, clutched the bottom rung of the ladder. He was complete but for the head. A headless corpse! The cigar dropped out of my gaping mouth with a tiny plop and a short hiss quite audible in the absolute stillness of all things under heaven. At that I suppose he raised up his face, a dimly pale oval in the shadow of the ship's side. But even then I could only barely make out down there the shape of his blackhaired head. However, it was enough for the horrid, frostbound sensation which had gripped me about the chest to pass off. The moment of vain exclamations was past, too. I only climbed on the spare spar and leaned over the rail as far as I could, to bring my eyes nearer to that mystery floating alongside.

As he hung by the ladder, like a resting swimmer, the sea lightning played about his limbs at every stir; and he appeared in it ghastly, silvery, fishlike. He remained as mute as a fish, too. He made no motion to get out of the water, either. It was inconceivable that he should not attempt to come on board, and strangely troubling to suspect that perhaps he did not want to. And my first words were prompted by just that troubled incertitude.

"What's the matter?" I asked in my ordinary tone; speaking down to the face upturned exactly under mine.

"Cramp," it answered, no louder. Then slightly anxious, "I say, no need to call anyone."

"I was not going to," I said.

"Are you alone on deck?"

"Yes."

I had somehow the impression that he was on the point of letting go the ladder to swim away beyond my ken—mysterious as he came. But, for the moment, this being appearing as if he had risen from the bottom of the sea (it was certainly the nearest land to the ship) wanted only to know the time. I told him. And he, down there, tentatively:

"I suppose your captain's turned in?"

"I am sure he isn't," I said.

He seemed to struggle with himself, for I heard something like the low, bitter murmur of doubt. "What's the good?" His next words came out with a hesitating effort.

"Look here, my man. Could you call him out quietly?"

I thought the time had come to declare myself.

"*I* am the captain."

I heard a "By Jove!" whispered at the level of the water. The phosphorescence flashed in the swirl of the water all about his limbs, his other hand seized the ladder.

"My name's Leggatt."

The voice was calm and resolute. A good voice. The self-possession of that man had somehow induced a corresponding state in myself. It was very quietly that I remarked:

"You must be a good swimmer."

"Yes. I've been in the water practically since nine o'clock. The question for me now is whether I am to let go this ladder and go on swimming till I sink from exhaustion, or—to come on board here."

I felt this was no mere formula of desperate speech, but a real alternative in the view of a strong soul. I should have gathered from this that he was young; indeed, it is only the young who are ever confronted by such clear issues. But at the time it was pure intuition on my part. A mysterious communication was established already between us two—in the face of that silent, darkened tropical sea. I was young, too; young enough to make no comment. The man in the water began suddenly to climb up the ladder, and I hastened away from the rail to fetch some clothes.

Before entering the cabin I stood still, listening in the lobby at the foot of the stairs. A faint snore came through the closed door of the chief mate's room. The second mate's door was on the hook, but the darkness in there was absolutely soundless. He, too, was young and could sleep like a stone. Remained the steward, but he was not likely to wake up before he was called. I got a sleeping suit out of my room and, coming back on deck, saw the naked man from the sea sitting on the main hatch, glimmering white in the darkness, his elbows on his knees and his head in his hands. In a moment he had concealed his damp body in a sleeping suit of the same gray-stripe pattern as the one I was wearing and followed me like my double on the poop. Together we moved right aft, barefooted, silent.

"What is it?" I asked in a deadened voice, taking the lighted lamp out of the binnacle, and raising it to his face.

"An ugly business."

He had rather regular features; a good mouth; light eyes under somewhat heavy, dark eyebrows; a smooth, square forehead; no growth on his cheeks; a small, brown mustache, and a well-shaped, round chin. His expression was concentrated, meditative, under the inspecting light of the lamp I held up to his face; such as a man thinking hard in solitude might wear. My sleeping suit was just right for his size. A well-knit young fellow of twenty-five at most. He caught his lower lip with the edge of white, even teeth.

"Yes," I said, replacing the lamp in the binnacle. The warm, heavy tropical night closed upon his head again.

"There's a ship over there," he murmured.

"Yes, I know. The *Sephora*. Did you know of us?"

"Hadn't the slightest idea. I am the mate of her—" He paused and corrected himself. "I should say I *was*."

"Aha! Something wrong?"

"Yes. Very wrong indeed. I've killed a man."

"What do you mean? Just now?"

"No, on the passage. Weeks ago. Thirty-nine south. When I say a man—"

"Fit of temper," I suggested, confidently.

The shadowy, dark head, like mine, seemed to nod imperceptibly above the ghostly gray of my sleeping suit. It was, in the night, as though I had been faced by my own reflection in the depths of a somber and immense mirror.

"A pretty thing to have to own up to for a *Conway* boy," murmured my double, distinctly.

"You're a *Conway* boy?"

"I am," he said, as if startled. Then, slowly . . . "Perhaps you too—"

It was so; but being a couple of years older I had left before he joined. After a quick interchange of dates a silence fell; and I thought suddenly of my absurd mate with his terrific whiskers and the "Bless my soul—you don't say so" type of intellect. My double gave me an inkling of his thoughts by saying:

"My father's a parson in Norfolk. Do you see me before a judge and jury on that charge? For myself I can't see the necessity. There are fellows that an angel from heaven— And I am not that. He was one of those creatures that are just simmering all the time with a silly sort of wickedness. Miserable devils that have no business to live at all. He wouldn't do his duty and wouldn't let anybody else do theirs. But what's the good of talking! You know well enough the sort of ill-conditioned snarling cur—"

He appealed to me as if our experiences had been as identical as our clothes. And I knew well enough the pestiferous danger of such a character where there are no means of legal repression. And I knew well enough also that my double there was no homicidal ruffian. I did not think of asking him for details, and he told me the story roughly in brusque, disconnected sentences. I needed no more. I saw it all going on as though I were myself inside that other sleeping suit.

"It happened while we were setting a reefed foresail, at dusk. Reefed foresail! You understand the sort of weather. The only sail we had left to keep the ship running; so you may guess what it had been like for days. Anxious sort of job, that. He gave me some of his cursed insolence at the sheet. I tell you I was overdone with this terrific weather that seemed to have no end to it. Terrific, I tell you—and a deep ship. I believe the fellow himself was half crazed with funk. It was no time for gentlemanly reproof, so I turned around and felled him like an ox. He up and at me. We closed just as an awful sea made for the ship. All hands saw it coming and took to the rigging, but I had him by the throat, and went on shaking him like a rat, the men above us yelling, 'Look out! Look out!' Then a crash as if the sky had fallen on my head. They say that for over ten minutes hardly anything was to be seen of the ship—just the three masts and a bit of the forecastle head and of the poop all awash driving along in a smother of foam. It was a miracle that they found us, jammed together behind the forebits. It's clear that I meant business, because I was holding him by the throat still when they picked us up. He was black in the face. It was too much for them. It seems they rushed us aft together, gripped as we were, screaming 'Murder!' like a lot of lunatics, and broke into the cuddy. And the ship running for her life, touch and go all the time, any minute her last in a sea fit to turn your hair gray only a-looking at it. I understand that the skipper, too, started raving like the rest of them. The man had been deprived of sleep for more than a week, and to have this sprung on him at the height of a furious gale nearly drove him out of his mind. I wonder they didn't fling me overboard after getting the carcass of their precious shipmate out of my fingers. They had rather a job to separate us, I've been told. A sufficiently fierce story to make an old judge and a respectable jury sit up a bit. The first thing I heard when I came to myself was the maddening howling of that endless gale, and on that the voice of the old man. He was hanging on to my bunk, staring into my face out of his sou'wester.

" 'Mr. Leggatt, you have killed a man. You can act no longer as chief mate of this ship.' "

His care to subdue his voice made it sound monotonous. He rested a hand on the end of the skylight to steady himself with, and all that time did not stir a limb, so far as I could see. "Nice little tale for a quiet tea party," he concluded in the same tone.

One of my hands, too, rested on the end of the skylight; neither did I stir a limb, so far as I knew. We stood less than a foot from each other. It occurred to me that if old "Bless my soul—you don't say so" were to put his head up the companion and catch sight of us, he would think he was seeing double, or imagine himself come upon a scene of weird witchcraft; the strange captain having a quiet confabulation by the wheel with his own gray ghost. I became very much concerned to prevent anything of the sort. I heard the other's soothing undertone.

"My father's a parson in Norfolk," it said. Evidently he had forgotten he had told me this important fact before. Truly a nice little tale.

"You had better slip down into my stateroom now," I said, moving off stealthily. My double followed my movements; our bare feet made no sound; I let him in, closed the door with care, and, after giving a call to the second mate, returned on deck for my relief.

"Not much sign of any wind yet," I remarked when he approached.

"No, sir. Not much," he assented, sleepily, in his hoarse voice, with just enough deference, no more, and barely suppressing a yawn.

"Well, that's all you have to look out for. You have got your orders."

"Yes, sir."

I paced a turn or two on the poop and saw him take up his position face forward with his elbow in the ratlines of the mizzen-rigging before I went below. The mate's faint snoring was still going on peacefully. The cuddy lamp was burning over the table on which stood a vase with flowers, a polite attention from the ship's provision merchant—the last flowers we should see for the next three months at the very least. Two bunches of bananas hung from the beam symmetrically, one on each side of the rudder casing. Everything was as before in the ship—except that two of her captain's sleeping suits were simultaneously in use, one motionless in the cuddy, the other keeping very still in the captain's stateroom.

It must be explained here that my cabin had the form of the capital letter L, the door being within the angle and opening into the short part of the letter. A couch was to the left, the bed-place to the right; my writing desk and the chronometers' table faced the door. But anyone opening it, unless he stepped right inside, had no view of what I call the long (or vertical) part of the letter. It contained some lockers surmounted by a book case; and a few clothes, a thick jacket or two, caps, oilskin coat, and such like, hung on hooks. There was at the bottom of that part a door opening into my bathroom, which could be entered also directly from the saloon. But that way was never used.

The mysterious arrival had discovered the advantage of this particular shape. Entering my room, lighted strongly by a big bulkhead lamp swung on gimbals above my writing desk, I did not see him anywhere till he stepped out quietly from behind the coats hung in the recessed part.

"I heard somebody moving about, and went in there at once," he whispered.

I, too, spoke under my breath.

"Nobody is likely to come in here without knocking and getting permission."

He nodded. His face was thin and the sunburn faded, as though he

THE SECRET SHARER / 323

had been ill. And no wonder. He had been, I heard presently, kept under arrest in his cabin for nearly seven weeks. But there was nothing sickly in his eyes or in his expression. He was not a bit like me, really; yet, as we stood leaning over my bed-place, whispering side by side, with our dark heads together and our backs to the door, anybody bold enough to open it stealthily would have been treated to the uncanny sight of a double captain busy talking in whispers with his other self.

"But all this doesn't tell me how you came to hang on to our side ladder," I inquired, in the hardly audible murmurs we used, after he had told me something more of the proceedings on board the *Sephora* once the bad weather was over.

"When we sighted Java Head I had had time to think all those matters out several times over. I had six weeks of doing nothing else, and with only an hour or so every evening for a tramp on the quarter deck."

He whispered, his arms folded on the side of my bed-place, staring through the open port. And I could imagine perfectly the manner of this thinking out—a stubborn if not a steadfast operation; something of which I should have been perfectly incapable.

"I reckoned it would be dark before we closed with the land," he continued, so low that I had to strain my hearing, near as we were to each other, shoulder touching shoulder almost. "So I asked to speak to the old man. He always seemed very sick when he came to see me—as if he could not look me in the face. You know, that foresail saved the ship. She was too deep to have run long under bare poles. And it was I that managed to set it for him. Anyway, he came. When I had him in my cabin—he stood by the door looking at me as if I had the halter around my neck already—I asked him right away to leave my cabin door unlocked at night while the ship was going through Sunda Straits. There would be the Java coast within two or three miles, off Angier Point. I wanted nothing more. I've had a prize for swimming my second year in the *Conway*."

"I can believe it," I breathed out.

"God only knows why they locked me in every night. To see some of their faces you'd have thought they were afraid I'd go about at night strangling people. Am I a murdering brute? Do I look it? By Jove! If I had been he wouldn't have trusted himself like that into my room. You'll say I might have chucked him aside and bolted out, there and then—it was dark already. Well, no. And for the same reason I wouldn't think of trying to smash the door. There would have been a rush to stop me at the noise, and I did not mean to get into a confounded scrimmage. Somebody else might have got killed—for I would not have broken out only to get chucked back, and I did not want any more of that work. He refused, looking more sick than ever. He was afraid of the men, and also of that old second mate of his who had been sailing with him for years—a gray-headed old humbug; and his steward, too, had been with him devil knows how long—seventeen years or more—a dogmatic sort of loafer who hated me like poison, just because I was the chief mate. No chief mate ever made more than one voyage in the *Sephora*, you know. Those two old chaps ran the ship. Devil only knows what the skipper wasn't afraid of (all his nerve went to pieces altogether in that hellish spell of bad weather we had)—of what the law would do to him—of his wife, perhaps. Oh, yes! she's on board. Though I don't think she would have meddled. She would have been only too glad to have me out of the ship in any way. The 'brand of Cain' business, don't you see. That's all right. I was ready enough to go off wandering on the face of the earth—and that was price enough to pay for an Abel of that sort. Anyhow, he wouldn't listen to me. 'This thing must take its course. I represent the law here.' He was shaking like a leaf. 'So you won't?' 'No!' 'Then I hope you will be able to sleep on that,' I said, and turned my back on him. 'I wonder that *you* can,' cries he, and locks the door.

"Well, after that, I couldn't. Not very well. That was three weeks ago. We have had a slow passage through the Java Sea; drifted about Carimata for ten days. When we anchored here they thought, I suppose, it was all right. The nearest land (and that's five miles) is the ship's destination; the consul would soon set about catching me; and there would have been no object in bolting to these islets there. I don't suppose there's a drop of water on them. I don't know how it was, but tonight that steward, after bringing me my supper, went out to let me eat it, and left the door unlocked. And I ate it—all there was, too. After I had finished I strolled out on the quarter-deck. I don't know that I meant to do anything. A breath of fresh air was all I wanted, I believe. Then a sudden temptation came over me. I kicked off my slippers and was in the water before I had made up my mind fairly. Somebody heard the splash and they raised an awful hullabaloo. 'He's gone! Lower the boats! He's committed suicide! No, he's swimming.' Certainly I was swimming. It's not so easy for a swimmer like me to commit suicide by drowning. I landed on the nearest islet before the boat left the ship's side. I heard them pulling about in the dark, hailing, and so on, but after a bit they gave up. Everything quieted down and the anchorage became as still as death. I sat down on a stone and began to think. I felt certain they would start searching for me at daylight. There was no place to hide on those stony things—and if there had been, what would have been the good? But now I was clear of that ship, I was not going back. So after a while I took off all my clothes, tied them up in a bundle with a stone inside, and dropped them in the deep water on the outer side of that islet. That was suicide enough for me. Let them think what they liked, but I didn't mean to drown myself. I meant to swim till I sank—but that's not the same thing. I struck out for another of these little islands, and it was from that one that I first saw your riding light. Something to swim for. I went on easily, and on the way I came upon a flat rock a foot or two above water. In the daytime, I dare say, you might make it out with a glass from your poop. I scrambled up on it and rested myself for a bit. Then I made another start. That last spell must have been over a mile."

His whisper was getting fainter and fainter, and all the time he stared straight out through the porthole, in which there was not even a star to be seen. I had not interrupted him. There was something that made comment impossible in his narrative, or perhaps in himself; a sort of feeling, a quality, which I can't find a name for. And when he ceased, all I found was a futile whisper: "So you swam for our light?"

"Yes—straight for it. It was something to swim for. I couldn't see any stars low down because the coast was in the way, and I couldn't see the land, either. The water was like glass. One might have been swimming in a confounded thousand-feet deep cistern with no place for scrambling out anywhere; but what I didn't like was the notion of swimming round and round like a crazed bullock before I gave out; and as I didn't mean to go back . . . No. Do you see me being hauled back, stark naked, off one of these little islands by the scruff of the neck and fighting like a wild beast? Somebody would have got killed for certain, and I did not want any of that. So I went on. Then your ladder—"

"Why didn't you hail the ship?" I asked, a little louder.

He touched my shoulder lightly. Lazy footsteps came right over our heads and stopped. The second mate had crossed from the other side of the poop and might have been hanging over the rail, for all we knew.

"He couldn't hear us talking—could he?" My double breathed into my very ear, anxiously.

His anxiety was an answer, a sufficient answer, to the question I had put to him. An answer containing all the difficulty of that situation. I closed the porthole quietly, to make sure. A louder word might have been overheard.

"Who's that?" he whispered then.

"My second mate. But I don't know much more of the fellow than you do."

And I told him a little about myself. I had been appointed to take charge while I least expected anything of the sort, not quite a fortnight ago. I didn't know either the ship or the people. Hadn't had the time in port to look about me or size anybody up. And as to the crew, all they knew was that I was appointed to take the ship home. For the rest, I was almost as much of a stranger on board as himself, I said. And at the moment I felt it most acutely. I felt that it would take very little to make me a suspect person in the eyes of the ship's company.

He had turned about meantime; and we, the two strangers in the ship, faced each other in identical attitudes.

"Your ladder—" he murmured, after a silence. "Who'd have thought of finding a ladder hanging over at night in a ship anchored out here! I felt just then a very unpleasant faintness. After the life I've been leading for nine weeks, anybody would have got out of condition. I wasn't capable of swimming round as far as your rudder chains. And, lo and behold! there was a ladder to get hold of. After I gripped it I said to myself, 'What's the good?' When I saw a man's head looking over I thought I would swim away presently and leave him shouting—in whatever language it was. I didn't mind being looked at. I—I liked it. And then you speaking to me so quietly—as if you had expected me—made me hold on a little longer. It had been a confounded lonely time—I don't mean while swimming. I was glad to talk a little to somebody that didn't belong to the *Sephora*. As to asking for the captain, that was a mere impulse. It could have been no use, with all the ship knowing about me and the other people pretty certain to be round here in the morning. I don't know—I wanted to be seen, to talk with somebody, before I went on. I don't know what I would have said. . . . 'Fine night, isn't it?' or something of the sort."

"Do you think they will be round here presently?" I asked with some incredulity.

"Quite likely," he said, faintly.

He looked extremely haggard all of a sudden. His head rolled on his shoulders.

"H'm. We shall see then. Meantime get into that bed," I whispered. "Want help? There."

It was a rather high bed-place with a set of drawers underneath. This amazing swimmer really needed the lift I gave him by seizing his leg. He tumbled in, rolled over on his back, and flung one arm across his eyes. And then, with his face nearly hidden, he must have looked exactly as I used to look in that bed. I gazed upon my other self for a while before drawing across carefully the two green serge curtains which ran on a brass rod. I thought for a moment of pinning them together for greater safety, but I sat down on the couch, and once there I felt unwilling to rise and hunt for a pin. I would do it in a moment. I was extremely tired, in a peculiarly intimate way, by the strain of stealthiness, by the effort of whispering and the general secrecy of this excitement. It was three o'clock by now and I had been on my feet since nine, but I was not sleepy; I could not have gone to sleep. I sat there, fagged out, looking at the curtains, trying to clear my mind of the confused sensation of being in two places at once, and greatly bothered by an exasperating knocking in my head. It was a relief to discover suddenly that it was not in my head at all, but on the outside of the door. Before I could collect myself the words "Come in" were out of my mouth, and the steward entered with a tray, bringing in my morning coffee. I had slept, after all, and I was so frightened that I shouted, "This way! I am here, steward," as though he had been miles away. He put down the tray on the table next the couch and only then said, very quietly, "I can see you are here, sir." I felt him give me a keen look, but I dared not meet his eyes just then. He must have wondered why I had drawn the curtains of my bed before going to sleep on the couch. He went out, hooking the door open as usual.

I heard the crew washing decks above me. I knew I would have been told at once if there had been any wind. Calm, I thought, and I was doubly vexed. Indeed, I felt dual more than ever. The steward reappeared suddenly in the doorway. I jumped up from the couch so quickly that he gave a start.

"What do you want here?"

"Close your port, sir—they are washing decks."

"It is closed," I said, reddening.

"Very well, sir." But he did not move from the doorway and returned my stare in an extraordinary, equivocal manner for a time. Then his eyes wavered, all his expression changed, and in a voice unusually gentle, almost coaxingly:

"May I come in to take the empty cup away, sir?"

"Of course!" I turned my back on him while he popped in and out. Then I unhooked and closed the door and even pushed the bolt. This sort of thing could not go on very long. The cabin was as hot as an oven, too. I took a peep at my double, and discovered that he had not moved, his arm was still over his eyes; but his chest heaved; his hair was wet; his chin glistened with perspiration. I reached over him and opened the port.

"I must show myself on deck," I reflected.

Of course, theoretically, I could do what I liked, with no one to say nay to me within the whole circle of the horizon; but to lock my cabin door and take the key away I did not dare. Directly I put my head out of the companion I saw the group of my two officers, the second mate barefooted, the chief mate in long india-rubber boots, near the break of the poop, and the steward halfway down the poop ladder talking to them eagerly. He happened to catch sight of me and dived, the second ran down on the main deck shouting some order or other, and the chief mate came to meet me, touching his cap.

There was a sort of curiosity in his eye that I did not like. I don't know whether the steward had told them that I was "queer" only, or downright drunk, but I know the man meant to have a good look at me. I watched him coming with a smile which, as he got into point-blank range, took effect and froze his very whiskers. I did not give him time to open his lips.

"Square the yards by lifts and braces before the hands go to breakfast."

It was the first particular order I had given on board that ship; and I stayed on deck to see it executed, too. I had felt the need of asserting myself without loss of time. That sneering young cub got taken down a peg or two on that occasion, and I also seized the opportunity of having a good look at the face of every foremast man as they filed past me to go to the after braces. At breakfast time, eating nothing myself, I presided with such frigid dignity that the two mates were only too glad to escape from the cabin as soon as decency permitted; and all the time the dual working of my mind distracted me almost to the point of insanity. I was constantly watching myself, my secret self, as dependent on my actions as my own personality, sleeping in that bed, behind that door which faced me as I sat at the head of the table. It was very much like being mad, only it was worse because one was aware of it.

I had to shake him for a solid minute, but when at last he opened his eyes it was in the full possession of his senses, with an inquiring look.

"All's well so far," I whispered. "Now you must vanish into the bathroom."

He did so, as noiseless as a ghost, and I then rang for the steward, and facing him boldly, directed him to tidy up my stateroom while I was having my bath—"and be quick about it." As my tone admitted of no excuses, he said, "Yes, sir," and ran off to fetch his dustpan and brushes. I took a bath and did most of my dressing, splashing, and whistling softly for the steward's edification, while the secret sharer of my life stood drawn up bolt upright in that little space, his face looking very sunken in daylight, his eyelids lowered under the stern, dark line of his eyebrows drawn together by a slight frown.

When I left him there to go back to my room the steward was finishing dusting. I sent for the mate and engaged him in some insignificant conversation. It was, as it were, trifling with the terrific character of his whiskers; but my object was to give him an opportunity for a good look at my cabin. And then I could at last shut, with a clear conscience, the door of my stateroom and get my double back into the recessed part. There was nothing else for it. He had to sit still on a small folding stool, half smothered by the heavy coats hanging there. We listened to the steward going into the bathroom out of the saloon, filling the water bottles there, scrubbing the bath, setting things to rights, whisk, bang, clatter—out again into the saloon—turn the key—click. Such was my scheme for keeping my second self invisible. Nothing better could be contrived under the circumstances. And there we sat: I at my writing desk ready to appear busy with some papers, he behind me, out of sight of the door. It would not have been prudent to talk in daytime; and I could not have stood the excitement of that queer sense of whispering to myself. Now and then, glancing over my shoulder, I saw him far back there, sitting rigidly on the low stool, his bare feet close together, his arms folded, his head hanging on his breast— and perfectly still. Anybody would have taken him for me.

I was fascinated by it myself. Every moment I had to glance over my shoulder. I was looking at him when a voice outside the door said:

"Beg pardon, sir."

"Well!" . . . I kept my eyes on him, and so, when the voice outside the door announced, "There's a ship's boat coming our way, sir," I saw him give a start—the first movement he had made for hours. But he did not raise his bowed head.

"All right. Get the ladder over."

I hesitated. Should I whisper something to him? But what? His immobility seemed to have been never disturbed. What could I tell him he did not know already? . . . Finally I went on deck.

II

The skipper of the *Sephora* had a thin red whisker all round his face, and the sort of complexion that goes with hair of that color; also the particular, rather smeary shade of blue in the eyes. He was not exactly a showy figure; his shoulders were high, his stature but middling—one leg slightly more bandy than the other. He shook hands, looking vaguely around. A spiritless tenacity was his main characteristic, I judged. I behaved with a politeness which seemed to disconcert him. Perhaps he was shy. He mumbled to me as if he were ashamed of what he was saying; gave his name (it was something like Archbold—but at this distance of years I hardly am sure), his ship's name, and a few other particulars of that sort, in the manner of a criminal making a reluctant and doleful confession. He had had terrible weather on the passage out—terrible—terrible—wife aboard, too.

By this time we were seated in the cabin and the steward brought in a tray with a bottle and glasses. "Thanks! No." Never took liquor. Would have some water, though. He drank two tumblerfuls. Terrible thirsty work. Ever since daylight had been exploring the islands round his ship.

"What was that for—fun?" I asked, with an appearance of polite interest.

"No!" He sighed. "Painful duty."

As he persisted in his mumbling and I wanted my double to hear every word, I hit upon the notion of informing him that I regretted to say I was hard of hearing.

"Such a young man, too!" he nodded, keeping his smeary blue, unintelligent eyes fastened upon me. What was the cause of it—some disease? he inquired, without the least sympathy and as if he thought that, if so, I'd got no more than I deserved.

"Yes; disease," I admitted in a cheerful tone which seemed to shock him. But my point was gained, because he had to raise his voice to give me his tale. It is not worth while to record that version. It was just over two months since all this had happened, and he had thought so much about it that he seemed completely muddled as to its bearings, but still immensely impressed.

"What would you think of such a thing happening on board your own ship? I've had the *Sephora* for these fifteen years. I am a well-known shipmaster."

He was densely distressed—and perhaps I should have sympathized with him if I had been able to detach my mental vision from the unsuspected sharer of my cabin as though he were my second self. There he was on the other side of the bulkhead, four or five feet from us, no more, as we sat in the saloon. I looked politely at Captain Archbold (if that was his name), but it was the other I saw, in a gray sleeping suit, seated on a low stool, his bare feet close together, his arms folded, and every word said between us falling into the ears of his dark head bowed on his chest.

"I have been at sea now, man and boy, for seven-and-thirty years, and I've never heard of such a thing happening in an English ship. And that it should be my ship. Wife on board, too."

I was hardly listening to him.

"Don't you think," I said, "that the heavy sea which, you told me, came aboard just then might have killed the man? I have seen the sheer weight of a sea kill a man very neatly, by simply breaking his neck."

"Good God!" he uttered, impressively, fixing his smeary blue eyes on me. "The sea! No man killed by the sea ever looked like that." He seemed positively scandalized at my suggestion. And as I gazed at him, certainly not prepared for anything original on his part, he advanced his head close to mine and thrust his tongue out at me so suddenly that I couldn't help starting back.

After scoring over my calmness in this graphic way he nodded wisely. If I had seen the sight, he assured me, I would never forget it as long as I lived. The weather was too bad to give the corpse a proper sea burial. So next day at dawn they took it up on the poop, covering its face with a bit of bunting; he read a short prayer, and then, just as it was, in its oilskins and long boots, they launched it amongst those mountainous seas that seemed ready every moment to swallow up the ship herself and the terrified lives on board of her.

"That reefed foresail saved you," I threw in.

"Under God—it did," he exclaimed fervently. "It was by a special mercy, I firmly believe, that it stood some of those hurricane squalls."

"It was the setting of that sail which—" I began.

"God's own hand in it," he interrupted me. "Nothing less could have done it. I don't mind telling you that I hardly dared give the order. It seemed impossible that we could touch anything without losing it, and then our last hope would have been gone."

The terror of that gale was on him yet. I let him go on for a bit, then said, casually—as if returning to a minor subject:

"You were very anxious to give up your mate to the shore people, I believe?"

He was. To the law. His obscure tenacity on that point had in it something incomprehensible and a little awful; something, as it were, mystical, quite apart from his anxiety that he should not be suspected of "countenancing any doings of that sort." Seven-and-thirty virtuous years at sea, of which over twenty of immaculate command, and the last fifteen in the *Sephora*, seemed to have laid him under some pitiless obligation.

"And you know," he went on, groping shamefacedly amongst his feelings, "I did not engage that young fellow. His people had some interest with my owners. I was in a way forced to take him on. He looked very smart, very gentlemanly, and all that. But do you know—I never liked him, somehow. I am a plain man. You see, he wasn't exactly the sort for the chief mate of a ship like the *Sephora*."

I had become so connected in thoughts and impressions with the secret sharer of my cabin that I felt as if I, personally, were being given to understand that I, too, was not the sort that would have done for the chief mate of a ship like the *Sephora*. I had no doubt of it in my mind.

"Not at all the style of man. You understand," he insisted superfluously, looking hard at me.

I smiled urbanely. He seemed at a loss for a while.

"I suppose I must report a suicide."

"Beg pardon?"

"Sui-cide! That's what I'll have to write to my owners directly I get in."

"Unless you manage to recover him before tomorrow," I assented, dispassionately. . . . "I mean, alive."

He mumbled something which I really did not catch, and I turned my ear to him in a puzzled manner. He fairly bawled:

"The land—I say, the mainland is at least seven miles off my anchorage."

"About that."

My lack of excitement, of curiosity, of surprise, of any sort of pronounced interest, began to arouse his distrust. But except for the felicitous pretense of deafness I had not tried to pretend anything. I had felt utterly incapable of playing the part of ignorance properly, and therefore was afraid to try. It is also certain that he had brought some ready-made suspicions with him, and that he viewed my politeness as a strange and unnatural phenomenon. And yet how else could I have received him? Not heartily! That was impossible for psychological reasons, which I need not state here. My only object was to keep off his inquiries. Surlily? Yes, but surliness might have provoked a point-blank question. From its novelty to him and from its nature, punctilious courtesy was the manner best calculated to restrain the man. But there was the danger of his breaking through my defense bluntly. I could not, I think, have met him by a direct lie, also for psychological (not moral) reasons. If he had only known how afraid I was of his putting my feeling of identity with the other to the test! But, strangely enough—(I thought of it only afterward)—I believe that he was not a little disconcerted by the reverse side of that weird situation, by something in me that reminded him of the man he was seeking—suggested a mysterious similitude to the young fellow he had distrusted and disliked from the first.

However that might have been, the silence was not very prolonged. He took another oblique step.

"I reckon I had no more than a two-mile pull to your ship. Not a bit more."

"And quite enough, too, in this awful heat," I said.

Another pause full of mistrust followed. Necessity, they say, is mother of invention, but fear, too, is not barren of ingenious suggestions. And I was afraid he would ask me point-blank for news of my other self.

"Nice little saloon, isn't it?" I remarked, as if noticing for the first time the way his eyes roamed from one closed door to the other. "And very well fitted out, too. Here, for instance," I continued, reaching over the back of my seat negligently and flinging the door open, "is my bathroom."

He made an eager movement, but hardly gave it a glance. I got up, shut the door of the bathroom, and invited him to have a look round, as if I were very proud of my accommodation. He had to rise and be shown round, but he went through the business without any raptures whatever.

"And now we'll have a look at my stateroom," I declared, in a voice as loud as I dared to make it, crossing the cabin to the starboard side with purposely heavy steps.

He followed me in and gazed around. My intelligent double had vanished. I played my part.

"Very convenient—isn't it?"

"Very nice. Very com . . ." He didn't finish, and went out brusquely as if to escape from some unrighteous wiles of mine. But it was not to be. I had been too frightened not to feel vengeful; I felt I had him on the run, and I meant to keep him on the run. My polite insistence must have had something menacing in it, because he gave in suddenly. And I did not let him off a single item; mate's room, pantry, storerooms, the very sail locker which was also under the poop—he had to look into them all. When at last I showed him out on the quarter-deck he drew a long, spiritless sigh, and mumbled dismally that he must really be going back to his ship now. I desired my mate, who had joined us, to see to the captain's boat.

The man of whiskers gave a blast on the whistle which he used to wear hanging round his neck, and yelled, "*Sephora* away!" My double down there in my cabin must have heard, and certainly could not feel more relieved than I. Four fellows came running out from somewhere forward and went over the side, while my own men, appearing on deck too, lined the rail. I escorted my visitor to the gangway ceremoniously, and nearly overdid it. He was a tenacious beast. On the very ladder he lingered, and in that unique, guiltily conscious manner of sticking to the point:

"I say . . . you . . . you don't think that—"

I covered his voice loudly:

"Certainly not. . . . I am delighted. Good-by."

I had an idea of what he meant to say, and just saved myself by the privilege of defective hearing. He was too shaken generally to insist, but my mate, close witness of that parting, looked mystified and his face took on a thoughtful cast. As I did not want to appear as if I wished to avoid all communication with my officers, he had the opportunity to address me.

"Seems a very nice man. His boat's crew told our chaps a very extraordinary story, if what I am told by the steward is true. I suppose you had it from the captain, sir?"

"Yes. I had a story from the captain."

"A very horrible affair—isn't it, sir?"

"It is."

"Beats all these tales we hear about murders in Yankee ships."

"I don't think it beats them. I don't think it resembles them in the least."

"Bless my soul—you don't say so! But of course I've no acquaintance whatever with American ships, not I, so I couldn't go against your knowledge. It's horrible enough for me. . . . But the queerest part is that those fellows seemed to have some idea the man was hidden aboard here. They had really. Did you ever hear of such a thing?"

"Preposterous—isn't it?"

We were walking to and fro athwart the quarter-deck. No one of the crew forward could be seen (the day was Sunday), and the mate pursued:

"There was some little dispute about it. Our chaps took offense. 'As if we would harbor a thing like that,' they said. 'Wouldn't you like to look for him in our coal hole?' Quite a tiff. But they made it up in the end. I suppose he did drown himself. Don't you, sir?"

"I don't suppose anything."

"You have no doubt in the matter, sir?"

"None whatever."

I left him suddenly. I felt I was producing a bad impression, but with my double down there it was most trying to be on deck. And it was almost as trying to be below. Altogether a nerve-trying situation. But on the whole I felt less torn in two when I was with him. There was no one in the whole ship whom I dared to take into my confidence. Since the hands had got to know his story, it would have been impossible to pass him off for anyone else, and an accidental discovery was to be dreaded now more than ever. . . .

The steward being engaged in laying the table for dinner, we could talk only with our eyes when I first went down. Later in the afternoon we had a cautious try at whispering. The Sunday quietness of the ship was against us; the stillness of air and water around her was against us; the elements, the men were against us—everything was against us in our secret partnership; time itself—for this could not go on forever. The very trust in Providence was, I suppose, denied to his guilt. Shall I confess that this thought cast me down very much? And as to the chapter of accidents which counts for so much in the book of success, I could only hope that it was closed. For what favorable accident could be expected?

"Did you hear everything?" were my first words as soon as we took up our position side by side, leaning over my bed-place.

He had. And the proof of it was his earnest whisper. "The man told you he hardly dared to give the order."

I understood the reference to be to that saving foresail.

334 / JOSEPH CONRAD

"Yes. He was afraid of it being lost in the setting."

"I assure you he never gave the order. He may think he did, but he never gave it. He stood there with me on the break of the poop after the maintopsail blew away, and whimpered about our last hope—positively whimpered about it and nothing else—and the night coming on! To hear one's skipper go on like that in such weather was enough to drive any fellow out of his mind. It worked me up into a sort of desperation. I just took it into my own hands and went away from him, boiling, and— But what's the use telling you? *You* know! . . . Do you think that if I had not been pretty fierce with them I should have got the men to do anything? Not it! The bosun perhaps? Perhaps! It wasn't a heavy sea—it was a sea gone mad! I suppose the end of the world will be something like that; and a man may have the heart to see it coming once and be done with it—but to have to face it day after day—I don't blame anybody. I was precious little better than the rest. Only—I was an officer of that old coal-wagon, anyhow—"

"I quite understand," I conveyed that sincere assurance into his ear. He was out of breath with whispering; I could hear him pant slightly. It was all very simple. The same strung-up force which had given twenty-four men a chance, at least, for their lives, had, in a sort of recoil, crushed an unworthy mutinous existence.

But I had no leisure to weigh the merits of the matter—footsteps in the saloon, a heavy knock. "There's enough wind to get under way with, sir." Here was the call of a new claim upon my thoughts and even upon my feelings.

"Turn the hands up," I cried through the door. "I'll be on deck directly."

I was going out to make the acquaintance of my ship. Before I left the cabin our eyes met—the eyes of the only two strangers on board. I pointed to the recessed part where the little campstool awaited him and laid my finger on my lips. He made a gesture—somewhat vague—a little mysterious, accompanied by a faint smile, as if of regret.

This is not the place to enlarge upon the sensations of a man who feels for the first time a ship move under his feet to his own independent word. In my case they were not unalloyed. I was not wholly alone with my command; for there was that stranger in my cabin. Or rather, I was not completely and wholly with her. Part of me was absent. The mental feeling of being in two places at once affected me physically as if the mood of secrecy had penetrated my very soul. Before an hour had elapsed since the ship had begun to move, having occasion to ask the mate (he stood by my side) to take a compass bearing of the Pagoda, I caught myself reaching up to his ear in whispers. I say I caught myself, but enough had escaped to startle the man. I can't describe it otherwise than by saying that he shied. A grave, preoccupied manner, as though he were in possession of some perplexing intelligence, did not leave him henceforth. A little later I moved away from the rail to look at the compass with such a stealthy gait that the helmsman noticed it—and I could not help noticing the unusual roundness of his eyes. These are trifling instances, though it's to no commander's advantage to be suspected of ludicrous eccentricities. But I was also more seriously affected. There are to a seaman certain words, gestures, that should in given conditions come as naturally, as instinctively as the winking of a menaced eye. A certain order should spring on to his lips without thinking; a certain sign should get itself made, so to speak, without reflection. But all unconscious alertness had abandoned me. I had to make an effort of will to recall myself back (from the cabin) to the conditions of the moment. I felt that I was appearing an irresolute commander to those people who were watching me more or less critically.

And, besides, there were the scares. On the second day out, for instance, coming off the deck in the afternooon (I had straw slippers on my bare feet) I stopped at the open pantry door and spoke to the steward. He was doing something there with his back to me. At the sound of my voice he nearly jumped out of his skin, as the saying is, and incidentally broke a cup.

"What on earth's the matter with you?" I asked astonished.

He was extremely confused. "Beg pardon, sir. I made sure you were in your cabin."

"You see I wasn't."

"No, sir. I could have sworn I had heard you moving in there not a moment ago. It's most extraordinary . . . very sorry, sir."

I passed on with an inward shudder. I was so identified with my secret double that I did not even mention the fact in those scanty, fearful whispers we exchanged. I suppose he had made some slight noise of some kind or other. It would have been miraculous if he hadn't at one time or another. And yet, haggard as he appeared, he looked always perfectly self-controlled, more than calm—almost invulnerable. On my suggestion he remained almost entirely in the bathroom, which, upon the whole, was the safest place. There could be really no shadow of an excuse for anyone ever wanting to go in there, once the steward had done with it. It was a very tiny place. Sometimes he reclined on the floor, his legs bent, his head sustained on one elbow. At others I would find him on the campstool, sitting in his gray sleeping suit and with his cropped dark hair like a patient, unmoved convict. At night I would smuggle him into my bed-place, and we would whisper together, with the regular footfalls of the officer of the watch passing and repassing over our heads. It was an infinitely miserable time. It was lucky that some tins of fine preserves were stowed in a locker in my stateroom; hard bread I could always get hold of; and so he lived on stewed chicken, paté de foie gras, asparagus, cooked oysters, sardines—on all sorts of abominable sham delicacies out of tins. My early morning coffee he always drank; and it was all I dared do for him in that respect.

Every day there was the horrible maneuvering to go through so that my room and then the bathroom should be done in the usual way. I came to hate the sight of the steward, to abhor the voice of that harmless man. I felt that it was he who would bring on the disaster of discovery. It hung like a sword over our heads.

The fourth day out, I think (we were then working down the east side of the Gulf of Siam, tack for tack, in light winds and smooth water)—the fourth day, I say, of this miserable juggling with the unavoidable, as we sat at our evening meal, that man, whose slightest movement I dreaded, after putting down the dishes ran upon deck busily. This could not be dangerous. Presently he came down again; and then it appeared that he had remembered a coat of mine which I had thrown over a rail to dry after having been wetted in a shower which had passed over the ship in the afternoon. Sitting stolidly at the head of the table I became terrified at the sight of the garment on his arm. Of course he made for my door. There was no time to lose.

"Steward," I thundered. My nerves were so shaken that I could not govern my voice and conceal my agitation. This was the sort of thing that made my terrifically whiskered mate tap his forehead with his forefinger. I had detected him using that gesture while talking on deck with a confidential air to the carpenter. It was too far to hear a word, but I had no doubt that this pantomime could only refer to the strange new captain.

"Yes, sir," the pale-faced steward turned resignedly to me. It was this maddening course of being shouted at, checked without rhyme or reason, arbitrarily chased out of my cabin, suddenly called into it, sent flying out of his pantry on incomprehensible errands, that accounted for the growing wretchedness of his expression.

"Where are you going with that coat?"

"To your room, sir."

"Is there another shower coming?"

"I'm sure I don't know, sir. Shall I go up again and see, sir?"

"No! Never mind."

My object was attained, as of course my other self in there would have heard everything that passed. During this interlude my two officers never raised their eyes off their respective plates; but the lip of that confounded cub, the second mate, quivered visibly.

I expected the steward to hook my coat on and come out at once. He was very slow about it; but I dominated my nervousness sufficiently not to shout after him. Suddenly I became aware (it could be heard plainly enough) that the fellow for some reason or other was opening the door of the bathroom. It was the end. The place was literally not big enough to swing a cat in. My voice died in my throat and I went stony all over. I expected to hear a yell of surprise and terror, and made a movement, but had not the strength to get on my legs. Everything remained still. Had my second self taken the poor wretch by the throat? I don't know what I would have done next moment if I had not seen the steward come out of my room, close the door, and then stand quietly by the sideboard.

Saved, I thought. But, no! Lost! Gone! He was gone!

I laid my knife and fork down and leaned back in my chair. My head swam. After a while, when sufficiently recovered to speak in a steady voice, I instructed my mate to put the ship round at eight o'clock himself.

"I won't come on deck," I went on. "I think I'll turn in, and unless the wind shifts I don't want to be disturbed before midnight. I feel a bit seedy."

"You did look middling bad a little while ago," the chief mate remarked without showing any great concern.

They both went out, and I stared at the steward clearing the table. There was nothing to be read on that wretched man's face. But why did he avoid my eyes I asked myself. Then I thought I should like to hear the sound of his voice.

"Steward!"

"Sir!" Startled as usual.

"Where did you hang up that coat?"

"In the bathroom, sir." The usual anxious tone. "It's not quite dry yet, sir."

For some time longer I sat in the cuddy. Had my double vanished as he had come? But of his coming there was an explanation, whereas his disappearance would be inexplicable. . . . I went slowly into my dark room, shut the door, lighted the lamp, and for a time dared not turn round. When at last I did I saw him standing bolt upright in the narrow recessed part. It would not be true to say I had a shock, but an irresistible doubt of his bodily existence flitted through my mind. Can it be, I asked myself, that he is not visible to other eyes than mine? It was like being haunted. Motionless, with a grave face, he raised his hands slightly at me in a gesture which meant clearly, "Heavens! what a narrow escape!" Narrow indeed. I think I had come creeping quietly as near insanity as any man who has not actually gone over the border. That gesture restrained me, so to speak.

The mate with the terrific whiskers was now putting the ship on the other tack. In the moment of profound silence which follows upon the hands going to their stations I heard on the poop his raised voice: "Hard alee!" and the distant shout of the order repeated on the maindeck. The sails, in that light breeze, made but a faint fluttering noise. It ceased. The ship was coming round slowly; I held my breath in the renewed stillness of expectation; one wouldn't have thought that there was a single living soul on her decks. A sudden brisk shout, "Mainsail haul!" broke the spell, and in the noisy cries and rush overhead of the men running away with the main brace we two, down in my cabin, came together in our usual position by the bed-place.

He did not wait for my question. "I heard him fumbling here and just managed to squat myself down in the bath," he whispered to me. "The fellow only opened the door and put his arm in to hang the coat up. All the same—"

"I never thought of that," I whispered back, even more appalled than before at the closeness of the shave, and marveling at that something unyielding in his character which was carrying him through so finely. There was no agitation in his whisper. Whoever was being driven distracted, it was not he. He was sane. And the proof of his sanity was continued when he took up the whispering again.

"It would never do for me to come to life again."

It was something that a ghost might have said. But what he was alluding to was his old captain's reluctant admission of the theory of suicide. It would obviously serve his turn—if I had understood at all the view which seemed to govern the unalterable purpose of his action.

"You must maroon me as soon as ever you can get amongst these islands off the Cambodje shore," he went on.

"Maroon you! We are not living in a boy's adventure tale," I protested. His scornful whispering took me up.

"We aren't indeed! There's nothing of a boy's tale in this. But there's nothing else for it. I want no more. You don't suppose I am afraid of what can be done to me? Prison or gallows or whatever they may please. But you don't see me coming back to explain such things to an old fellow in a wig and twelve respectable tradesmen, do you? What can they know whether I am guilty or not—or of *what* I am guilty, either? That's my affair. What does the Bible say? 'Driven off the face of the earth.' Very well. I am off the face of the earth now. As I came at night so I shall go."

"Impossible!" I murmured. "You can't."

"Can't? . . . Not naked like a soul on the Day of Judgment. I shall freeze on to this sleeping suit. The Last Day is not yet—and . . . you have understood thoroughly. Didn't you?"

I felt suddenly ashamed of myself. I may say truly that I understood —and my hesitation in letting that man swim away from my ship's side had been a mere sham sentiment, a sort of cowardice.

"It can't be done now till next night," I breathed out. "The ship is on the offshore tack and the wind may fail us."

"As long as I know that you understand," he whispered. "But of course you do. It's a great satisfaction to have got somebody to understand. You seem to have been there on purpose." And in the same whisper, as if we two whenever we talked had to say things to each other which were not fit for the world to hear, he added, "It's very wonderful."

We remained side by side talking in our secret way—but sometimes silent or just exchanging a whispered word or two at long intervals.

And as usual he stared through the port. A breath of wind came now and again into our faces. The ship might have been moored in dock, so gently and on an even keel she slipped through the water, that did not murmur even at our passage, shadowy and silent like a phantom sea.

At midnight I went on deck, and to my mate's great surprise put the ship round on the other tack. His terrible whiskers flitted round me in silent criticism. I certainly should not have done it if it had been only a question of getting out of that sleepy gulf as quickly as possible. I believe he told the second mate, who relieved him, that it was a great want of judgment. The other only yawned. That intolerable cub shuffled about so sleepily and lolled against the rails in such a slack, improper fashion that I came down on him sharply.

"Aren't you properly awake yet?"

"Yes, sir! I am awake."

"Well, then, be good enough to hold yourself as if you were. And keep a lookout. If there's any current we'll be closing with some islands before daylight."

The east side of the gulf is fringed with islands, some solitary, others in groups. On the blue background of the high coast they seem to float on silvery patches of calm water, arid and gray, or dark green and rounded like clumps of evergreen bushes, with the larger ones, a smile or two long, showing the outlines of ridges, ribs of gray rock under the dark mantle of matted leafage. Unknown to trade, to travel, almost to geography, the manner of life they harbor is an unsolved secret. There must be villages—settlements of fishermen at least—on the largest of them, and some communication with the world is probably kept up by native craft. But all that forenoon, as we headed for them, fanned along by the faintest of breezes, I saw no sign of man or canoe in the field of the telescope I kept on pointing at the scattered group.

At noon I gave no orders for a change of course, and the mate's whiskers became much concerned and seemed to be offering themselves unduly to my notice. At last I said:

"I am going to stand right in. Quite in—as far as I can take her."

The stare of extreme surprise imparted an air of ferocity also to his eyes, and he looked truly terrific for a moment.

"We're not doing well in the middle of the gulf," I continued, casually. "I am going to look for the land breezes tonight."

"Bless my soul! Do you mean, sir, in the dark amongst the lot of all them islands and reefs and shoals?"

"Well—if there are any regular land breezes at all on this coast one must get close inshore to find them, mustn't one?"

"Bless my soul!" he exclaimed again under his breath. All that afternoon he wore a dreamy, contemplative appearance which in him was a mark of perplexity. After dinner I went into my stateroom as if I meant to take some rest. There we two bent our dark heads over a half-unrolled chart lying on my bed.

"There," I said. "It's got to be Koh-ring. I've been looking at it ever since sunrise. It has got two hills and a low point. It must be inhabited. And on the coast opposite there is what looks like the mouth of a biggish river—with some town, no doubt, not far up. It's the best chance for you that I can see."

"Anything. Koh-ring let it be."

He looked thoughtfully at the chart as if surveying chances and distances from a lofty height—and following with his eyes his own figure wandering on the blank land of Cochin-China, and then passing off that piece of paper clean out of sight into uncharted regions. And it was as if the ship had two captains to plan her course for her. I had been so worried and restless running up and down that I had not had the patience to dress that day. I had remained in my sleeping suit, with straw slippers and a soft floppy hat. The closeness of the heat in the gulf had been most oppressive, and the crew were used to see me wandering in that airy attire.

"She will clear the south point as she heads now," I whispered into his ear. "Goodness only knows when, though, but certainly after dark. I'll edge her in to half a mile, as far as I may be able to judge in the dark—"

"Be careful," he murmured, warningly—and I realized suddenly that all my future, the only future for which I was fit, would perhaps go irretrievably to pieces in any mishap to my first command.

I could not stop a moment longer in the room. I motioned him to get out of sight and made my way on the poop. That unplayful cub had the watch. I walked up and down for a while thinking things out, then beckoned him over.

"Send a couple of hands to open the two quarter-deck ports," I said, mildly.

He actually had the impudence, or else so forgot himself in his wonder at such an incomprehensible order, as to repeat:

"Open the quarter-deck ports! What for, sir?"

"The only reason you need concern yourself about is because I tell you to do so. Have them open wide and fastened properly."

He reddened and went off, but I believe made some jeering remark to the carpenter as to the sensible practice of ventilating a ship's quarter-deck. I know he popped into the mate's cabin to impart the fact to him because the whiskers came on deck, as it were by chance, and stole glances at me from below—for signs of lunacy or drunkenness, I suppose.

A little before supper, feeling more restless than ever, I rejoined, for a moment, my second self. And to find him sitting so quietly was surprising, like something against nature, inhuman.

I developed my plan in a hurried whisper.

"I shall stand in as close as I dare and then put her round. I shall presently find means to smuggle you out of here into the sail locker, which communicates with the lobby. But there is an opening, a sort of square for hauling the sails out which gives straight on the quarter-deck and which is never closed in fine weather, so as to give air to the sails. When the ship's way is deadened in stays and all the hands are aft at the main braces you shall have a clear road to slip out and get overboard through the open quarter-deck port. I've had them both fastened up. Use a rope's end to lower yourself into the water so as to avoid a splash—you know. It could be heard and cause some beastly complication."

He kept silent for a while, then whispered, "I understand."

"I won't be there to see you go," I began with an effort. "The rest . . . I only hope I have understood, too."

"You have. From first to last," and for the first time there seemed to be a faltering, something strained in his whisper. He caught hold of my arm, but the ringing of the supper bell made me start. He didn't, though; he only released his grip.

After supper I didn't come below again till well past eight o'clock. The faint, steady breeze was loaded with dew; and the wet, darkened sails held all there was of propelling power in it. The night, clear and starry, sparkled darkly, and the opaque, lightless patches shifting slowly against the low stars were the drifting islets. On the port bow there was a big one more distant and shadowily imposing by the great space of sky it eclipsed.

On opening the door I had a back view of my very own self looking at a chart. He had come out of the recess and was standing near the table.

"Quite dark enough," I whispered.

He stepped back and leaned against my bed with a level, quiet glance. I sat on the couch. We had nothing to say to each other. Over our heads the officer of the watch moved here and there. Then I heard him move quickly. I knew what that meant. He was making for the companion; and presently his voice was outside my door.

"We are drawing in pretty fast, sir. Land looks rather close."

"Very well," I answered. "I am coming on deck directly."

I waited till he was gone out of the cuddy, then rose. My double moved too. The time had come to exchange our last whispers, for neither of us was ever to hear each other's natural voice.

"Look here!" I opened a drawer and took out three sovereigns. "Take this, anyhow. I've got six and I'd give you the lot, only I must keep a little money to buy some fruit and vegetables for the crew from native boats as we go through Sunda Straits."

He shook his head.

"Take it," I urged him, whispering desperately. "No one can tell what—"

He smiled and slapped meaningly the only pocket of the sleeping jacket. It was not safe, certainly. But I produced a large old silk handkerchief of mine, and tying the three pieces of gold in a corner, pressed it on him. He was touched, I suppose, because he took it at last and tied it quickly round his waist under the jacket, on his bare skin.

Our eyes met; several seconds elapsed, till, our glances still mingled, I extended my hand and turned the lamp out. Then I pased through the cuddy, leaving the door of my room wide open. . . . "Steward!"

He was still lingering in the pantry in the greatness of his zeal, giving a rub-up to a plated cruet stand the last thing before going to bed. Being careful not to wake up the mate, whose room was opposite, I spoke in an undertone.

He looked round anxiously. "Sir!"

"Can you get me a little hot water from the galley?"

"I am afraid, sir, the galley fire's been out for some time now."

"Go and see."

He fled up the stairs.

"Now," I whispered, loudly, into the saloon—too loudly, perhaps, but I was afraid I couldn't make a sound. He was by my side in an instant—the double captain slipped past the stairs—through the tiny dark passage—a sliding door. We were in the sail locker, scrambling on our knees over the sails. A sudden thought struck me. I saw myself wandering barefooted, bareheaded, the sun beating on my dark poll. I snatched off my floppy hat and tried hurriedly in the dark to ram it on my other self. He dodged and fended off silently. I wonder what he thought had come to me before he understood and suddenly desisted. Our hands met gropingly, lingered united in a steady, motionless clasp for a second. . . . No word was breathed by either of us when they separated.

I was standing quietly by the pantry door when the steward returned.

"Sorry, sir. Kettle barely warm. Shall I light the spirit lamp?"

"Never mind."

I came out on deck slowly. It was now a matter of conscience to shave the land as close as possible—for now he must go overboard whenever the ship was put in stays. Must! There could be no going back for him. After a moment I walked over to leeward and my heart flew into my mouth at the nearness of the land on the bow. Under any other circumstances I would not have held on a minute longer. The second mate had followed me anxiously.

I looked on till I felt I could command my voice.

"She will weather," I said, then in a quiet tone.

"Are you going to try that, sir?" he stammered out incredulously.

I took no notice of him and raised my tone just enough to be heard by the helmsman.

"Keep her good full."

"Good full, sir."

The wind fanned my cheek, the sails slept, the world was silent. The strain of watching the dark loom of the land grow bigger and denser was too much for me. I had shut my eyes—because the ship must go closer. She must! The stillness was intolerable. Were we standing still?

When I opened my eyes the second view started my heart with a thump. The black southern hill of Koh-ring seemed to hang right over the ship like a towering fragment of the everlasting night. On that enormous mass of blackness there was not a gleam to be seen, not a sound to be heard. It was gliding irresistibly toward us and yet seemed already within reach of the hand. I saw the vague figures of the watch grouped in the waist, gazing in awed silence.

"Are you going on, sir?" inquired an unsteady voice at my elbow.

I ignored it. I had to go on.

"Keep her full. Don't check her way. That won't do now," I said warningly.

"I can't see the sails very well," the helmsman answered me, in strange, quavering tones.

Was she close enough? Already she was, I won't say in the shadow of the land, but in the very blackness of it, already swallowed up as it were, gone too close to be recalled, gone from me altogether.

"Give the mate a call," I said to the young man who stood at my elbow as still as death. "And turn all hands up."

My tone had a borrowed loudness reverberated from the height of the land. Several voices cried out together: "We are all on deck, sir."

Then stillness again, with the great shadow gliding closer, towering higher, without a light, without a sound. Such a hush had fallen on the ship that she might have been a bark of the dead floating in slowly under the very gate of Erebus.

"My God! Where are we?"

It was the mate moaning at my elbow. He was thunderstruck, and as it were deprived of the moral support of his whiskers. He clapped his hands and absolutely cried out, "Lost!"

"Be quiet," I said sternly.

He lowered his tone, but I saw the shadowy gesture of his despair. "What are we doing here?"

"Looking for the land wind."

He made as if to tear his hair, and addressed me recklessly.

"She will never get out. You have done it, sir. I knew it'd end in something like this. She will never weather, and you are too close now to stay. She'll drift ashore before she's round. O my God!"

I caught his arm as he was raising it to batter his poor devoted head, and shook it violently.

"She's ashore already," he wailed, trying to tear himself away.

"Is she? . . . Keep good full there!"

"Good full, sir," cried the helmsman in a frightened, thin, childlike voice.

I hadn't let go the mate's arm and went on shaking it. "Ready about, do you hear? You go forward"—shake—"and stop there"—shake—"and hold your noise"—shake—"and see these head sheets properly over-hauled"—shake, shake—shake.

And all the time I dared not look toward the land lest my heart should fail me. I released my grip at last and he ran forward as if fleeing for dear life.

I wondered what my double there in the sail locker thought of this commotion. He was able to hear everything—and perhaps he was able to understand why, on my conscience, it had to be thus close—no less. My first order, "Hard alee!" re-echoed ominously under the towering shadow of Koh-ring as if I had shouted in a mountain gorge. And then I watched the land intently. In that smooth water and light wind it was impossible to feel the ship coming-to. No! I could not feel her. And my second self was making now ready to slip out and lower himself overboard. Perhaps he was gone already . . . ?

The great black mass brooding over our very mastheads began to pivot away from the ship's side silently. And now I forgot the secret stranger ready to depart, and remembered only that I was a total stranger to the ship. I did not know her. Would she do it? How was she to be handled?

I swung the mainyard and waited helplessly. She was perhaps stopped, and her very fate hung in the balance, with the black mass of Koh-ring like the gate of the everlasting night towering over her taffrail. What would she do now? Had she way on her yet? I stepped to the side swiftly, and on the shadowy water I could see nothing except a faint phosphorescent flash revealing the glassy smoothness of the sleeping surface. It was impossible to tell—and I had not learned yet the feel of my ship. Was she moving? What I needed was something easily seen, a piece of paper, which I could throw overboard and watch. I had nothing on me. To run down for it I didn't dare. There was no time. All at once my strained, yearning stare distinguished a white object floating within a yard of the ship's side. White on the black water. A phosphorescent flash passed under it. What was that thing? . . . I recognized my own floppy hat. It must have fallen off his head . . . and he didn't bother. Now I had what I wanted—the saving mark for my eyes. But I hardly thought of my other self, now gone from the ship, to be hidden forever from all friendly faces, to be a fugitive and a vagabond on the earth, with no brand of the curse on his sane forehead to stay a slaying hand . . . too proud to explain.

And I watched the hat—the expression of my sudden pity for his mere flesh. It had been meant to save his homeless head from the dangers of the sun. And now—behold—it was saving the ship, by serving me for a mark to help out the ignorance of my strangeness. Ha! It was drifting forward, warning me just in time that the ship had gathered sternway.

"Shift the helm," I said in a low voice to the seaman standing still like a statue.

The man's eyes glistened wildly in the binnacle light as he jumped round to the other side and spun round the wheel.

I walked to the break of the poop. On the overshadowed deck all hands stood by the forebraces waiting for my order. The stars ahead seemed to be gliding from right to left. And all was so still in the world that I heard the quiet remark "She's round," passed in a tone of intense relief between two seamen.

"Let go and haul."

The foreyards ran round with a great noise, amidst cheery cries. And now the frightful whiskers made themselves heard giving various orders. Already the ship was drawing ahead. And I was alone with her. Nothing! no one in the world should stand now between us, throwing a shadow on the way of silent knowledge and mute affection, the perfect communion of a seaman with his first command.

Walking to the taffrail, I was in time to make out, on the very edge of a darkness thrown by a towering black mass like the very gateway of Erebus—yes, I was in time to catch an evanescent glimpse of my white hat left behind to mark the spot where the secret sharer of my cabin and of my thoughts, as though he were my second self, had lowered himself into the water to take his punishment: a free man, a proud swimmer striking out for a new destiny.

THE DEAD
by James Joyce
(1882–1941)

Lily, the caretaker's daughter, was literally run off her feet. Hardly had she brought one gentleman into the little pantry behind the office on the ground floor and helped him off with his overcoat than the wheezy hall-door bell clanged again and she had to scamper along the bare hallway to let in another guest. It was well for her she had not to attend to the ladies also. But Miss Kate and Miss Julia had thought of that and had converted the bathroom upstairs into a ladies' dressing-room. Miss Kate and Miss Julia were there, gossiping and laughing and fussing, walking after each other to the head of the stairs, peering down over the banisters and calling down to Lily to ask her who had come.

It was always a great affair, the Misses Morkan's annual dance. Everybody who knew them came to it, members of the family, old friends of the family, the members of Julia's choir, any of Kate's pupils that were grown up enough and even some of Mary Jane's pupils too. Never once had it fallen flat. For years and years it had gone off in splendid style as long as anyone could remember; ever since Kate and Julia, after the death of their brother Pat, had left the house in Stoney Batter and taken Mary Jane, their only niece, to live with them in the dark gaunt house on Usher's Island, the upper part of which they had rented from Mr Fulham, the corn-factor on the ground floor. That was a good thirty years ago if it was a day. Mary Jane, who was then a little girl in short clothes, was now the main prop of the household for she had the organ in Haddington Road. She had been through the Academy and gave a pupils' concert every year in the upper room of the Ancient Concert Rooms. Many of her pupils belonged to better-class families on the Kingstown and Dalkey line. Old as they were, her aunts also did their share. Julia, though she was quite grey, was still the leading soprano in Adam and Eve's, and Kate, being too feeble to go about much, gave music lessons to beginners on the old square piano in the back room. Lily, the caretaker's daughter, did housemaid's work for them. Though their life was modest they believed in eating well; the best of everything: diamond-bone sirloins, three-shilling tea and the best bottled stout. But Lily seldom made a mistake in the orders so that she got on well with her three mistresses. They were fussy, that was all. But the only thing they would not stand was back answers.

Of course they had good reason to be fussy on such a night. And then it was long after ten o'clock and yet there was no sign of Gabriel and his wife. Besides they were dreadfully afraid that Freddy Malins might turn up screwed. They would not wish for worlds that any of Mary Jane's pupils should see him under the influence; and when he was like that it was sometimes very hard to manage him. Freddy Malins always came late but they wondered what could be keeping Gabriel: and that was what brought them every two minutes to the banisters to ask Lily had Gabriel or Freddy come.

"O, Mr Conroy," said Lily to Gabriel when she opened the door for him, "Miss Kate and Miss Julia thought you were never coming. Goodnight, Mrs Conroy."

"I'll engage they did," said Gabriel, "but they forget that my wife here takes three mortal hours to dress herself."

He stood on the mat, scraping the snow from his goloshes, while Lily led his wife to the foot of the stairs and called out:

"Miss Kate, here's Mrs Conroy."

Kate and Julia came toddling down the dark stairs at once. Both of them kissed Gabriel's wife, said she must be perished alive and asked was Gabriel with her.

"Here I am as right as the mail, Aunt Kate! Go on up. I'll follow," called out Gabriel from the dark.

He continued scraping his feet vigorously while the three women went upstairs, laughing, to the ladies' dressing-room. A light fringe of snow lay like a cape on the shoulders of his overcoat and like toecaps on the toes of his goloshes; and, as the buttons of his overcoat slipped with a squeaking noise through the snow-stiffened frieze, a cold fragrant air from out-of-doors escaped from crevices and folds.

"Is it snowing again, Mr Conroy?" asked Lily.

She had preceded him into the pantry to help him off with his overcoat. Gabriel smiled at the three syllables she had given his surname and glanced at her. She was a slim, growing girl, pale in complexion and with hay-coloured hair. The gas in the pantry made her look still paler. Gabriel had known her when she was a child and used to sit on the lowest step nursing a rag doll.

"Yes, Lily," he answered, "and I think we're in for a night of it."

He looked up at the pantry ceiling, which was shaking with the stamping and shuffling of feet on the floor above, listened for a moment to the piano and then glanced at the girl, who was folding his overcoat carefully at the end of a shelf.

"Tell me, Lily," he said in a friendly tone, "do you still go to school?"

"O no, sir," she answered. "I'm done schooling this year and more."

"O, then," said Gabriel gaily, "I suppose we'll be going to your wedding one of these fine days with your young man, eh?"

The girl glanced back at him over her shoulder and said with great bitterness:

"The men that is now is only all palaver and what they can get out of you."

Gabriel coloured as if he felt he had made a mistake and, without looking at her, kicked off his goloshes and flicked actively with his muffler at his patent-leather shoes.

He was a stout tallish young man. The high colour of his cheeks pushed upwards even to his forehead where it scattered itself in a few formless patches of pale red; and on his hairless face there scintillated restlessly the polished lenses and the bright gilt rims of the glasses which screened his delicate and restless eyes. His glossy black hair was parted in the middle and brushed in a long curve behind his ears where it curled slightly beneath the groove left by his hat.

When he had flicked lustre into his shoes he stood up and pulled his waistcoat down more tightly on his plump body. Then he took a coin rapidly from his pocket.

"O Lily," he said, thrusting it into her hands, "it's Christmas-time, isn't it? Just . . . here's a little. . . ."

He walked rapidly towards the door.

"O no, sir!" cried the girl, following him. "Really, sir, I wouldn't take it."

"Christmas-time! Christmas-time!" said Gabriel, almost trotting to the stairs and waving his hand to her in deprecation.

The girl, seeing that he had gained the stairs, called out after him:

"Well, thank you, sir."

He waited outside the drawing-room door until the waltz should finish, listening to the skirts that swept against it and to the shuffling of feet. He was still discomposed by the girl's bitter and sudden retort. It had cast a gloom over him which he tried to dispel by arranging his cuffs and the bows of his tie. Then he took from his waistcoat pocket a little paper and glanced at the headings he had made for his speech. He was undecided about the lines from Robert Browning for he feared they would be above the heads of his hearers. Some quotation that they could recognise from Shakespeare or from the Melodies would be better. The indelicate clacking of the men's heels and the shuffling of their soles reminded him that their grade of culture differed from his. He would only make himself ridiculous by quoting poetry to them which they could not understand. They would think that he was airing his superior education. He would fail with them just as he had failed with the girl in the pantry. He had taken up a wrong tone. His whole speech was a mistake from first to last, an utter failure.

Just then his aunts and his wife came out of the ladies' dressing-room. His aunts were too small plainly dressed old women. Aunt Julia was an inch or so the taller. Her hair, drawn low over the tops of her ears, was grey; and grey also, with darker shadows, was her large flaccid face. Though she was stout in build and stood erect her slow eyes and parted lips gave her the appearance of a woman who did not know where she was or where she was going. Aunt Kate was more vivacious. Her face, healthier than her sister's, was all puckers and creases, like a shrivelled red apple, and her hair, braided in the same old-fashioned way, had not lost its ripe nut colour.

They both kissed Gabriel frankly. He was their favourite nephew, the son of their dead elder sister, Ellen, who had married T. J. Conroy of the Port and Docks.

"Gretta tells me you're not going to take a cab back to Monkstown to-night, Gabriel," said Aunt Kate.

"No," said Gabriel, turning to his wife, "we had quite enough of that last year, hadn't we. Don't you remember, Aunt Kate, what a cold Gretta got out of it? Cab windows rattling all the way, and the east wind blowing in after we passed Merrion. Very jolly it was. Gretta caught a dreadful cold."

Aunt Kate frowned severely and nodded her head at every word.

"Quite right, Gabriel, quite right," she said. "You can't be too careful."

"But as for Gretta there," said Gabriel, "she'd walk home in the snow if she were let."

Mrs Conroy laughed.

"Don't mind him, Aunt Kate," she said. "He's really an awful bother, what with green shades for Tom's eyes at night and making him do the dumb-bells, and forcing Eva to eat the stirabout. The poor child! And she simply hates the sight of it! . . . O, but you'll never guess what he makes me wear now!"

She broke out into a peal of laughter and glanced at her husband, whose admiring and happy eyes had been wandering from her dress to her face and hair. The two aunts laughed heartily too, for Gabriel's solicitude was a standing joke with them.

"Goloshes!" said Mrs Conroy. "That's the latest. Whenever it's wet underfoot I must put on my goloshes. To-night even he wanted me to put them on, but I wouldn't. The next thing he'll buy me will be a diving suit."

Gabriel laughed nervously and patted his tie reassuringly while Aunt Kate nearly doubled herself, so heartily did she enjoy the joke. The smile soon faded from Aunt Julia's face and her mirthless eyes were directed towards her nephew's face. After a pause she asked:

"And what are goloshes, Gabriel?"

"Goloshes, Julia!" exclaimed her sister. "Goodness me, don't you know what goloshes are? You wear them over your . . . over your boots, Gretta, isn't it?"

"Yes," said Mrs Conroy. "Guttapercha things. We both have a pair now. Gabriel says everyone wears them on the continent."

"O, on the continent," murmured Aunt Julia, nodding her head slowly.

Gabriel knitted his brows and said, as if he were slightly angered:

"It's nothing very wonderful but Gretta thinks it very funny because she says the word reminds her of Christy Minstrels."

"But tell me, Gabriel," said Aunt Kate, with brisk tact. "Of course, you've seen about the room. Gretta was saying . . ."

"O, the room is all right," replied Gabriel. "I've taken one in the Gresham."

"To be sure," said Aunt Kate, "by far the best thing to do. And the children, Gretta, you're not anxious about them?"

"O, for one night," said Mrs Conroy. "Besides, Bessie will look after them."

"To be sure," said Aunt Kate again. "What a comfort it is to have a girl like that, one you can depend on! There's that Lily, I'm sure I don't know what has come over her lately. She's not the girl she was at all."

Gabriel was about to ask his aunt some questions on this point but she broke off suddenly to gaze after her sister who had wandered down the stairs and was craning her neck over the banisters.

"Now, I ask you," she said, almost testily, "where is Julia going? Julia! Julia! Where are you going?"

Julia, who had gone halfway down one flight, came back and announced blandly:

"Here's Freddy."

At the same moment a clapping of hands and a final flourish of the pianist told that the waltz had ended. The drawing-room door was opened from within and some couples came out. Aunt Kate drew Gabriel aside hurriedly and whispered into his ear:

"Slip down, Gabriel, like a good fellow and see if he's all right, and don't let him up if he's screwed. I'm sure he's screwed. I'm sure he is."

Gabriel went to the stairs and listened over the banisters. He could hear two persons talking in the pantry. Then he recognised Freddy Malins' laugh. He went down the stairs noisily.

"It's such a relief," said Aunt Kate to Mrs Conroy, "that Gabriel is here. I always feel easier in my mind when he's here. . . . Julia, there's Miss Daly and Miss Power will take some refreshment. Thanks for your beautiful waltz, Miss Daly. It made lovely time."

A tall wizen-faced man, with a stiff grizzled moustache and swarthy skin, who was passing out with his partner said:

"And may we have some refreshment, too, Miss Morkan?"

"Julia," said Aunt Kate summarily, "and here's Mr Browne and Miss Furlong. Take them in, Julia, with Miss Daly and Miss Power."

"I'm the man for the ladies," said Mr Browne, pursing his lips until his moustache bristled and smiling in all his wrinkles. "You know, Miss Morkan, the reason they are so fond of me is—"

He did not finish his sentence, but, seeing that Aunt Kate was out of earshot, at once led the three young ladies into the back room. The middle of the room was occupied by two square tables placed end to end, and on these Aunt Julia and the caretaker were straightening and smoothing a large cloth. On the sideboard were arrayed dishes and plates, and glasses and bundles of knives and forks and spoons. The top of the closed square piano served also as a sideboard for viands and sweets. At a smaller sideboard in one corner two young men were standing, drinking hop-bitters.

Mr Browne led his charges thither and invited them all, in jest, to some ladies' punch, hot, strong and sweet. As they said they never took anything strong he opened three bottles of lemonade for them. Then he asked one of the young men to move aside, and, taking hold of the decanter, filled out for himself a goodly measure of whisky. The young men eyed him respectfully while he took a trial sip.

"God help me," he said, smiling, "it's the doctor's orders."

His wizened face broke into a broader smile, and the three young ladies laughed in musical echo to his pleasantry, swaying their bodies to and fro, with nervous jerks of their shoulders. The boldest said:

"O, now, Mr Browne, I'm sure the doctor never ordered anything of the kind."

Mr Browne took another sip of his whisky and said, with sidling mimicry:

"Well, you see, I'm like the famous Mrs Cassidy, who is reported to have said: *Now, Mary Grimes, if I don't take it, make me take it, for I feel I want it.*"

His hot face had leaned forward a little too confidentially and he had assumed a very low Dublin accent so that the young ladies, with one instinct, received his speech in silence. Miss Furlong, who was one of Mary Jane's pupils, asked Miss Daly what was the name of the pretty waltz she had played; and Mr Browne, seeing that he was ignored, turned promptly to the two young men who were more appreciative.

A red-faced young woman, dressed in pansy, came into the room, excitedly clapping her hands and crying:

"Quadrilles! Quadrilles!"

Close on her heels came Aunt Kate, crying:

"Two gentlemen and three ladies, Mary Jane!"

"O, here's Mr Bergin and Mr Kerrigan," said Mary Jane. "Mr Kerrigan, will you take Miss Power? Miss Furlong, may I get you a partner, Mr Bergin. O, that'll just do now."

"Three ladies, Mary Jane," said Aunt Kate.

The two young gentlemen asked the ladies if they might have the pleasure, and Mary Jane turned to Miss Daly.

"O, Miss Daly, you're really awfully good, after playing for the last two dances, but really we're so short of ladies to-night."

"I don't mind in the least, Miss Morkan."

"But I've a nice partner for you, Mr Bartell D'Arcy, the tenor. I'll get him to sing later on. All Dublin is raving about him."

"Lovely voice, lovely voice!" said Aunt Kate.

As the piano had twice begun the prelude to the first figure Mary Jane led her recruits quickly from the room. They had hardly gone when Aunt Julia wandered slowly into the room, looking behind her at something.

"What is the matter, Julia?" asked Aunt Kate anxiously. "Who is it?"

Julia, who was carrying a column of table-napkins, turned to her sister and said, simply, as if the question had surprised her:

"It's only Freddy, Kate, and Gabriel with him."

In fact right behind her Gabriel could be seen piloting Freddy Malins across the landing. The latter, a young man of about forty, was of Gabriel's size and build, with very round shoulders. His face was fleshy and pallid, touched with colour only at the thick hanging lobes of his ears and at the wide wings of his nose. He had coarse features, a blunt nose, a convex and receding brow, tumid and protruded lips. His heavy-lidded eyes and the disorder of his scanty hair made him look sleepy. He was laughing heartily in a high key at a story which he had been telling Gabriel on the stairs and at the same time rubbing the knuckles of his left fist backwards and forwards into his left eye.

"Good-evening, Freddy," said Aunt Julia.

Freddy Malins bade the Misses Morkan good-evening in what seemed an offhand fashion by reason of the habitual catch in his voice and then, seeing that Mr Browne was grinning at him from the sideboard, crossed the room on rather shaky legs and began to repeat in an undertone the story he had just told to Gabriel.

"He's not so bad, is he?" said Aunt Kate to Gabriel.

Gabriel's brows were dark but he raised them quickly and answered:

"O no, hardly noticeable."

"Now, isn't he a terrible fellow!" she said. "And his poor mother made him take the pledge on New Year's Eve. But come on, Gabriel, into the drawing-room."

Before leaving the room with Gabriel she signalled to Mr Browne by frowning and shaking her forefinger in warning to and fro. Mr Browne nodded in answer and, when she had gone, said to Freddy Malins:

"Now, then, Teddy, I'm going to fill you out a good glass of lemonade just to buck you up."

Freddy Malins, who was nearing the climax of his story, waved the offer aside impatiently but Mr Browne, having first called Freddy Malins' attention to a disarray in his dress, filled out and handed him a full glass of lemonade. Freddy Malins' left hand accepted the glass mechanically, his right hand being engaged in the mechanical readjustment of his dress. Mr Browne, whose face was once more wrinkling with mirth, poured out for himself a glass of whisky while Freddy Malins exploded, before he had well reached the climax of his story, in a kink of high-pitched bronchitic laughter and, setting down his untasted and overflowing glass, began to rub the knuckles of his left fist backwards and forwards into his left eye, repeating words of his last phrase as well as his fit of laughter would allow him.

Gabriel could not listen while Mary Jane was playing her Academy piece, full of runs and difficult passages, to the hushed drawing-room. He liked music but the piece she was playing had no melody for him and he doubted whether it had any melody for the other listeners, though they had begged Mary Jane to play something. Four young men, who had come from the refreshment-room to stand in the doorway at the sound of the piano, had gone away quietly in couples after a few minutes. The only persons who seemed to follow the music were Mary Jane herself, her hands racing along the key-board or lifted from it at the pauses like those of a priestess in momentary imprecation, and Aunt Kate standing at her elbow to turn the page.

Gabriel's eyes, irritated by the floor, which glittered with beeswax under the heavy chandelier, wandered to the wall above the piano. A picture of the balcony scene in *Romeo and Juliet* hung there and beside it was a picture of the two murdered princes in the Tower which Aunt Julia had worked in red, blue and brown wools when she was a girl. Probably in the school they had gone to as girls that kind of work had been taught, for one year his mother had worked for him as a birthday present a waistcoat of purple tabinet, with little foxes' heads upon it, lined with brown satin and having round mulberry buttons. It was strange that his mother had had no musical talent though Aunt Kate used to call her the brains carrier of the Morkan family. Both she and Julia had always seemed a little proud of their serious and matronly sister. Her photograph stood before the pierglass. She held an open book on her knees and was pointing out something in it to Constantine who, dressed in a man-o'-war suit, lay at her feet. It was she who had chosen the names for her sons for she was very sensible of the dignity of family life. Thanks to her, Constantine was now senior curate in Balbriggan and, thanks to her, Gabriel himself had taken his degree in the Royal University. A shadow passed over his face as he remembered her sullen opposition to his marriage. Some slighting phrases she had used still rankled in his memory; she had once spoken of Gretta as being country cute and that was not true of Gretta at all. It was Gretta who had nursed her during all her last long illness in their house at Monkstown.

He knew that Mary Jane must be near the end of her piece for she was playing again the opening melody with runs of scales after every bar and while he waited for the end the resentment died down in his heart. The piece ended with a trill of octaves in the treble and a final deep octave in the bass. Great applause greeted Mary Jane as, blushing and rolling up her music nervously, she escaped from the room. The most vigorous clapping came from the four young men in the doorway who had gone away to the refreshment-room at the beginning of the piece but had come back when the piano had stopped.

Lancers were arranged. Gabriel found himself partnered with Miss Ivors. She was a frank-mannered talkative young lady, with a freckled face and prominent brown eyes. She did not wear a low-cut bodice and the large brooch which was fixed in the front of her collar bore on it an Irish device.

When they had taken their places she said abruptly:

"I have a crow to pluck with you."

"With me?" said Gabriel.

She nodded her head gravely.

"What is it?" asked Gabriel, smiling at her solemn manner.

"Who is G. C.?" answered Miss Ivors, turning her eyes upon him.

Gabriel coloured and was about to knit his brows, as if he did not understand, when she said bluntly:

"O, innocent Amy! I have found out that you write for *The Daily Express*. Now, aren't you ashamed of yourself?"

"Why should I be ashamed of myself?" asked Gabriel, blinking his eyes and trying to smile.

"Well, I'm ashamed of you," said Miss Ivors frankly. "To say you'd write for a rag like that. I didn't think you were a West Briton."

A look of perplexity appeared on Gabriel's face. It was true that he wrote a literary column every Wednesday in *The Daily Express*, for which he was paid fifteen shillings. But that did not make him a West Briton surely. The books he received for review were almost more welcome than the paltry cheque. He loved to feel the covers and turn over the pages of newly printed books. Nearly every day when his teaching in the college was ended he used to wander down the quays to the second-hand book-sellers, to Hickey's on Bachelor's Walk, to Webb's or Massey's on Aston's

Quay, or to O'Clohissey's in the by-street. He did not know how to meet her charge. He wanted to say that literature was above politics. But they were friends of many years' standing and their careers had been parallel, first at the University and then as teachers: he could not risk a grandiose phrase with her. He continued blinking his eyes and trying to smile and murmured lamely that he saw nothing political in writing reviews of books.

When their turn to cross had come he was still perplexed and inattentive. Miss Ivors promptly took his hand in a warm grasp and said in a soft friendly tone:

"Of course, I was only joking. Come, we cross now."

When they were together again she spoke of the University question and Gabriel felt more at ease. A friend of hers had shown her his review of Browning's poems. That was how she had found out the secret: but she liked the review immensely. Then she said suddenly:

"O, Mr Conroy, will you come for an excursion to the Aran Isles this summer? We're going to stay there a whole month. It will be splendid out in the Atlantic. You ought to come. Mr Clancy is coming, and Mr Kilkelly and Kathleen Kearney. It would be splendid for Gretta too if she'd come. She's from Connacht, isn't she?"

"Her people are," said Gabriel shortly.

"But you will come, won't you?" said Miss Ivors, laying her warm hand eagerly on his arm.

"The fact is," said Gabriel, "I have already arranged to go—"

"Go where?" asked Miss Ivors.

"Well, you know, every year I go for a cycling tour with some fellows and so—"

"But where?" asked Miss Ivors.

"Well, we usually go to France or Belgium or perhaps Germany," said Gabriel awkwardly.

"And why do you go to France and Belgium," said Miss Ivors, "instead of visiting your own land?"

"Well," said Gabriel, "it's partly to keep in touch with the languages and partly for a change."

"And haven't you your own language to keep in touch with—Irish?" asked Miss Ivors.

"Well, said Gabriel, if it comes to that, you know, Irish is not my language."

Their neighbours had turned to listen to the cross-examination. Gabriel glanced right and left nervously and tried to keep his good humour under the ordeal which was making a blush invade his forehead.

"And haven't you your own land to visit," continued Miss Ivors, that you know nothing of, your own people, and your own country?"

"O, to tell you the truth," retorted Gabriel suddenly, "I'm sick of my own country, sick of it!"

"Why?" asked Miss Ivors.

Gabriel did not answer for his retort had heated him.

"Why?" repeated Miss Ivors.

They had to go visiting together and, as he had not answered her, Miss Ivors said warmly:

"Of course, you've no answer."

Gabriel tried to cover his agitation by taking part in the dance with great energy. He avoided her eyes for he had seen a sour expression on her face. But when they met in the long chain he was surprised to feel his hand firmly pressed. She looked at him from under her brows for a moment quizzically until he smiled. Then, just as the chain was about to start again, she stood on tiptoe and whispered into his ear:

"West Briton!"

When the lancers were over Gabriel went away to a remote corner of the room where Freddy Malins' mother was sitting. She was a stout feeble old woman with white hair. Her voice had a catch in it like her son's and she stuttered slightly. She had been told that Freddy had come and that he was nearly all right. Gabriel asked her whether she had had a good crossing. She lived with her married daughter in Glasgow and came to Dublin on a visit once a year. She answered placidly that she had had a beautiful crossing and that the captain had been most attentive to her. She spoke also of the beautiful house her daughter kept in Glasgow, and of all the nice friends they had there. While her tongue rambled on Gabriel tried to banish from his mind all memory of the unpleasant incident with Miss Ivors. Of course the girl or woman, or whatever she was, was an enthusiast but there was a time for all things. Perhaps he ought not to have answered her like that. But she had no right to call him a West Briton before people, even in joke. She had tried to make him ridiculous before people, heckling him and staring at him with her rabbit's eyes.

He saw his wife making her way towards him through the waltzing couples. When she reached him she said into his ear:

"Gabriel, Aunt Kate wants to know won't you carve the goose as usual. Miss Daly will carve the ham and I'll do the pudding."

"All right," said Gabriel.

"She's sending in the younger ones first as soon as this waltz is over so that we'll have the table to ourselves."

"Were you dancing?" asked Gabriel.

"Of course I was. Didn't you see me? What words had you with Molly Ivors?"

"No words. Why? Did she say so?"

"Something like that. I'm trying to get that Mr D'Arcy to sing. He's full of conceit, I think."

"There were no words," said Gabriel moodily, "only she wanted me to go for a trip to the west of Ireland and I said I wouldn't."

His wife clasped her hands excitedly and gave a little jump.

"O, do go, Gabriel," she cried. "I'd love to see Galway again."

"You can go if you like," said Gabriel coldly.

She looked at him for a moment, then turned to Mrs Malins and said:

"There's a nice husband for you, Mrs Malins."

While she was threading her way back across the room Mrs Malins, without adverting to the interruption, went on to tell Gabriel what beautiful places there were in Scotland and beautiful scenery. Her son-in-law brought them every year to the lakes and they used to go fishing. Her son-in-law was a splendid fisher. One day he caught a fish, a beautiful big big fish, and the man in the hotel boiled it for their dinner.

Gabriel hardly heard what she said. Now that supper was coming near he began to think again about his speech and about the quotation. When he saw Freddy Malins coming across the room to visit his mother Gabriel left the chair free for him and retired into the embrasure of the window. The room had already cleared and from the back room came the clatter of plates and knives. Those who still remained in the drawing-room seemed tired of dancing and were conversing quietly in little groups. Gabriel's warm trembling fingers tapped the cold pane of the window. How cool it must be outside! How pleasant it would be to walk out alone, first along by the river and then through the park! The snow would be lying on the branches of the trees and forming a bright cap on the top of the Wellington Monument. How much more pleasant it would be there than at the supper-table!

He ran over the headings of his speech: Irish hospitality, sad memories, the Three Graces, Paris, the quotation from Browning. He repeated to himself a phrase he had written in his review: *One feels that one is listening to a thought-tormented music.* Miss Ivors had praised the review. Was she sincere? Had she really any life of her own behind all her propagandism? There had never been any ill-feeling between them until that night. It unnerved him to think that she would be at the supper-table, looking up at him while he spoke with her critical quizzing eyes. Perhaps she would not be sorry to see him fail in his speech. An idea came into his mind and gave him courage. He would say, alluding to Aunt Kate and Aunt Julia: *Ladies and Gentlemen, the generation which is now in the wane among us may have had its faults but for my part I think it had certain qualities of hospitality, of humour, of humanity, which the new and very serious and hypereducated generation that is growing up around us seems to me to lack.* Very good: that was one for Miss Ivors. What did he care that his aunts were only two ignorant old women?

A murmur in the room attracted his attention. Mr Browne was advancing from the door, gallantly escorting Aunt Julia, who leaned upon his arm, smiling and hanging her head. An irregular musketry of applause escorted her also as far as the piano and then, as Mary Jane seated herself on the stool, and Aunt Julia, no longer smiling, half turned so as to pitch her voice fairly into the room, gradually ceased. Gabriel recognised the prelude. It was that of an old song of Aunt Julia's —*Arrayed for the Bridal*. Her voice, strong and clear in tone, attacked with great spirit the runs which embellish the air and though she sang very rapidly she did not miss even the smallest of the grace notes. To follow the voice, without looking at the singer's face, was to feel and share the excitement of swift and secure flight. Gabriel applauded loudly with all the others at the close of the song and loud applause was borne in from the invisible supper-table. It sounded so genuine that a little colour struggled into Aunt Julia's face as she bent to replace in the music-stand the old leather-bound song-book that had her initials on the cover. Freddy Malins, who had listened with his head perched sideways to hear her better, was still applauding when everyone else had ceased and talking animatedly to his mother who nodded her head gravely and slowly in acquiescence. At last, when he could clap no more, he stood up suddenly and hurried across the room to Aunt Julia whose hand he seized and held in both his hands, shaking it when words failed him or the catch in his voice proved too much for him.

"I was just telling your mother," he said, "I never heard you sing so well, never. No, I never heard your voice so good as it is to-night. Now! Would you believe that now? That's the truth. Upon my word and honour that's the truth. I never heard your voice sound so fresh and so . . . so clear and fresh, never."

Aunt Julia smiled broadly and murmured something about compliments as she released her hand from his grasp. Mr Browne extended his open hand towards her and said to those who were near him in the manner of a showman introducing a prodigy to an audience:

"Miss Julia Morkan, my latest discovery!"

He was laughing very heartily at this himself when Freddy Malins turned to him and said:

"Well, Browne, if you're serious you might make a worse discovery. All I can say is I never heard her sing half so well as long as I am coming here. And that's the honest truth."

"Neither did I," said Mr Browne. "I think her voice has greatly improved."

Aunt Julia shrugged her shoulders and said with meek pride:

"Thirty years ago I hadn't a bad voice as voices go."

"I often told Julia," said Aunt Kate emphatically, "that she was simply thrown away in that choir. But she never would be said by me."

She turned as if to appeal to the good sense of the others against a refractory child while Aunt Julia gazed in front of her, a vague smile of reminiscence playing on her face.

"No," continued Aunt Kate, "she wouldn't be said or led by anyone, slaving there in that choir night and day, night and day. Six o'clock on Christmas morning! And all for what?"

"Well, isn't it for the honour of God, Aunt Kate?" asked Mary Jane, twisting round on the piano-stool and smiling.

Aunt Kate turned fiercely on her niece and said:

"I know all about the honour of God, Mary Jane, but I think it's not at all honourable for the pope to turn out the women out of the choirs that have slaved there all their lives and put little whipper-snappers of boys over their heads. I suppose it is for the good of the Church if the pope does it. But it's not just, Mary Jane, and it's not right."

She had worked herself into a passion and would have continued in defence of her sister for it was a sore subject with her but Mary Jane, seeing that all the dancers had come back, intervened pacifically:

"Now, Aunt Kate, you're giving scandal to Mr Browne who is of the other persuasion."

Aunt Kate turned to Mr Browne, who was grinning at this allusion to his religion, and said hastily:

"Oh, I don't question the pope's being right. I'm only a stupid old woman and I wouldn't presume to do such a thing. But there's such a thing as common everyday politeness and gratitude. And if I were in Julia's place I'd tell that Father Healy straight up to his face . . ."

"And besides, Aunt Kate," said Mary Jane, "we really are all hungry and when we are hungry we are all very quarrelsome."

"And when we are thirsty we are also quarrelsome," added Mr Browne.

"So that we had better go to supper," said Mary Jane, "and finish the discussion afterwards."

On the landing outside the drawing-room Gabriel found his wife and Mary Jane trying to persuade Miss Ivors to stay for supper. But Miss Ivors, who had put on her hat and was buttoning her cloak, would not stay. She did not feel in the least hungry and she had already overstayed her time.

"But only for ten minutes, Molly," said Mrs Conroy. "That won't delay you."

"To take a pick itself," said Mary Jane, "after all your dancing."

"I really couldn't," said Miss Ivors.

"I am afraid you didn't enjoy yourself at all," said Mary Jane hopelessly.

"Ever so much, I assure you," said Miss Ivors, "but you really must let me run off now."

"But how can you get home?" asked Mrs Conroy.

"O, it's only two steps up the quay."

Gabriel hesitated a moment and said:

"If you will allow me, Miss Ivors, I'll see you home if you really are obliged to go."

But Miss Ivors broke away from them.

"I won't hear of it," she cried. "For goodness sake go in to your suppers and don't mind me. I'm quite well able to take care of myself."

"Well, you're the comical girl, Milly," said Mrs Conroy frankly.

"Beannacht libh," cried Miss Ivors, with a laugh, as she ran down the staircase.

Mary Jane gazed after her, a moody puzzled expression on her face, while Mrs Conroy leaned over the banisters to listen for the hall-door. Gabriel asked himself was he the cause of her abrupt departure. But she did not seem to be in ill humour: she had gone away laughing. He stared blankly down the staircase.

At that moment Aunt Kate came toddling out of the supper-room, almost wringing her hands in despair.

"Where is Gabriel?" she cried. "Where on earth is Gabriel? There's everyone waiting in there, stage to let, and nobody to carve the goose!"

"Here I am, Aunt Kate!" cried Gabriel, with sudden animation, "Ready to carve a flock of geese, if necessary."

A fat brown goose lay at one end of the table and at the other end, on a bed of creased paper strewn with sprigs of parsley, lay a great ham, stripped of its outer skin and peppered over with crust crumbs, a neat paper frill round its shin and beside this was a round of spiced beef. Between these rival ends ran parallel lines of side-dishes: two little minsters of jelly, red and yellow; a shallow dish full of blocks of blancmange and red jam, a large green leaf-shaped dish with a stalk-shaped handle, on which lay bunches of purple raisins and peeled almonds, a companion dish on which lay a solid rectangle of Smyrna figs, a dish of custard topped with grated nutmeg, a small bowl full of chocolates and sweets wrapped in gold and silver papers and a glass vase in which stood some tall celery stalks. In the centre of the table there stood, as sentries to a fruit-stand which upheld a pyramid of oranges and American apples, two squat old-fashioned decanters of cut glass, one containing port and the other dark sherry. On the closed square piano a pudding in a huge yellow dish lay in waiting and behind it were three squads of bottles of stout and ale and minerals, drawn up according to the colours of their uniforms, the first two black, with brown and red labels, the third and smallest squad white, with transverse green sashes.

Gabriel took his seat boldly at the head of the table and, having looked to the edge of the carver, plunged his fork firmly into the goose. He felt quite at ease now for he was an expert carver and liked nothing better than to find himself at the head of a well-laden table.

"Miss Furlong, what shall I send you?" he asked. "A wing or a slice of the breast?"

"Just a small slice of the breast."

"Miss Higgins, what for you?"

"O, anything at all, Mr Conroy."

While Gabriel and Miss Daly exchanged plates of goose and plates of ham and spiced beef Lily went from guest to guest with a dish of hot floury potatoes wrapped in a white napkin. This was Mary Jane's idea and she had also suggested apple sauce for the goose but Aunt Kate had said that plain roast goose without apple sauce had always been good enough for her and she hoped that she might never eat worse. Mary Jane waited on her pupils and saw that they got the best slices and Aunt Kate and Aunt Julia opened and carried across from the piano bottles of stout and ale for the gentlemen and bottles of minerals for the ladies. There was a great deal of confusion and laughter and noise, the noise of orders and counter-orders, of knives and forks, of corks and glass-stoppers. Gabriel began to carve second helpings as soon as he had finished the first round without serving himself. Everyone protested loudly so that he compromised by taking a long draught of stout for he had found the carving hot work. Mary Jane settled down quietly to her supper but Aunt Kate and Aunt Julia were still toddling round the table, walking on each other's heels, getting in each other's way and giving each other unheeded orders. Mr Browne begged of them to sit down and eat their suppers and so did Gabriel but they said there was time enough so that, at last, Freddy Malins stood up and, capturing Aunt Kate, plumped her down on her chair amid general laughter.

When everyone had been well served Gabriel said, smiling:

"Now, if anyone wants a little more of what vulgar people call stuffing let him or her speak."

A chorus of voices invited him to begin his own supper and Lily came forward with three potatoes which she had reserved for him.

"Very well," said Gabriel amiably, as he took another preparatory draught, "kindly forget my existence, ladies and gentlemen, for a few minutes."

He set to his supper and took no part in the conversation with which the table covered Lily's removal of the plates. The subject of talk was the opera company which was then at the Theatre Royal. Mr Bartell D'Arcy, the tenor, a dark-complexioned young man with a smart moustache, praised very highly the leading contralto of the company but Miss Furlong thought she had a rather vulgar style of production. Freddy Malins said there was a negro chieftain singing in the second part of the Gaiety pantomime who had one of the finest tenor voices she had ever heard.

"Have you heard him?" he asked Mr Bartell D'Arcy across the table.

"No," answered Mr Bartell D'Arcy carelessly.

"Because," Freddy Malins explained, "now I'd be curious to hear your opinion of him. I think he has a grand voice."

"It takes Teddy to find out the really good things," said Mr Browne familiarly to the table.

"And why couldn't he have a voice too?" asked Freddy Malins sharply. "Is it because he's only a black?"

Nobody answered this question and Mary Jane led the table back to the legitimate opera. One of her pupils had given her a pass for *Mignon*. Of course it was very fine, she said, but it made her think of poor Georgina Burns. Mr Browne could go back farther still, to the old Italian companies that used to come to Dublin—Tietjens, Ilma de Murzka, Campanini, the great Trebelli, Giuglini, Ravelli, Aramburo. Those were the days, he said, when there was something like singing to be heard in Dublin. He told too of how the top gallery of the old Royal used to be packed night after night, of how one night an Italian tenor had sung five encores to *Let Me Like a Soldier Fall*, introducing a high C every time, and of how the gallery boys would sometimes in their enthusiasm unyoke the horses from the carriage of some great *prima donna* and pull her themselves through the streets to her hotel. Why did they never play the grand old operas now, he asked, *Dinorah, Lucrezia Borgia*? Because they could not get the voices to sing them: that was why.

"O, well," said Mr Bartell D'Arcy, "I presume there are as good singers to-day as there were then."

"Where are they?" asked Mr Browne defiantly.

"In London, Paris, Milan," said Mr Bartell D'Arcy warmly. "I suppose Caruso, for example, is quite as good, if not better than any of the men you have mentioned."

"Maybe so," said Mr Browne. "But I may tell you I doubt it strongly."

"O, I'd give anything to hear Caruso sing," said Mary Jane.

"For me," said Aunt Kate, who had been picking a bone, "there was only one tenor. To please me, I mean. But I suppose none of you ever heard of him."

"Who was he, Miss Morkan?" asked Mr Bartell D'Arcy politely.

"His name," said Aunt Kate, "was Parkinson. I heard him when he was in his prime and I think he had then the purest tenor voice that was ever put into a man's throat."

"Strange," said Mr Bartell D'Arcy. "I never even heard of him."

"Yes, yes, Miss Morkan is right," said Mr Browne. "I remember hearing of old Parkinson but he's too far back for me."

"A beautiful pure sweet mellow English tenor," said Aunt Kate with enthusiasm.

Gabriel having finished, the huge pudding was transferred to the table. The clatter of forks and spoons began again. Gabriel's wife served out spoonfuls of the pudding and passed the plates down the table. Midway down they were held up by Mary Jane, who replenished them with raspberry or orange jelly or with blancmange and jam. The pudding was of Aunt Julia's making and she received praises for it from all quarters. She herself said that it was not quite brown enough.

"Well, I hope, Miss Morkan," said Mr Browne, "that I'm brown enough for you because, you know, I'm all brown."

All the gentlemen, except Gabriel, ate some of the pudding out of compliment to Aunt Julia. As Gabriel never ate sweets the celery had been left for him. Freddy Malins also took a stalk of celery and ate it with his pudding. He had been told that celery was a capital thing for the blood and he was just then under doctor's care. Mrs Malins, who had been silent all through the supper, said that her son was going down to Mount Melleray in a week or so. The table then spoke of Mount Melleray, how bracing the air was down there, how hospitable the monks were and how they never asked for a penny-piece from their guests.

"And do you mean to say," asked Mr Browne incredulously, "that a chap can go down there and put up there as if it were a hotel and live on the fat of the land and then come away without paying a farthing?"

"O, most people give some donation to the monastery when they leave," said Mary Jane.

"I wish we had an institution like that in our Church," said Mr Browne candidly.

He was astonished to hear that the monks never spoke, got up at two in the morning and slept in their coffins. He asked what they did it for.

"That's the rule of the order," said Aunt Kate firmly.

"Yes, but why?" asked Mr Browne.

Aunt Kate repeated that it was the rule, that was all. Mr Browne still seemed not to understand. Freddy Malins explained to him, as best he could, that the monks were trying to make up for the sins committed by all the sinners in the outside world. The explanation was not very clear for Mr Browne grinned and said:

"I like that idea very much but wouldn't a comfortable spring bed do them as well as a coffin?"

"The coffin," said Mary Jane, "is to remind them of their last end."

As the subject had grown lugubrious it was buried in a silence of the table during which Mrs Malins could be heard saying to her neighbour in an indistinct undertone:

"They are very good men, the monks, very pious men."

The raisins and almonds and figs and apples and oranges and chocolates and sweets were now passed about the table and Aunt Julia invited all the guests to have either port or sherry. At first Mr Bartell D'Arcy refused to take either but one of his neighbours nudged him and whispered something to him upon which he allowed his glass to be filled. Gradually as the last glasses were being filled the conversation ceased. A pause followed, broken only by the noise of the wine and by unsettlings of chairs. The Misses Morkan, all three, looked down at the tablecloth. Someone coughed once or twice and then a few gentlemen patted the table gently as a signal for silence. The silence came and Gabriel pushed back his chair and stood up.

The patting at once grew louder in encouragement and then ceased altogether. Gabriel leaned his ten trembling fingers on the tablecloth and smiled nervously at the company. Meeting a row of upturned faces he raised his eyes to the chandelier. The piano was playing a waltz tune and he could hear the skirts sweeping against the drawing-room door. People, perhaps, were standing in the snow on the quay outside, gazing up at the lighted windows and listening to the waltz music. The air was pure there.

In the distance lay the park where the trees were weighted with snow. The Wellington Monument wore a gleaming cap of snow that flashed westward over the white field of Fifteen Acres.

He began:

"Ladies and Gentlemen."

"It has fallen to my lot this evening, as in years past, to perform a very pleasing task but a task for which I am afraid my poor powers as a speaker are all too inadequate."

"No, no!" said Mr Browne.

"But, however that may be, I can only ask you to-night to take the will for the deed and to lend me your attention for a few moments while I endeavour to express to you in words what my feelings are on this occasion."

"Ladies and Gentlemen. It is not the first time that we have gathered together under this hospitable roof, around this hospitable board. It is not the first time that we have been the recipients—or perhaps, I had better say, the victims—of the hospitality of certain good ladies."

He made a circle in the air with his arm and paused. Everyone laughed or smiled at Aunt Kate and Aunt Julia and Mary Jane who all turned crimson with pleasure. Gabriel went on more boldly:

"I feel more strongly with every recurring year that our country has no tradition which does it so much honour and which it should guard so jealously as that of its hospitality. It is a tradition that is unique as far as my experience goes (and I have visited not a few places abroad) among the modern nations. Some would say, perhaps, that with us it is rather a failing than anything to be boasted of. But granted even that, it is, to my mind, a princely failing, and one that I trust will long be cultivated among us. Of one thing, at least, I am sure. As long as this one roof shelters the good ladies aforesaid—and I wish from my heart it may do so for many and many a long year to come—the tradition of genuine warm-hearted courteous Irish hospitality, which our forefathers have handed down to us and which we in turn must hand down to our descendants, is still alive among us."

A hearty murmur of assent ran round the table. It shot through Gabriel's mind that Miss Ivors was not there and that she had gone away discourteously: and he said with confidence in himself:

"Ladies and Gentlemen."

"A new generation is growing up in our midst, a generation actuated by new ideas and new principles. It is serious and enthusiastic for these new ideas and its enthusiasm, even when it is misdirected, is, I believe, in the main sincere. But we are living in a skeptical and, if I may use the phrase, a thought-tormented age: and sometimes I fear that this new generation, educated or hypereducated as it is, will lack those qualities of humanity, of hospitality, of kindly humour which belonged to an older day. Listening to-night to the names of all those great singers of the past it seemed to me, I must confess, that we were living in a less spacious age. Those days might, without exaggeration, be called spacious days: and if they are gone beyond recall let us hope, at least, that in gatherings such as this we shall still speak of them with pride and affection, still cherish in our hearts the memory of those dead and gone great ones whose fame the world will not willingly let die."

"Hear, hear!" said Mr Browne loudly.

"But yet," continued Gabriel, his voice falling into a softer inflection, "there are always in gatherings such as this sadder thoughts that will recur to our minds: thoughts of the past, of youth, of changes, of absent faces that we miss here tonight. Our path through life is strewn with many such sad memories: and were we to brood upon them always we could not find the heart to go on bravely with our work among the living. We have all of us living duties and living affections which claim, and rightly claim, our strenuous endeavours."

"Therefore, I will not linger on the past. I will not let any gloomy moralising intrude upon us here to-night. Here we are gathered together for a brief moment from the bustle and rush of our everyday routine. We are met here as friends, in the spirit of good-fellowship, as colleagues, also to a certain extent, in the true spirit of *camaraderie*, and as the guests of—what shall I called them?—the Three Graces of the Dublin musical world."

The table burst into applause and laughter at this sally. Aunt Julia vainly asked each of her neighbours in turn to tell her what Gabriel had said.

"He says we are the Three Graces, Aunt Julia," said Mary Jane.

Aunt Julia did not understand but she looked up, smiling, at Gabriel, who continued in the same vein:

"Ladies and Gentlemen."

"I will not attempt to play to-night the part that Paris played on another occasion. I will not attempt to choose between them. The task would be an invidious one and one beyond my poor powers. For when I view them in turn, whether it be our chief hostess herself, whose good heart, whose too good heart, has become a byword with all who know her, or her sister, who seems to be gifted with perennial youth and whose singing must have been a surprise and a revelation to us all to-night, or, last but not least, when I consider our youngest hostess, talented, cheerful, hard-working and the best of nieces, I confess, Ladies and Gentlemen, that I do not know to which of them I should award the prize."

Gabriel glanced down at his aunts and, seeing the large smile on Aunt Julia's face and the tears which had risen to Aunt Kate's eyes, hastened to his close. He raised his glass of port gallantly, while every member of the company fingered a glass expectantly, and said loudly:

"Let us toast them all three together. Let us drink to their health, wealth, long life, happiness and prosperity and may they long continue to hold the proud and self-won position which they hold in their profession and the position of honour and affection which they hold in our hearts."

All the guests stood up, glass in hand, and, turning towards the three seated ladies, sang in unison, with Mr Browne as leader:

> For they are jolly gay fellows,
> For they are jolly gay fellows,
> For they are jolly gay fellows,
> Which nobody can deny.

Aunt Kate was making frank use of her handkerchief and even Aunt Julia seemed moved. Freddy Malins beat time with his pudding-fork and the singers turned towards one another, as if in melodious conference, while they sang, with emphasis:

> Unless he tells a lie,
> Unless he tells a lie.

Then, turning once more towards their hostesses, they sang:

> For they are jolly gay fellows,
> For they are jolly gay fellows,
> For they are jolly gay fellows,
> Which nobody can deny.

The acclamation which followed was taken up beyond the door of the supper-room by many of the other guests and renewed time after time, Freddy Malins acting as officer with his fork on high.

The piercing morning air came into the hall where they were standing so that Aunt Kate said:

"Close the door, somebody. Mrs Malins will get her death of cold."

"Browne is out there, Aunt Kate," said Mary Jane.

"Browne is everywhere," said Aunt Kate, lowering her voice.

Mary Jane laughed at her tone.

"Really," she said archly, "he is very attentive."

"He has been laid on here like the gas," said Aunt Kate in the same tone, "all during the Christmas."

She laughed herself this time good-humouredly and then added quickly:

"But tell him to come in, Mary Jane, and close the door. I hope to goodness he didn't hear me."

At that moment the hall-door was opened and Mr Browne came in from the doorstep, laughing as if his heart would break. He was dressed in a long green overcoat with mock astrakhan cuffs and collar and wore on his head an oval fur cap. He pointed down the snow-covered quay from where the sound of shrill prolonged whistling was borne in.

"Teddy will have all the cabs in Dublin out," he said.

Gabriel advanced from the little pantry behind the office, struggling into his overcoat and, looking round the hall, said:

"Gretta not down yet?"

"She's getting on her things, Gabriel," said Aunt Kate.

"Who's playing up there?" asked Gabriel.

"Nobody. They're all gone."

"O no, Aunt Kate," said Mary Jane. "Bartell D'Arcy and Miss O'Callaghan aren't gone yet."

"Someone is strumming at the piano, anyhow," said Gabriel.

Mary Jane glanced at Gabriel and Mr Browne and said with a shiver:

"It makes me feel cold to look at you two gentlemen muffled up like that. I wouldn't like to face your journey home at this hour."

"I'd like nothing better this minute," said Mr Browne stoutly, "than a rattling fine walk in the country or a fast drive with a good spanking goer between the shafts."

"We used to have a very good horse and trap at home," said Aunt Julia sadly.

"The never-to-be-forgotten Johnny," said Mary Jane, laughing.

Aunt Kate and Gabriel laughed too.

"Why, what was wonderful about Johnny?" asked Mr Browne.

"The late lamented Patrick Morkan, our grandfather, that is," explained Gabriel, "commonly known in his later years as the old gentleman, was a glue-boiler."

"O, now, Gabriel," said Aunt Kate, laughing, "he had a starch mill."

"Well, glue or starch," said Gabriel, "the old gentleman had a horse by the name of Johnny. And Johnny used to work in the old gentleman's mill, walking round and round in order to drive the mill. That was all very well; but now comes the tragic part about Johnny. One fine day the old gentleman thought he'd like to drive out with the quality to a military review in the park."

"The Lord have mercy on his soul," said Aunt Kate compassionately.

"Amen," said Gabriel. "So the old gentleman, as I said, harnessed Johnny and put on his very best tall hat and his very best stock collar and drove out in grand style from his ancestral mansion somewhere near Back Lane, I think."

Everyone laughed, even Mrs Malins, at Gabriel's manner and Aunt Kate said:

"O now, Gabriel, he didn't live in Back Lane, really. Only the mill was there."

"Out from the mansion of his forefathers," continued Gabriel, "he drove with Johnny. And everything went on beautifully until Johnny came in sight of King Billy's statue: and whether he fell in love with the horse King Billy sits on or whether he thought he was back again in the mill, anyhow he began to walk round the statue."

Gabriel paced in a circle round the hall in his goloshes amid the laughter of the others.

"Round and round he went," said Gabriel, "and the old gentleman, who was a very pompous old gentleman, was highly indignant. *Go on, sir! What do you mean, sir? Johnny! Johnny! Most extraordinary conduct! Can't understand the horse!*"

The peals of laughter which followed Gabriel's imitation of the incident were interrupted by a resounding knock at the hall-door. Mary Jane ran to open it and let in Freddy Malins. Freddy Malins, with his hat well back on his head and his shoulders humped with cold, was puffing and steaming after his exertions.

"I could only get one cab," he said.

"O, we'll find another along the quay," said Gabriel.

"Yes," said Aunt Kate. "Better not keep Mrs Malins standing in the draught."

Mrs Malins was helped down the front steps by her son and Mr Browne and, after many manoeuvres, hoisted into the cab. Freddy Malins clambered in after her and spent a long time settling her on the seat, Mr Browne helping him with advice. At last she was settled comfortably and Freddy Malins invited Mr Browne into the cab. There was a good deal of confused talk, and then Mr Browne got into the cab. The cabman settled his rug over his knees, and bent down for the address. The confusion grew greater and the cabman was directed differently by Freddy Malins and Mr Browne, each of whom had his head out through a window of the cab. The difficulty was to know where to drop Mr Browne along the route and Aunt Kate, Aunt Julia and Mary Jane helped the discussion from the doorstep with cross-directions and contradictions and abundance of laughter. As for Freddy Malins he was speechless with laughter. He popped his head in and out of the window every moment, to the great danger of his hat, and told his mother how the discussion was progressing till at last Mr Browne shouted to the bewildered cabman above the din of everybody's laughter:

"Do you know Trinity College?"

"Yes, sir," said the cabman.

"Well, drive bang up against Trinity College gates," said Mr Browne, "and then we'll tell you where to go. You understand now?"

"Yes, sir," said the cabman.

"Make like a bird for Trinity College."

"Right, sir," cried the cabman.

The horse was whipped up and the cab rattled off along the quay amid a chorus of laughter and adieus.

Gabriel had not gone to the door with the others. He was in a dark part of the hall gazing up the staircase. A woman was standing near the top of the first flight, in the shadow also. He could not see her face but he could see the terracotta and salmonpink panels of her skirt which the shadow made appear black and white. It was his wife. She was leaning on the banisters, listening to something. Gabriel was surprised at her stillness and strained his ear to listen also. But he could hear little save the noise of laughter and dispute on the front steps, a few chords struck on the piano and a few notes of a man's voice singing.

He stood still in the gloom of the hall, trying to catch the air that the voice was singing and gazing up at his wife. There was grace and mystery in her attitude as if she were a symbol of something. He asked himself what is a woman standing on the stairs in the shadow, listening to distant music, a symbol of. If he were a painter he would paint her in that attitude. Her blue felt hat would show off the bronze of her hair against the darkness and the dark panels of her skirt would show off the light ones. *Distant Music* he would call the picture if he were a painter.

The hall-door was closed; and Aunt Kate, Aunt Julia and Mary Jane came down the hall, still laughing.

"Well, isn't Freddy terrible?" said Mary Jane. "He's really terrible."

Gabriel said nothing but pointed up the stairs towards where his wife was standing. Now that the hall-door was closed the voice and the piano could be heard more clearly. Gabriel held up his hand for them to be silent. The song seemed to be in the old Irish tonality and the singer seemed uncertain both of his words and of his voice. The voice, made plaintive by distance and by the singer's hoarseness, faintly illuminated the cadence of the air with words expressing grief:

> O, the rain falls on my heavy locks
> And the dew wets my skin,
> My babe lies cold . . .

"O," exclaimed Mary Jane. "It's Bartell D'Arcy singing and he wouldn't sing all the night. O, I'll get him to sing a song before he goes."

"O do, Mary Jane," said Aunt Kate.

Mary Jane brushed past the others and ran to the staircase but before she reached it the singing stopped and the piano was closed abruptly.

"O, what a pity!" she cried. "Is he coming down, Gretta?"

Gabriel heard his wife answer yes and saw her come down towards them. A few steps behind her were Mr Bartell D'Arcy and Miss O'Callaghan.

"O, Mr D'Arcy," cried Mary Jane, "it's downright mean of you to break off like that when we were all in rapture listening to you."

"I have been at him all the evening," said Miss O'Callaghan, and Mrs Convoy too and he told us he had a dreadful cold and couldn't sing."

"O, Mr D'Arcy," said Aunt Kate, "now that was a great fib to tell."

"Can't you see that I'm as hoarse as a crow?" said Mr D'Arcy roughly.

He went into the pantry hastily and put on his overcoat. The others, taken aback by his rude speech, could find nothing to say. Aunt Kate wrinkled her brows and made signs to the others to drop the subject. Mr D'Arcy stood swathing his neck carefully and frowning.

"It's the weather," said Aunt Julia, after a pause.

"Yes, everybody has colds," said Aunt Kate readily, "everybody."

"They say," said Mary Jane, "we haven't had snow like it for thirty years; and I read this morning in the newspapers that the snow is general all over Ireland."

"I love the look of snow," said Aunt Julia sadly.

"So do I," said Miss O'Callaghan. "I think Christmas is never really Christmas unless we have the snow on the ground."

"But poor Mr D'Arcy doesn't like the snow," said Aunt Kate, smiling.

Mr D'Arcy came from the pantry, fully swathed and buttoned, and in a repentant tone told them the history of his cold. Everyone gave him advice and said it was a great pity and urged him to be very careful of his throat in the night air. Gabriel watched his wife who did not join in the conversation. She was standing right under the dusty fanlight and the flame of the gas lit up the rich bronze of her hair which he had seen her drying at the fire a few days before. She was in the same attitude and seemed unaware of the talk about her. At last she turned towards them and Gabriel saw that there was colour on her cheeks and that her eyes were shining. A sudden tide of joy went leaping out of his heart.

"Mr D'Arcy," she said, "what is the name of that song you were singing?"

"It's called *The Lass of Aughrim*," said Mr D'Arcy, "but I couldn't remember it properly. Why? Do you know it?"

"*The Lass of Aughrim*," she repeated. "I couldn't think of the name."

"It's a very nice air," said Mary Jane. "I'm sorry you were not in voice to-night."

"Now, Mary Jane," said Aunt Kate, "don't annoy Mr D'Arcy. I won't have him annoyed."

Seeing that all were ready to start she shepherded them to the door where good-night was said:

"Well, good-night, Aunt Kate, and thanks for the pleasant evening."

"Good-night, Gabriel. Good-night, Gretta!"

"Good-night, Aunt Kate, and thanks ever so much. Good-night, Aunt Julia."

"O, good-night, Gretta, I didn't see you."

"Good-night, Mr D'Arcy. Good-night, Miss O'Callaghan."

"Good-night, Miss Morkan."

"Good-night, again."

"Good-night, all. Safe home."

"Good-night. Good-night."

The morning was still dark. A dull yellow light brooded over the houses and the river; and the sky seemed to be descending. It was slushy underfoot; and only streaks and patches of snow lay on the roofs, on the parapets of the quay and on the area railings. The lamps were still burning redly in the murky air and, across the river, the palace of the Four Courts stood out menacingly against the heavy sky.

She was walking on before him with Mr Bartell D'Arcy, her shoes in a brown parcel tucked under one arm and her hands holding her skirt up from the slush. She had no longer any grace of attitude but Gabriel's eyes were still bright with happiness. The blood went bounding along his veins; and the thoughts went rioting through his brain, proud, joyful, tender, valorous.

She was walking on before him so lightly and so erect that he longed to run after her noiselessly, catch her by the shoulders and say something foolish and affectionate into her ear. She seemed to him so frail that he longed to defend her against something and then to be alone with her. Moments of their secret life together burst like stars upon his memory. A heliotrope envelope was lying beside his breakfast-cup and he was caressing it with his hand. Birds were twittering in the ivy and the sunny web of the curtain was shimmering along the floor: he could not eat for happiness. They were standing on the crowded platform and he was placing a ticket inside the warm palm of her glove. He was standing with her in the cold, looking in through a grated window at a man making bottles in a roaring furnace. It was very cold. Her face, fragrant in the cold air, was quite close to his; and suddenly she called out to the man at the furnace:

"Is the fire hot, sir?"

But the man could not hear her with the noise of the furnace. It was just as well. He might have answered rudely.

A wave of yet more tender joy escaped from his heart and went coursing in warm flood along his arteries. Like the tender fires of stars moments of their life together, that no one knew of or would ever know of, broke upon and illumined his memory. He longed to recall to her those moments, to make her forget the years of their dull existence together and remember only their moments of ecstasy. For the years, he felt, had not quenched his soul or hers. Their children, his writing, her household cares had not quenched all their souls' tender fire. In one letter that he had written to her then he had said: *Why is it that words like these seem to me so dull and cold? Is it because there is no word tender enough to be your name?*

Like distant music these words that he had written years before were borne towards him from the past. He longed to be alone with her. When the others had gone away, when he and she were in their room in the hotel, then they would be alone together. He would call her softly:

"Gretta!"

Perhaps she would not hear at once: she would be undressing. Then something in his voice would strike her. She would turn and look at him. . . .

At the corner of Winetavern Street they met a cab. He was glad of its rattling noise as it saved him from conversation. She was looking out of the window and seemed tired. The others spoke only a few words, pointing out some building or street. The horse galloped along wearily under the murky morning sky, dragging his old rattling box after his heels, and Gabriel was again in a cab with her, galloping to catch the boat, galloping to their honeymoon.

As the cab drove across O'Connell Bridge Miss O'Callaghan said:

"They say you never cross O'Connell Bridge without seeing a white horse."

"I see a white man this time," said Gabriel.

"Where?" asked Mr Bartell D'Arcy.

Gabriel pointed to the statue, on which lay patches of snow. Then he nodded familiarly to it and waved his hand.

"Good-night, Dan," he said gaily.

When the cab drew up before the hotel Gabriel jumped out and, in spite of Mr Bartell D'Arcy's protest, paid the driver. He gave the man a shilling over his fare. The man saluted and said:

"A prosperous New Year to you, sir."

"The same to you," said Gabriel cordially.

She leaned for a moment on his arm in getting out of the cab and while standing at the curbstone, bidding the others good-night. She leaned lightly on his arm, as lightly as when she had danced with him a few hours before. He had felt proud and happy then, happy that she was his, proud of her grace and wifely carriage. But now, after the kindling again of so many memories, the first touch of her body, musical and strange and perfumed, sent through him a keen pang of lust. Under cover of her silence he pressed her arm closely to his side; and, as they stood at the hotel door, he felt that they had escaped from their lives and duties, escaped from home and friends and run away together with wild and radiant hearts to a new adventure.

An old man was dozing in a great hooded chair in the hall. He lit a candle in the office and went before them to the stairs. They followed him in silence, their feet falling in soft thuds on the thickly carpeted stairs. She mounted the stairs behind the porter, her head bowed in the ascent, her frail shoulders curved as with a burden, her skirt girt tightly about her. He could have flung his arms about her hips and held her still for his arms were trembling with desire to seize her and only the stress of his nails against the palms of his hands held the wild impulse of his body in check. The porter halted on the stairs to settle his guttering candle. They halted too on the steps below him. In the silence Gabriel could hear the falling of the molten wax into the tray and the thumping of his own heart against his ribs.

The porter led them along a corridor and opened a door. Then he set his unstable candle down on a toilet-table and asked at what hour they were to be called in the morning.

"Eight," said Gabriel.

The porter pointed to the tap of the electric-light and began a muttered apology but Gabriel cut him short.

"We don't want any light. We have light enough from the street. And I say, he added, pointing to the candle, you might remove that handsome article, like a good man."

The porter took up his candle again, but slowly for he was surprised by such a novel idea. Then he mumbled good-night and went out. Gabriel shot the lock to.

A ghostly light from the street lamp lay in a long shaft from one window to the door. Gabriel threw his overcoat and hat on a couch and crossed the room towards the window. He looked down into the street in order that his emotion might calm a little. Then he turned and leaned against a chest of drawers with his back to the light. She had taken off her hat and cloak and was standing before a large swinging mirror, unhooking her waist. Gabriel paused for a few moments, watching her, and then said:

"Gretta!"

She turned away from the mirror slowly and walked along the shaft of light towards him. Her face looked so serious and weary that the words would not pass Gabriel's lips. No, it was not the moment yet.

"You looked tired," he said.

"I am a little," she answered.

"You don't feel ill or weak?"

"No, tired: that's all."

She went on to the window and stood there, looking out. Gabriel waited again and then, fearing that diffidence was about to conquer him, he said abruptly:

"By the way, Gretta!"

"What is it?"

"You know that poor fellow Malins?" he said quickly.

"Yes. What about him?"

"Well, poor fellow, he's a decent short of chap after all," continued Gabriel in a false voice. "He gave me back that sovereign I lent him and I didn't expect it really. It's a pity he wouldn't keep away from that Browne, because he's not a bad fellow at heart."

He was trembling now with annoyance. Why did she seem so abstracted? He did not know how he could begin. Was she annoyed, too, about something? If she would only turn to him or come to him of her own accord! To take her as she was would be brutal. No, he must see some ardour in her eyes first. He longed to be master of her strange mood.

"When did you lend him the pound?" she asked, after a pause.

Gabriel strove to restrain himself from breaking out into brutal language about the sottish Malins and his pound. He longed to cry to her from his soul, to crush her body against his, to overmaster her. But he said:

"O, at Christmas, when he opened that little Christmas-card shop in Henry Street."

He was in such a fever of rage and desire that he did not hear her come from the window. She stood before him for an instant, looking at him strangely. Then, suddenly raising herself on tiptoe and resting her hands lightly on his shoulders, she kissed him.

"You are a very generous person, Gabriel," she said.

Gabriel, trembling with delight at her sudden kiss and at the quaintness of her phrase, put his hands on her hair and began smoothing it back, scarcely touching it with his fingers. The washing had made it fine and brilliant. His heart was brimming over with happiness. Just when he was wishing for it she had come to him of her own accord. Perhaps her thoughts had been running with his. Perhaps she had felt the impetuous desire that was in him and then the yielding mood had come upon her. Now that she had fallen to him so easily he wondered why he had been so diffident.

He stood, holding her head between his hands. Then, slipping one arm swiftly about her body and drawing her towards him, he said softly:

"Gretta dear, what are you thinking about?"

She did not answer nor yield wholly to his arm. He said again, softly:

"Tell me what it is, Gretta. I think I know what is the matter. Do I know?"

She did not answer at once. Then she said in an outburst of tears:

"O, I am thinking about that song, *The Lass of Aughrim*."

She broke loose from him and ran to the bed and, throwing her arms across the bed-rail, hid her face. Gabriel stood stock-still for a moment in astonishment and then followed her. As he passed in the way of the cheval-glass he caught sight of himself in full length, his broad, well-filled shirt-front, the face whose expression always puzzled him when he saw it in a mirror and his glimmering gilt-rimmed eyeglasses. He halted a few paces from her and said:

"What about the song? Why does that make you cry?"

She raised her head from her arms and dried her eyes with the back of her hand like a child. A kinder note than he had intended went into his voice.

"Why, Gretta?" he asked.

"I am thinking about a person long ago who used to sing that song."

"And who was the person long ago?" asked Gabriel, smiling.

"It was a person I used to know in Galway when I was living with my grandmother," she said.

The smile passed away from Gabriel's face. A dull anger began to gather again at the back of his mind and the dull fires of his lust began to glow angrily in his veins.

"Someone you were in love with?" he asked ironically.

"It was a young boy I used to know," she answered, "named Michael Furey. He used to sing that song, *The Lass of Aughrim*. He was very delicate."

Gabriel was silent. He did not wish her to think that he was interested in this delicate boy.

"I can see him so plainly," she said after a moment. "Such eyes as he had: big dark eyes! And such an expression in them—an expression!"

"O then, you were in love with him?" said Gabriel.

"I used to go out walking with him," she said, "when I was in Galway."

A thought flew across Gabriel's mind.

"Perhaps that was why you wanted to go to Galway with that Ivors girl?" he said coldly.

She looked at him and asked in surprise:

"What for?"

Her eyes made Gabriel feel awkward. He shrugged his shoulders and said:

"How do I know? To see him perhaps."

She looked away from him along the shaft of light towards the window in silence.

"He is dead," she said at length. "He died when he was only seventeen. Isn't it a terrible thing to die so young as that?"

"What was he?" asked Gabriel, still ironically.

"He was in the gasworks," she said.

Gabriel felt humiliated by the failure of his irony and by the evocation of this figure from the dead, a boy in the gasworks. While he had been full of memories of their secret life together, full of tenderness and joy and desire, she had been comparing him in her mind with another. A shameful consciousness of his own person assailed him. He saw himself as a ludicrous figure, acting as a pennyboy for his aunts, a nervous well-meaning sentimentalist, orating to vulgarians and idealising his own clownish lusts, the pitiable fatuous fellow he had caught a glimpse of in the mirror. Instinctively he turned his back more to the light lest she might see the shame that burned upon his forehead.

He tried to keep up his tone of cold interrogation but his voice when he spoke was humble and indifferent.

"I suppose you were in love with this Michael Furey, Gretta," he said.

"I was great with him at that time," she said.

Her voice was veiled and sad. Gabriel, feeling now how vain it would be to try to lead her whither he had purposed, caressed one of her hands and said, also sadly:

"And what did he die of so young, Gretta? Consumption, was it?"

"I think he died for me," she answered.

A vague terror seized Gabriel at this answer as if, at that hour when he had hoped to triumph, some impalpable and vindictive being was coming against him, gathering forces against him in its vague world. But he shook himself free of it with an effort of reason and continued to caress her hand. He did not question her again for he felt that she would tell him of herself. Her hand was warm and moist: it did not respond to his touch but he continued to caress it just as he had caressed her first letter to him that spring morning.

"It was in the winter," she said, "about the beginning of the winter when I was going to leave my grandmother's and come up here to the convent. And he was ill at the time in his lodgings in Galway and wouldn't be let out and his people in Oughterard were written to. He was in decline, they said, or something like that. I never knew rightly."

She paused for a moment and sighed.

"Poor fellow," she said. "He was very fond of me and he was such a gentle boy. We used to go out together, walking, you know, Gabriel, like the way they do in the country. He was going to study singing only for his health. He had a very good voice, poor Michael Furey."

"Well; and then?" asked Gabriel.

"And then when it came to the time for me to leave Galway and come up to the convent he was much worse and I wouldn't be let see him so I wrote a letter saying I was going up to Dublin and would be back in the summer and hoping he would be better then."

She paused for a moment to get her voice under control and then went on:

"Then the night before I left I was in my grandmother's house in Nuns' Island, packing up, and I heard gravel thrown up against the window. The window was so wet I couldn't see so I ran downstairs as I was and slipped out the back into the garden and there was the poor fellow at the end of the garden, shivering."

"And did you not tell him to go back?" asked Gabriel.

"I implored of him to go home at once and told him he would get his death in the rain. But he said he did not want to live. I can see his eyes as well as well! He was standing at the end of the wall where there was a tree."

"And did he go home?" asked Gabriel.

"Yes, he went home. And when I was only a week in the convent he died and he was buried in Oughterard where his people came from. O, the day I heard that, that he was dead!"

She stopped, choking with sobs, and, overcome by emotion, flung herself face downward on the bed, sobbing in the quilt. Gabriel held her hand for a moment longer, irresolutely, and then, shy of intruding on her grief, let it fall gently and walked quietly to the window.

She was fast asleep.

Gabriel, leaning on his elbow, looked for a few moments unresentfully on her tangled hair and half-open mouth, listening to her deep-drawn breath. So she had had that romance in her life: a man had died for her sake. It hardly pained him now to think how poor a part he, her husband, had played in her life. He watched her while she slept as though he and she had never lived together as man and wife. His curious eyes rested long upon her face and on her hair: and, as he thought of what she must have been then, in that time of her first girlish beauty, a strange friendly pity for her entered his soul. He did not like to say even to himself that her face was no longer beautiful but he knew that it was no longer the face for which Michael Furey had braved death.

Perhaps she had not told him all the story. His eyes moved to the chair over which she had thrown some of her clothes. A petticoat string dangled to the floor. One boot stood upright, its limp upper fallen down: the fellow of it lay upon its side. He wondered at his riot of emotions of an hour before. From what had it proceeded? From his aunt's supper, from his own foolish speech, from the wine and dancing, the merry-making when saying good-night in the hall, the pleasure of the walk along the river in the snow. Poor Aunt Julia! She, too, would soon be a shade with the shade of Patrick Morkan and his horse. He had caught that haggard look upon her face for a moment when she was singing *Arrayed for the Bridal.* Soon, perhaps, he would be sitting in that same drawing-room, dressed in black, his silk hat on his knees. The blinds would be drawn down and Aunt Kate would be sitting beside him, crying and blowing her nose and telling him how Julia had died. He would cast about in his mind for some words that might console her, and would find only lame and useless ones. Yes, yes: that would happen very soon.

The air of the room chilled his shoulders. He stretched himself cautiously along under the sheets and lay down beside his wife. One by one they were all becoming shades. Better pass boldly into that other world, in the full glory of some passion, than fade and wither dismally with age. He thought of how she who lay beside him had locked in her heart for so many years that image of her lover's eyes when he had told her that he did not wish to live.

Generous tears filled Gabriel's eyes. He had never felt like that himself towards any woman but he knew that such a feeling must be love. The tears gathered more thickly in his eyes and in the partial darkness he imagined he saw the form of a young man standing under a dripping tree. Other forms were near. His soul had approached that region where dwell the vast hosts of the dead. He was conscious of, but could not apprehend, their wayward and flickering existence. His own identity was fading out into a grey impalpable world: the solid world itself which these dead had one time reared and lived in was dissolving and dwindling.

A few light taps upon the pane made him turn to the window. It had begun to snow again. He watched sleepily the flakes, silver and dark, falling obliquely against the lamplight. The time had come for him to set out on his journey westward. Yes, the newspapers were right: snow was general all over Ireland. It was falling on every part of the dark central plain, on the treeless hills, falling softly upon the Bog of Allen and, farther westward, softly falling into the dark mutinous Shannon waves. It was falling, too, upon every part of the lonely churchyard on the hill where Michael Furey lay buried. It lay thickly drifted on the crooked crosses and headstones, on the spears of the little gate, on the barren thorns. His soul swooned slowly as he heard the snow falling faintly through the universe and faintly falling, like the descent of their last end, upon all the living and the dead.

part four
beyond the safety zone: new directions in experimental fiction

Eugene Ionesco, playwright of the "theater of the absurd," once declared that he wanted to take his audience "beyond the safety zone," where the old traditional rules that once governed literature do not apply. Here the reader must grope his way through the labyrinth of the chaotic modern world, deprived of the lights of the past and confused by dead-ends, cul-de-sacs, and detours that lead nowhere. In a sense, traditional literature, though it was often discomfiting, pivoted on a fixed relationship between reader and work; the reader sympathized with or scorned characters with clearly drawn personalities impelled by definable motives, characters who walked a realistic, exterior world, in conflict with themselves or others, driven through a related series of incidents to destruction or enlightenment. We approached these characters and their worlds on beaten paths: they remained in their world, and we stayed in our armchairs. This comfortable relationship, whose basic premise was that fiction is an artificial construction with a beginning, a middle, and an end, and which took its parts from a fixed external reality, seems over. Because we lack historical perspective on the present course of fiction, we shall consider it, here, at greater length than was devoted to earlier periods.

A modern writer may confuse his reader deliberately; he may talk to him, lie to him, assault or berate him (as in John Barth's "life story"), or even leave him with the rubble of an unfinished story. Joyce's *Ulysses*,

Pirandello's *Each in His Own Way*, and Eliot's *The Wasteland* (to take an example from each of the three genres) are not so much finished pieces of literature as the raw materials with which we must build our own constructions. Perhaps the most interesting recent experiment in "plastic" or malleable fiction is Julio Cortázar's novel *Hopscotch*, the chapters of which need *not* be read in sequence. This novel comes with a set of instructions together with a key that indicates many possible arrangements, not one unique novel. But *Hopscotch*, although it contains but 155 chapters, is virtually millions of books. To be exact, it is $155 \times 154 \times 153 \times 152$, etc., for each new ordering of chapters changes the basic structure of the novel and the course and development of the themes and characters who make up the book. In the three modes, then—fiction, drama, and poetry— the reader/viewer is often an active participant in a concept of literature as process; he is a co-author, a conspirator.

It is difficult today to account for this new and convoluted state of affairs, but at least we can provide a brief overview of how it came about. In the neoclassical period (*ca.* 1660–1800) the artist's universe was fixed, ruled over by a deistic god. The artist's function was to *imitate* that stable exterior pattern and to find his own place in the scheme of things. His telescope, as it were, was directed outward, and his function was to instruct or delight. Literature was a vehicle of instruction and entertainment. But with the Romantics, particularly Wordsworth and Coleridge, the universe came to be seen as perpetually changing, imperfect; and our interaction with it became a fit subject matter for the artist. His own responses, his feelings and emotions, his imagination at work, were now the subject matter of his art; he himself became his central metaphor and the organizing principle of his work. In effect, he turned inwards. Despite the fact that Coleridge said that art grew out of the "coalescence" of the perceiver and the external world, gradually the focus would be shifted to himself, and the imitative or mimetic function of art would be lost. And lost with it, in time, would be the harmonious world vision.(This is the theme of Cortázar's "Blow-up" and Landolfi's "Gogol's Wife.") This is what R. Buckminster Fuller means when he titles his autobiography *I Seem to Be a Verb* and says "there is no such thing as a thing," for everything is process, unfixed, perpetually kinetic. Given this range in external reality, the artist found refuge in history, mythology, art, his own creative imagination. Eventually, however, the chaos outside filtered into these sanctuaries and became a central theme of modern literature.

The shift in the artist's perspective of reality thus reverberated into his relation to himself, to his art, to the world outside him, and to society. In *The Mirror and the Lamp* (neoclassicism is the mirror and Romanticism the lamp), M. H. Abrams outlines four pivotal areas of art together with their schools of literature and criticism: the mimetic theory, in which the primary pivot is the phenomenal world whose pattern must be imitated;

the pragmatic theory, in which the audience is the primary pivot and must be elevated and instructed; the expressionistic theory, in which the artist's feelings and emotions are the focal points; and the objective theory, in which the work of art—higher than the raw materials from which it came and the hand that shaped it and with no immediate debt to society—is the primary pivot. Of course every period mixes all these matters to some extent, but beginning with the Romantics, the expressionistic and objective theories received greater emphasis than the mimetic or pragmatic that had reigned before. If, as Bunyan says, there are three requirements for communication—a speaker, a listener, and a convention—we must wonder at the nature and size of the artist's audience once the underpinning of art was moved off center in the nineteenth century, especially since "convention" implies not only a common language but a common set of symbols, norms, and goals.

With the decline of a broadly based art liberated from representationalism (from the eye of the camera, from depicting things as they appear), the face of art underwent a radical metamorphosis. That face became visible even before the end of the last century, and it is a strikingly unique and unfamiliar face. One widely distributed collection of recent experimental fiction is aptly titled *Anti-Story*, and its contents are doubly interesting in the context of the artist's changing role and new perspecive. Its eight sections are: "Against Mimesis" (subtitled "fiction about fiction"), "Against 'Reality' " ("the uses of fantasy"), "Against Event" ("the primacy of voice"), "Against Subject" ("fiction in search of something to be about"), "Against the Middle Range of Experience" ("new forms of extremity"), "Against Analysis" ("the phenomenal world"), "Against Meaning" ("forms of the absurd"), and finally, "Against Scale" ("the minimal story"). Obviously these categories overlap, and some of the anthologized stories seem improperly classified. Cortázar's "Blow-up," for example, inflates our conception of reality, yet is not so classified; and Michel Butor's "Welcome to Utah," which appears in the "Against Analysis" section, is really a work of social criticism. The key to Butor's story, which along with "Blow-up" is contained in the present collection, lies in its assault on the historical, political, geographical, social, idealistic, and even temporal makeup of the United States. America, charges Butor, has no singleness of identity or purpose; and its past, like its present, is marred by hypocrisy.

The interesting thing about a great deal of experimental fiction is that once we have a general context and are given a clue to the theme, the story under study surrenders itself in toto surprisingly easily. Indeed, there is often very little to say about experimental fiction from a rational standpoint because it does not subscribe to conventional rules of structure and organization. The logical links, the transitions and connectives that are prerequisites of rational discourse, are left out. We must supply them ourselves or bump into unintelligible material. The keys to traditional fiction, character and plot, often will not open the doors of avant-garde literature.

Hopscotch exemplifies the multiplication or explosion of formal structures. Two other subcategories of recent contemporary fiction trace the opposite pattern, toward implosion: the *tropism* and the *minimal story*. The minimal story is easier to understand, or, rather, to fit into context precisely because of what it is *not*; it is not a story with a beginning, a middle, and an end, with characters who move from one emotional state to another. The minimal story does not have time or scope for such luxuries. Like the minimal painting (an empty white canvas, with perhaps a spot on it), the minimal story is illustrative of the *reduction* of conventional structures to the barest elements of the form. The results of such minimalization are predictable: first there is confusion, then the reader constructs character, discovers plot (or the lack of it), and finds or fails to find a clear, logical theme. The discovery of meaninglessness is itself the theme of much such fiction.

To date, no good, clear, widely distributed definition of a tropism exists, and a dictionary provides no help with the term. Basically, a tropism is a quick, fleeting camera shot of an action, character, or incident. It is the word-maker's attempt to approximate a visual form. The author in traditional fiction often served as our guide, pointing out things of significance for us, often prejudging character and foreshadowing events. The tropist does not do this: he is objectified out of the work, while stating that the surface of personality and event are more interesting than inner or inherent meaning; if we dive deep, we do so at our peril. Yet everything the artist constructs has meaning, even when he claims otherwise. The difficulty in determining that meaning is compounded here by the restricted length of the tropism. Often we must piece together a series of snapshots to find that meaning, but if we are patient we will discover it.

Probably the foremost exponent of the so-called new novel is Alain Robbe-Grillet, who posits a rather frightening conception of literature as a scientific exercise. Literature and science, he maintains, are not incompatible; indeed, they must intersect if fiction is to have a resurgence. The "old novel" presupposed an affinity between man and the phenomenal world, the world reached through the senses, yet this premise, Robbe-Grillet maintains, has become fallacious. Man is not a related part of the universe he inhabits. Things are merely things, removed from man and apart from him, existing in a universe beyond "signification" and without inherent meaning. The artist-scientist must reduce language to its *denotative* level, stripping away the connotative and symbolic veneer. Syntax is direct, bald, straightforward. All the devices of the rhetorician are abandoned, for the new novelist is interested in as pure a descriptive literature as he can achieve. Robbe-Grillet's conception of literature, variously called "aliterature," "thingism," and "anti-literature," is but the latest manifestation of a form in perpetual change, yet always vital and alive.

Literature beyond the safety zone is noteworthy for its diversity of moods, types, and intents. Some pieces are long, others very short; some are chaotic, others closely manicured; some are grotesque, others extremely funny; still others telescope the comic and the serious. What unifies them is the belief that modern fiction cannot and will not reside in the old, walled house of past fiction. New fiction is not a static but an organic process, and the reader is part of that process.

ACTION WILL BE TAKEN
by Heinrich Böll
(b. 1917)

Probably one of the strangest interludes in my life was the time I spent as an employee in Alfred Wunsiedel's factory. By nature I am inclined more to pensiveness and inactivity than to work, but now and again prolonged financial difficulties compel me—for pensiveness is no more profitable than inactivity—to take on a so-called job. Finding myself once again at a low ebb of this kind, I put myself in the hands of the employment office and was sent with seven other fellow-sufferers to Wunsiedel's factory, where we were to undergo an aptitude test.

The exterior of the factory was enough to arouse my suspicions: the factory was built entirely of glass brick, and my aversion to well-lit buildings and well-lit rooms is as strong as my aversion to work. I became even more suspicious when we were immediately served breakfast in the well-lit, cheerful coffee shop: pretty waitresses brought us eggs, coffee and toast, orange juice was served in tastefully designed jugs, goldfish pressed their bored faces against the sides of pale-green aquariums. The waitresses were so cheerful that they appeared to be bursting with good cheer. Only a strong effort of will—so it seemed to me—restrained them from singing away all day long. They were as crammed with unsung songs as chickens with unlaid eggs.

Right away I realized something that my fellow-sufferers evidently failed to realize: that this breakfast was already part of the test; so I chewed away reverently, with the full appreciation of a person who knows he is supplying his body with valuable elements. I did something which normally no power on earth can make me do: I drank orange juice on an empty stomach, left the coffee and egg untouched, as well as most of the toast, got up, and paced up and down in the coffee shop, pregnant with action.

As a result I was the first to be ushered into the room where the questionnaires were spread out on attractive tables. The walls were done in a shade of green that would have summoned the word "delightful" to the lips of interior decoration enthusiasts. The room appeared to be empty, and yet I was so sure of being observed that I behaved as someone pregnant with action behaves when he believes himself unobserved: I ripped my pen impatiently from my pocket, unscrewed the top, sat down at the nearest table and pulled the questionnaire toward me, the way irritable customers snatch at the bill in a restaurant.

Question No. 1: Do you consider it right for a human being to possess only two arms, two legs, eyes, and ears?

Here for the first time I reaped the harvest of my pensive nature and wrote without hesitation: "Even four arms, legs and ears would not be adequate for my driving energy. Human beings are very poorly equipped."

Question No. 2: How many telephones can you handle at one time?

Here again the answer was as easy as simple arithmetic: "When there are only seven telephones," I wrote, "I get impatient; there have to be nine before I feel I am working to capacity."

Question No. 3: How do you spend your free time?

My answer: "I no longer acknowledge the term free time—on my fifteenth birthday I eliminated it from my vocabulary, for in the beginning was the act."

I got the job. Even with nine telephones I really didn't feel I was working to capacity. I shouted into the mouthpieces: "Take immediate action!" or: "Do something!—We must have some action—Action will be taken—Action has been taken—Action should be taken." But as a rule—for I felt this was in keeping with the tone of the place—I used the imperative.

Of considerable interest were the noon-hour breaks, when we consumed nutritious foods in an atmosphere of silent good cheer. Wunsiedel's factory was swarming with people who were obsessed with telling you the story of their lives, as indeed vigorous personalities are fond of doing. The story of their lives is more important to them than their lives, you have only to press a button, and immediately it is covered with spewed-out exploits.

Wunsiedel had a right-hand man called Broschek, who had in turn made a name for himself by supporting seven children and a paralyzed wife by working night shifts in his student days, and successfully carrying on four business agencies, besides which he had passed two examinations with honors in two years. When asked by reporters: "When do you sleep, Mr. Broschek?" he had replied: "It's a crime to sleep!"

Wunsiedel's secretary had supported a paralyzed husband and four children by knitting, at the same time graduating in psychology and German history as well as breeding shepherd dogs, and she had become famous as a nightclub singer where she was known as *Vamp Number Seven*.

Wunsiedel himself was one of those people who every morning, as they open their eyes, make up their minds to act. "I must act," they think as they briskly tie their bathrobe belts around them. "I must act," they think as they shave, triumphantly watching their beard hairs being washed away with the lather: these hirsute vestiges are the first daily sacrifices to their driving energy. The more intimate functions also give these people a sense of satisfaction: water swishes, paper is used. Action has been taken. Bread gets eaten, eggs are decapitated.

With Wunsiedel, the most trivial activity looked like action: the way he put on his hat, the way—quivering with energy—he buttoned up his overcoat, the kiss he gave his wife, everything was action.

When he arrived at his office he greeted his secretary with a cry of "Let's have some action!" And in ringing tones she would call back: "Action will be taken!" Wunsiedel then went from department to department, calling out his cheerful: "Let's have some action!" Everyone would answer: "Action will be taken!" And I would call back to him too, with a radiant smile, when he looked into my office: "Action will be taken!"

Within a week I had increased the number of telephones on my desk to eleven, within two weeks to thirteen, and every morning on the streetcar I enjoyed thinking up new imperatives, or chasing the words *take action* through various tenses and modulations: for two whole days I kept saying the same sentence over and over again because I thought it sounded so marvelous: "Action ought to have been taken;" for another two days it was: "Such action ought not to have been taken."

So I was really beginning to feel I was working to capacity when there actually was some action. One Tuesday morning—I had hardly settled down at my desk—Wunsiedel rushed into my office crying his "Let's have some action!" But an inexplicable something in his face made me hesitate to reply, in a cheerful gay voice as the rules dictated: "Action will be taken!" I must have paused too long, for Wunsiedel, who seldom raised his voice, shouted at me: "Answer! Answer, you know the rules!" And I answered, under my breath, reluctantly, like a child who is forced to say: I am a naughty child. It was only by a great effort that I managed to bring out the sentence: "Action will be taken," and hardly had I uttered it when there really was some action: Wunsiedel dropped to the floor. As he fell he rolled over onto his side and lay right across the open doorway. I knew at once, and I confirmed it when I went slowly around my desk and approached the body on the floor: he was dead.

Shaking my head I stepped over Wunsiedel, walked slowly along the corridor to Broschek's office, and entered without knocking. Broschek was sitting at his desk, a telephone receiver in each hand, between his teeth a ballpoint pen with which he was making notes on a writing pad, while with his bare feet he was operating a knitting machine under the desk. In this way he helps to clothe his family. "We've had some action," I said in a low voice.

Broschek spat out the ballpoint pen, put down the two receivers, reluctantly detached his toes from the knitting machine.

"What action?" he asked.

"Wunsiedel is dead," I said.

"No," said Broschek.

"Yes," I said, "come and have a look!"

"No," said Broschek, "that's impossible," but he put on his slippers and followed me along the corridor.

"No," he said, when we stood beside Wunsiedel's corpse, "no no!" I did not contradict him. I carefully turned Wunsiedel over onto his back, closed his eyes, and looked at him pensively.

I felt something like tenderness for him, and realized for the first time that I had never hated him. On his face was that expression which one sees on children who obstinately refuse to give up their faith in Santa Claus, even though the arguments of their playmates sound so convincing.

"No," said Broschek, "no."

"We must take action," I said quietly to Broschek.

"Yes," said Broschek, "we must take action."

Action was taken: Wunsiedel was buried, and I was delegated to carry a wreath of artificial roses behind his coffin, for I am equipped with not only a penchant for pensiveness and inactivity but also a face and figure that go extremely well with dark suits. Apparently as I walked along behind Wunsiedel's coffin carrying the wreath of artificial roses I looked superb. I received an offer from a fashionable firm of funeral directors to join their staff as a professional mourner. "You are a born mourner," said the manager, "your outfit would be provided by the firm. Your face— simply superb!"

I handed in my notice to Broschek, explaining that I had never really felt I was working to capacity there; that, in spite of the thirteen telephones, some of my talents were going to waste. As soon as my first professional appearance as a mourner was over I knew: This is where I belong, this is what I am cut out for.

Pensively I stand behind the coffin in the funeral chapel, holding a simple bouquet, while the organ plays Handel's *Largo*, a piece that does not receive nearly the respect it deserves. The cemetery café is my regular haunt; there I spend the intervals between my professional engagements, although sometimes I walk behind coffins which I have not been engaged to follow, I pay for flowers out of my own pocket and join the welfare worker who walks behind the coffin of some homeless person. From time to time I also visit Wunsiedel's grave, for after all I owe it to him that I discovered my true vocation, a vocation in which pensiveness is essential and inactivity my duty.

It was not till much later that I realized I had never bothered to find out what was being produced in Wunsiedel's factory. I expect it was soap.

Translated by Leila Vennewitz

BLOW-UP
by Julio Cortázar
(b. 1914)

It'll never be known how this has to be told, in the first person or in the second, using the third person plural or continually inventing modes that will serve for nothing. If one might say: I will see the moon rose, or: we hurt me at the back of my eyes, and especially: you the blond woman was the clouds that race before my your his our yours their faces. What the hell.

Seated ready to tell it, if one might go to drink a bock over there, and the typewriter continue by itself (because I use the machine), that would be perfection. And that's not just a manner of speaking. Perfection, yes, because here is the aperture which must be counted also as a machine (of another sort, a Contax 1.1.2) and it is possible that one machine may know more about another machine than I, you, she—the blond—and the clouds. But I have the dumb luck to know that if I go this Remington will sit turned to stone on top of the table with the air of being twice as quiet that mobile things have when they are not moving. So, I have to write. One of us all has to write, if this is going to get told. Better that it be me who am dead, for I'm less compromised than the rest; I who see only the clouds and can think without being distracted, write without being distracted (there goes another, with a grey edge) and remember without being distracted, I who am dead (and I'm alive, I'm not trying to fool anybody, you'll see when we get to the moment, because I have to begin some way and I've begun with this period, the last one back, the one at the beginning, which in the end is the best of the periods when you want to tell something).

All of a sudden I wonder why I have to tell this, but if one begins to wonder why he does all he does do, if one wonders why he accepts an invitation to lunch (now a pigeon's flying by and it seems to me a sparrow), or why when someone has told us a good joke immediately there starts up something like a tickling in the stomach and we are not at peace until we've gone into the office across the hall and told the joke over again; then it feels good immediately, one is fine, happy, and can get back to work. For I imagine that no one has explained this, that really the best thing is to put aside all decorum and tell it, because, after all's done, nobody is ashamed of breathing or of putting on his shoes; they're things that you do, and when something weird happens, when you find a spider in your shoe or if you take a breath and feel like a broken window, then you have to tell what's happening, tell it to the guys at the office or to the doctor. Oh, doctor, every time I take a breath . . . Always tell it, always get rid of that tickle in the stomach that bothers you.

And now that we're finally going to tell it, let's put things a little bit in order, we'd be walking down the staircase in this house as far as Sunday, November 7, just a month back. One goes down five floors and stands then in the Sunday in the sun one would not have suspected of Paris in November, with a large appetite to walk around, to see things, to take photos (because we were photographers, I'm a photographer). I know that the most difficult thing is going to be finding a way to tell it, and I'm not afraid of repeating myself. It's going to be difficult because nobody really knows who it is telling it, if I am I or what actually occurred or what I'm seeing (clouds, and once in a while a pigeon) or if, simply, I'm telling a truth which is only my truth, and then is the truth only for my stomach, for this impulse to go running out and to finish up in some manner with this, whatever it is.

We're going to tell it slowly, what happens in the middle of what I'm writing is coming already. If they replace me, if, so soon, I don't know what to say, if the clouds stop coming and something else starts (because it's impossible that this keep coming, clouds passing continually and occasionally a pigeon), if something out of all this . . . And after the "if" what am I going to put if I'm going to close the sentence structure correctly? But if I begin to ask questions, I'll never tell anything, maybe to tell would be like an answer, at least for someone who's reading it.

Roberto Michel, French-Chilean, translator and in his spare time an amateur photographer, left number 11, rue Monsieur-le-Prince Sunday November 7 of the current year (now there're two small ones passing, with silver linings). He had spent three weeks working on the French version of a treatise on challenges and appeals by José Norberto Allende, professor at the University of Santiago. It's rare that there's wind in Paris, and even less seldom a wind like this that swirled around corners and rose up to whip at old wooden venetian blinds behind which astonished ladies commented variously on how unreliable the weather had been these last few years. But the sun was out also, riding the wind and friend of the cats, so there was nothing that would keep me from taking a walk along the docks of the Seine and taking photos of the Conservatoire and Sainte-Chapelle. It was hardly ten o'clock, and I figured that by eleven the light would be good, the best you can get in the fall; to kill some time I detoured around by the Isle Saint-Louis and started to walk along the quai d'Anjou. I stared for a bit at the hôtel de Lauzun, I recited bits from Apollinaire which always gets into my head whenever I pass in front of the hôtel de Lauzun (and at that I ought to be remembering the other poet, but Michel is an obstinate beggar), and when the wind stopped all at once and the sun came out at least twice as hard (I mean warmer, but really it's the same thing), I sat down on the parapet and felt terribly happy in the Sunday morning.

One of the many ways of contesting level-zero, and one of the best, is to take photographs, an activity in which one should start becoming an adept very early in life, teach it to children since it requires discipline, aesthetic education, a good eye and steady fingers. I'm not talking about waylaying the lie like any old reporter, snapping the stupid silhouette of the VIP leaving number 10 Downing Street, but in all ways when one is walking about with a camera, one has almost a duty to be attentive, to not lose that abrupt and happy rebound of sun's rays off an old stone, or the pigtails-flying run of a small girl going home with a loaf of bread or a bottle of milk. Michel knew that the photographer always worked as a permutation of his personal way of seeing the world as other than the camera insidiously imposed upon it (now a large cloud is by, almost black), but he lacked no confidence in himself, knowing that he had only to go out without the Contax to recover the keynote of distraction, the sight without a frame around it, light without the diaphragm aperture or 1/250 sec. Right now (what a word, *now*, what a dumb lie) I was able to sit quietly on the railing overlooking the river watching the red and black motorboats passing below without it occurring to me to think photographically of the scenes, nothing more than letting myself go in the letting go of objects, running immobile in the stream of time. And then the wind was not blowing.

After, I wandered down the quai de Bourbon until getting to the end of the isle where the intimate square was (intimate because it was small, not that it was hidden, it offered its whole breast to the river and the sky), I enjoyed it, a lot. Nothing there but a couple and, of course, pigeons; maybe even some of those which are flying past now so that I'm seeing them. A leap up and I settled on the wall, and let myself turn about and be caught and fixed by the sun, giving it my face and ears and hands (I kept my gloves in my pocket). I had no desire to shoot pictures, and lit a cigarette to be doing something; I think it was that moment when the match was about to touch the tobacco that I saw the young boy for the first time.

What I'd thought was a couple seemed much more now a boy with his mother, although at the same time I realized that it was not a kid and his mother, and that it was a couple in the sense that we always allegate to couples when we see them leaning up against the parapets or embracing on the benches in the squares. As I had nothing else to do, I had more than enough time to wonder why the boy was so nervous, like a young colt or a hare, sticking his hands into his pockets, taking them out immediately, one after the other, running his fingers through his hair, changing his stance, and especially why was he afraid, well, you could guess that from every gesture, a fear suffocated by his shyness, an impulse to step backwards which he telegraphed, his body standing as if it were on the edge of flight, holding itself back in a final, pitiful decorum.

All this was so clear, ten feet away—and we were alone against the parapet at the tip of the island—that at the beginning the boy's fright didn't let me see the blond very well. Now, thinking back on it, I see her much better at that first second when I read her face (she'd turned around suddenly, swinging like a metal weathercock, and the eyes, the eyes were there), when I vaguely understood what might have been occurring to the boy and figured it would be worth the trouble to stay and watch (the wind was blowing their words away and they were speaking in a low murmur). I think that I know how to look, if it's something I know, and also that every looking oozes with mendacity, because it's that which expels us furthest outside ourselves, without the least guarantee, whereas to smell, or (but Michel rambles on to himself easily enough, there's no need to let him harangue on this way). In any case, if the likely inaccuracy can be seen beforehand, it becomes possible again to look; perhaps it suffices to choose between looking and the reality looked at, to strip things of all their unnecessary clothing. And surely all this is difficult besides.

As for the boy I remember the image before his actual body (that will clear itself up later), while now I am sure that I remember the woman's body much better than the image. She was thin and willowy, two unfair words to describe what she was, and was wearing an almost-black fur coat, almost long, almost handsome. All the morning's wind (now it was hardly a breeze and it wasn't cold) had blown through her blond hair which pared away her white, bleak face—two unfair words—and put the world at her feet and horribly alone in front of her dark eyes, her eyes fell on things like two eagles, two leaps into nothingness, two puffs of green slime. I'm not describing anything, it's more a matter of trying to understand it. And I said two puffs of green slime.

Let's be fair, the boy was well enough dressed and was sporting yellow gloves which I would have sworn belonged to his older brother, a student of law or sociology; it was pleasant to see the fingers of the gloves sticking out of his jacket pocket. For a long time I didn't see his face, barely a profile, not stupid—a terrified bird, a Fra Filippo angel, rice pudding with milk—and the back of an adolescent who wants to take up judo and has had a scuffle or two in defense of an idea or his sister. Turning fourteen, perhaps fifteen, one would guess that he was dressed and fed by his parents but without a nickel in his pocket, having to debate with his buddies before making up his mind to buy a coffee, a cognac, a pack of cigarettes. He'd walk through the streets thinking of the girls in his class, about how good it would be to go to the movies and see the latest film, or to buy novels or neckties or bottles of liquor with green and white labels on them. At home (it would be a respectable home, lunch at noon and romantic landscapes on the walls, with a dark entryway and a mahogany umbrella stand inside the door) there'd be the slow rain of time, for studying, for being mama's hope, for looking like dad, for writing to his aunt in Avignon. So that there was a lot of walking the streets, the whole of the river for him (but without a nickel) and the mysterious city of fifteen-year-olds with its signs in doorways, its terrifying cats, a paper of fried potatoes for thirty francs, the pornographic magazine folded four ways, a solitude like the emptiness of his pockets, the eagerness for so much that was incomprehensible but illumined by a total love, by the availability analogous to the wind and the streets.

This biography was of the boy and of any boy whatsoever, but this particular one now, you could see he was insular, surrounded solely by the blond's presence as she continued talking with him. (I'm tired of insisting, but two long ragged ones just went by. That morning I don't think I looked at the sky once, because what was happening with the boy and the woman appeared so soon I could do nothing but look at them and wait, look at them and . . .) To cut it short, the boy was agitated and one could guess without too much trouble what had just occurred a few minutes before, at most half-an-hour. The boy had come onto the tip of the island, seen the woman and thought her marvelous. The woman was waiting for that because she was there waiting for that, or maybe the boy arrived before her and she saw him from one of the balconies or from a car and got out to meet him, starting the conversation with whatever, from the beginning she was sure that he was going to be afraid and want to run off, and that, naturally, he'd stay, stiff and sullen, pretending experience and the pleasure of the adventure. The rest was easy because it was happening ten feet away from me, and anyone could have gauged the stages of the game, the derisive, competitive fencing; its major attraction was not that it was happening but in foreseeing its denouement. The boy would try to end it by pretending a date, an obligation, whatever, and would go stumbling off disconcerted, wishing he were walking with some assurance, but naked under the mocking glance which would follow him until he was out of sight. Or rather, he would stay there, fascinated or simply incapable of taking the initiative, and the woman would begin to touch his face gently, muss his hair, still talking to him voicelessly, and soon would take him by the arm to lead him off, unless he, with an uneasiness beginning to tinge the edge of desire, even his stake in the adventure, would rouse himself to put his arm around her waist and to kiss her. Any of this could have happened, though it did not, and perversely Michel waited, sitting on the railing, making the settings almost without looking at the camera, ready to take a picturesque shot of a corner of the island with an uncommon couple talking and looking at one another.

Strange how the scene (almost nothing: two figures there mismatched in their youth) was taking on a disquieting aura. I thought it was I imposing it, and that my photo, if I shot it, would reconstitute things in their true stupidity. I would have liked to know what he was thinking, a man in a grey hat sitting at the wheel of a car parked on the dock which led up to the footbridge, and whether he was reading the paper or asleep. I had just discovered him because people inside a parked car have a tendency to disappear, they get lost in that wretched, private cage stripped of the beauty that motion and danger give it. And nevertheless, the car had been there the whole time, forming part (or deforming that part) of the isle. A car: like saying a lighted streetlamp, a park bench. Never like saying wind, sunlight, those elements always new to the skin and the eyes, and also the boy and the woman, unique, put there to change the island, to show it to me in another way. Finally, it may have been that the man with the newspaper also became aware of what was happening and would, like me, feel that malicious sensation of waiting for everything to happen. Now the woman had swung around smoothly, putting the young boy between herself and the wall, I saw them almost in profile, and he was taller, though not much taller, and yet she dominated him, it seemed like she was hovering over him (her laugh, all at once, a whip of feathers), crushing him just by being there, smiling, one hand taking a stroll through the air. Why wait any longer? Aperture at sixteen, a sighting which would not include the horrible black car, but yes, that tree, necessary to break up too much grey space. . . .

I raised the camera, pretended to study a focus which did not include them, and waited and watched closely, sure that I would finally catch the revealing expression, one that would sum it all up, life that is rhythmed by movement but which a stiff image destroys, taking time in cross section, if we do not choose the essential imperceptible fraction of it. I did not have to wait long. The woman was getting on with the job of handcuffing the boy smoothly, stripping from him what was left of his freedom a hair at a time, in an incredibly slow and delicious torture. I imagined the possible endings (now a small fluffy cloud appears, almost alone in the sky), I saw their arrival at the house (a basement apartment probably, which she would have filled with large cushions and cats) and conjectured the boy's terror and his desperate decision to play it cool and to be led off pretending there was nothing new in it for him. Closing my eyes, if I did in fact close my eyes, I set the scene: the teasing kisses, the woman mildly repelling the hands which were trying to undress her, like in novels, on a bed that would have a lilac-colored comforter, on the other hand she taking off his clothes, plainly mother and son under a milky yellow light, and everything would end up as usual, perhaps, but maybe everything would go otherwise, and the initiation of the adolescent would not happen, she would not let it happen, after a long prologue wherein the awkwardnesses, the exasperating caresses, the running of hands over bodies would be resolved in who knows what, in a separate and solitary pleasure, in a petulant denial mixed with the art of tiring and disconcerting so much poor innocence. It might go like that, it might very well go like that; that woman was not looking for the boy as a lover, and at the same time she was dominating him toward some end impossible to understand if you do not imagine it as a cruel game, the desire to desire without satisfaction, to excite herself for someone else, someone who in no way could be that kid.

Michel is guilty of making literature, of indulging in fabricated unrealities. Nothing pleases him more than to imagine exceptions to the rule, individuals outside the species, not-always-repugnant monsters. But that woman invited speculation, perhaps giving clues enough for the fantasy to hit the bullseye. Before she left, and now that she would fill my imaginings for several days, for I'm given to ruminating, I decided not to lose a moment more. I got it all into the view-finder (with the tree, the railing, the eleven-o'clock sun) and took the shot. In time to realize that they both had noticed and stood there looking at me, the boy surprised and as though questioning, but she was irritated, her face and body flat-footedly hostile, feeling robbed, ignominiously recorded on a small chemical image.

I might be able to tell it in much greater detail but it's not worth the trouble. The woman said that no one had the right to take a picture without permission, and demanded that I hand her over the film. All this in a dry, clear voice with a good Parisian accent, which rose in color and tone with every phrase. For my part, it hardly mattered whether she got the roll of film or not, but anyone who knows me will tell you, if you want anything from me, ask nicely. With the result that I restricted myself to formulating the opinion that not only was photography in public places not prohibited, but it was looked upon with decided favor, both private and official. And while that was getting said, I noticed on the sly how the boy was falling back, sort of actively backing up though without moving, and all at once (it seemed almost incredible) he turned and broke into a run, the poor kid, thinking that he was walking off and in fact in full flight, running past the side of the car, disappearing like a gossamer filament of angel-spit in the morning air.

But filaments of angel-spittle are also called devil-spit, and Michel had to endure rather particular curses, to hear himself called meddler and imbecile, taking great pains meanwhile to smile and to abate with simple movements of his head such a hard sell. As I was beginning to get tired, I heard the car door slam. The man in the grey hat was there, looking at us. It was only at that point that I realized he was playing a part in the comedy.

He began to walk toward us, carrying in his hand the paper he had been pretending to read. What I remember best is the grimace that twisted his mouth askew, it covered his face with wrinkles, changed somewhat both in location and shape because his lips trembled and the grimace went from one side of his mouth to the other as though it were on wheels, independent and involuntary. But the rest stayed fixed, a flour-powdered clown or bloodless man, dull dry skin, eyes deepset, the nostrils black and prominently visible, blacker than the eyebrows or hair or the black necktie. Walking cautiously as though the pavement hurt his feet; I saw patent-leather shoes with such thin soles that he must have felt every roughness in the pavement. I don't know why I got down off the railing, nor very well why I decided to not give them the photo, to refuse that demand in which I guessed at their fear and cowardice. The clown and the woman consulted one another in silence: we made a perfect and unbearable triangle, something I felt compelled to break with a crack of a whip. I laughed in their faces and began to walk off, a little more slowly, I imagine, than the boy. At the level of the first houses, beside the iron footbridge, I turned around to look at them. They were not moving, but the man had dropped his newspaper; it seemed to me that the woman, her back to the parapet, ran her hands over the stone with the classical and absurd gesture of someone pursued looking for a way out.

What happened after that happened here, almost just now, in a room on the fifth floor. Several days went by before Michel developed the photos he'd taken on Sunday; his shots of the Conservatoire and of Sainte-Chapelle were all they should be. Then he found two or three proof-shots he'd forgotten, a poor attempt to catch a cat perched astonishingly on the roof of a rambling public urinal, and also the shot of the blond and the kid. The negative was so good that he made an enlargement; the enlargement was so good that he made one very much larger, almost the size of a poster. It did not occur to him (now one wonders and wonders) that only the shots of the Conservatoire were worth so much work. Of the whole series, the snapshot of the tip of the island was the only one which interested him; he tacked up the enlargement on one wall of the room, and the first day he spent some time looking at it and remembering, that gloomy operation of comparing the memory with the gone reality; a frozen memory, like any photo, where nothing is missing, not even, and especially, nothingness, the true solidifier of the scene. There was the woman, there was the boy, the tree rigid above their heads, the sky as sharp as the stone of the parapet, clouds and stones melded into a single substance and inseparable (now one with sharp edges is going by, like a thunderhead). The first two days I accepted what I had done, from the photo itself to the enlargement on the wall, and didn't even question that every once in a while I would interrupt my translation of José Norberto Allende's treatise to encounter once more the woman's face, the dark splotches on the railing. I'm such a jerk; it had never occurred to me that when we look at a photo from the front, the eyes reproduce exactly the position and the vision of the lens; it's these things that are taken for granted and it never occurs to anyone to think about them. From my chair, with the typewriter directly in front of me, I looked at the photo ten feet away, and then it occurred to me that I had hung it exactly at the point of view of the lens. It looked very good that way; no doubt, it was the best way to appreciate a photo, though the angle from the diagonal doubtless has its pleasures and might even divulge different aspects. Every few minutes, for example when I was unable to find the way to say in good French what José Norberto Allende was saying in very good Spanish, I raised my eyes and looked at the photo; sometimes the woman would catch my eye, sometimes the boy, sometimes the pavement where a dry leaf had fallen admirably situated to heighten a lateral section. Then I rested a bit from my labors, and I enclosed myself again happily in that morning in which the photo was drenched, I recalled ironically the angry picture of the woman demanding I give her the photograph, the boy's pathetic and ridiculous flight, the entrance on the scene of the man with the white face. Basically, I was satisfied with myself; my part had not been too brilliant, and since the French have been given the gift of the sharp response, I did not see very well why I'd chosen to leave without a complete demonstration of the rights, privileges and prerogatives of citizens. The important thing, the really important thing was having helped the kid to escape in time (this in case my theorizing was correct, which was not sufficiently proven, but the running away itself seemed to show it so). Out of plain meddling, I had given him the opportunity finally to take advantage of his fright to do something useful; now he would be regretting it, feeling his honor impaired, his manhood diminished. That was better than the attentions of a woman capable of looking as she had looked at him on that island. Michel is something of a puritan at times, he believes that one should not seduce someone from a position of strength. In the last analysis, taking that photo had been a good act.

Well, it wasn't because of the good act that I looked at it between paragraphs while I was working. At that moment I didn't know the reason, the reason I had tacked the enlargement onto the wall; maybe all fatal acts happen that way, and that is the condition of their fulfillment. I don't think the almost-furtive trembling of the leaves on the tree alarmed me, I was working on a sentence and rounded it out successfully. Habits are like immense herbariums, in the end an enlargement of 32×28 looks like a movie screen, where, on the tip of the island, a woman is speaking with a boy and a tree is shaking its dry leaves over their heads.

But her hands were just too much. I had just translated: "In that case, the second key resides in the intrinsic nature of difficulties which societies . . ." —when I saw the woman's hand beginning to stir slowly, finger by finger. There was nothing left of me, a phrase in French which I would never have to finish, a typewriter on the floor, a chair that squeaked and shook, fog. The kid had ducked his head like boxers do when they've done all they can and are waiting for the final blow to fall; he had turned up the collar of his overcoat and seemed more a prisoner than ever, the perfect victim helping promote the catastrophe. Now the woman was talking into his ear, and her hand opened again to lay itself against his cheekbone, to caress and caress it, burning it, taking her time. The kid was less startled than he was suspicious, once or twice he poked his head over the woman's shoulder and she continued talking, saying something that made him look back every few minutes toward that area where Michel knew the car was parked and the man in the grey hat, carefully eliminated from the photo but present in the boy's eyes (how doubt that now) in the words of the woman, in the woman's hands, in the vicarious presence of the woman. When I saw the man come up, stop near them and look at them, his hands in his pockets and a stance somewhere between disgusted and demanding, the master who is about to whistle in his dog after a frolic in the square, I understood, if that was to understand, what had to happen now, what had to have happened then, what would have to happen at that moment, among these people, just where I had poked my nose in to upset an established order, interfering innocently in that which had not happened, but which was now going to happen, now was going to be fulfilled. And what I had imagined earlier was much less horrible than the reality, that woman, who was not there by herself, she was not caressing or propositioning or encouraging for her own pleasure, to lead the angel away with his tousled hair and play the tease with his terror and his eager grace. The real boss was waiting there, smiling petulantly, already certain of the business; he was not the first to send a woman in the vanguard, to bring him the prisoners manacled with flowers. The rest of it would be so simple, the car, some house or another, drinks, stimulating engravings, tardy tears, the awakening in hell. And there was nothing I could do, this time I could do absolutely nothing. My strength had been a photograph, that, there, where they were taking their revenge on me, demonstrating clearly what was going to happen. The photo had been taken, the time had run out, gone; we were so far from one another, the abusive act had certainly already taken place, the tears already shed, and the rest conjecture and sorrow. All at once the order was inverted, they were alive, moving, they were deciding and had decided, they were going to their future; and I on this side, prisoner of another time, in a room on the fifth floor, to not know who they were, that woman, that man, and that boy, to be only the lens of my camera, something fixed, rigid, incapable of intervention. It was horrible, their mocking me, deciding it before my impotent eye, mocking me, for the boy again was looking at the flour-faced clown and I had to accept the fact that he was going to say yes, that the proposition carried money with it or a gimmick, and I couldn't yell for him to run, or even open the road to him again with a new photo, a small and almost meek intervention which would ruin the framework of drool and perfume. Everything was going to resolve itself right there, at that moment; there was like an immense silence which had nothing to do with physical silence. It was stretching it out, setting itself up. I think I screamed, I screamed terribly, and that at that exact second I realized that I was beginning to move toward them, four inches, a step, another step, the tree swung its branches rhythmically in the foreground, a place where the railing was tarnished emerged from the frame, the woman's face turned toward me as though surprised, was enlarging, and then I turned a bit, I mean that the camera turned a little, and without losing sight of the woman, I began to close in on the man who was looking at me with the black holes he had in place of eyes, surprised and angered both, he looked, wanting to nail me onto the air, and at that instant I happened to see something like a large bird outside the focus that was flying in a single swoop in front of the picture, and I leaned up against the wall of my room and was happy because the boy had just managed to escape, I saw him running off, in focus again, sprinting with his hair flying in the wind, learning finally to fly across the island, to arrive at the footbridge, return to the city. For the second time he'd escaped them, for the second time I was helping him to escape, returning him to his precarious paradise. Out of breath, I stood in front of them; no need to step closer, the game was played out. Of the woman you could see just maybe a shoulder and a bit of the hair, brutally cut off by the frame of the picture; but the man was directly center, his mouth half open, you could see a shaking black tongue, and he lifted his hands slowly, bringing them into the foreground, an instant still in perfect focus, and then all of him a lump that blotted out the island, the tree, and I shut my eyes, I didn't want to see any more, and I covered my face and broke into tears like an idiot.

Now there's a big white cloud, as on all these days, all this untellable time. What remains to be said is always a cloud, two clouds, or long hours of a sky perfectly clear, a very clean, clear rectangle tacked up with pins on the wall of my room. That was what I saw when I opened my eyes and dried them with my fingers: the clear sky, and then a cloud that drifted in from the left, passed gracefully and slowly across and disappeared on the right. And then another, and for a change sometimes, everything gets grey, all one enormous cloud, and suddenly the splotches of rain cracking down, for a long spell you can see it raining over the picture, like a spell of weeping reversed, and little by little, the frame becomes clear, perhaps the sun comes out, and again the clouds begin to come, two at a time, three at a time. And the pigeons once in a while, and a sparrow or two.

Translated by Paul Blackburn

TITLE
by John Barth
(b. 1930)

Beginning: in the middle, past the middle, nearer three-quarters done, waiting for the end. Consider how dreadful so far: passionlessness, abstraction, pro, dis. And it will get worse. Can we possibly continue?

Plot and theme: notions vitiated by this hour of the world but as yet not successfully succeeded. Conflict, complication, no climax. The worst is to come. Everything leads to nothing: future tense; past tense; present tense. Perfect. The final question is, Can nothing be made meaningful? Isn't that the final question? If not, the end is at hand. Literally, as it were. Can't stand any more of this.

I think she comes. The story of our life. This is the final test. Try to fill the blank. Only hope is to fill the blank. Efface what can't be faced or else fill the blank. With words or more words, otherwise I'll fill in the blank with this noun here in my prepositional object. Yes, she already said that. And I think. What now. Everything's been said already, over and over; I'm as sick of this as you are; there's nothing to say. Say nothing.

What's new? Nothing.

Conventional startling opener. Sorry if I'm interrupting the Progress of Literature, she said, in a tone that adjective clause suggesting good-humored irony but in fact defensively and imperfectly masking a taunt. The conflict is established though as yet unclear in detail. Standard conflict. Let's skip particulars. What do you want from me? What'll the story be this time? Same old story. Just thought I'd see if you were still around. Before. What? Quit right here. Too late. Can't we start over? What's past is past. On the contrary, what's forever past is eternally present. The future? Blank. All this is just fill in. Hang on.

Still around. In what sense? Among the gerundive. What is that supposed to mean? Did you think I meant to fill in the blank? Why should I? On the other hand, why not? What makes you think I wouldn't fill in the blank instead? Some conversation this is. Do you want to go on, or shall we end it right now? Suspense. I don't care for this either. It'll be over soon enough in any case. But it gets worse and worse. Whatever happens, the ending will be deadly. At least let's have just one real conversation. Dialogue or monologue? What has it been from the first? Don't ask me.

What is there to say at this late date? Let me think; I'm trying to think. Same old story. Or. Or? Silence.

This isn't so bad. Silence. There are worse things. Name three. This, that, the other. Some choices. Who said there was a choice?

Let's try again. That's what I've been doing; I've been thinking while you've been blank. Story of Our Life. However, this may be the final complication. The ending may be violent. That's been said before. Who cares? Let the end be blank; anything's better than this.

It didn't used to be so bad. It used to be less difficult. Even enjoyable. For whom? Both of us. To do what? Complicate the conflict. I am weary of this. What, then? To complete this sentence, if I may bring up a sore subject. That never used to be a problem. Now it's impossible; we just can't manage it. You can't fill in the blank; I can't fill in the blank. Or won't. Is this what we're going to talk about, our obscene verbal problem? It'll be our last conversation. Why talk at all? Are you paying attention? I dare you to quit now! Never dare a desperate person. On with it, calmly, one sentence after another, like a recidivist. A what? A common noun. Or another common noun. Hold tight. Or a chronic forger, let's say; committed to the pen for life. Which is to say, death. The point, for pity's sake! Not yet. Forge on.

We're more than halfway through, as I remarked at the outset: youthful vigor, innocent exposition, positive rising action—all that is behind us. How sophisticated we are today. I'll ignore her, he vowed, and went on. In this dehuman, exhausted, ultimate adjective hour, when every humane value has become untenable, and not only love, decency, and beauty but even compassion and intelligibility are no more than one or two subjective complements to complete the sentence. . . .

This is a story? It's a story, he replied equably, or will be if the author can finish it. Without interruption I suppose you mean? she broke in. I can't finish anything; that is my final word. Yet it's these interruptions that make it a story. Escalate the conflict further. Please let me start over.

Once upon a time you were satisfied with incidental felicities and niceties of technique: the unexpected image, the refreshingly accurate word-choice, the memorable simile that yields deeper and subtler significances upon reflection, like a memorable simile. Somebody please stop me. Or arresting dialogue, so to speak. For example?

Why do you suppose it is, she asked, long participial phrase of the breathless variety characteristic of dialogue attributions in nineteenth-century fiction, that literate people such as we talk like characters in a story? Even supplying the dialogue-tags, she added with wry disgust. Don't put words in her mouth. The same old story, an old-fashioned one at that. Even if I should fill in the blank with my idle pen? Nothing new about that, to make a fact out of a figure. At least it's good for something. Every story is penned in red ink, to make a figure out of a fact. This whole idea is insane.

And might therefore be got away with.

No turning back now, we've gone too far. Everything's finished. Name eight. Story, novel, literature, art, humanism, humanity, the self itself. Wait: the story's not finished. And you and I, Howard? whispered Martha, her sarcasm belied by a hesitant alarm in her glance, flickering as it were despite herself to the blank instrument in his hand. Belied indeed; put that thing away! And what does flickering modify? A person who can't verb adverb ought at least to speak correctly.

A tense moment in the evolution of the story. Do you know, declared the narrator, one has no idea, especially nowadays, how close the end may be, nor will one necessarily be aware of it when it occurs. Who can say how near this universe has come to mere cessation? Or take two people, in a story of the sort it once was possible to tell. Love affairs, literary genres, third item in exemplary series, fourth—everything blossoms and decays, does it not, from the primitive and classical through the mannered and baroque to the abstract, stylized, dehumanized, unintelligible, blank. And you and I, Rosemary? Edward. Snapped! Patience. The narrator gathers that his audience no longer cherishes him. And conversely. But little does he know of the common noun concealed for months in her you name it, under her eyelet chemise. This is a slip. The point is the same. And she fetches it out nightly as I dream, I think. That's no slip. And she regards it and sighs, a quantum grimlier each night it may be. Is this supposed to be amusing? The world might end before this sentence, or merely someone's life. And/or someone else's. I speak metaphorically. Is the sentence ended? Very nearly. No telling how long a sentence will be until one reaches the stop. It sounds as if somebody intends to fill in the blank. What *is* all this nonsense about?

It may not be nonsense. Anyhow it will presently be over. As the narrator was saying, things have been kaput for some time, and while we may be pardoned our great reluctance to acknowledge it, the fact is that the bloody century for example is nearing the three-quarter mark, and the characters in this little tale, for example, are similarly past their prime, as is the drama. About played out. Then God damn it let's ring the curtain. Wait wait. We're left with the following three possibilities, at least in theory. Horseshit. Hold onto yourself, it's too soon to fill in the blank. I hope this will be a short story.

Shorter than it seems. It seems endless. Be thankful it's not a novel. The novel is predicate adjective, as is the innocent anecdote of bygone days when life made a degree of sense and subject joined to complement by copula. No longer are these things the case, as you have doubtless remarked. There was I believe some mention of possibilities, three in number. The first is rejuvenation: having become an exhausted parody of itself, perhaps a form— Of what? Of anything—may rise neoprimitively from its own ashes. A tiresome prospect. The second, more appealing I'm sure but scarcely likely at this advanced date, is that moribund what-have-yous will be supplanted by vigorous new: the demise of the novel and short story, he went on to declare, needn't be the end of narrative art, nor need the dissolution of a used-up blank fill in the blank. The end of one road might be the beginning of another. Much good that'll do me. And you may not find the revolution as bloodless as you think, either. Shall we try it? Never dare a person who is fed up to the ears.

The final possibility is a temporary expedient, to be sure, the self-styled narrator of this so-called story went on to admit, ignoring the hostile impatience of his audience, but what is not, and every sentence completed is a step closer to the end. That is to say, every day gained is a day gone. Matter of viewpoint, I suppose. Go on. I am. Whether anyone's paying attention or not. The final possibility is to turn ultimacy, exhaustion, paralyzing self-consciousness and the adjective weight of accumulated history. . . . Go on. Go on. To turn ultimacy against itself to make something new and valid, the essence whereof would be the impossibility of making something new. What a nauseating notion. And pray how does it bear upon the analogy uppermost in everyone's mind? We've gotten this far, haven't we? Look how far we've come together. Can't we keep on to the end? I think not. Even another sentence is too many. Only if one believes the end to be a long way off; actually it might come at any moment; I'm surprised it hasn't before now. Nothing does when it's expected to.

Silence. There's a fourth possibility, I suppose. Silence. General anesthesia. Self-extinction. Silence.

Historicity and self-awareness, he asseverated, while ineluctable and even greatly to be prized, are always fatal to innocence and spontaneity. Perhaps adjective period Whether in a people, an art, a love affair, on a fourth term added not impossibly to make the third less than ultimate. In the name of suffering humanity cease this harangue. It's over. And the story? Is there a plot here? What's all this leading up to?

No climax. There's the story. Finished? Not quite. Story of our lives. The last word in fiction, in fact. I chose the first-person narrative viewpoint in order to reflect interest from the peculiarities of the technique (such as the normally unbearable self-consciousness, the abstraction, and the blank) to the nature and situation of the narrator and his companion, despite the obvious possibility that the narrator and his companion might be mistaken for the narrator and his companion. Occupational hazard. The technique is advanced, as you see, but the situation of the characters is conventionally dramatic. That being the case, may one of them, or one who may be taken for one of them, make a longish speech in the old-fashioned manner, charged with obsolete emotion? Of course.

I begin calmly, though my voice may rise as I go along. Sometimes it seems as if things could instantly be altogether different and more admirable. The times be damned, one still wants a man vigorous, confident, bold, resourceful, adjective, and adjective. One still wants a woman spirited, spacious of heart, loyal, gentle, adjective, adjective. That man and that woman are as possible as the ones in this miserable story, and a good deal realer. It's as if they live in some room of our house that we can't find the door to, though it's so close we can hear echoes of their voices. Experience has made them wise instead of bitter; knowledge has mellowed instead of souring them; in their forties and fifties, even in their sixties, they're gayer and stronger and more authentic than they were in their twenties; for the twenty-year-olds they have only affectionate sympathy. So? Why aren't the couple in this story that man and woman, so easy to imagine? God, but I am surfeited with clever irony! Ill of sickness! Parallel phrase to wrap up series! This last-resort idea, it's dead in the womb, excuse the figure. A false pregnancy, excuse the figure. God damn me though if that's entirely my fault. Acknowledge your complicity. As you see, I'm trying to do something about the present mess; hence this story. Adjective in the noun! Don't lose your composure. You tell me it's self-defeating to talk about it instead of just up and doing it; but to acknowledge what I'm doing while I'm doing it is exactly the point. Self-defeat implies a victor, and who do you suppose it is, if not blank? That's the only victory left. Right? Forward! Eyes open.

No. The only way to get out of a mirror-maze is to close yours eyes and hold out your hands. And be carried away by a valiant metaphor, I suppose, like a simile.

There's only one direction to go in. Ugh. We must make something out of nothing. Impossible. Mystics do. Not only turn contradiction into paradox, but *employ* it, to go on living and working. Don't bet on it. I'm betting my cliché on it, yours too. What is that supposed to mean? On with the refutation; every denial is another breath, every word brings us closer to the end.

Very well: to write this allegedly ultimate story is a form of artistic fill in the blank, or an artistic form of same, if you like. I don't. What I mean is, same idea in other terms. The storyteller's alternatives, as far as I can see, are a series of last words, like an aging actress making one farewell appearance after another, or actual blank. And I mean literally fill in the blank. Is this a test? But the former is contemptible in itself, and the latter will certainly become so when the rest of the world shrugs its shoulders and goes on about its business. Just as people would do if adverbial clause of obvious analogical nature. The fact is, the narrator has narrated himself into a corner, a state of affairs more tsk-tsk than boo-hoo, and because his position is absurd he calls the world absurd. That some writers lack lead in their pencils does not make writing obsolete. At this point they were both smiling despite themselves. At this point they were both flashing hatred despite themselves. Every woman has a blade concealed in the neighborhood of her garters. So disarm her, so to speak, don't geld yourself. At this point they were both despite themselves. Have we come to the point at last? Not quite. Where there's life there's hope.

There's no hope. This isn't working. But the alternative is to supply an alternative. That's no alternative. Unless I make it one. Just try; quit talking about it, quit talking, quit! Never dare a desperate man. Or woman. That's the one thing that can drive even the first part of a conventional metaphor to the second part of same. Talk, talk, talk. Yes yes, go on, I believe literature's not likely ever to manage abstraction successfully, like sculpture for example, is that a fact, what a time to bring up that subject, anticlimax, that's the point, do set forth the exquisite reason. Well, because wood and iron have a native appeal and first-order reality, whereas words are artificial to begin with, invented specifically to represent. Go on, please go on. I'm going. Don't you dare. Well, well, weld iron rods into abstract patterns, say, and you've still got real iron, but arrange words into abstract patterns and you've got nonsense. Nonsense is right. For example. On, God damn it; take linear plot, take resolution of conflict, take third direct object, all that business, they may very well be obsolete notions, indeed they are, no doubt untenable at this late date, no doubt at all, but in fact we still lead our lives by clock and calendar, for example, and though the seasons recur our mortal human time does not; we grow old and tired, we think of how things used to be or might have been and how they are now, and in fact, and in fact we get exasperated and desperate and out of expedients and out of words.

Go on. Impossible. I'm going, too late now, one more step and we're done, you and I. Suspense. The fact is, you're driving me to it, the fact is that people still lead lives, mean and bleak and brief as they are, briefer than you think, and people have characters and motives that we divine more or less inaccurately from their appearance, speech, behavior, and the rest, you aren't listening, go on then, what do you think I'm doing, people still fall in love, and out, yes, in and out, and out and in, and they please each other, and hurt each other, isn't that the truth, and they do these things in more or less conventionally dramatic fashion, unfashionable or not, go on, I'm going, and what goes on between them is still not only the most interesting but the most important thing in the bloody murderous world, pardon the adjectives. And that my dear is what writers have got to find ways to write about in this adjective adjective hour of the ditto ditto same noun as above, or their, that is to say our, accursed self-consciousness will lead them, that is to say us, to here it comes, say it straight out, I'm going to, say it in plain English for once, that's what I'm leading up to, me and my bloody anticlimactic noun, we're pushing each other to fill in the blank.

Goodbye. Is it over? Can't you read between the lines? One more step. Goodbye suspense goodbye.

Blank.

Oh God comma I abhor self-consciousness. I despise what we have come to; I loathe our loathesome loathing, our place our time our situation, our loathsome art, this ditto necessary story. The blank of our lives. It's about

over. Let the *dénouement* be soon and unexpected, painless if possible, quick at least, above all soon. Now now! How in the world will it ever
GLOSSOLALIA
Still breathless from fending Phoebus, suddenly I see all—and all in vain. A horse excreting Greeks will devour my city; none will heed her Apollo loved, and endowed with clear sight, and cursed when she gainsaid him. My honor thus costlily purchased will be snatched from me by soldiers. I see Agamemnon, my enslaver, meeting death in Mycenae. No more.

Dear Procne: your wretched sister—she it is weaves this robe. Regard it well: it hides her painful tale in its pointless patterns. Tereus came and fetched her off; he conveyed her to Thrace . . . but not to see her sister. He dragged her deep into the forest, where he shackled her and raped her. Her tongue he then severed, and concealed her, and she warbles for vengeance, and death.

I Crispus, a man of Corinth, yesterday looked on God. Today I rave. What things my eyes have seen can't be scribed or spoken. All think I praise His sacred name, take my horror for hymns, my blasphemies for raptures. The holy writ's wrongly deciphered, as beatitudes and blessings; in truth those are curses, maledictions, and obscenest commandments. So be it.

Sweet Sheba, beloved highness: Solomon craves your throne! Beware his craft; he mistranslates my pain into cunning counsel. Hear what he claims your hoopoe sang: that its mistress the Queen no longer worships Allah! He bids you come now to his palace, to be punished for your error. . . . But mine was a love song: how I'd hymn you, if his tongue weren't beyond me—and yours.

Ed' pélut', kondó, nedóde, ímba imbá imbá. Singé erú. Orúmo ímbo ímpe ruté sceléte. Ímpe re scéle lee lutó. Ombo té scele té, beré te kúre kúre. Sinté te lúté sinte kúru, te ruméte tau ruméte. Onkó keere scéte, tere lúte, ilee léte leel' lúto. Scélé.

Ill fortune, constraint and terror, generate guileful art; despair inspires. The laureled clairvoyants tell our doom in riddles. Sewn in our robes are horrid tales, and the speakers-in-tongues enounce atrocious tidings. The prophet-birds seem to speak sagely, but are shrieking their frustration. The senselessest babble, could we ken it, might disclose a dark message, or prayer.

GOGOL'S WIFE
by Tommaso Landolfi
(b. 1908)

At this point, confronted with the whole complicated affair of Nikolai Vassilevitch's wife, I am overcome by hesitation. Have I any right to disclose something which is unknown to the whole world, which my unforgettable friend himself kept hidden from the world (and he had his reasons), and which I am sure will give rise to all sorts of malicious and stupid misunderstandings? Something, moreover, which will very probably offend the sensibilities of all sorts of base, hypocritical people, and possibly of some honest people too, if there are any left? And finally, have I any right to disclose something before which my own spirit recoils, and even tends toward a more or less open disapproval?

But the fact remains that, as a biographer, I have certain firm obligations. Believing as I do that every bit of information about so lofty a genius will turn out to be of value to us and to future generations, I cannot conceal something which in any case has no hope of being judged fairly and wisely until the end of time. Moreover, what right have we to condemn? Is it given to us to know, not only what intimate needs but even what higher and wider ends may have been served by those very deeds of a lofty genius which perchance may appear to us vile? No indeed, for we understand so little of these privileged natures. "It is true," a great man once said, "that I also have to pee, but for quite different reasons."

But without more ado I will come to what I know beyond doubt, and can prove beyond question, about this controversial matter, which will now—I dare to hope—no longer be so. I will not trouble to recapitulate what is already known of it, since I do not think this should be necessary at the present stage of development of Gogol studies.

Let me say it at once: Nikolai Vassilevitch's wife was not a woman. Nor was she any sort of human being, nor any sort of living creature at all, whether animal or vegetable (although something of the sort has sometimes been hinted). She was quite simply a balloon. Yes, a balloon; and this will explain the perplexity, or even indignation, of certain biographers who were also the personal friends of the Master, and who complained that, although they often went to his house, they never saw her and "never even heard her voice." From this they deduced all sorts of dark and disgraceful complications—yes, and criminal ones too. No, gentlemen, everything is always simpler than it appears. You did not hear her voice simply because she could not speak, or to be more exact, she could only speak in certain conditions, as we shall see. And it was always, except once, in tête-à-tête with Nikolai Vassilevitch. So let us not waste time with any cheap or empty refutations but come at once to as exact and complete a description as possible of the being or object in question.

Gogol's so-called wife was an ordinary dummy made of thick rubber, naked at all seasons, buff in tint, or as is more commonly said, flesh-colored. But since women's skins are not all of the same color, I should specify that hers was a light-colored, polished skin, like that of certain brunettes. It, or she, was, it is hardly necessary to add, of feminine sex. Perhaps I should say at once that she was capable of very wide alterations of her attributes without, of course, being able to alter her sex itself. She could sometimes appear to be thin, with hardly any breasts and with narrow hips more like a young lad than a woman, and at other times to be excessively well-endowed or—let us not mince matters—fat. And she often changed the color of her hair, both on her head and elsewhere on her body, though not necessarily at the same time. She could also seem to change in all sorts of other tiny particulars, such as the position of moles, the vitality of the mucous membranes and so forth. She could even to a certain extent change the very color of her skin. One is faced with the necessity of asking oneself who she really was, or whether it would be proper to speak of a single "person"—and in fact we shall see that it would be imprudent to press this point.

The cause of these changes, as my readers will already have under-stood, was nothing else but the will of Nikolai Vassilevitch himself. He would inflate her to a greater or lesser degree, would change her wig and her other tufts of hair, would grease her with ointments and touch her up in various ways so as to obtain more or less the type of woman which suited him at that moment. Following the natural inclinations of his fancy, he even amused himself sometimes by producing grotesque or monstrous forms; as will be readily understood, she became deformed when inflated beyond a certain point or if she remained below a certain pressure.

But Gogol soon tired of these experiments, which he held to be "after all, not very respectful" to his wife, whom he loved in his own way— however inscrutable it may remain to us. He loved her, but which of these incarnations, we may ask ourselves, did he love? Alas, I have already indicated that the end of the present account will furnish some sort of an answer. And how can I have stated above that it was Nikolai Vassilevitch's will which ruled that woman? In a certain sense, yes, it is true; but it is equally certain that she soon became no longer his slave but his tyrant. And here yawns the abyss, or if you prefer it, the Jaws of Tartarus. But let us not anticipate.

I have said that Gogol obtained with his manipulations *more or less* the type of woman which he needed from time to time. I should add that when, in rare cases, the form he obtained perfectly incarnated his desire, Nikolai Vassilevitch fell in love with it "exclusively," as he said in his own words, and that this was enough to render "her" stable for a certain time—until he fell out of love with "her." I counted no more than three or four of these violent passions—or, as I suppose they would be called today, infatuations—in the life (dare I say in the conjugal life?) of the great writer. It will be convenient to add here that a few years after what one may call his marriage, Gogol had even given a name to his wife. It was Caracas, which is, unless I am mistaken, the capital of Venezuela. I have never been able to discover the reason for this choice: great minds are so capricious!

Speaking only of her normal appearance, Caracas was what is called a fine woman—well built and proportioned in every part. She had every smallest attribute of her sex properly disposed in the proper location. Particularly worthy of attention were her genital organs (if the adjective is permissible in such a context). They were formed by means of ingenious folds in the rubber. Nothing was forgotten, and their operation was rendered easy by various devices, as well as by the internal pressure of the air.

Caracas also had a skeleton, even though a rudimentary one. Perhaps it was made of whalebone. Special care had been devoted to the construction of the thoracic cage, of the pelvic basin and of the cranium. The first two systems were more or less visible in accordance with the thickness of the fatty layer, if I may so describe it, which covered them. It is a great pity that Gogol never let me know the name of the creator of such a fine piece of work. There was an obstinacy in his refusal which was never quite clear to me.

Nikolai Vassilevitch blew his wife up through the anal sphincter with a pump of his own invention, rather like those which you hold down with your two feet and which are used today in all sorts of mechanical workshops. Situated in the anus was a little one-way valve, or whatever the correct technical description would be, like the mitral valve of the heart, which, once the body was inflated, allowed more air to come in but none to go out. To deflate, one unscrewed a stopper in the mouth, at the back of the throat.

And that, I think, exhausts the description of the most noteworthy peculiarities of this being. Unless perhaps I should mention the splendid rows of white teeth which adorned her mouth and the dark eyes which, in spite of their immobility, perfectly simulated life. Did I say simulate? Good heavens, simulate is not the word! Nothing seems to be the word, when one is speaking of Caracas! Even these eyes could undergo a change of color, by means of a special process to which, since it was long and tiresome, Gogol seldom had recourse. Finally, I should speak of her voice, which it was only once given to me to hear. But I cannot do that without going more fully into the relationship between husband and wife, and in this I shall no longer be able to answer to the truth of everything with absolute certitude. On my conscience I could not—so confused, both in itself and in my memory, is that which I now have to tell.

Here, then, as they occur to me, are some of my memories.

The first and, as I said, the last time I ever heard Caracas speak to Nikolai Vassilevitch was one evening when we were absolutely alone. We were in the room where the woman, if I may be allowed the expression, lived. Entrance to this room was strictly forbidden to everybody. It was furnished more or less in the Oriental manner, had no windows and was situated in the most inaccessible part of the house. I did know that she could talk, but Gogol had never explained to me the circumstances under which this happened. There were only the two of us, or three, in there. Nikolai Vassilevitch and I were drinking vodka and discussing Butkov's novel. I remember that we left this topic, and he was maintaining the necessity for radical reforms in the laws of inheritance. We had almost forgotten her. It was then that, with a husky and submissive voice, like Venus on the nuptial couch, she said point-blank: "I want to go poo poo."

I jumped, thinking I had misheard, and looked across at her. She was sitting on a pile of cushions against the wall; that evening she was a soft, blonde beauty, rather well-covered. Her expression seemed commingled of shrewdness and slyness, childishness and irresponsibility. As for Gogol, he blushed violently and, leaping on her, stuck two fingers down her throat. She immediately began to shrink and to turn pale; she took on once again that lost and astonished air which was especially hers, and was in the end reduced to no more than a flabby skin on a perfunctory bony armature. Since, for practical reasons which will readily be divined, she had an extraordinarily flexible backbone, she folded up almost in two, and for the rest of the evening she looked up at us from where she had slithered to the floor, in utter abjection.

All Gogol said was: "She only does it for a joke, or to annoy me, because as a matter of fact she does not have such needs." In the presence of other people, that is to say of me, he generally made a point of treating her with a certain disdain.

We went on drinking and talking, but Nikolai Vassilevitch seemed very much disturbed and absent in spirit. Once he suddenly interrupted what he was saying, seized my hand in his and burst into tears. "What can I do now?" he exclaimed. "You understand, Foma Paskalovitch, that I loved her?"

It is necessary to point out that it was impossible, except by a miracle, ever to repeat any of Caracas' forms. She was a fresh creation every time, and it would have been wasted effort to seek to find again the exact proportions, the exact pressure, and so forth, of a former Caracas. Therefore the plumpish blonde of that evening was lost to Gogol from that time forth forever; this was in fact the tragic end of one of those few loves of Nikolai Vassilevitch, which I described above. He gave me no explanation;

he sadly rejected my proffered comfort, and that evening we parted early. But his heart had been laid bare to me in that outburst. He was no longer so reticent with me, and soon had hardly any secrets left. And this, I may say in parenthesis, caused me very great pride.

It seems that things had gone well for the "couple" at the beginning of their life together. Nikolai Vassilevitch had been content with Caracas and slept regularly with her in the same bed. He continued to observe this custom till the end, saying with a timid smile that no companion could be quieter or less importunate than she. But I soon began to doubt this, especially judging by the state he was sometimes in when he woke up. Then, after several years, their relationship began strangely to deteriorate.

All this, let it be said once and for all, is no more than a schematic attempt at an explanation. About that time the woman actually began to show signs of independence or, as one might say, of autonomy. Nikolai Vassilevitch had the extraordinary impression that she was acquiring a personality of her own, indecipherable perhaps, but still distinct from his, and one which slipped through his fingers. It is certain that some sort of continuity was established between each of her appearances—between all those brunettes, those blondes, those redheads and auburn-headed girls, between those plump, those slim, those dusky or snowy or golden beauties, there was a certain something in common. At the beginning of this chapter I cast some doubt on the propriety of considering Caracas as a unitary personality; nevertheless I myself could not quite, whenever I saw her, free myself of the impression that, however unheard of it may seem, this was fundamentally the same woman. And it may be that this was why Gogol felt he had to give her a name.

An attempt to establish in what precisely subsisted the common attributes of the different forms would be quite another thing. Perhaps it was no more and no less than the creative afflatus of Nikolai Vassilevitch himself. But no, it would have been too singular and strange if he had been so much divided off from himself, so much averse to himself. Because whoever she was, Caracas was a disturbing presence and even—it is better to be quite clear—a hostile one. Yet neither Gogol nor I ever succeeded in formulating a remotely tenable hypothesis as to her true nature; when I say formulate, I mean in terms which would be at once rational and accessible to all. But I cannot pass over an extraordinary event which took place at this time.

Caracas fell ill of a shameful disease—or rather Gogol did—though he was not then having, nor had he ever had, any contact with other women. I will not even try to describe how this happened, or where the filthy complaint came from; all I know is that it happened. And that my great, unhappy friend would say to me: "So, Foma Paskalovitch, you see what lay at the heart of Caracas; it was the spirit of syphilis."

Sometimes he would even blame himself in a quite absurd manner; he was always prone to self-accusation. This incident was a real catastrophe as far as the already obscure relationship between husband and wife, and the hostile feelings of Nikolai Vassilevitch himself, were concerned. He was compelled to undergo long-drawn-out and painful treatment—the treatment of those days—and the situation was aggravated by the fact that the disease in the woman did not seem to be easily curable. Gogol deluded himself for some time that, by blowing his wife up and down and furnishing her with the most widely divergent aspects, he could obtain a woman immune from the contagion, but he was forced to desist when no results were forthcoming.

I shall be brief, seeking not to tire my readers, and also because what I remember seems to become more and more confused. I shall therefore hasten to the tragic conclusion. As to this last, however, let there be no mistake. I must once again make it clear that I am very sure of my ground. I was an eyewitness. Would that I had not been!

The years went by. Nikolai Vassilevitch's distaste for his wife became stronger, though his love for her did not show any signs of diminishing. Toward the end, aversion and attachment struggled so fiercely with each other in his heart that he became quite stricken, almost broken up. His restless eyes, which habitually assumed so many different expressions and sometimes spoke so sweetly to the heart of his interlocutor, now almost always shone with a fevered light, as if he were under the effect of a drug. The strangest impulses arose in him, accompanied by the most senseless fears. He spoke to me of Caracas more and more often, accusing her of unthinkable and amazing things. In these regions I could not follow him, since I had but a sketchy acquaintance with his wife, and hardly any intimacy—and above all since my sensibility was so limited compared with his. I shall accordingly restrict myself to reporting some of his accusations, without reference to my personal impressions.

"Believe it or not, Foma Paskalovitch," he would, for example, often say to me: "Believe it or not, *she's aging!*" Then, unspeakably moved, he would, as was his way, take my hands in his. He also accused Caracas of giving herself up to solitary pleasures, which he had expressly forbidden. He even went so far as to charge her with betraying him, but the things he said became so extremely obscure that I must excuse myself from any further account of them.

One thing that appears certain is that toward the end Caracas, whether aged or not, had turned into a bitter creature, querulous, hypocritical and subject to religious excess. I do not exclude the possibility that she may have had an influence on Gogol's moral position during the last period of his life, a position which is sufficiently well known. The tragic climax came one night quite unexpectedly when Nikolai Vassilevitch and I were celebrating his silver wedding—one of the last evenings we were to spend together. I neither can nor should attempt to set down what it was that led to his decision, at a time when to all appearances he was resigned to tolerating his consort. I know not what new events had taken place that day. I shall confine myself to the facts; my readers must make what they can of them.

That evening Nikolai Vassilevitch was unusually agitated. His distaste for Caracas seemed to have reached an unprecedented intensity. The famous "pyre of vanities"—the burning of his manuscripts—had already taken place; I should not like to say whether or not at the instigation of his wife. His state of mind had been further inflamed by other causes. As to his physical condition, this was ever more pitiful, and strengthened my impression that he took drugs. All the same, he began to talk in a more or less normal way about Belinsky, who was giving him some trouble with his attacks on the *Selected Correspondence*. Then suddenly, tears rising to his eyes, he interrupted himself and cried out: "No. No. It's too much, too much. I can't go on any longer," as well as other obscure and disconnected phrases which he would not clarify. He seemed to be talking to himself. He wrung his hands, shook his head, got up and sat down again after having taken four or five anxious steps around the room. When Caracas appeared, or rather when we went in to her later in the evening in her Oriental chamber, he controlled himself no longer and began to behave like an old man, if I may so express myself, in his second childhood, quite giving way to his absurd impulses. For instance, he kept nudging me and winking and senselessly repeating: "There she is, Foma Paskalovitch; there she is!" Meanwhile she seemed to look up at us with a disdainful attention. But behind these "mannerisms" one could feel in him a real repugnance, a repugnance which had, I suppose, now reached the limits of the endurable. Indeed . . .

After a certain time Nikolai Vassilevitch seemed to pluck up courage. He burst into tears, but somehow they were more manly tears. He wrung his hands again, seized mine in his, and walked up and down, muttering: "That's enough! We can't have any more of this. This is an unheard of thing. How can such a thing be happening to me? How can a man be expected to put up with *this?*"

He then leaped furiously upon the pump, the existence of which he seemed just to have remembered, and, with it in his hand, dashed like a whirlwind to Caracas. He inserted the tube in her anus and began to inflate her. . . . Weeping the while, he shouted like one possessed: "Oh, how I love her, how I love her, my poor, poor darling! . . . But she's going to burst! Unhappy Caracas, most pitiable of God's creatures! But die she must!"

Caracas was swelling up. Nikolai Vassilevitch sweated, wept and pumped. I wished to stop him but, I know not why, I had not the courage. She began to become deformed and shortly assumed the most monstrous aspect; and yet she had not given any signs of alarm—she was used to these jokes. But when she began to feel unbearably full, or perhaps when Nikolai Vassilevitch's intentions became plain to her, she took on an expression of bestial amazement, even a little beseeching, but still without losing that disdainful look. She was afraid, she was even committing herself to his mercy, but still she could not believe in the immediate approach of her fate; she could not believe in the frightful audacity of her husband. He could not see her face because he was behind her. But I looked at her with fascination, and did not move a finger.

At last the internal pressure came through the fragile bones at the base of her skull, and printed on her face an indescribable rictus. Her belly, her thighs, her lips, her breasts and what I could see of her buttocks had swollen to incredible proportions. All of a sudden she belched, and gave a long hissing groan; both these phenomena one could explain by the increase in pressure, which had suddenly forced a way out through the valve in her throat. Then her eyes bulged frantically, threatening to jump out of their sockets. Her ribs flared wide apart and were no longer attached to the sternum, and she resembled a python digesting a donkey. A donkey, did I say? An ox! An elephant! At this point I believed her already dead, but Nikolai Vassilevitch, sweating, weeping and repeating: "My dearest! My beloved! My best!" continued to pump.

She went off unexpectedly and, as it were, all of a piece. It was not one part of her skin which gave way and the rest which followed, but her whole surface at the same instant. She scattered in the air. The pieces fell more or less slowly, according to their size, which was in no case above a very restricted one. I distinctly remember a piece of her cheek, with some lip attached, hanging on the corner of the mantelpiece. Nikolai Vassilevitch stared at me like a madman. Then he pulled himself together and, once more with furious determination, he began carefully to collect those poor rags which once had been the shining skin of Caracas, and all of her.

"Good-by, Caracas," I thought I heard him murmur. "Good-by! You were too pitiable!" And then suddenly and quite audibly: "The fire! The fire! She too must end up in the fire." He crossed himself—with his left hand, of course. Then, when he had picked up all those shriveled rags, even climbing on the furniture so as not to miss any, he threw them straight on the fire in the hearth, where they began to burn slowly and with an excessively unpleasant smell. Nikolai Vassilevitch, like all Russians, had a passion for throwing important things in the fire.

Red in the face, with an inexpressible look of despair, and yet of sinister triumph too, he gazed on the pyre of those miserable remains. He had seized my arm and was squeezing it convulsively. But those traces of what had once been a being were hardly well alight when he seemed yet again to pull himself together, as if he were suddenly remembering something or taking a painful decision. In one bound he was out of the room.

A few seconds later I heard him speaking to me through the door in a broken, plaintive voice: "Foma Paskalovitch, I want you to promise not to look. *Golubchik*, promise not to look at me when I come in."

I don't know what I answered, or whether I tried to reassure him in any way. But he insisted, and I had to promise him, as if he were a child, to hide my face against the wall and only turn round when he said I might. The door then opened violently and Nikolai Vassilevitch burst into the room and ran to the fireplace.

And here I must confess my weakness, though I consider it justified by the extraordinary circumstances. I looked round before Nikolai Vassilevitch told me I could; it was stronger than me. I was just in time to see him carrying something in his arms, something which he threw on the fire with all the rest, so that it suddenly flared up. At that, since the desire to *see* had entirely mastered every other thought in me, I dashed to the fireplace. But Nikolai Vassilevitch placed himself between me and it and pushed me back with a strength of which I had not believed him capable. Meanwhile the object was burning and giving off clouds of smoke. And before he showed any sign of calming down there was nothing left but a heap of silent ashes.

The true reason why I wished to see was because I had already glimpsed. But it was only a glimpse, and perhaps I should not allow myself to introduce even the slightest element of uncertainty into this true story. And yet, an eyewitness account is not completely without a mention of that which the witness knows with less than complete certainty. To cut a long story short, that something was a baby. Not a flesh-and-blood baby, of course, but more something in the line of a rubber doll or a model. Something, which, to judge by its appearance, could have been called *Caracas' son*.

Was I mad too? That I do not know, but I do know that this was what I saw, not clearly, but with my own eyes. And I wonder why it was that when I was writing this just now I didn't mention that when Nikolai Vassilevitch came back into the room he was muttering between his clenched teeth: "Him too! Him too!"

And that is the sum of my knowledge of Nikolai Vassilevitch's wife. In the next chapter I shall tell what happened to him afterward, and that will be the last chapter of his life. But to give an interpretation of his feelings for his wife, or indeed for anything, is quite another and more difficult matter, though I have attempted it elsewhere in this volume, and refer the reader to that modest effort. I hope I have thrown sufficient light on a most controversial question and that I have unveiled the mystery, if not of Gogol, then at least of his wife. In the course of this I have implicitly given the lie to the insensate accusation that he ill-treated or even beat his wife, as well as other like absurdities. And what else can be the goal of a humble biographer such as the present writer but to serve the memory of that lofty genius who is the object of this study?

Translated by Wayland Young

WELCOME TO UTAH
by Michel Butor
(b. 1927)

the sun is setting in
WELLINGTON, Mountain Time.
After having walked for months and months through the desert, the Latter-Day Saints came in sight of Great Salt Lake.

Kings Peak, highest point in the state.
　　　　　WELLINGTON, NEV., the Far West,—the Summit
　　　　　Lake Indian Reservation.

HUNTSVILLE, Weber County.

In July 1847, Brigham Young decided that it was in this place that the city was to be built.

Deadman and Thousand Lake Mountain.

CLEVELAND, Emery County, UTAH,—The Shivwits Indian
Reservation.

In 1889, some Oceanians from Hawaii, converted to the Morman religion, founded the city of Iosepa.

A gray Pontiac driven by an old Negro passes an old black Hudson driven by a young white man going much faster than the daytime speed limit, "go straight ahead."

MILFORD, Mormon state,—the Koosharem Indian Reservation.

In 1893, leprosy broke out among the Hawaiian Mormons of Iosepa.

Through Sears, Roebuck & Co., you can obtain the new "Map of the United States" school bag, "now it is so easy for children to learn something about their country! Bright colored map on the back. Seals of eighteen governmental departments, photographs of the Capitol and the White House on the front . . ."

MILFORD, WYOMING, the least heavily populated
            state after Alaska and Nevada,—the Wind
River Indian Reservation.

Still a little red sunlight on the mountain tops.

Shoshone National Forest.

On a dead branch, a sharp-shinned hawk, tearing apart a small bird with a
purple breast.

NEWCASTLE.

NEWCASTLE, Iron County, UTAH, a desert state.—the Ute
            Indian Reservation.

*In 1916, when a Mormon temple was built in Hawaii, the last survivors of
the Iosepa colony returned to their country, abandoning the town to its
ghosts.*

Sand Pass, Thomas Pass.

            NEW CASTLE, COLO.,—Southern Ute Indian Res-
                ervation.

ALPINE, UTAH.

*In Mountain Meadows, in September 1857, a group of 140 emigrants from
Arkansas were stopped by the Federal troops about to invade the Mormon
state because the Easterners were scandalized by the practice of polygamy.
After a siege lasting several days, the emigrants were massacred. The only
survivors, 17 children, were taken back to Arkansas.*

Indian Peak.—When it is seven P.M. in

RANDOLPH,
            already nine P.M. in
RANDOLPH, Eastern Time.

Are you asleep?

            RANDOLPH.

*The trial of Susanna Martin, Salem, June 29, 1692:
"11) Jervis Ring testified that about seven or eight years ago he*

had ben severall times afflicted in the night time by some body or some thing coming up upon him when he was in bed and did sorely afflict by Laying upon him and he could neither move nor speak while it was upon him but sometimes made a kind of noyse; but one time in the night it came upon me as at other times and I did then see the person of Susanna Martin of Amesbury, and she came to this deponent and took him by the hand and bitt him by the finger by force and the print of the bite is yet to be seen on the little finger of his right hand . . ."

CHESTER, Windsor County.

Asleep . . .

CHESTER, MASS., New England.

"12) But beyond all these evidences there was a very marvelous testimony of one Joseph Ring produced upon this occasion. This man had been strangely transported by demons into unknown places where he saw meetings and feastings and many strange sights and from August Last he was Dum and could not speake till this last Aprill. He also relates that there was a certain Thos. Hardy which said Hardy demanded of this deponent two shillings and with that dreadfull noyse and hideous shapes of creatures and fireball. About Oct following coming from Hampton in Salsbury pine plane a company of horses with men and women upon them overtook this deponent and the aforsead Hardy being one of them came to this deponent as before and demanded his two shillings of him and threatened to tear him to pieces to whom this deponent made no answer and so he and the rest went away and left this deponent. After this this deponent had divers strange appearances which did force him away with them into unknown places where he saw meetings and he also relates that there did use to come to him a man that did present him a book to which he would have him sett his hand with promise of anything that he would have and there were presented all Delectable things and persons. And places imaginall, but he refusing it would usually and with most dreadful shapes noyses and screeking that almost scared him out of his witts and this was the usuall manner of proceeding with him and one time the book was brought and a pen offered him and to his apprehension there was blod in the Ink horne but he never toucht the pen. He further say that they never told him what he should writt nor he could not speak to ask them what he should writ. He farther say in several their merry meetings he have seen Susanas Martin appear among

*them. And in that house did also appear the aforesayd Hardy
and another female person which the deponent did not know,
there they had a good fire and drink it seemed to be sider their
continued most part of the night said Martin being then in her
natural shape and talking as shee used to do, but toward the
morning the said Martine went from the fire made a noyse and
turned into the shape of a black hog and went away and so did
the other to persons go away and this deponent was strangely
caryed away also and the first place he knew was by Salmuel
woods house in Amsbury . . ."*

CHESTER, CONN., New England.

RICHMOND.

RICHMOND, Chittenden County, VERMONT, New England,—
    the border of the Canadian province of Quebec, one
of the least heavily populated states.

The woods at night.

An old overloaded jeep parked beside the highway; another jeep passes,
"turn left."

RICHMOND.
53,000 Norwegians,
    410,000 Poles,
the Greeks who read the "National Herald,"
    the Hungarians who read the "Amerikai
    Magyar Nepszava,"
        the Italians who read "Il Pro-
        gresso."
SATURDAY EVENING POST SATURDAY EVENING POST SATUR

Colombo's steaks,
    Quo Vadis, French cuisine,
        East of Suez, Indonesian,
White Turkey, American specialties,
    Schine's, Irish
        Grotta Azzurra, Italian.

The planes leaving for Munich,
    for Léopoldville,
    coming from Beirut,
        from Athens.

418 / MICHEL BUTOR

WBNX, Ukranian broadcasts,
   WEVD, Norwegian broadcasts,
     WFUV-FM, Polish broadcasts.

The ships sailing for Boston,
   for Mobile,
    arriving from Philadelphia,
     from Providence.

Even cheaper clothes for women at Macy's, Saks-34th,
Gimbels and Ohrbach's.

The Empire State Building: the most powerful search-
   lights in the world, a city of shops on the
   street floor.

Loew's Commodore,
   Art Theater,
     Academy of Music.

The subways coming from the far ends of the Bronx,
Brooklyn and Queens:
     Northern Boulevard,
   Atlantic Avenue,
Intervale Avenue,
     46 Street,
   De Kalb Avenue,
Prospect Avenue,
     Steinway Street,
   Myrtle Avenue,
Jackson Avenue.
     36 Street,
   (crossing the East River)
   Broadway.
     Queens Plaza.
Museum of Natural History: superb wax reproduction
(life size) of a flowering magnolia.

   Alone tonight, baby?
     Thirsty?
   Terribly!
     Do you know them?
That's what he said on television.
   I can't remember their names.
     Great!
   Not bad . . .

Bronx Zoo:
griffon vultures,
> *bearded vultures,*
>> *Pondicherry vultures.*

Drink Coca-Cola!
> *Drink Pepsi-Cola!*
>> *Kleenex!*

CHESTER, Orange County.

85,000 Rumanians,
the Hungarians who read "Az Ember,"
Sea Fare, fish,
the planes leaving for Chicago,
for Istanbul,
WEVD, Spanish broadcasts,
Danny's Hide-a-way, steaks,
the ships leaving for Naples,
for Tangiers,
Irving Place Theater.

> *950,000 Russians,*
> *the Italians who read the "Corriere degli*
> *Italiani,"*
> *Twenty-One, French cuisine,*
> *the planes coming from Kansas City,*
>> *from Teheran,*
> *WFUV-FM, Russian broadcasts,*
> *Shanghai, Chinese dishes,*
> *the ships coming from Genoa,*
>> *from Madeira,*
> *Gramercy Theater.*

>> *The Portuguese who read, "A*
>> *Luta,"*
>> *San Marino, Italian cuisine,*
>> *WHOM, Polish broadcasts,*
>> *Giovanni, Italian specialties,*
>> *the Empire State Building: 35,-*
>> *000 visitors a day, coming from*
>> *every country in the world,*
>> *Murray Hill Theater.*

HOLIDAY HOLIDAY HOLIDAY HOLIDAY HOLIDAY HOLIDA

Cheapest clothes for women, at Klein's.
The subways coming from the Bronx, lower Manhat-
tan, Queens:
                    Courthouse Square,
          Prince Street,
Third Avenue,
                    Ely Avenue,
          Eighth Street,
149 Street,
                         (crossing the East River)
                    Lexington Avenue,
          Union Square,
(crossing the Harlem River)
135 Street.
                    Fifth Avenue,
          23 Street.
               Seventh Avenue.

Museum of Natural History: Audubon Gallery: collection of
objects relating to the life and work of John James Audubon;
Audubon's original paintings and drawings, and those of his
son; some bronze and copper plates used in printing "Birds of
America"; portrait of the engraver Robert Havell; plates showing
Audubon armed with his rifle.

Bronx Zoo:
white-headed vulture,
          white Egyptian vulture,
                    black East African vulture.

Smoke Chesterfield,
          Smoke Lucky Strike,
                    Smoke Salem!
          There must be a mistake.
                    Not too tired?
          I've reserved a room.
                    Did you hear?
They had to send a bill.
                    Shut up!
          She still hasn't come in.
                    What can she do?
          I've rarely been so bored.

New York Historical Society: sleds and prints of New
York winter scenes.

RANDOLPH, Chattaraugus, N.Y.,—the Saint Regis Indian Reservation.

65,000 Scots,
the Japanese who read "Hokubei Shimpo,"
Stouffer's, American specialties,
the planes leaving for Detroit,
                for Karachi,
WEVD, Swedish broadcasts,
Hickory House, steaks,
the ships leaving for the Bahamas,
                for Bermuda,
Cameo Theater,
the subway coming from Harlem:
125 Street,
116 Street,
110 Street,
Bronx Zoo: mountain zebra,
Fly Air France!
THE NEW YORKER THE NEW YORKER THE NEW YORKER THE NEW YO
                25,000 Spaniards
                the Lithuanians who read "Tevyne,"
                Voisin, French cuisine,
                the planes coming from Montreal,
                                from Honolulu,
                WFUV-FM, Spanish broadcasts,
                Miyako, Japanese dishes,
                the ships coming from the Azores,
                                from the Windward Islands,
                Loew's Lexington,
                the subway coming from downtown New
                York:
                28 Street,
                33 Street,
                49 Street,
                57 Street,
                Bronx Zoo: Grant's zebra,
                Fly Pan American!
Fruits and vegetables: Washington, Fulton and Vesey
Streets.

                        The Norwegians who read the
                        "Nordisk Tidende,"
                        Café Geiger, German cuisine,
                        Empire State Building: 16,000

> *tenants,*
> *WHOM, Russian broadcasts,*
> *Alamo, Mexican specialties,*
> *New York Historical Society:*
> *old fire pumps,*
> *R.K.O. 58 Street Theater,*
> *the subway from uptown New*
> *York:*
> *50 Street,*
> *42 Street,*
> *Pennsylvania Station,*
> *23 Street,*
> *14 Street,*
> *Bronx Zoo: Grevy's zebra,*
> *Fly TWA!*

Museum of Natural History: hall of human biology: growth and development of the individual, racial classification of man; genetics and mixture of races; population problems; development of a human embryo; life-size figures showing the chief racial types.

New York City Museum: gallery devoted to the history of the fire department of New York.

> *Have you been here long?*
> *Just a minute.*
> *When are you leaving?*
> *I was late.*
> *A last glass.*
> *He had to sell his car.*
> *Not another.*
> *We're coming.*
> *I'd never have believed it.*
> *What will you have?*

Shell,—a huge Nash collides with an old one already going much faster than the 50-mile speed limit,—through Montgomery Ward, you can obtain the booklet "Sports Cars of the Future," by Strother MacMinn, "deals with the cars of your dreams planned by European and American builders," as well as the prototypes of the makes:
—Corvette,

WINDSOR, Green Mountain State.

La Salle II,

The covered bridges at night.

—Oldsmobile F 88,

Through Sears, Roebuck & Co., a "Lady Kenmore" sewing machine, "stitches with inconceivable daintiness. The 20 styles illustrated on the dial can be modified and combined to produce countless intricate decorative variations. You can embroider in two colors thanks to twin needles . . . vary the size of the stitch with the regulator . . ."

—Chrysler Gran Turismo. Also discusses mechanical elements and body design likely to appear in future cars.

WINDSOR, Broome County.

> *Hep!*
> > *Miss!*
> *This isn't for you?*
> > *Oh, thank you!*
> *Don't you feel well?*
> *They had to sell their apartment.*
> *Go home.*
> > *Go home!*
> *Sleep.*
> > *If you think . . .*
> *Did you think . . .*

55,000 Swedes,
> *15,000 Swiss,*
> > *32,000 Turks,*
the Poles who read the "Nowy Swiat,"
> *the Spanish who read "La Prensa,"*
> > *the Swedes who read "Norden,"*
Keen's, steaks and chops,
> *Côte Basque, French cuisine,*
> > *Berkowitz, Rumanian,*
the planes leaving for Lima,
> *for Helsinki,*
> > *coming from Bogotá,*
> > *from Oslo,*
> > *Chrysler Building, 77 floors,*
> > *60 Wall Street, 66 floors,*

WEVD, Ukrainian broadcasts,
  WHOM, Spanish broadcasts,
    WWRL, Greek broadcasts,
Pen and Pencil, steaks,
  Balalaika, Russian cooking,
    Sevilla, Spanish specialties,
the ships leaving for Bristol,
  for Barcelona,
    coming from Cardiff,
      from Piraeus,
        the Seagram Building, like a
        huge block of solidified whis-
        key.
        On top of the Mutual Life In-
        surance Building, the green star
        if the weather is going to be
        fair, orange for cloudy, winking
        orange for rain, white for snow.
THE MAGAZINE OF FANTASY AND SCIENCE FICTION THE M
     EBONY EBONY EBONY EBONY EBONY EBONY EB
         MAD MAD MAD MAD MAD MAD M

Flowers, 28 Street and Sixth Avenue,
  · linen, Grand Street,
        silver, Lexington Avenue be-
        tween 56 and 58 Street, and on
        Nassau Street,
Plaza Theater,
  Baronet Theater,
        Trans-Lux 52 Street Theater,
the subways going to the Bronx, Queens and Brooklyn:
86 Street,
      Fifth Avenue,
        West Fourth Street,
96 Street,
    Lexington Avenue,
      Spring Street,
103 Street.
      (crossing the East River)
      Queensboro Plaza,
        Canal Street,
      Beebe Avenue.
        Chambers Street,
        Broadway, Nassau Street.
Bronx Zoo: cassowaries,

      yaks,
              ornithorynchus,
New York Historical Society: Audubon Gallery: all the
original drawings for "Birds of America,"
            New York City Museum: 1920 doll's house, made by
            Varrie Walter Stettheimer; note the ballroom painting
            which is a real Marcel Duchamp,
                   Museum of Natural History:
                   Planetarium: a new show each
                   month:
                   Trip to Mercury,
                   Trip to the Moon,
                   The End of the World . . .
Fly Sabena,
     Fly BOAC,
        Fly KLM.

In April 1524, The Florentine navigator Verrazzano piloted the French caravel Dauphine *to the discovery of the port of New York and named the place Angoulême in honor of François I, King of France.*

The drive-in movie is over.

NEWPORT.

NEWPORT, county seat of Orleans County, VT., ski state.

The mountains at night.

NEWPORT.

O night!

NEWPORT.

The sea at night.

BRISTOL, Addison County.

The streams at night.

BRISTOL, Grafton County.

Mother night!

> BRISTOL, ME.,—the border of the Cana-
> dian provinces of Quebec and
> New Brunswick,—the Penobscot Indian
> Reservation.

> *The rocks at night.*

> RICHMOND, Cheshire County, N.H.

The highway at night.

> Texaco,—a Kaiser passes a shiny Hudson.

The movement of the windshield wipers.

> RICHMOND.

The water streaming over the glass.

> CHESTER, Rockingham County.

> *The street lamp at night.*

The water streaming over the highway.

> DANVILLE.—When it is ten P.M. in

DANVILLE,

> ten P.M. in
DANVILLE.

"Notes on the State of Virginia":
". . . The improvement of the blacks in body and mind, in the first instance of their mixture with the whites, has been observed by every one, and proves that their inferiority is not the effect merely of their condition of life. We know that among the Romans, about the Augustan age especially, the condition of their slaves was much more deplorable than that of the blacks on the continent of America. The two sexes were confined in separate apartments, because to raise a child cost the master more than to buy one. Cato, for a very restricted indulgence to his slaves in this particular, took from them a certain price. But in this country the slaves multiply as fast as the free inhabitants. Their situation and manners place the commerce between the two sexes almost without restraint . . ."

Thomas Jefferson.

At Monticello, Thomas Jefferson set a light stucco frieze around the ceiling of his hall: griffons, vases, foliage and torches.

DANVILLE.

Sleep.

DANVILLE.

Sleep.

DANVILLE, KANS.

GLASGOW, Rockbridge County.

At Monticello, Thomas Jefferson installed the first parquet flooring in the United States in his salon.

". . . The same Cato, on a principle of economy, always sold his sick and superannuated slaves. He gives it as a standing precept to a master visiting his farm, to sell his old oxen, old wagons, old tools, old and diseased servants, and everything else become useless . . . The American slaves cannot enumerate this among the injuries and insults they receive . . ."

Thomas Jefferson.

GLASGOW, KY.

The falls at night.

GLASGOW, MO.

The insomnia.

FRANKLIN.

Green light.

FRANKLIN.

FRANKLIN, Southampton County, VIRGINIA.

". . . It was the common practice to expose in the island Aesculapius, in the Tyber, diseased slaves whose cure was like to become tedious. The emperor Claudius by an edict, gave freedom to such of them as should recover, and first declared that if any person chose to kill rather than to expose them, it should not be deemed homicide. The exposing them is a crime of which no

instance has existed with us; and were it to be followed by death, it would be punished capitally. We are told of a certain Vedius Pollio, who, in the presence of Augustus, would have given a slave as food to his fish, for having broken a glass. With the Romans, the regular method of taking the evidence of their slaves was under torture. Here it has been thought better never to resort to their evidence. When a master was murdered, all his slaves, in the same house, or within hearing, were condemned to death. Here punishment falls on the guilty only, and as precise proof is required against him as against a freeman. Yet notwithstanding these and other discouraging circumstances among the Romans, their slaves were often their rarest artists. They excelled too in science, insomuch as to be usually employed as tutors to their masters' children. Epictetus, Terence, and Phaedrus were slaves. But they were of the race of whites . . ."

Thomas Jefferson.

Thomas Jefferson,
        at Monticello, above the door from the salon to the dining room, under an elegant pediment, set a light stucco frieze of bucrania, vases, shields, helmets, whose elements were repeated over the mantelpiece.

FRANKLIN.

The smells of the night.

FRANKLIN, ALA.

BRISTOL, where you can order apple ice cream in the Howard Johnson Restaurant.

At Monticello, Thomas Jefferson had a white stucco eagle set in the entrance hall ceiling, surrounded by eighteen gold stars and holding in its talons the suspension pulleys of a lamp to be raised and lowered which he had purchased in Paris.

Thomas Jefferson.

". . . It is not their condition then, but nature, which has produced the distinction. Whether further observation will or will not verify the conjecture, that nature has been less bountiful to them in the endowments of the head, I believe that in those of the heart she will be found to have done them justice. That disposition to theft with which they have been branded, must be ascribed to their situation, and not to any depravity of the moral sense. The man in whose favor no laws of property exist, probably feels himself less bound to respect those made in favor of others. When arguing for ourselves, we lay it down as a fundamental, that laws, to be just, must give a

reciprocation of right; that, without this, they are mere arbitrary rules of conduct, founded in force, and not in conscience; and it is a problem which I give to the master to solve, whether the religious precepts against the violation of property were not framed for him as well as his slave? And whether the slave may not as justifiably take a little from one who has taken all from him, as he may slay one who would slay him? That a change in the relations in which a man is placed should change his ideas of moral right or wrong, is neither new, nor peculiar to the color of the blacks. Homer tells us it was so two thousand six hundred years ago:

> *'Jove fix'd it certain, that whatever day*
> *Makes man a slave, takes half his worth away.'*

But the slaves of which Homer speaks were whites . . ."

Thomas Jefferson.

Through Sears, Roebuck & Co., you can obtain painting equipment that will give hours of pleasure to your whole family: "merely follow the numbers to have fun and relax. Our finest selection: 2 large prepared panels, 30 numbered colors, 3 washable brushes, instructions; choose from:

—bouquet of flowers,
       roses,
—Madonna and Child,

BRISTOL, TENN.

       the Good Shepherd,
—winter shadows,
       fisherman's luck,

If you're not asleep . . .

—the Last Supper,
       Christ with children,
—decorative owls,

NEWPORT.

       decorative raccoons,
—the fisherman up in his tree,
       the fisherman on the bank."

NEWPORT, Giles County, VA.

"... *Notwithstanding these considerations which must weaken their respect for the laws of property, we find among them numerous instances of the most rigid integrity, and as many as among their better instructed masters, of benevolence, gratitude, and unshaken fidelity. The opinion that they are inferior in the faculties of reason and imagination, must be hazarded with great diffidence. To justify a general conclusion, requires many observations, even where the subject may be submitted to the anatomical knife, to optical glasses, to analysis by fire or by solvents. How much more then where it is a faculty, not a substance, we are examining; where it eludes the research of all the senses; where the conditions of its existence are variously combined; where the effects of those which are present or absent bid defiance to calculation; let me add too, as a circumstance of great tenderness, where our conclusion would degrade a whole race of men from the rank in the scale of beings which their Creator may perhaps have given them . . ."*

Thomas Jefferson.

Thomas Jefferson,
        at Monticello, over the mantelpiece of the dining room set exquisite panels of blue-and-white Wedgwood representing Apollo and the Muses.

Or a group of three panels, eighteen jars of paint; choose from "Distant lands:
        —Chinese pagoda,
        —the old mill,
        —lofty mountains,

NEWPORT.

—Biblical subjects:
        —Christ,
        —the Good Shepherd,
        —Jesus in meditation,
        Thieves . . .

—Seascapes:
        —Clipper ship,
        —rocks and beaches,
        —harbor scene,

NEWPORT, S.C.

—Horses:
        —pride of the stable,

—out to grass,
—Derby winner,

Prowlers . . .

—Far West:
—majestic canyons,
—heavenly waterfalls,
—enchanted valleys,

WINDSOR. State Flower: dogwood.

—Holland:
—Delft,
—windmills,
—canals," page 1037.

At Monticello, in the dining room, on each side of the mantelpiece, Thomas Jefferson ingeniously concealed small bottle elevators connecting with the wine cellar.

". . . To our reproach it must be said, that though for a century and a half we have had under our eyes the races of black and of red men, they have never yet been viewed by us as subjects of natural history. I advance it, therefore, as a suspicion only, that the blacks, whether originally a distinct race, or made distinct by times and circumstances, are inferior to the whites in the endowments both of body and mind. It is not against experience to suppose that different species of the same genus, or varieties of the same species, may possess different qualifications . . ."
Thomas Jefferson.

Or a group of four small panels framed in black plastic; choose from: "Birds,

WINDSOR, N.C.

—Dogs,

Murderers . . .

—Parisian scenes,

WINDSOR.

—Horses."

FRANKLIN.

RICHMOND, where you can order pear ice cream in the Howard
        Johnson Restaurant, county seat of Henrico County,
capital of the state, VA.

"... Will not a lover of natural history then, one who views the gradations
in all the races of animals with the eye of philosophy, excuse an effort to
keep those in the department of man as distinct as nature has formed them?
This unfortunate difference of color, and perhaps of faculty, is a powerful
obstacle to the emancipation of these people ..."
                                                        Thomas Jefferson.

Thomas Jefferson,
        at Monticello, situated the slaves' quarters under the southern
terrace, so that their comings and goings would not spoil the view.

VIENNA, Fairfax County.

"... Many of their advocates, while they wish to vindicate the liberty of
human nature, are anxious also to preserve its dignity and beauty. Some of
these, embarrassed by the question, 'What further is to be done with them?'
join themselves in opposition with those who are actuated by sordid avarice
only. Among the Romans emancipation required but one effort. The slave,
when made free, might mix with, without staining the blood of his master.
But with us a second is necessary, unknown to history. When freed, he is to
be removed beyond the reach of mixture ..."
                                                        Thomas Jefferson.

Thomas Jefferson,
        on January 10, 1806, being then President of the United States,
wrote to the chiefs of the Cherokee Nation:
"... Tell all your chiefs, your men, women and children, that I take them
by the hand and hold it fast. That I am their father, wish their happiness
and well-being, and am always ready to promote their good. My children, I
thank you for your visit and pray to the Great Spirit who made us all and
planted us all in this land to live together like brothers that He will conduct
you safely to your homes, and grant you to find your families and your
friends in good health."

VIENNA, MD.—When it is eleven P.M. in

CHESTER, where you can order pistachio ice cream in the How-
        ard Johnson Restaurant,

IN THE CORRIDORS OF THE UNDERGROUND: THE ESCALATOR
by Alain Robbe-Grillet
(b. 1922)

A motionless group, at the bottom of the long, iron-gray staircase, whose steps become level, one after the other, as they get to the top, and disappear, one by one, with a sound of well-oiled machinery, and with a heavy, and yet at the same time abrupt, regularity, which gives the impression of being quite rapid at the place where the steps disappear, one after the other, beneath the horizontal surface, but which seems, on the contrary, to be of extreme slowness, and also to have lost all its jerkiness, to the eye which travels down the series of successive steps, and rediscovers, right at the bottom of the long, rectilinear staircase, as if in the same place, the same group, whose position hasn't varied in the slightest degree—a motionless group, standing on the bottom steps, which has only just got on to the escalator, has immediately become petrified for the duration of the mechanical journey, has suddenly come to a standstill in the midst of its bustle and rush—as if the fact of setting foot on the moving steps had suddenly paralyzed the bodies forming the group, one after another, into positions both relaxed and tense, in suspense, representing a temporary halt in the midst of an interrupted journey, while the whole rectilinear staircase continues its climb, ascends regularly with a movement that is uniform, slow, almost imperceptible, and, in relation to the vertical bodies, oblique.

These bodies are five in number, grouped on three or four steps, on the left-hand side of these steps, at a greater or lesser distance from the handrail, which is also moving at the same speed, though here the movement is made even more imperceptible, more uncertain, by the very shape of the handrail, an ordinary thick strip of black rubber which has a smooth surface, two rectilinear edges, and no fixed point against which it is possible to determine its speed, unless it is the two hands which are placed on it, about a yard apart, at the very bottom of the narrow, oblique strip whose immobility everywhere else seems obvious, and which yet advances continuously, smoothly, at the same time as the whole of the rest of the system.

The higher of these two hands belongs to a man in a gray suit, a gray that is rather pale, uncertain, yellowish under the yellow light, who has a step to himself at the head of the group, and who holds his body very erect, with his legs together, his left arm bent round close against his chest, the hand holding a newspaper folded in four, over which his face is inclined in what seems a somewhat excessive fashion, so exaggerated is the downward flexion of his neck, the chief effect of which is to bring well into view not his forehead and nose, but the top of his cranium and his large bald patch, a big circle of pink and shining scalp which is transversally intersected by a breakaway wisp of thin red hair sticking to the skin.

But the face is suddenly raised, in the direction of the top of the staircase, showing the forehead, the nose, the mouth—all the features, which, however, are expressionless, and it stays there for a few instants, certainly for longer than would be necessary to make sure that the ascent is still by no means at an end and so allows the continuance of the reading of the article that has been begun, which the person finally decides to do, abruptly lowering his head again, though his countenance, now hidden once more, has not given the slightest sign of the kind of attention that has been paid for a moment to the surroundings, which perhaps were not even noticed by those wide-open, staring eyes with the blank look. In their place, in the same position as it was at the beginning, the round cranium, with its bald zone in the middle, now reappears.

As if the man, in the middle of the reading to which he has returned, has then suddenly thought about the enormous, empty, rectilinear staircase, which he has just contemplated without seeing, and wants, by a sort of delayed-action reflex, to look behind him, to find out whether there is a similar desert in that direction, he turns round, as abruptly as he just now raised his head, and without moving the rest of his body any more than he did then. He can thus observe that there are four people behind him, that they are motionless, and gently ascending at the same speed as he, and he immediately returns to his original position and to his perusal of the newspaper. The other passengers haven't budged.

In the second row, after an empty step, come a woman and a child. The woman is exactly behind the man with the paper, but she hasn't put her right hand on the rail; her arm hangs down at her side and is holding a kind of handbag, or string shopping bag, or spheroid parcel, the precise nature of whose brownish mass cannot be determined, as it is almost completely hidden behind the man's gray trouser leg. The woman is neither young nor old; her face looks tired. She is dressed in a red mackintosh and on her head is a multi-colored scarf which is knotted beneath her chin. On her left, the child, a boy of about twelve, wearing a high-necked sweater and tight blue jeans, holds his head either tilted to one side, against his shoulder, with his face raised toward his right, toward the profile of the woman, or else slightly further round toward the bare wall, which is completely covered with small white ceramic rectangles and which is passing by at an even speed, above the handrail, between the woman and the man with the paper.

Next, and still at the same speed, against this shiny white background cut up into countless little rectangles, all identical and drawn up in methodical lines, the horizontal joins being continuous and the vertical joins alternate, come the silhouettes of two men in dark lounge suits, the first standing behind the woman in red, two steps lower down, with his right hand on the rail, then, after three empty steps, the second, standing behind the child, his head coming very little higher than the child's thonged sandals, in other words, a bit lower than his knees, which are indicated at the back of his blue jeans by numerous horizontal puckers creasing the material.

And the rigid group continues to ascend, and each individual's pose remains as invariable as his position in the group. But, as the man in front has turned round to look behind him, the man at the bottom, who is probably wondering what the object of this abnormal interest is, also turns round. All he can see is the long series of successive steps and, at the very bottom of the rectilinear, iron-gray staircase, standing on the bottom steps, a motionless group that has only just got on to the escalator, is ascending at the same slow and sure speed, and stays the same distance away.

Translated by Bruce Morrissette

ANTI-FICTION AND TROPISMS
by Carlos Fontana
(b. 1937)

MANDALA

an anti-story

n he wondered if he dared do it ev
eryone was against it what would h
is wife say and the brother the un
iversity administrators   out there
the city the world but the thought
of it intrigued and disturbed him
it would not let him rest finally
after drawing mandalas at work for
an hour he resolved to do it i sha
ll never know or find my limits or
who i am until i do he said he did
it then his wife and the universit
y administrators called the police
then they took him away hes still
there thats where he wrote this st
ory now read it again and put in t
he pu n c t u a t i   o

FAREWELL TO ARMS AND LEGS

an anti-novel not by hemingway

Should he claim to be a c.o. or just let them take him? Besides, he would get the g.i. bill and it would pay for his last year of school. It was a difficult and knotty problem. "What the hell," he said and finally decided to go ahead and go. He was killed in some kind of mission. Search and destroy they call it, I think.

TROPISM I: A MOTH FOR STRINDBERG

All is silence in the jar whose partially unscrewed jelly top has eleven irregular holes punched with a Phillips screwdriver. The mantis systematically separates the cricket's parts, first removing its head, the decapitated body twitching sporadically, its hind legs embracing the mantis. With flying insects the mantis first removes the tissue wings, then the head. The mantis has difficulty with the hard inedible cricket's skull. He contemplates it for several seconds, turning it around, looking for a place of entry. He picks away the eyes, leaving inverted black bowls. Then he turns the head over and consumes the contents of the skull, leaving it hard and shiny and black and clean. He drops the empty cavity by a leaf at the bottom of the jar. Because the mantis will not eat what it has not killed itself, there are two dead intact flies beside the leaf nearest the twig, whose color and configuration the mantis closely approximates. Yesterday he was green because the twig was not there, but the leaves were. He draws the dull yellow jelly-like fluid from the cricket's neck cavity as with a straw. Almost satiated, he rests, the cricket's body moving from time to time, but less than before. The mantis turns his head to observe the kneeling man and two boys who observe him. The man thinks. All is silence. Separation. Assignment. The distribution and redistribution of parts. The older boy asks, "Does Strindberg know I am his master? Does he think I am his father as you are mine? I must catch a moth for Strindberg."

TROPISM V: ELM TREE

The light is after all still red and the children are still there and the confused branches reach for the sureness of the ground for the sky is very far away. The man waits inside his automobile as the schoolchildren pass in front of him, the large diseased elm tree weighted down by the first snow arching out beyond above him branching down, now one centimeter. It is marked with a large yellow chalked X for cutting. Many trees down the street are similarly marked except for a single tree at the opposite end of the street some of whose diseased limbs have been removed from an otherwise healthy trunk, the sawdust still peppering the rosebushes underneath. For these it is too late. Yet they have not been set to the teeth of onehanded saws. He watches as the children delay the beginning of the school day, one child dropping books after having been pushed by another but he is not angry and tries to snowball the wet snow and misses when he throws it but laughs. Slowly, infinitesimally, one centimeter, now two, the huge, arched blackness of the tree's dead limbs weigh out beyond, above the automobile. The man waits. They will be late he thinks. I will be late. But we all do these things. All of us and then he thinks what do they know of life. It is better to know he thinks. The sky is overcast and the dark skinlike bark of the tree cannot reach for the saving rays of the sun and the children are still there and the light is after all still red and the confused branches reach surely for the sureness of the ground for the sky is very far away. For these trees it is too late. On someone's desk the cutting orders wait. Now they are picked up. Where can they go? They will wait. The trees will wait. The man waits inside. And slowly, infinitesimally, one centimeter, now two, now three the huge arched blackness of the tree's releasing and inverting distance, and dark skin, and heavy weight press down upon the automobile. Soon the hard and dark skin of the dead disease inevitable and destined only for one time and one place and this and this the painted metal skin will become one again. The man waits inside. What do they know of death or they would not play with snow he thinks as slowly infinitesimally one centimeter now two now three now four now more the huge and heavy blackness of the tree's dead and diseased and insistent and burdened limbs weigh on the air it cannot hold and moves from underneath it has itself to care for and it groans. No. It is better to be young he

AN OPERA
by Emmett Williams
(b. 1925)

AUTHOR'S NOTE

"An Opera" is a mystery story—among other things—in which the object of search, the dot on an i, is presented visually throughout the progress of the story. The story not only illustrates itself, but the "illustration"—the basic metaphor—is also used as a percussion score when the work is performed.

It was first published in a German translation in 1960, and in March of that year first performed as a farce ("Der verlorene i-Punkt") at the Keller-Festspiele in the artists' cellar club in Darmstadt. The actor Gerd Winter

*attempted to read aloud a microcard version of the text,
Claus Bremer and Daniel Spoerri held up a giant score that
extended from one end of the stage to the other, I pretended
to interpret the wobbly score with a collapsing tenor
recorder, and the audience tried to follow the tiny libretti
in flickering candlelight.*

*The first "legitimate" performance took place at the
Städtisches Museum in Wiesbaden in 1962, during the first
"Festum Fluxorum" or Fluxus Festival. The performance
was all but broken up by students who jumped up on the
stage and sang college songs, and a brave lad who set fire
to the 15-foot-long score.*

*The most dramatic performance was at Aachen on
the 20th of July, 1964, which turned out to be the 20th
anniversary of the plot to assassinate Adolf Hitler. This
deluxe version, with narrator, actors, and the author as
drummer all comfortably installed in plush chairs and a
sofa, and placards to indicate scene changes, would have
lasted close to 3 hours; but the performance was halted by
the police 30 minutes along in the confusion and rioting
that followed a bloody attack on artist Joseph Beuys by a
student from the Technical University. The elaborate
multicolored score that I had painstakingly drawn out by
hand, and the placards, were destroyed by students, some
of whom mistook my steady bongo-drumming for a
comment pro or con Hitlerism, militarism, fascism,
communism, Americanism, pacifism, or some such thing,
or combination of things.*

yes, it was still there. shutting his eyes would not make it flee
once he opened them again. it had no father, no mother, yet there it was, just
as he had conceived it between the unwritten sheets. he stroked it gently,
then lifted it tenderly to the night table, where he placed it, without spilling a
drop of its efficacy, plop in the middle of a folded kleenex. it was sweating,
so he wiped it with his index finger. alas! the dot was gone. there was no
mistaking it as he bent closer and saw the stump, the bare stump of the i
without its head. it had lost itself in the grain of the wood. he sprang out of
bed and switched on the overhead light. covering his nakedness from the
newborn invalid with his left hand, he lifted everything off the table with his
right and placed the objects, one by one, as they were on the tabletop, onto
the bed. with his free hand he went over every inch of the tabletop. to no
avail. he bent down and licked the table, licking from left to right, right to
left, up and down and back again, slowly, then frantically, feverishly, in and
out faster and faster, coating the surface with saliva and sweat. he pulled his

tongue back in suddenly. he rushed up to the mirror and thrust it out. he could see nothing unusual. but the painful throbbing spread. he looked at it again. no dot. now his teeth hurt, too. his lower jaw. left ear. he fled to the end of the hall, where the young woman lived, and entered without knocking.

"wake . up . . wake . . . up . . . .," he implored.

her left eye opened, then the right. "what do you want at this ungodly hour?"

"you . . . . . must . . . . . . come . . . . with . . . . me . . . .
. . quickly . . . .," he pleaded.

"pull yourself together, man. get under the cover and catch a little sleep."

"but . . . . you . . . . must . . . . come
. . . . with . . . . me . . . . at . .
. . . . once . . . . "

"you can't be that hard up."

"you . . . . don't . . . . understand . . . . its . . . . my . . . . .
. . . . tongue . . . . my . . . .
. . . . teeth . . . . my . . . . . .
. . . . gums . . . . my .
. . . . left . . . .
. . . ear . . . . and . . . .
. . . . it's . . . . spreading
. . . . to . . . .
. . . . my . . . . throat
. . . . help! . . . .
. . . . me . . . .
. . . . . do . . . . something . .
. . . . pull . . . .
. . . . it . . . .
. . . . out . . . .
. . . . pull . . . .
. . . . it . . . .
. . . . out . . . . please
. . . . help . . . . . .
. . . . me . . . .
. . . . "

"calm down a bit, for pity's sake. what is it you want me to pull out?"

"look . . . .
. at . . . . it .
. . . . do . . . .
. . . . you . . . . .
. . . . see . . . . .
. . . . it . . . . . .
. . . . ?"

"i see a tongue, that's all i see. now look, i don't even know who you are. either cool off and get in bed with me for a little while or go back where you came from. i just hit the pad and i intend to get some more sleep." she rolled over and pulled the pillow over her head.

"you're . . . .
. . . . a . . . .
. . . . murderer . . . .
. . . ."

she sat up suddenly. "how do you know?"

"how . . . .
. . . . do . . . .
. . . . i . . . .
. . . . know . . . .
. . . . what . . . .
. . . . ?"

"how do you know that i killed him?"

"i . . . .
. . . . couldn't . . . .
. . . . care . . . .
. . . . less . . . .
about . . . .
. . . . whom . . . .
. . . . you've . . . .
. . . . killed .
. . . .
. . . . but . . . .
. . . . unless . . . .
. . . . you .
. . . . help . . . .
. . . . me . . . .
. . . get . . . .
. . . . the . . . .
. . . . dot . . .
. . . . off . . . .
. . . . my . . . .
. . . .
. . . . tongue . . . .
. . . . it . . . .
. . . .
. . . . will . . . .
. . . . die . . . .

. . . .
. . . ."

"what are you talking about? what will die?"

"come . . . .
. . . . with . . . .
. . . .
. . . . me . . . .
. . . . and . . . . .
. . . .
. . . . i'll . . . .
. . . .
. . . . show . . . .
. . . . you . . . .
. . . .
. . . ."

she pulled herself out of bed. "all right, let's go", she said wearily. "i won't get any peace with you in this state of mind."

"but . . . . , ...
. . . . you're . . . .
. . . .
. . . . naked . . . .
. . . .
. . . . !"

"so are you."

"but . . . .
. . . . you're . . . . . .
. . . .
. . . . a . . . .
. . . .
. . . . woman . . . .
. . . .
. . . . !"

"and so? you've got more to hide than i have, if that's what's worrying you. and why on earth do you keep your left hand down there? cold?"

"we'd . . . .
. . . . better .
. . . .
. . . . hurry . . . .
. . . .
. . . ."

she followed him down the hall.

"here . . . .
. . . . it . .
. . . .
. . . . is . . . .

. . . .
. . . ."

    "it's lovely. good-looking. well proportioned. sleek. graceful, too. it's lovable and pettable. succulent and rapturous. winning and winsome. it's bewitching, fascinating, captivating, enervating—and so gallant. it's adorable, wooable, kissable, clutchable, eatable, hearable, feelable, yearnable. why, it's almost discernible. what is it?"

    "don't . . . .
. . . .
you . . . .
. . . . see . .
. . . .
. . . . anything .
. . . .
. . . . wrong . .
. . . .
. . . . with . . .
. . . .
. . . . it . . . . . .
. . . .
. . . . ?"

    "offhand, i don't. it looks all right, and it feels all right, though it's a little slippery, and a mite rough to touch. like a sparrow. the sweet little thing. may i kiss it?"

    "look . . . .
. . . .
. . . . . . closely . . . .
. . . .
. . . ."

    "o dear, it is strange, isn't it, when you get closer to it. it smells like —like cheese, maybe? or nasturtiums? dried nasturtium leaves, perhaps? but it's a clean smell. and look right there. it looks like it lacks something. yes, i'm sure it isn't exactly the way it ought to be."

    "do . . . .
. . . .
. . . . . . you . . . .
. . . .
. . . . see . . . .
. . . .
. . . . that . . . .
. . . .
. . . . ?"

    "that?"

    "that . . . .

. . . ."
. . . ."
        "what happened there?"
        "well . . . .
. . . .
. . . . as . . . .
. . . .
. . . . i . . . .
. . . .
. . . . was . . . .
. . . .
. . . . wiping . . . .
. . . .
. . . . it . . . .
. . . .
. . . . . the . . . .
. . . .
. . . . dot . . . .
. . . .
. . . . fell . . . .
. . . .
. . . . off . . . . .
. . . .
. . . ."
        "you say the dot fell off?"
        "yes . . . .
. . . .
. . . ."
        "i don't believe it."
        "it's . . . .
. . . .
. . . . on . . . .
. . . .
. . . . my . . . .
. . . .
. . . . tongue . . . .
. . . .
. . . . and . . . .
. . . .
. . . . the . . . .
. . . .

. . . .
. . . . pain . . . .
. . . .
. . . . is . . . .
. . . .
. . . . killing . . . .
. . . .
. . . . me . . . .
. . . .
. . . . "
. . . . . .

"let me look again". she pushed back his head and bent down to him.
"open wide, now, like a good boy. stick it out as far as you can. more. as
far as you can". she pinched it.
"ouch . . . .
. . . .
. . . . "

"did i hurt you? i didn't mean to. hold on to me if it hurts. see, it's
better now. keep it there. no, stick it out as far as you can. ah, that's better,
that's better, that's wonderful, keep it there, that's perfect. keep it there,
keep it there, there. ah, that's it, that's the boy. don't breath on me so hard,
it clouds up my glasses".
"hurry . . . .
. . . .
. . . . up . . . .
. . . .
. . . . "
. . . .

"i was right, i was right. there's no dot on your tongue at all. What
did i tell you?"
"look . . . . '
. . . .
. . . . again . . . .
. . . .
. . . .
. . . . "

"it's no use, i tell you, there's no dot there. but it is a peculiar color."
"red . . . .
. . . .
. . . . ?"
"black."
"good . . . .
. . . .

. . . . god . . . .
. . . .
. . . .
. . . . then . . . .
. . . .
. . . . it . .
. . . .
. . . .
. . . . is . . . .
. . . .
. . . .
. . . . serious . . . .
. . . .
. . . . but . .
. . . .
. . . .
. . . . what . . . .
. . . .
. . . . do . . . .
. . . .
. . . . i . . . .
. . . .
. . . . care . . . .
. . . .
. . . . about . . . .
. . . .
. . . . me . . . .
. . . .
. . . . it's . . . .
. . . . the
. . . .
. . . . poor . . . .
. . . .
. . . . stump . . . .
. . . .

. . . .
. . . . i'm . . . .
. . . .
. . . .
. . . . worried . . . .
. . . .
. . . .
. . . . about . . . .
. . . .
. . . .
. . . ."

"if that's all that's worrying you, then you might as well go on back to
sleep, because there's nothing radically wrong with the stump at all."

"but . . . .
. . . .
. . . .
its . . . .
. . . .
. . . . head
. . . .
. . . .
. . . .
. . . . fell . .
. . . .
. . . .
. . . . off . . .
. . . .
. . . .
. . . ."

"nonsense. the head couldn't possibly have fallen off. it couldn't have
fallen off because it wasn't attached to it. how could it possibly have fallen
off? now if it had been the crossbar of the t, the hole of the o, the spine of
the h or the ball of the b, then you'd really have something to worry about.
but the dot of the i? nothing, absolutely nothing to get hot and bothered
about."

"are . . . .
. . . .
. . . .
. . . . . you . . . .
. . . .
. . . .
. . . . certain . . . .
. . . .
. . . .
. . . . ?"

"of course i'm certain. the only thing you have to worry about is your tongue. but i think i know what the trouble is and what we can do about it."

"what . . . .

. . . .

. . . .

. . . .?"

"well, you say you licked up the dot. that's a. b, there's no doubt about it because the color itself is symptomat'c. c, your tongue can distinguish the forest from the trees, to put it bluntly, because, d, how can you tell the dancer from the dance, to call a spade a spade? e, the dot, consequently, is nondot and the nondot dot, in which case, f, quis custodiet ipsos custodes? for surely, g, your tongue is the dot and the dot your tongue. consequently, h, it is a tongue-dot and a dot-tongue:

that is why, k, it is black and not red, black and not green, black and not blue, black, not aquamarine, not mauve, but black, not pistachine, nor, l, can you blame it for doing what it did, because, m, you freed it; n, it freed itself; o, the stump freed it and in freeing it lost it—which you found, although it was never, p, yours nor, q, his nor, r, hers nor, s, theirs. which makes it clear, t, that, putting two and two together, you reproduced it, and, u, it reproduced you! for, v, although the mere duality of its totality is all that infected you, it is necessary, w, to embrace its absolute before, x, its absolute embraces you, thus, y, drying up the sap, the lymph, the elastic fluid, so to speak, that can build the bridge over which you will be free to cross and be made whole again. before which, of course, you must, z, take my hand in yours to seal a gentleman's agreement. no, your left hand. that's the boy."

"why the pain's all gone! it doesn't hurt at all! not an iota! it feels better than ever before. you're great, you're wonderful, you're marvelously efficacious. and i don't even know your name. isn't that delicious—after all you've done for me i don't even know your name. but tell me one thing —why didn't you stick in the i and the j?"

"oh dear   bel eve someth ng b t me t's t ckl ng me t burns t's eat ng

                    i
                         i
                              i
                                   i
                                        i
                                             i
                                                  i
                                                       i
                                                            i
                                                                 i

ts way nto me t's scratch ng t's k ll ng me qu ck qu ck do someth ng
i
       i
            i
                   i
                      i
                            i
                                i
                                    i
                                        i

stop t stop t."

     i
       i

    "i'm coming, i'm coming."

part five
the writer's workshop

How to Read the Story:
Guide Questions to Fiction

1. Can you isolate and paraphrase the plot of the work? Can you draw a triangular representation of the work, placing its turning point at the apex of the diagram? How many preparatory incidents are there before the climactic point? Does the author fully exploit these incidents? Are there any extraneous incidents or episodes? Which? Explain how or how not.

2. What point of attack does the author employ? That is, at what juncture in the sequence of events does he choose to begin? Why? What alternatives suggest themselves to you?

3. Is the author primarily interested in plot, character, context, time, or structure? What is he least concerned with?

4. What point of view has the author selected? Why? Does he fully

exploit the strengths of this point of view? Does he skirt its inherent weaknesses? Does he shift point of view? Why? What alternatives might he have considered? What changes would these alternatives have occasioned?

5. Is the story best suited to treatment in a short story, novella, or novel? Why?

6. Into how many parts or chapters is the work subdivided? Does the author employ dramatic principles of structure and composition? Musical principles? How is the structure suited (or ill-suited) to elucidation of character and/or theme? If the structure appears fragmented, is the fragmentation revelatory of theme?

7. What is the narrative-dramatic mix? That is, what is the relation of narration to dialogue? If narration is stressed, is the work unduly slowed? If the dramatic mode is dominant, does the author provide sufficient detail and attention to context and thought?

8. How much time is covered in the work? Too much? What time of day or year? Why? What particular span of time? Is this time of historical significance?

9. Identify the central characters; the minor or secondary characters. What motivates the characters? Are they flat or round characters? Are their actions consistent with the pictures the author gives us? What methods of characterization does the author employ? Can the author be identified with any of his characters? Is the author's gallery too crowded?

10. What contexts or settings does the author employ? How does setting shape or elucidate character or theme? What alternative settings suggest themselves? Is there a change of setting during the work? Of what thematic significance is the change? Is the geographical movement symbolic? Is there a movement east or west? Is this significant? Is the context merely a backdrop or is it moving and alive?

11. Is the author principally concerned with the inner world of thought and reflection, or the outer world of thing and event? Is the one to the exclusion of the other?

12. Does the author enter into his story? Does he editorialize, or judge his characters? Is the author intrusive?

13. Does the work make use of Greek/Roman myths? the Bible? history? If so, how does the author adapt his source to fit his own needs?

14. What recurrent words, phrases, images, symbols do you note? What are the key images and symbols? What do they symbolize?

15. How would you characterize the author's style? Is his diction Latinate or Anglo-Saxon? What about his sentence length? Is his language heavily metaphorical? Check his verbs. Are they strong and forceful action verbs, as Hemingway wanted them?

16. What is the author's intent or objective? Is it pure entertainment, satire, general social criticism?

17. Is this an early or late work in the artist's canon? Put it into context in that canon. Is it typical or atypical in theme, character, imagery, symbol?

18. Using this work as empirical evidence, determine how the author conceives the nature of fiction and the artist's role.

19. Did you enjoy the work? Why or why not? What are its particular strengths? What are its weaknesses?

20. Where does the work fall on the following scale:

Mimetic	History	Naturalism	Realism	Romance	Allegory	Expressionism	Surrealism
a factual representational world						a subjective and/or unrepresentational world	

The Criticism of Fiction: Statements and Questions

The Critics

1. On the Nature of Art

The Preface to
THE PICTURE OF DORIAN GRAY
by Oscar Wilde

The artist is the creator of beautiful things.

To reveal art and conceal the artist is art's aim.

The critic is he who can translate into another manner or a new material his impression of beautiful things.

The highest, as the lowest, form of criticism is a mode of autobiography.

Those who find ugly meanings in beautiful things are corrupt without being charming. This is a fault.

Those who find beautiful meanings in beautiful things are the cultivated. For these there is hope. They are the elect to whom beautiful things mean only Beauty.

There is no such thing as a moral or an immoral book. Books are well written, or badly written. That is all.

The nineteenth century dislike of Realism is the rage of Caliban seeing his own face in a glass.

The nineteenth century dislike of Romanticism is the rage of Caliban not seeing his own face in a glass.

The moral life of man forms part of the subject-matter of the artist, but the morality of art consists in the perfect use of an imperfect medium. No artist desires to prove anything. Even things that are true can be proved.

No artist has ethical sympathies. An ethical sympathy in an artist is an unpardonable mannerism of style.

No artist is ever morbid. The artist can express everything.

Thought and language are to the artist instruments of an art.

Vice and virtue are to the artist materials for an art.

From the point of view of form, the type of all the arts is the art of the musician. From the point of view of feeling, the actor's craft is the type.

All art is at once surface and symbol. Those who go beneath the surface do so at their peril. Those who read the symbol do so at their peril.

It is the spectator, and not life, that art really mirrors.

Diversity of opinion about a work of art shows that the work is new, complex, and vital.

When critics disagree the artist is in accord with himself.

We can forgive a man for making a useful thing as long as he does not admire it. The only excuse for making a useless thing is that one admires it intensely.

All art is quite useless.

Preface to
THE NIGGER OF THE "NARCISSUS"
by Joseph Conrad

A work that aspires, however humbly, to the condition of art should carry its justification in every line. And art itself may be defined as a single-minded attempt to render the highest kind of justice to the visible universe, by bringing to light the truth, manifold and one, underlying its every aspect. It is an attempt to find in its forms, in its colors, in its light, in its shadows, in the aspects of matter and in the facts of life, what of each is fundamental, what is enduring and essential—their one illuminating and convincing quality—the very truth of their existence. The artist, then, like the thinker or the scientist, seeks the truth and makes his appeal. Impressed by the aspect of the world the thinker plunges into ideas, the scientist into facts—whence, presently, emerging they make their appeal to those qualities of our being that fit us best for the hazardous enterprise of living. They speak authoritatively to our common sense, to our intelligence, to our desire of peace or to our desire of unrest; not seldom to our prejudices, sometimes to our fears, often to our egoism—but always to our credulity. And their words are heard with reverence, for their concern is with weighty matters: with the cultivation of our minds and the proper care of our bodies, with the attainment of our ambitions, with the perfection of the means and the glorification of our precious aims.

It is otherwise with the artist.

Confronted by the same enigmatical spectacle the artist descends within himself, and in that lonely region of stress and strife, if he be deserving and fortunate, he finds the terms of his appeal. His appeal is made to our less obvious capacities: to that part of our nature which, because of the warlike conditions of existence, is necessarily kept out of sight within the more resisting and hard qualities—like the vulnerable body within a steel armor. His appeal is less loud, more profound, less distinct, more stirring—and sooner forgotten. Yet its effect endures forever. The changing wisdom of successive generations discards ideas, questions facts, demolishes theories. But the artist appeals to that part of our being which is not dependent on wisdom: to that in us which is a gift and not an acquisition—and, therefore, more permanently enduring. He speaks to our capacity for delight and wonder, to the sense of mystery surrounding our lives; to our sense of pity, and beauty, and pain; to the latent feeling of fellowship with all creation—and to the subtle but invincible conviction of solidarity that knits together the loneliness of innumerable hearts, to the solidarity in dreams, in joy, in sorrow, in aspirations, in illusions, in hope, in fear, which binds men to each other, which binds together all humanity—the dead to the living and the living to the unborn.

It is only some such train of thought, or rather of feeling, that can in a measure explain the aim of the attempt, made in the tale which follows, to present an unrestful episode in the obscure lives of a few individuals out of all the disregarded multitude of the bewildered, the simple and the voiceless. For, if any part of truth dwells in the belief confessed above, it becomes evident that there is not a place of splendor or a dark corner of the earth that does not deserve if only a passing glance of wonder and pity. The motive then, may be held to justify the matter of the work; but this preface, which is simply an avowal of endeavor, cannot end here—for the avowal is not yet complete.

Fiction—if it at all aspires to be art—appeals to temperament. And in truth it must be, like painting, like music, like all art, the appeal of one temperament to all the other innumerable temperaments whose subtle and resistless power endows passing events with their true meaning, and creates the moral, the emotional, atmosphere of the place and time. Such an appeal to be effective must be an impression conveyed through the senses; and, in fact, it cannot be made in any other way, because temperament, whether individual or collective, is not amenable to persuasion. All art, therefore, appeals primarily to the senses, and the artistic aim when expressing itself in written words must also make its appeal through the senses, if its high desire is to reach the secret spring of responsive emotions. It must strenuously aspire to the plasticity of sculpture, to the color of painting, and to the magic suggestiveness of music—which is the art of arts. And it is only through complete, unswerving devotion to the perfect blending of form and substance; it is only through an unremitting never-discouraged care for the shape and ring of sentences that an approach can be made to plasticity, to color, and that the light of magic suggestiveness may be brought to play for an evanescent instant over the commonplace surface of words: of the old, old words, worn thin, defaced by ages of careless usage.

The sincere endeavor to accomplish that creative task, to go as far on that road as his strength will carry him, to go undeterred by faltering, weariness or reproach, is the only valid justification for the worker in prose. And if his conscience is clear, his answer to those who in the fullness of a wisdom which looks for immediate profit, demand specifically to be edified, consoled, amused; who demand to be promptly improved, or encouraged, or frightened, or shocked, or charmed, must run thus: My task which I am trying to achieve is, by the power of the written word to make you hear, to make you feel—it is, before all, to make you see. That—and no more, and it is everything. If I succeed, you shall find there according to your deserts: encouragement, consolation, fear, charm—all you demand—and, perhaps, also that glimpse of truth for which you have forgotten to ask.

To snatch in a moment of courage, from the remorseless rush of time, a passing phase of life, is only the beginning of the task. The task approached in tenderness and faith is to hold up unquestioningly, without choice and without fear, the rescued fragment before all eyes in the light of a sincere mood. It is to show its vibration, its color, its form; and through its movement, its form, and its color, reveal the substance of its truth— disclose its inspiring secret: the stress and passion within the core of each convincing moment. In a singleminded attempt of that kind, if one be deserving and fortunate, one may perchance attain to such clearness of sincerity that at last the presented vision of regret or pity, of terror or mirth, shall awaken in the hearts of the beholders that feeling of unavoidable solidarity; of the solidarity in mysterious origin, in toil, in joy, in hope, in uncertain fate, which binds men to each other and all mankind to the visible world.

It is evident that he who, rightly or wrongly, holds by the convictions expressed above cannot be faithful to any one of the temporary formulas of his craft. The enduring part of them—the truth which each only imperfectly veils—should abide with him as the most precious of his possessions, but they all: Realism, Romanticism, Naturalism, even the unofficial sentimentalism (which like the poor, is exceedingly difficult to get rid of), all these gods must, after a short period of fellowship, abandon him—even on the very threshold of the temple—to the stammerings of his conscience and to the outspoken consciousness of the difficulties of his work. In that uneasy solitude the supreme cry of Art for Art itself loses the exciting ring of its apparent immorality. It sounds far off. It has ceased to be a cry, and is heard only as a whisper, often incomprehensible, but at times and faintly encouraging.

Sometimes, stretched at ease in the shade of a roadside tree, we watch the motions of a laborer in a distant field, and, after a time, begin to wonder languidly as to what the fellow may be at. We watch the movements of his body, the waving of his arms, we see him bend down, stand up, hesitate, begin again. It may add to the charm of an idle hour to be told the purpose of his exertions. If we know he is trying to lift a stone, to dig a ditch, to uproot a stump, we look with a more real interest at his efforts; we are disposed to condone the jar of his agitation upon the restfulness of the landscape; and even, if in a brotherly frame of mind, we may bring ourselves to forgive his failure. We understood his object, and, after all, the fellow has tried, and perhaps he had not the strength—and perhaps he had not the knowledge. We forgive, go on our way—and forget.

And so it is with the workman of art. Art is long and life is short, and success is very far off. And thus, doubtful of strength to travel so far, we talk a little about the aim—the aim of art, which, like life itself, is inspiring, difficult—obscured by mists. It is not in the clear logic of a triumphant conclusion; it is not in the unveiling of one of those heartless secrets which are called the Laws of Nature. It is not less great, but only more difficult.

To arrest, for the space of a breath, the hands busy about the work of the earth, and compel men entranced by the sight of distant goals to glance for a moment at the surrounding vision of form and color, of sunshine and shadows; to make them pause for a look, for a sigh, for a smile—such is the aim, difficult and evanescent, and reserved only for a very few to achieve. But sometimes, by the deserving and the fortunate, even that task is accomplished. And when it is accomplished—behold!—all the truth of life is there: a moment of vision, a sigh, a smile—and the return to an eternal rest.

WILLIAM FAULKNER'S
NOBEL ADDRESS
December 10, 1950

I feel that this award was not made to me as a man, but to my work—a life's work in the agony and sweat of the human spirit, not for glory and least of all for profit, but to create out of the materials of the human spirit something which did not exist before. So this award is only mine in trust. It will not be difficult to find a dedication for the money part of it commensurate with the purpose and significance of its origin. But I would like to do the same with the acclaim too, by using this moment as a pinnacle from which I might be listened to by the young men and women already dedicated to the same anguish and travail, among whom is already that one who will some day stand here where I am standing.

Our tragedy today is a general and universal physical fear so long sustained by now that we can even bear it. There are no longer problems of the spirit. There is only the question: When will I be blown up? Because of this, the young man or woman writing today has forgotten the problems of the human heart in conflict with itself which alone can make good writing because only that is worth writing about, worth the agony and the sweat.

He must learn them again. He must teach himself that the basest of all things is to be afraid; and, teaching himself that, forget it forever, leaving no room in his workshop for anything but the old verities and truths of the heart, the old universal truths lacking which any story is ephemeral and doomed—love and honor and pity and pride and compassion and sacrifice. Until he does so, he labors under a curse. He writes not of love but of lust, of defeats in which nobody loses anything of value, of victories without hope and, worst of all, without pity or compassion. His griefs grieve on no universal bones, leaving no scars. He writes not of the heart but of the glands.

Until he relearns these things, he will write as though he stood among and watched the end of man. I decline to accept the end of man. It is easy enough to say that man is immortal simply because he will endure: that when the last ding-dong of doom has clanged and faded from the last worthless rock hanging tideless in the last red and dying evening, that even then there will still be one more sound: that of his puny inexhaustible voice, still talking. I refuse to accept this. I believe that man will not merely endure: he will prevail. He is immortal, not because he alone among creatures has an inexhaustible voice, but because he has a soul, a spirit capable of compassion and sacrifice and endurance. The poet's, the writer's, duty is to write about these things. It is his privilege to help man endure by lifting his heart, by reminding him of the courage and honor and hope and pride and compassion and pity and sacrifice which have been the glory of his past. The poet's voice need not merely be the record of man, it can be one of the props, the pillars to help him endure and prevail.

2. The Relationship Between Art and Life

The realist, if he is an artist, will seek to give us not a banal photographic representation of life, but a vision of it that is fuller, more vivid and more compellingly truthful than even reality itself.

To give an account of everything would be impossible, for we should need at least one volume for each day in order to record the multitude of insignificant incidents that fill our lives.

Selection is therefore necessary,—and that is the first blow to the theory of "the whole truth."

Life, moreover, is made up of elements that are utterly different from each other, of things utterly unexpected, contrary and incongruous; it is harsh, inconsequent, incoherent, and filled with disasters which, inexplicable, illogical and contradictory as they are, must be gathered together under the heading "sundry happenings."

That is why the artist, having made his choice of subject, should select from this life, crowded as it is with accidents and trivialities, only those characteristic details that are useful for his theme; all the rest, all the incidentals, he must reject.

—*Guy de Maupassant*

3. The Pace of Fiction

I find I can explain my view of the nature of narrative in fiction, its varieties and the place it occupies between the reader and the imaginary world of the novel most easily if I translate a psychological fact into a physical metaphor, and say that the reader is divided from the imaginary world of the novel by a high wall over which he cannot see. On the top of the wall is perched the novelist. He looks down into the world of his imagination and then turns to the reader and tells him what is going on there. The novelist does not, like the dramatist, pick up bits of his world and set them down on the near side of the wall for actors to animate and his audience to see; the novelist narrates; he tells what he sees.

What is it that he sees? The world of the particular novel which is at present engaging him; a tremendous three-dimensional pageant of life, not endless, but rolling continuously past the novelist's mental eye. A seething flux of phenomena, continually changing, continually transmuting as to some of its items, continually rolling, sweeping, surging, sparking and banging by.

Since this world, this moving pageant, is the novelist's creation, he is of course omniscient and omnipotent with regard to it.

He is omniscient—the cries of its birds, the thuds of its battles, the thoughts of its people, its clouds, its sunsets, its leaves, its deepest emotions and vastest plains, are all part of its seething flux and he knows them all.

He is omnipotent—he can alter his pageant at will, he can survey any part, in any way, at will. He can look at it or not look at it, as he likes, whenever he likes. He can look at parts of it and not at other parts, if he likes. He can hold it at a distance, he can draw it close. He has its progress, its rolling, completely under his control; he can make it go past him swiftly or slowly, as he likes; he can reverse it backwards, and bring it up again with a jerk, if he chooses. And he does so choose; he delights in handling his pageant variously. Before he begins to tell about his pageant to his readers, he has rolled it backwards and forwards many a score of times, trying to improve its interest and its beauty, trying, too, to decide how he shall handle it on that final occasion when he tells it to his readers.

There are as many ways of rolling a pageant as there are human minds, but in our metaphor the speed of the process is the operative factor in the type of narrative we receive. Sometimes the novelist rolls the pageant by swiftly, so swiftly that details are not discernible. Sometimes the novelist rolls it slowly, so that he sees (and tells) each specific action, hears each actual word. Sometimes he halts it altogether for a moment.

Suppose, for example, a part of the novelist's imaginary world concerns the journey of his hero Dick and his villain Tom from a village in Central Africa to London. The rolling pageant brings in its course Dick and Tom to a long stretch of desert. The desert (this is in Victorian times) is all the same and not very important, and so the novelist rolls it swiftly by. He does *not* say: "Dick and Tom raised their right foot and put it down, striding over a yard of sand, and then raised their left foot and put it down, striding over another yard of sand," and go on saying that or something like it until Tom and Dick have marched two hundred miles, and at last reach a palm tree. At the same time he is bound to give an impression of the two hundred miles, for the remoteness, the loneliness, of Dick and Tom is highly important. He therefore holds his pageant at a distance so that he can see its full breadth and rolls it quickly by; he tells us in a few paragraphs about the distant mountains, the burning sun, the sand, the heat of the day, how the feelings of loneliness of Dick and Tom heightened with the journey, and so on. Then when he has created a sufficient impression of the vast stretch of desert lying between the travellers and civilisation, he goes on:

The sun was just sinking as Dick and Tom entered the Zazifa oasis.

Something important in his story is going to happen in this oasis, he knows; so he slows up the pageant, and looks very intently at this one portion of it. Now that it is going so slowly, instead of a blur of sound he can hear voices, instead of a white blank he can see the nose and eyes and cheeks of a face, instead of a pulsating ribbon of cerebration he can perceive the thoughts of Dick and Tom at this single moment. And so, instead of telling us summaries of speech and personality and behaviour, he tells us specific words and actions. We read his account of the exact words in which Dick and Tom quarrel, the exact knife-blow with which

Tom murders Dick, the exact thoughts, horrified yet rejoicing, with which Tom buries the body.

But the rest of Tom's journey to England isn't important in the least, so the novelist simply declines to look at it; he whizzes it by in a flash, so fast that he does not see it at all. He ends his chapter, that is to say; he breaks off his narrative, begins it again only when the liner carrying Tom approaches Southampton. Tom's landing in England isn't very important, so we have a fairly swift narrative of the disembarkation—with one slower view perhaps at the bookstall, where Tom sees an account of Dick's death in a travel magazine. The pageant rolls by fairly swiftly as Tom travels up to London—we must have an impression of farms and green fields, to convey that this is civilisation, but do not need to travel the journey mile by mile.

But now Tom arrives at the London terminus, and is met by Ellen, the girl to whom Dick was engaged, the girl whom Tom hopes to marry. This meeting is of the first importance. The novelist therefore slows up the pageant and takes a long slow look, and tells us everything that happened in minute detail—Tom's struggles to play a part in look and word, Ellen's candid grief presently becoming shadowed by distrust.

When the novelist halts his moving world and tells us what he sees, we term that type of narrative a *description*. When he moves it slowly and tells us single specific actions (including of course those specific actions we call speech and thought), we have learned to term that type of narrative a *scene*. When he rolls his fictitious world by rapidly, so that he gives us, not each specific moment of many battles but the integrated campaign, not the single impressions of a character but the sum of that character, not the minute by minute thoughts of a man but a summarised account of his gradual conversion to a new course of life—what is the term for that type of narration? Unfortunately there is no generally accepted term. Percy Lubbock calls these summaries *retrospect* when they refer to the past, but that covers only one of their functions. I myself have adopted the term *summary* to express these condensations, these integrations, but I am not at all satisfied with it. The words *scene* and *summary, description* and *summary*, are not proper antitheses. Though indeed—and this is the crux of the argument—the kinds of narrative described above are not antitheses, but distant points in a scale of subtle gradations, stretching from the specific to the integrated.

For all narrative is in fact a summary to some degree. The most specific scene does not narrate the contraction of the muscles, the rush of the impulse along the grey ganglions of the mind, which produces speech or smile. When Virginia Woolf, devotee of the specific, writes: "Thick wax candles stand upright; young men rise in white gowns; while the subservient eagle bears up for inspection the great white book" (*Jacob's Room*), she is summarising the complex interactions of systems of internal stresses subjected to external forces, the involved activity of muscular tissue, which makes the candles hold upright in their sconces, the book rest on the eagle, the young men rise. Kipling in his short story *The Ship That Found Herself* specificised (if the word may be forgiven) the movement of a ship; but to state: "a steel girder quivered" is still to summarise the play of conflicting tensions. James Joyce records the swift succession of thought association, but even he does not detail the physical nerve processes of which they are a result. Still, for practical purposes the place on the scale of the specific of the scene and the summary are sufficiently far apart to justify different names.

The metaphor of the wall and the rolling pageant is a metaphor only, and metaphors though often illuminating are in the last resort untrue, being metaphors and not the thing itself. The story of Dick and Tom and Ellen was a crude invented instance. The truth or falsity of the suggested definition of scene and summary must be tested in the actual narratives of fiction.

—*Phyllis Bentley*

4. The Distinction Between Plot and Story

Let us define a plot. We have defined a story as a narrative of events arranged in their time sequence. A plot is also a narrative of events, the emphasis falling on causality. "The king died and then the queen died" is a story. "The king died, and then the queen died of grief" is a plot. The time sequence is preserved, but the sense of causality overshadows it. Or again: "The queen died, no one knew why, until it was discovered that it was through grief at the death of the king." This is a plot with a mystery in it, a form capable of high development. It suspends the time sequence, it moves as far away from the story as its limitations will allow. Consider the death of the queen. If it is in a story we say "and then?" If it is in a plot we ask "why?" That is the fundamental difference between these two aspects of the novel. A plot cannot be told to a gaping audience of cavemen or to a tyrannical sultan or to their modern descendant the movie public. They can only be kept awake by "and then—and then"—they can only supply curiosity. But a plot demands intelligence and memory also.

—*E. M. Forster*

5. Characterization

I think that actual life supplies a writer with characters much less than is thought. Of course there must be a beginning to every conception, but so much change seems to take place in it at once, that almost anything comes to serve the purpose—a face of a stranger, a face seen in a portrait, almost a face in the fire. And people in life hardly seem definite enough to appear in print. They are not good or bad enough, or clever or stupid enough, or comic or pitiful enough. They would have to be presented by means of detailed description, and would not come through in talk.

—Ivy Compton Burnett

You can't put the whole of a character into a book, unless the book were of inordinate length and the reader of inordinate patience. You must select traits. You must take many traits for granted, and refer to them, in a way to show that they are conventionalized. If you wanted to get at a total truth you'd only get a confused picture. Question: Does a novelist want his characters to remain in the mind of the reader? Some novelists don't. But I do, for one. Dickens's characters remain in the mind. They may perhaps be too conventionalized, too simplified. Same for Thackeray—Dobbin and Amelia. But they remain in the mind. No novelist can always be creating absolutely new, or fresh, characters.

—Arnold Bennett

The poor novelist constructs his characters, he controls them and makes them speak. The true novelist listens to them and watches them function; he eavesdrops on them even before he knows them. It is only according to what he hears them say that he begins to understand who they are.

I have put "watches them function" second—because for me, speech tells me more than action. I think I should lose less if I went blind than if I became deaf. Nevertheless I do see my characters—not so much in their details as in their general effect, and even more in their actions, their gait, the rhythm of their movements. I do not worry if the lenses of my glasses fail to show them completely "in focus"; whereas I perceive the least inflections of their voices with the greatest sharpness.

I wrote the first dialogue between Olivier and Bernard and the scenes between Passavant and Vincent without having the slightest idea what I was going to do with those characters, or even who they were. They thrust themselves upon me, despite me. . . .

—*André Gide*

When one says picture, one says of character, when one says novel, one says of incident, and the terms may be transposed. What is character but the determination of incident? What is incident but the illustration of character? What is a picture or a novel that is not of character? What else do we seek in it and find in it?

—*Henry James*

6. The Nature of Modern Fiction

From Virginia Woolf's
MODERN FICTION

We have to admit that we are exacting, and, further, that we find it difficult to justify our discontent by explaining what it is that we exact. We frame our question differently at different times. But it reappears most persistently as we drop the finished novel on the crest of a sigh—Is it worth while? What is the point of it all? Can it be that owing to one of those little deviations which the human spirit seems to make from time to time Mr. Bennett has come down with his magnificent apparatus for catching life just an inch or two on the wrong side? Life escapes; and perhaps without life nothing else is worth while. It is a confession of vagueness to have to make use of such a figure as this, but we scarcely better the matter by speaking, as critics are prone to do, of reality. Admitting the vagueness which afflicts all criticism of novels, let us hazard the opinion that for us at this moment the form of fiction most in vogue more often misses than secures the thing we seek. Whether we call it life or spirit, truth or reality, this, the essential thing, has moved off, or on, and refuses to be contained any longer in such ill-fitting vestments as we provide. Nevertheless, we go on perseveringly, conscientiously, constructing our two and thirty chapters after a design which more and more ceases to resemble the vision in our minds. So much of the enormous labour of proving the solidity, the likeness to life, of the story is not merely labour thrown away but labour misplaced to the extent of obscuring and blotting out the light of the conception. The writer seems constrained, not by his own free will but by some powerful and unscrupulous tyrant who has him in thrall to provide a plot, to provide comedy, tragedy, love, interest, and an air of probability embalming the whole so impeccable that if all his figures were to come to life they would find themselves dressed down to the last button of their coats in the fashion of the hour. The tyrant is obeyed; the novel is done to a turn. But sometimes, more and more often as time goes by, we suspect a momentary doubt, a spasm of rebellion, as the pages fill themselves in the customary way. Is life like this? Must novels be like this?

Look within and life, it seems, is very far from being "like this." Examine for a moment an ordinary mind on an ordinary day. The mind receives a myriad impressions—trivial, fantastic, evanescent, or engraved with the sharpness of steel. From all sides they come, an incessant shower of innumerable atoms; and as they fall, as they shape themselves into the life of Monday or Tuesday, the accent falls differently from of old; the moment of importance came not here but there; so that if a writer were a free man and not a slave, if he could write what he chose, not what he must, if he could base his work upon his own feeling and not upon convention, there would be no plot, no comedy, no tragedy, no love interest or catastrophe in the accepted style, and perhaps not a single button sewn on as the Bond Street tailors would have it. Life is not a series of gig lamps symmetrically arranged; but a luminous halo, a semi-transparent envelope surrounding us from the beginning of consciousness to the end. Is it not the task of the novelist to convey this varying, this unknown and uncircumscribed spirit, whatever aberration or complexity it may display, with as little mixture of the alien and external as possible? We are not pleading merely for courage and sincerity; we are suggesting that the proper stuff of fiction is a little other than custom would have us believe it.

It is, at any rate, in some such fashion as this that we seek to define the quality which distinguishes the work of several young writers, among whom Mr. James Joyce is the most notable, from that of their predecessors. They attempt to come closer to life, and to preserve more sincerely and exactly what interests and moves them, even if to do so they must discard most of the conventions which are commonly observed by the novelist. Let us record the atoms as they fall upon the mind in the order in which they fall, let us trace the pattern, however disconnected and incoherent in appearance, which each sight or incident scores upon the consciousness. Let us not take it for granted that life exists more fully in what is commonly thought big than in what is commonly thought small. Any one who has read *The Portrait of the Artist as a Young Man* or, what promises to be a far more interesting work, *Ulysses*,* now appearing in the *Little Review*, will have hazarded some theory of this nature as to Mr. Joyce's intention. On our part, with such a fragment before us, it is hazarded rather than affirmed; but whatever the intention of the whole there can be no question but that it is of the utmost sincerity and that the result, difficult or unpleasant as we may judge it, is undeniably important. In contrast with those whom we have called materialists Mr. Joyce is spiritual; he is concerned at all costs to reveal the flickerings of that innermost flame which flashes its messages through the brain, and in order to preserve it he disregards with complete courage whatever seems to him adventitious, whether it be probability, or coherence or any other of these signposts which for generations have served to support the imagination of a reader when called upon to imagine what he can neither touch nor see. The scene in the cemetery, for instance, with its brilliancy, its sordidity, its incoherence, its sudden lightning flashes of significance, does undoubtedly come so close to the quick of the mind that, on a first reading at any rate, it is difficult not to acclaim a masterpiece. If we want life itself here, surely we have it. Indeed, we find ourselves fumbling rather awkwardly if we try to say what else we wish, and for what reason a work of such originality yet fails to compare, for we must take high examples, with *Youth* or *The Mayor of Casterbridge*. It fails because of the comparative poverty of the writer's mind, we might say simply and have done with it. But it is possible to press a little further and wonder whether we may not refer our sense of being in a bright yet narrow room, confined and shut in, rather than enlarged and set free, to some limitation imposed by the method as well as by the mind. Is it the method that inhibits the creative power? Is it due to the method that we feel neither jovial nor magnanimous, but centred in a self which, in spite of its tremor of susceptibility, never embraces or creates what is outside itself and beyond? Does the emphasis laid, perhaps didactically, upon indecency, contribute to the effect of something angular and isolated? Or is it merely that in any effort of such originality it is much easier, for contemporaries especially, to feel what it lacks than to name what it gives? In any case it is a mistake to stand outside examining "methods." Any method is right, every method is right, that expresses what we wish to express, if we are writers; that brings us closer to the novelist's intention if we are readers. This method has the merit of bringing us closer to what we were prepared to call life itself; did not the reading of *Ulysses* suggest how much of life is excluded or ignored, and did it not come with a shock to open *Tristram Shandy* or even *Pendennis* and be by them convinced that there are not only other aspects of life, but more important ones into the bargain.

However this may be, the problem before the novelist at present, as we suppose it to have been in the past, is to contrive means of being free to

* Written April 1919.

set down what he chooses. He has to have the courage to say that what interests him is no longer "this" but "that": out of "that" alone must he construct his work. For the moderns "that," the point of interest, lies very likely in the dark places of psychology. At once, therefore, the accent falls a little differently; the emphasis is upon something hitherto ignored; at once a different outline of form becomes necessary, difficult for us to grasp, incomprehensible to our predecessors.

Questions on the Criticism of Fiction

1. Wilde contends that "no artist has ethical sympathies," that "there is no such thing as a moral or an immoral book," that "all art is quite useless." Compare and contrast his conception of art with that of Conrad and Faulkner.

2. Which story (or stories) in this collection best reflects Oscar Wilde's conception of art? Why? Which story best reflects Conrad's view? Faulkner's? Why?

3. According to Bentley, the writer is "omniscient" and "omnipotent." What *point of view* do you think best utilizes or exploits this omniscience or omnipotence: first person? third person? stream of consciousness? dramatic? How will the *pace* of a story be affected by the selection of *point of view*? Would Virginia Woolf agree with Bentley's ideas of fiction? Explain.

4. In Phyllis Bentley's view, what devices does the writer use to control the pace of his story? What is the difference between *description* and *scene*?

5. Apply Bentley's terms—*description, scene,* and *summary*—to any story in this collection. Would these terms be applicable to the stories in Part 4, "Beyond the Safety Zone"? Why or why not?

6. Do Burnett and Gide agree or disagree on the relationship of the writer to his characters? Explain. What does Gide mean when he says that the "true novelist" "listens to [his characters] and watches them function"? What would Burnett say of this statement?

7. What is the distinction between *plot* and *story* in E. M. Forster's view? What does Forster mean by "causality"? Demonstrate the structural causality that exists in a story such as Hawthorne's "Young Goodman Brown."

8. How would *character* (as Henry James, Arnold Bennett, or Ivy Compton Burnett conceive of it) be changed in modern fiction, if

we accept Virginia Woolf's theses? James says that *character* is *incident*. Would this still be true?

9. According to Ivy Compton Burnett, what does a writer have to do to a real-life person in order to make him an effective, believable, character? Would Arnold Bennett agree or disagree? Why?

10. Apply Henry James' concept of the interaction of character and incident to his story "Paste." He contends, for example, that "incident . . . is the illustration of character." Is this true in his story? Explain why or why not.

11. De Maupassant contends that one of the chief functions of the artist is to select "the characteristic details that are useful to his theme." How does he apply this principle in his story "A Coward?" Would this same principle apply to stories such as "Gogol's Wife" or "Action Will Be Taken?"

12. Why does de Maupassant maintain that good art should not provide us with a photographic representation of life? In making this comment, what position is de Maupassant taking on the function of the artist? How does this position differ (if it does) from the positions of Joyce, Virginia Woolf, Conrad, or Faulkner?

13. In Virginia Woolf's conception, how does modern fiction differ from the fiction of previous periods? That is, how has the face of contemporary fiction changed?

14. Conrad says in the Preface to *The Nigger of the "Narcissus"* that "all art . . . appeals primarily to the senses." What senses does Conrad appeal to in his short novel *The Secret Sharer*? He says, further, that the writer's task is to make us hear, feel, and, above all, *see*. How does he accomplish these aims in his short novel?

15. Apply Virginia Woolf's theories of modern fiction to the avant-garde fiction in part 4, "Beyond the Safety Zone." Is this the kind of fiction she had in mind? Would she approve or disapprove of "Welcome to Utah"? "Mandala"? "Blow-up"?

Dateline: The Newspaper and Fiction

A good deal of fiction is directly adapted from real life, either from an artist's personal experiences or from recorded incidents and events involving people he may not even know. Joseph Conrad built his novel *Lord Jim* from a thin newspaper account of fraud on the high seas. The following newspaper accounts are based on real events and real people, although the editors have "polished" the truth in several instances to enhance fictional possibilities. Determine which of the following accounts are suitable for fiction. Would they best be treated in short story, novella, or novel form? What point of view would be most effective in each case? What point of attack would be most effective? Approach these accounts as if you were a writer. Later, you may choose to review your own newspaper for other potentially rich accounts.

1. Dateline: The Mediterranean, 1797*

On the tenth of the last month a deplorable occurrence took place on board H.M.S. *Indomitable*. John Claggart, the ship's master-at-arms, discovering that some sort of plot was incipient among an inferior section of the ship's company, and that the ringleader was one William Budd; he, Claggart in the act of arraigning the man before the Captain was vindictively stabbed to the heart by the suddenly drawn sheath-knife of Budd.

The deed and the implement employed, sufficiently suggest that though mustered into the service under an English name the assassin was no Englishman, but one of those aliens adopting English cognomens whom the present extradorinary necessities of the Service have caused to be admitted into it in considerable numbers.

The enormity of the crime and the extreme depravity of the criminal appear the greater in view of the character of the victim, a middle-aged man respectable and discreet, belonging to that minor official grade, the petty-officers, upon whom, as none know better than the commissioned gentlemen, the efficiency of His Majesty's navy so largely depends. His function was a responsible one; at once onerous and thankless and his fidelity in it the greater because of his strong patriotic impulse. In this instance as in so many other instances in these days, the character of this unfortunate man signally refutes, if refutation were needed, that peevish saying attributed to the late Dr. Johnson, that patriotism is the last refuge of a scoundrel.

The criminal paid the penalty of his crime. The promptitude of the punishment has proved salutary. Nothing amiss is now apprehended aboard H.M.S. *Indomitable*.

2. Dateline: Rome, 1972

Vittorio Federici, Chief of Research for Vatican museums, reports that a secret signature, a small "m," has been found in the left palm of the

* From a work by H. Melville, noted American cetologist. All other newspaper accounts were prepared by the editors from actual newspaper stories.

Madonna in Michelangelo's famous Pietá. The signature, which has gone unnoticed for centuries, was found by Paolo Michaeli, one of several artists repairing damage inflicted by a religious fanatic several months ago.

3. Dateline: Jardín de Pirañas, Paraguay, South America, 1972

For almost two hundred years the villagers in Jardín de Pirañas, a small village of 2,000 inhabitants located at the southern tip of Paraguay, knew that they were squatters on land owned by an unknown landowner possessing the deed to the 20 square miles on which the village is located. It was not until this week that the mystery was cleared up. Jesús María Sanchez, an eccentric local peddler, laughingstock of the village, and allegedly the village idiot, died. When his son, also a peddler, went through his effects, he found the deed to the land in his father's Bible. The son says that he will not force the villagers to leave if they submit to his rule. Asked by reporters what kind of system he will enforce, he was quoted as saying, "benevolent despotism."

4. Dateline: The Moon, July 19, 1969

Astronaut Neil Armstrong became the first man to set foot on an alien stellar body today. An hour later, Astronaut Buzz Aldrin followed him onto lunar soil, while Astronaut Michael Collins circled the moon in the command module. The successful landing culminated an effort of almost ten years to beat the Russians to the moon.

5. Dateline: The Philippines, 1971

A tribe of Stone Age men, virtually untouched by civilization, has been revealed in the Tasaday watershed in the Philippine Islands. Dr. Eusebio Martínez, credited with the discovery of the tribe, is considered a god by the tribesmen. The tribe has virtually no tools. He communicates to the tribesmen through a native he befriended on his first trip into the watershed, two years ago. They do have a language and are primarily vegetarians, supplementing their diet with fish and whatever small animals they can trap. Dr. Martínez, who refuses to reveal the exact location of the tribe, says that "the people are docile and extraordinarily kind. Violence is a concept they do not understand."

6. Dateline: Addis Ababa, Ethiopia, 1972

Ethiopian sky marshals killed seven hijackers today, the highest death toll in a long series of airplane hijackings. Nine people were injured. Professor Roderick Hilsinger, 40, a philosophy professor at Temple University, was cited for bravery by authorities for preventing additional deaths by picking up an unpinned grenade and throwing it into an unoccupied portion of the plane. He was injured by flying shrapnel. A conflicting report said that one of the hijackers disposed of the grenade. Dr. Hilsinger is described by colleagues as a "retiring and scholarly man." He was quoted as saying that "it wasn't heroism, it was survival."

7. Dateline: The Andes, Christmas, 1972

It was confirmed today that some of the sixteen survivors of the October 13 plane crash in the Chilean Andes had committed what one survivor called "unspeakable practices and unnatural acts" to sustain life once limited food supplies were exhausted. Twenty-nine Uruguayan rugby players, relatives, and friends died in the crash and subsequent 70-day ordeal. According to one survivor, the acts of cannibalism were performed "only after extended philosophical debate." No relatives of the survivors were eaten. Another survivor likened the acts to a transplant. Another survivor was quoted as saying that "just as Christ gave his body and blood for the salvation of humanity, some of our dead companions helped us to survive." A Roman Catholic theologian in Rome said that he felt the acts were not immoral, "given the unique circumstances of a most unusual case."

8. Dateline: London, *London Times* Want Ads, anytime

Middle-aged, middle-class female eunuch, tired of life alone with 13-year-old boy, appalled by looming vista of life with aging mother, would like to contact others, possibly men also, to discuss possibility of semi-communal establishment, in or near London.

The Stream-of-Consciousness Technique

Although "civilized" people have always been intrigued by their thought processes, we do not know with certainty the origin of the literary record of the mind at work, the stream-of-consciousness technique and its related forms, some of which are illustrated herein. The three most celebrated modern proponents of the technique are James Joyce (who said that he found the form in Michel Dujardin's French novel *Les lauriers sont coupés*, 1888), Virginia Woolf, and William Faulkner. The seed they brought to flower may have grown from the ancient Greek monody, or from the soliloquy (such as Iago's soliloquy from *Othello*, below), but it is more recognizable in the dramatic monologue, particularly as practiced by Robert Browning (one of whose poems appears below). Except for the remarkable eighteenth-century novel *Tristram Shandy*, then, we can say that the stream-of-consciousness technique is a nineteenth-century fiction development perfected in the twentieth century, with related forms in both poetry and drama. In addition, we can, as did Robert Humphrey in *Stream of Consciousness in the Modern Novel*, classify two kinds of stream of consciousness: (1) the indirect method, which is typified by the use of the third-person pronoun, and in which thoughts are transmitted to the reader in logical and coherent grammatical and rhetorical form through a filtering presence; and (2) the direct method, which gives the reader raw images and bits and pieces of seemingly unrelated impressions, thoughts, and reflections, all with apparent disregard for the rules of grammar. Despite the two major subcategories of this literary technique, the form is as diverse as the people who employ it. William Faulkner, in his *The Sound and the Fury*, sets apart by italics past conversations and thoughts which impinge upon present ones in a disarming fashion. Sometimes the thoughts of a character are neatly manicured for us, as in the fiction of Virginia Woolf. And sometimes, as in Joyce's *Ulysses*, recorded images, impressions, and memories flood the reader. The range of this technique is wide indeed, and the general term implies varied forms, some of which— together with parent forms—are illustrated below.

Iago's Soliloquy from
OTHELLO (Act I, Scene 3)
(Oct. 1, 1604?)
by William Shakespeare

Thus do I ever make my fool my purse;
For I mine own gained knowledge should profane,
If I would time expend with such a snipe,
But for my sport and profit. I hate the Moor,
And it is thought abroad, that 'twixt my sheets

Has done my office. I know not if't be true,
But I for mere suspicion in that kind
Will do as if for surety. He holds me well;
The better shall my purpose work on him.
Cassio's a proper man. Let me see now;
To get his place, and to plume up my will
In double knavery—how, how? Let's see.
After some time, to abuse Othello's ear
That he is too familiar with his wife—
He hath a person, and a smooth dispose
To be suspected; framed to make women false.
The Moor is of a free and open nature,
That thinks men honest, that but seem to be so,
And will as tenderly be led by th' nose
As asses are.
I have it; it is engendered. Hell and night
Must bring this monstrous birth to the world's light.

SOLILOQUY OF THE
SPANISH CLOISTER
by Robert Browning

Gr-r-r—there go, my heart's abhorrence!
    Water your damned flower-pots, do!
If hate killed men, Brother Lawrence,
    God's blood, would not mine kill you!
What? your myrtle-bush wants trimming?
    Oh, that rose has prior claims—
Needs its leaden vase filled brimming?
    Hell dry you up with its flames!

At the meal we sit together:
    Salve tibi![1] I must hear
Wise talk of the kind of weather,
    Sort of season, time of year:
Not a plenteous cork-crop: scarcely
    Dare we hope oak-galls, I doubt:
What's the Latin name for "parsley"?
    What's the Greek name for Swine's Snout?

---

[1] Hail, or God save thee.

Whew! We'll have our platter burnished,
    Laid with care on our own shelf!
With a fire-new spoon we're furnished,
    And a goblet for ourself,
Rinsed like something sacrificial
    Ere 'tis fit to touch our chaps—
Marked with L for our initial!
    (He-he! There his lily snaps!)

Saint, forsooth! While brown Dolores
    Squats outside the Convent bank
With Sanchicha, telling stories,
    Steeping tresses in the tank,
Blue-black, lustrous, thick like horsehairs,
    —Can't I see his dead eye glow,
Bright as 'twere a Barbary corsair's?
    (That is, if he'd let it show!)

When he finishes refection,
    Knife and fork he never lays
Cross-wise, to my recollection,
    As do I, in Jesu's praise.
I the Trinity illustrate,
    Drinking watered orange-pulp—
In three sips the Arian[2] frustrate;
    While he drains his at one gulp.

Oh, those melons? If he's able
    We're to have a feast! so nice!
One goes to the Abbot's table,
    All of us get each a slice.
How go on your flowers? None double?
    Not one fruit-sort can you spy?
Strange!—And I, too, at such trouble,
    Keep them close-nipped on the sly!

There's a great text in Galatians,
    Once you trip on it, entails
Twenty-nine distinct damnations,
    One sure, if another fails:
If I trip him just a-dying,
    Sure of heaven as sure can be,
Spin him round and send him flying
    Off to hell, a Manichee?[3]

---

[2] An anti-Trinitarian heretic.
[3] Again, a heretic, believing the universe to be comprised of two opposing principles: light and dark, or good and evil.

Or, my scrofulous French novel
    On grey paper with blunt type!
Simply glance at it, you grovel
    Hand and foot in Belial's gripe:
If I double down its pages
    'At the woeful sixteenth print,
When he gathers his greengages,
    Ope a sieve[4] and slip it in't?

Or, there's Satan—one might venture
    Pledge one's soul to him, yet leave
Such a flaw in the endenture
    As he'd miss till, past retrieve,
Blasted lay that rose-acacia
    We're so proud of! *Hy, Zy Hine* . . .
'St, there's Vespers! *Plena gratiâ*
    Ave, Virgo![5] Gr-r-r—you swine!

from MRS. DALLOWAY
and TO THE LIGHTHOUSE
by Virginia Woolf

> *Samples 1, 2, and 3 are from Virginia Woolf's novel (1925) in which Mrs. Dalloway, an aging aristocrat of tenuous physical substance, prepares for a party. The entire novel, uninterrupted by chapter breaks, is enclosed by one day, the movement from day to night. Recalling the past and reflecting on her own mortality, Mrs. Dalloway searches for some absolute truth or thing in a fluid and chaotic world. Note in particular Woolf's use of the parenthesis and punctuation.*

1

And everywhere, though it was still so early, there was a beating, a stirring of galloping ponies, tapping of cricket bats; Lords, Ascot, Ranelagh and all the rest of it; wrapped in the soft mesh of the grey-blue morning air, which, as the day wore on, would unwind them, and set down

---

[4] A basket.
[5] Hail, Virgin (Mary), full of grace.

on their lawns and pitches the bouncing ponies, whose forefeet just struck the ground and up they sprung, the whirling young men, and laughing girls in their transparent muslins who, even now, after dancing all night, were taking their absurd woolly dogs for a run; and even now, at this hour, discreet old dowagers were shooting out in their motor cars on errands of mystery; and the shopkeepers were fidgeting in their windows with their paste and diamonds, their lovely old sea-green brooches in eighteenth-century settings to tempt Americans (but one must economise, not buy things rashly for Elizabeth), and she, too, loving it as she did with an absurd and faithful passion, being part of it, since her people were courtiers once in the time of the Georges, she, too, was going that very night to kindle and illuminate; to give her party.

2

Did it matter then, she asked herself, walking towards Bond Street, did it matter that she must inevitably cease completely; all this must go on without her; did she resent it; or did it not become consoling to believe that death ended absolutely? but that somehow in the streets of London, on the ebb and flow of things, here, there, she survived, Peter survived, lived in each other, she being part, she was positive, of the trees at home; of the house there, ugly, rambling all to bits and pieces as it was; part of people she had never met; being laid out like a mist between the people she knew best, who lifted her on their branches as she had seen the trees lift the mist, but it spread ever so far, her life, herself.

3

Only for a moment; but it was enough. It was a sudden revelation, a tinge like a blush which one tried to check and then, as it spread, one yielded to its expansion, and rushed to the farthest verge and there quivered and felt the world come closer, swollen with some astonishing significance, some pressure of rapture, which split its thin skin and gushed and poured with an extraordinary alleviation over the cracks and sores! Then, for that moment, she had seen an illumination; a match burning in a crocus; an inner meaning almost expressed. But the close withdrew; the hard softened. It was over—the moment.

> *Sample 4 is from Woolf's* To the Lighthouse *(1927),*
> *which shares many themes with* Mrs. Dalloway, *chiefly the*
> *transience and insignificance of human life and event*
> *(here reduced to brackets) amid the flux of time. The novel*
> *is divided into three major parts: in the first, the Ramsay*
> *family plans a trip to the lighthouse, only to have it aborted*
> *by bad weather; in part two, "Time Passes," from which*
> *this excerpt is taken, ten years pass, during which several*
> *of the original party die; in part three, those who remain*
> *complete the pilgrimage to the lighthouse.*

4

The spring without a leaf to toss, bare and bright like a virgin fierce in her chastity, scornful in her purity, was laid out on fields wide-eyed and watchful and entirely careless of what was done or thought by the beholders. [Prue Ramsay, leaning on her father's arm, was given in marriage. What, people said, could have been more fitting? And, they added, how beautiful she looked!]

As summer neared, as the evenings lengthened, there came to the wakeful, the hopeful, walking the beach, stirring the pool, imaginations of the strangest kind—of flesh turned to atoms which drove before the wind, of stars flashing in their hearts. Of cliff, sea, cloud, and sky brought purposely together to assemble outwardly the scattered parts of the vision within. In those mirrors, the minds of men, in those pools of uneasy water, in which clouds for ever turn and shadows form, dreams persisted, and it was impossible to resist the strange intimation which every gull, flower, tree, man and woman, and the white earth itself seemed to declare (but if questioned at once to withdraw) that good triumphs, happiness prevails, order rules; or to resist the extraordinary stimulus to range hither and thither in search of some absolute good, some crystal of intensity, remote from the known pleasures and familiar virtues, something alien to the processes of domestic life, single, hard, bright, like a diamond in the sand, which would render the possessor secure. Moreover, softened and acquiescent, the spring with her bees humming and gnats dancing threw her cloak about her, veiled her eyes, averted her head, and among passing shadows and flights of small rain seemed to have taken upon her a knowledge of the sorrows of mankind.

[Prue Ramsay died that summer in some illness connected with childbirth, which was indeed a tragedy, people said, everything, they said, had promised so well.]

And now in the heat of summer the wind sent its spies about the house again. Flies wove a web in the sunny rooms; weeds that had grown close to the glass in the night tapped methodically at the window pane. When darkness fell, the stroke of the Lighthouse, which had laid itself with such authority upon the carpet in the darkness, tracing its pattern, came now in the softer light of spring mixed with moonlight gliding gently as if it laid its caress and lingered stealthily and looked and came lovingly again. But in the very lull of this loving caress, as the long stroke leant upon the bed, the rock was rent asunder: another fold of the shawl loosened; there it hung, and swayed. Through the short summer nights and the long summer days, when the empty rooms seemed to murmur with the echoes of the fields and the hum of flies, the long streamer waved gently, swayed aimlessly; while the sun so striped and barred the rooms and filled them with yellow haze that Mrs. McNab, when she broke in and lurched about, dusting, sweeping, looked like a tropical fish oaring its way through sunlanced waters.

But slumber and sleep though it might there came later in the summer ominous sounds like the measured blows of hammers dulled on felt, which, with their repeated shocks still further loosened the shawl and cracked the tea-cups. Now and again some glass tinkled in the cupboard as if a giant voice had shrieked so loud in its agony that tumblers stood inside a cupboard vibrated too. Then again silence fell; and then, night after night, and sometimes in plain mid-day when the roses were bright and light turned on the wall its shape clearly there seemed to drop into this silence, this indifference, this integrity, the thud of something falling.

[A shell exploded. Twenty or thirty young men were blown up in France, among them Andrew Ramsay, whose death, mercifully, was instantaneous.]

At that season those who had gone down to pace the beach and ask of the sea and sky what message they reported or what vision they affirmed had to consider among the usual tokens of divine bounty—the sunset on the sea, the pallor of dawn, the moon rising, fishing-boats against the moon, and children making mud pies or pelting each other with handfuls of grass, something out of harmony with this jocundity and this serenity. There was the silent apparition of an ashen-coloured ship for instance, come, gone; there was a purplish stain upon the bland surface of the sea as if something had boiled and bled, invisibly, beneath. This intrusion into a scene calculated to stir the most sublime reflections and lead to the most comfortable conclusions stayed their pacing. It was difficult blandly to overlook them; to abolish their significance in the landscape; to continue, as one walked by the sea, to marvel how beauty outside mirrored beauty within.

Did Nature supplement what man advanced? Did she complete what he began? With equal complacence she saw his misery, his meanness, and his torture. That dream, of sharing, completing, of finding in solitude on the beach an answer, was then but a reflection in a mirror, and the mirror itself was but the surface glassiness which forms in quiescence when the nobler powers sleep beneath? Impatient, despairing yet loth to go (for beauty offers her lures, has her consolations), to pace the beach was impossible; contemplation was unendurable; the mirror was broken.

[Mr. Carmichael brought out a volume of poems that spring, which had an unexpected success. The war, people said, had revived their interest in poetry.]

from Molly Bloom's Soliloquy
from ULYSSES
by James Joyce

*Perhaps the most famous stream-of-consciousness passage
in modern literature is Molly Bloom's forty-page rambling
soliloquy just prior to the end of the day in James Joyce's
Ulysses (1922), a novel of Everyman, everything, and
all time. Here Molly recalls, in seemingly random fashion,
the day Mr. Bloom proposed to her. In reality, the passage
is tightly knit by the logic of association and by the careful
repetition of key images, motifs, and words. This great
novel, covering one day, encloses all time as a record
of human experience.*

. . . the sun shines for you he said the day we were lying among the
rhododendrons on Howth head in the grey tweed suit and his straw hat the
day I got him to propose to me yes first I gave him the bit of seedcake out
of my mouth and it was leapyear like now yes 16 years ago my God after
that long kiss I near lost my breath yes he said I was a flower of the
mountain yes so we are flowers all a womans body yes that was one true
thing he said in his life and the sun shines for you today yes that was why I
liked him because I saw he understood or felt what a woman is and I knew
I could always get round him and I gave him all the pleasure I could
leading him on till he asked me to say yes and I wouldnt answer first only
looked out over the sea and the sky I was thinking of so many things he
didnt know of Mulvey and Mr Stanhope and Hester and father and old
captain Groves and the sailors playing all birds fly and I say stoop and
washing up dishes they called it on the pier and the sentry in front of the
governors house with the thing round his white helmet poor devil half
roasted and the Spanish girls laughing in their shawls and their tall combs
and the auctions in the morning the Greeks and the jews and the Arabs
and the devil knows who else from all the ends of Europe and Duke street
and the fowl market all clucking outside Larby Sharons and the poor
donkeys slipping half asleep and the vague fellows in the cloaks asleep in
the shade on the steps and the big wheels of the carts of the bulls and the
old castle thousands of years old yes and those handsome Moors all in
white and turbans like kings asking you to sit down in their little bit of a
shop and Ronda with the old windows of the posadas glancing eyes a
lattice hid for her lover to kiss the iron and the wineshops half open at
night and the castanets and the night we missed the boat at Algeciras the

watchman going about serene with his lamp and O that awful deepdown torrent O and the sea the sea crimson sometimes like fire and the glorious sunsets and the figtrees in the Alameda gardens yes and all the queer little streets and pink and blue and yellow houses and the rosegardens and the jessamine and geraniums and cactuses and Gibraltar as a girl where I was a Flower of the mountain yes when I put the rose in my hair like the Andalusian girls used or shall I wear a red yes and how he kissed me under the Moorish wall and I thought well as well him as another and then I asked him with my eyes to ask again yes and then he asked me would I yes to say yes my mountain flower and first I put my arms around him yes and drew him down to me so he could feel my breasts all perfume yes and his heart was going like mad and yes I said yes I will Yes.

Saints and Sinners:
Character Types in Fiction

The following gallery of archetypes and fictional models is a representative handful of character types. It does not pretend to be comprehensive, nor does it tap the wealth of archetypes found in poetry and drama. It suggests how various characters—some old, some new—reveal themselves in Western thought and literature. The gallery is a crowded one; with this limited collection of portraits we merely sample some of the categories of human personality which manifest themselves again and again in fiction.

The Fallen Adam

Billy Budd from
BILLY BUDD
by Herman Melville

Yes, Billy Budd was a foundling, a presumable by-blow, and, evidently, no ignoble one. Noble descent was as evident in him as in a blood horse.

For the rest, with little or no sharpness of faculty or any trace of the wisdom of the serpent, nor yet quite a dove, he possessed a certain degree of intelligence along with the unconventional rectitude of a sound human creature—one to whom not yet has been proffered the questionable apple of knowledge. He was illiterate; he could not read, but he could sing, and like the illiterate nightingale was sometimes the composer of his own song.

480 / THE WRITER'S WORKSHOP

Of self-consciousness he seemed to have little or none, or about as much as we may reasonably impute to a dog of St. Bernard's breed.

Habitually being with the elements and knowing little more of the land than as a beach, or, rather, that portion of the terraqueous globe providentially set apart for dance-houses, doxies and tapsters, in short, what sailors call a "fiddlers' green," his simple nature remained unsophisticated by those moral obliquities which are not in every case incomparable with that manufacturable thing known as respectability. But are sailor frequenters of fiddlers' greens without vices? No; but less often than with landsmen do their vices, so-called, partake of crookedness of heart, seeming less to proceed from viciousness than exuberance of vitality after long restraint, frank manifestations in accordance with natural law. By his original constitution, aided by the co-operating influences of his lot, Billy in many respects was little more than a sort of upright barbarian much such perhaps as Adam presumably might have been ere the urbane Serpent wriggled himself into his company.

.   .   .

Though our Handsome Sailor had as much of masculine beauty as one can expect anywhere to see; nevertheless, like the beautiful woman in one of Hawthorne's minor tales, there was just one thing amiss in him. No visible blemish, indeed, as with the lady; no, but an occasional liability to a vocal defect. Though in the hour of elemental uproar or peril, he was everything that a sailor should be, yet under sudden provocation of strong heart-feeling his voice, otherwise singularly musical, as if expressive of the harmony within, was apt to develop an organic hesitancy,—in fact, more or less of a stutter or even worse. In this particular Billy was a striking instance that the arch-interpreter, the envious marplot of Eden, still has more or less to do with every human consignment to this planet of earth. In every case, one way or another, he is sure to slip in his little card, as much as to remind us—I too have a hand here.

A Modern Eve

Fayaway from
TYPEE
by Herman Melville

Fearful lest some fatal calamity had overtaken him, I sought out young Fayaway, and endeavoured to learn from her, if possible, the truth.

This gentle being had early attracted my regard, not only from her extraordinary beauty, but from the attractive cast of her countenance, singularly expressive of intelligence and humanity. Of all the natives she alone seemed to appreciate the effect which the peculiarity of the circumstances in which we were placed had produced upon the minds of my companion and myself. In addressing me—especially when I lay reclining upon the mats suffering from pain—there was a tenderness in her manner which it was impossible to misunderstand or resist. Whenever she entered the house, the expression of her face indicated the liveliest sympathy for me; and moving towards the place where I lay, with one arm slightly elevated in a gesture of pity, and her large glistening eyes gazing intently into mine, she would murmur plaintively, "Awha! awha! Tommo," and seat herself mournfully beside me.

Her manner convinced me that she deeply compassionated my situation, as being removed from my country and friends, and placed beyond the reach of all relief. Indeed, at times I was almost led to believe that her mind was swayed by gentle impulses hardly to be anticipated from one in her condition; that she appeared to be conscious there were ties rudely severed, which had once bound us to our homes; that there were sisters and brothers anxiously looking forward to our return, who were, perhaps, never more to behold us.

In this amiable light did Fayaway appear in my eyes; and reposing full confidence in her candour and intelligence, I now had recourse to her, in the midst of my alarm, with regard to my companion.

. . .

At this place the waters flowed between grassy banks, planted with enormous breadfruit-trees, whose vast branches, interlacing overhead, formed a leafy canopy; near the stream were several smooth black rocks. One of these, projecting several feet above the surface of the water, had upon its summit a shallow cavity, which, filled with freshly gathered leaves, formed a delightful couch.

Here I often lay for hours, covered with a gauze-like veil of tappa, while Fayaway, seated beside me, and holding in her hand a fan woven from the leaflets of a young coco-nut bough, brushed aside the insects that occasionally lighted on my face, and Kory-Kory, with a view of chasing away my melancholy, performed a thousand antics in the water before us.

As my eye wandered along this romantic stream, it would fall upon the half-immersed figure of a beautiful girl, standing in the transparent water, and catching in a little net a species of diminutive shell-fish, of which these people are extravagantly fond. Sometimes a chattering group would be seated upon the edge of a low rock in the midst of the brook, busily engaged in thinning and polishing the shells of coco-nuts, by rubbing them briskly with a small stone in the water, an operation which soon converts them into a light and elegant drinking-vessel, somewhat resembling goblets made of tortoiseshell.

But the tranquillizing influences of beautiful scenery, and the exhibition of human life under so novel and charming an aspect, were not my only sources of consolation.

The Serpent in the Garden

Claggart from
BILLY BUDD
by Herman Melville

Claggart was a man of about five-and-thirty, somewhat spare and tall, yet of no ill figure upon the whole. His hand was too small and shapely to have been accustomed to hard toil. The face was a notable one; the features, all except the chin, cleanly cut as those on a Greek medallion; yet the chin, beardless as Tecumseh's, had something of the strange protuberant heaviness in its make that recalled the prints of the Rev. Dr. Titus Oates, the historical deponent with the clerical drawl in the time of Charles II, and the fraud of the alleged Popish Plot. It served Claggart in his office that his eye could cast a tutoring glance. His brow was of the sort phrenologically associated with more than average intellect; silken jet curls, partly clustering over it, making a foil to the pallor below, a pallor tinged with a faint shade of amber akin to the hue of time-tinted marbles of old.

This complexion singularly contrasting with the red or deeply bronzed visages of the sailors, and in part the result of his official seclusion from the sunlight, though it was not exactly displeasing, nevertheless seemed to hint of something defective or abnormal in the constitution and blood. But his general aspect and manner were so suggestive of an education and career incongruous with his naval function, that when not actively engaged in it he looked like a man of high quality, social and moral, who for reasons of his own was keeping incognito.

. . .

In a list of definitions included in the authentic translation of Plato, a list is attributed to him, occurs this: "Natural Depravity: a depravity according to nature." A definition which, though savouring of Calvinism, by no means involves Calvin's dogma as to total mankind. Evidently its intent makes it applicable but to individuals. Not many are the examples of this depravity which the gallows and jail supply. At any rate, for notable instances—since these have no vulgar alloy of the brute in them, but invariably are dominated by intellectuality—one must go elsewhere. Civilisation, especially if of the austerer sort, is auspicious to it. It folds itself in the mantle of respectability. It has its certain negative virtues serving as silent auxiliaries. It is not going too far to say that it is without vices or small sins. There is a phenomenal pride in it that excludes them from anything—never mercenary or avaricious. In short, the depravity here meant partakes nothing of the sordid or sensual. It is serious, but free from acerbity. Though no flatterer of mankind, it never speaks ill of it.

But the thing which in eminent instances signalises so exceptional a nature is this: though the man's even temper and discreet bearing would seem to intimate a mind peculiarly subject to the law of reason, not the less in his soul's recesses he would seem to riot in complete exemption from that law, having apparently little to do with reason further than to employ it as an ambidexter implement for effecting the irrational. That is to say: toward the accomplishment of an aim which is wantonness of malignity would seem to partake of the insane, he will direct a cool judgment sagacious and sound.

These men are true madmen, and of the most dangerous sort, for their lunacy is not continuous, but occasional; evoked by some special object; it is secretive and self-contained, so that when most active it is to the average mind not distinguished from sanity, and for the reason above suggested that whatever its aim may be, and the aim is never disclosed, the method and the outward proceeding is always perfectly rational.

Now something such was Claggart, in whom was the mania of an evil nature, not engendered by vicious training or corrupting books or licentious living, but born with him and innate, in short, "a depravity according to nature."

The Intellectual Sinner

Aylmer from
THE BIRTHMARK
by Nathaniel Hawthorne

In the latter part of the last century there lived a man of science, an eminent proficient in every branch of natural philosophy, who not long before our story opens had made experience of a spiritual affinity more attractive than any chemical one. He had left his laboratory to the care of an assistant, cleared his fine countenance from the furnace smoke, washed the stain of acids from his fingers, and persuaded a beautiful woman to become his wife. In those days when the comparatively recent discovery of electricity and other kindred mysteries of Nature seemed to open paths into the region of miracle, it was not unusual for the love of science to rival the love of woman in its depth and absorbing energy. The higher intellect, the imagination, the spirit, and even the heart might all find their congenial aliment in pursuits which, as some of their ardent votaries believed, would ascend from one step of powerful intelligence to another, until the philosopher should lay his hand on the secret of creative force and perhaps make new worlds for himself. We know not whether Aylmer possessed this degree of faith in man's ultimate control over Nature. He had devoted himself, however, too unreservedly to scientific studies ever to be weaned from them by any second passion. His love for his young wife might prove the stronger of the two; but it could only be by intertwining itself with his love of science, and uniting the strength of the latter to his own.

Such a union accordingly took place, and was attended with truly remarkable consequences and a deeply impressive moral. One day, very soon after their marriage, Aylmer sat gazing at his wife with a trouble in his countenance that grew stronger until he spoke.

"Georgiana," said he, "has it never occurred to you that the mark upon your cheek might be removed?"

"No, indeed," said she, smiling; but perceiving the seriousness of his manner, she blushed deeply. "To tell you the truth it has been so often called a charm that I was simple enough to imagine it might be so."

"Ah, upon another face perhaps it might," replied her husband; "but never on yours. No, dearest Georgiana, you came so nearly perfect from the hand of Nature that this slightest possible defect, which we hesitate whether to term a defect or a beauty, shocks me, as being the visible mark of earthly imperfection."

"Shocks you, my husband!" cried Georgiana, deeply hurt; at first reddening with momentary anger, but then bursting into tears. "Then why did you take me from my mother's side? You cannot love what shocks you!"

To explain this conversation it must be mentioned that in the centre of Georgiana's left cheek there was a singular mark, deeply interwoven, as it were, with the texture and substance of her face. In the usual state of her complexion—a healthy though delicate bloom—the mark wore a tint of deeper crimson, which imperfectly defined its shape amid the surrounding rosiness. When she blushed it gradually became more indistinct, and finally vanished amid the triumphant rush of blood that bathed the whole cheek with its brilliant glow. But if any shifting motion caused her to turn pale, there was the mark again, a crimson stain upon the snow, in what Aylmer sometimes deemed an almost fearful distinctness. Its shape bore not a little similarity to the human hand, though of the smallest pygmy size. Georgiana's lovers were wont to say that some fairy at her birth hour had laid her tiny hand upon the infant's cheek, and left this impress there in token of the magic endowments that were to give her such sway over all hearts. Many a desperate swain would have risked life for the privilege of pressing his lips to the mysterious hand. It must not be concealed, however, that the impression wrought by this fairy sign manual varied exceedingly, according to the difference of temperament in the beholders. Some fastidious persons—but they were exclusively of her own sex—affirmed that the bloody hand, as they chose to call it, quite destroyed the effect of Georgiana's beauty, and rendered her countenance even hideous. But it would be as reasonable to say that one of those small blue stains which sometimes occur in the purest statuary marble would convert the Eve of Powers to a monster. Masculine observers, if the birthmark did not heighten their admiration, contented themselves with wishing it away, that the world might possess one living specimen of ideal loveliness without the semblance of a flaw. After his marriage,—for he thought little or nothing of the matter before,—Aylmer discovered that this was the case with himself.

Had she been less beautiful,—if Envy's self could have found aught else to sneer at,—he might have felt his affection heightened by the prettiness of this mimic hand, now vaguely portrayed, now lost, now stealing forth again and glimmering to and fro with every pulse of emotion that throbbed within her heart; but seeing her otherwise so perfect, he found this one defect grow more and more intolerable with every moment of their united lives. It was the fatal flaw of humanity which Nature, in one shape or another, stamps ineffaceably on all her productions, either to imply that they are temporary and finite, or that their perfection must be wrought by toil and pain. The crimson hand expressed the ineludible gripe in which mortality clutches the highest and purest of earthly mould, degrading them into kindred with the lowest, and even with the very brutes, like whom their visible frames return to dust. In this manner, selecting it as the symbol of his wife's liability to sin, sorrow, decay, and death, Aylmer's sombre imagination was not long in rendering the birthmark a frightful object, causing him more trouble and horror than ever Georgiana's beauty, whether of soul or sense, had given him delight.

The Middle-Class Gentleman

Mr. Podsnap from
OUR MUTUAL FRIEND
by Charles Dickens

Mr. Podsnap was well to do, and stood very high in Mr. Podsnap's opinion. Beginning with a good inheritance, he had married a good inheritance, and had thriven exceedingly in the Marine Insurance way, and was quite satisfied. He never could make out why everybody was not quite satisfied, and he felt conscious that he set a brilliant social example in being particularly well satisfied with most things, and, above all other things, with himself.

Thus happily acquainted with his own merit and importance, Mr. Podsnap settled that whatever he put behind him he put out of existence. There was a dignified conclusiveness—not to add a grand convenience—in this way of getting rid of disagreeables, which had done much towards establishing Mr. Podsnap in his lofty place in Mr. Podsnap's satisfaction. "I don't want to know about it; I don't choose to discuss it; I don't admit it!" Mr. Podsnap had even acquired a peculiar flourish of his right arm in often clearing the world of its most difficult problems, by sweeping them behind him (and consequently sheer away) with those words and a flushed face. For they affronted him.

Mr. Podsnap's world was not a very large world, morally; no, nor even geographically: seeing that although his business was sustained upon commerce with other countries, he considered other countries, with that important reservation, a mistake, and of their manners and customs would conclusively observe, "Not English!" when, PRESTO! with a flourish of the arm, and a flush of the face, they were swept away. Elsewise, the world got up at eight, shaved close at a quarter-past, breakfasted at nine, went to the City at ten, came home at half-past five, and dined at seven. Mr. Podsnap's notions of the Arts in their integrity might have been stated thus. Literature; large print, respectively descriptive of getting up at eight, shaving close at a quarter-past, breakfasting at nine, going to the City at ten, coming home at half-past five, and dining at seven. Painting and Sculpture; models and portraits representing Professors of getting up at eight, shaving close at a quarter-past, breakfasting at nine, going to the City at ten, coming home at half-past five, and dining at seven. Music; a respectable performance (without variations) on stringed and wind instruments, sedately expressive of getting up at eight, shaving close at a quarter-past, breakfasting at nine, going to the City at ten, coming home at half-past five, and dining at seven. Nothing else to be permitted to those same vagrants the Arts, on pain of excommunication. Nothing else To Be— anywhere!

As a so eminently respectable man, Mr. Podsnap was sensible of its being required of him to take Providence under his protection. Consequently he always knew exactly what Providence meant. Inferior and less respectable men might fall short of that mark, but Mr. Podsnap was always up to it. And it was very remarkable (and must have been very comfortable) that what Providence meant, was invariably what Mr. Podsnap meant.

The Writer's Laboratory

This section provides for experimentation with aspects of the creative process in a laboratory situation. The central purpose here is not to train writers, but to attune readers to the many alternatives, factors, and elements that the professional writer must weigh and evaluate before, during, and after the creative act. Ideally, this exercise will convince the student that a good writer uses not only his heart but also his head. In doing so, he sets into operation the basic principles of fiction discussed in "The Roots of Fiction," the introductory essay in this book. A quick review of that essay may be good preparation for the problems that follow. The student-writer will doubtless benefit most from this section if he carefully studies the following questions before composing: What theme or controlling ideas does he propose to treat? What is the desired relationship of author to narrator? narrator to work? narrator to reader? What basic motivation guides the characters in the frame-story as he conceives of it? How is that motivation most effectively illustrated? Is the material in the frame-story most effectively treated in short or long fiction? How should time be treated in the work? chronologically? How much description should the writer give? What balance of narration and dialogue most effectively treats the fictional possibilities of the material? What methods of characterization should you employ? What use should you make of Lajos Egri's breakdown of character anatomy into physiology, sociology, and psychology? What other factors covered in the introductory essay should be further considered? The student must be careful not to attempt to do too much; that is, he should not attempt to write an entire story for each problem, but instead limit himself to the immediate problem, "solving" the frame-story, step by step, in natural progression.

APARTMENT FOR RENT
a Frame-Story
by Carlos Fontana

SEQUENCE OF EVENTS IN CHRONOLOGICAL ORDER

1. A young man rents a basement apartment and learns from the landlady that the room adjoining his bedroom is occupied by a very old man "who stays in his own room and don't bother nobody."

2. Alone in his room for the first time, he carefully examines the apartment he has rented, noticing minute and particular details, such as a crack in the ceiling, a fly caught in a small spider web, the water pipes which run up through the floor through the ceiling. He lies down to rest and hears the old man cough.

3. Repeatedly during the week that follows he hears the old man moving about and coughing, but he does not see the old man until a week later, when he bumps into him on the stairway leading out of the basement.

4. That evening he can think only of his encounter with the old man. Very early in the morning he is awakened by the old man's cough and is unable to sleep.

5. He resolves to kill the old man and carefully plots a crime "whose exactness and intellectual precision will be its justification."

6. There is at least one aborted entry into the old man's room, but finally he enters the old man's apartment and kills him.

7. The story is told after the killing from the point of view of someone not directly involved in the action, perhaps at a trial, at the landlady's home, at a neighbor's home, etc.

EXPERIMENTS

1. Determine if the story is—given these materials—a short story, novella, or novel. Why?

2. Use each of the basic points of view on one or more parts of the frame-story. Can you successfully alternate points of view to piece

together a "mosaic" story? Do you get a fragmented effect? Is that undesirable? Explain. Which point of view was most effective? Why? Which part of the story might lend itself best to the use of stream of consciousness? Why?

3. Use first person central point of view in developing part seven of the frame-story. Now use first person peripheral. What character might you consider for the latter?

4. How is your story affected if you begin your point of attack with part seven of the frame story? With each of the other parts? Which strikes you as most effective? Why? Which part, if any, does not lend itself to treatment as a point of attack? Why not?

5. Give a physical description of any of the characters in the story. Now use some gesture, habit, physical act, or movement to depict and make your character distinctive.

6. Depict any one of the characters in the story through what he/she says and, perhaps, by some peculiarity of speech.

7. Depict any one of the characters through his/her environment.

8. Depict any one of the characters through his/her effect on another character.

9. Write a brief exchange of dialogue between any two characters in the frame-story about a third character.

10. What senses can you appeal to most effectively in any of the above experiments to draw your reader into the story? What sense or senses are least helpful? Why?

11. Are there enough basic parts in the frame-tale to make for a viable plot? If not, what could you add to strengthen the plot?

12. Can you experiment with time here as Faulkner does in "A Rose for Emily"? If so, in what order would you arrange the elements of the frame-story?

13. Write a section in which the central character talks out his thoughts.

14. Use the indirect stream of consciousness technique to reveal the protagonist's thoughts, perhaps treating the material in problem

thirteen. Now use the direct stream of consciousness technique. Which most effectively treats the material?

15. Write a section in which the narrator enters the story, as Melville does in *Billy Budd*. Where in the sequence of events can you most effectively do this? Now rewrite the same section objectifying the narrator out of the story. Which of the two methods is most effective? Why?

16. Write a section in which you treat some object, incident, event, or person from multiple perspectives; that is, as seen by different people.

17. Write a short scene in which you work in a diary entry or letter.

18. Take any basic situation you have written and, if it is mostly narration, recast it into dialogue and vice versa. What adjustments must you make? What do you gain or lose in making the two changes?

19. Take any basic situation or phase of the frame tale and write it, copying the style of any one of the authors in this text.

20. Match the following leads to the various stages or elements of the frame-story, and then finish one or more of them:

   A. Carefully, knowingly, as if he had done this many times before, his hand encircled the doorknob as if it were a hand; yet, it felt like a cold pear in his sweaty palm. He was calm, almost objectified out of himself and watching a twin or double doing his deeds.

   B. I closed the apartment since it happened. Who would rent it now anyhow?

   C. It was him! There he was, a face of white bark, with a handkerchief to his coughing mouth and what looked like jellied blood in the handkerchief.

   D. There it was again. And then again! Disgusting and sickening, the sound of raised and expelled phlegm! And once again!

   E. Slowly he approached the half-frame half-redbrick house, the cement chipping away into dust on the second of three concrete steps. A rubber mat, the letters "w," "e," and "l" worn away, was set at an angle on the step. Bird droppings from the large Chinese elms spotted the driveway where the peonies had been torn by someone. Where the droppings and the flowers mixed, the deep pink changed to a blood-like color in a spot just before him and his shoes picked up flakings of the mixture.

21. Do you note any parallels between this story and Poe's "The Tell-Tale Heart"?

22. Can you piece your most effective examples together into a unified whole or entity, filling in whatever gaps remain to complete a story? What changes must you make in the parts as written to make them fit together?

23. Lastly, evaluate and criticize the following exercises. Which are not particularly good? Why not? Which are effective? Why? (Remember that these accounts were prepared in an introduction to fiction course by freshmen with no previous creative writing experience.)

A. Never before had I seen anything that could match the sight I saw at that moment. He was barely five feet, but his height seemed to diminish as he grew closer. His age ranged from sixty-five to a hundred, leaning toward a hundred. The antiquity of the man became more apparent the closer he approached. His wardrobe was a dominant brown, a drab pair of beaten brown leather shoes with a complementing pair of outstretched elastic brown socks. His mahogany shirt was untucked over his food-stained, baggy chestnut pants. His flat head was covered by a ratted mud-colored hat. The gaffer walked with a slight but distinguishable limp and it appeared to me that his right leg was longer than his left.

His total ugliness did not strike me until I saw him face to face on the stairs. His hateful eyes were peering at me out of the slits in his eyelids. His twisted face gave him a sneer for a smile from his crooked mouth. A dirty toothpick was sticking from the geezer's mouth, revealing a set of distorted decaying teeth. A wheezing sound came from the old man's throat. A layer of dirt lay under his long fingernails, and his appearance suggested the old man had not bathed that month. His very sight was repulsive. He smelled of cough medicine and a pill case was escaping from his right pocket. He clutched a dirty handkerchief in his right hand and his left hand moved to wipe a thin line of scarlet trickling from his mouth.

B. His ear picked it up again, there it was! And again! And again! When would that infernal coughing cease. The student uneasily tapped his pen on his papers. His mind went blank, he broke into a cold sweat and his body began to tremble. His physical nervousness could not control his emotional desire to cease the diligent coughing, violently he thrashed his fist upon the study table, beating it, trying to relieve his emotional frustration. He grabbed for the miniature "Rock of Gibraltar" paper weight, stirring his class assignments. Clutching this close to his chest, he envisioned a hundred people coughing at each other in the next room, he wanted to break through the wall and gag every one of them. Unconsciously he thrust the paper weight, knocking over and breaking his only lighted lamp. Darkness swelled in his small apartment. His mind began to hallucinate, the coughing turned to laughing. "Why?" he cried. "Why are they laughing?" His mad attempt of escape from the room that endured the hysterical laughter was delayed in his search for the doorknob. Finding it locked, his only alternative was to break the latch. The door snapped, light trickled into his room, he was free. Running into the narrow hallway he stopped abruptly, there in the grimness of the hall stood an old and crippled man. This was his neighbor. The initial encounter was frightening, the only sound was the student's heavy breathing. The old man began to cough again, he reached into his pocket for a small bottle, suddenly he vomited blood and collapsed limply to the cold cement floor. The young man fell to his knees and cried. It had stopped.

C. The diseased are a burden he said. The diseased breathe and foul the air of the young he said. They should not live he said. They have the stench of bloated sheep about them. The diseased should not live. He watches his hand move slowly, independently of the rest of his body, slowly slowly reach for the doorknob where the infirm are kept and then he pulls back his hand and repeats the movements several times. It pleases him. He smiles. The movements of my hand please me. The fingers dance in unison for they are pleased at what they will do. Slowly he takes his handkerchief from his pocket and covers the doorknob where the infirm are kept for the infirm leave their germs and the diseased are a burden and those who cough phlegm, phlegm is ugly. The work of the mind brings pleasure to the parts of the body. And those who cough disturb the walls. The movement of the opening door reminds him of his moving hand and he smiles. In all things there is movement and stillness and the young must resolve the infirm he says. For the diseased are a burden and the white bark of the face of the infirm must be crushed and spread among the grass and the cough stopped so the walls can have silence. That way the flowers can grow, for the diseased are a burden.

D. As she retold the hideous tale of that damned evening several weeks in the past, I couldn't help but notice the three-sided dimension that seemed to envelope her like a closed black glove. But to my dismay no one else there saw it. They all sat on cushions of sympathy, including that evilly mustached judge—a recreated Midas of death. Only I could see through her atmosphere of sorrowful thinness and faulting calmness to the evil naked soul that hid within her. While my eyes pleaded with the frequent sentencing glares she shot at me for her life-saving mercy, she was all too convincing in shaping the mold that only I could fit. My creation was God's first mistake. Visions of sickening, horror flooded the background of my mind as she continued about how I not only did it one time to that poor old man, but again and again and again until she could share his suffering no longer and fainted. When she finished no one moved or spoke at first, but slowly every head in the room turned in my direction as if watching someone walking my way. Then I saw it again.

E. Slowly his hand encircled the doorknob; it felt like a cold pear in his sweaty palm. As he struggled to turn the rusty knob, the sudden noise of a blasting television upstairs caused him to drop his hand and jump back into the shadow of the nearby stairwell. After what seemed an eternity, he cautiously stepped out into the dim light of the hallway and his hand once again slowly encircled the doorknob. This time the knob turned more easily and he pushed open the door with a slight jar, as if it hadn't been opened in quite some time. At the threshold of the room he stopped, held his breath and listened. No noise, except that of the television above, could be heard. Entering the room, his eyes darted back and forth from side to side as if to survey the contents. It was a dingy room.

F. There was nothing clumsy about Ernst Hausman's movements. He walked with easy coordination, the very motion
of his body giving him pleasure. His tall figure was muscular
and even his large hands were supple from strenuous work.
One had only to glance at him to see the virility bound in
his little body but his even greater intellectual frustration was
masked in his face.

God, he'd be damned if he was going to be stuck in a hole
like that basement room for the rest of his life. Oh, no, he
was meant for *better* things than working as a janitor in a
warehouse. He'd be laughed out of the university if anyone
ever found out that the great mathematical genius was
forced to push a broom to pay his tuition. And to think he
had to live next to some kind of old, diseased derelict. What
had the old man done with his life, anyway? What had he
contributed? He had no friends, no family, and obviously no
money. He didn't even have good health. Just that damned
coughing, night after night. No sir, Ernst Hausman was
never going to become a failure like the old man. The possibility of his ever becoming frail and sick was appalling and
upsetting to think about. No, Ernst Hausman was one young
man who would be powerful and sturdy in his old age, that's
for sure.

G. Look, if you are *really* interested, I'll tell you. Not everything. But what I think you really need to study and weigh
the—the, well, let's call it the trip and the . . . the incident.
I can't think of a better word right off hand that won't
prejudice you from the beginning. I don't want that. I want
you to see it from my vantage point. To understand the
situation as it evolved, and how I felt. That's the only way
to guarantee *me* a fair deal. But if you're reading this because your teacher asked you or told you. If that's your only
reason, then close the damn book. Right now. Go ahead. I
dare you. Now you either did, in which case you came back,
or you didn't, in which case you probably should. I'm not
going to be a test, a history for anybody, or at least for anybody who isn't interested.

part six
a critical
glossary

Allegory   A narrative in which characters and their actions are abstract personifications, representing meanings which lie outside the story. An allegory differs from a parable in that the narrative in a parable attempts to draw parallels between its events or theme and the particular lesson that the speaker is trying to convey. Among the stories included in this collection, Hawthorne's "Young Goodman Brown" may be classified as an allegory. The Biblical story of the Good Samaritan is a parable.

Antagonist   From the Greek, meaning "that which struggles against" —the force (internal, familial, social, natural, or cosmic) against which the chief character in a story, the protagonist, struggles in order to create the tension of the literary work. Examples of antagonists or antagonistic forces in this collection are: the self and one's own ignorance in Joyce's *The Dead*; de Signoles' cowardice in de Maupassant's "A Coward"; natural forces in Crane's "The Open Boat." *Compare* Protagonist.

Anti-Fiction   A comparatively recent and unorganized type of fiction, Anti-Fiction repudiates conventional literature and conventional approaches. As the term implies, anti-fictionists assume an argumentative stance, rejecting character, plot, structure, and time as they are found in traditional fiction. Almost every selection in part 4, "Beyond the Safety Zone," can serve as an example of anti-fiction. See the preliminary essay to part 4 for a discussion of experimental fiction.

Atmosphere   Atmosphere in fiction is the mood, or complex of moods, ranging from the tragic to the comic, which conditions the attitude of the reader. Atmosphere is conditioned by the time of day and year, by the weather, by the incidents that make up a story, by the characters we meet, and by the images the writer uses. Joyce blunts the party atmosphere of *The Dead* with a snowstorm, and with repeated incidents of minor friction.

Characterization   Characterization deals not only with the participants in a story, but also with the manner in which the author reveals their personalities to the reader. The author may reveal *directly* what we must know about his characters. Alternately, he may have one or more characters discuss the personality of a second character, or he may accentuate that personality through use of a contrasting character, or *foil*. Another approach is to have a character reveal his own personality, as through his words or deeds. Finally, we may judge a character's personality by his effect on others.

Depending on the size of his cast, the writer may choose not to give equal attention to all of his characters. Those he allows us to see as fully developed, tridimensional, realistic characters are called by E. M. Forster *round characters*; characters presented in outline form and who usually embody a single principle or facet, are, in Forster's terminology, *flat characters*. In Joyce's *The Dead,* Gabriel is a *round character*, while the maid and aunts are all *flat characters*. In either case, the idea or principle which impels or drives the character (greed, lust, power) to deeds which can be justified by the ground is *motivation*. That is, the basic motivation must reside in the personality of the character and give rise to deeds and actions which are appropriate to and consistent with that motivation. If Miss Emily in Faulkner's "A Rose for Emily" is to be revealed for what she is, the reader must be attuned—as he is—to her mental condition.

Climax   *See* Plot.

Conflict   *See* Plot.

Epiphany   In fiction, the term *epiphany* is almost exclusively used with regard to the work of James Joyce. Strictly speaking, it is the moment at which a deity reveals itself to externalize the inner state of mind of a character. A moment of high emotional intensity, the epiphany invests some common thing or person with uncommon, even religious, significance. In Joyce's *A Portrait of the Artist as a Young Man*, a girl sunbathing becomes the angel of art, calling Stephen, the protagonist, to his true vocation, the priesthood of art. In *The Dead*, which is contained in this collection, Gabriel realizes in a moment of blinding awareness the true significance and universality of death; this knowledge is prefigured by his wife, whom he does not recognize as she stands at the head of the stairs listening to a haunting song which reminds her of a dead lover.

Foreshadowing   A hint or suggestion given early in a narrative of some significant event that will occur later. It can be simply a song as in Joyce's *The Dead*, or a strand of gray hair, as in Faulkner's "A Rose for Emily."

Incident   In common terms, incident implies a chance encounter or occurrence of little importance. In fiction such encounters invariably unfold the theme, as does the meeting between Brown and the old man in Hawthorne's "Young Goodman Brown," or between the captain and Leggatt in *The Secret Sharer.*

Irony   Irony takes many forms, but all varieties have one important element in common: they contrast appearance and reality. Verbal irony is a figure of speech in which the speaker's words convey the opposite of what he says. Thus Hawthorne employs irony when he entitles his story "Young Goodman Brown." Irony may also manifest itself in situations or events, a classic example being Oedipus' decision in Sophocles' *Oedipus Rex* not to return to Corinth, his adoptive home, but to go to Thebes (which is, unknown to him, his real home) after an oracle tells him that he will murder his father and marry his mother. An example of irony of situation is found in our text in Joyce's *The Dead* when Gabriel learns the real meaning of death at a festive party. Dramatic irony is a special term with a special meaning. It is knowledge held by the audience but hidden from the characters in a play.

Naturalism   Naturalism, which some critics consider akin to *determinism*, is a school of the nineteenth and twentieth centuries which contends that man is the pawn of social, psychological, biological, and genetic forces over which he has no control. Like the tragic hero, the naturalistic hero has a rendezvous with fate, usually leading to his destruction. Unlike the tragic hero, however, the naturalistic hero does not transcend the forces which decimate him. Thus, he does not grow in a work of fiction, but instead is revealed as the object of larger, destructive forces. Although naturalism supposedly offers a *tranche de vie*, or *slice of life*, in actuality the slice comes from only the lowest layer of the cake. There is no comedy, no joy, no growth. (*Compare* Realism.)

Parable   *See* Allegory.

Plot   As E. M. Forster has said (page 461), *plot* is the events and incidents of a story placed in a cause and effect relationship. Some critics prefer to call these important events, thus arranged, the *action* of the story. The story as a whole is, in a sense, the spine of the body; the incidents which comprise the story are the discs which maintain the spine. Some stories, usually long stories, contain subordinate plots which echo or contrast with the major plot. These secondary plots are called *subplots*. Because fiction always contains tension, some element of *conflict* must be introduced, in which opposing forces are juxtaposed. The forces must either push against each other, or pull away from each other. The point of highest tension may be called the *climax*, while the point at which one force or set of forces overrides the other, where the protagonist's fate is determined (though not necessarily unfolded), can be called the *turning point*. The number of major and minor parts or subdivisions in a story, and the scheme of their arrangement (episodic, causal, chronological), can properly be termed the *structure* of a story.

Point of View   Point of view in fiction departs from its usual meaning of "opinion," and instead signifies the angle of vision that the reader has with respect to the story and characters in a work. In *third-person-omniscient*, the most often-used point of view, the narrator is not bound by time or space. He knows everything that happens and is not reluctant to reveal this information. In particular, he knows and reveals the thoughts of his characters. Sometimes he will confine himself to the mind of a single character, as in Joyce's *The Dead*. In *third-person limited* the author, while using the pronouns "he," "she," and "it," does not reveal all the information at his disposal, but restricts it, usually for ironic effect. In *first-person-central*, as in Poe's "The Tell-Tale Heart," the protagonist tells the story, while in *first-person-peripheral* a person somehow connected with the protagonist does so. *Stream of consciousness* is, fundamentally, an attempt to put the reader into the thought processes of a character's mind, where the central "logic" is the process of association. Here, punctuation is often slighted, as is discursive logic. Point of view, lastly, is often governed by the relationship the author desires between his reader and his characters, and reveals the author's desire to immerse himself in his own narrative or to withdraw from it in the sense that a dramatist does.

Protagonist   The protagonist is the central character or force in a work, the figure the story is centrally concerned with or about. Ordinarily the protagonist is "the hero," and engages our allegiance, but this need not always be true. Indeed, villains make good protagonists but poor heroes, as is the case in Poe's "The Tell-Tale Heart." Groups, crowds, mobs, etc., can also act as the central force in a work. In recent fiction, the protagonist is often anti-heroic, a bungler, failure, or outsider. Gogol in Landolfi's "Gogol's Wife" is such an anti-hero, while the unnamed ship's captain in *The Secret Sharer* is a more conventional protagonist. *Compare* Antagonist.

Realism   Realism has been called both a technique and a school. Strictly speaking, realism attempts to depict in close detail the immediate world as it is or appears. It is preoccupied with everyday matters, particularly in the lives of the lower and middle classes. In part, realism is a reaction against techniques or schools, such as sentimentalism or romanticism, which refuse to mirror the real world, choosing to gloss it over with feelings, fantasy, or dreams. Realism differs from naturalism in that naturalism, while employing realism, is confined by the philosophical theory that man's destiny is governed by biological, social, and environmental forces over which he has little control. The naturalistic hero inevitably moves toward destruction; this is not necessarily true of the hero in realism. Henry James is considered the great realist of modern times. Crane's "The Open Boat" is an example of naturalism. See the diagram (page 451) in "The Writer's Workshop." *Compare* Naturalism.

Romance   Unlike the realistic work, the romance does not pretend to render a close and exact imitation of "real" people and events. The romance, of which Hawthorne's "Young Goodman Brown" is an example, uses stylized or allegorical characters who are far removed from the real world to create an evanescent, dreamlike quality. Often, the motivation of the character in a romance is ill-defined and far removed from everyday affairs. Often, the romancer is less concerned with a context per se than with the mood or atmosphere it evokes. Time is often indeterminate, so that the lessons of the romance can be applied in all times. It is in the romance that the psychology of the Bible finds its fictional analogue.

Setting   The background, physical and spiritual, against which the action of a story takes place. Elements of a story which may be considered as part of the setting are (1) the geographical or merely physical location of a story (thus setting can be confined to a world as small as a lifeboat in Crane's "The Open Boat" or as expansive and complex as the Dublin of Joyce's *The Dead*); (2) the time or historical period in which the action occurs (seventeenth-century New England, as in Hawthorne's "Young Goodman Brown") and, finally, the religious, ethical, social, and economic environment and circumstances in which the characters move (the ethos of a post-Civil War southern town, as in Faulkner's "A Rose for Emily").

Structure   *See* Plot.

Style   To define style briefly, it is necessary to simplify a complex subject. Some critics claim that, basically, there are two impulses in writing: the *plain* style and the *ornate* style. The plain style prefers a bare, simple vocabulary; denotation; simple and short sentences; and spareness, direct-ness, and lucidity. Perhaps Hemingway is the best example of such a style. The ornate style, of which James is a practitioner, prefers long and often syntactically complex sentences; a polysyllabic vocabulary or Latinate sen-tences; and extensive use of adjectives and adverbs. Often the style of a work reflects not only the author but also the themes of a work. When Joseph Conrad wants his reader to progress without interruption, as in *The Secret Sharer*, the style poses few obstacles; but when his protagonist strug-gles up the Congo in another work, *Heart of Darkness*, Conrad employs a thick, obstacle-ridden narrative. Thus, a writer employs the style or com-bination of styles that best suits his work.

Theme   The central idea in a piece of literature is its theme. In the short story and novel, the theme is usually an abstract idea that is given a particular expression or representation in a person, action, or symbol in the work. Some of the more conventional themes are the lust for power or money, and the search for love.

Turning Point   See Plot.